Sons and Brothers

Bill Ridgway

CHURNET VALLEY BOOKS
6 Stanley Street, Leek, Staffordshire. ST13 5HG 01538 399033

www.leekbooks.co.uk

ISBN 9780992887926

For my family

Acknowledgements

The author wishes to acknowledge the following hymn writers, poets and lyricists, extracts from whose work have been used in this novel:

Hymns:
Rejoice the Lord is King, Charles Wesley
All things bright and beautiful, Mrs C F Alexander
Thou whose almighty word, John Marriott
There is a land of pure delight, Isaac Watts
God moves in a mysterious way, William Cowper
There's a home for little children, A Midlane

Poems and verse:
A Shropshire Lad XXXII and XI, A E Housman
The Lady of Shalott, Alfred, Lord Tennyson
Hamlet Act V, II. William Shakespeare
The Rubaiyat of Omar Khayyam translated by Edward Fitzgerald
The Rime of the Ancient Mariner, S T Coleridge
Up-Hill, Christina Rossetti
The Fairies, William Allingham
There's a land, by Charles Mackay
Here's a leaf with nine points on, Traditional

Songs:
We all go the same way home, Harry Castling
Trial by Jury, W.S. Gilbert
Our place we know, Ernest Jones
Sumer is icumen in. Anon.
The man who is born to a nation. Anon.
Book of Common Prayer.

OTHER BOOKS BY BILL RIDGWAY

Potteries Lad
More Potteries Lad
Biddulph Moor within Living Memory
Knypersley Recalled
Bateman's World
Church for the Moor

SONS AND BROTHERS

PART ONE
EXPECTATIONS 1870-1882
Page 5

PART TWO
REALITIES 1882-1900
Page 181

PART THREE
RESOLUTIONS 1900-1924
Page 345

EPILOGUE
THE GRANGE, MILLENNIUM EVE, 1999
IN MEMORIAM
Page 523

Author's Note

The Tanbrey brothers are a product of the writer's imagination. They're not based on anyone named Tanbrey, living or past, or on anyone else of another name. Their wives, children, friends and relations are also fictional, and any similarity to anyone living or dead is coincidence.

The Heaths and Batemans, the schoolmaster Harry Caulton and the rectors of Moor Top did exist, but their characters and beliefs are conjecture and their dealings with fictional characters and with each other are fictitious.

Of the politicians and the politically motivated, only David Lloyd George, Bonar Law, Edward Grey and Mrs Pankhurst and her children were real. Their involvement with other characters remains a figment of the writer's imagination, and their response to actual and imaginary events supposition.

The towns and places referred to in the novel did, and do, exist, and their names have been retained - apart from Moor Top whose name is an invention. It was here the Moel could once have been located, but it would not have been called the Moel. And the Tanbreys who lived there never lived there.

Bill Ridgway 2012

The Author

After grammar school, Bill Ridgway did a variety of jobs before gaining a teaching certificate. He subsequently combined schools' writing with his teaching career, producing almost 100 books. On leaving teaching, he became a free-lance journalist, a series editor for Nelson Thornes and a local history writer. The Moorlands has inspired his debut novel, *Sons and Brothers*, as it continues to inspire his life. Bill Ridgway is married with two children.

PART ONE

EXPECTATIONS
1870-1882

From far, from eve and morning
And yon twelve-winded sky,
The stuff of life to knit me
Blew hither: here am I
A E Housman: *A Shropshire Lad*

A spiteful wind tugged at the lantern as Bevis ran his hand across the cow's flank. It began a relentless lowing, its eyes pricked yellow in the flickering light. He rose awkwardly to his feet. Nat moved into the light, a hook of hair plastered to his forehead. He held out the rope to his father, who made a fumbling knot.

'You might've cut it something like. Come on, Charlie, give us a hand.' Nat stood vacantly in the doorway. 'Hold on to her, Charlie. And watch she doesn't 'ave you in the mire while I tie the legs up.' The rope tautened. 'Don't just stand there proppin' up the door, Nat, get hold. You too, Charlie.'

Rain bounced across the slates. There was a distant thunder and the faint tinkle of brasses. 'Pull harder, put your back in it.' Bevis shook his head. Charlie held on. 'Fetch the horse, Nat. Calf's to come out one way or the other.'

Nat hung his head, as if struggling with the words, then went off. Charlie looked up at the farmer.

'Why won't the calf come out, Mr Benersley?'

'It's lodged in. The cow's too small, her's already lost one.'

'Will she lose this?'

'If Nat doesn't get the horse up sharp we're likely lose both of 'em.'

Nat held the shire by the halter. Bevis backed the horse into the open doorway. 'Pass us the rope, Charlie.' Bevis slipped it round the horse's withers and tied it to the calf's legs.

'Right, Nat, take him out slow, no galloping .'

'Beast'll hurt.'

'It'll hurt a sight more with the calf stuck half in. Charlie, keep the rope steady.'

A nearer thunder echoed across the hills. Nat tugged the horse forward, and the rope grew taut.

'Dead slow. Now, go again.'

Charlie steadied the rope as the horse moved away. The calf's shanks emerged like bound faggots. The cow began to low, its neck bulging against the chain.

'Dead slow, Nat, ease it out slow as you can.'

Charlie's foot slid under him, carrying him into the gully. The calf was half out, its lifeless legs dragging across the setts. The shire took a pace forward, dragging the calf after it. The cow sank down into the stall, mooing feebly. Benersley ran his knuckles down the animal's spine. 'Well, that's about it far as the beast's concerned. It's the knacker's for her.'

The calf lay in the straw like a discarded toy.

'I can see him breathing, Mr Benersley. His chest's going up and down.'

The farmer prized back the lolling head. 'Take the horse back, Nat - and get some milk from the dairy.'

'Cow'll have milk.'

'Have you ever tried milk a cow from the floor? Be lucky to last the night, both of 'em.'

Nat returned with a pan. Benersley took it roughly, splashing the floor. Sliding his hand under the calf's head, he lifted it until the animal lay in the crook of his arm.

'Now, Charlie, ladle some in. Take your time, don't want him choking.'

He prized open the calf's mouth and Charlie tilted the pan forward. The animal made a feeble attempt to swallow, then lay still.

Doris looked through the easing rain into the yard. Her husband came from the cowshed with Charlie, Nat trailing behind.

'Charlie's mother'll be wondering what he's up to. What time is it, Ellen?'

A girl bent over her darning in the weak light. She was about to answer when Benersley came into the outer kitchen and removed his boots. 'Well, it'll have to take its chance, not much I can do now one way or the other.'

Charlie followed him into the room. Doris smiled. 'Sit down, Charlie. Ellen - budge up and let Charlie sit down.' Bevis threw a log on the fire and lit his pipe. He tamped in a worm of twist and eased back. 'I think you'd best be getting back, Charlie,' Mrs Benersley said, setting a mug by her husband's chair. 'Your mother'll be wondering where you've got to.'

'She knows where he's got to. Here, Charlie, while I think on' - Bevis fumbled a penny from his pocket, caught the boy's wrist and pressed the coin into his palm. 'A present for you. 1870, fresh minted this year. It'll bring you luck.' Charlie muttered his thanks and put it in his pocket. 'You must tell your mother you've been a big help when you get in. Better'n that soft sod o' mine.'

Doris said: 'It's a tidy leg back. Ellen'll go with you as far as the gate, won't you, Ellen?' The girl nodded without looking up. 'Well, I do believe it's stopped raining'

Mrs Benersley pressed a wrap of butter into his hand as he left. From the upward-climbing track he looked back. A candle-lit rectangle glimmered from Nat's room. He tightened his muffler against the chill and buttoned his jacket. Ellen walked a little away from him, holding a lantern. He opened the gate and looped it behind him with a length of chain.

'I'll be off, then.'

'Father reckons we'll lose the calf an' all.'

He tugged at his muffler. 'We pulled it out with the horse. Cow weren't too happy.'

She laughed and he felt himself redden. 'You're funny, Charlie.'

Grey clouds raced across the hills. She stood at the gate, her lamp resting on the post.

'See you tomorrow, Charlie.'

She went back, singing a hymn she'd learnt at school that week.

The rector swept an eye over their upturned faces. It came to rest on the bell-rope, a Sunday ritual that never failed to inspire him for his sermon. 'And as I look about me, what do I see? The faces of the saved, or of those who spend a few hasty minutes in God's House away from what they consider their *real* life? And what, pray, is this real life? The life of the shepherd tending his flock, is that what we mean? Perhaps it is. Indeed, the land on which this House is fixed is tended by some of those strong yeomen, custodians of the Lord's domain. Or some might think the strike of pick on coal is real life. Fire to stoke the furnaces. Power to work the mighty engines which have made England great. Iron and steel. The forging of great chains for the steamships which carry our wares to the far-flung reaches of the Empire.'

His gaze trailed to the vestry door.

'My friends, that may indeed be true life. The life of crook and plough, of collier and herdsman. I am certain Mr Bateman, that God-fearing benefactor unstinting in his service to our small community, would be the first to agree. And yet – ' the questioning cadence drew Charlie's head upwards – 'and yet: is this all that comprises real life? Is it the sum total? The eternal cycle of birth, marriage, toil, progeny and decease, is that all? Or is there more? Is there more?'

A ray broke across the chancel rubric, *Come Unto Me And I Will Give You Rest* above an arch of pale plaster. Charlie lowered his head to avoid being asked to provide the answer. 'Yes, there is more. I can tell you there is much more than the swinging of scythes and the wielding of picks. Important they are, but they are not the reality our Lord knew. They are not the reality contained in that perpetual life which awaits us beyond the grave. For death is life's one certainty. No picks and shovels there. No ploughs, no furrows. And beyond it do we all hope one day to be drawn. Into that life of glory; everlasting, indestructible, without end. Amen.' He drew his eyes from the cord, his face transfixed by a personal vision of paradise. The vestry clock struck the hour. 'Rejoice the Lord is King. Hymn 210.'

Lift up your heart, lift up your voice;
Rejoice, again, I say rejoice

Charlie ran along the lane and crawled under a hawthorn canopy. A blackbird began a strident call and flew out through the leaves. Splinters rasped his knuckles, making them bleed. He pulled his sleeve over the torn skin and reached into a cavity where a nest lay, tracing the curve of an egg with his finger tips. He delved into the confusion of moss and bark, teased the egg upwards and held it against the light. A bough sprang forward and he flexed back, letting go the egg while the mother wheeled overhead.

'Nestin' not allowed.'

At the sound of his brother's voice, Charlie came out backwards. 'I bet it's smashed now. How am I to find it in the nettles? It needs to be back in the nest.' He retreated into the thicket. 'It's cracked, I knew it would be.' He emerged again, the crazed egg cupped in his palm. 'There's only two left, now. It's nowt to laugh at.'

'I'm not laughin'. Tell you what, I'll shoot all them cats then there'll be plenty of birds. Every cat round here'll end up as mittens.'

Charlie eased the egg into the verge and went home.

Will pushed his empty plate away and picked at his teeth. His wife looked threadbare even in her Sunday Best. Charlie resembled neither. Will had once been dark; Edna still was. Bill had inherited their colouring, but Charlie had mousy hair, and John, the middle brother, was fair. Now Will had turned flabby and Bill was heir to the muscular frame he once had.

Bill took a mouthful of tea. 'Sup up, then, young Charlie. I dare say the bird'll still be singin' come spring. You should've been there, mother, he flew out of the bush quicker than a jack rabbit.'

Edna carried the plates to the stand. 'You're best keepin' out of them nests, you'll be tearin' your jacket.' She scraped the scraps into a bowl. 'Pig has more than us, I don't know what the world's comin' to.' Speaking to her husband's reflection in the window: 'And you'd best get some ash under that tile before somebody breaks their neck. I've told you before, they all want relaying.'

John pushed back his chair and took a book from the shelf. Will's eyes slid down the wall to Charlie. 'Down Benersley's again?'

'I was helping him out.'

'We could do with a spot of help here. Why should you be helpin' when he's got that youth of his? Doesn't he like gettin' his hands dirty?'

'He's a bit on the slow side.'

'He'll speed up a bit chance he has to run everythin' himself.'

'I mean he's not all there.'

'I hope you're not callin' Nat an idiot,' Bill cut in with mock severity. 'Say that in front of Benersley and he'll have your guts for garters.'

'Well, I didn't mean -'

Charlie took a corkwool from the mantelpiece. He'd fixed four nails to a reel and twined them with thread, then picked the thread over each nail in turn, the resulting cord tugged through the hole in the base. When the cord was long enough, he'd sew it into a spiral to make a teapot stand. Restless, he put the corkwool on the arm of his chair and went over to the window.

The sky had cleared. He pulled on his cap and muffler, unlatched the door and left the house, John following. An empty bottle of Owbridge's Lung Tonic lay in the verge, and he stuffed it into a hole in the wall.

'Where shall we go, John?'

'Down the woods.'

'I aren't sure.'

The woods and most of the farms about belonged to Mr Bateman, a local colliery owner. They could see his flag staff jutting above the trees from their house.

'No one'll see.'

'What about the gamekeeper?'

'He's nobody.'

'It's trespassing.'

John moved on. 'That's right.'

The sky was fading to white. A lark sprinkled song across the pasture. Below them a narrow bridge spanned the brook. From the parapet they peered down into the water.

'The rector's in with the nobs,' John said. 'Bateman, Heath, they're both as rich as Croesus.'

'Have you ever seen Mr Heath?'

'Only Bateman. One day I'll be richer than either of them. Richer than Bateman at any rate.'

'Mr Benersley says Bateman spent all his money on his gardens.'

'How does *he* know?'

'That's what he said, anyhow. Mr Bateman was thinking of selling his house 'cos he were broke.'

John moved away. 'It's just talk. What does Benersley know? He's only a farmer.'

The lane ran by a stand of birch. A path threaded through the trees, emerging at intervals into brakes. Sunlight dappled the ground with golden tints, and a resinous scent floated on the air. Charlie found a stick in the undergrowth and swung it against a rhododendron. A wood pigeon flew out, cooing. He watched it settle, its breast swollen against the light. The path narrowed, and they climbed to a secret hollow. Charlie slid inside, scuffing the marl as he settled. John came in after him and they sat for a time in silence.

'Suppose we'd better be gettin' back,' Charlie said at last.

'Let's take a look around Bateman's gardens first, see this Chinese pagoda he's supposed to have.'

'His gamekeepers'll set the dogs on us. Let's go down the leat instead, see if there's a kingfisher.'

But John was already moving away. 'I'm not scared of Bateman. You go down the leat if you want, I'm going for a look around.'

Martha had looked after the pub near the pit for five years since her husband died. In Jack's time she seldom went behind the bar, but now she had no choice. Worry had etched premature spiders across her face and shrivelled her figure. At first they'd whispered behind her back; now they called across the saloon.

'What d'you call this?'

'I dare say you'll get it down.'

'Tell you what, Martha. I'd rather get this down than you.'

'You flatter yourself.'

A derisive laugh broke through the din. She passed the change across and unlatched the cellar door. As she went down, their voices faded amid the wheezing barrels.

The speaker drummed the floor with his clogs. 'All right down there, Martha? Fancy a spot o' company?'

She'd learnt to judge her time. When she came up, they'd be stupid with ale and leave her in peace.

Bill shared the bar with the local cronies. His height and build marked him out. He earned good money at the pit face, and a mediocre wage on the farms during lay-offs. But behind his banter lurked a more restless character. He wondered how long it would be before he grew tired of dragging a chair through Martha's sawdust.

She reappeared and pulled mechanically at the pump.

'Stick one in there, Martha.'

'Somethin' with a head on it, not your usual pap.'

A skittle clattered against the table. She took a rag and began to wipe the glasses.

Charlie paid his pence and joined a group by the stove. The only time the room was warm was on hot summer days; melt-snow slicked the yard in winter, and on clear days icicles clung like stalactites to the gutters. On those days the weather would strike through worsted as if it were muslin.

'I was here first, Tanbrey, sling your hook.'

Charlie hunched his shoulders. 'You don't own the stove.'

'D' you think you do?'

'I bet you take it in turns gettin' warm down your house, first you, then your John.'

'Bloody swat, your John.'

'If you mean he can read and write, he is.'

'He'll still end up down the pit chance he can read or not.'

'He's not cut out for the pit.'

'Oh, and what's he to be, then, King o' England?'

His eyes followed his fingers stroking the guard. He'd avoid the stove in future, get to school on the bell when he could sidle into lines and avoid them. As he moved away from the guard he saw the Reverend Francis Gordon coming through the door at the far end of the room, his wife just behind with a man he'd never seen before. The rector swept to the front and waited for them to settle.

'Good morning, children. I depart from my usual duties to introduce your new master, Mr Caulton. I need not tell you he is to be shown every courtesy, and I do not expect any of you to let down either myself or Mr Caulton in this regard.' Eyes briefly moved to the new arrival before returning to stare blankly at Gordon. 'You will find Mr Caulton a trusty friend to those willing to grasp the opportunities we offer, and you'll want to join me in wishing him well here at Moor Top School.'

Mrs Gordon whispered to him behind a raised hymnal. 'Ah, yes. I am also reminded of Mrs Gordon's duty to the school over the past weeks, where she has looked forward to helping you with your catechism.'

His last words slowed as he noticed an inattentive face. 'You, boy! Stand!' A red-headed scholar wearing torn hand-me-downs shuffled to his feet. 'What were you whispering about?' The lad lowered his eyes. 'Come out.'

The hall stilled. There was a draught from the part-open door. The rector seemed to rise like a genie, eclipsing Mr Caulton in its shadow. The boy approached with lowered head. 'I don't know whether Mr Caulton is aware of the standards we expect of a Church School pupil. I know that Mrs

Gordon has adopted strict measures in order to maintain good order. However' - his grip on the offender's shoulder tightened - 'it appears there are some who wilfully choose to ignore what they have been taught. What is your name, boy?' The child gave an inaudible reply. 'Speak up, I can't hear you.' He cupped an ear to the boy's lips. 'Alexander Booth, is that it? Well, Alexander Booth, your manners are fit only for infidels. Are you an infidel?'

'No, sir.'

'I should hope not. In future, you will oblige me by making no comment unless you are required to do so. Do I make myself clear?'

'Sir.'

'Perhaps this once we can forgive your indiscretion.' He lowered himself to the boy's height. 'Do I make myself clear?'

'Sir.'

The rector uncurled. A vicarious relief rippled through the room. 'Before I leave you in Mr Caulton's care, let us bow our heads. 'O God, we call upon Thee to bless our school and those who work in it. We ask Thy help in moulding Thy charges into Godfearing examples of Thyself, and humbly beseech Thee to cause Thy servant Mr Caulton to deal wisely and' – a crack appeared beneath the fluttering lids – 'firmly with Thy charges. Thou hast taught us to suffer little children and to forbid them not; yet, lest we spare the rod and in so doing deliver to Thy care a child spoiled beyond human aid, we beg Thee to endow Mr Caulton with the gift of authority, and his class with the gift of obedience. Amen.'

He turned and followed his wife out of the room, leaving the new master to face them.

'Good morning, boys. I hope we can get along together. If you work well, I'll do my best to give you the benefit of my experience in dealing with boys like yourselves. If you do your best by me, I'll strive to do likewise by you. I'd be obliged if you'd call me sir. While we're working here, Mrs Caulton will be instructing the girls in sewing, music and cookery next door.'

He moved from the window into the shade and back to the light. Eyes and ears fixed on his face, assembling clues and cadences, measuring his potential for attack and retaliation. From the girls' room came the first verse of a hymn.

All things bright and beautiful,
All creatures great and small,
All things wise and wonderful,
The Lord God made them all

He opened his mouth to complete his introduction, but turned instead to the adjoining door and opened it. The singing petered out.

'My dear, I wonder if you could move the piano to the other side of the room?'

A seditious muttering broke out from the boys' side. A desk lid crashed, adding to the disturbance next door. Through the part-open door Charlie could see his new teacher helping his wife push the piano under the window. The girls were talking behind their hymn books; two of the boys had launched into a mock battle. Then the outside door swung back and the rector stood there. A hush fell on both rooms. Mrs Caulton dislodged her music book, which struck a discord as it fell to the floor.

'I must beg forgiveness,' the rector began expansively. 'I thought I was leaving the school, then I discover I've blundered into a cage of monkeys. I think I must be in a zoo, a human zoo full of foul-mouthed and noisome creatures -'

'Maybe I can explain –' Caulton began.

' – base creatures to whom God did not grant the gift of self-discipline. Unfortunately, you are favoured otherwise, and since you choose to forget His gift, I must jog your memory. Form a line!'

He jabbed a space at the front with his finger. As he stood with the rest, Charlie was aware of Caulton standing undecided by the door, and of the Reverend Gordon at the cane cupboard. The rector turned with his selection, slashing imaginary palms before levering up the first boy's hand.

'Reverend Gordon, there's been some mistake, I only went to ask Mrs Caulton if –'

The first stroke curtailed Caulton's plea. The boy paled, hugging his swollen fingers to his armpit. A second due was paid, followed by the whip of arm and cane to the end of the line. Charlie saw nothing but a moving mouth as the rector issued a final warning and strode out. They remained silent until the bell at end of the lesson. Before the last clang died, those nearest the exit had reached the yard or the privvies. Charlie hovered by the wall which split the boys' yard from the girls' as their voices rose and dipped around him. Ellen was swinging a rope, whipping the ground in time to a rhyme, her pinafore billowing in the slight breeze. She gave way to a bystander and came over to the wall arm in arm with the other girl.

'This is Charlie Tanbrey from up Moel.'

The girl began preening Ellen's hair.

'What's your new teacher like?' Charlie said.

'Mrs Caulton lives up Alton.' They laughed secretively in unison, and the girl went back to her rope. Ellen said: 'How many did you have, Charlie?'

'One. I weren't doing nothing neither.'

'Let's see your fingers.' He held them out for inspection. 'They seem all right to me. You'd be hard put to see owt.'

'It wasn't you had the stick.'

She pushed his hand back in feigned disappointment. The caretaker had left the gate open, and spikes of willow-herb bent across the gap.

'Ee, you're funny, Charlie.' The bell clanged for the end of play. He felt for Mr Benersley's coin and fished it out, holding it like a lens against the sun. 'You're rich, now, like King Midas, whoever he was.'

'It's the penny your dad gave me.'

'You can buy us a liquorice.'

'I aren't sure but I should keep it. It's supposed to be lucky.'

He scraped it across the coping, and a powdery deposit blew into the yard. Looking up, he saw Ellen join the girl and go in. He ran to catch the tail-enders.

A cock disturbed the early morning calm. Will spat into a bowl, got out of bed and pulled on his work clothes. The valley lay wreathed in fog, the ridge beyond rising as from a flat, grey sea. He turned from the window and went downstairs. The air tasted of smuts, but down by the hen runs it had the strong, clear scent of dawn. He took five eggs from the shed and looked to the sturks. When he got in, his wife was at the range. He scattered chunks of bread into a bowl of warm milk, ate noisily and took a mouthful of sweet tea before pulling on his cap and leaving the house. The mist cleared as the sun strengthened, leaving steam-white tendrils through which the hawthorn rose. Pulling his cap tight, he set off for Jacobs' Pit, a hundred yards from Bateman's boundary. Bags of coal were already being loaded on to a cart ready for the morning deliveries. Jack Jacobs appeared at the mouth of an adit, a spare figure speckled with grit.

'We lost some roof in the night. Give us a hand with the props.' Will followed him to a pile of old timbers. 'It's a stanchion I'm after, six foot o' thereabouts.'

A stove burnt dully in the corner of the shed and a bun-legged table stood in the centre of an earth floor. There were planks running the length of a wall, and a single arched window, translucent with grime.

'How're your lads?' Jack asked, pouring boiling water into a battered pot.

'I've nowt to complain of.'

'How old's your Bill now?'

'Comin' up to eighteen, this time.'

'Still down Whitfield, is he?'

'Ay, still on the face.' Jack hovered by the stove, swilling tea around his mouth.'And our John's still down at the dye works, though I've a mind he's cut out for better things.'

Jack drained his mug and left it on a shelf. 'If he doesn't want to get his hands dirty, send him over the wall.'

'I'm not with you.'

'Your John.' Jacobs thumbed at Bateman's flag staff, just visible through the window. 'I hear they're lookin' for a lad in the office. See Urias Ball, he's a friend of the wife's cousin.' He moved towards the open door. 'Well, we're not goin' to shift much stood here, better get this roof seen to.'

Whitfield Colliery rose from a plain of grey waste. A hawser hissed against the flat cloud, bringing up a loaded cage. Bill stepped into the light, his teeth shining in the dust-blackened face he took back to Moor Top at the end of a shift. George Dixon, the butty, was waiting for them and began to undo the clasps of his satchel with deliberate slowness.

'I'll be laying off tomorrow. You can blame the manager, all I do is dole out the brass.' He delved into the carrier and began a slow count of coins while reading names from a stub. The first collier pushed through the knot and stepped up the incline. They hung on as the last wage was paid, Dixon taking his time with the empty satchel, clipping the buckles and testing their hold. He jabbed at various heads. 'You. You. You. Take the rest of the week off. Might be something come the middle o' next if you trouble to turn up.'

'Bloody hell, George –'

The butty brushed the dust from his jacket. 'And you, Tanbrey - best find yourself something else.'

Across the shale came a shout of coarse laughter. At the edge of the waste women waited.

'Why have I been singled out?'

'Because it suits me.' The first drops of rain sent oily spirals across the pools. 'Tell you what, they think I'm a bastard and they're right, for to be a boss you've to be a bastard. Now I'll tell you something concerning me and my missus. I don't give a tuppenny damn what you do with other women, but take a word of advice. Keep yourself off my patch or you'll be waking up with your teeth in a bag - and not only your teeth. Is that plain enough?'

'I don't know what sort of a cock and bull tale you've picked up, George. I've got all I can handle without spendin' my time grubbin' about down there.' He flicked his head towards the grubby terrace where Dixon lived.

The butty's eyes widened, and he closed in on the taller man. 'Remember what I said. One more tale and I'll be paying you a visit, and not just me.' He held Bill's eyes for a moment, looped the strap of his satchel over his shoulder and began to move off. 'You can whistle for work as long as I'm on the bank. Try the fustian, I hear the wenches there aren't too fussy.'

Bill watched him walk off through the drizzle. As he climbed to Moor Top, the light rain washed coal dust into the neck of his shirt. Ladling water into the bath, he stepped in. The soap stung his eyes, and he chafed them vigorously, sluicing himself with the soiled water. Who'd been spreading tales? There'd never been any love lost between George Dixon and himself, yet he sensed the butty was unsure. At thirty-four he'd married a girl of nineteen, there were no children, and they shared a house with Dixon's widowed mother. Bill had sometimes seen his wife waiting with the others at the end of a shift. She reminded him of a butterfly on a sooty wall. He levered himself out of the tub, put on a collarless shirt, swilled the yard and hung the bath from a nail. The gossip about Dixon's life had been of no consequence until now. Was she really kept under lock and key? Was Dixon as big in chapel as someone once told him? A weariness came over him, and he went upstairs and slumped on to the bed. As he hoisted up the blanket, the butty's face had already begun to fade.

2

The bell was clanging as Charlie reached the yard. Caulton counted them into the room and left the register to be completed later. 'Please raise your hand if you've forgotten to bring a pencil. Hands up those without a pencil!' Twenty hands were raised. 'I'd have thought buying a simple black lead wouldn't provoke a family crisis.' His voice rose against the din. He took a tin box from his desk. 'Keep your hands raised while the monitor gives them out.' A boy gave out sheets of coarse paper and pads. 'I don't care whether the pads are creased or not, they will serve. Please be quiet. QUIET!' He thumped his desk, catching the remaining pads, which cartwheeled to the floor. 'Now, those who still want their pencils sharpened step smartly forward.'

He opened his clasp knife and began whittling. When it was Charlie's turn, the teacher smiled faintly. 'There you are, lad, good as new. Remember, revere the artist and not his tools. Don't worry, one of my useless aphorisms. Be a good fellow and ask Mrs Caulton if she's ready, will you?'

The bedlam now extended to both sides of the partition. Mrs Caulton stood in front, adjusting her bonnet.

'It's Charlie Tanbrey!' shouted one of the girls.

He shrank back into Mr Caulton, who'd come up behind. 'I sent young Tanbrey to say we're ready, my dear, but I suspect the sight of so many beautiful young ladies has proved too much for him.' The girls shrieked and made a parody of slapping each other. Mrs Caulton waited for the din to die down. Eventually the boys spilled on to the yard and formed a straggly line by the gate. Mrs Caulton lined the girls up alongside the wall.

'Now,' said Caulton, trying to inject an air of authority into his voice, 'today we're going to try an experiment involving the use of hand and eye - in short, observation. I hope this afternoon you'll learn something. Now keep together, boys first, the girls to follow.'

He struck out under the tumbling clouds, his walking cane flashing, his wife trailing behind with a hand to her bonnet. Before they'd covered fifty yards the lines fell into disarray. Mrs Caulton tried to hold her class in check while her husband continued oblivious to the boys straggling the width of the lane. At the crossroads he halted the line.

'What's wrong, Harry?'

'A change of plan.'

'Aren't we going to Trent Head?'

'I thought a little further.'

'Where do you suggest?'

He studied his pocket watch. 'How about the finger post?'

'But it's a mile away.'

'There's time.'

She ordered the girls to wait while the boys moved off. As they marched past the rectory, a curtain twitched.

The meadow glistened with buttercups. To the east, patches of woodland climbed the hills, the fields between furrowed by ragged lines of darker green. Caulton stood on the height sniffing the air, the children grouped around him on the grass. His wife came up, jolting him from his reverie.

'What d'you think of Polly's work?' she asked.

Caulton reached for the girl's pad. Heavy pencil marks scored a sheet of stick trees and smiling stick figures.

'Don't you think it shows merit? Especially the hills. Don't you think they look life-like?'

'Hills, what hills? I thought they were washing lines.' Caulton squinted against the light. 'I see no washing today, do you?'

'You're not to take Mr Caulton too seriously, Polly, he must have his little joke. Let's ask him what he thinks of your figures. I think they're excellent.'

'If Mrs Caulton thinks them excellent, then excellent they must be,' he said, passing the sketch back, 'but they may not be as excellent as other people's figures, and I include among them Mrs Caulton's. I must walk about and compare.'

His wife led the girl away. The boys began to throw grass, and he made an attempt to restore order. 'I'm really disappointed in you. I shudder to think what Mr Millais would make of your work. No, he is not a schools inspector, but a man of vision whose work delights the eye. You have a country wrought by angels and not one of you can see past a handful of thrown grass.' He was speaking to himself. The land fell around him in tatters. 'Perhaps if I speak to the farmer he'll let you use his farm to leap about in, like colts. It seems I have no choice but to take you back to school.'

He'd managed to reduce them to a manageable silence, when a girl's hand sprang up. ‘This is our farm, Mr Caulton.’

‘Your father won’t gaol us for trespassing?’

‘This is Ellen Benersley,’ his wife said.

‘I’m very pleased to hear it.’

‘We’ve got two shires and a mare but no colts. Father won’t mind us playing, though, we only live down the bank.’

He followed the line of her finger, then turned to face the classes. ‘Very well, you may give your drawings to Mrs Caulton and your pencils to me. When you hear the whistle, wait by the finger post. He was talking to their backs. ‘Aren’t you going, Charlie?’

‘Can I finish the picture, sir?’

‘By all means.’

Charlie bent to it, oblivious to a coal cart creaking up the lane behind them.

As dusk settled, Caulton sat on his garden bench puffing a small Havana. The plot which came with School House had remained untended since he took the job. He felt at ease with the nettles and groundsel which had encroached into the shrinking area of grass. Arcing the butt across the cinder path, he went inside. His wife had spread the afternoon’s efforts across the floor and she passed a sheet to him.

‘What d’you make of that?’

He angled the drawing, looking for a name. ‘Oh, Charlie Tanbrey. You don’t know our Charlie, do you? A solitary sort.’

‘I thought you’d like it.’

‘Leaves the others standing. Look at the detail. I’d say it shows a precocious talent. Yes, definitely precocious.’ He tapped a point here and there. ‘You see how he’s drawn in these flowers, making them larger than life? D’you know, I think our Charlie has a taste for the elemental.’

He put the drawing down and watched her sorting through the diminishing pile. ‘You work too hard.’

‘Mm?’

‘I said let’s go to bed.’

‘I don’t feel tired.’

‘Well, you will when I’ve finished with you.’

She gave a cry of protest and struggled against him. The papers spilled across the room as he chased after her, whooping into the darkened hall.

'Pray forgive me, Mrs Caulton. The door was open.'

She made an effort to straighten her dress. 'Darling, it's the rector, would you turn up the lamp?

Urias Ball arranged his papers and gestured towards a bench. Eventually he looked up. 'Can you read?'

'He can read better than –'

'I'm asking the boy.'

'Quite well, thank you.'

He handed John a copy of *Bartlet's Accountancy Practice*. 'Here, read that.'

'What page shall I choose?'

'Suit yourself.'

'*The ground rules a novice or trainee accountant would be well advised to remember –* '

'All right, you can read. Now, how's your figuring? Can you tackle sums?'

'What sort, Mr Ball?'

'What have you done up at the school, owt or nowt?'

'Length, weight, capacity, time, number; some algebra and Euclid.'

'You won't find much use for algebra when they're trying to short change you for a pile of sand. 'What's five loads o' stone at £5.10.6d a load?'

Ball watched him mouth the calculation.

'£27.12.6d.'

'Seems they've taught you something after all. And why d'you want to leave the dye works?'

'He's wasted there, skivvying,' Will put in. 'If you take him on, Mr Ball, you'll not regret it.'

Urias coughed into his handkerchief. 'Hours from seven till we've done with you, Monday to Saturday morning. You've an entitlement to a week off over and above Wakes and Christmas Day.'

'You're setting him on, then?'

'I'll have to clear it with Bateman. He'll no doubt make a few enquiries of his own.' He removed his glasses and polished them with slow, deliberate movements before looping them over his ears. Will extended a hand, which the estate manager held limply for a second before returning to his papers.

As he was leaving, Will asked: 'What kind of a wage might the boy expect, Mr Ball? If he's here permanent, like?'

'I'm not in a position to say.'

'Just so the lad knows where he stands.'

Urias dropped his sheets into a drawer and banged it shut. Will shuffled uneasily, wringing his cap. 'Well – I know you'll do the best you can.'

John followed his father out. It was early June, and the scents of summer wafted across the ornamental lake. As they were leaving, John turned to look at Bateman's grand house. One day he'd live in a house like that.

Men grouped around a lamp-lit depression. The two wicker cages each contained gamecock.

'Here's a sovereign on Satan's Blood.'

'Match it with this.'

'Put two on Killer.'

Agitated by the mood of the men, one of the cocks began to squawk. Bill put a finger close to the cage and the bird snapped forward, impaling the space with its beak. He looked across at the other. In size and weight they were a match. He nodded to Satan's Blood. 'Put five on this.'

'I thought you were out of work.'

'What're the odds?'

'Treble that, if you're lucky.'

Bill counted over the money. The cages were sprung and the spurred birds emerged, probing like prize-fighters while their keepers flapped hessian sacks. An onlooker began a dance macabre, fluttering against a bird's tail. It flew, clawing at the air, into the path of its opponent. Maddened by the growing tumult, the bird rushed forward, jabbing at its assailant and drawing blood. The wounded bird gave a piercing shriek, backed towards the flailing clogs and ran haphazardly around the enclosure before mounting the other's back and striking through the feathers. The bird convulsed as its attacker struck at the grey skin.

'Come on, Killer –'

'Finish it, Blood.'

A fox barked, and a bright moon appeared between scudding grey cloud. Now the cocks flew at each other with splayed feathers. A dark stain seeped through Satan's plumage. Spurs twice bit into Bill's bird, scattering its feathers across the pit. Satan's Blood lunged in retaliation, taking out its opponent's eye and gashing a deep furrow across the maimed bird's sternum. Killer faltered. A leg crumpled. The other cock savaged it, its spurs entangled in a visceral ribbon. The golden cock lay on its side, its comb trembling. Satan's Blood perched on the breast, and with a swift, indifferent movement burrowed its beak into the dying brain. The bird jerked for the last time. The victor crowed to the moonlit sky. The losers blamed blunted spurs, a starved bird, chicanery. Some set off down the track for Leek. The farmer who'd presided over the contest climbed into the ring to scuff out the evidence of fighting. Bill pocketed his winnings, a bloodshot eye on the farmer.

'What's up now, Joss?'

'You're not too drunk to know it's banned.' The man held up the lamp so that its light fell across their stupid faces. 'Do me a favour – take him off.'

He went in, bolting the door behind him. The others left Bill to make his own way home. Drink had befuddled him. He stopped to take stock of his winnings, then replaced his purse, squinting down at his fingers fiddling with the button. A crack sounded behind. He made a sluggish half-turn, then the ground seemed to rise up. It may have been only seconds later that he felt a pulpy swelling at his temple. He winced in pain and examined his hand like a child puzzling the answer to a sum. At length he managed to stagger a few yards into the bushes. His head seemed to be made of lead. He fumbled awkwardly inside his jacket pocket. The purse was still there, but the money had gone. In its place he found a scrap of paper. He crumpled it into his fob and staggered back against a gate post. When he reached the Moel, the eastern sky was paling.

James Bateman formed his fingers into an arch. 'Would you care to elaborate?' he asked

The rector cleared his throat. 'It may be no more than a settling-in period, but there are matters which have come to my attention which I feel should be put before the committee.' He turned to the others in the room while Bateman examined his newly-gilded cornice. 'First there's the question of Mr Caulton's garden. The fact is, School House garden has been allowed to degenerate into a bed of weeds. The last time I looked that way, I saw a brood of capons and a ruined hen hut. Is this the standard we wish to set for our scholars?'

'I should think not,' agreed a joiner named Bourne. 'His agreement was to keep the land in sound fettle.'

The rector closed his eyes and nodded. 'Quite so. And there's another, more serious point. My wife informs me she saw the entire school making an excursion up to the moor. On the evidence of my coal man, their destination was Benersley's Farm. He tells me he saw the scholars romping in the fields while our employees paid not the slightest heed.'

Bateman said: 'I suppose there might be some reasonable explanation.'

Bourne sought guidance in the ceiling. Another member of the committee, a thin-lipped butcher, looked suitably aghast: 'Frolicking and running amock? Correct me if I'm wrong, I was under the impression they were paid to educate, not gad about the countryside taking the air.' He turned his beefy face to the rector. 'Caulton seemed well enough set up when we gave him the job. Maybe he was doing something beneficial, like -'

'Counting cobwebs?' Bateman murmured, shaking his head.

A deferential titter passed between them. A local grocer, Fallows, commented: 'Happen Mr Wilbraham could be right. Whether being right represents a return on outlay's another matter. I'd like to ask the rector if he's any further light to throw on it.'

The rector stretched out his chin, pulling the skin taut. 'As you will appreciate, my duties afford me little time to look into the school as often as I would wish. There is one other point, and I mention it only inasmuch as it might help shed some light on Mr Caulton's character. As I've said, my wife saw the children go past the window. I thought I might look into the matter further and in the evening I stopped by at School House. The door stood open, and I surprised Caulton in the act of chasing his wife. It seemed to be some sort of a game. As you can imagine, I made my excuses and left. As I say, time has been unkind to me of late. However, the committee is now aware of matters, such as they are.'

Bourne stared at the wall, Fallows and Wilbraham at each other. Bateman stroked his beard thoughtfully. 'Mr Caulton is a young man, and we must take the charitable view. The new Education Acts may well have encouraged him to experiment with progressive methods of teaching. As regards his private life, I can only say that as far as I'm aware he's not a drunkard and the rector tells me Mrs Caulton is a regular attender at church. The question of the garden must, of course, be looked into. I wouldn't like us to be over-hasty before we find out more about the matter.' He turned to the rector, whose envy of Bateman's kindness was tempered by a desire for justice. 'Francis, perhaps you could look into the school again. I know Mr Caulton had some difficulties at first with his control of the class. I know you'll exercise your usual discretion.'

'Rest assured I shall do my best.'

The meeting broke up. Urias Ball saw them leaving from the office window. Bateman stood for a few minutes, looking across the gardens it had taken him years to create. An intense satisfaction settled on him, and the trivia of the meeting was lost in clouds of orchids. He left the room and emerged outside in gum boots and waistcoat. His wife watched him for a few minutes, then drew the blind against the sun and lay back on the counterpane.

'So Bill lost his job down at the pit?'

Charlie watched the smoke drift lazily upwards from Benersley's briar, while kittens squeaked in the hearth. 'Have they got names yet, Mr Benersley?'

'Well, that's Sultan, least that's what Ellen calls him. The others are Prince and Rajah. I think it were somethin' they were doin' at school about the darkies.'

'They're Indian names.'

'Well, that's what I just told you.' He knocked out his pipe against the mantelpiece. 'It's only a fad, next week it'll be Tiger or some such. Has he got anything else, then?'

'Who?'

'Who we were talkin' about before these cats – and don't let the bugger climb on the table, Charlie, I don't want it messin' all over the place – your Bill.'

'He hasn't been feeling too well.'

'What's up with him?'

'He's been in bed.'

'Flu', is it?'

'I don't rightly know.' Before the next question could be put, he added: 'Our John might have a job down the Grange.'

'Moving in society, is he?'

'He'll be in the office.'

Benersley puffed reflectively. 'Tell your Bill I can put a spot of work his way. I'm not up to all I should be, maybe old age creepin' up. Nat's gettin' no better – worse, truth be known.' The clock chimed the hour. Around it the wallpaper had begun to peel, revealing a patch of crazed plaster. 'Anyroad, Ellen'll be leaving school in a week or two, so there'll be another pair of hands, least till she gets wed. And how's school treating you, Charlie? Are you top of the class yet?'

'Not yet, Mr Benersley.'

'Well, if you've learnt to read and write it'll be a step in the right direction. I never learnt, though the missus can turn out a fair hand when'er needs to. Just farmin', that's all we had.' His eyes softened. 'Have you still got your penny?' Charlie fished it out of his pocket. 'Muck for luck eh?'

'I keep it by me.'

'Well, they've gone off shoppin' and I can't say what time they'll be back. Tell you what, get a bit of cake from the tin, then I'll show you how to use a sickle. Have you handled a sickle before?' The boy shook his head. 'It's the year for thistles. They all want cuttin' down and burnin'.' Charlie went into the scullery and came out with a plate. The cake disintegrated, and he caught the crumbs with his free hand.

After he'd eaten, they went out into the sun and the farmer gave him a rag so the shaft wouldn't bring up the blisters. At first he flattened as many thistles as he cut, but he soon learned to angle the blade. He cut hard by fallen stones, drawing sparks from the quoins, laid bare a rusting bucket and broken slates. Dense nettles hid the debris and he cut them down, raising a haze of pollen. The air fluttered with moths, which rose up from the masonry. Benersley called him in for a mug of elderberry, and when he went back he saw Ellen on the crest.

'Charlie! What're you doing?'

'Your dad's asked me to clear the ground.'

'By, you're getting to be a real man now, using all these new-fangled tools. Show us how it's done.' He lifted the blade and began to swish. 'No, show us proper, show me where to put me hands.'

A wisp of hair hung from her bonnet. He moved her hand up the haft, and she opened her eyes wide in feigned surprise.

'You just do it in a circle,' he said, as she swung the blade and more thistles crumpled. 'Haven't you done it before?'

'Hey, I could do this all day. You're a real handyman, Charlie. Come in and see what mam bought me from up Leek.' It was a bag of humbugs. She offered him one, then went up to her room.

Benersley dallied with him on the step before he went home.' I bet you can't remember the first time you come here, can you, Charlie?' He said he couldn't. 'Mrs Benersley used to make buttons for Stonier's and your mother did the same thing. She used to come here once in a while, sometimes gave the wife a bit o' company. They'd work side by side. Has her told you?'

He shook his head. Benersley stroked his moustache thoughtfully. 'She didn't come down again much after you were born. I dare say she were busy. When she started up again she brought her buttons down to Doris to take in with her own. Then she started sending you down with 'em. Can't you remember?'

'Not really, Mr Benersley.

'You'd be about five or six. You only paid us a couple o' visits, then the work began to dry up.'

'She gets stuff from somewhere else, now.'

Benersley chuckled. 'I thought she might. Anyhow, that's how you come to be payin' me these visits.' He looked up curiously. 'Does your father mind you comin'?'

'He hasn't said.'

Charlie sensed a sort of relief in him. He went in as Ellen came out. 'Are you off now, Charlie?'

'I've to get back. I promised John I'd play football for a bit.'

She walked with him, preening her hair. At the gate she picked at the lichen, her eyes close to the weathered wood. 'He's not me real father, you know, and she's not me real mother neither. Me real mam were a lady o' leisure, or so I've been told.' She looked over her shoulder at the farm, then turned and pecked his cheek. 'That's for teaching me how to use a sickle,' she said, bouncing away.

'But you call them mum and dad,' he shouted after her.

'In name only.'

The world didn't seem solid after all. His thoughts turned to Bill. Where had the bruises really come from? Behind one wall lay another; Ellen, Bill, Mr Benersley - all secrets, like a mask behind a mask. When he reached the finger post he lifted his hand to his cheek, as if to feel the imprint of her mouth there.

John opened the letter. Bateman had agreed a wage of twelve shillings and sixpence a week on a month's trial. He was to present himself neatly dressed at seven on Monday. He handed the letter to his mother.

'Make sure you use your manners when you speak to your betters, and only open your mouth when you're spoken to.'

'Only Charlie, then that's it, all earnin'.'

Edna frowned. 'Our Bill hasn't earned a brass farthing in two weeks.'

'He seems to have got by well enough.'

She replaced an iron on the hob and spat on the other. The spittle hissed across the plate. 'Struck by a cart? Struck by a fist, more like!'

She clumped the iron down. Will went to attend to the fowl.

'Mr Benersley can fix Bill up,' Charlie said.

But her face was threadbare, and instead Mrs Benersley rose through the steam. He saw her in red, then melting into his mother's colourless form. He turned another thread. The corkwool was now long enough to make a plate stand. He cut it free, twisted it into a spiral, dropped the bobbin in a drawer, put the corkwool and scissors on the sideboard and took an unfinished sketch of a sycamore leaf from between the pages of *The Coral Island.* He began to ghost in the veins, running his tongue across his upper lip in concentration.

3

At a quarter to seven John rang the bell. There was no answer, so he settled by the wall to wait. Soon he heard the sound of crunching gravel, and Urias came around a corner wearing a tweed paletot. Making no sign he'd noticed the new employee, he pushed the door open and stood before his cluttered desk adjusting his glasses.

'Best get things right now as later. You can refer to me as Mr Ball. If you meet Bateman it's the same, always Mr Bateman to his face, or Sir if you've a mind.' He fitted a nib to the stock. 'Later this morning he'll no doubt be sending for you. Now, you can make yourself useful. Have you ever lit up a stove before?'

'At home.'

'At home Mr Ball.'

'At home, Mr Ball.'

'Well you can light that bugger so I've something to brew on. You'll find it's already been set up by the night staff. Here-' He threw over a box of vestas. John picked them up from the floor and lit a ball of paper. A thin smoke curled into the office. 'Hey up! You're not smoking out a warren o' bloody rabbits. I thought you'd handled one of these.'

Urias banged down a lever. 'That's how it's done, get the smoke going up, not down!'

He moved behind his desk, glancing back at the stove as he sat. 'Now, of a morning we set up shop, make sure the pens have good nibs and there's ink in the pot. Post comes at eight and by that time you've lit the stove, made a brew and got everything put by. There's no need for haste. A steady pace day by day, that's what's called for.' He slid a spike of bills across the desk. 'I'm going to start you off with these. First you'll need somewhere to work. See that desk under the window? That's yours. Put all the junk on the sill. Right, let's get down to business.'

He left John to enter the paid bills in a ledger. The post came shortly after eight, and Ball gathered Bateman's correspondence and took personal letters through the connecting door into the house. Below the balustrade, a gardener's lad was edging the lawn. John put down his pen and let his eyes wander over the office paraphernalia, the softly hissing stove, the papers and ledgers. After a time he applied himself again to the sheet, and was completing the entries as Ball returned.

'Leave that. Bateman wants a word.'

The manager led him through the hall and up a sweeping staircase.

Bill eased back on the bolster. His mother's comfrey had helped reduce the swelling at his temple and now she came in with a bowl of stew, putting it down on a bed-side chair.

'What's this?'

'I've made some rabbit broth.'

He reached out an arm and she passed him the bowl. His eye fell on the mug she was holding.

'It's only daisy water. The comfrey's finished. It'll help your eye.' She bent to touch the inflamed skin, but he jerked away. 'It's still blood-shot. I don't know why you don't want the doctor in.'

'And what good would he do?'

She stood by the bed until he'd finished. When she'd gone downstairs he took the scrap from his pocket and unfolded it. Something in the scrawled invective stirred his memory. His sight blurred, and he gave up and lay back. The place was beginning to sicken him. He'd earned well at the pit and put aside money against the day he decided to leave. Every week for over a year he'd unscrewed a jar and dropped in a few more coins. Out of work, he'd thrown caution to the winds and put part of what remained into the cock fight.

His memory suddenly sharpened, and he sprang out of bed and waited for his mother to leave the house before he went downstairs. He took a tin of receipts from the cupboard and leafed through them, making a pile across the table until he found what he was looking for. He laid his scrap alongside it and compared the writing.

Item: dozen yards silk thread/jasmine

Item: fifty button blanks, polished hardwood

The letters were identically formed, the same hand, the same writer. He'd often seen such receipts lying about the house and wondered how his memory could have held on to them. Now he noticed the fragment of print edging the torn scrap matched that on the paper from the drawer. He returned the tin, putting the receipt and scrap into his pocket. He didn't go back to bed, but sat by the fire, waiting for his mother to return from the shop and settle down to her work again.

'D'you ever get fed up making buttons?'

'Did you ever get fed up working down the pit?'

'Where d'you get all this stuff from?'

'Vale Mill, where else am I to get it?'

'But who signs it out when you collect it?'

'I thought you were supposed to be sick. Are you thinkin' of startin' up yourself?'

'I was just curious. I chanced to look through the tin and came across a receipt. I thought the prices looked a bit steep. I wondered if somebody was trying to make a bit on the side. Look, I'll show you.'

He handed her the receipt, and she gave it a cursory glance. 'Looks fine to me. I wouldn't put it past Jud, mind. He's mean as muck.'

'Jud?'

'You wouldn't know him.' She drew a twist of silk through the blank. 'Jud Cowlishaw. Any the wiser?'

He knew the name. Someone's face came to mind. He said, 'D'you know, mother, I suddenly feel a lot better.'

A week passed before he went out. The bruising had almost faded, and he felt well enough to start the investigation that had been on his mind. It struck him there was still a chance his winnings were intact if Cowlishaw had taken them and if Jud was as mean as his mother had said. Vale Mill was a short walk through the fields, but when he reached the town he turned instead into a narrow street and knocked at a house. There was no answer, and he approached a neighbour who was scrubbing her step.

'I was told I'd find Jud Cowlishaw here.'

'You've come to the wrong place, that's his sister's. You'll find Jud down Vale Mill.'

'He's not there, he's been off all week and I was going to pay him a visit. Any idea where he lives?'

'I've an idea he's down Brindley.' She put down her brush.'You'll have no trouble, it's only a couple of streets, anyone'll tell you.'

The village was twenty minutes away. He'd have a drink – his first since the night of the cock fight – then he'd sort things out.

Jud Cowlishaw's hair had thinned almost to baldness, the remaining strands combed across his scalp like a twine-wrapped egg. He'd worked at Vale Mill since his twelfth birthday and at forty-six he'd made it as far as the office. He'd never married. His only social activity was attending the

Methodist Chapel on a Sunday morning and again at night. Years of living alone had made him peculiar, and as he grew older his behaviour had become more erratic. He stole packing to block holes in his boots, and took a short cut home along the railway to save leather. He risked sacrificing his job to pilfer a small, unnoticed amount each week from the firm's orders. He suspected everyone of talking behind his back and his suspicions were slowly turning to delusions. But at work he was in control and no one knew. He sometimes visited his sister. Over the last year he'd had disturbing dreams where Jane appeared, naked, at his door. He was full of self-loathing and desire. His dreams began to merge with his day-time world. He spent dark hours in the alley opposite her house, following her moves. One night she'd come home with a young man, and Jud had watched the gas light flicker in her bedroom. At midnight the visitor had left, unaware he was being followed back to the Moel.

Bill left the pub and found a boy who pointed out Cowlishaw's house at the end of the row. A cinder track bore the imprint of cart wheels, and an entry ran between the yard walls. He eased the gate open and walked cautiously up to the locked back door. A loosely-tacked board had been fitted across a broken window and it gave to a jab of his hand. He hooked an arm inside, twisted the casement catch, threw a leg over the sill and climbed in.

It was seven before Jud returned. As he closed the door, the tiles leapt up at him and the room quivered into darkness. Someone was speaking to him. He tried to raise himself but a slow, throbbing ache broke through the fog. He lifted a finger to his swollen lips. A red froth dribbled down his chin, and he broke into a spasm of coughing. Groaning, he levered himself onto the chaise longue and slumped. A shadow moved against the window-light. He looked up as if he had neither the interest nor will to help himself, and saw Bill flicking a wad of notes in his face.

'I'll have this back for a start, you thieving bastard. I might've been drunk, but I'm not soft in the head. You thought I was too gone to stand upright, but that's something else you got wrong.'

Jud stared at the ceiling like a sickly child. Bill pulled up a chair and folded the money into his pocket. A thin ribbon oozed from Cowlishaw's broken mouth. The room fell silent.

'Jud Cowlishaw? I never knew there was a Jud Cowlishaw, but I felt him here.' He touched the side of his head.' I never knew any Cowlishaw but one, and that was a woman. I didn't know she was your sister till today, then you turn up. I don't recall seein' you at the cock ring, but I wasn't lookin' for a weedy runt like you so like as not I missed you – unless you were out prowling the lanes, spying your chance. Was that it, Jud?'

The man lay rigid, his chest heaving.

'Nice girl, your sister Jane, nice body. She didn't mind showin' it off, neither. I can't vouch for her dyeing cloth, but she was pretty good in other directions.'

Cowlishaw's eyes rolled emptily. From outside came the faint cries of children at play. Bill looked at him as if he were a curiosity. It had taken him less than an hour to discover Jud's hoard. Where had it all come from? Had he been up to something at work? Like other misers, he'd been careless of his hiding place. Instead of the bank, he'd used the case of a broken clock. He felt strangely detached from the man on the couch. Jane came into his mind, a brief flirtation. He hadn't seen her in five months, and this little man with the bleeding mouth was the brother who'd tracked him down and focused his delusions on him.

'Beware of jealousy, Jud. I suppose you thought you'd grab my winnings and teach me a lesson at the same time. But tell me this, if you can speak with a gob full o' teeth – why bother with the note? Did you know I'd get around to recognising your scrawl from my mother's bills of sale, was that part of it?' Cowlishaw turned his eyes on him, but there was nothing behind them. 'Tit for tat, now, Jud. I didn't even thieve the rest of your money, chance how much you've got or where you got it. Only what you owed.' He moved to the door. 'D'you know, I've a mind you wanted to get found out. You wanted to punish yourself. Tell you what, I noticed a bottle of whisky hidden away in the other room. I didn't know Methodists were partial to a glass, but it seems there's a lot I don't know. I'll bring it in, you can console yourself with it.'

He suddenly felt the urge to be rid of the dirt, the smell of soot in the empty grate. It had been on his mind to ask the man if he'd put Dixon up to giving him the sack. Maybe they knew each other. He didn't care, had to get out. Instead of turning into the street, he found himself climbing the scree behind the house. From the top he could strike back across the fields and breathe fresh air again.

*

The rector slid his eyes from the bell-rope and focused on his flock. 'You will no doubt have heard of the death of Dr David Livingstone. And what, do you think, was his mission? Some might think he merely wished to explore that sombre continent of Africa. It was only last year that Mr Stanley brought back word of the discovery of a mighty waterfall which now bears the name of our Queen. We are given to understand Dr Livingstone suffered tremendous hardship in his efforts to reveal to us the mysteries of this alien place. But I ask again: *was this his mission*?

'It was not. The fruits of his journeyings are there for all who care to read about them, but they pale into insignificance compared with his true mission – to convert the heathen to the glory of Christ; to scatter the spirit of our Saviour upon the dark reaches of their lands; to help them perceive the divinity of the True God, who sees into every heart and lights every chamber. I've no doubt the doctor was an excellent man. He explored the vast Zambezi and witnessed trees which as yet bear no name. He shielded himself from the ravages of beasts and a sun which can shrivel a man within the hour.

'All these wonders, all these mysteries. Yet the mission seldom spoken of was Dr Livingstone's true mission: to bring God to the godless; to bring light to the darkness; to bring hope to the helpless and help to the hopeless. To seek out the untutored savage and bring him to the Glory. The London Missionary Society. Here is the true explorer, not jungle and mountain, the brutes of the forest, the awesome Victoria Falls. Rather, the discoverer of the Way to Everlasting Truth in the Body of Christ Jesus. Amen.'

Rain drummed the church roof. The rector leafed through his papers. 'God said Let there be Light: and there was Light. Hymn number 333.'

The congregation rose, hymnals spread.

Hear us we humbly pray
And where the gospel day
Sheds not its glorious ray

Let there be light, thought Caulton as he stood with his wife on the platform with a raised umbrella. A dark plume rose beyond the curve of the track. The train clanked to a halt, hissing steam against the lowering sky. He swung open the door and hoisted his luggage to the rack.

'Terrible weather,' he remarked to a woman sitting opposite. 'It certainly doesn't bode well for the holidays.' He ignored his wife's embarrassment. 'I've read somewhere farmers have lost half their wheat, but I dare say Mr

Gladstone will have something up his sleeve.'

The passenger got off at the next station. They made their connection, catching a London express which rumbled into Euston five hours later. At Victoria they spent an hour in the buffet, waiting for the Eastbourne train. Late in the afternoon they took a cab to the West Rocks Hotel where he'd booked a two weeks' stay. While his wife indulged in a bath, he unpacked their cases and fell on to the bed. The Downs beckoned, away from the rector, the school and the moor.

It was November and Bateman stood at his window watching a rook flapping across the drizzle-shrouded gardens. He'd had the best of everything. Oxford educated and an authority on the propagation of orchids, how many others had the means to create a fantasy garden of ravines, tunnels, glens and cascades from an undrained bog? How many had the money to cart stone, dig out lakes, commission carvings, indulge themselves in temples and fund the import of rare plants? He'd been blessed with good health and an active mind; he'd served as a Justice of the Peace and as chairman of a dozen local committees - yet he no longer wished to stay. The money he'd spent maintaining his house and garden nagged at him like a constant toothache. In fact, he was making arrangements for its sale at that moment.

At sixty, public office was no longer expected of him, and if he took care he might earn himself another twenty years in the balmy South Coast air. A weak light filtered through the blinds. He could hear his wife coughing and started up the stairs, then changed his mind and turned instead into the quiet of his library.

Caulton found the letter waiting on his return from Eastbourne. His frown deepened as he read the rector's note a second time:

> 'Dear Mr Caulton,
> It causes me some embarrassment having to write this letter. Under the terms of your agreement, you were obliged to keep up the schoolmaster's garden. However, I find that the land has been allowed to run wild. Moreover a number of fowl and a hen-hut now occupy the greater part of the site. I can only suppose you are unaware of this breach, and will soon bring the land back to its former state.
>
> It saddens me to remark on a more serious matter. I understand your control of the class has again been allowed to

deteriorate. I am of the opinion this has caused an increase in the number of children absent from the school, and so a falling off of pence. According to my sources, there have been occasions when those who attended have not been entered as having paid. I need not remind you that, again, under the terms of your contract, your diligence in this matter is essential. I trust that a speedy resolution to these matters be made at the start of the new term. I hope you enjoyed your holiday.

My Regards to Mrs Caulton,
Yours Sincerely,
Rev Francis Gordon'

Caulton crumpled the letter and threw it in the hearth. His wife heard him bellow from the hall and came out on to the landing. 'Can't it wait, Harry? I'm sorting through my materials.'

'You've enough cloth up there to supply an army.' She came down, by which time he'd retrieved the letter. 'Here, read that! I tell you this, Louisa, I don't like that fellow. I've always found him pompous. What does he mean, control allowed to deteriorate? Does he expect me to bind them with wain rope? Does he have any notion what we're about with these urchins? They're not coming to school because I'm too lenient, because I don't gag them every second? All he cares about is his bloody pence. There's one thing for certain, I've no friend there!'

He sank exhausted into a chair, leapt up, snatched the paper from her and hurled it in the fire. 'If he hasn't the common courtesy to see me himself, why should I bother with it?' His anger spent, he smiled and held out his hand to her. 'Anyway, who cares? He should be exhibited in a museum. People would pay their pence just to see him.'

She gave a restrained smile. No matter what her feelings regarding the rector, she recognised his power in the district. He had influence with Bateman and the school managers, and he was responsible for their living. Their house was adequate, they had no children, they could live a pleasant life.

'I'll get us something to eat, then we'll talk about it.'

'About what, my love? Is there a case to answer?'

'Things can't be left in the air, Harry.'

After dinner she sat with her embroidery as her husband blew smoke rings.

'I'm told he was a teacher himself,' she began.

'Who?'

'The rector, of course. Mrs Pattinson told me.'

'Pattinson?'

'She sits on the front pew.'

'I didn't know she was an authority on parish history.'

'She said he'd taught in a private school down south.' She put down her needle and regarded him thoughtfully. 'We need to think about this letter, Harry.'

'I have thought. I'll write tomorrow and explain that the reason children stay away is that their parents see little value in an education which prepares them neither for cows nor coal.'

She pushed her needle into the cambric. 'I think we need to answer the letter in a more circumspect way.'

'I intend to give him the plain truth of it.'

'No, you need to take it seriously. I did tell you about the garden...'

The blood rose to his face. 'Whose side are you on?'

'I'm on your side my love, but I can't let you lose your job. Why don't you get rid of the poultry and buy a scythe? Come spring we can get the ground neatened up. That's one problem out of the way.'

'I like a wilderness.'

'But Mr Gordon clearly doesn't. And it is in the agreement.'

'The Devil take the agreement. The man has no aesthetic sense.'

'If you wish, I will take over the register. I know how you hate filling in columns of figures.'

'If that is what you want.'

'I think that as long as the money is collected methodically the rector will have less to quibble about.'

'And if they still don't turn up?'

'I hardly think we can hold ourselves responsible for that. At the same time we shouldn't allow ourselves to fall into a trap.'

'What kind of trap?'

'Harry, you well know what kind of a school they want – catechisms to order and blind obedience. I know it's not your way, and neither is it mine. The difference is I'm willing to play their game and see how it goes. If things become too uncomfortable we can go elsewhere. We've no ties. Your friend's school in Devon, perhaps, even France. But we can't move as soon as we've arrived. Let's just try and fit in for a while.'

He rose from his chair and stood for a moment, gazing into the fire. 'Do you remember the day we took them out sketching, all those miscreants up to their necks in muck and daisies, knowing nothing, going nowhere....' He paused, caught up in his reminiscence. 'You remember young Charlie Tanbrey, that sketch of his? It *did* mean something. I *did* help him. I helped him to see things.'

'Perhaps he could see them already.'

'But now he knows what he's looking at.'

She fell silent. The scholars couldn't be allowed to run wild, neither could they be parcelled into desks and whipped for breathing. She said, 'Harry, we need money to live. If you're unhappy here, we must move, and that could break our contract and lose us a wage. Can I suggest you write back to the rector and assure him you have the school's best interests at heart – which, indeed, you do.' She smiled winsomely. 'It would please me enormously if you would. Not for Francis Gordon, but for me.'

She thought he was set, then he turned, smiling. 'Does it matter? Anything my cherub wishes.'

Bateman took his seat at the head of the table. 'I think we can begin, gentleman. Rector, I believe you were going to look at our Mr Caulton. Have you been able to make any progress?'

The Reverend Gordon cleared his throat. 'I believe I can offer a little more information. The last meeting was towards the end of the school term and as you will appreciate the time available to me has been limited. However, I did have the opportunity to examine the registers over the holiday, and since the start of the new term I have been able to visit Mr Caulton in the classroom on three occasions. I must tell the committee that irregularities in the accounts have come to light.'

Wilbraham's lips shrunk to a pale line. 'You mean the man's been falsifying the scholars' money?'

The rector shook his head. 'I believe the issue is one of negligence. Mr Caulton has been as lax in his collection of money as in the tending of his garden and keeping order in his class.' He took an envelope from his inside pocket. 'I took it upon myself to write to Mr Caulton, putting before him the facts as I see them. Two days ago I received this reply:

"Thank you for your letter. I have now considered it and I hope this note will reassure both yourself and the managers that whatever talents I possess reside firmly in Moor School. When one takes up an appointment, it is some time before he is fully acquainted with the tasks to hand. In the case of the scholars, there is often a lapse before the master and his pupils become used to one another, and during that period respect will naturally grow. I defer to your comments on the matter of the School House grounds, and assure you that I shall put matters to rights at the first opportunity. Your Obedient Servant, Harry Caulton." '

'Well, at least he seems to have had the decency to apologise,' Wilbraham said. 'Happen we should give him another month to sort himself out.'

Bateman cast his eyes over the letter. 'I agree with Mr Wilbraham. Let's take this young man at his word. I'm sure the rector will be able to give us more promising news in a month or so. Now, gentlemen, can we pass to the costs of school coking?'

John looked across from Ball's office at the lamp-lit windows. He'd watched the managers arrive and knew their names by heart.

Charlie put down his pencil. The class burst up on either side of him, crashing back the hinged desk seats. Caulton's voice had risen above the din, but his efforts were wasted. By the time the monitors had collected the papers, the room was deserted.

A change had come over the teacher. He'd been harsher, and there'd been no more outside visits though the winter had been mild. At first he'd given out new copy-books for forming letters and slates were handed out for table practice, but by degrees, he'd reverted to his former self. Today was the third art lesson in a week, and he'd asked them to draw the articles he'd laid out on the table – a sickle, a pitcher, a quern. He'd called the collection Rural Life and spoke to them about the beauty of the land which masked the poverty of those who worked on it. The collection was part of the countryside, showing its tending, its bounty and the new machines which had made it possible to feed the people. He talked about the ships which brought wheat from the America and beef from Argentina and how this was taking its toll on farmers' livelihoods. But people needed more than just bread, he said. They needed nourishment for the spirit and time to look at a sunset or an apple, stained red across the green. He talked of form and texture. They had to know that nothing lasted, neither sickle nor quern, Queen or Empire, perhaps not even God, and he'd held them at last. Bedlam had broken out when drawing started. The teacher had tried to quell it, but the class had left forty sheets of scribble while Charlie had only just begun to draw the pitcher.

'Now, that's beginning to look well.' Caulton squeezed into his seat, bunching his legs to fit under the desk. 'What you need is a little shading. You see where the light falls, from the windows there, and the lamps there? We take our pencil, and' – he began to apply the lead to the side of the pitcher – 'you see? And we usually have an area of light here' – he indicated the extreme edge – 'reflected light, we call it.' Charlie stole a glance at Caulton's absorbed face, the tongue nudging the sandy moustache he'd started to grow. 'There, you see? Roundness and solidity, then the essence of the thing comes out in all its glory.'

He leaned back, contemplating the finished result. 'D'you know, I'm rather pleased with that.'

'It's better now, sir.'

'But it was already roughed out by your good self.' He linked his fingers loosely below the desk.'Tell me, do you enjoy school?'

'We have to come, sir.'

'I dare say neither Mrs Caulton nor I would choose to come if we had enough to live on without it. Unfortunately we don't, so we must be grateful for a stroll across the Downs and leave the Temple of Luxor to those who can afford it.'

Charlie rubbed his nose.

'Your brother John was quite bright, I'm told. I came too late to help him in any special way, but.... I wonder if your father would agree to your having, shall we say, a special lesson a week? You can have a drink of lemonade into the bargain.'

'I don't know, sir.'

Dusk was closing in, and already the pitcher was in shadow. 'Talk it over with him. There'll be no fee.' He got up and began attending to the remaining pencils and papers, putting them in the high desk he rarely used. 'See what they say, let me know.'

*

Will looked to Edna for confirmation.

'I don't care about his going. Pity our John here couldn't have had the chance.'

Charlie thought she might be right. 'Mr Caulton says everything will go in time, even Queen Victoria, even God.'

John glanced up, then returned to his book.

A haze of smoke clung to the ceiling. A glass had been spilt, and sawdust trapped the stain of spreading porter. The din of Christmas sounded muffled in Martha's room, but it was still loud enough to know what they were shouting. Jack had died five years ago and it had been Christmas then, and she'd hated the season ever since. They weren't like that when he was alive. Now he'd gone she was something to shy at, a bundle of rags along with the peeling limewash. Snow slid down the glass and collected in a corner of the pane. Jack's face was there, his mouth twisted in a remembered smile. There had been a carousel, rowing in the park, beef tea. She'd left her umbrella behind at the Great Exhibition. Fully grown trees under the glass! And the heat! She could still feel it, striking through her frock. He'd always remembered the Crystal Palace. Four year later, they'd lost their son at Sevastopol.

The clock chimed. Soon the last of them would be gone. She took a counterpane from a drawer and spread it over the bed, carefully smoothing out the wrinkles. She poured water from the ewer into a bowl, set out a towel and soap, removed her smock and slowly washed her face, neck and arms. She put on a muslin chemise. There was a pendant, too, with a lock of her mother's hair and a darker strand of her father's. Fumbling awkwardly with the clasp, she eased the pendant over her scrub of hair and rouged her lips, rubbing them together as she used to. She took her pearl earrings from the box they shared with Jack's links and tie pin, clipped them on and stepped in front of the cheval. Her rheumy eyes widened in a smile. She heard the last of the revellers singing down the lane and bolted the door.

4

Benersley was leaving the milking parlour as Bill came over. 'I hear you might have work, thought I'd stop by on the off chance.' The farmer invited him in as Charlie went with Ellen to fill the mangers. Doris had polished the room and pinned sprigs of holly above the doors.

'I hear you've been suffering,' Benersley said.

'I see the word's spread. You've got it nice in here,'

The farmer nodded. 'Father still down with Jack Jacobs?'

'Ay, still diggin'.'

'Chest any better?'

'So - so.'

A chill clung to the room despite the glowing fire. The farmer spread his hands to its warmth.

'Mother keepin' well, is she?' chimed Doris from the skullery.

'She's fine.' Bill took a mouthful of cake, dusted the crumbs into the grate. 'Happy as a lark.'

'That's nice to know.'

They'd grown up together, but even as a child there'd been a barrier. Edna's looks had seemed to fade once she'd married Will. They'd always seemed an ill-assorted pair, no spark. Edna had walked over to Three Elms once in a while, not saying much when she came, then she stopped coming. Doris gave an inward shrug. It was all water under the bridge.

'And how's Nat?' Bill asked.

Bevis puffed at his pipe. 'He's coping. Tell the truth, I'm beginning to feel my age, Bill. I'm not getting about like I used to.'

'You look hale enough to me.'

'It's his joints,' piped up his wife from the other room. 'Sometimes his back locks solid, doesn't it, Bevis? And his hands swell up so he's a job to handle the beasts. Ellen's not old enough for the really heavy work and Nat's not got the nous, I'm not being unkind to the lad, neither.'

Bevis pulled on his coat and scarf. 'Best come and look around.'

The cattle had pock-marked the yard and churned the ground to slush by the gate. Bevis took a woollen hat from his pocket and pulled it on. The cows were silent, their legs encrusted in frozen dung. Ellen wheeled a barrow into the byre, while Charlie pitched hay into a manger.

'Keep up the good work,' Benersley said, passing with Bill through the far door.

Ellen watched them through a window slit as they disappeared behind the outbuildings. Her cheeks glowed against her pale eyes and she brushed away the errant wisps straying from her bonnet. 'A good day's work, Charlie, don't you think?'

'I can't feel the cold any more.'

She picked at a spot on her chin. 'It's all them muscles o' yours.'

'Where d'you come from, Ellen?'

'What d'you mean, where d'you think I come from?'

'You said Benersleys weren't your real mum and dad.'

'That's history.'

'Do you know?'

'Of course I know.' She picked at a splint in the stall. 'Well, I know what I was told.'

'What was that?'

'That me mother were one o' the nobs and I were a disgrace to her.'

'But who was she? Who was your dad?'

'Me mother had a position. I don't know about me dad.'

'But how did you come to be with Mrs Benersley?'

'She says she met somebody in the mill, and they wanted someone to give me a home. I aren't bothered, anyroad. Come on, Charlie, let's go inside, I'm starvin' to death out here.'

Bill left Charlie to make his own way back. The hedges were no longer stock proof, and on the higher land the walls had collapsed. Bevis could pay only a small wage, but Bill could stay as long as he wanted and there was his keep if he cared to live in. It only needed a fire to thaw out one of the unused rooms. He told Benersley he'd let him know within the next few days, and was still turning things over as he passed the rector by the lych gate. He raised his cap and received a cursory nod, which he put down to not attending the Advent Service.

Within striking distance of home, he changed his mind and took the road into Bradley Green. He felt restless, felt a need to be moving somewhere, anywhere. He'd read some tale about a tiger which had leapt into the tender of a moving engine near Midnapore. He'd never seen a tiger, and he wanted a drink. More than a drink, he wanted company.

It was growing dark as he knocked at Jane's window and waited.

Pulling open the letter box, he hooked away a drape and looked along the passage. The house seemed deserted, but as he turned to go the door opened and she stood there.

'Bill Tanbrey? What're you doing here?

'I thought you were out.'

'I was dozing. You'd best step in.'

She struck a vespa and reached up to the lamp. There was a soft plop of flame, which she adjusted to a bright pennant. He took a seat on the sofa while she closed the curtain.

'I didn't expect to see you again.'

'I thought I'd pop down for a spot of festivity.'

She wore a plain dress and a shawl which she held at the hem so that it accentuated her body. He was aware of the scent of dye, carried on her clothes from the mill.

'If you've come for what I think you've come for, I'm not in the mood.'

He got up from the sofa, pulled her to him and tried to kiss her but she twisted her head away, so that he left a slobbering trail across her cheek. He'd partly dragged the shawl from her shoulders and begun to knead her breast, but she jerked her hand free and caught his hair. With a vague look of surprise he reeled back against the chair. He sat morosely while she tugged her shawl into place and repinned her broach.

'Maybe you should go.'

'Maybe I should. I doubt it was worth waiting for anyway.'

She began a retort, then broke off. 'My brother died last week.'

Her news shocked him. She'd never mentioned Jud before, and if she suspected Bill knew of him, she might also know about his visit to Brindley. He was wondering what to say when she added: 'Of course, you never met Jud. He suffered a minor stroke. He was off work a couple of weeks, but he wasn't right when he went back. Then he had another, Monday just gone. That was it.' He heard himself offer his condolences. 'He kept himself to himself. The family were C of E, but he had a bee in his bonnet. He used to go down Whitfield Chapel. I've been told he never missed a week.'

He remembered Dixon's words, *I'll tell you something concerning you and my missus....* Jud. George.... Whitfield Chapel....

'Would you care for some tea?'

'Got anything stronger?'

'As it's the festive season.'

He'd almost forgotten why he came. She poured him a brandy. He took a sip and felt the first flush of heat. 'You've done well for yourself. House, free drink, all the vices o' good living. You must tell me how it's done.'

'Take care of the pennies and the pounds take care of themselves.'

'Is that it?'

She stared into the fire, but after a moment got up and reached for her coat. 'If you're in no hurry to get back you can make yourself useful.'

'Where're we going?'

'I've not had a chance to sort through Jud's things.' She turned down the lamp. Away from the fire, the air from the passage chilled the room. 'I don't want to be walking the streets by myself in the dead of night. I'll have no chance till next Sunday, and I don't want it hanging on.'

He went to help her down the steps, but she checked him. It suddenly occurred to him he'd been wrong about her. He'd thought she was there for the use men might make of her, but it struck him now she'd been the one with the whip hand, and for some reason it amused him. They walked through the town, past the church and smithy. He felt awkward, and walked a little apart from her. He still couldn't reconcile himself to Jud's death, wondered if he'd brought it on. For the sake of something to say, he asked, 'What was that you said earlier about being careful with pennies?'

'It's just words. I don't want my business broadcasting to all and sundry.'

'So it's not just the pennies then?'

They reached the first houses. 'There was a bit of money on mother's side. Her sister's husband was involved in carting for the fustians. When mum and dad died aunt Cissie brought us up. She'd no children of her own, and when my uncle passed on she made a will out to Jud and me. She died a few years back. I bought the house with my share, but Jud carried on renting. I dare say he hoarded it up somewhere. That's why I could do with a hand, it'd not be wise leaving the house empty.'

Eruptions of flame shot into the sky, the slag wagons clanking rhythmically across the road.

'Maybe he gave it all to chapel, passed some on to George Dixon while he was at it.'

She looked at him curiously. 'I didn't know you were acquainted with George Dixon?'

'He was the butty down Whitfield. I'd an idea he went to the same chapel as your brother.'

'I heard Jud mention him once. You sounded a bit put out just then.'

'Nothing to do with your Jud. Just a work feud, that's all.'

It was almost dark, and the burning slag threw silver spears across the rooftops. She took a key from her bag and he followed her into Jud's house. She lit the lamps and their breath rose like candle-smoke in the unheated rooms. Nothing had changed since his visit.

'What d'you want me to do?'

'Just keep me company while I have a look around.' She took off her hat and brought a chair to reach the shelves. 'I dare say most of his stuff'll end up on the fire. I came down for an hour after the funeral to find the landlord nosing about, Jud not cold and he's telling me there's somebody wanting to move in next week.' She grabbed a pile of old newspapers and handed them down. 'Here, dump these in the yard.'

He wondered if she knew he'd seen Jud, if she were toying with him. Did she know about the clock, that when he'd left Jud there was still money hidden inside? Was she really there to sift through the worthless flotsam of her brother's life, or had she already found his hoard and removed it during a previous visit? Now she was taking down empty jars, a Brummagem cocoa tin containing a stub of candle on a bed of burnt matches. She removed the debris from each shelf, tipping the contents on to an old curtain she'd found in the parlour. The last thing was a mug decorated with a newly-wed Victoria and Albert. He looked up at the clock. What if she didn't know and he took the rest of the money? You couldn't steal from a corpse.

'The mug's the only thing worth keeping. Let's sort through the sideboard.'

The drawers yielded a pack of playing cards, a tarnished candle-holder and a dead cockroach. She glanced once more around the room, her eyes resting on her brother's rocking chair. In the scullery they found a blackened saucepan, which he threw into the yard along with a broken dolly peg and rubbing board. She went into the parlour, leaving him taunted by the clock with its store of notes and coins.

She was prizing the lid off a biscuit box. Inside, were bundles of papers. She replaced them and took a final glance around the room. 'I don't know about hoarding money, he could have done with spending some on a cleaning woman.' She shook the curtain, turning away from the flying dust. 'I'll leave the couch here for the removal man.' Warmed by her exertions, she unfastened her coat and stood looking about the room. 'Have you been in the attic?'

'I poked my head through the hatch,' he said. 'Just dust.'

She looked up at the clock. 'That can go, too, I've never once heard it strike.' She stood on a chair and tugged at it, but couldn't free it from the wall. 'Here, you have a go.'

It came away unexpectedly, and he clamped it to his chest so that the face wouldn't spring open. 'I wouldn't put it past Jud to have given it away to charitable causes. You're clutching that clock like a baby. You'd best sling it out with the rest.'

'If it's all the same, I'll keep it. I know somebody handy, might be able to do something with it.'

'Hadn't you better see if it's got any works inside, first?'

'I've already done that. If he can't get it going it'll still do for ornament. Are we done, now?'

She began to laugh. As he laughed with her, he wondered if she knew. She kissed him spontaneously and he felt her yield beneath the heavy coat, the soft contours of her stomach against his groin.

'I don't suppose I'll be rich after all,' she said.

He put the clock under the scullery table and when he came back she'd slipped off her coat. Somewhere in the darkness a cat squealed.

It was not far off first light when he left her to sort through the remaining shreds of her brother's life. He picked up the clock and walked up the street with it under his arm, and it was only when he'd left the rows behind that the cold struck him. Unable to restrain himself longer, he hunted for the clasp and pressed it. The face swung out, capturing the dawn light. He reached into the cavity. There was nothing. He scrabbled in the void. The money had gone. She'd had him for a fool. The rumble of a passing train jarred him. With all his strength he dashed the clock against the side of a wagon. Again and again he struck, splintering the wood and shearing it from the casting. As the last truck went by, he hurled the remains into the sky. The face caught the bright glow of slag, and by the time he'd reached the rise, Jud's hiding place lay buried under the cooling mound.

'There was no need for it,' Edna was saying, 'no need for a Christian body to do that.'

Will knotted his muffler and began to pull on his work coat. 'She'd had enough.'

'At Christmastide, too.'

'I suppose when you've of a mind to do that you don't worry about the season.'

He went out as John came downstairs. Catching the tone of their voices, he asked his mother what it was about.

'It's Martha. They found her last night. She's done away with herself.' She made a gesture of impatience. 'They say she took something.'

'What?'

'How should I know? She's been having nerve tonics ever since her husband died. Her soul must have been in torment, poisonin' herself like that. I know things are sent to try us, I've been there myself more than once, but...'

'How did they find her?'

'She'd been laid up there the best part of a week. They thought she'd gone strange and wouldn't open up. It were the postman noticed the curtains drawn and snow piled up at the window. He got the bobby and they found her lying on top of the bed, all decked out in her best.'

Upstairs, Bill strained to hear their voices. As a result of Jud's delusions he'd lost his job and been cheated out of the price of retribution. He should have forgotten his scruples and taken the lot while he had the chance. Why not? Jud had stolen from him. And now this woman had killed herself. He pulled up the blankets. Jane wouldn't need to trouble herself with his company again. There were plenty of willing women. Before he drifted to sleep, he resolved never to set foot in the pub again.

As the months passed, Urias came to see John as someone to be wary of. He still had ten years left, and hoped he'd be well-placed to continue when Bateman moved, which wouldn't be long. He wasn't yet ready to lay down his pen, neither did he want to antagonise his underling. He decided a less formal approach wouldn't come amiss, especially at the end of each month, a fact which hadn't escaped John's notice.

John was already at work on the Monday when Urias arrived. He gave the manager a cursory glance before resuming work on the sales' catalogue for the house. The printer had asked for the information by the end of the month, and the list of internal fixtures was almost complete. Urias spread his hands before the stove and looked over John's shoulder at the boldly written columns, each numbered item bearing a brief description. Pouring himself a mug of tea, he studied John through steam-narrowed eyes.

'You've no need to be at it every minute of the day and night, you know. It's like the old women used to say, all work and no play make Jack a dull boy.' John continued to write. 'I've a mind you'll be getting a call later. Bateman wants to make a start on the outside now the inside's all but done.'

He stroked his chin absently, then made a show of getting his papers together. 'Papers, papers everywhere and all the desks did shrink.' He gave a chuckle. 'Now I see we're having problems with the schoolmaster up on the moor. The rector's got it in for him by all accounts. They don't get on, according to Jimmy Stanton. I don't suppose you've met Jimmy?' John said he hadn't. 'You've to realise, this place is more full o'gossip than a woman's knitting parlour. Bateman passes the tittle-tattle to his wife, and she confides in Jimmy, seeing as how they're both gardening wallahs. Jimmy and me get together over the occasional glass, and you're the privileged beneficiary.'

'What's the schoolmaster supposed to have done?'

'Story goes he's been gallivanting on the moor, letting the buggers run riot. Then there's been a few goings-on up at the School House. He's let the garden run riot for a start, which won't bode well with the boss, I can tell you.' Why did he feel the urge to take the younger man into his confidence? Perhaps his week-end adventures had loosened his tongue. 'I'll tell you something, young man, chance how much you're worth, you can spend the lot. Look at this place. It costs a fortune to keep up. The heating alone's more than your old man'll earn in a lifetime. They don't stint themselves, you know. They don't, by jingo. He's down London half the time, Jimmy reckons he's been and bought a house down Hyde Park from his pal Cooke.' He lowered his voice and looked towards the door. 'Truth be known, Cooke had as much a hand in what's through that window as Bateman, though I suppose he'll take the credit. You can't go carting tons o' rock about without paying a bob or two. That's one of the reasons he's got to move to a smaller place, I reckon. He's garden mad. What is it he wrote, *Orchidaceae of Mexico and Guatemala*? There'll be no orchids left in Mexico nor anywhere else, chance him and his pals have had their pick, they'll all be in the greenhouses down here. And this is not his only place, you know, not by a long chalk. Knype, the Old Hall and all the land between. Him and Heath, they own the air you breathe between them. I'm told he won't even entertain the idea of hybrids in his glasshouses. Not part of God's plan, according to him!'

An image of his employer in his britzka faded, and he forced a smile. 'Ah, well, neither of us might be here come next month. I reckon Heath'll take over this lot. He's the only one as can afford it.' He edged back in his seat. 'Wonder what he'll make of fifty humming birds and a load of Roman pots? Not our concern, Johnny, lad. We're just the hired help.' His cheeks flushed behind the wisps of beard as he rose with a clip of papers and went to the door. 'This place'd fall apart without me. I'm the one keeps it on an even keel, I do, that.'

He went, whistling, down the passage. John sat for a moment, sucking his pencil. Urias still hadn't returned when the office door opened and Bateman strode in. 'I suppose you've no idea of Mr Ball's whereabouts?'

'He said he had to attend to some business, Mr Bateman. Is there anything I can do?'

Bateman studied him for a minute. 'Mr Ball tells me your work is first rate. I shall put a word in at the right quarter when the time comes.... incidentally, he tells me you're fond of the gardens.'

John nodded enthusiastically, pleased his lie to Urias had borne fruit.

'They're splendid, Mr Bateman. I wish I knew all the plants in them.'

'Has Mr Ball said anything to you about the need to complete the inventory as a matter of urgency?'

'I came in early this morning to work on it, sir.'

Bateman gave a lop-sided smile. 'Perhaps he's mentioned your working with me this morning?'

'Sir?'

'We need an assessment of the grounds. Do you feel up to the task?'

'Certainly, sir.' He reached for his pad and followed his employer out to the terrace.

'Have you explored the gardens?'

'I wasn't sure it was allowed, sir. I knew there were public visits, but

I wasn't sure staff could take advantage.' He snapped back the cover.

'I see you're keen to make a start. Come, we'll begin by the lake.' When they reached the water's edge, Bateman put a hand on his shoulder. 'You'll have to indulge me if I bore you. What I say might help with the inventory. After we've finished you mustn't be afraid to ask the head gardener to go over any detail I've missed. The important thing is to get the information right.'

'I see that, sir.'

Bateman gazed across the lake. 'What you see has cost me a great deal of time and effort. I shall regret having to leave it. However, Mrs Bateman's health is delicate and the best cure for bronchitis is southern air.' John nodded gravely. 'Now, a friend and I set about devising a series of world gardens. What we have here is Italy, China, Egypt, Scotland, mountains and dells, valleys and caves; a temple, a tower, a Cheshire cottage. Exotic plants, all growing in their accustomed place, an image of the world in rock, leaf and water. D'you understand?'

'I'm sorry not to have taken the trouble before, sir.'

'Come,' said Bateman, briskly. 'Keep your pencil sharpened.'

A leaden band hung over the trees. The temperature had fallen, making the air damp and still. They entered Egypt through a pyramid of clipped yew. Stone Sphinxes guarded the entrance to the tunnel where the Ape of Thoth bathed in a ruby light. They came out below the Cheshire cottage on to a path flanked by cedar and chamaecyparis. Another tunnel led to thickets of rhododendron, a cleft in the rocks to a glen. They passed a stone frog, dragons cut from the turf, a gilded ox gazing across a pool of still water. Bateman pointed out the Great Wall of China, with its watch-tower and joss house.

'Of course, the plants are best in their season. They're still quite young. The maple over there, for instance. Acer Palmatum Rubrum. Nothing more beautiful. Copper red leaves, burnished with sunshine. Then we have our golden larches, bamboos and japonica - I won't trouble you with all their names. Then there's Thuja, Weigela, Juniper, Salix Purpurea Pendula, gold amid purple, red against green. Mr Stanton will help you with the spelling.'

'Could you tell me the depth of the water, Mr Bateman?'

'That's not important as far as the catalogue is concerned. You see the banks where the plants have been set? The men who dug out the lake made those mounds from the spoil. Very economic work, don't you think?'

John bent again to his writing. 'I'm taken by the stone frog, sir,' he said, as the Grange's façade rose again above the trees.

'You have Mr Waterhouse Hawkins to thank for that.' He gave a soft, inward laugh, as if at some private joke. 'Now you mustn't reveal this confidence, but I got the idea for my Chinese Temple from a book called *Wanderings in China*.'

John feigned a nod of interest, and gave an uneasy cough. 'If you'll excuse me, something's been nagging at me, Mr Bateman, and I don't know who to see about it... about gardens... about finding God's heart in a garden.'

'Well?'

'It feels like that, as if I were cut off from the outside world.'

'And what's the puzzle?'

'Maybe I should speak to the rector about it, whether God is in every leaf, even in the stone monsters, to ward off evil.'

'Like gargoyles on church spouts? It's something that hadn't struck me. If I could answer you in this way: God is the highest of all head gardeners. He created our natural world and ordered the plants in it. The flowerless plants, like ferns, he made early, so the coal they produced would be ready to serve man in due course. The orchids came later, to soothe man with their fragrance and beauty. It is certainly not as Mr Darwin would have us believe, that living things are there merely to suit their desire for survival. You need puzzle no further. God's heart in a garden is an excellent way of putting things.'

They were back on the terrace, and the band of grey cloud had grown more oppressive. John looked across at the path striking through the plantations. 'I think it's a pity more people can't be helped to see things like that, sir. In their education, I mean.'

'Oh, I'm sure now that the new boards have been set up, schoolmasters will be forging ahead with their instruction. Did you not learn your catechism at Moor Top?'

'When we had Mrs Gordon, sir.'

'Well, there you are.'

'But then it's not right to my mind sir, that the master doesn't believe. That was another thing I was puzzled about.'

'Which master?'

'The schoolmaster, sir, Mr Caulton.'

'You're saying Mr Caulton doesn't believe in God?'

'That's what he said to my brother, and I don't understand it. I'm sorry, Mr Bateman, I hope I'm not talking out of turn. I'll go and complete the inventory now you've shown me the grounds.'

He turned towards the office, but Bateman restrained him. 'He actually told your brother he was a non believer?'

'Yes, sir, unless our Charlie heard wrong.' His pained look intensified. 'I just thought it my Christian duty to pass on what I'd heard.'

'But how did your brother come to tell you this?'

'He wasn't speaking to me in particular, sir. He told my mother everything would go in time. Queen Victoria, even God. He said Mr Caulton had told the class.'

'I see.' Bateman plucked at his beard, running the straggly wisps through his fingers. 'Well, you've done the right thing in telling me this. Now you may go about your work.'

5

When Charlie had left, Caulton stood with his back to the fire, stretching himself.

'His mathematics is weak, but he writes with flair, and, of course, his art is outstanding.' He lit one of his small Havanas. 'If I can help him, I shall feel I've not laboured in vain.'

His wife looked up from her embroidery, remembering the letter which had arrived for him that morning. It was from Bateman. Would he favour them with his attendance at the Managers' Meeting on Wednesday at seven o'clock?

He squinted through the smoke. 'Wonder what's afoot?'

'I can't say, Harry. It can't be the registers, they're right enough now.'

'Since you've been doing them, you mean?' There was an edge to his voice which he regretted. His wife bent again to her frame, and he ran through his last weeks at school. 'It can't be the garden. It won't grow until spring, whatever Gordon ordains. I tell you, Luisa, this place has been a bad move for me. I'm beginning to wish we'd gone down to Devon.'

'Before you jump to conclusions, why not just turn up and see what it's about?'

'I bet it's the fowl again. I suppose they expect me to conjure up a buyer out of thin air.'

'Wait and see, Harry, there's a dear.'

'I'll tell you this, Luisa, if they think I'm someone to be pushed around like a station trolley, they're in for a big surprise.' A sudden smile lit his face, and he threw the remains of his cigar into the fire. 'In fact, I may be forced to abandon schoolmastering and try for something more ghoulish,' he said, baring his teeth to her neck.

He approached Bateman's house along the dimly-lit drive, and had an uncomfortable wait in the vestibule before the maid showed him into a room at the end of the passage. Each face but the rector's turned towards him as he went in. Bateman half rose and indicated a seat at the end of the table.

'Ah, Mr Caulton, a wretched night to bring you from your hearth. Perhaps if you hang your coat on one of the pegs?'

Apart from Bateman's show of courtesy, a chill hung over the room. The rector cleared his throat. 'Mr Caulton, I'll come straight to the point:

the managers wish to know the extent of your commitment to Moor Top School.'

'I'm not sure I understand.'

'The managers are aware of the correspondence that has passed between us. However, a more serious matter has come to our attention which we've asked you here to answer.'

'Then you'd better make me as wise as your good selves.'

'It's not a matter of wisdom, Mr Caulton; it concerns your religious commitment to the school.'

'My religious commitment?'

'Your belief in God, man,' chimed Bourne, with the moral intensity of the practising non-believer.

'I think I made my views plain at my interview.'

'And are we to take it they're unaltered since then?'

'You can take it how you will.'

'Now, Mr Caulton, perhaps if I could explain a little more fully what we're about,' Bateman said. 'We have a strong Christian ethos, and when you secured your post we were given to understand you were a believer. We are, of course, aware of your occasional attendance at church, and of your help with various choral activities alongside your wife.... the fact is, it has come to our notice that you have confessed atheism to a scholar.'

'I don't know where this so-called confession has come from, but I should think the word would have as little impact on my charges as on that clock, since for the most part they are unable to understand anything with more than a syllable to it.'

The rector looked sharply up. 'You have no call to be facetious, sir. You seem unable to grasp the effect such an allegation could have on your future here.'

'Who's made it?'

'It's not for us to tell you anything, young man,' Wilbraham said, his pale lips twitching, 'remember you're in our employ and we can terminate it whenever we've a mind.'

'I was under the impression the agreement was for three months on either side.'

'Ay, and more on ours than yours, if you persist in antagonising this table,' said Fallows. 'You've been asked a civil question. Are we to take it you're declining to answer?'

An angry buzz coursed through the room. Caulton sat, seething and immobile. Gordon addressed his linked fingers. 'Mr Caulton, there has in the past been some unpleasantness between us. You broke the terms of your agreement in respect of the garden, and you have only recently begun to mend your registers. I believe you are now coaching a pupil privately.'

'That is my concern, and since it is done without payment, opprobrium is the last thing I expect.'

'It is expressly stated in your agreement that scholars cannot be admitted into the schoolmaster's quarters.'

'I hope you're not suggesting anything untoward happened?'

'I'm suggesting, sir, that you'd do us a great favour - and yourself - if you'd answer the complaint against you. Do you deny the existence of God?'

Bateman stroked his beard. Gordon appraised Caulton in silence, his jaw set in an uncompromising line.

'If the God you represent is an ally of people like yourselves, then not only do I not believe in Him, I'm amazed He found the road to Calvary.'

The rector gave a sudden lurch. 'This is blasphemy. Mr Chairman, I believe we are entitled to demand this man's resignation as someone totally unfit to hold office here.'

'Please, Mr Caulton,' Bateman pleaded, uncomfortable at the eruption of hostility towards the schoolmaster, 'you do yourself no good.'

Caulton's face had set in a hard mask. 'I came to this school with the best of intentions. I work hard to little avail. We went out sketching, and even that small diversion is akin to sin. Does it really matter if bantams overrun the garden, or the nettles are ten feet high? Do I complain if the hovel you provide has peeling paper and rotting windows?'

'You'd only to ask –' began Bourne.

'And this religion, so narrow I'd be hard put to drive a pin through it. I have a religion. I have a belief. It's not the belief of one who feels it his Christian duty to flog children to within an inch of their lives. My belief is that the spirit exists in all living things, including your good selves, and can't be pinned down to cosy parochial chats. I believe the beauty of a butterfly's wing is more a testimony to the miracle of life than any artifice contrived by the Church. I believe in the sanctity of nature and the glory of a sunset. If you expect me to respect the notion of some benevolent Intelligence when men are treated worse than pit ponies and daily sent to their deaths at the hands of some Bismarck or other, then you expect too much.'

A buzzing silence followed his outburst. The clock's slow tick sounded loud in the room. He felt a great swell of ease within him, seemed to see their faces as through a distorting prism.

'Mr Caulton,' said Bateman, hesitantly, 'you will appreciate the difficulties you place us under. I speak for the table in asking for your resignation.'

'You won't get it.'

'It would be better for you to resign than for us to dismiss you.'

'On what grounds?'

'Your pantheistic beliefs will suffice,' the rector snapped.

'I repeat, my agreement was for three months either side.'

Wilbraham made a gesture with his hand. 'Mr Chairman, if I could be allowed a word? I think what this young man has told us warrants a prompt response. Forget the agreement, he's broken it. He should hand in his keys tonight. The sooner he goes the better.' He aimed his pencil at Caulton. 'I shouldn't like to think you were in charge of no son of mine.'

'If he were anything like his father, neither would I.'

Wilbraham's face seemed to swell with anger. 'I find you insolent, sirrah.'

The schoolmaster regarded him with indifference. Bateman made a faint gesture of reconciliation. 'Mr Caulton, would you be good enough to wait outside?'

The teacher left the room and stood with his back to the wall in the dim light. The moonlit wainscot glimmered down the passage, and he allowed his eyes to wander over the fuzzy outlines of paintings as voices rumbled faintly on the other side of the door. Yes, he'd bitten off his nose to spite his face. They'd be doing him a favour if they kicked him out. But they'd not break the agreement. They'd not wipe their feet on him.

A ribbon of light sprang across the tiles, and he went in. 'We've decided on a course of action,' Bateman said. 'We believe you should continue at a reduced quarterly fee for the next three months, at which time you are required to resign.'

'And what kind of reduced fee am I to expect?'

'You are entitled to the grant paid as part of your wage by the government. The manager's levy will not be forthcoming. We see no reason to alter our decision, particularly since the results of the examinations at the end of last term do not justify it.'

'So now we drop my religious beliefs and concentrate instead on my academic shortcomings.'

'We had no wish to bring them up,' the rector interjected. 'We are sensible of the fact you have only been with us a brief while, and...'

Caulton held up his hand as if to still a raging in his head. 'You are breaking an officially drawn up agreement and I shall take the matter further if you reduce my wage in any way. Since the quarterly fee was carried jointly by my wife and myself, you are also penalising a third party.' He reached for his coat. 'I shall leave you gentlemen to talk among yourselves. Any reduction in my wage over the next three months will secure your appearance in court. And don't think I'm not in earnest. In the meantime I shall look for other employment. I'll let myself out.'

They listened in silence to his fading footsteps. The vestibule door clanged shut. Fallows tattooed the table with his pencil. 'Well, what's to do now?'

Bateman took comfort from the knowledge that a buyer had been found for the Grange. By the time anything came of this Caulton affair, he'd be far away.

It was a bright Sunday in spring, and church bells pealed faintly from the valley. Bill took a path through the fields and thought over his decision as he walked. He'd spend no more than a year on the moor, then he'd go to America. He'd need more money, and there was more to be made in the pit than in attending to Benersley's sturks. He couldn't pretend the situation between Dixon and himself would improve, but they were setting on again and there was a chance that if enough men were needed, Dixon might relent. He stopped for a quart at Brindley before taking the lane to Whitfield. When he knocked on Dixon's door, a woman he hadn't seen before answered.

'He's not lived here close on three months. I was going to say you'll find him up the chapel, but he'll have gone back by now. He lives down Hesketh Lane – he's left us for the nobs.'

It took Bill twenty minutes to reach the house she'd named, and it wasn't what he expected. A flash of surprise showed in Dixon's face as he answered the door.

'Morning, George. I heard they were setting on again. I've come about a job.'

'Sorry, I can't help.'

Bill put his foot against the door as it swung to. 'There's something else. Something concerning a mutual acquaintance by the name of Cowlishaw.'

The butty hesitated, then pulled open the door. Bill followed him into a large parlour, with good quality furniture arranged around a Winton square. 'Looks as if you've come up in the world, George.'

'Say what you came to say.'

'Was it Jud Cowlishaw fed you that line about me and your wife?'

'You'll leave her out of it.'

'You mean you've not asked her the truth of it?' Bill sensed he'd hit a raw nerve, and tried for a more conciliatory tone. 'Look, what you tell your wife's your own concern, I aren't bothered either way. What I came here for is work, but you need to know about Cowlishaw as well. He was the one told you the cock and bull story, wasn't he?'

Dixon's eyes narrowed. 'What d'you know of him?'

'Let's say I met him and leave it at that. Look, if Jud fed you scandal, he did it for his own benefit, not yours. Bloody hell, George, who cares? All I want to do is use a pick.'

Dixon dropped his voice. 'Trouble is, he's no longer here to tell us any different, is he?'

'See reason, for Christ's sake. The man was feeding you a line. Get your wife in here and confront her with it. It's a load o' lies from top to bottom.'

'I've told you, leave my missus out of it.'

Bill fought against a rising anger, and he was about to speak when his eyes fell on the expensive swirls under his feet. An idea erupted with such force it swept his gaze from the carpet to Dixon's thick-skinned face as if seeing it for the first time.

'*It was you.*'

'What was me?'

'This place. All this lot. It was you. You stole Cowlishaw's money.'

'You're not making sense.'

'I must've been blind. You're down Whitfield in a two up, two down, hardly a stick to your name and suddenly you're living like gentry. You helped yourself to his bloody cash!'

In a low voice Dixon said: 'How come you know so much about all this so-called money? It couldn't be you were after rich picking's yourself, could it? Maybe more than one was seeking something to his gain. I can't think of names off the top of my head, but it could be a stroke of luck, who's to say?'

'Folk might be interested as to how a collier can afford all this for a start,' Bill said, his heat dying as he saw his advantage slipping away. 'Butties don't usually run to frills and fancies.' Dixon wouldn't know a chair from a pit-prop. What had he told his wife? How much did Cowlishaw have in the clock? Enough for all this? He should have taken the lot when he'd had the chance. 'What did you tell your wife, George?'

Dixon took a step forward. 'I've nothing to bother myself about with you, Tanbrey. You know nothing, you can prove nothing. Don't come again.' He flicked Bill's waistcoat with the back of his hand, like a tailor pleased with his handiwork. 'If you try to meddle in my business again, they'll be fishin' you out of the brook.' He threw a smile. 'Find another pit if you've a mind. Don't come here again.'

A sound made him turn. His wife was standing in the doorway.

'Is everything all right, George?'

'Perfectly fine,' Dixon beamed, draping his arm around Bill's shoulders. 'I was just showing Mr Tanbrey out.'

'Your mother says she heard voices.'

'Tell her it were a spot o' pit talk.'

She hesitated, then walked away. On the step Dixon turned to Bill. 'Take my advice and stay on the moor.' He opened the door, revealing a shillelagh which lay against the wall.

'I'll bide my time, George. Don't fret, I'll bide my time.'

The butty stood on the threshold until the younger man had passed from view.

Urias looked at his watch. The afternoon train was ten minutes late, and he greeted the distant plume with relief. A fellow passenger might have taken him for a clerk, or a family man from one of the villas thrusting into the countryside around Congleton or Macclesfield. He hid behind his copy of the *Times*, thinking about the delights awaiting him on his arrival at Manchester but trying to concentrate on the jogging lines: Disraeli, Victoria, Ireland, South Africa, Suez – the words drifted across the page, ousted by thoughts of Pol. As the train drew into London Road Station, he tossed the paper aside, hailed a cab, climbed inside and considered his good fortune. The previous week it had been confirmed that Robert Heath would indeed take over the Grange, and true to his word Bateman had agreed with the new owner that Urias and John be kept on. And office skills weren't the only ones he was good at, he tittered, as he browsed through the smut-smeared window at a waif huddled in the Exchange doorway. Yes, he'd fared better than many, but it was no more than he deserved.

He halted the cab outside the Barton Arcade and handed the cabbie a tip. Glancing furtively about, he set off in the direction of Castlefield. Pushing through the crowds streaming into the city, he crossed the road into a labyrinth of back streets and turned into the gateless entrance of a villa. The door opened before he rang and a middle-aged woman came out to greet him, her tight red curls exposing the scalp at the root of each tuft.

'Mr Blank, so nice to see you again.'

'Nice to be here, my dear.'

'She's upstairs waiting for you, same place as always.'

She turned into her room and a half-drunk gin. The place had an air of dingy grandeur. Framed prints hung from the faded wallpaper, which bore a tide-mark following the line of the stairs. A passage led off at the top, and he bent his ear to a door before giving his knock.

'Urias!' Pol opened her arms to him with feigned enthusiasm. Her chemise had fallen open, revealing the charms he'd travelled thirty miles to see. She led him to the couch. 'How's my saucy boy?'

'Very well, thank you.'

'Good. Well, first a little brandy, then naughty Mr Blank and his Pol is going to have some fun.'

She dug him playfully in the ribs, then poured him a generous measure. He was beginning to sweat. An iron bed stood under the window, a decorated bowl and ewer on the commode. On a shelf sat a carrara venus, above it a sampler. For six years she'd made her living selling flowers outside the Peter Street Music Halls. A friend had suggested there were other things she could do which paid more, so Pol, taking note of her unsupported breasts and well-turned legs, took her advice. Her body was greatly appreciated by those who could afford it and Urias, dribbling with anticipation, was one of her monthly regulars, money in hand. As he drank he ran his pudgy hand over her crotch.

'Now, give yourself time,' she chided him, 'none of your naughty games until you're nice and relaxed.'

He drained his glass and pulled her on to his knee. Her gown had fallen across the couch in gauzy waves, and she smiled down at him, her auburn hair framing her startled grey eyes. She was plumper now, but her thighs were as firm as alabaster. He let his glass fall and drew his wet lips across her cheek as he moved his hand to the hem of her gown, bunching it up until he was wrapped in the material like a seaside photographer. He tore at her drawers, ripping the fabric and kissing her half-exposed breasts. She went through a moaned repertoire as he extricated himself, making a note to add the cost of new underwear to his bill. In less than a minute it was over. He toppled like a rag doll to the couch and fumbled his wilted manhood back into his trousers. Pol helped him with his jacket as a tap on the door announced tea. She lit his cigar, and he leaned back into the cushions, his small eyes travelling appreciatively over her body.

'I've had a right week, my dear. The gardener's been off sick and we're up to our neck in grass.' Pol gave a pout of consolation. 'I've got a good man in the manager, mind. He keeps everything on an even keel. And that lad he set on's shaping up, though I can't say I altogether trust him.'

She toyed with his thinning hair. 'It must grind you into the ground, keeping your estate on the go. How many acres did you say you got?'

'Nigh on three hundred, with woods and farmland. And I'm hoping to acquire a bit more before the year's out.'

'You'll have to take me to see it some time.'

'The wife won't be best pleased.'

Pol chuckled along with him. Urias Blank! One of her most able performers, a Mr Wilfred Price, had told her he worked for the *Manchester Evening News*. She'd found out he was a bishop, who used to pray for forgiveness before sex. She tried to prolong Urias's delusions and handed him another drink. Soon, he attempted to lift her on to the bed, but his legs crumpled. She spread herself luxuriously on the sheet. He struggled out of his shirt, trousers and drawers. He was slower this time and grew flaccid. Eventually he came with a grunt and drifted off to sleep with his short, hairy arm across her stomach. She extricated herself, dressed, and looked disinterestedly down into the empty street. As he was leaving, he pressed a week's wage into her hand and kissed her wrist.

'Very debonair, Urias.' She gave a knowing wink and opened a drawer. 'Here's a present for you to remember me by. No need to look at it now. Keep it till you get home. It'll show you what you're missing.'

He slid it into his pocket and went downstairs. When he'd gone, she sponged herself down. He treated himself to roast veal at the Sawyer's Arms and caught the train back. The light was fading as he opened the envelope and drew out a photograph of a naked girl poised against a pillar. At the bottom was a scrawled message: 'Many kisses for Urias, from your own Polly.'

He sat contentedly back, blind to the fact that Pol was keeping her options open.

'He wants to see you,' Urias told John the following Monday.

John tapped his papers straight and went to Bateman's room. A harsh morning light flooded the passage and the exhibition cases alongside the wall. Urias, who'd overslept and missed his breakfast, threw his coat over a chair and followed him.

Bateman and another man were seated by a dull fire.

'Where's Mr Ball?' Bateman inquired.

'He's coming directly, sir.'

The owner nodded and continued a conversation he'd begun before John arrived. John studied the other man, his side whiskers, strong nose, the alert eyes under their pouched lids. There was a hardness about his mouth, with the thick lower lip thrust defiantly out from a firm chin. A second knock sounded, and the manager stepped in.

'Ah, Mr Ball, I won't keep you long. I expect you already know Mr Heath?'

'Certainly, Mr Bateman.' Urias held out his hand. 'I swear I've never heard bells peal like them you donated to the church, Mr Heath.'

'I thought you should meet your new employer,' Bateman was saying. 'I'm sure you'll wish to thank him for having retained your services in these straitened times.'

'I'm sure Mr Heath knows we're in his debt. And I'm sure Master

John, here –'

'Pleased to meet you, sir,' John interrupted.

A flicker of amusement sparked in Heath's eyes. 'Where're you from?'

'Moor Top, sir.'

Heath turned to Bateman. 'He's not much of a Moor wallah in speech is he, Jim?'

'I think young John's taking pains to improve himself,' Bateman said.

Urias, irked at being excluded, consoled himself with comparisons. The two richest men in the locality stood there, Heath richer than Bateman now, with his coal and ironstone mines linked by private railway lines. Yet, thought Urias, he, Urias Ball, had kept Bateman ticking, just as he would Heath. He was indispensible.

'Can I make so bold as to ask when you'll be moving in, Mr Heath?' he asked.

'Shortly, I dare say.'

After a moment's strained silence, Bateman said: 'Well, John, we won't keep you from your duties. Urias, if you can outline your responsibilities, Mr Heath will have a clearer idea of the way we run things at the Grange – not, perhaps, the way Mr Heath might wish to run them....'

John closed the door and went back to the office. He sat for a time wondering about the new master. He'd ingratiated himself with Bateman – could he do the same with Heath? He picked up a sheet from the sales catalogue and ran his eye down the entries: the Rhododendron Ground, the Pinetum, Glen and Stumpery, the parterres and all the other areas of Bateman's domain. As he read, his mood changed, and he screwed the sheet into a ball and threw it across the desk. He looked around at the rows of ledgers and the hissing stove and the reality of his own position hit him. He was no more than an office lackey, slaving for a pittance while they drank port upstairs. Going over to the cupboard, he ladled a spoonful of tea into the chipped pot. It was then he saw the envelope by Urias' chair. It must have fallen out of his pocket in his morning rush. He picked it up and took out the photograph. The only nudes he'd seen before were the bronze nymphs on his mother's commode. Pol was no bronze nymph, and she was smiling up at him. Reading the line at the bottom, he felt the threads of his life begin to twist. He put the photograph back in its envelope and let it drop, then changed his mind and slid it into his coat pocket.

Jacobs spoke through the wisps rising from his tea mug. 'Been a spot of bother your way of late.'

'How d'you mean, Jack?' Will asked.

'Trouble with the schoolmaster, I'm told.'

'I've heard nothing of it.'

'According to the wife he's suing the school managers, reckons they're underpayin' him.'

'It's the first I've heard of it. Where's she got it from?'

Jack pulled on his cap. 'She's picked it up from some woman works for Hand, the attorney.' Will joined him at the door. An old grey stood in the sorting shed, its nose in a feed bag. Jack said: 'I can't see as he can sue Bateman. I've heard he'll be gone by this week.'

The tunnel swallowed the pool of summer light. Will bunched his muffler to his throat and followed the other man into the darkness.

From his room, Bateman looked down at their familiar faces. Urias stood at the end, the gardener next to him in his canvas apron and leather gaiters. Bateman noticed that John hung back from the rest. Perhaps he should have paid them more, but he hadn't enough to indulge everyone who came to his door, and now it would shortly belong to Robert Heath. Soon his gardens would be hidden behind the deodars and redwoods he'd had shipped in from the far side of the globe. His son John was comfortably settled at Brightlingsea, Rowland had taken up missionary work in the Punjab, Robert had already exhibited at the Royal Academy. Then there was Katharine, after whom a white clematis had been named. Katharine and her barrister husband, all settled, all well....

His wife stood at the door, waiting. 'Are you ready, James?'

He followed her into the vestibule. Most of their effects had already been auctioned. Their London home would be much smaller. They'd given some thought as to what to take and had at last agreed that space be found for his hummingbirds. As they went out into the sunshine, his hands closed on an envelope in his pocket.

The housekeeper smiled. 'Well, sir, we trust you'll have a pleasant journey. Looks set for a fine day.'

'You'll have no problems on that score,' Stanton said, priming Bateman's hand like a water pump.

'You'll have to send us a letter, make sure you've arrived in one piece,'

Urias threw in, causing a flurry of exaggerated laughter, 'care of Mr Heath, that is.'

There followed a chorus which Bateman rode, holding up his hand to cries of 'Speech!'

'You had all the speeches you're likely to get last night,' he said, referring to an earlier celebration. 'I'd just like to say that Mrs Bateman and I will not forget your kindness to us over the years, and we trust your future under Mr Heath will be just as agreeable. At Urias' suggestion I shall write to Mr Heath in due course and he will no doubt let you know how we're faring at Hyde Park Gate.'

'And you must stand up for your marvellous garden and not allow Stanton to start ripping everything to pieces,' Bateman's wife quavered, overcoming her reluctance to speak. 'Tell him to jolly well leave it alone.'

As Bateman followed his wife into the waiting landau, John kept in the background. The place already seemed nothing more to him than walls and pretty gardens, and as the noise of wheels faded, so did the Batemans. He saw instead the dominant figure of the new owner. He had Pol's picture safely hidden and Urias, who'd never hinted at having lost anything, would help him along. He went back into the house before the rest, and it was some time before Urias returned to the office. John looked up from his desk as the manager came in.

'What do you know of Heath, Mr Ball?'

'It all depends what you want to find out.'

'Is he as well off as Bateman was?'

'A sight richer, I should think. And he married well, like they all do. Her family owned a pot-bank.'

John absorbed the facts expressionlessly. As Bateman handed his letter to the coachman to post before catching the London train, Urias warmed to his subject.

Caulton went over the correspondence he hoped would prepare him for his case, to be heard at the County Court later that year. He'd committed the letters from Francis Gordon to memory, and there were copies of his own letters to the rector and one to Bateman informing him of 'certain charges the rector has preferred affecting my reputation'. There were copies of his letters to the managers in which he'd made clear he'd been advised not to accept any reduction in salary and that he'd claim whatever money was due to make up the deficit. Hasty sorting had left other papers mixed with the correspondence, including one from Gordon's gardener, stating that the garden was in a poorer condition since Caulton took it over, and that 'the large number of fowls he kept have eaten every herb and flower left.' And now the letter from Bateman, delivered earlier that day:

'Dear Caulton,

I hoped you could be dissuaded from proceeding with any legal activities in respect of the reduction in your salary which the managers have proposed. Whilst I realise you feel you have been unfairly treated, I do beg you to reconsider this action since there must be a strong possibility you will lose your case and not only will you have to find a considerable sum, but your future will be blighted no matter what the outcome. My advice is that you resign your position and seek employment elsewhere. You can rely on me to furnish you with any references.

I write this note in a private capacity and no one but yourself is aware of its contents. I now have nothing at stake in the matter and the reason for this letter resides purely in my hopes for your welfare. I am convinced that you are, at heart, a Christian, though there are others who would adopt a less charitable view. I beg you therefore, for your wife's sake as much as your own, to seek an end to this matter and to resign your post in good faith.

I remain your obedient servant,
James Bateman
Hyde Park Gate, Wednesday'

Caulton folded the letter with his other correspondence. The thing had gone too far now. There was only one place where the right of the matter could be addressed, and if he were unsuccessful it would confirm the opinion he'd already formed of the place he'd had the misfortune to choose for a living. They'd have to sue for costs. He wouldn't be able to pay and he had nothing of value to sell. Hand had said he'd a good chance of winning. Others hoped he'd lose. What were they but nobodies from a town of back-to-backs. At least he'd expose them. They wouldn't enjoy a muck-rake through the local paper. He'd go down flags flying if he had to.

The next day the County Court required him to produce 'all books, letters, writings and documents relating to the matter in question'. For a moment his resolution deserted him, and he felt an overwhelming urge to be free of it all. Telling his wife he was going for a walk, he put on his old jacket and shut the door on his worries. The sun was warm on his face, and a soft breeze drew mares' tails across the sky. He followed them, whistling. As he passed the rectory he raised his hat to Mrs Gordon, who acknowledged him by drawing the curtain. Cupping his hands to a vespa, he lit his small cigar. As the village fell behind, his mood grew lighter, and his heart sang to the tom-tits flitting through the hedgerow and the air that danced with the scents of summer.

6

Ellen watched Bevis go over to the sheds where Bill was working. Seeing Bill disturbed her, and she'd become aware of an awakening interest when he was around. She caught Doris looking at her, spilt some elderberry juice and mopped it with her apron.

'You'll be spilling the rest if you don't hold it right. I think you should be keeping the house tidy, time enough for other things later.'

She went out, leaving Ellen to go to her room. The cheval picked up the brightness from the window, and she stood before it, studying her body, fanning her hair into a peacock's tail. She pouted and pushed out her small breasts, admiring her profile as the men's voices rose through the glass. She hoisted her dress tentatively to her thighs, running her fingers across the taut skin. A growing warmth brushed her stomach, and the farm sounds faded into silence.

'Ellen?'

She spun around. 'Charlie! What're you doing here?' She tugged her dress straight, her face on fire as he stood silent in the doorway. 'You've no right to come creeping up on folk like that, you gave me a right turn.'

'Your mam told me you'd be upstairs.'

'You've no business in my room. Anyway, what're you going to do now you've found me?'

'I thought -' he began, but the distance between them yawned. He held out a shrivelled bag. 'Would you like some toffee?'

She peeled her laugh, and his spirits rose. 'I'd better watch my teeth or I won't look beautiful no more.' She dipped into the bag. 'Tell you what, let's go and pick a bunch o' flowers.'

Nat was scraping at a crust of manure which caked the farmyard, and he looked up briefly as they passed. 'He's getting worse,' she said cheerily. 'Dad says he can't see no hope, and neither can anyone else, either.'

'Can he read?'

'He's a job to speak, let alone fiddle with letters. He likes looking at pictures, though. He's got one he likes special, he's always studying it.'

'What is it?'

'It's an imp dancin' on a haystack in the dead o' night. Fancy him liking that! It's nowt but a story-book picture – and Nat, getting to be a grown man.'

They pushed through the stile. Unripe berries hung in clusters against the thorns. 'I've still got the penny.'

'And has it brought you luck yet?'

'Well, it's brought me nothing bad.' He struggled for something else to say, adding: 'I'm having private lessons an' all.'

'Who from?'

'Mr Caulton.'

'My, maybe that's your luck. Maybe you're cut out to be a man o' letters.'

'What's that?'

'You can bet it's something important.'

The hardened ruts made walking hazardous. They continued across a strip of untended land. The air seemed bathed in a luminous green.

'What were you doing in your bedroom, Ellen?'

'If you must know, I was looking for ringworm.'

'I thought you got that in your hair.'

'You can get it anywhere. Hey, Charlie, maybe that's it! Maybe you're going to be a doctor and cure the ringworm.' She pushed under a canopy of leaves. A marshy pond with sides of weathered clay lay hidden in an arabesque of roots. Forget-me-nots clouded the slope, and beyond, creamy drifts of meadowsweet.

'Go on, Charlie, pick us some flowers.'

He plunged into the dappled shade where campion grew while she looked towards the byres. 'We've got a fair lot between us now, Charlie. All them forget-me-nots, shepherd's purse and whatnot. The only thing missing's ragwort, and they're like weeds in our field. We have to take'em out 'cos the beasts get sick if they eat them. Just pick us a daisy or two from near the wall.'

'It's a marguerite.'

'It's an ox-eye.'

'It's got another name.'

'What business have lads with flowers, anyway? I bet your Bill doesn't know a heartsease from a buttercup.'

She smiled at a game going well. In the shed, Bill finished rolling out the rest of the churns, stripped to the waist and sluiced himself under the pump. The shock knocked out his breath, and he felt the heat drain from him. He caught Ellen looking at him and grinned. Bevis called to him.

Would he help get the Angus out of the stall? It had been brought in to service the herd and had to be returned to pasture.

'You'll need to keep tight hold on him. Put the stick in his nose from the other stall while I pull him out. Have you dealt with one o' these before?'

'Can't say I have.'

'Well, they're crafty buggers.' Benersley exhaled wearily and passed Bill a length of hickory. Bill brought his eyes to the level of the bull's and probed the animal's snout. The head reared irritably and he tried again, capturing the ring and twisting the stick. 'Got him?'

'I reckon so.'

Benersley pushed the bull's forehead with the flat of his hand. It took a step back, flicking its tail and spinning Bill's arm upwards. 'He's coming. Keep your stick straight.' The bull began to nod, slow sweeps of its head from roof to floor as the farmer reddened his palm against its flanks. 'When he comes out lead him up the field and he'll follow you like a lamb.'

Bill struggled to grip the rod with his sweating hands. 'I wouldn't mind swapping places, Bevis. It's not something I'm used to.'

Benersley's eyes lit with amusement. 'All right, I can't have you in the mire. Come round and we'll swap.'

The bull emerged at the end of the farmer's arm and stood impassively facing the end of the shippon. He twisted the stick, bending the bull's head towards the gate in an effort to drive it out. 'It wants a kick up the arse.' Bill slapped its haunches. 'Bang it again. Come out, damn you!'.

The animal let out a bellow and began to hoof the floor, dipping its head and wrenching the stick from Benersley's grasp. As he bent to pick it up the horns thrust upwards without warning and he was momentarily aware of flight, then a drawn thread of silence. Charlie heard the commotion and looked across at the byre. Nat stumbled towards them, his mouth ugly and mobile. Ellen broke into a run, Charlie at her heels. As they reached the door, the bull ran out and Ellen halted them by the wall, the forgotten flowers dangling from her hand. 'Get down, Nat. Down!' She held tight to his shoulder as the bull careered through the vegetable patch.

They found Bevis by the wall, Bill fanning the farmer's face with his cap. 'Charlie, tell the missus there's been an accident.' He reared back helplessly. 'The beast threw him clean across the shippon, I never saw the like, one minute he's got it by the ring, next bang against the wall.'

Doris pushed through, her skirt flecked with straw. Dropping to her knees, she reached for Benersley's hand. 'Ee, lad, what've you been up to now?' He tried to speak, but his breath came in whispers and he lay still, like a discarded sack. 'Come on, wake up, open your eyes.'

'I'll get a blanket,' Ellen said.

As they reached the door, the farmer's eyes blinked open. He slowly focused on his wife, then the boy. 'Charlie, isn't it?'

'Yes, that's Charlie, and this is our Nat. You know Nat, don't you? Ellen's gone for a blanket.'

'Where - where's..?'

'You've taken a tumble. It's nothin' to worry about. Look, here's Ellen now.'

She wrapped him as best she could and stroked back his hair.

'I'll get the doctor.' Bill saddled Benersley's horse and rode off. When he got back the farmer was sitting blanketed in his armchair, puffing his pipe. The doctor pronounced a lucky escape. The horn had lodged under the belt of Bevis's trousers, winding him and bruising his stomach. He'd struck the wall and his cap, miraculously in place, had saved his skull. Yet despite the assurance, the fall had knocked something besides breath out of him.

When Charlie awoke, the sun was streaming through his bedroom window. He dressed hurriedly and went downstairs. His mother wasn't there, and he wondered if she'd gone down to the hens. But in place of his breakfast bowl he found a scrap of paper on which she'd scrawled a message: Gone to Three Elms.

He was late, and the class was busy with recitation when he got in. Caulton directed him with a nod to his desk and continued to conduct the group with his ruler.

On either side the river lie
Long fields of barley and of rye
That clothe the wold and meet the sky
And thro' the field the road runs by
To many towered Camelot
And up and down the people go
Gazing where the lilies blow

Round an island there below
The island of Shalott

'The muse is on us today,' he told them.'No doubt Mr Tennyson will soon make a point of visiting the school.'

A rare tranquillity had settled on them and he wondered if it had anything to do with the weather. He returned to the poem, this time marking the rhythm with his cane. 'Now that is what a poem should be, full of romance and mystery, throwing rainbows into the mind. Think of it, a knight in magic lands, his golden helmet aflame in the setting sun.' He doubted they could see further than the mullions. The anticipated din came when writing began, and he struggled as always to subdue it until the bell clanged, and he came over to Charlie.

'I've something to tell you.' The boy looked up at him, caught the chestnut streak in the clipped moustache. 'Mrs Caulton and I will shortly be leaving Moor Top. Have you ever been to Devon, Charlie? A magnificent county. Sea top and bottom, and a pleasanter climate than hereabouts.' He hesitated a moment. 'The place is Bideford. It's famous for its bridge. I've not seen the school yet, but I'm told it was built for the sons of gentlefolk, in other words money folk.' He laughed lightly as one shout or another rang out from the playground.

'I hope you do alright, sir.'

'You must practice hard, especially your painting. Try not to waste yourself.'

'No, sir.'

Caulton turned away and began to clean the board with a scrap of flannel. 'In a sense, the decision was not of my making.'

'I've heard about the court,' Charlie ventured, overcoming his embarrassment that the schoolmaster should confide in him.

'Oh, from whom?'

'I heard my dad talk about it.'

'What else do you know?'

'Nothing else, sir.' The master rubbed the chalk dust from his hands and gazed through the window at the greying sky. The wind began to sough against a wall. 'I did hear something, sir.'

Caulton asked what, his face still turned away.

'My father was asking our John questions. I thought he said something about religion.'

'Your brother, he was working for Mr Bateman, wasn't he?'

'He's in the office, sir.'

'And he mentioned my religious beliefs? Strange.'

'I aren't sure what was said. I didn't think it was important.'

'And neither is it, Charlie. Not now, at any rate.'

They fell silent, but an echo of something said lodged in Caulton's mind. He struggled to recall it but gave up and turned instead to the impending court hearing and his luck at receiving the letter from an old friend offering him a job at the Bideford school. The ways of the Almighty were indeed mysterious. The Almighty.... *Now he had it*! Sickle and quern.... all things would end.... the Empire, perhaps even God. That was it! It was there he'd said it, to the class. He began to laugh. The boy looked up, startled.

'I must congratulate you Charlie, you lost me my job,' He laughed again, dabbing at his tear-stained eyes, 'but take heart, I'm sure you meant nothing by it. You don't know what I'm talking about, do you?' He moved to his high desk and began to tidy the contents. 'It doesn't matter. Think of my departure as an accident of fate and all for the best.' He brushed at his sleeve. The bell began to clang. 'You've missed your break. Do you want to pay a private visit to the lavvies?'

As he went off, Caulton reversed the blackboard to show Sir Lancelot in coloured chalks. 'The Lady of Shalott. And how does brave Sir Lancelot find his way into our tale? If you care to listen.... if you care to listen carefully, you might be as wise as myself. Stop this bedlam. Stop it at once!'

The sky paled with the coming autumn. Heath had begun to refurbish his new home, and to make plans to re-route the road which skirted the grounds.

'Best be on your mettle now,' Urias told John. 'He's got the energy of a lion, has Heath. Don't run away with the idea he's another Bateman. This bugger hasn't had the edges knocked off. The only trouble is, he expects everybody else to put in a thirty hour day, like himself. That's not likely, seeing as I'm only earning in a year what he picks up in a day.'

At the end of October, Heath told John he could take next Saturday morning off with pay, since he and his family had a function to attend in London. Once he'd got over his surprise, John decided to do something he'd been wanting to do since he found Pol's photograph. In the afternoon, when Urias was waiting at Congleton Station, he didn't notice a figure by the crossing gate. When the Manchester train came in, John got into an empty compartment. He remained in his seat at London Road, watching the manager make his way towards the station exit. When he was sure he wouldn't be seen, he left the carriage and trailed him. The traffic through Piccadilly was slow and it wasn't difficult to keep Urias's cab in view.

The manager alighted at the Barton Arcade and set out on foot, John following at a distance. Much of Deansgate was being rebuilt, and a constant thud of machinery accompanied him up the street. As the crowds thinned he hung back, occasionally dodging into the doorways of shops which hadn't yet been swept away. He felt a growing excitement as he saw Urias cross the road, and quickened his pace. Waiting for a wagon to pass, he crossed into Liverpool Road. Newly-built warehouses rose amid soot-blackened older buildings and railway lines. He began to hurry. A narrow road led off to the right, and he caught sight of Urias at the corner and followed him quickly, reaching the end a few seconds later. Now the manager was less than fifty yards in front, walking more assuredly, with none of the wary half-turns he'd made on the main road. John hid behind a hay cart and watched him pass into a cul-de-sac. Almost at the bottom he climbed a short flight of steps and disappeared through a part-open door. John waited a minute, then followed, continuing directly past the house. An entry led from the cul-de-sac back to the main road. Taking out a notebook and pencil, he jotted down 'Back Sage Street' and the house number, watched by a girl holding a hoop.

'What district is this?'

'It's Manchester, mister.'

'I know that. What's this part called?'

She began to clatter her hoop over the cobbles. He caught what he thought was Castlefield and wrote it down.

There was no need to hurry back. He spent some time watching bargees unload coal by the Rochdale Canal amid the thunder of wagons along the viaduct, then retraced his steps through Deansgate. Hackneys wove between the carts, and the stench of manure filled the air. He turned into St Mary's Gate, where the Exchange towered above Georgian houses which had survived the demolition and continued through narrow thoroughfares to emerge in Albert Square. He found himself marching,

marching in pride to the music of life pulsing about him. Ignore beggars under the empty terrace, the crones at their handcarts. Here was the future. His future. He turned back at last, past the Portland Street warehouses and the Piccadilly Infirmary, with its statues of Peel and Wellington. Reaching the station in a bouyant mood, he spent his last penny at the buffet.

In the evening, he sat at his diary. Putting down his pen, he rubbed at his ink-stained finger and recalled the article he'd read in the paper. Caulton's court appearance represented his first success. Because of him, Caulton had been called to the manager's meeting. He was the reason for the reduction in the schoolmaster's salary which had brought about the court action and now Caulton had lost the case. Cutting out the clip, he pasted it into his diary, blotted his entry and locked the book away.

Some time earlier, the rector had scrutinised the same article. Caulton had been obliged to pay legal costs, of course, but where on earth would he find the money? He should never have appointed him. Caulton had misled the managers as to his professed belief and had justly suffered. Gordon had given the matter a great deal of thought. He still had his notes to support the managers' case, written in his own shorthand. The court had called upon him to reveal the facts of the matter. Fallows, Wilbraham and Bourne had remained silent during the hearing as a letter was read, sent by Bateman from London, citing ill-health as a reason for his non-attendance. The rector had expected the case to be adjourned, but the magistrate had ruled otherwise. As he reflected on the triumph of truth over duplicity, his spirits rose. Taking a sheet from his bureau, he wrote a brief note:

'My Dear Bateman,

I trust this finds you in good health, and that Mrs Bateman finds your new life to her taste. The main point in writing this is to inform you that Caulton has lost his case, and will need to find eighty guineas. I am sure he could have spared himself this burden by adopting an attitude more fitting his profession, or he could have resigned honourably, with none of the stigma he has brought upon himself. I doubt he has private means, neither do I know where he will find employment when his agreement expires. No doubt he will reflect more seriously on any action of the kind in future.

As far as I am aware, Mr Heath has settled well at the Grange, although I must confess I'm disappointed that he hasn't followed yourself as Chair of the School Committee. I'm sure your son is quite up to the task, however, and has conducted his first business in a most workmanlike manner. I believe he, too, intends a move shortly, so we may be forced to look again for a Chair. Little else changes here, and I look forward to news from Hyde Park Gate.

Until then, I remain your humble friend

Francis'

He blotted the note and sat back. As if to still a nagging doubt, he took another sheet and wrote a second note, this time to Caulton:

'Dear Mr Caulton,

Will you please do me the favour of leaving your keys with the caretaker not later than noon on the day of your departure?' He was about to sign, when a lingering sense of charity forced him to add: 'May you find employment elsewhere to your liking. My regards to your wife and yourself.

Yours Faithfully,

Rector.'

The last words came uneasily to him, but he brushed them aside and sealed the flap.

Caulton had left Hand's office a worried man. The fact the magistrate was a friend of Wilbraham's had proved a bad omen. The only shred of comfort was that he'd been given six months in which to find costs. The agreement maintained three months right of dismissal, but said nothing of the right to reduce salary, a technicality for which he must pay. He'd been given notice to quit, and welcomed it. Luisa had stood by him, and the Devon job had come miraculously out of nowhere. It was simply a case of money. He cursed himself for his stubbornness. He cursed himself for having taught there at all. Gordon had the right idea. Cane with catechism. Anything less was weakness. He'd thought he could do something different, and his idealism had tripped him up. But there was Charlie, at least. Why shouldn't he have coached the lad in the privacy of his own quarters? Another rule broken, another veto.

Talking to himself helped lift the gloom which had fallen on him since the trial. On an impulse he pushed open a pub door. Settling in the empty snug, he grew more optimistic. He ordered another drink, and when he left his debt had become a fleeting annoyance. He smiled to himself as he began to climb the hill. Had it been wrong to admit misgivings about the kind of creator the rector wished him to believe in? Had it been wrong to hint his beliefs to the class, for Charlie to pass them on until they came to rest in Bateman's ear? Could anything anyone said be wrong if the sayer believed it to be true? He wondered if there would still be time for such musings in a hundred years, when men's lust for goods had gouged the greenness from the land and the land itself had ceased to exist. When he reached Moor Top, he felt uncomfortably hot. He tipped his hat to a passer-by, wishing the days gone so he could be rid of the place. He immediately announced to his wife his intention to invite the Tanbreys to a farewell meal.

'But Harry, we can't afford it. What about the costs of court?'

'What of them? They can wait, wait and whistle.'

He began a tuneless piping, pulled her to her feet and danced her around the furniture. At the window he waved to one of Gordon's sidesmen, who answered with a sneer.

That evening a knock sounded, and Caulton went to the door. 'Mrs Tanbrey, let me take your coat.'

She undid her buttons while her husband stood under the oil lamp holding his cap. Luisa showed them into the room, Charlie following. His parents settled on the chaise longue as Caulton produced a decanter and glasses. 'And for you, Charlie, barley water.'

An awkward silence followed. Caulton lit his cigar while his wife went to attend to the meal. He began to wonder if he'd done the right thing inviting them to his home. He skirted around Will's employment and Edna's button-making; mentioned Gladstone's resignation, the situation in Ireland. Mrs Tanbrey remembered wearing a new frock for a party in honour of Victoria's accession. He tried to draw her out, but only drew a reticent smile. Luisa called him to help bring in the food, and it was towards the end of the meal that he sparked a response.

'Well, Mr Tanbrey, how does it feel to have a scholar in our midst?'

Will chewed his potatoes, the folds of his neck trapped inside a stiffly-starched collar. 'We've already got one scholar at home, I can't see as there's room for two.'

'I'm not quite with you.'

'Booklearning's all right for some. Our John's bright, he might have made something of it.' He tilted his plate and spooned up the gravy.

'But surely, if Charlie has potential, it's in his best interest to cultivate it?'

'That's what I keep telling him,' his wife agreed, with feeble obstinacy. 'My health isn't all it should be, Mr Caulton, though it's good as wealth if you've got it. I'd like Charlie to make something of himself if he's a mind. It's all luck, isn't it, Mrs Caulton?'

Luisa glanced at her husband and nodded brightly.

'But surely you'd not deny your son a chance,' Caulton persisted reasonably. 'That would mean his private lessons have been a waste of time. I'm sure you'd like him to have the opportunities you've missed.'

'My husband's never seen the use of it, Mr Caulton. He's to have a job when he leaves, see?'

Caulton fiddled with his napkin, then began to pour, leaving a stain on the cloth. Luisa ran to fetch a rag.

'But surely you'd agree Charlie deserves more. It's all very well to think of the pit or what have you for those suited to them, but Charlie's not and I doubt he ever will be.' A hush fell across the table. Caulton looked at Charlie's lowered head and felt a vicarious embarrassment for him. He was about to say more when Luisa put a restraining hand on his arm.

'Darling, what about your surprise?'

He'd forgotten. He went over to the cupboard and took out a package. 'Charlie, if I make a speech you'd have to make one in return, and I know you wouldn't want that. I'll simply say the very best to you, and I hope your future will be a little less bleak than your Pa thinks it should be. I hope when you use it you'll think of your tutor sometimes, slaving away to give you what has been denied the rest of the rabble –'

'Harry!'

'I mean, the other eager members of class. You may open it if you wish.'

Charlie peeled off the wrapping to reveal a polished hardwood box. Tentatively he swivelled the two brass clasps and lifted the lid. There were thirty six paints in all and three brushes, one as thin as a hair. There was a miniature water container, with tubes of colour recessed at either end, burnt ochre, vermilion, ultramarine, Mars Black. He ran his finger over the pointed sables.

'Could I trouble you for another cup, Mrs Caulton?' Will asked.

Charlie lowered the lid and fixed the clasps.

'I take it everything's in order?' Caulton said.

He nodded.

'Remember your manners. Say thank-you,' said Mrs Tanbrey.

'Thank you.'

Will poured his tea into his saucer and blew. A sort of pride showed through his wife's veiled expression. 'You'll have to send Mr Caulton a picture, Charlie. I'm not one to take notice o' gossip, Mr Caulton, you've taken pains with the lad and it's best speak as you find.'

'Now you can turn out masterpieces by the score,' Caulton was saying. 'Look after it and it'll last a lifetime.'

Will put down the saucer and nudged his wife. Caulton thought of Luisa, who might never bear a child, and checked a surge of anger towards him.

'I think we'd best be making a move.'

'Don't forget to keep the brushes well washed,' Caulton warned as their coats were brought in. 'I don't expect to find the dog has sunk its teeth into them when I'm next up this way.'

Mrs Tanbrey moved towards the door. 'Well, Charlie, you'd better write down the Master's new address, let him know how you're getting on.'

'A capital idea! Luisa – a pen.'

They took their leave. Dense clouds hid the moon, and a wind stirred the leaves. Charlie walked through the dark between them. The paints were never mentioned, and when they reached the Moel, Will went straight to bed.

Two days later, the Caultons left. As their cab passed the rectory, the schoolmaster signalled it to stop. The rector's gardener was cutting back a lilac when he heard Caulton call. Would he inform the rector the school keys were in the horse trough? Throwing down his shears, he rapped on the window. Mrs Gordon appeared.

'What is the meaning of this?'

'The meaning is that the key your husband requested is now sunk in a foot of murky water.'

'I shouldn't bother with him, ma'am, I think it's a touch o' the sun.'

'You're probably right,' Caulton said, sweeping out an arm in an exaggerated farewell.

The cab moved off, leaving his regards to the rector booming across the lane. A week later, he received a letter bearing a London postmark:

'Dear Caulton,

My son forwarded your Devon address. I believe you are in debt to the courts to the extent of the sum enclosed, and I hope you will not feel any obligation if I assist you in this. I am sorry you did not take my earlier advice. Nevertheless, I am impressed that you had the courage of your convictions. If you feel unable to accept what you may see as charity, please donate the sum to an organisation of your choice.

I hope you are successful in your new position, and wish both yourself and Mrs Caulton many happy years.

Yours Faithfully,
James Bateman'

7

The rector's robes were bright in the nave. Charlie and his family sat in the first pew; other figures, his mother's sister from Tunstall, the Benersleys, people from the village. Could his mother really be in that coffin under the chancel arch? What if she were still alive and they'd shut her in by mistake?

Rain drummed faintly on the roof. The rector was coming to the end. Humble maker of buttons.... beloved mother.... devoted wife. 'I am the resurrection and the Life, saith the Lord. He that believeth in me, though he were dead, yet shall he live.' His robes seemed incongruous against the water-washed burial ground. 'I know that my Redeemer liveth, and that He shall stand at the latter day upon the Earth....' The coffin was lowered, watched by their wind-bent faces. The first sod crumbled against the lid. 'We brought nothing into this world, and it is certain we can carry nothing out. The Lord gave, and the Lord hath taken away; blessed be the name of the Lord.'

The words still rang in Charlie's ears as the room began to fill.

'You'll miss her, Will.'

'Could be a blessing she went when she did. Father went at the same time, just gone forty. If you're born with a good heart, you're born to last.'

'It'll be a comfort, the lads being at home. Least you'll not be on your own. And what about you, Charlie? You'll soon be leaving school, won't you?'

The rain had slackened and he crept out unseen and ran down the lane until it dipped towards Spring Wood, then followed the leat and began to climb through the pines. Only when he'd gained the rise did the first sobs come, and even then he stifled them. The hollow where he'd sat with John had filled with water. He let fall a stone and watched his mother's face floating in the spirals. He wiped his cheeks with his sleeve and cooed to a passing pigeon. Raindrops plopped from the leaves and her face faded. He followed the bird's call across the brake. When he reached home, all but the Benersleys had left.

'You're a fine one. I wonder what your mother'd say?'

Doris laid a hand on his arm. 'Never mind, Charlie, you can come and work on the farm whenever you like.'

'There's enough to be done here,' Will said, his voice drained of expression, 'long as it doesn't effect his painting.'

Bevis smiled. 'You'll be able to see clear this time next year, Charlie. You must turn to other matters now.'

By the time they left, the sky had cleared. Will damped the fire and left the unwashed dishes on the board. Upstairs Charlie lay awake, waiting for the stairs to creak.

Urias strode into the office in his usual Monday mood and clapped John on the back. 'You don't know when your luck's in. First you land this job, now you've got a girl on your shirt tails. I can already hear the church bells ringing.'

Of late, John had grown tired of the manager's patronising breeziness, and now there was the business of the girl. Despite his earlier assurances, Heath had given notice to a number of staff since Bateman's departure. One of the first to go had been Stanton, the head gardener, his place taken by Luke Pointon. A new chambermaid had also arrived, and Urias had caught her in an idle moment with her eyes on John. John thought she was quite pretty, though the most she could hope for would be a housekeeper's post. On the other hand, he'd learned from the footman that Ginny Leadbetter had become a favourite with Mrs Heath, given the job of putting out the flowers and laying out the mistress's clothes.

He mulled over what he'd been told. Bateman had thwarted his ambitions by moving away, but it was not too late to bring himself to the new master's attention, and Ginny might be the means to do it.

The next day he saw her in the gardens, and went to meet her. The sound of his approaching footsteps startled her.

'I've to pick a basket for the tables, she explained, blushing.

'You've not worked here long.'

'Only since February. Mrs Holly set me on.'

'Where were you before?'

'Up Porthill. They were butchers. They had five shops.'

'Why did you leave?'

'I have my own room here. There's only my brother and me, and he's gone to London for work.'

She was wearing a calico dress which flattered her modest figure. He thought of her as a girl of fourteen, though he knew her to be three years older.

'Are you taking messages?' she ventured, seeing his papers.

'You've noticed.'

'I didn't think there'd be anybody to take messages to, down here.'

'I thought I'd go the long way for a breath of air. There's some good blossom near the bowling green.'

'She expressly told me flowers, I'd best do as she says.'

'Mrs Heath?'

'She loves flowers.' She began walking towards the building. 'Your name's John Tanbrey, isn't it?' She added quickly: 'It were Mrs Holly told us. She told me and Cathy everybody's name, she's the other girl they set on. Then there's Urias Ball, he's the estate manager you work with and Luke's the new gardener -'

'I'd better be on my way,' he said. 'Heath will think I'm idling.' She walked with him until the house came into view. He pretended to study his papers, then turned along the path.

When he got back, he caught Urias kicking the stove.

'Bloody scrapings, it's nowt but slack! Just what you'd expect from the bugger who owns half the pits in England.' With the damper drawn, he managed to coax a feeble flame. 'There's something else landed on the desk – as if there isn't enough to do.' John glanced down. There was to be a Summer Ball, and Urias was to help organise it. 'And where am I supposed to get up a band from? You'd be hard put to get a bloody organ grinder around here. Bloody band! For what he pays I'd be better off piping myself.' He took a pippin from his pocket and sank his teeth into it. 'Reach me down the oddments book from that top shelf there, we'd best make a start with that.'

He whipped over the pages, tut-tutting to himself. Ginny Leadbetter popped briefly into John's mind, then disappeared with her flowers into the ledgers.

After her midday meal, Dixon's mother's rocking chair stilled and she began to snore. Priscilla went quickly up to her room and took a dress from her wardrobe. Her jewellery box lay open on the dressing table and she picked at her rings and pinchbeck broaches, undecided what to take out. Unclipping her earrings, she dropped them into the box, chose a belt, handkerchiefs, a basque, a camisole and put her jewellery box along with her clothes into a case in the passage. At the door she paused. Colliery clatter came faintly into the room. She took down her coat and pinned her hat in place; then, taking a last look at the bed she'd once shared with Dixon, she picked up her case and crept downstairs.

The old lady muttered in her sleep. Priscilla waited for her to settle, then moved into the drawing room and opened a rosewood desk. She drew out a velvet bag, which she put in her coat pocket. A tense excitement gripped her as she picked up the case. She closed the door gently behind her and waited by the gate. At the sound of the approaching cab, she took a step forward. It drew to a halt, and she struggled with the handle. The passenger came to her aid. The vehicle passed from sight down the lane.

For some reason, Dixon had been uneasy throughout the day. When he'd married Priscilla he'd been confident of the strength which had first attracted her to him, but it hadn't taken her long to discover that wherever his power lay, it wasn't in the bedroom. At first she'd put up with his jealous tirades because he'd been kind to her. Her father had died when she was young, and George had shown concern for her mother and been generous with his money. She'd tried to ignore his constant demands as to where she'd been, who she'd spoken to, but even before their first year she found her denials futile. She felt an increasing need to escape the net he was drawing around her – to escape his mother, who she'd come to believe had been brought into the house to spy on her.

It had been Jud Cowlishaw who'd come close to the truth. Calling on chapel matters when Dixon and his wife were out, George's mother had invited him in. Loose-tongued with stout, she'd told him things between George and Priscilla were 'not as they should be'. She seemed to increase Jud's own paranoia, and his lies regarding Bill had come at a low point in the butty's life. He struck his wife for the first time that night, raising a bruise under an eye that kept her in the house for a fortnight. Whatever feeling she'd had for him left her at that moment and Dixon knew it.

Jud Cowlishaw had confided to him in an off-guarded moment that 'he had a bit put by'. One Sunday he hadn't been to chapel, and George had called around. The back door lay open, and he found Jud spread-eagled across the couch smelling of drink. For half an hour he'd tried unsuccessfully to rouse him. Then he heard Cowlishaw's boast echoing in his ears and felt his spirits lift. He'd searched the room and was amazed, as he counted the money, at how much Jud had managed to hoard. It hadn't taken him long to buy and furnish the cottage, with a sizeable amount put by. Jud no longer came to chapel, and there was nothing of the robbery in the papers. Maybe it hadn't been Jud's money to begin with. That was it! Jud had confided he dealt with the money side of things at work. He must have been helping himself. Having reached his conclusion, Dixon brushed the matter aside and began spending lavishly on Priscilla, telling her he'd invested in railway stock. For a while he'd managed to shore up the rift between them, but his efforts hadn't lasted. Cut off from her old home and the few people she knew, she found herself lonelier than before.

A young doctor had prescribed laudanum to help her sleep. As she regained her confidence she began to look upon him as a support, then as a friend. By the coming spring, they were lovers. She'd already made up her mind to leave when Tanbrey called at the cottage. Pressing her ear to the wall, she'd heard enough to understand the real source of their new-found wealth and the connection between Tanbrey, Jud and her husband. By early summer the doctor had received a letter from New South Wales offering him a post in the St Teresa Sanatorium, Melbourne. He advertised his practice and received two replies, one of which he accepted. He booked a passage on the *SS Sumatra*, sailing from Southampton at the end of July. When Priscilla, clutching her case and with her husband's stolen sovereigns in her pocket, closed the cab door, she felt an overwhelming sense of release. By the time he discovered her gone, she'd be a face at the dockside.

Dixon watched the shift pick their way across the lines, then took the path home. His foreboding deepened as he approached his house, and when he opened the door an unusual silence engulfed him. He hung up his coat, unable to make his fingers work on the loop.

'Where's Prissy?'

His mother, befuddled with sleep, repeated the words stupidly. He ran upstairs. His wife's wardrobe lay open, and he threw back the door with such force it split against the wall.

'I asked where Prissy's gone.'

'How should I know where she's gone? Gone up the doctor's I dare say.'

'She was up the doctor's not twenty four hours since.'

'Well, if you must keep shelling out –'

'She can't be up at the doctor's lest she's had a bloody relapse, can she?'

'Well she were in earlier.'

'And what's earlier – dawn?'

'It's no use falling out with me, George. You're man and wife, it's not my place to interfere.'

He left the room and stood at the window fancying her with someone else, hearing the moans he'd never been able to raise. A brooding hatred threatened to suffocate him, against his mother, his wife, most of all himself. His mother came in as he was wrenching open the desk.

'Is it your money? Has she taken your money?'

A storm of self pity raged over him. He let out a cry and fell to his knees.

'Don't take on, son, you're too good for her. She'll be back, don't you fret. She knows the way her bread's buttered – '

She jerked back as the drawer smashed against the wall. 'I did it for her. She was all I ever cared about!' A violent sob convulsed him, but the self-control he'd exerted year in, year out, stifled the sound. 'Well, mother, I'm treading dirt all over the house. Best heat up a bath.'

She turned dumbly from the room. An hour later he left the house. They brought him back in a dog cart and he slept throughout the next day. In the evening he got drunk again.

Mrs Gordon called the leavers to one side and handed Charlie his book: *Tales of Adventure in a Christian Land* by the Rev T S Hawtry, BA. Awarded to Charles Tanbrey, Moor Top School. He ran his fingers along the spine, then examined the coloured plate. St George held a lance to the dragon's throat. There was a lick of red on the scales, a brown tower on a green hill.

'It's a pity the rector is away on business today. I'm sure he would have taken great pleasure in presenting your books himself. However, let me say I hope you've enjoyed your time at Moor Top School and I trust you will remember our Lord's teachings. I know many of you will work on farms and some of you might become colliers. Either way you will be serving God with your hands. Remember that the righteous need never fear want, for their nourishment is in the word of God. You may dismiss.'

They charged to the door. Charlie walked out after them, leaving the rector's wife rigid at the board. Since his mother died, a wall had grown between Will and himself. His brothers didn't share the sense of isolation he felt. Will gave his leaving book no more than a cursory glance.

'A book's not going to put jam on your bread.'

'John had one when he left.'

'I shouldn't waste your time reading, it might give you ideas.'

Regular mealtimes and wash-days had fallen apart. His mother had always set store by her routines; she'd stitched in time to save nine, made hay while the sun shone, never shed salt without tears. Will was a rudderless boat, drifting. Charlie wondered if she was still in the house somewhere, at the range, dollying in the yard.

'I've been speaking to somebody might be able to put some work your way. He'll see you tomorrow.'

'What is it?'

'Wait and see.'

He slept to the quaverings of a hunting owl until early light splashed the curtain. John was already out of bed when he awoke. He heard the door scrape as his father went out to feed the hens.

'D'you know anything about this job of mine?'

John sat at the foot of his bed, tying his laces. 'It'll be general, potting up and the like.'

'What will?'

'Don't you know about Luke Pointon?'

'Who?'

'Luke Pointon, head gardener down the Grange. I heard he was looking for someone and he said he'd give you a try.'

'And you told father?'

'Didn't he say?'

'He doesn't tell me much.'

John shrugged. 'You can come down with me.'

Will had come in. He glanced up as Charlie came downstairs and was about to speak but went back to boiling milk instead. Charlie buttered some bread. It seemed like yesterday Caulton had stood at the easel, tapping out *The Lady of Shalott* with his cane. Now school had finished with both of them. And what did he want with gardening any more than the pit? He'd have been happier working for Mr Benersley on the farm, except Bill was there. Perhaps when his brother left he could take his place.

He followed John through the door.

'You go along to Spring Grove, the big house opposite the church.'

'Does he know I'm coming?'

'You'll be all right, just tell him Master John made the arrangement.'

John left him near the Grange. Charlie stood undecided for a moment, then took the path which skirted Heath's coach houses and came out on the Congleton road. But for a wagon, the way was deserted. He was about to ring the bell when he heard a barrow squeak and turned to find a man half hidden behind a pile of weeds.

'Is there anything you want?'

'I've to see Mr Pointon about a job.'

'And what did you say your name was?'

'Master John made the arrangement.... he's my brother.'

'If you go down the path 'ere you'll come to a shed. You'll find him in there.'

Charlie gave a hesitant knock, which pushed the door open. Luke Pointon was scribbling in a notebook, occasionally stroking the lead across his tongue. Charlie began to deliver his message, but Luke cut him short.

'So John's your brother, is he?' He replaced the pencil and notebook in the pocket of his jacket. 'He's a rum'un, I must say. I always see him as an old man with a beard. Is he like that at home?'

'Sometimes.'

'Give him a couple of years, he'll be giving Heath a run for his money.' He relapsed into silence. Charlie wondered if he'd forgotten he was there. 'He's not told you about his girl-friend yet, then?'

'I didn't know he had one.'

'Proper dark horse, your John.'

Charlie found he was no longer twisting Benersley's penny in his pocket, and grew bold enough to ask: 'Am I to work under you, Mr Pointon?'

'Have you had any experience of gardening before?'

'I planted a bush at home.'

'Well, you'll have more than a bush to plant here.'

'I help Mr Benersley out some weekends.'

'Who's he when he's home?'

'A farmer. I help him clean out the byres and do odd jobs around the farm. I sometimes give my dad a hand, too.'

'Is he a farmer too?'

'He's got a couple of sturks and a few chickens, that's all.'

Pointon fixed his soft brown eyes on a cobwebbed sieve hanging from the window. 'It wasn't you lost your mother a bit back, was it? I seem to recall reading it in the paper. Moel, is that your house?'

Charlie nodded, wondering why his brother hadn't said anything. 'There's just me, John and father now. There were our Bill, but he's moved down Benersley's while he's working for him.'

'So there's another one like you and your John? Your father must feel well blessed.'

He jabbed a thumb into the pocket of his jacket as if to reassure himself his book was still there. 'Well this won't buy the baby a new bonnet, let's find you a bit of something to be getting on with. You can leave your snapping tin on the bench 'long as it's mouse-proof.'

He left the door swinging in the current. Charlie was given a hoe, rake and barrow and directed to the cabbage patch.

GL to serve drinks Heath's ball. Musicians play for servants after guests leave. G asked me if I want to go. I agreed – it might be to my advantage. Delivery of new suit. Shall purchase shoes when money allows.

John put his diary away and lay back on his bed. He hadn't practised much dancing, apart from a few steps he'd picked up the year before from Bill. He felt he was moving into uncharted waters. He had Urias's photograph, and other possibilities might present themselves. Yes, he'd go to the dance and see what came up.

Next morning he paid a rare visit to church. He'd been told the rector knew Heath as well as he'd known Bateman. It might be worth his while coming more often – as a sidesman, perhaps, or a churchwarden. He took a stroll out with Charlie before they parted and made his way back to get ready for the evening.

He borrowed the links his father kept in a drawer, and chose dark blue socks to match his new suit. When he took the socks out of the drawer, he found a hole at the heel. His mother's darning needle still lay under a paraphernalia of bobbins and thread, but he found a length of wool approximating the colour and bent resentfully over his task, working the wool between strands until the darned heel formed the focal point of the stocking. His shoes, too, were showing signs of wear. He began to brush them, trusting that a highly waxed cap would draw any curious glances from the scuffed heels. When he'd finished, he stood before the mirror to admire his new suit, lifting his wrists to the glass to display the links to himself. Running a little macassar oil through his hair, he left the house.

The night was warm, with a thin scattering of cloud. A distant throb of music reached his ears as he walked down the avenue of deodars which led to the Grange. Music lilted through the dusk, and he could make out the shapes of revellers from the path, the girls' dresses luminous against the dusky woodland. The tips of cigars studded the darkness, their smoke mingling with the scent of gillyflowers wafting across the grass. As he drew near, he saw two young men cavorting by the sphinxes, a third emerging from an underground lair.

'Oh, Roddy, don't be an utter ass.'

'Savaged by the ruby-eyed monster.'

'Oh, Roddy, you talk such awful drivel.'

They'd be packed off to their schools tomorrow, recounting their adventures to others who'd had similar adventures at other balls and neither would give a tinker's cuss for the skivvies like him who kept it all going. A Promotionen Valse came through the open windows, the quintet busy under an aspidistra. He decided to wait in the office until the clamour died down and the band was left to the servants, but changed his mind and on an impulse entered the glittering ballroom.

A galop was in progress, and couples were taking their places on the floor. He moved to a more inconspicuous place as one of Heath's factotums came towards him with a tray.

'Have you taken leave of your senses? If the old man claps eyes on you you'll be off the bank by tomorrow. I'd wait for the servants' dance if I were you.'

John ignored him and helped himself to wine as the band-leader stepped forward. 'Now, ladies, the moment you've been waiting for. Time to chose your partner for the Kate Kearney Valse.' From various parts of the hall girls were leading young men to the floor. John looked on from the corner of the room. He was about to take the waiter's advice when he heard a voice from behind. The girl had a faint but assertive smile, and her grey eyes wavered mischievously between him and her party. He dimly noted the modest swell of her breasts, flattered by the blue dress she was wearing, the rouged cheeks framed by auburn ringlets.

'My dancing's not all it should be.'

'Oh, nonsense. I can't bear to see you alone with no one to talk to.'

'I've not come dressed for dancing.'

A chord was struck and she hauled him to his feet, leaving him no time to do up his jacket. A flurry of clapping broke out from her table. She guided him towards the band. The room steadied. For the first time he heard the music and realised his feet were following hers across the floor. His grip on the girl's waist tightened, and by the time the final chord struck he'd managed his first waltz. He led her back to her table, made an awkward bow and collided with Roddy, who'd returned to the dance the worse for drink. The accident dislodged John's shoe, which came to rest under the girls' feet. A whoop of laughter drowned Roddy's apology, one of the girls pointing to John's darned sock. He remembered pulling his shoe back on and pushing through the French windows, then fumbling for the office key to let himself in.

A rocket whooshed over the lake, throwing a silver cascade across the water. There was a distant cheer, a faint vibration of music. He wasn't aware it had stopped until he felt a presence in the room and turned to see Ginny standing in the doorway.

'I came to see if you were all right.'

'Why shouldn't I be?'

She stood a little way from his desk. 'I thought I'd find you in here. They've gone, now. I thought you might come along to the servants' do.'

'So they can share another joke at my expense?'

'We've all had darned socks.'

'I'm not all.'

'No one hardly noticed,' she said. 'I was serving. I saw the young man bump into you and a few heads turn, nothing more.'

'They were laughing at me!'

'You're worth any two of them,' she said with sudden passion as he sat in sullen silence. 'I don't suppose Mr Heath would mind, he were playing billiards all night with some other gentlemen, I'd to take drinks in to them as well.' She lowered her eyes. 'Do you know Miss Nerissa?'

'Who's Nerissa?'

'The one you were dancing with in the ladies' *Excuse Me*, Nerissa Birkenshaw, I do believe her father owns a mill up Macclesfield.'

'Am I supposed to be impressed?'

'She must've taken a shine to you.'

'She probably danced with me because of a wager with her friends. I don't suppose she has dealings with the lower classes.'

She was no longer wearing her maid's apron, but a light cotton dress. She stood in the cooling air, gently rubbing her arms. The band struck up *The Lancers*. 'I like this one, John. Shall we go in? Mrs Heath has done us proud, you ought to see the spread.'

'I've had enough. Go on your own.'

He hated her for being there. She lingered for a moment in silence, then left him to brood in the shadows. He went home shortly after, taking a different path to avoid being seen. When he got back he went directly to his room, opened his diary and scribbled a stream of invective across the page.

'I hear you created a bit of a stir last night,' Urias greeted him. 'Does Heath know you were invited to his private ball?'

'Is there to be a sermon?'

'More a word of advice, John. I know you're anxious to put yourself about, and I know you'd like to strike a chord with the Heaths of this world. There's nothing wrong with healthy ambition and I wish I'd had a touch more when I was your age, but there are ways and ways. See what I'm driving at?'

'Tell me.'

'How old are you, nineteen? You've got a lot going for you – that Ginny, you couldn't hope for a nicer lass. This job, it might not be worth a king's ransom but it's better than burrowing down the pit like a mole, up to your legs in shit. You never know, play your cards right and you could eventually end up in my job. Think of it. You've got a good eye for the work and you can get folk to do what you want better than ever I could at your age.' He leaned forward and stuck out his finger. 'You've to learn there's the Heaths of this world and there's us. I'm not saying they're better. Some have less nous than that stove. What I'm saying is keep to your station, don't try to muscle in, or they'll spit you out with less thought than putting a guinea on a Derby nag. D'you see what it is I'm trying to tell you?'

John studied the week's invoices. He was being lectured to by a man who consorted with whores. What other secrets did he keep up his frayed sleeves?

'From what you've said before I should think I did something close to your own heart.'

'Poking your face in at Heath's private do, what d'you mean, close to my heart?'

'You've always said we're equal in God's eyes.'

'Ay, and some more equal than others.' Urias continued in a more conciliatory tone: 'Look, lad, I don't want to berate you. We rub along well enough together – in fact, we run this bloody place between us. Take it how it's meant, with your best interests at heart.'

John excused himself, leaving Urias to contemplate the real reason for his advice was less a concern for John's welfare than his need to reaffirm his own status, which he felt was slowly ebbing away. When, a week later, a package arrived at the office addressed to 'Mr John Tanbrey, Estate Manager, The Grange' Urias demanded to know why he hadn't been notified of John's 'promotion' and stormed out of the room.

Under the layers of wrapping he found three pairs of socks and a note:
'Dear John Tanbrey,

So you won't think too badly of me the other night, I send you a small token of my regard. I hope the size is right, and that grey will prove more suitable than the blue shade you seem to favour.

Yours Sincerely,

Nerissa Birkenshaw

PS I did enjoy the dance. And you?'

He re-read the letter, then sent a brief reply to the address on the note:
'Dear Miss Birkenshaw,

Thank you for the socks. It's a pity you weren't able to present them to me formally. If you had, you'd have found I'm not really a manager but a lackey worthy of no more than the socks I was wearing.

PS I can't say I enjoyed the dance, because I'm not very good at dancing. Perhaps you will teach me how to extend my repertoire?

Yours,

John'

He slid the note into one of Heath's monogrammed envelopes and left it ready for the morning post.

8

Bill removed his money from its hiding place at the Moel and sat with his savings piled across the dresser at Benersley's house. As he ran his eye across the mound of sovereigns he was conscious of a chill in the room. With the onset of winter, his impatience to leave the moor had grown, and he consoled himself with the thought he'd soon be free of it. He'd not seen Jane since their visit to Cowlishaw's house. He'd heard she'd moved to Leek and felt that, in any case, she'd outgrown him or they'd outgrown each other. He swept the coins into a pouch and had just eased the bag into a space behind the skirting when he heard the boards creak and saw Ellen standing at the door.

'Is there something you wanted?'

She flushed. 'I've just been up to my room, there's no law against it, is there? I went up for this.' She held up a penny dreadful. 'I wasn't spying, if that's what you think.'

'Who said you were?'

'Every board creaks, it's to be expected of a house this age.'

Bevis had gone with his wife to Leek, Nat was in the barns. He faced her across the landing, her hand on the newel, her body outlined against the window-lit fabric of her dress.

'You might show me your book now you've got it.'

'Haven't you seen one before?'

'We were more for high brow stuff at our house.'

A watchful silence had settled on her. She took a step forward. 'There's nothing much in 'em anyway,' she said, giggling a little as he flicked through the pages.

'This is rubbish.'

'It isn't.'

'Rubbish from front to back. I've a mind to drop it through the window.'

He raised the sash and dangled the magazine over the yard. She clambered after him, and he held her off with his free hand. Her hair tumbled loose, obscuring her face, and she pushed it back with pouting indignation, pushing between him and the window. He let the magazine fall, and trapped her arms as she made a display of reaching out for it, his body hard against her back. He reached with quiet confidence for her breasts and pulled her gently towards the bed. She lay still as he kissed her and began to unfasten her dress. He resisted the urge to quicken until the last button had been freed and her exposed breasts rose under his hand. He began to kiss her throat as she lay pliant beneath him.

'Ellen, are you there?'

She rolled off the bed and ran behind the door, snatching up her clothes. Bill came out on to the landing and leaned over the rail.

'She's not here, Nat. Have you looked outside?' Nat reached the top, his eyes turned shiftily away. Bill caught sight of a line of blood across the back of his hand. 'Where've got all them scratches from?' Nat drew his hand back. 'You'll be needing a spot o' soap and water, else they're likely to turn septic. Come on, put your hand out.'

Ellen listened behind the door as Bill reached around Nat's back and pulled out his clenched fist. The skin was ribboned with congealed blood, the eyes stricken with anxiety. 'It was the bird, the bird had 'em.'

'Was it the rooster?'

'Bird in the loft.'

'What were you doing up in the loft? You're a cunning old sod, trying to lead me up the garden path like your sister.'

They went downstairs. Ellen heard their receding voices and the clank of the pump and went out by the back door. A few minutes later she came back into the house holding her penny dreadful. Nat followed Bill into the kitchen and stood staring at the rack.

'Hello, Nat, Bill tells me a bird scratched your hand. It were no rooster, though, was it? Dad's told you before, hasn't he? What did he say? Go on, tell Bill what he told you.' Nat mumbled under his breath. 'We can't hear. Tell Bill what your father told you.'

Nat seemed to sink further into himself. 'Father'll be 'ere in a minute, father'll be'ere.'

'I know he'll be here, but you still haven't said nothing about that big barn owl. You weren't to go disturbing her, were you?'

'I'm goin' to fork hay.'

'Yes, fork hay but you mustn't go after the owl again or it'll scratch your eyes out.'

When he'd gone, she said: 'We've had the owls these past two years. Bevis took Nat up to see them and he's been making the trip ever since. He thinks there's a ruck of eggs to be had. The season's neither here nor there with Nat.'

'He doesn't learn very quick, does he?'

'There's no harm in him.'

'Not like his sister, then.'

She turned away. A cart was rumbling down the track. Bevis, wrapped like a mummy, sat at the reins. 'I've to begin tea,' she said, leaving him unsatisfied.

Benersley weathered the mild winter, but by early spring his health had begun to fail. He'd lost some of his strength since the accident, though the cows still had to be milked, the hedges layered, the track mended, the gates repaired. He'd been spared the poor harvests suffered by the grain farmers, but his land had never yielded enough for comfort. It was no use telling the queues at the butcher's to buy local beef when imported meat was cheaper, and although the demand for milk held up, its low price would mean a larger herd if he were to make a better living; and that would mean more capital. He had nothing else. The world would run its course and the house would rot and the wallpaper turn to mould while he shrouded himself in pipe smoke as his wife whirred about him.

It was on a wet February afternoon that Bill caught him holding his side in the dairy. The farmer had passed it off as a 'touch o' rheumatics', but for the first time Bill noticed the grizzled stubble about his cheeks and a waxy skin which presaged illness.

'Go and take the weight off your legs, Bevis, I can handle this.'

The farmer nodded. 'I'll just bide my time an hour, see if I can get down later.' He went into the house and bent his thin hands to the fire. The dull ache in his side intensified with every breath. He thought he might have torn a muscle and began to run over the jobs he'd done that day, but the effort proved too much and he settled back in his chair and turned vacantly to the window-light.

When Doris came in the sight of him shocked her. His eyes were the colour of tarnished china, and he seemed to have shrunk into himself like a paper figure wrapped in rag. She plumped the cushions needlessly. 'You should have left the heavy work to Bill. What d'you think we pay him for?' She pulled a blanket over his shoulders as the kettle chuckled in the hearth. 'Ellen, get a mug of tea for father.'

Ellen had been listening from the back room and came in. The sight of the farmer slumped into his chair alarmed her.

'It's here.' He rubbed his side, slow sweeps of his hand. 'It's like a razor when I catch breath.'

He put the mug to his lips while Doris brought in the bed brick and put it in the range to warm. His tea dribbled from the corner of his mouth, and she wiped it away. She tried to persuade him to go to bed, but he craved the warmth of the fire. When she mentioned the doctor he shook his head.

'You'll have to have him, Bevis, you're not well.' She turned to Ellen, still standing at the door. 'Go fetch Dr McEvoy.'

'What if he's not at home?'

'Then wait till he gets back. Take the dog cart.'

'Couldn't Bill do it? I could be more use here.'

'We can't keep asking Bill to do this, do that, he's not family. Any road, he's still down the dairy. Get your coat on or there'll be two sick.'

She started up the track. When she reached the height a squall brought the first splinters of sleet, and she stopped to pull up her hood. To the west the hills drove into the fading light. She jerked the rein and the horse moved forward sluggishly. The wind strengthened along the ridge, and through the icy rain she saw the sprinkling of lights in the valley. She reached the deserted town and drove directly into McEvoy's yard. A gust blew a scrap of sacking against her legs, and from an upstairs room came the faint wail of a violin. She hammered at the door, and a pool of light lit the cobbles. The doctor's wife stood on the step, a hand closing her shawl. McEvoy put down his instrument and came downstairs. He listened briefly as the girl told him Bevis's symptoms, then turned back into the house. She waited until he emerged in his outdoor clothes and went to attend to his trap.

He found the farmer sunk into his chair. Every slight breath caused him to wince in pain.

'How long has he been like this?'

'He'd just came up from the dairy,' Doris said. 'He's not looking good, is he doctor?'

McEvoy draped his coat over the chair and took a stethoscope from his bag. Benersley coughed feebly. 'Look at him, doctor, he's all done in. How do you feel, Bevis? I think he's trying to tell us he's warm enough already. I wonder if he's sickenin' after the fever?'

McEvoy eased up Benersley's shirt and put his stethoscope to his ears, holding the chest piece between the farmer's shoulders, moving to his lower back, across to his chest and stomach. The farmer's breathing was hardly more than a sigh, and he listened at each site, his eyes narrowed in concentration. Below the whisper of air he could hear the rub of the pleural surfaces. He placed his palm lightly on the farmer's chest.

'What is it, doctor?'

'How long since he had the argument with the bull?'

'That'd be nearly two years since. He's not been right since.'

'Any subsequent injury?'

'None that I know of.' She searched her memory. 'You remember the bull only caught him a glancing blow. Most of the bruising were down below.'

'Has he been shivering?'

'He looked feverish when he came in.'

McEvoy had already formed a diagnosis on the doorstep of his home. His examination confirmed the onset of pleurisy, but what concerned him more was the inevitability of pneumonia.

'Has your husband ever suffered from bronchitis?'

'He's been worn out from time to time, though for the most part he's managed to keep going. We've a man helping now, so it's easier, though I must say he'd be better finishing altogether. He's never been strong, as you might say. There's always something to do on a farm.'

Beckoning her into the scullery, he took a vial and tapped half the powder it contained into an envelope. 'I'm giving you this to ease the pain.' He wondered if she could read the note he'd handed her and repeated the instructions. 'It's a little Dover's Powder to help him sleep. I see you've got a hot brick to warm him up.'

'I thought it best now the weather's turned.'

'If we're to get your husband on the mend we're going to need more than a brick. Hot fomentations are the order of the day.'

'You mean poultices?'

'Just plain hot water, you know how it's done.'

Her voice fell to a whisper. 'He's got inflammation, hasn't he, doctor? Inflammation o' the lung.'

'Your husband has pleuritis, and the powders I have prescribed are for that condition. You must do as I say, make him a bed downstairs, get him comfortable.' He gave a smile of reassurance. 'Plenty of nourishing broth.'

He buttoned his ulster.

'About your fee?'

'I'll call the day after tomorrow. If he deteriorates, send for me.'

'But, your – '

'Let's get him well first.' He moved to the door.'I'll let myself out.'

He took a moment to light his carriage lamp. Ellen watched him climbing the farm track from her window.

He was sent for at dawn. A hasty bed had been set up near the fire, and the room lay in disorder, with blankets and clothing scattered over the chairs and towels strewn across the floor. Benersley's small head rose from the blankets, the outline of his body hidden under a greatcoat. He was shivering violently, his head twitching from side to side. Doris brushed the stiff, grey hair from his forehead. A weak retching came from the pillow, followed by a rapid breathing. His face was tinged with a dusky flush, his lips dark and his eyes sunk in violet sockets. McEvoy confirmed the build up of fluid on the lung. Could the girl obtain sufficient powder from the druggist for ten days, together with an expectorant?

'What are his chances, doctor?'

Like so many others, the house was squalid and damp. The man had no obvious access either to the money that could pay for good nursing or the robust constitution which could put up a fight against the illness. Like mill workers with weakening sight, bronchitic stone masons and an army of consumptives, the man was old before his time.

'Oh, I don't think we'll allow him to hang up his clogs just yet.'

Bevis made an involuntary snatch at the blanket as his wife stroked his brow. His eyes rolled beneath their lids, and he began to retch. 'This is how it was shortly after you left, doctor. I thought he was going to be sick. He's only had soup since last night, and only half a bowl at that.'

McEvoy led her to one side. 'You must prepare yourself for the worst. But don't cross your bridges yet.'

'What d'you want me to do?'

'You need help. You mentioned a man yesterday. The crisis will be soon, perhaps a week, but your husband will need constant care, night and day.'

'He's a friend of the family, I don't like to impose on his time. In any event, the farm needs tending, coming at the busy time -'

'Then he must carry out only essential tasks. Can he cook?'

'Our Ellen's good in the kitchen, she can do anything round a house.'

'Then I shall leave you to organise things. He must be nursed. You and Ellen can do it. Take turns. Don't forget to keep on with the fomentations, the heat will draw the illness out of him. Keep on with the Dover's Powder, five grains every six hours. Double it if necessary. It will help his coughing. The druggist will have my note. And don't be alarmed at the rubbish he coughs up. It's normal when the lungs are inflamed.'

'Shall I use horehound to bring his heat down?'

'A cloth with tepid water is all that's needed. And you must feed him whether he wants food or not. Plenty of milk. Plenty of soups. I'll call every day. If you're really worried, send your girl to fetch me.' She stood silent, watching Bevis' tongue loll about his blue lips. 'Take heart, Mrs Benersley, I've seen cripples dance, and he's not a cripple, is he?'

He made a quick check of the medicines and swung his bag into the carriage. The sky was a pale aquamarine, and the finches were already flitting across the hedgerows. The track cut up between heather banks, and behind him the fields were shining with the glowing emerald of early spring. He felt the air fresh on his face. What better than that glorious country to practice his music? That song – how did it go?

I am now a respectable chap
And shine with a virtue resplendent
And, therefore, I haven't a rap,
Of sympathy with the defendant!

Three Elms lay blanched in moonlight. Ellen stood at the window, looking out across the dark fields. Bevis was not her real father any more than Doris was her mother, but they were the only family she had. She couldn't imagine his chair empty. She turned into the room, where Doris was snoring in a chair. The fire had burnt to redness, the lamp by the farmer's bed sending oily spirals to the ceiling. She wrung out a cloth and sponged his face and chest. He was sleeping better under sedation, but his skin was still on fire though she changed the fomentations every few hours. After the second day the rise and fall of his chest became uneven, as if he were labouring under a great strain.

Then it was Doris' turn, and Bill was called upon to make tea, bring in water and empty the bucket. Benersley's bristles grew to a beard, but he was too ill to be shaved and his wash was no more than a cool sponging to bring down the heat which surged through every tissue. By the fourth day he was making a thick, blood-speckled sputum which stuck to the sides of the bowl. Doris sat stroking his hand, drifting in and out of sleep as the fire crackled and the lamps burnt low. By the sixth day he seemed to be giving up. His arms had grown thin, the veins in his neck standing out from the flesh in violet seams, his cheeks sunk in a spectral face. He became delirious, his legs and arms flailing wildly, the iris of his eyes a hot, intense blue under the pink-rimmed lids. He called for Nat, reprimanded Charlie for leaving the birds, stared wide-eyed into the disjointed ends of nightmares until the drugs did their work and he relapsed into sleep.

'The next hours will decide,' McEvoy told her, his voice betraying nothing of the frustration he felt watching good men die. Expectorants, fomentations and soup – it was like trying to stave off the tide with matchsticks. But that was all there was. And even if a cure were to be discovered, he doubted the wise old men of medicine would agree its benefits until a thousand took up their beds and walked.

It was Ellen, waking from a doze, who noticed the change and shook Doris awake. Their voices aroused Bill, who ran downstairs.

She turned her face towards him, her eyes brimming. 'He's breathing again.'

'He's all right?'

'It was only a minute ago.'

'I thought he were gone,' Doris wept. 'Oh, you've done well, lad, I'm right proud of you.' She pushed back the stubborn grey hair. 'I'm glad, right glad. Come in now, Nat, come in. I think your dad's goin' to be all right. Feel his wrist, Ellen, his heart's calming to nothing. Oh, and look at the sweat, it's pouring out.' They stood amid the debris of disease as the anguish lifted from Bevis' eyes. He moved his hand slowly towards his wife. 'I think he's trying to tell us something. What is it? What are you after?' She pressed her ear to his mouth. 'He wants something to eat, Ellen.' The sudden release made her laugh, and she wiped her eyes on her apron. 'Get him a bowl o' stock. Beef stock, with plenty o' lumps in it.'

Her tiredness vanished with the coming day.

Charlie was too restless to finish his watercolour. Pulling on his jacket, he cut a crust and set off for Benersley's farm. The dusk of early evening had settled over the fields, and the sky glowed like a blue pearl. Along the track clumps of holly made a silhouette against the fading light. He stood for a moment listening to the distant beat of Heath's forge hammers, then climbed the rise as night closed in. The lane shone bone-white along the ridge and it was there he saw a fox in the shadow of a wall, its ears alert, its eyes beaded, tracking up the hummocks towards Rudyard. When he reached the top it had gone, and the land lay before him folded in sweeping pools of mist. He sat with a straw to his lips, looking across the fields. Was his mother part of the atoms that made the Earth? Could she see him sitting alone in the dark, or was she nothing, only blackness? He saw the windows of Three Elms had been lit, and went down to the house. Doris was standing in the doorway.

'Oh, it's you, Charlie. I thought it was your Bill come back.'

'I heard about Mr Benersley. I thought I'd come and see how things are.'

'He's much better now. Must be divine providence, that's all I can say. I'll tell you what, though, whatever the tittle tattle about your Bill, we couldn't have done without him. He even helped pay the doctor. It's only a loan, mind, I want no charity.' She clucked into the back room, Charlie following. 'Sit down, he's only dozing. My, it's a treat to see the spring again, all the buds comin' out.'

A snuffle broke from the pillow and he found Bevis looking up at him.

'You're getting to be a man, Charlie. You're like a spotted dick.'

The unfamiliar face with its hollow eyes startled him. Bevis strained to raise himself, but slumped back.

'Are you feeling better, Mr Benersley?'

'Better than them in the churchyard, I expect.'

'I would've come sooner, only Bill told us it were best to keep away. Father sends his regards.'

'You must thank him for me.'

'Maybe he could come and see you when you're well enough.'

'You must tell him.'

'It won't be long before you're up and about, will it?'

'I doubt it'll be a touch longer yet, it's not something you get over in a hurry.'

Doris bustled in with a tray. 'Here, throw a cobble on the fire then come and have a drink.'

She manhandled Benersley up, plumping the pillows. He took slow, loud sips from his mug. 'Well, nothing's changed since you were last down, Charlie –apart from Bevis, that is. It's been a struggle to keep things going.' Her eyes darted across at him. 'I heard you've a job with Heath's gardener.'

He nodded. 'Ay, that's right.... how's Ellen?'

'She's a bonny lass, our Ellen. She's a proper nurse, isn't she, Bevis? Sixteen now. Wait till she starts getting down to Leek. All them farmers! There'll be queues all the way up the square and back.' She could already see her decked out, and shook her head at the pride of it. 'You must go and find her, Charlie, she's about somewhere. She were helpin' Bill the last time I saw her.' Charlie glanced down at Bevis. 'Oh, don't bother yourself about him, he's glad you come. He's always glad to see you.'

Benersley's eyes drooped. He dozed for a second, then woke again. 'You mustn't leave it so long next time,' he murmured.

Doris took the empty mug and he sank down.

'I'll just see if I can find her then, Mrs Benersley.'

The moon had brightened and the yard was bathed in a silver light. He called out, but there was no answer. A lantern hung by the byre, and he picked his way past the cows pulling quietly at their mangers. Cautiously, he climbed the ladder at the far end. The air was full of the sweet, warm scent of hay. Hay lay in ridges across the boards, and in bails piled crosswise to the rafters. Behind the first, others spanned the length of the loft like dunes, with bluffs and coves crossed by walkways. He felt his way, heard a faint fluttering and listened intently, remembering what Bill had told him about the owl. It came again, a rhythmic pulse which grew louder as he crept through the pools of shadow. Then a grotesque phantom seemed to hurl itself at him, and he lifted his hand to his eyes. In the hay lay Bill and Ellen, their naked bodies luminous against the backwash of straw. There was a movement as she lifted a coat to her breast, Bill twisting in the half-light.

The owl flashed across the rafters, and he found himself on the ladder, then running across the yard. He'd reached the finger post when the stitch bent him. When the pain cleared he looked back at the lit doorway and saw Ellen there and heard the rector's voice thundering across the hedgerows *Woe unto you, for ye are like unto whited sepulchres which outwardly appear beautiful, but inwardly are unclean.*

Ginny handed John a clutch of letters. 'I brought these in from Mrs Heath.

She says to post them tonight since they're urgent.... what're you doing?'

'Working.'

She gave a shy giggle and hovered behind him. He felt he'd been tricked again into taking her out. The first time had been shortly after the summer ball, when he'd met her on a Sunday by chance and grudgingly agreed to take her to a concert for which she'd bought two tickets. Other times had followed; an outing to Leek, a staff party at Christmas when she'd bought him a monogrammed case which cost her a week's wages. He'd given her a packet of plain handkerchiefs in return.

'Will you be walking out this Sunday, John?'

'I might be busy.'

'It's a long time since I've been up the Cloud. I could get us a picnic if you like.'

'I'll think about it.'

She went out. He finished the accounts he'd been working on and put his feet up. Urias was out for the morning and he wouldn't be disturbed. He took an envelope from his pocket and opened the folded sheet.

'Dear John,

Thank you for your letter. We seem to have worked up quite a correspondence over the past months. I do enjoy reading the little snippets you send me about daddy's friend Mr Heath. I'm sure you know more about the Grange than I do about our own house, and certainly more than daddy knows about our mill. Do you know I have an admirer? You must recall Roderick Davenport – he was the reason for your displaced shoe, remember? He hopes to go up to Oxford this year, or is it Cambridge? He wrote to me to ask if I'd agree to meet him over Easter, when he'll be down for the vacation. He's another of daddy's acquaintances, or, rather, his father is, being involved in the Derbyshire mines, I believe.

Perhaps I shall see you if we come down to the Heaths again later this year. Of course, you will understand if I get too caught up in the social whirl and can't see you. You must acquaint me further with other interesting tit-bits when you have the time. I remain your good friend,

Nerissa.'

It had surprised him when she'd sent the socks, even more when she'd replied to his note. He'd written to suggest she teach him how to dance better, and she'd responded. Perhaps he interested her, as a moth might a lepidopterist – or was it the illicit friendship that intrigued her? Her mention of Roddy had been wilful. She'd probably guessed that John saw as a threat anyone who came in the way of a closer relationship with her and to whatever chances she could put his way. The gardeners had hung up lumps of fat for the starlings. As he watched them squabbling under the rhododendrons, something of his recklessness at the ball came over him again. Taking a sheet, he wrote:

'Dear Nerissa,

Thank you for your letter. I shall feel abandoned if you meet this Roderick. If anyone is to trifle with your affections, it should be me. I'm pleased you find my remarks about Mr Heath of interest and hope you will give him my regards through your father, so that he might better favour me in future.' He read his message through, before adding: 'I know I'm not the correspondent you would normally have chosen, but you can't stop me from admiring you.' He put the envelope in his pocket to post later.

He'd nothing better to do than to go on the Sunday outing with Ginny. She carried the bag and adjusted her steps to his as they climbed the path to the Cloud, a local landmark which had been a favourite of her father's. At the summit they sat in a cleft away from the breeze which carried the scent of heather across the hill. The day was clear, and he scanned the countryside disinterestedly as she spread a cloth and brought out a bottle of elderflower and sandwiches. Far below, a train trundled over the viaduct on its journey to Manchester.

'Would you have some lettuce, John?'

'How boring,' he said, leaning against a rock.

She nibbled at her sandwich. 'You shouldn't have come, if you didn't want to. Don't you like it up here?'

'It's fine if you're a bird.'

'People come from miles around to admire the view. Dad said on a clear day you can see Liverpool docks.'

'At least there's something happening in Liverpool, which is more than you can say about this place.' He took a sandwich and ate in silence.

'They used to live up here in the olden days, so they say. Stone Age folk, the teacher once told us.' She munched her sandwich contemplatively. 'They found stone axes. Their huts were somewhere about, though I've yet to discover where.'

'I shouldn't bother yourself with ancient history, it's no use in a kitchen.'

Why did he persevere, why did she? She reached for the bottle, but he poured for himself.

'I found an interesting thing out,' she said, giggling as if at a joke told against herself. 'I found out the secret of Mr Heath's wealth.'

'Found a seam of coal, did you?'

'It were when I was cleaning Mrs Heath's jewellery. You ought to see what she has, John. Such a necklace, pearls as big as marbles, jewellery boxes full to overflowing, everything you can think of. Solid gold and silver broaches, bracelets, rings - she even has a diamond band for her hair - for special occasions, like.' Her eyes lit. 'Rubies, sapphires, I lost count. I had to separate the gold from the silver and clean 'em all. The silver had to be dipped in something, holding it with tweezers. It's the silver tarnishes, you see. Then there was a box of paste stuff on her dresser, I had to use that an' all.'

'So you think Heath's wealth lies in his wife's diamonds?'

'No, I've not finished my tale yet. I emptied her jewel box and I got a little brush to dust over the velvet inside. I was real careful, but the bottom got snagged and the velvet came up. There was a slip of paper under it, with the number of the safe on it. See? I told you I knew the secret of Mr Heath's wealth, didn't I?'

'And how do you know it was the number of the safe?'

'I couldn't think what else it could be. I never saw her take her things out, but I know where the safe is.' She smiled proudly. 'It's surprising what you find, cleanin' and dustin'.'

'Go on.'

'It's outside the butler's pantry. Most everything's kept in there.'

'I wouldn't put it past Heath to have safes all over the house. What you probably saw was where he keeps his cuff links.'

She opened her eyes in innocent surprise. 'No, John, you're wrong on that score. When I'd finished shining the jewellery, I helped her put it back in the safe. All except the box with the number in it. She keeps that on her dressing table.'

'And I suppose if Heath's burgled it'll be you who's to blame?'

'Not me, John, I forgot the number. Only I didn't forget where it's kept, mind.'

Later in the afternoon, they returned by another path. He left her in the lane to make her own way back.

A month later, Nerissa Birkenshaw came down to the Grange with her father and called at the office. John was quick to conceal his surprise.

'I take it you've called with another pair of socks. You'd better leave them on Ball's desk while he's out on business, mine's too cluttered.' She folded her parasol and sat. 'Would you like some tea? I'm afraid we don't run to Wedgwood.'

'I'm not thirsty, thank you.' A beam fell across her eyes and she moved her chair to see him without squinting. 'I've decided to help you,' she said. 'I'm going to tell Mr Heath the truth.'

'What truth?'

'That I met you at the ball last year and that you have shown how committed you are to your work and how much you know about the running of the house. I shall tell him I count you as one of my friends and that I'm disappointed you have only an office position.'

'Don't mock me, Nerissa.' His outburst startled her into laughing. 'It's just a game with you, isn't it? You, your Roddy, the lot of you, just a bloody game.' He was gripping her arm, then he found himself kissing her and pulled away. A high colour had risen to her cheeks. 'You shouldn't antagonise me,' he said, his voice hoarse. 'If it's any consolation, I'm sorry. Blame the heat of the moment. I apologise.'

It seemed she might leave in a huff, but when she looked at him the smile in her eyes was at odds with her reproach. 'Perhaps I should tell Mr Heath you tried to seduce me, then where would you be?'

'On the parish or in court.'

'A servant kissing his master's guest, whatever would he think?' She came close, her dress dappled with light from the window. 'You mustn't worry, I'm used to intrigue. It makes life so much more exciting.'

'And Roddy?'

'What of him?'

'Is he to kiss you too?'

She twisted a ringlet. 'I don't know that that's any concern of yours. Anyway, you'll be too busy in your office to find out.' She was leaving as

Ginny Leadbetter came up. They exchanged a glance and Nerissa walked away, unfurling her parasol.

'It seems I've come at an awkward time,' Ginny said, going off in the opposite direction.

A few days later, as he passed through the vestibule on his way to deliver a message, he ran into Heath. As always, the man's bulk made him think of an indestructible warship.

'Good morning, sir. I hope Mrs Heath is getting better.'

'On the mend,' Heath grunted, referring to his wife's recent stomach upset and resentful of having to speak on any matter unconnected with his business. 'I've had a report in your favour, Tanbrey. I've been told you're sticking to your work, and that's something, I think.'

'Thank you, sir.'

'I heard from a good source, though how that source knows I aren't rightly sure.' He gave John a curious stare and continued heavily across the hall. 'Anyway, you seem to have made your mark, so there must be something in the moorland air after all.'

When John returned to the office, Urias caught his mood. 'You look like a man who fell in the midden and come up with a gold watch.'

'I've just been speaking to Heath.'

'And what's he got to say for himself?'

'He wants to be remembered to you.'

'You want to keep out of his road, he'll have you on toast for breakfast.'

'I'm cultivating him so I can take over when he dies.'

'Buggers like Heath don't die.'

Urias flicked through a calendar, making notes in his jotter and mumbling answers to questions he put to himself, a habit growing more entrenched as he got older. John worked with an exhilaration which went unnoticed by the older man, who had his head sunk in ledgers for much of the day. When John returned to the Moel, he went upstairs and took out Pol's photograph. He spent a minute examining her plump curves, then turned over the picture and wrote:

YOU MIGHT CARE TO LOOK AT THIS SO YOU KNOW WHAT KIND OF PERSON YOU HAVE IN YOUR EMPLOY. SOMEONE WHO IS NOT FIT

> TO HOLD AN OFFICE OF TRUST. IF YOU THINK THIS IS NONSENSE SEND A MAN TO THE ADDRESS BELOW AND HE WILL LEAVE YOU IN NO DOUBT. MR URIAS BALL DOES NOT DESERVE HIS POSITION AND WHEN THE TIME COMES FOR US TO ADMIT OUR SINS BEFORE GOD HE WOULD DO WELL TO STAND BEFORE THE HOST AND REPENT FOR THE GOOD OF HIS SOUL. GO TO 14 BACK SAGE STREET CASTLEFIELD IN MANCHESTER WHERE YOU WILL ENCOUNTER A DEN OF VICE KNOWN ONLY TOO WELL TO MR BALL. I FEEL IT MY CHRISTIAN DUTY TO GIVE YOU THESE FACTS

Written by a religious zealot, perhaps? Nothing could ever be proved. He sealed the envelope and addressed it to Mr Heath, the Grange, then changed his mind and added an 's' to 'Mr'. Heath might be a man of the world, but not his wife. The photograph would go to her. He pictured Urias taking the morning post with his own execution warrant in his hand. He thought he'd send it from Leek, that was far enough away to make them wonder. He'd go that weekend, might even take Ginny. The notion amused him. Everything amused him. He went downstairs and into the garden, ate an apple, threw the core into the bushes and laughed out loud.

Less than a week later, Urias found himself on the Manchester train. Oblivious to the riot of leaves behind the glass, his thoughts were on Pol. She faded at the next bridge and re-emerged at Stockport like a mischievous spirit. A pod of venom exploded in him. Not the letter, nor the sender, not even Heath, but Pol was responsible. She'd given him the picture to trap him, and now his position, the fingers pointed, the whispered asides - it was all her fault. He joined the crowd leaving the train and clambered into a waiting cab. Leaving it, he ran through streets he couldn't remember taking to her house.

The nets flicked. 'Mr Blank! I hope you had a pleasant journey.'

'Is she upstairs?'

'I do believe she is.'

His tone alerted the woman, who, instead of turning to her room opened a door further down the passage. Urias gained the landing. Pol's door was locked. He heard bolts being drawn and saw the flicker of a smile, a pink gown, a protrusive knee. There were words, perhaps his own, before his hands found her neck. Her nails scored his forearm before she toppled back, her robe open at the legs and breast. As she buckled he fell on top of her. Her hand groped for the fire-iron and she spat in his face and brought her knee up, making him grunt. Then her fingers closed on the poker and she arced it across his back. A bolt of pain shot through him and she scrambled for the table bell, but before she could reach it he'd launched himself on her, dislodging the carrara venus which smashed beside them. Two thickly-muscled men ran from the downstairs room, clearing the steps two at a time. Urias remembered the door bursting open, a nerve-wrenching pain in his arm, his sweating face thrust unnaturally backwards.

'He tried to kill me, the bastard!'

She pulled at her chemise as they manhandled him to the head of the stairs. Fear thrust through the fog in his brain as the tiled hall swam far below and their grip on his arm tightened. Screams seemed to follow him all the way to the front door, and he felt himself being hurled down the steps and into the gateless entrance. The noise of the door being slammed came to him as he rose shakily to his feet. He reached a tavern and sat huddled in a corner of the saloon. An Irish bargee was decrying the heathen Turks, a crone cackled by the bar, the landlord rattled a tray of glasses, a regular spat into a spittoon while his terrier dozed under the table.

'Know what they say, Enoch, Cross by name and cross by nature.'

'He wants to get the bloody drains sorted out afore he starts on the water. What's the good o' bringing in fresh water when you have your middens emptied in it seven days a week?

'He's best seeing to our bread, bloody maggots in it, chalk, anythin' they can lay their hands to. It's about time some bugger gave the bakers a run for their money.'

Cross's recent reforms were lost on Urias. He didn't know even now why the girl had been the focus of his anger when a more rational man would have blamed whoever had got him dismissed. And he knew who it was. *He knew*. He cast his mind back to when John's father had brought him in. He'd had it in for him even then. Something behind the eyes. Something to be wary of. He'd sent it to Heath, he'd sent it to do him down, to wipe his nose in the dirt. He'd somehow got hold of the photograph, bided his time. Urias remembered losing it, remembered being worried about it. Tanbrey had taken it. He knew it. But that had been long since. Why send it to Heath's wife now, why not then? *It's my job he wants, my job*. But was it Tanbrey? Where was the proof?

'Sit yourself down, Ball. I've something to show you.'

Through his glass he saw again the envelope reflected in Heath's writing desk.

'What would that be, Mr Heath?'

'Look inside.'

'What's it about?'

'Don't you know?'

The girl's mocking smile swam before him.

'Somebody's out to to get me, Mr Heath.'

'It's your name across it.'

'Anybody could've put it there.'

'D'you want me to send a man up to this Back Sage Street? I've never been one to pry into a man's private life. If you wanted to indulge some tart you should've been more circumspect, like the rest of us. I can't quarrel with your work. If I'd been sent it I'd have put it on the fire and had a quiet word. Unfortunately it was my wife saw it. Do you get my drift?'

He left the pub, clutching the wall while the street reeled. There was a a jingle of reins, and he lurched forward.

'I'm giving you notice. I'm wearing my magistrate's cap. I'm supposed to keep a sound house, no malarkey. Whoever wrote that seems in a position to do us all a bit of damage.'

He watched the flames lick Pol's image through a blur of hackneys and omnibuses, his employer breaking up the blackened fragments with a poker.

'What am I to do now Mr Heath? Who's going to look at me at fifty-seven?'

Heath poked at the disintegrated remains. 'Get yourself up to the forge Monday. We'll see if we can't find you something to tide you over.'

He teetered on the edge of the pavement. All he'd had was his job. What was he to be, a common labourer leading donkeys up the sytch? A brakeman on the wagons? A foundry cleaner, working for men thirty years his junior. D'you know who that is? That's Ball, Heath's old estate manager, fond of the wenches, though you'd never think so to look at him.... He could hear them now, could still hear them as he lurched into the gutter.

He hadn't seen the dray. The first wheel struck him a glancing blow, and the following wheel passed over his foot. Featureless faces gathered around him as he went down. He didn't care.

9

The sky was a hot, clear blue. Charlie found some shade and sat for his lunch. He hadn't been to Three Elms since he saw Ellen and Bill together. He'd expected her always to be there, but now she belonged to a different world and her cornflower eyes were doors to a place he couldn't reach. He contented himself with his pictures, sketching the guelder rose which grew in the hedge and the heartsease which sprung like weeds below his window. Some he colour-washed using the brushes Caulton had given him, which brought to mind the teacher's advice and urged him look afresh at the lupins' tessellated petals and the candles of syringa growing along the path.

When Ellen called in early September, he was working at the table and didn't hear her knock. When he looked up she was standing in the doorway.

'I've not seen you in months, Charlie. I came to see how you're getting on.'

'I've been busy of late.' He bent again to his work, adding dribbles in an agony of embarrassment.

'What're you up to?'

'Just practising.'

'You were always one for flowers. Remember that time we had words about daisies, when you said they were marguerites?' She peered over his shoulder. 'What are they, buttercups? I like the way you've arranged them. You've got just the right shade of yellow an' all.' He mixed a cerulean ground, added white. 'Everybody's out, are they?'

'They've gone down Bradley Green.'

'Well, you know what they say, artists don't need to eat.' He could sense her restlessness and hoped she'd make her excuses and leave. He wanted her to stay.

'D'you fancy a walk,' she asked, 'while the weather holds?' She waited by the door while he put on his jacket and muffler and didn't speak again until they were away from the house. 'Can you keep a secret?'

'It depends.'

'On what?'

'On what it is.'

'I've a secret about you, but I shan't tell it, not yet any road.'

'Please yourself.'

'I've another, Charlie, I've to tell somebody or I'll go mad.'

'Why don't you tell our Bill?'

'It's about your Bill.'

'I don't know why you want to talk to me when you've got him.'

'I'm telling you 'cos I'm not sure Bill's ready to be a father yet.' Her voice had risen, and when she looked at him he could see she was close to tears. 'It were the first time, Charlie, I was nowt but headstrong.'

'Are you saying you're in the family way?'

'Don't let on to Doris, will you? You mustn't tell, promise you won't tell.' Struggling with himself, he asked if she was sure. 'What d'you think I am, Charlie, a cow in calf? They take time, you know. It won't be long before I start to get looks. It's Bevis as much as me, I don't want him upset.' She swished absently at the grass. 'D'you remember how simple it all seemed, you on one side o' the playground and me on the other? Why do we have to grow up, why can't we stay at school till we're ninety?'

'You'll have to tell him,' he said.

'And what then?'

'I suppose you'll have to get wed.'

Her chin began to quiver. 'You know what I found when I was cleaning his room? A bag of sovereigns stuck in a hole behind the skirting. I moved back the cupboard to dust and hit the board with the broom. It just fell off. But what's it all for?'

'I suppose for when he has a wife.'

'Has he been with lots of girls?'

'He'd always one or the other.'

'I think he's saving for something.' Her sudden brightness evaporated. 'Where would we live, I'm hardly seventeen.'

'I don't suppose you're the first to have a baby,' he said, feeling older than his years. 'I dare say things'll sort themselves out one way or another.'

'You're a good sort, Charlie. I knew I'd be able to tell you. You're a real friend. It's you I should be getting wed to.' She dabbed at her eyes. 'It's as well to have somebody to talk to, it helps sort things out inside. Things could be worse, couldn't they? I could be dead, couldn't I? You won't tell?'

'No, I won't tell.'

'Not even Will, nobody.'

They'd walked almost to Moor Edge. A stiff breeze sprung from the greying sky. As they took the road to the finger post, he felt the first stirrings of age.

She told Bill the following month. His wild plans led nowhere, and she felt helpless. She was afraid she might become hysterical and frighten him off. She didn't want a child and she didn't want to marry him or anyone and she knew he felt the same.

'Just for the baby's sake?'

'Ay.'

'When?'

'Soon as I can arrange things.'

'Shall I tell them?'

'Let me arrange things first.'

'What is there to arrange?'

'You can't expect to drop this on my doorstep without giving it some thought.'

'I suppose you weren't responsible for puttin' it there?'

'I suppose you were somewhere else at the time. Look,' he said, trying to console himself as well as her, 'you can't just turn it out to grass like a sturk. Maybe we should've thought on while we were enjoyin' ourselves. I'll talk to your folks.'

'Now?'

'I'll sleep on it.'

Already she felt a stranger to him. She avoided Doris and went straight to her room, where she lay awake listening to the faint strain of voices downstairs. He'd done nothing to allay her fears. Babies born out of wedlock were bastards even to those born bastards themselves. The word would spread disorder through the ordered landscape, something to be whispered behind turned backs and closed doors. She wished she'd never set eyes on him.

That night, as the hay glimmered against the dark sweeps of woodland, Nat climbed the stack as he'd seen the manikin do in his book when he spun straw into gold. Around him shone belladonna, red with a prince's blood and a turret with a flag flying over the waveless sea.

'Nat!' A head had risen above the ladder. 'Nat, what're you doing up there in the dead o' night?'

'Spot o' mendin''. Wind springs up, have hay in the brook.'

'There's no wind and the brook's two fields off. Look, Nat, I want you to do me a favour. I can't talk loud or they'll hear inside, right? And I can't talk to you stuck up on top o' the rick, for Christ's sake.' Nat moved to the ladder and slowly climbed down. 'I want you to do me a favour. I want you to give this to Ellen tomorrow, and don't let your father or mother see it. It's for Ellen on her own, understand? You're to give it to Ellen and nobody else. Give it her when she's in the shed. Now don't forget or you'll get me in a bother.' Bill pushed a small bag into his hand and Nat took it, his eyes opaque. 'I'm trusting you, Nat. I don't want it squirrelin' away so she can't find it. He pressed a florin into the youth's palm. 'Come on, put it in your pocket.' He patted Nat's jacket, his voice hoarse with frustration. 'You mustn't forget – where're you going?'

'I've seen rabbits up by th' barns.'

'Nat, I've to go now. You're to say nothing to Bevis or Doris, eh?'

'Owl's gone.'

'Must've been his bloody brother in the loft, then.'

Bill was already moving away. He turned by the byres to find Nat looking at him quizzically, and when he turned again he'd gone back up the ladder. At the finger post he took a deep breath. The lane stretched palely before him. A sense of release grew with the steady beat of his footsteps. Soon he'd be leaving Moor Top to its shadows. He thought of his father, his brothers, the rector, the swinging pub sign and the owl calling from the lea. It was midnight by the time he reached the valley and walked past Heath's pit and forge, with the hammers still pounding.

At the same time, George Dixon lurched into a table, sending the glasses spinning. The landlord and his son got him to the door and left him on the step. Brindley lay still in a dusky hollow. Dixon blinked at the veils of cloud before scrambling to his feet and turned towards the hill of slag. He'd show them! He'd fight every single one of them. 'Bastards!' The hill echoed his shouts. He shadow-boxed it, then saw Priscilla in the moon's face in her white blouse, with her white skin. Rainwater had weathered the shale into gullies and he stumbled from gulley to ridge. His house was five minutes over the tip, and he lurched across, swearing, breaking into snatches of raucous song. He'd nothing to go back to, only the whispers that had begun with the doctor's housekeeper. Even his mother was dead, now. Nothing to go back to.

He was in sight of the lane when a movement caught his eye. Something in the shape, the way it moved. He struggled to build a pattern he could recognise as it glided across the debris. Slowly, a name came to him. The man drew level.

'Tanbrey? Come to pay your respects to my Missus?'

'Why, is she waiting up for anybody that happens to be slogging over the tips in the middle o' the night?'

'You always were a cheeky bastard. I should've laid you out long since.'

Bill could smell ale on Dixon's breath, the rage simmering behind the small, vindictive, eyes.

'Are you wanting to start a fight in the middle of nowhere at one in the morning? Why don't you go home and sober up, George?' He moved down the runnel, but the butty lurched after him like an ape, seized him by the shoulder and swung him around. Bill saw the hook coming and jerked away. The momentum carried Dixon into the slack.

'Take another swing and I'll put you off your feet.'

Dixon scrambled up, cursing. They were all in it together, Tanbrey, the doctor, all of them, trying to destroy him. 'I might be drunk but I'm not so drunk I can't sort you out.'

He lurched forwards and Bill went down, trapped under Dixon's bulk. Dixon pinned his wrists to the dirt and was awkwardly trying to butt him. Bill dodged and gathered a gob of spit which he spat full at the unhinged face. As Dixon momentarily relaxed his grip, Bill brought up his forearm, striking the man's windpipe and jerking back his head. On his feet, he aimed a kick at Dixon's groin, catching the inside of his thigh and dragging himself off balance. He got up as Dixon gripped him from the back and kicked back, but the older man had his legs apart. The fug in Dixon's brain was beginning to clear. He felt the man weaken. He'd squeeze the blood from him and trample on his carcass in revenge for all the insults paid him.

Bill grew dizzy and nauseous. Gathering the last of his strength, he smashed his elbow against the butty's chest. The man toppled back, and Bill rolled away, fighting for breath. The older man lay still, staring up with a questioning expression and a sticky thread oozing from the corner of his mouth. Bill bent and cracked him sharply about the face. 'You're too old for games, George, get up and go home.' It was then he saw the blood-stained spike which had broken through the breast of the jacket Jud Cowlishaw's money had paid for. He stared at it, touching the point with a dull curiosity, wondering how it came to be there.

'George!'

He struggled to think. About his plan, a plan that nobody was going to scotch, least of all Dixon. He heaved the body into the scree and began to bury it under rubble, clinker, shale, higher and higher until nothing remained. The distant panting of pit engines broke through the fog of his brain. He forced himself to stand and walked slowly away, looking over his shoulder. At the edge of the mound he began to stride out.

He reached the city a little before dawn and hovered under a canal bridge, cooling his face with the murky water before catching the first train to Liverpool. He managed to purchase a late steerage for the *Bothnia*, sailing that evening and due in New York eight days later. He bought a new coat, Derby shoes, a shirt and tie. Packing his other purchases into a waterproof railway valise, he spent a long afternoon in a hotel lounge awaiting his departure.

The mild autumn had given way to the first snows of winter, and in Leek the cobbled streets were already blanketed. From an upstairs room, Ellen looked down on a woman struggling with a bassinet. The window would normally have provided a bright morning light, but the oppressive afternoon made her bedroom look squalid.

Four months had passed since Bill's departure. She'd been to the Moel a score of times, but they'd heard nothing from him. She'd taken pains to hide her pregnancy from Bevis and his wife, and they'd put her upset down to Bill's leaving. By October she told them she wanted to move away from the farm, saying she felt too cut off, wanted to earn her own money and seek companionship in town. She knew nothing of the money Bill had left her, nor of his note advising her to spend it at some back-street abortionist's. Nat had pocketed the ten sovereigns, then, convinced he'd be hung for thieving, had hid them down a rabbit hole. As Bill was sailing towards a new life, Ellen was examining the cavity behind the skirting board. The vacant space had convinced her he wasn't coming back. She was in turmoil, plodding the lanes with Charlie, wondering what to do. She'd heard they wanted silk winders at Leek, and that seemed to provide a temporary solution to her problems.

'But you can't work with a baby coming.'

'Some carry a full nine months and you'd hardly know. Look at me hair!' She lowered her face, parting the strands. 'It's all lank, dandruff all over the place. Do I look pale?' He said she didn't. Brightening, she said: 'How would you like to come to the farm regular, take over from your brother?'

'I aren't sure.'

'You'll do it for me, Charlie?' He shrugged. 'For Bevis, then?'

'I'll have to give it some thought.'

'You'll get paid.'

'I don't like letting folks down.'

'Luke Pointon won't miss you! Gardening's for old men.'

'They'd have to be fit mauling the barrow I have to contend with.'

She pealed her laugh, her problems for the moment forgotten. 'Have you still got your penny, the one that's supposed to bring you luck?'

'It's sat at home in the drawer.'

'Keep it for me, Charlie, maybe it'll bring me luck as well one day.'

'It's brought me none yet. Not even a good homecoming of an evening.'

'What d'you mean?'

'It doesn't matter.'

'Tell me.'

He rubbed at his brow. 'I get the feeling father doesn't want to know me, especially since mother died.' She turned towards him as if there was something she'd wanted to say. The look passed. 'Anyway, I can't run the farm, I wouldn't know where to start.'

'You've done it before.'

'Ay, with your old man doing most o' the work. Anyway, I've been thinking things over. I've been wondering if I could get a painting job at some time.'

'You can start by painting our house.'

'I mean proper painting, what I do now.'

'You mean you want to be an artist! Maybe one of these days I'll be able to say I knew Charlie Tanbrey, the famous painter. And how d'you set about that? There's not many round here have money to spend on pictures. They're hard put to buy boot leather.'

He gave his shrug. 'I dare say there'll be somebody as knows.'

'How about Dr McEvoy, or the rector? Happen they'll know how to go about it....'

But he'd remained with Luke Pointon while Bevis struggled with itinerant labourers and the constant worry he might have to sell some of his land to keep insolvency at bay. Ellen felt for them, cut off in the snow. But she was determined not to inflict the shame of a child born out of wedlock on them . Not until she'd made her own way.

Late in the afternoon, Heath summoned John to his office. After a calculated interval, he faced the younger man.

'How long have you been with us, Tanbrey?'

'Almost five years, sir.'

'How have you found it? Speak plain, I won't bite your head off.'

'I think I'm equal to any demand you might make of me.'

Heath tittered to himself. 'Any demand I might make, eh?' He leaned suddenly forward. 'You'd like Urias' job, wouldn't you?'

'Obviously, if such a position were offered –'

The industrialist tittered again, tensing his chin as if to stifle an urge to laugh. 'You're a queer fish, Tanbrey. You speak like a politician. I bet you could teach Disraeli a thing or two.' He bent to examine a list on his desk. 'Let's see, you've done Ball's job since he left.'

'Since September last, along with my own.'

'And?'

'I'd taken the trouble to learn the work, sir. Mr Ball was very kind. I was sorry to see him go.'

'That's neither here nor there. D'you think you're ready to creep into his boots on a permanent basis?'

'I'm confident I could manage.'

'I bet you are, too.' Heath paused, beating a tattoo on the desk. 'That brother of yours, have you heard of his whereabouts?'

'Bill? No, sir, I'm afraid we haven't.'

'I got the story from one of the gardeners. There's always a nark of one sort or another, Tanbrey. One had his knife in Ball, but that's another tale. Urias can thank his stars he's not in the workhouse.' A heavy silence had fallen across the room. John tried to gauge the man's thoughts, but Heath was inscrutable. At length he focused his eyes on the younger man. 'How do you fancy the Bull?'

'The colliery and ironworks? In what capacity, Mr Heath?'

'Don't get the belly-ache, there's plenty down under without you joining them. I've a notion to put you with Jock Duggan. You won't know him. He's got two years left, then he's out to grass. If you can pick up what he's about, I can't see any good reason why you shouldn't take over where he leaves off.'

'Doing what, Mr Heath?'

'Call him my right-hand man, if you like. What are you, gone twenty? Just the right age to be thinking about making your way. What d'you say?'

'I could give you a fairer answer if I knew what it was about.'

Heath faced him stonily, his eyes alert behind the expressionless face. 'You worked hard on your speech. I'm told when you started you were full of the moor. Why take all the trouble?'

'I wanted to make something of myself.'

Heath muttered the words back at him, making faint rattles of amusement in his throat. 'Tell you what, you go to the same lengths with this work and you'll be opening your own front door before two years are up. Canny as only a Scot can be, Jock Duggan, doesn't miss a trick. You'll find him a touch dour at first, but he's straight as a die. Go on letting him think he runs the place and he'll be your friend for life.'

'And what about my work here?'

Heath leaned forward and linked his hands across the desk. 'I'm doing you a favour. I keep you in Ball's old job, what have I got? An errand boy. Is that what you want? I don't think it is, and I flatter myself I can read folks right. Anyway, I've already got somebody in mind for that. I'll double your wage. Mind you earn every last penny and keep your nose clean. Consider it an apprenticeship if you like.' He'd already immersed himself in new correspondence, leaving John to make his way out of the room. As he opened the door, Heath looked up. 'You never know, with that kind of wage you could afford to get wed.'

When he got back to the office he put his feet on the desk and sat beaming at the desolate winter gardens through the window. He was already contemplating his future as Heath's new man. He'd played for Urias' job and got another. Fate had dealt him a winning hand. He had a sudden feeling of benevolence towards other less fortunate souls, and to get rid of it he took up his pen.

'Dear Nerissa,

Mr Heath has offered me a position on his colliery and ironworks at the Bull, working with one Jock Duggan, who seems to be a mainstay of the place. I'm told Duggan will shortly be retiring and I can expect his job. I see this as an opportunity to become a force in the district, which would suit me very well. When you next come over, perhaps we could accidentally meet in a secluded part of the gardens.

Yours Affectionately,
John'

He put the note in an envelope and and settled once more to his papers. Within a week he'd received a reply, congratulating him and asking that she in turn be congratulated on her engagement to Roddy Davenport. She hoped that if she brought Roddy over to the Grange, he'd not allow himself to be jealous. He shredded the page and dropped the pieces into the stove. He'd deluded himself into thinking he was something more to her than an interesting pastime. Let her have her Roddy, or any of the other fops he'd seen lounging by the walls at the ball. They deserved each other. What was she but the heiress to a floor of clapped-out looms? Seizing a sheet, he jabbed his pen into the inkwell and scrawled a reply.

'Dear Nerissa,

You couldn't have made a wiser choice. You need not concern yourself on my account. At present I'm still only the office boy. I hope to have the chance of meeting your fiance on a better 'footing' than before. I'm sure we'll get on like a house on fire.

Congratulations,
John'

He sat brooding in the fading light and looking out across the ornamental lake. It was exceptionally mild, with something of the air of spring. The water reflected the grey of the sky, with streaks of pallid light etched across its surface. It took him a moment to realise the figure against the dark foliage was Ginny. Pushing back his chair, he went out to her. She turned, startled, as she heard him approach.

'Why, John! I'd to run an errand for the Mistress. It's not like winter at all, is it?'

'Where are you going?'

'Back to the house. It's Molly Mills' new baby - you know Sammy Mills, don't you? He tends the horses. Mrs Heath sent me with a parcel, a tin of sweetmeats for Molly and a nice rattle. What have you been up to?'

'This and that.'

'It must be more than three weeks since we walked out together.'

'Perhaps you'd like to walk out now?'

'I have to get back,' she said doubtfully. 'I could see you this weekend, if you like?'

'Either we go now, or not at all.'

She considered, downcast. 'All right, but not for long, or I'll be in a bother. Where shall we walk to?'

'We'll take a turn in the Chinese Garden. Don't worry, you won't be seen, you'll be hard put to see your hand in ten minutes.'

She walked uncertainly a step ahead. A feeling of reckless power gripped him. 'We'll go through the passage, no one will see us there.'

'Are you sure?'

'You'll be back before we've started.'

Clipped yews cut into the threatening sky. He led the way past the sphinxes guarding the underground passage. A fungal smell rose from the floor, and he pushed towards the glimmering figure of the Ape of Thoth.

'I've never liked it down here, John, I feel all shut in.'

'There's no danger.'

'I'd rather go.' In the grey half-light, he found himself gripping her wrist. She struggled against him, but he'd seized her other wrist, pistoning her arms to break their strength. 'Stop it, John, you're hurting me.'

'That's right, I'm hurting you.' He spat the words at the pale shadow of her face, mocking her speech, making her arms jerk like a marionette's.

'Don't! Stop it!'

'You're nothing but a skivvy. I'll show you how little you're worth.'

Her maid's cap fell to the floor, her hair caught in his fingers. He trapped her scream with his hand and kicked her legs from under her, bringing her down. He raised his hand to hit her but tangled it in her flailing arms. She was emptily crying, but he'd trapped her under his hip and held her head to the floor. He felt a growing arousal, sought her face with wet, open lips. She strained her head away like a dying fish and lay beneath him, whimpering as he dug his fingers into her flesh. She felt nothing but a yawning void as he lunged into her and lay, sprawled across the bricks. The silence lasted no more than a minute. He lay listening to last season's leaves crackling against the base of the figure, then began to button his fly.

'Ginny - I've not hurt you, have I?'

'You forced yourself on me, I didn't want this, I didn't want this - '

She spoke through a convulsion of sobs, and he could scarcely make out what she said. The enormity of what he'd done began to dawn on him. He held her by the shoulders but she shook him off. 'Ginny, listen to me, it's been pent up in me all these months. You mustn't feel badly of me. I couldn't help it, I couldn't help it.' Moved by his own words, the tears coursed down his cheeks. 'Promise you won't tell, Ginny, promise.'

'How could you do it, you had no need.'

She struggled, still sobbing, to her feet. He followed her out into the darkness. 'I'll go and see Mrs Heath, I'll tell her you didn't feel well and had to go to your room.'

'It's like cattle, even the beasts –' She ran her hand across her swollen cheek. 'I'm none of those things you said, and now I'm ruined. I'd have hoped for more than that from you. I might have hoped you loved me.'

'I do, I do love you,' he heard himself say, the promised job too precious to be lost for want of a lie.

'I don't want your love, I want to go.'

'For God's sake, Ginny, I didn't know what I was doing. I - I thought you were going out with somebody else, that's why I hadn't seen you in weeks. It was all jealousy, I didn't mean it. Don't say anything. I don't want us to part like this, don't bring trouble on us.'

'You love that Nerissa Birkenshaw. I bet you've never done that to her.'

'She's nobody. I didn't know what I was doing!' He hid his face from her, believing what he heard himself say, feeling the wet against his fingers. She'd sunk into a deep well of sadness and he couldn't reach her. He played his last card. 'If you tell anyone, I'll kill myself.'

She turned towards him with a curious disinterest. When he raised his head she was moving away along the path.

'Tell me what to do,' he called after her.

'You must do what you will.'

He stood in silence looking after her, then went home.

10

The rector examined his pocket watch. 'So you wish to pursue an artistic career. Have you heard of Uccello?' Charlie said he hadn't. 'You can do worse than study the masters. D'you know the works of Michelangelo? His *Pieta*; I've never seen it in the life, but I once saw a plaster-cast. There's an engraving at the rectory you can look at, but I'm afraid there's no time today.'

'I've been doing a lot of flowers of late, but they seem more like designs. I can't fathom it right.'

'I'm not sure I understand your problem,' he said, moving away. 'Take my advice and stick to gardening. Art is a precarious way to earn a living. I suppose,' he added, creaking open the nave door, 'that is the reason only the gentry have been able to indulge in it.' He hoisted his vestments to avoid the pockets of uncleared snow. 'Observe the achievements of others – that's a good place to begin. In the meanwhile carry on gardening.' Turning at the rectory gate, he added: 'You could do worse than study Mr Bateman's *Orchidaceae of Mexico and Guatemala*. 'There's all the plant paintings you could wish for. Come and see me later if you want to see it, I can fix that up for you.'

Charlie lingered for a moment, then turned for home.

The following Sunday was cold and fine, and he decided to walk over to Three Elms. When he got there, Doris was working hard at the butter churn.

'We've had a letter from our Bill. He's gone off to America.' He gave the information with pride, enjoying the roll of the word on his tongue.

'And what's he have to say for himself?'

'He's going out West, he says there are opportunities. He asks after Ellen.'

Doris uncorked the butter barrel and poured out the residue. 'Could do with a touch more turning. Here, Charlie, give this to the pigs.'

She passed him the pan, and he poured the buttermilk into the squealing trough. When he returned to the dairy, she'd gone into the house. A downspout had come away from the wall since his last visit, and the windows were rotting in the mullion. Benersley looked up as he came in, his finger tamping the unlit bowl.

'I'm surprised you've found us, it's been so long. Doris says you've heard from that brother of yours.'

Charlie took out the letter and offered it, but Benersley waved him away. 'Read it to me, let's hear what he's got to say for himself.'

He unfolded the sheets: "You'll be wondering what I've been doing since I went away. I arrived at Castle Garden where all the new arrivals go, now I'm staying at a place in New York. It's not too smart, but it's all I can afford. In due course I intend to go out West. I'm sorry I didn't let you know, and you can apologise to the Benersleys as well for leaving them in the lurch. There's space to breathe here. There are a lot of Irish, Germans as well, and Swedish, all the old countries mixed up. Some are on their own like me, but there are families too. Please tell Ellen where I am and give her my regards and don't think amiss of me. I've done some bad things, but no worse than anybody else. I'm going to try and make something of myself out here, and if I don't it won't be for want of trying. Don't forget to tell Ellen, and please thank the Benersleys for their kindness.

Your loving son and brother,

Bill." '

Benersley squinted at the post mark. 'Why, it's taken near ten weeks to get here.'

'He'd no need to put himself on the other side of the world just to spare the girl's feelings,' Doris interrupted. 'He could just as well have told her, couldn't he? He's a tongue in his head, hasn't he, Charlie?'

They obviously knew nothing about Ellen's condition, and thought he'd left to prevent her from getting more 'involved'.

'I suppose so, Mrs Benersley.'

'What d'you mean, you suppose so? You should know. Anyway,' she added, her sharpness forgotten, 'if you're staying you can empty that pot into a couple of mugs before it gets stewed.' Benersley poured his tea into a saucer, blowing ripples as if involved in some magical rite. 'You've no idea where Ellen's living, have you?' she asked from the door. 'I know it's Leek, but last time we met she seemed cagey about it. I can't make her out, she were always open in 'er ways. It's more than four weeks since she was last down. It doesn't bother him,' she castigated her husband. 'If the devil himself popped in, he'd pull up a chair.'

Benersley puffed contentedly, his eyes shining like beads. 'And how's your John? Still down the Grange, is he?'

'He seems all right.'

'And the gardening? Not much doing this time o' the year, I expect?'

'We do repairs, then there's veg to lift and the greenhouses to attend to.'

'Who is it you work for, d'you say?'

'Luke Pointon. I was telling the rector, I can't see myself gardening for ever.'

'You want to be grateful you've not got beasts to look after. Chance what you do in life, there are drawbacks, Charlie. You've to take the rough with the smooth, though it's more rough than smooth much of the time. By the by, how's Will these days?'

'He doesn't say much.'

'He never was much for conversation.'

His wife brought in a bowl of pobs, which he began to eat, mashing butter into the milk-sodden crusts and sprinkling them with brown sugar.

'You care for a bowl, Charlie?' called Doris from the back room.

'I'm not hungry at the moment, Mrs Benersley.'

'You don't know what's good for you,' Benersley chided. 'Them and lumpy tums - they'll put hairs on your chest.' Charlie watched him in silence, his rough hand holding the nickel-worn spoon in a clenched fist as if it were a farming implement, stroking the milk from his moustache with the back of a finger as the contents dwindled. 'I didn't tell you, I got a labourer down the hiring fair. For a year, like. Happen I'll keep him on if we suit each other. A young lad, bit older than yourself. He's in Bill's old room. You'll have to get acquainted when you come again. He's doing a spot o' wallin' with Nat at the moment; taught him how to dress stone, he reckons, which is more'n I was ever able to do.'

The farmer's voice rose and dipped in the fire-lit room. Charlie's eyes drifted to a decorated vase on the sill. Maybe he knew where he was going after all, despite what he'd told the rector....

'Are you listening to what I'm telling you? He's costing me. Mind, I can't grumble. Good lads are hard to come by. I dare say we'll cope.'

It was spitting snow as he started back. He'd missed not seeing Ellen and wondered if he should go to Leek and find out where she was living. He wondered about his brother in America, then the empty vase popped into his mind again, with the satisfying thought that here was something that would fulfil him in a way working for Luke Pointon never could. By the time he reached Top Road he saw himself as a designer of fine ware, his pieces crated and dispatched; cups to India, plates to Ohio, teapots and sugar basins to Bechuanaland and all the other places he'd heard of, signed with his name. The driving flakes stung his face as he reached the hill and he stuck his hands deep into his pockets feeling that, although he'd yet to tread the rung, at least he'd found the ladder.

Ellen woke to the mill bell clanging through the early morning dark and ran her hand down her stomach. It was bitterly cold in the room. She could hear others getting ready and hauled herself up to the edge of the bed. At length the pain subsided and she pulled on a loose-fitting smock and went out to the privy which served the tenants living in the terrace. A cough came from behind the door and a lodger came out, fastening his belt. She clenched her nostrils and went inside. A woman's head appeared over the door. 'Could you hurry up, love, else I'm goin' to be shut out?' Ellen adjusted her smock and lifted the bucket from a nail with the intention of swilling out the privy, but another stab of pain forced her to relinquish the pan to the next user.

A whiskering of snow smothered the alley. She came out opposite the mill and joined a group of girls walking through the gate, their chatter drowned by the throb of engines. A child was manhandling a consignment of silk from a cart as she crossed the yard. The din grew louder as she climbed the steps from the dyeing shop to the looms above. She took them slowly, supporting herself with a hand to the glazed brick. At the top she took a deep breath.

A beamed room spanned the length of the building, and bolted to the floor were rows of winding machines with girls in attendance. The windows to either side threw a wintry light across the room, aided by flares fixed at intervals to the walls. She made her way across to her place. The sight of the books of silk sickened her. She stooped to unfasten the uppermost parcel, labelled in Italian with a copperplate weight tariff made out by some railway clerk. Cutting the twine which bound the silk together, she fitted the first skein to the winding machine and attached the thread to a bobbin. The noise seemed to act like a pestle on her brain. The bobbins danced on their spools and she replaced them mechanically. She wanted rest. She wanted to be back at Three Elms, breathing fresh air and laughing with Charlie.

She'd bent to a fresh skein when something gave inside her, and she brought her legs together, trapping a wetness between her thighs. She left the skein where it had fallen and gripped the edge of the winder. The overlooker came and took her arm, and she found herself being led through the ranks of machinery towards the stairwell. The outside air struck her, and the factory noise subsided to a hollow drumming as the overseer leaned her against the wall.

'How far to home?'

'I'll make my own way.'

'What, both of you? I'll see Jervis.'

Ellen closed her eyes. The overlooker came back.

'They all know, do they?'

'Jervis knows there's a winder off sick.'

'What about the others?'

'He'll tell Kinnersley, the others can keep guessing. If they know, they'll gossip and if they don't they'll gossip. Close by, are you?'

'Just down Chorley Street.'

She'd thought she could have the child in the seclusion of her room. Now, for the first time, she was afraid. She'd never planned for next week because it didn't seem important. Perhaps she could have moved further away, to Ashbourne, or Cheadle. No one would know her there. But it might have been harder to find work. She'd made up some tale about losing her husband; farm accidents were ten a penny, people were always getting maimed or killed. With luck she'd be all right. There was many a man willing to marry a pretty girl, child or not. She'd be all right.

The house was empty. As she climbed the stair the first contractions made her cry out. She gained her attic room and fell on to the palliasse, her face beaded in sweat. The room dissolved into blurred images, a patch of laths, an oak-grained door, a square of sky. Her skirts fell to either side the bed, the discarded smock ruckled under her arched legs.

'Push!'

'I am. I am.'

'Harder.'

She stifled the scream and when it came didn't recognise it as her own.

'Come on, Ellen, you've got to push. Put all you've got into it. Push!'

There was a haystack, Mrs Caulton pinning her hat, a spinning bobbin, a thread twisting round and round and round her throat.... 'Is it coming?'

'Stuck....stuck....knife.'

'Who?'

The sound of a drawer being opened.

'I can feel the head. Keep pushing.'

'I'm -'

'Nearly there. One more. One last one.'

Her body was on fire. She thought she heard water gushing from the garden pump, the garden itself damp with sorrel, the roots shining and water burbling into the trough....

The overlooker was looking down at her.

'Is it all right?'

The woman seemed far away. Ellen closed her eyes and a great weariness overtook her. When she awoke, shadows had crept into the room. She reached for the blanket and pulled it under her chin and lay still for a while, then tried to turn, sending a jab of pain across her stomach.

'Go back to sleep.'

'The baby....'

'Asleep, as you should be.'

'Let me look at him.'

'It's a her.'

'I want to hold her. Give her to me.'

A bundle was lowered into her arms. 'I did the best I could. You're a rum'un, not so much as a cot or cloth, let alone a mid-wife. How did you think you were going to manage?'

'Isn't she tiny?'

'And who's the father?'

'Look, her hands are frozen.'

'When was the fire last lit?'

'I'm not lugging coal,' purred Ellen, holding the baby's hand between her thumb and finger and gazing down at the shrouded head in the half-dark, 'but we'll have fires now, won't we? We'll be all right, won't we?' She addressed the package in plaintive whispers, lifting it to her breast, rocking it gently to and fro.

'I'll get you something to eat.'

She clucked at the bundle as the door opened, threading light across the room. When the woman returned, she put a bowl on the trestle. Ellen gave her the baby and the overseer placed it in an open drawer.

'What time is it?'

'Gone six. Get it down, it'll do you good.'

'Fancy you looking after me and I've not spoken more than a dozen words to you all the time I've been at the Wellington.'

'There's been no need.'

Sobs rose uncontrollably to her throat. For a time she was incoherent. 'They won't send me to the workhouse, will they?'

'I wouldn't think you'd be much use picking oakum, the state you're in.'

'But they won't send us, will they?'

'No, they won't send you the workhouse.'

'But I've hardly anything put by.' She began to weep 'I don't want to go back home in this state, I don't want to go back, I don't want them to find out.'

The woman released her hand and stood over the baby. 'Who was it, a mill hand?'

'You wouldn't know him. He ran off soon as I told him.'

'Most do.'

'You're not married....'

'Never met anybody who came up to my expectations.'

She said with defiance, 'He were the first, you know!' Sobs gushed again. 'A lot of girls get away with it, don't they, why is it me gets saddled, what have I done?'

'Where's he gone?'

'He never left me so much as a sovereign.' She dried her eyes on the blanket and gathered herself. 'He had money, stored up in a hole in the wall. I never knew a farm hand before but spent it carousing. Bill had another side to him. I never properly got to workin' him out....'

'You said Bill. His other name – was it Tanbrey?'

'You know him?'

'I know him, and I can tell you where he's gone. America. He spoke about it when I knew him. He wasn't one for responsibilities. Happen it's just the thing as would make him start packing.'

'But....'

'The world's full of Bills. Once you've got the hang of it you can make your own way without benefit of any of them. I don't think I've seen him in over three years. I moved here shortly after my brother died.' Voices rose faintly below, a shout, a laugh. 'I reckon he thought I was a bit of a girl, but

I've never been other than Jane Cowlishaw and that's the name I'll keep, unless I meet someone with something between the ears as well as the legs.'

'But you lay with him?'

'I eat, too, but that doesn't mean I'm in love with lobby.'

'You've not ended up like me.'

Jane's voice droned through sleep and wakefulness and slowly stilled. When dawn came she was still asleep, wrapped in her coat. Ellen reached for the drawer and in the weak light saw her child's face, half hidden. Carefully, she picked her up. There was no cry or movement. Perhaps day-old babies didn't cry or move. Maybe it would be better fed. She began to undo herself, pulling the baby's face free of the coverings. The mouth looked strangely puckered in the gloom, and she went over to the window where the light was stronger. The upper lip was riven to the nose.

Jane had woken and was watching from the chair. 'Ellen, your baby's dead. I - I didn't know how to tell you.'

The texture of the room had altered. It was darker, somehow. Ellen reached for the bundle and pressed her lips to the pale forehead. She didn't feel Jane's hand on her shoulder. 'I'll stay with you. I'll not go in for a few days. Jervis can whistle.' From below came the clatter of clogs, a door being slammed. The house was silent. 'I have to go out for a minute. I'll get you something to eat when I come back.'

When she'd left the room, Ellen put her baby gently into her work bag and pulled on her boots. Each step was painful, and when she reached the door she had to lean against the wall. She rested by a post, sucking the morning air into her lungs, then shuffled across the road and leaned by a trough. She dragged herself down the deserted street and past the jumble of yards skirting the church. The lych gate lay open and she entered the building through a side door and saw the pews, their numbers painted in black, the pillars and stained windows in planes of white and brown with vivid stabs of red. Someone was speaking somewhere, *Mary, Mother of God, turn not thine eyes from this Thy child which hath sinned, but rather grant her everlasting salvation so that her days shall not be wearisome, but that her soul shall find God's grace*. The words were her own. She turned at the chancel screen, listening for a moment to the far-off cooing of pigeons, took the bundle from the bag and went over to the font. Dipping her finger into the empty bowl, she made the sign of the cross.

'I christen this child Sarah Benersley. May God look after her in the world to come. Amen.'

She left the bag on a pew. Taking a stub of pencil from her coat, she tore the last, blank page from a hymnal and printed: Please give my child a Christian burial.

In the clear light magpies wheeled, croaking, above the road. A thin smoke was rising above the town. She climbed the stairs to her room and immersed herself in the under-blanket dark.

'Miss Nerissa Elizabeth Birkenshaw, daughter of Mr Francis Birkenshaw, the proprietor of a Macclesfield textile mill of national repute, was married to Mr Roderick Davenport on May Day. Miss Birkenshaw wore a silk gown made for the occasion at her father's works. The bridegroom is the son of a well-known Derbyshire family, whose interests reside in the extraction of limestone. He recently came down from Oxford University, where he read palaeontology. The happy couple were escorted from the church by a party of the groom's friends, who made a bridge to the waiting landau. Thence to the bride's former residence, for the wedding luncheon and an address by the Best Man, a Mr Percival Winnock, of Winchester. Among guests present were Lord Brocklehurst, a landowner, and Mr Robert Heath Esq., mine owner and ironmaster.'

John threw the paper aside. Heath had sent for him, and he cleared his head as he went to his room. As usual, the master was bent over his papers and indicated the seat without looking up. Eventually he raised his head. 'You're packing up here this week. I want you to make a start up at the Bull come Monday. You've had young Hassop under your wing these last five months. What d'you think, can he cope?'

'I think he's competent enough,' John said, making no reference to his subordinate's struggle to draft a letter.

'I expect we'll sort him out one way or the other. Now to this other business: you're to take yourself up to the main office at seven sharp. I've seen Jock Duggan, he'll put you right regarding your duties.' He got up and stood for a time at the window. 'Let me say this to you. You're not there to take over, you're not there to give advice. If you make your mark, that'll come in due course. Jock might seem long in the tooth, but he's nobody's fool. Just learn the ropes and see what the good Lord sends you.'

John walked back to his office. Hassop was settled in his chair, and

John watched as he laboriously entered an invoice in the copy-book.

'You'll be on your own from next week.'

'From next week?'

'From Monday.'

'So I'll be doing the lot?'

'The lot.'

A shadow passed over the youth's eyes. The news would mean sleepless nights as he fretted over his responsibilities. 'And where are you off to?' Hassop asked reproachfully.

'The Bull.'

He had his eyes fixed on the wall calendar. 'Well, all the best, Master John,' he said, offering a limp hand.

'Don't worry, you'll be an asset to the household.'

John awoke to a clear morning and took a short cut across the fields to the colliery and ironworks. The gateman pointed out the offices and he made his way past a high-sided shed, watching the clouds of acrid smoke drift above the roofs. He crossed the yard and entered the office under a covered way. The door he wanted was half way down the corridor, and he went in without knocking. The room was large and dingy, the lower wall painted a dull brown. In an attempt to brighten it, a potted plant had been placed in a corner. Rows of desks ran from side to side, mostly occupied by women. A speaking tube fixed above the nearest desk communicated with the adjacent room.

'Can I be of assistance?'

'I have an appointment to see a Mr Duggan. My name is John Tanbrey.'

'If you could wait here, Mr Tanbrey?'

The woman ushered him into a smaller office containing a writing desk and a pair of wooden filing cabinets. To either side the clock were Farquarson prints, unseen by the workers whose shadows passed behind the frosted glass. In due course the door opened and a raw-boned man strode in, hung his hat from the stand and moved behind the desk.

'So you're the new body?' Duggan shouted, rummaging in his drawer for a primer and paper. 'I want ye to do the first five. I'll be back in a quarter of an hour.' He pushed the primer over. 'Ye may begin.'

He shut the door, giving an order that the man in the next room was not to be disturbed. Returning punctual to the minute, he looked over John's shoulder. 'Ye've still to do the fifth. No matter, I can see ye're already acquainted with substantial arithmetic.' He leaned back in his chair. 'I dinna know what the master's told ye about this place. It's a big concern, and if the shipping lines go and buy their chains from Germany, half the folk hereabouts will be hard put tae buy bread.'

'I understand Mr Heath's contribution to the local economy.'

'I wonder if ye do? The business is like an octopus, with tentacles all over the place. There's hauliers and railwaymen and an army of clerks just to keep it on an even keel. It's more than an industry; it's an institution, and if ye're to be part of it ye'll need tae sink a portion of your life in tae making sure the cogs keep turning. Now I've a mind the master's considering ye for ma job. Well, at least ye'll be inheriting an organisation built up by myself, and not the lot inflicted on me when I first came. They'd a job tae read and write.' He glowered from his desk. 'I'm to take it ye dinna fit in tae that category o' sinners, sir?'

'I don't think Mr Heath has anything to complain of.'

Duggan held his gaze. 'I've learned nothing to the contrary. I wouldnae like to see the running of the office fall in tae the wrong hands, worse still incompetent hands. Now, what d'ye know about this side o' the business?'

'I was hoping you'd show me.'

'I'll be blunt, and Heath's aware of ma feelings: it would've been fairer to get someone from the big office than your good self. He's left me with a headache. What am I to tell them? Folk I've worked with all these years not even considered, whereas you're an unknown quantity here. Nothing personal, ye understand, but it's bound tae stir up a hornets' nest.'

'I shall have to prove myself.'

'I've tae smuggle ye in like any other hand, and I dinna mind telling ye I dinna like subterfuge. Be that as it may, if Heath has made up his mind you're tae be ma successor, then that's how it's tae be.' Duggan gave him an eccentric stare. 'This is the administration side of things. Fifty people work here, and I'm answerable to Heath for any decisions I might take regarding the day-to-day running o' the offices. We deal with costings, all that's needed tae dig anthracite and produce fine quality steel. The stuff that comes in is weighed, and everything that goes through the gate has to be tallied. We pride ourselves on good book-keeping, Mr Tanbrey. We're involved with litigation from time to time and Mr Hand acts for Mr Heath in legal matters. The acquisition of other concerns is made binding by the lawyers, but in the first place passes through this office. There's very little goes on here I don't know about. Wages are made out by the clerks, and fixed by Mr Heath dependent on age and position. Accuracy is the keynote. If the men perceive their hours tae be in error, there's hell to pay, and rightly so. We're also deliberating the merits of a sick-pay scheme. It was at ma own instigation, and as yet I haven't any notion o' Heath's intentions. If I bring him 'round tae ma way o' thinking, each man will pay a small sum a week out o' his wage. If McEvoy - that's the doctor we use - is able tae confirm a man's illness, the worker will receive enough tae keep him from the debtor's gaol till he's on the mend.'

'Won't the men feign sickness?'

'Ye're not the first tae throw that at me. Will it encourage sloth and penalise the men of integrity, ye ask? I expect if ye'd seen bairns with their stomachs bulging through lack of food, yer might take a more charitable view. Where I come from men only ate when there was a ship tae be built. It's a scheme that might have merit to it, and I hope Heath gives it the chance it deserves.'

'And will he?'

'We'd best wait and see. Now, we'll make a tour o' the works, and after I'll introduce ye tae some o' the staff.' His tone changed, and his eyes lit up. 'Ever seen the making o' steel before, Mr Tanbrey? A wonderful sight, better than the Northern Lights. It's nae use the Earth having all the bounty, we can make far better use of it here.'

John followed him out. Railway sidings criss-crossed an enclosure between the wagon yard and foundry. Sets had been laid in places across the tracks, providing cart routes to the buildings. Engines laboured with truck loads of girders, and Duggan held out a restraining arm as they entered the foundry. The glowing cavern brought a smile to the Scotsman's face, his eyes moving over the floor as if to miss nothing. A great number of men were at work, dark against the glare of molten metal. Along the roof sprang ribbons of yellow light. Duggan picked his way over chains with surprising agility, and the din faded as they left the building.

'Well? What d'ye make o' that, Mr Tanbrey? That's what puts the *great* in Britain.'

John listened with half an ear. His attention had been drawn to a figure painting numbers on a wagon. As he watched, the man hobbled towards a hut and disappeared inside.

'Ye'll know Urias,' Duggan said, following his eyes. 'He fell from grace, as ye'll nae doubt be aware. He'll have work here – as long as he doesn't blot his copy book again. Now, back tae business. Have ye ever ventured down a pit before?'

'That's to be my next treat?'

'Indeed it is, ye're about tae visit another part o' Mr Heath's enterprise. Ye might not like what ye see, but the Bull's a sight better run than many. Come on, I'll show ye what we're about.'

When he got back home he was surprised to find Ginny waiting for him.

'I've come up to see you.... your father's been keepin' me company.'

'So I see.'

He removed his jacket and draped it over a chair. He'd taken pains to avoid her. He was no longer sure what she would do, if she could harm him still. There had been nothing between them since that time, and the only reason he tolerated her now was to keep in Heath's favour. He thought that after he'd made himself indispensable to Duggan, he'd let her go.

'I'd like to walk out, John.'

He picked up his coat without a word and followed her. It was a fine, still evening in June, and as they walked along the field path scythes were already at work. She nibbled her lower lip, as was her habit when something preyed on her mind.

'Well? What is it?'

'I've - I've been to see Madam.'

'About what?'

'It isn't my fault,' she cried, suddenly, her eyes brimming. 'I had to take much o' the blame, what else could I do? I couldn't say – I couldn't .... You don't understand. You don't want to understand.'

He took hold of her arm. 'What did you say?'

'I didn't want to tell you, I didn't want to tell you.' She buried her face, fought to regain her composure. 'She says she'll be seein' the master about it. I feel it's all my fault. I wish I'd never been born!'

A hay cart was moving towards them from the edge of the field.

'You're expecting! Do you know what you've done, you stupid bitch?

You've wrecked my chances, you -'

The volley of blows took him by surprise and shocked him into silence. She pummelled him distractedly about the chest, shoulders, face, until exhaustion overtook her and she fell by the stile, gulping air. She'd stopped crying, but her face was like putty, the features bloated and unrecognisable. 'You'll have to see him.' she said, distantly. 'She wanted to know if you'd make a responsible father, and I said I didn't know.' She gave a bitter laugh. 'Don't worry, I won't tie you down, you needn't do nothin' you don't want to.'

He turned away. 'I always knew you'd do for me.'

Later that week, Heath faced him across his desk. 'I'm not concerned with your private life, Tanbrey. I've set you up when I could just as easy have given half a dozen others the chance. Now I'm wondering: can I trust a man as would leave a girl in the lurch? If he can play fast and loose with her, will he play fast and loose with me? My wife tells me she's a good lass, and there's no complaints as far as her work goes. Is there anything you want to say?'

'I'll not shirk my responsibilities.'

'See you don't.' He toyed for a moment with a marbled ledger. 'You're as hard as gritstone, Tanbrey, and I don't think you're most folks' cup of tea. That's why I'd rather have you in the wagon spitting out than outside spitting in. It's an unfortunate fact of life, but there it is. If you do well, maybe we can do something about accommodation. Where will you live when you get wed?'

'I haven't thought that far ahead, sir.'

'It's up to you. I dare say there'll be some arrangement.' He drew in his breath. 'Now, to other matters. Jock's told me you've fared well since you arrived. He mentioned this insurance scheme of his, did he?'

'Yes, he did say something about it.'

'Bloody harebrained idea, but I'm bound to listen to all manner of suggestions and this is no worse than the rest.' He firmed his jaw. 'I reckon you might as well fly before you walk. Get involved, look into the possibilities of it.'

'But Mr Duggan –'

'I've already had a word with Jock. You'll not be putting him out. We both agree you should get your teeth into it first as last.'

'And you want me to work out what is to be paid in and the benefits accruing?'

'Duggan'll put you in touch with the right people.'

'Will that be all, sir?'

Heath grunted at the ceiling. 'Don't let me down. In either matter.'

Three weeks later John and Ginny were married. They rented cheap rooms and on their wedding night slept apart.

11

Francis Birkenshaw gazed across the Macclesfield roof tops. The Victoria had seen better times. There were more mills now than fifty years ago, when his father had set up an engineering works in a rented wagon shed. With the growth of steam looms he'd begun to specialise in the maintenance of machinery. He'd been lucky enough to be at the forefront when the silk industry expanded in the Forties, and set up new premises in response to the need to make repairs which would keep the looms running. When a local mill went bankrupt he was offered it at a price which would offset the money owed him in unpaid bills. Able now to produce his thread and service his own machinery, he'd paid off the capital within a decade and expanded. By the time Francis had been ready to take over, the old man had built a thriving concern. Unfortunately, his son hadn't inherited his father's business sense, and the Victoria's reputation had suffered. Instead of investment in new equipment, Francis had purchased a run-down Georgian mansion and spent a fortune on its renovation. He'd moved in with his new wife, the daughter of a building contractor, with the aim of consolidating his business. Shortly after, the contractor had left his wife and departed with his money and mistress to South America. As a result, Francis' reaction to his daughter's match was less his liking of Roddy Davenport than Roddy's family money.

Now demand for silk had fallen, and his out-of-date looms had given the edge to his competitors. He'd managed to maintain his lifestyle by selling off plots of land for 'gentlemen's residences' and auctioning half a dozen houses on his estate. But the bulk of his father's fortune had been spent on his hall, his continental holidays, visits to the races and whatever else was needed to keep up appearances. Shortly after Nerissa's tenth birthday, when his wife died, he also found himself supporting a number of female friends.

He had no intention of stinting himself as long as the money lasted. The mill was still producing orders which called for a traditional touch at a rate discerning patrons could afford to pay. He'd never been impressed by Roddy Davenport, who he considered a waste of time. Were it not for his father's fortune, made from quarrying limestone at a time the railways needed all the ballast they could get, he'd have dismissed him out of hand. He couldn't really understand what Nerissa saw in him, apart from the clink of sovereigns. Even so, he'd felt he must offer Roddy a position. Roddy was already well provided for through a dividend paid from his father's business, and the Davenports had bought him a place at Oxford which he'd left three years later with a useless degree in palaeontology. But a daughter of Francis wouldn't be married to a do-nothing. It wasn't right and it didn't look right. Against his better judgement he'd offered Roddy the position of merchandising manager. Very little was expected of him except a good accent, the right contacts and a grasp of the social niceties which might enhance the status of the company.

A rap on the door broke into Francis's reverie. It was the overseer, Jackson.

'Your daughter called to say Mr Davenport won't be in today, sir.'

'Did she say why?'

'She gave me to understand he was indisposed.'

'I dare say we'll see him tomorrow.' The irony in Birkenshaw's tone hadn't been lost on Jackson. Davenport's fondness for drink was well known. Birkenshaw had thought that marriage would cure him, and he'd been wrong. 'And where is Mrs Davenport now?'

'I believe she said she was going to the station later on.'

'Manchester, eh? Another load of hat boxes in the attic.'

Jackson went out, leaving Nerissa's father at the window wondering if her marriage would last the year.

The same thought struck Nerissa as her train pulled into London Road. She'd made the journey often over the last six months. The streets were snarled with traffic, and it was twenty minutes before she stepped into the lobby of the Queen's Hotel. John had a newspaper to his face, and when he turned she saw he'd grown a thin moustache. He rose to embrace her, but she stepped back, reluctant to attract the attention of the guests scattered about the room. He took her coat and hung it from a stand which, together with the pillar, screened them.

'And how's my clerk?'

'Well, thank you.'

'And what excuses did you give this time?'

'I'm supposed to be here on business. It was settled quite quickly, as it happens.'

'Nothing's more important than business.'

'I'm glad you came. I don't know what sort of a rein Mr Davenport has on you.'

'Much the same as Mrs Tanbrey has on you, I should imagine.'

He called a waiter and ordered coffee.

'I prefer wine.'

'Would you bring a bottle of Chablis?' He poured two measures. 'I'm supposed to take the five o'clock train back. That is, unless I'm delayed.'

'And is that is a possibility?'

'There's a later train, I believe. What about you? What time are you expected back?'

She studied her wine. 'Do you know, I really can't be sure. If my lady friend and I are too tired to catch the evening train after the tiresome business of shopping, I might have to spend the night at her house.'

'Will Mr Davenport object?'

'I left a note under the ormolu clock.'

'And can he read?'

'He has a degree in palaeontology.'

'I don't suppose your friend would be too put out if you were to prefer an hotel room? Apparently,' he said, speaking more loudly, 'they're expecting war with the Zulus. Well, I won't detain you further, Mrs Orville.' He stood, clicking the clasps of his brief case and leaving his newspaper folded on the table. 'I'm sure you have nothing to fear as far as your portfolio is concerned. If only the rest of my clients were as astute in financial matters.... well, good day.'

He left while Nerissa perused the paper, memorising the room number he'd written in the margin. After a decent interval she got up. The reception clerk was bent over his counter, studying a pamphlet through wire-rimmed glasses, and didn't see her climb the stairs. John's door was ajar and she closed it behind her and leaned against it. He'd taken off his jacket and came across and stood over her, sliding his eyes across the base of her neck, watching the rise and fall of her breasts. He turned her head towards him and thrust her lips apart with his mouth. He felt her yield and pulled her to him, licking the suggestion of cleavage, running his tongue across her neck. She'd became pliant, and he carried her awkwardly to the bed. With her tumbled hair, she looked less a lady, more like a chambermaid, more like his own wife. Roddy! The poor bastard deserved all his wife was about to get.

She reached up to him, her bodice open to the waist. He laid her on the counterpane and stood off, drawn by the play of light on her stockings, then lay down beside her and began to kiss her, imagined her arranging the house, instructing the keeper. The sounds she made were almost of pain as he stroked the yielding flesh of her breasts and hips. She tumbled forward, her arms collapsing under his final lunge. A feeling of great lethargy swept over him, and his desire for her blew away like dandelion seed.

When he awoke it was growing dark. Nerissa stood at the window, looking down into the hurly-burly of lit carriages. Gas-light pooled the cobbles, and the clip-clop of horses came faintly through the sash. She sat on the edge of the bed and began to tidy her hair.

'Leave him.'

'For you?'

'Is there someone else?'

She clicked her bag shut. 'But it would upset Roddy.'

'I couldn't give a tinker's cuss for Roddy.'

'Yes, but he has money and you don't.'

'You don't love him.'

'What's that got to do with it? He can be quite pleasant when he's sober. Anyway, what about that little woman of yours, your Ginny? And the imminent arrival?'

'I'm sure we can sort something out.'

'This is boring. Tell me what you've been up to since you got your new job.'

He left the bed and dressed. A brooding silence had settled on him, which she found amusing.

'Get dressed, we're going somewhere else for dinner.'

She left first, gliding past the clerk when his back was turned. John followed a minute later, handing in his key. She knew a restaurant and they took a light meal while a trio played in the adjacent room.

'I've been working on the figures for three months,' he was explaining, his mood now mellow in the after-dinner glow. 'It seems Heath's warming to the idea. That's why I'm in Manchester. One of the reasons.' He toyed with his glass. He seemed to have aged since they last met and she thought he could have passed for thirty, or more. 'The men will pay a fixed rate each week to make the scheme work. I clashed with

Duggan over the terms. He had it in his head to pay a man for up to six months off. It couldn't be done, unless Heath chipped in, and he was against it. He thinks the men would be less likely to abuse a system they own, and I agree. We're about to put names to paper. The amount they get will be just enough to keep them off the breadline if they use their wits. The money will attract 12% interest, which can be reinvested for the pot.'

'What about wives and children, do they have anything?'

'We're looking into it. Duggan wants an allowance to be paid in the event of a man's death. We're working on the details.'

'And who will be in control of the plan – and the money?'

He leaned forward and stubbed out his cigar. 'Duggan will shortly be retiring. When he does, I shall be the sole administrator,' he said.

Bill leaned on the rail of the Albatross. Beyond the Hudson, the Adirondack foothills blazed with the first vermilion tints of autumn. They moored overnight at Buffalo, and in the morning sailed past forests of maple and yellow birch. Now Lake Erie shone against the distant uplands, and lights twinkled through the dusk. Toledo, Monroe, then the slow tramp up the Detroit to Lake St Clair, then Lake Huron in the pink of another dawn, a stiff breeze whipping the surface.

At Duluth he left the boat. It was mid afternoon when he found a shack announcing a Shave and Cut for ten cents. In the evening he found a bar. A girl brought him steak and he ate greedily, swilling down the food with a carafe of water. He returned to his lodgings to find the room had chilled. A soiled buffalo skin lay across the bunk and he slapped out the bugs and pulled it up. He awoke at first light and checked the money he'd hidden under his bolster. Mosquitoes had bitten his arms and neck, raising the skin in red blotches. While he waited for the Minneapolis train, he found a place overlooking the harbour. He sensed someone at his side, and turned to find an elderly man studying the same view as himself.

'They come, they go, every day, every year. Sometimes I wonder why they don't stop awhile, get all that travellin' outa their system.'

'The ships?'

'Sure, the ships.' The man narrowed his eyes. 'Where you from?'

'England.'

'You mean London?'

'You wouldn't know if I told you.'

'Try tellin' me.'

'Near Manchester. You've heard of Manchester?'

'Manchester England or Manchester New Hampshire?'

'I've never been to New Hampshire.'

'So what're you doin' here?'

'Seeking my fortune.'

The man took a mouthful of drink. 'Wish I had a dollar for every Jack goin' to make his fortune. I'd be rich as Johnny D.'

'Who's that?'

'You not heard o' Rockefeller? He got more in the bank than you got hairs on your head. What're you drinkin'?'

'Beer.'

'I'll get you a real drink.' He returned with two glasses of whiskey and sat in silence appreciating the view from the window. 'You jest come across the lakes and you're headin' West, my guess the Badlands - right?'

'How d'you know?'

'Cos they're all headin' for the hills – ain't that so, Chester?'

The barman nodded, making the glasses squeak with his rag. 'Black Hills fever, Ephraim, they all got it.'

Ephraim winked. 'You got more chance bein' eat by a grizzly than strikin' a lode.'

Bill pushed his glass away. He still had a little money left from his savings, together with the dollars he'd earned fish packing in New York.

'I dare say I've the same chance as anybody else.'

'Jest hope them redskins don't go stickin' things in you,' the barman called across. 'Them Sioux, they think nothin' o' flayin' a man alive.' He replaced the glasses, talking into the mirror. 'Mind, they've lived in them hills for generations, some'n sacred to their ancestors, stands to reason they don't take kindly to the Whites movin' in.'

Ephraim agreed. 'They'll all be in reservations by the time you get there. That old Sittin' Bull's mutton, dead as a lamb chop.' A double hoot sounded. 'Well, sounds like your train, mister. Sure hope you're successful, but if you're not – why, see you this time next year.'

Bill left with the man's laugh ringing in his ears as the train came in, puffing wood smoke above the high-gabled station. The ground bordering the track was strewn with travellers' trunks and wicker cases. He stepped through them and joined the crowd; plainly dressed women, young girls in straw bonnets clutching china dolls, prospectors, itinerants. A group of railroad men lifted baggage up to the car at the rear. He hoisted what luggage he had and took a seat by the window. A woman scolded her child in German. Others spoke in American accents or American English in which traces of Scouse, Irish or Scots could be heard. Some of the men were already asleep by the time he began to nod.

'Mind if I join you?'

Bill moved his hat from the seat and the newcomer sank down heavily, pinning his satchel between his feet. A curtain of smoke blew past the window. He drifted into sleep, then shuddered awake and looked at his pocket watch. He'd been out for over two hours. A mournful note wailed at the window, and he looked out at the moonlit prairie. A surge of emotion coursed through him, and for some reason he found himself remembering the mountain of slag near Jud Cowlishaw's house and George Dixon's lifeless body buried under it.

'Now you're awake - care for a cigar?' Still drowsy with sleep, he took the offered cheroot. 'Name's M Scott McGoohan. Since we're likely to be travelling all the way to Minneapolis, I thought we'd best get acquainted.'

Bill held out his hand. 'Bill Tanbrey, newly arrived.'

'From England, uh, going by your manner of speech? My grandfather was from Scotland, which is pretty close I think. You ever been there, Mr Tanbrey?'

'The border's over two hundred miles from where I come from.'

'Why, you're practically on the doorstep.' He leaned back. 'You don't look like no farmsteader and you don't look like no prospector either. You got the advantage of me.'

His good-natured curiosity disarmed Bill's reserve. 'I heard about the gold strike in South Dakota four years back. I decided to travel out there.'

'So I was wrong. Guess I'm losing my edge.'

'I'm not a prospector.'

Bill outlined his idea. Sparks blew past the window. Under the swaying oil-lamps passengers slept.

'Well, Mr Tanbrey, maybe we can do business.' McGoohan fished a card from his case. 'If you carry your plan through, and I must say it's the sort of thing that might just work if you don't go bust first – you write me and I'll be right over.' Bill read the card in the weak light, picked out McGoohan's name and that of his director, Aaron Montgomery Ward. 'Only a small outfit yet, Mr Tanbrey, but I tell you this, the mail order business will burst through these plains like a prairie fire. You'll see if I'm not right.'

'D'you have a list?'

'Well, it so happens I have a sales catalogue right here.' He burrowed in his case. 'Everything can be got immediately, the rest'll take a little longer.' His boom of laughter sounded suddenly loud in the sleeping car, and he lowered his voice conspiratorially. 'We're adding to the stock all the time. You want a parlour organ or a portable printing press? Here's where you find it. You don't suffer from piles, do you?'

'Not so's you'd notice.'

'We got stuff for them too, right here under medicines and ointments. Star collars, hair dye, champagne, glassware – it's all here for the taking at a very competitive rate. Satisfaction guaranteed or your money back.'

Bill glanced around. Perhaps he'd been unwise to confide in a stranger. There was no sign of movement, however, and unlike the others McGoohan didn't seem to need rest. Bill steered him into small talk, and as dawn broke the catalogue slipped to the floor.

McGoohan got off at Minneapolis with some other travellers. Their places were taken by groups of men with round-blade spades and picks strung over their shoulders. Water courses criss-crossed the land, with stars of sunlight suggesting lakes far out on the horizon. Plains of needle-grass dotted with buffalo rose from outcrops of rock and met the cloud-wisped sky. A track-side post announced South Dakota, land of the ring-necked pheasant. Through the window stretched limitless vistas of sun-bleached grass.

He left the train and lodged at the Silver Bullet. In the morning, he shared a coach with two nuns and a Frenchman. Now arroyos crossed the land and buttes jagged the clear sky. After putting down to water the horses, the faint outline of the Black Hills smudged the horizon fifty miles away. The coach drew into Deadwood as the light was fading. He climbed down and immediately went in search of a bed.

12

Charlie hadn't seen Ellen since the previous June. She'd told him she'd lost her baby, and given up her attic for a rented room at the house of a friend of hers, Jane Colishaw. He should have learned her address, and now the letter he was reading had brought new disappointments. 'We found your designs interesting, though we feel they are not sufficiently commercial to use in the foreseeable future. Whilst we hope you will have success in placing them elsewhere, we must warn you that the more avant garde designers have had difficulty in the past, although they have been able to obtain employment when they reworked their ideas to address customers' tastes. It might be in your interests to write to the Wedgwood Institute in Burslem, which exists principally to further the work of local artists who wish to make a career in ceramic design. We trust this letter will be of some help to you. W.R. Hollinsworth'

Charlie put it in his portfolio, pushed the portfolio behind the dresser and pulled on his coat. As he walked through the winter fields, his disappointment faded. The men were warming themselves at the stove before the day's work when he reached the nurseries. Luke Pointon stood with his hands to the ironwork, then went with him to the vegetable gardens.

'Are you used to lifting sprouts in the cold?'

'Fairly, Mr Pointon.'

'Sometimes I think it's colder here than where you come from, top o' them hills.'

'I know how to keep warm, I've had plenty of practice.

'I hear your brother's a father.'

He realised the reference was to John and not Bill. 'Ay. I haven't seen it yet, like.'

'So you've no idea how the mother's faring?' Charlie steadied his barrow. 'Well, I'll leave you to it, then. When you find something out, let us know, the wife'll get a parcel up.'

Charlie began plucking at the frozen stalks as Luke walked away. The area was a waste of part-cleared plots and the remains of marigolds which had been planted in with the lettuce over summer. As he worked, he made up his mind to follow the letter's advice and write to the institute. Bevis's coin could still bring him luck. After tea he composed his letter and readdressed it. The portfolio came back a fortnight later.

'Dear Mr Tanbrey,

Thank you for giving me the opportunity to look at your work. Unfortunately, to secure a place at the institute it is necessary to satisfy one of the local manufacturers as to the commercial merit of your work. I suggest you acquaint them with your ideas, and should any consider them suitable, a course of study might be arranged. I return your package together with a list of pottery firms who might be interested in the designs you have submitted.

Yours Faithfully,

G Theaker'

The company heading the list was the firm he'd last sent his material to, having exhausted all the rest. By the end of winter he'd made a decision, and went to see Luke Pointon.

Luke scratched his head in puzzlement. 'Well, Charlie, you're old enough to make up your own mind, though I must say the pit's not to my liking.'

'Nor mine, Mr Pointon. I'm hoping it won't be for long.'

'Well, if you decide different at any time you can count on a bit o' work here. Let's see – your brother Bill was down Whitfield, wasn't he?'

'For a while, before he went farming.'

'And now he's off with the Yankees.' He gave his quiet laugh, as if at some private joke. 'You could always join him if you get restless down below.'

'It's only for money, otherwise I'd stick to me barrow. It's just that they pay a touch more down there, and I want to try and save a bit.'

Luke patted him on the back and went off, whistling.

Charlie left on the first warm day of spring, and the men plied him with enough ale to send him into the shrubs. The idea of working in the pit had come to him over winter. Despite the refusals he'd received, an inner voice told him to plod on. What they called commercial restraints was a way of getting him to tow the line, but that was no use. He wanted the freedom to produce his own designs and to set his own pace. Independence would give him belief in what he was doing, and he could only achieve it if he had money. He heard Caulton's voice caution him but shook it off. Like Bill, he'd put some by until he had enough to strike out, and meanwhile he'd practise, practise, practise....

*

Urias Ball peered out from behind a wagon at the late meeting which had been convened at the ironworks to celebrate Duggan's retirement. He should have been one of them, but instead he was a nobody. He recognised Tanbrey's head behind the glass and thought he'd look well between the sights of the Enfield his cousin had brought back from the Crimea. He'd make his escape in the dark, hiding the rifle under a pile of bricks by the boundary wall. 'Good riddance, Mr Tanbrey.'

He awoke from his reverie and lowered the illusory weapon. He'd been a fool to attack Pol when it was Tanbrey's fault. He knew it was Tanbrey's fault. His crushed foot, his mauling at the hands of pimps, the loss of his job. Now he spent his days sweating over pots of paint and bags of nails, whispered about in the office and mocked by the men. Only a simmering hatred of Tanbrey kept him alive. He wrenched himself away and walked over the lines to the gateman's hut.

Duggan's retirement had been a cause for celebration in the boardroom, and Heath smiled his approval before continuing his speech. 'What can you say about Jock? Well, I suppose there's a lot you could say if you knew him as I do. I reckon there's a lot his wife could tell us too, especially about his marrow growing activities. But I aren't one to intrude into Jock's marital difficulties. I'm here to say thank you for his service to this business and to the way he's grafted his fingers to the bone for it. I did once consider calling it Heath and Duggan, but he wouldn't hear of it.' He paused for the anticipated laugh. 'And we find him going on sixty-six still working his fingers to the bone, still coming up with one harebrained scheme or another. Jock, you've never thrown in the towel and we're grateful to you for it. You've shown me the error of my ways more than once, and I can speak for all when I say I'm sorry to see you go.'

The Scotsman raised a hand to still the clapping which broke out as Heath took his seat. 'Far be it for me tae take issue with the man who's fed me ma bread o'er the years, but I question his use o' the term harebrained, as I'm sure those working yonder will question it. However, be that as it may, I'd not be telling the truth if I was tae say I'm pleased tae be leaving. The place holds too many memories for me tae give it up that easy, and you've tae mind I had my feet under the desk before some of ye were a glint in your father's eye. I'm sure Mr Heath will go from strength tae strength, knowing the time and energy he's devoted tae his various concerns, and I trust my successor will find his time here as rewarding as myself.' John rode their glances with a feigned smile of amusement. Officially a shortlist had been drawn up for interviews the following Monday; unofficially, Duggan's job was his, and everyone knew it. 'So I thank ye all for putting up wi' me over the years, and especially I'd like to thank Mr Heath for his support of my harebrained schemes and for being a vital link in the chain – no pun intended – which has helped these islands forge ahead of its rivals and become the envy of the world.'

John walked back under the fizzing lamps with Duggan's voice still ringing in his ears. People had worked well for the Scotsman because they'd respected him. The most he could expect was a grudging acceptance. He wanted to be rid of the shoddy streets, the emaciated dogs and the down-and-outs lurching between bars. He detested the hovel his wife called home, now that she'd left the Heath's employ. He reached the door in a low mood and fumbled for his key. The tiled passage was in deep shadow, and he felt his way to the small back room and sat on the sofa with his back to the moonlit wall. His fingers brushed his son's rattle, and he toyed morosely with it. The sofa was second-hand, and Ginny had covered it in cheap fabric to hide the holes. The table was second-hand, and the joint-loosened chairs, and the faded print, and the cutlery they ate with and the plates they ate from. He had an urge to smash everything, to keep on smashing until nothing remained but a shower of particles borne away on the wind.

She was standing at the door. 'John? Did your meetin' go all right?' His face was in shadow, but she felt his eyes upon her. She began again: 'Matthew's not been sleepin' well –' when he grabbed the throat of her gown with such force she gasped for air. She tried to free herself, but his fingers closed around her neck. Abruptly he discarded her like a used toy. She rose shakily to her feet as he began to climb the stairs. He heard her go to her room some time after, quietly sobbing.

She lay awake until morning light then dressed, leaving her son still sleeping while she went to attend to the fire. A bowl of oats steamed on the table as her husband appeared. Her face was pale from lack of sleep, and her hand shook as she lifted the kettle. He sat in his waistcoat without speaking. She'd put Matthew in a high chair, where he rapped his spoon on the bowl as she fed him with another. He was the buoy which kept her afloat. Without him there would be no point.

'Get this mess cleared up by the time I get back,' he said, pushing back his chair, 'and get yourself sorted out – you look like a skivvy.'

The sky was brightening as she dressed her son in his outdoor clothes. She had no idea at first where to go; her only wish was to escape the house, to get it out of her sight. 'I know, we'll take a walk up the Cloud, shall we? We'll have them legs as fat as sausages in no time at all.'

A dray rumbled past. The waggoner, who lived in the next street, doffed his cap.

'Up with the larks, Mrs Tanbrey?'

'Where're you going, Joe?'

'I've to be up at Bosley afore dinner.'

'Can I beg a lift?'

He stopped at a shop while she bought some apples. Perched high above the road, she watched the last houses slide back.

'Not working down the Grange no more?'

'Not since Matthew came along.'

'And mister, still up at Heath's works, is he?'

She nodded and pointed upwards. 'Look, Matthew, a kestrel, he's goin' to eat a poor mouse. Watch him!'

The bird swooped, and her eyes tumbled with it. At length she lifted the boy down and the dray rumbled off. The land was bright with new leaf, and they took a path through the pines up to the crest. A quilt of greens fell to the far distance, the pale green of early barley, the vivid green of meadow grass, the denser woodland greens rising to the foot of heather hills which met the sky in water-washed lines. She stood in the cool uprush of air and looked out over the cloud-shadowed land. She remembered being there before with John. Climbing to the edge, she stood on a projecting lip of rock. Far below, tumbled boulders stood like chessmen amid the coarse grass. *They used to live up here in the olden days, Stone Age folk. I've yet to discover where....* Her insignificance devastated her, and she felt helpless amid the years of other lives lived in that place. She was nothing more than an atom of peat, to be blown away in the gusts. She took a step towards the edge. There was a tug at her dress, and she looked down at her son. The breeze tousled his fine hair, and blew the tears from her chin in shining droplets. There was no one but herself and Matthew. No one. She lifted him up and pressed him to her.

'Mummy had a nasty thought,' she said, 'but it's gone now.'

'Shall we go home?'

'Let's have a walk first.'

They meandered between the rocks as a lark trilled on the rise.

Jane Cowlishaw took a last look around her room before sliding the key under her landlord's mat. Wellington Mill had provided her with the essentials of life, and the rent she earned from her house in Bradley Green had paid the rent on the more convenient rooms in Leek, with money left over. She was content and solvent, and as she walked to the station she went over the circumstances which had made her departure inevitable. Jervis, the boss's right-hand man, saw it as his duty to take tittle-tattle up the steps and leave it at Kinnersley's door. Jervis had never liked her because she'd never been impressed by him, and for a long time he'd sought ways to get rid of her. Unfortunately, she was good at her job, and her section enjoyed an easy camaraderie, which was to Kinnersley's advantage. Jervis had told him Jane and the Benersley girl had taken unofficial leave of absence, and he was disappointed the manager had decided not to act on the information, rather than sack them on the spot. It was not until Jane began to take an interest in workers' causes – not only the complaints of the twisters with whom she worked, but the dyers, weavers, cutters and the rest – that an opportunity presented itself. Kinnersley detested unions and had in the past dismissed any he felt could be a threat to his firm. Knowing this, Jervis had followed her moves with growing interest. There was talk of the need for better pay and shorter working hours. At first snippets reached him, bar room gossip. Now a group of employees were beginning to argue their rights, and it was only a short step from Friday gatherings over a glass to talk of unions. Jervis knew the landlord of the inn where they met, and a small bribe secured him a room above the vaults. With his ear pressed to the boards, it became clear Jane Cowlishaw had a lot to say. Now he was able to give Kinnersley names, with Jane's at the top. Over the next few days the 'ringleaders' received notices of dismissal, and Kinnersley had sent warnings to other local mills should they apply for work there. The last to go had been Jane, charged with leaving her employment without permission with one Ellen Benersley, now no longer in the company's employ. She'd been expecting it. 'It's not that, is it Mr Kinnersley? It's the idea of a union. Well, unions are here to stay. We're mushrooms, pick us in the morning, by night we're up again. It's a battle you can't win.'

Her words came back to her as she got on the Macclesfield train. Settling herself into a seat, she wondered what tomorrow would bring.

Bevis thought Ellen coming back to the farm had been a good omen. Prices had risen, and he felt more at ease. She'd only come back, she said, because the work in Leek had dried up, but she'd stayed on at Three Elms, and grown back into the work. He thought she'd be a credit to any of the local farmers looking for a wife. She'd put on weight, but she was still attractive, with her clear skin and the pale golden hair which curled in wisps from the fringes of her bonnet.

Only Charlie and Jane Cowlishaw knew of her circumstances. She'd always be grateful to Jane for taking her in, and she'd miss her now she'd gone. She missed the mill too, but not enough to leave the easy familiarity of Three Elms and go back. For the present, work about the farm calmed her, and she was glad of it. She was glad of her own company, and she'd learned to keep the casual labourers that came and went at a distance. But the same was not true of Charlie. One Sunday she decided on an impulse to see him again.

'Charlie! Where've you been hiding?'

'I've been busy.'

'Too busy to pay a visit?'

'I thought you were still in Leek. How're your folks?'

'Much the same, and yours?'

'John's doing all right, as far as I know.'

'What about Bill, have you heard ?'

He took a letter from the dresser and handed it to her. She examined the stamp and passed it back. 'No, tell me what it says.'

'It's not all that private.'

She leafed through the sprawl. 'So he's gone into business. I thought he might.' She handed it back.

'When he's got a settled address I'll pass it on, then you can write and tell him what happened.'

'Why?'

'He asked about it.'

'If he's that concerned he shouldn't 've run off in the first place.' A tense silence followed, her mood ruffled like the surface of a pond. It passed. 'Charlie, I know what it is! It's your eyes, they're all black-rimmed.'

'That's what you get working down the pit. I gave Pointon notice, I'm down Whitfield now.'

'You, a collier?'

His admission had brought the old reticence to his tongue, making him feel a fool. 'I've had correspondence myself,' he said to change the subject. 'I thought I might strike out on my own when the time comes.'

'What're you on about?'

'You know about tiles?'

'What of them?'

'I've been thinking things over. I reckon it's tiles that are going to be the thing. People're teeming into the towns, they'll all be wanting tiles with a pattern to show off their halls.'

'Tiles don't break, cups do. If it's patterns you're after, you'd be better off with cups. Once you've sold a tile you've sold it. Trouble with you is you've no sense of where you're going.' He looked away, stroking his upper lip in discomfort. 'Don't take on, I was only speaking in jest. What's this latest bee in your bonnet? D'you want to make tiles or something?'

'I've been wondering if I could set up on my own, in a shed or something. I had a notion to do the whole thing, me and one or two others. If we could make something a touch different than anybody else for them as can afford it– well, it was an idea, it can bear some thinking about yet.'

He was still sailing close to land, where a sudden squall could hurl him on the rocks.

'You need somebody behind you, you need to be asking around before you make a move. You can't go spending against a whim. You'd be better off working in a pot bank, to see how things are done.' She stifled an urge to shake him. 'Why Whitfield, when you could've worked at the Bull with your John? I bet he could've fixed you up with a job in the office, none of them rings round your eyes.'

'I need to put something by if I'm to set up on my own. The only way is face work, nothing else pays well enough. If I give it a couple of years - well, I just wanted to fend for myself for once, like my brothers have had to do.'

She studied his face, the silky stubble across his upper lip. She felt a sudden urge to protect him. Perhaps she'd always had it, even as a girl skipping on the far side of the school wall. He wouldn't have left her like his brother. He'd have worn himself to the quick for her.

'Shall I come again or will you come down and see us? Bevis is always asking after you.'

'I'll come down tell him, next Sunday.'

'What's the matter with now? Come on, you can have a bite to eat. If you're too worn out with the excitement I'll see if I can't bring you back in the trap.'

He hesitated. 'All right, I'll come.'

The girl was seventeen, but could have passed for thirty. Her unrouged cheeks were unnaturally pale, the hawkish eyes staring up at him from sepia pouches. She put down her glass and led him out to the covered wagon behind the saloon, cocking an ear to the side before climbing up. Bill handed her a dollar and she stuffed it in her belt. He felt awkward. The girls he'd known at home had been loose or weak, but this girl sold herself like a sack of soya. She pulled aside a canvas and undressed in silence with her back to him. He took off his jacket and boots and began to undo his breeches while she lay on a mattress, biting a nail. A stink of sweat and perfume rose to his nose, and he struggled to stifle it. He bent to kiss her but she snatched her head away. Despite her rebuff he drove into her, the creaking wagon and his frustration vanishing like snuff on a fire.

She pushed him off with an oath and he drew back the canvas and climbed down. His mood had lifted. The girl, now on her way back to the saloon, meant no more to him than the tin bath hanging on a nail at Moor Top. He rode back to his quarters, took off his boots and lay on his bunk listening to the breeze through the open widow.

The sun was already bright when he awoke. He took a bucket from the corner and opened the door. A resinous scent filled the air, and from the forest came the rush of moving water. He lowered the bucket down the well, brought it up brimming and washed outside before lowering it again for cooking. Hanging out his suit to rid it of the stink of tobacco, he breakfasted, smoothed his bunk and read through the uncrossed lists ready for McGoohan's visit: Merrick's Six Cord Thread, Mennen's Sure Corn Killer, Hovey's Starch, a Crown Sewing Machine. He wondered about the new safety razor he'd heard about, and added it below the Eastman camera. There was still ten minutes to go before he opened the door. He picked up an out-of-date copy of the *New York Times* and browsed through the pages. Paddy Ryan had knocked out Joe Goss after eighty-seven bare-knuckle rounds. An English baker had given New York its first muffin. There'd been further wrangling over the Panama Canal. He skipped the rest and looked around his store. The man at Duluth had been right. Black Hills fever sent thousands on a goose chase and most were lucky to come back with their fare. But the adventurers who traded their future on a promise had to eat. They needed blankets and boots and sewing thread and tents. They couldn't dig without spades and the ones they'd bought had to be replaced. The idea he'd had, to be a supplier rather than a digger, had been more successful than he'd dared hope. The other merchants had set up in the towns, but he'd acquired a disused shack for a song and brought the store to the prospectors. With a loan he'd arranged in Deadwood added to what he still had of his own, he was able to repair the roof, put in windows and block up the holes with new timber and newsprint. As the first chill winds blew, he'd opened for business.

He'd telegraphed Montgomery Ward and McGoohan had appeared within the week, a beaverskin hat hiding his thinning hair and a fur coat to his knees. They'd worked on an order for the next few months and before winter he had blankets to the rafters, stoves, fur-lined boots and mittens, tools, sacks of flour and rice, root beer powder and fifty copies of Henry James' *The American* to help wile away the nights. Before his first Christmas, the blankets, boots and mittens had been sold, and though Henry James still stood in a corner, there was only eight copies left. He'd tried to telegraph again, but blizzards had brought down the lines and no train could get further than Minneapolis. He'd learnt to live with the season. Although the well-water waxed with ice in the twenty strides back to his shack, he had enough logs to last until the spring thaw and beans and oats to see him through the weather. He'd slept and ate in his coat, and when a fitful sun shone, rode his horse out to the camps. At night, with the wind shrieking across the land and the fragrance of smouldering pine blown into the room, the ghosts of the place would haunt him. Custer and his troopers on the banks of the Little Big Horn, the failed gold diggers at French Creek, Whitewood Gulch and Black Trail, the gun fighters outside the saloon doors, the Sioux and Cheyenne. He listened to them all and wondered at his new life. He'd extended the store in the spring and written home saying he'd exchanged a fishing rod for a pair of moccasins brought in by a native...

He heard a knock and went to open the door. A woman came in and put out her hand.

'Mr Tanbrey? I'm Elizabeth Schmelling from Montgomery Ward. I'm afraid Mr McGoohan won't be doing any more business in these parts - indeed, in any parts. He fell victim to a robbery.'

He shook his head. 'What happened?'

'You know how it is, Mr Tanbrey. These young men, they drink it all and then there's nothing left but a round and a gun. It happened in Chicago. He wouldn't hand over the case, so they shot him. All they got was samples and a catalogue. Can you believe that?'

He pointed to a seat near the open window, and she began to fan herself with her hand. She was in her mid thirties, of average height, a neat figure with swept-back chestnut hair. Her face was still pretty, but the faint lines of age had begun to mark the skin. He felt shabby in his work clothes and tugged self-consciously at his collar.

'Well, I hope I don't get shot too. I'm Mr McGoohan's replacement.'

'You?'

'We women sometimes have to earn a dollar too, you know.' A spark had passed between them, and he laughed with her. A group of prospectors walked in. 'You go right on ahead, I'll just make myself at home while you serve these gentlemen.'

He was busy for most of the morning. At lunch he stuck up a notice saying the store was closed and carried her bag through to the office. 'We were on first name terms, Scott and me,' he said.

'Well, we might as well carry on the same. You can call me Elizabeth, and you're Bill, right? He spoke about you.' As she pushed the lists across the table, he noticed her ring and felt a pang of disappointment. 'So,' she said, running once more through the lists, 'you're happy with these?'

'I think so.'

'I'll leave you another catalogue and some more order forms. Mail them on to us whenever you like, you'll get your stuff usually within a couple of weeks.' She held out her hand. 'Well, Bill, I'm pleased to have done business with you.'

'With you, too.'

She pushed the door open. A far-off crump of explosives dulled the air.

'The goldmen are at it again,' she said.

'Where are you going now?'

'I have another customer down at Lead. I told the feller who drove me here I'd see him by Jancey's place as near noon as he can make it.'

'It's too hot to wait. I'll take you.'

'It's more than fifty miles.'

'We'll drop a note with Jancey, say you've had to leave early.'

'What if he's not there?'

'We'll pin it to a post.'

He locked the store and she waited for him to tack the horse and hoist a shade above the seat. He lifted her bag inside, mounted the gig and gave her a hand up. The trail to Lead was a mile away, and the dust flurried behind them. By mid afternoon, the track broiled under a shimmering sun.

'Jancey says your store's a bigger gold mine than a gold mine.'

'Only twice as hot.'

'You get used to it in the end,' she said, noting his discomfort. 'My father always said there isn't much difference between the summers at Rosenheim and Indiana. The winters neither. They're both pretty brutal.'

'Where's Rosenheim?'

'Well, I've never been there. It's a town in Germany, pretty near the Austrian border. You've come from somewhere else –'

'England.'

'Where in England?'

When he told her she nodded like a happy bird. 'My father came over in forty one. He married a girl from Rzeszow. There weren't many Poles in those days. More now, I guess. She died of smallpox when I was eight. It was a long time ago. D'you know this country lost more through smallpox than all the Indian wars put together? It's just that the Indians got the bad news.' She turned to look at him as if anticipating a reaction. 'We're trespassers in a sense, don't you think, Bill? The Black Hills belonged to the Plains Indians for centuries. The Fort Laramie Treaty was intended to protect them, but gold got in the way. I suppose I shouldn't really be talking this way. I hope you don't object to me speaking my mind?' He thought she'd speak it whether he objected or not. 'I lost my husband through gold,' she said in her matter-of-fact way.

He joggled the reins more briskly. 'How did it happen?'

'He had a job in the Homestake Mining Company. There was a roof fall and he got buried.'

'When was that?'

'Oh, that would be in sixty-six, ten years after the lode was found. We'd only been married three years.'

'And you've not married since?'

'Never found anyone good enough.' Cicadas trilled and the air bore a faint scent of honey. 'It's a beautiful country, don't you think? There are places in the Black Hills where you can walk in flowers. The air's full of bees humming, birds singing – makes you glad to be alive. No wonder it was a sacred place.'

'So how did you go on after your husband died? Do you have children?'

'I would have liked children. No, I did this and that. My father's uncle gave me some work, making shirts. It was a real sweatshop. I suppose I got a better deal than most, being family. Then I came out here nursing for a spell.'

He felt easy with her. She might have been some years his senior, but that was a figure in a stockbook. Oil lamps glimmered in the dusk as they approached Lead. He'd stay the night and return the following morning to attend to his business. He left her with a family she knew and took a cheap hotel room. Despite the journey, sleep came slowly.

13

Roddy rapped at Nerissa's bedroom door and pushed it open. She was sitting at the cheval in her underwear, flushing her cheeks with a powder brush. He came in and slumped a leg over the arm of her chair. 'Where are you off to again?' he demanded with childish petulance. 'You're always going out, we hardly ever go through the door together.'

'I've already told you,' she explained to the mirror, rubbing her lips together experimentally, 'Angelica wants to go to the theatre'

'I don't believe you. What are you going to see?'

'Don't be tiresome, darling.' She opened a wardrobe. 'Let's see: the black or the green? The black, I think. No–the green.' She took out a silk dress.

'Don't pretend you haven't heard. What are you going to see?'

'If you must know, we're going to see a new play called *Hearts of Oak*, and I hope it will be worth all the trouble.' She put a foot on the bed, smoothing a stocking up her thigh. He felt a stirring of desire, came up awkwardly behind her and ran his hand up her leg. She pushed him away with casual annoyance, causing him to lose his balance and topple on to the quilt. 'No time for that, Roddy, dear, the cab will be here in a moment.'

'There's never time, never time for anything except your excursions. A chap might go as far as to think you were seeing someone else.' He paused for the comfort of a denial, but she was taking a fan from the drawer and didn't answer. 'Well, are you?'

'I've told you, I'm going to see a play. You've never liked the theatre, so I'm going with Angelica.' She stepped into the passage. 'There's no need to wait up. I may stay the night at her house.'

He heard a goodnight from the maid, poured himself a brandy and fell back in his chair. He downed the glass and returned to the chiffonier, where he'd hidden another bottle. As he drank a well of hurt opened up in him. He'd show her a thing or two. She treated her dog better than him. He wasn't up to much in bed, but neither were a lot of fellows, especially those who liked a tot now and again, and what was the harm in that? Any man would drink himself stupid married to Nerissa, with her damned patronising attitude. He was beginning to think she'd married him just for his money. When did she last tell him she loved him? He set up a mumbling dialogue between himself and the decanter. 'Appearances? What the devil do I care about appearances? Not that much!' He clicked his fingers soundlessly, glowering at them as if they were spiteful demons. 'She thinks she can come and go as she pleases, but she'll find out who's master here! I'm more than her equal in all sorts of ways. No, by God, in every way! Look at that – doesn't that prove anything?' His alter-ego had noticed the quartz egg in the display cabinet. 'Doesn't she realise she's married to a paleontologist?'

He glared morosely into the glass, the fact the egg had been purchased from a London dealer and his degree had more to do with a donation made by his father, forgotten. The voices faded and he began to snore. The maid eased the decanter from the cushion and he awoke with a start.

'What time is it? How long have I been asleep?

'It's gone eight, sir. I'm not sure how long, I only just come into the room.'

'No matter. You can pay a visit to Angelica – if she's in.'

'Go where, sir?'

'To Ang – to the Mullineux' house. You know her, don't you? Mrs Mullineux and her husband? They've been here for dinner – don't fret, I'll call a cab. This will earn you a florin, Lucy. Just get me a pencil and paper.'

The maid had grown used to his drunken outbursts and the companions who called themselves friends as long as he had money to treat them. She'd suspected from the smell of tobacco smoke on Nerissa's clothes the purpose of her 'visits'. She could hardly blame her. She herself found the master weak and repugnant, but a florin was a florin and she was happy to enter into an intrigue which would be all over the town by tomorrow. She handed him the paper. He rested it on the display box and scribbled a couple of lines.

'Take this to the Mullineux. When the maid answers the door, hand her the note. You're not to go until you get a reply. Do you understand, Lucy? Don't set off back until you get an answer. I'll sort her out, the brazen hussy!'

Tanbrey was waiting in the lobby when Nerissa arrived. Since their first meeting they'd settled into a routine and become more reckless. He no longer contrived excuses to explain his overnight stops in Manchester to Heath, and it was immaterial to him whether Ginny knew or not, just as Davenport's guessing games were irrelevant to Nerissa. Betrayal was irresistible to her, her feelings for Tanbrey trammelled in it like a fish in a net. They corresponded by letter. Roddy had a pact with her father to begin work no earlier than ten, and he was never up before nine, by which time the mail had been delivered and her own letters brought up to her room. Her letters to John were marked 'confidential', and sent to his workplace in a plain envelope. She knew, as she crossed the hotel lobby, that Roddy would be slumped at home. Moreover, she thought as she followed Tanbrey to his room, her secret life was safe with Angelica.

'Be a dear and undo me,' she said later.

He undid the knots and watched her dress. Later she lay on the bed, filing her nails.

'I had a dream last night,' he said. 'I dreamed I was in a fire.'

'Perhaps you are going to join the Fire Brigade.'

He lit a cigar and inhaled. 'The place was in flames and the roof was falling in. I can smell it now, the stench of smoke.' He turned to her, faintly mocking. 'Can you smell it?'

'The only thing I can smell is your cigar. Move it away, it gets in my hair.' She slid off the bed. 'Let's go downstairs and have a drink.'

'Do you think that's wise?'

'I'm not sure. And what were you up to in this fire of yours?'

'I was looking for something. Something that would make me a lot of money.'

'Like my father. He dreams of buying land and selling it for housing at an enormous profit.'

'And does he have an area in mind?'

'Indeed he does. Unfortunately he's running out of money. I've even asked my husband to consider the purchase, but I don't think he's up to it.'

'I thought he could have bought up all the land in England.'

'I don't mean he's short, I mean if I wanted him to buy, he wouldn't. "Leave investments to the money men. My grandfather once told me about a fellow who laid down a fortune in roadside hotels, then the railwaymen started up and he was bankrupt within the year." That's Roddy.'

'And am I to know where this goldmine is?'

'I can't see it will do you any good. You're not exactly rich, are you?'

'Then you'll be safe telling me.'

She smiled, pleased at having drawn his anger. 'There's a farm on the Macclesfield road which produces a few ducks a year, but as building land it's worth ten times its present value. It only needs a line on the county surveyor's map. The county surveyor, of course, knows people who know people who know my papa who, in turn, told me. Nothing has been decided yet, but it will be, and farmer Brown will end up rich. Unless someone makes him an offer he can't refuse, in which case that someone else will end up rich. Oh dear, that someone could have been my Roddy.'

'And would this man sell?'

'Everyone has their price.'

He toyed reflectively with his glass. His mood grew bitter as he thought of chances like this, dropping on his lap and out of reach. No wonder they could afford their carriages and villas. When would his turn come?

'Now you're sulking.'

He drained his glass and lay back on the bed.

His mood persisted as he travelled back on the early morning train and took a cab directly to the Bull. In the year he'd worked there he'd overhauled the office procedures while Duggan had looked forward to his retirement. Duggan had risen to a decent position and his reward had been a good wage and a steady job, but John wasn't the sort to reconcile himself to a steady job. He resented Heath's not providing him with 'his own front door' as he'd promised. He deserved more than a rented end-of-terrace. Duggan had retired before he could get involved in the benevolent fund, and now it was up and working no one gave Tanbrey credit. He paced his office, weighed down by the injustice. It was then an idea came to him with such force he reached for his chair.

Over the next few days he refined his plan. He had to restrain his excitement, bide his time. Then, working late one night he came across an envelope addressed to Heath and bearing the familiar embossed stamp of Heath's stockbroker. He'd pushed it into a drawer with other correspondence which had arrived that morning to attend to later. Usually such letters were taken to the coalmaster's office, or to the Grange for Heath to look at if he was at home. Now he retrieved it and took it into a store where the stove used for tea by the office staff was still hot. With coals from the hopper he coaxed a flame, partly filled a kettle and waited for it to boil. When the first wisps appeared, he steamed open the flap. The brief note inside provided the key he'd been looking for. Suddenly, there were omens in everything he saw; in the grimy windows, the calendar on the desk, the chiming of the hour. All he had to do was reach out and play the cards he'd been dealt. He had to act quickly. Tonight. No, tomorrow. It would have to be tomorrow. He looked again at the sheet in his hand and mouthed thanks to whatever gods had delivered it to him.

Charlie scratched a clear patch on the iced window and peered out. The iron-grey land plunged from a sky stippled with stars. He went downstairs, ate a slow supper and left the house. Congealed mud formed stone-hard corrugations of moonlight along the path and jarred his feet. When he reached the valley, he walked along the railway using the sleepers as stepping stones. A train clanked by, and he climbed on to the last truck as it passed through the pricks of light.

He joined the night shift, ducked under the guard and felt the familiar uprush of air against his face as the cage descended. They left the cage and passed into a whitewashed vault. From a recess came the sweet smell of hay. One of the men produced an apple and held it across the planking; a pony nuzzled his outstretched hand.

A barrier spanned the passage, with a door cut into it just wide enough for a man to step through. The roof dipped, and rails ran along a tunnel part-buried in debris. Now the dip narrowed, the roof supported on columns of uncut coal and pit props. As he waded through the darkness a lump rose to his throat and he fought against his habitual dread of being trapped. The gallery ended in a seam worked by a series of tunnels which climbed at intervals to new levels, the coal brought down with shot and pony-hauled to the shaft bottom. Already the men were removing their jackets, making piles on a shelf alongside their snap tins. He brought up a tub, spat in his palms and raised his pick.

Freezing weather frosted the colliery buildings. As his shift went to work, another group took a break around an underground smithy which had recently been moved from the base of the downcast shaft and away from the cooling air. A flue led into a cross-cut, and from there a draught vented the fumes to the surface by way of an upcast shaft. Moving the smithy meant the flue had been shortened by some ten yards, causing it to glow duskily with the increased heat. Charlie had been working less than an hour when two of the miners drew up the smithy fire using lumps of coal and cotton. A scrummage of boys gathered around it for warmth, then went with the two men to their work, leaving it unattended. One returned briefly to burn the grease off his safety lamp. By the time he'd gone to his work, the flue had started to glow, and now a wisp snaked into the airway.

A quarter of a mile away, Charlie stopped to wipe his brow, smearing a mask across his eyes. He put down his pick and drank a mouthful of cold tea. There was a faint scrape of shovels, a flicker of lamps, a song floating through the blackness.

'They won't have you in the Methy choir, Cain.'

'Maybe he'll get a place in the celestial choir instead.'

Charlie took another swig.

'You'll be getting drunk, Charlie.'

'He'd be drunk on water, him.'

'He wants t' get himself fixed up with a woman. He wouldn't have need o' this tea he keeps drinkin'.'

'Ever had a woman, Charlie?'

Dust thickened his reply. He felt somehow uneasy, different than before, a mood, a foreboding he couldn't understand.

At half past twelve Ginny left her bed and peered through the window at the flakes of snow squalling against the glass. Matthew coughed and fidgeted on to his back. She'd begun to realise that whatever John said, she'd nothing to blame herself for. She had Matthew, she could endure. As the ledge whitened, she was thinking there were others worse off. She wondered about Charlie, so different from the others, so unsure of himself. She saw him underground, hewing coal. Colliers could be worse off than her. At least she wasn't down the pit. Her son started in his sleep, and she stroked his cheek.

Tom Viggars stumbled over a line. He took off his jacket and rubbed his swollen arm. He'd need to go to the lit gallery at the shaft bottom and take a closer look. As he walked, he didn't immediately notice the smell of burning. When he did, he froze. His mind's eye saw the page of rules: *If at any time the pit should be reported unsafe....* Smoke wreathed in the light of his lamp and he broke into a spasm of coughing.... *suspend all operations until special directions from the manager have been received....*The manager. Where was he? Where the bloody hell was Thompson?

'You want to get off that moor, Charlie. Just think, if you weren't down here you'd be up above, forced to breath fresh air. Where's Arthur with that bloody horse? Here, load this on the tub.'

A cage clanged to the surface. Flakes whitened the winding towers. A loaded train clanked mournfully up the incline.

Viggars buried his face in his sleeve. Through the thickening smoke he saw the forge pipe glowing red and the roof veined with bright threads of fire. Tongues of flame licked the wall, driving him back towards the dip. He stumbled again, sieving his breath through a rag. There were lights a short way off. He blundered towards them, calling, but his voice had lost its force and he called again through cupped hands. 'The pit's afire. Get the lads up top.' He caught a youth by the sleeve and blasted the words in his ear 'Get the men, tell'em to get up top. Anyone you find.'

'What if they think I'm in jest, Tom?'

'In jest, you stupid bastard, does it look as if I'm bloody joking?'

'But they're miles down the goaf –'

'Get anybody you can find, tell'em to get the bosses, any bugger long as he's got a tub o' water.' He blundered towards the shaft. Lights already pricked the bottom, and he pushed among them into the cage. With agonising slowness, it began to rise.

'What d'you mean, the pit's on fire?'

Viggars found himself explaining to Thompson's back. As he ran to the pit-head, he gathered anyone he passed. A bitter wind blustered snow into their faces. Candles flickered from the bedrooms of the nearby terraces. 'Get over the Middle Pit, bring horse boxes, many as you can get. Let's get the bloody horses out.'

'We're wanting water, Ted, not boxes.'

'Who's in charge, you or me?'

'If we don't get water sharp there'll be no bloody horse boxes and no pit neither.'

Viggars left him running towards the cage and began to give orders of his own.

Thompson's son came up. 'We're in trouble,' he said.

*

The haft gave with a crack. Charlie shouted across to Joe Dale for a spare pick. There'd be a spare in the lamp room, no doubt. Charlie swung the tool over his shoulder and started back as a faint cry rang down the tunnel. Ahead he could make out the blink of lamps and as he neared the cross-cut he smelt the first drifts. He quickened. The air grew hot and bitter, and he stumbled blindly through the smoke.

An arm shot out of the darkness. It was Thompson's. 'Where've you come from?'

'Down the face.'

'Who's there now?'

'Dick Cottonbury and Arthur -'

'Go tell'em the pit's afire, get'em up on the bank. Don't stand there gawpin', get'em up.' Thompson changed his mind. 'No, you can help with water. Get some tubs down. Go on, bugger yourself off and bring the tubs.'

Charlie let the pick go and ran to the cage. A confusion of shapes bore water to the cross-cut. By the stables men wrestled with the ponies. By a quarter to two the fire had spread into the travelling dip and a hazy smoke was seeping into the nearest galleries.

A crowd of onlookers were scattered across the surface. Men rolled water tubs through the sleet towards the pit-head. The cage clanged up and clanged down. Sam Viggars fought the fire below, his eyebrows singed, his hair smouldering.

Lights shone from the houses below the waste. Christopher Beech's son was already up and dressed. 'Father, you've been sent for, the pit's afire.'

The older man's snores ended in a snuffle, and he woke to feel his son shaking him by the shoulder. He waited for the words to sink in, his throat tight with sleep. The wind whipped his coat as he went out. He got to the bank, and saw agitated figures silhouetted against the colliery lamps. He recognised his other son, Joe; and Atherton, rolling butts. Simcock, Dawson, Jolley; crowds hovering. He joined the men at the next cage and went down.

In the far galleries, picks struck through the pools of pallid light.

'And what were you up to last night, Deanie?'

'None o' your business.'

'I bet you were with that wench - what's 'er called, the Whitfield Wanderer? Her's seen more tassels than a midwife.'

'Where's bloody Tanbrey? I bet he broke his pick deliberate, so 'e wouldn't 'ave to work.'

Jolley and Dawson backed away from the heat. The manager ranted orders to bring the horses to the top.

'If we stay here we're all going to be smothered,' Jolley said.

Dawson left the confusion to go up with some others. More followed; James Simcock, Arthur Lowe, leaving Thompson smashing the forge flue with a sledge hammer.

Quarter to three. Joe Beech had caught up with his father close to the face.

'Father, get out and save your life.'

'There's men down here. What about theirs?'

'Leave them to Thompson. It's not your concern.'

'Thompson!' The older man spat into the dust.

'You're goin' no further. It's madness, the bloody pit'll go up any time.'

'Then you'd better save yourself.'

'D'you want t' see mother a widow?'

His father yelled into the darkness. James Fletcher and John Davis were nearest and his call reached them as a faint whisper of urgency. It sounded again.

Fletcher paused. 'Best see what's afoot.'

Thompson's lips worked soundlessly. An inner voice screamed the ruination of the company, the loss of the mine. He heard himself call for barrels, horse boxes, as the tendrils swirled upwards from the shaft. His head knew the orders, but the words flapped around his throat. Where were they, why hadn't they heard, why weren't they up?

Charlie was sweating despite the cold, rolling tubs.

'Get over the cage, bring Boulton and Billy Lockett – and that youth over by there, bring him an' all.'

He followed them to the cage, Edward Thompson, Henry Boulton, then Lockett and the boy. He looked aghast at their faces in the flares.

*

Ginny returned to bed and managed to doze. She thought she'd heard a thud, or maybe she'd dreamed it. She got up again and peered out. A glow hung over the roof tops to the south. There was a far-off clamour of bells. She crossed to John's room and shook him. The oath died on his lips as an urgent clanging broke from the street below.

The manager's son, John, lay unconscious at the pit head, a thick stream of blood oozing from his ears and mouth. His brother lay close by, a bone protruding from his thigh. Flame poured from the mine, enveloping the headgear and a row of wagons in a flaring arc. Fire had caught the engine house, igniting the grease tubs. Edward Thompson had been blown across the tracks by the force of the explosion, the cage blasted into the tower. It would be two hours before Henry Boulton's torso was discovered, entwined in the winding gear. William Lockett and the lad had been blown out and fell into the pit on their descent. The moment was a date on paper to Charlie; a broken pick, what he was doing, thinking, hidden as deep below the surface as the seam which had almost killed him.

The rector swept his eyes across the pews. 'Seven days ago, twenty four colliers perished at the Chatterley Whitfield mine, a mine which took pride in its men; hewers of coal, engineers, jiggers, carpenters – all who worked steadfastly for their masters, for their country. The manager, one of his sons, both were cruelly injured. As if this were not enough his other son, John, was snatched from him. Others too, hurled into the pit, leaving fifty two children without a father, eighteen widows who will grieve till the end of their days.' A spate of muffled sobbing broke out. Some lifted their eyes to the chancel arch, and the rector drew their observations into his sermon. 'Yes, look upon those words: *Come Unto Me and I Will Give You Rest.* Many among you must now be wondering what this rest is. How can a benevolent God allow this to happen? To snuff out a man like a candle flame as he toils in the bowels of the earth, do they not deserve better of this God? Why did God– if He is kindly disposed towards us– strike down those whose duty it was to serve Him in the only way they knew– with their hands? William Gidman, a jigger from Chell Heath; Robert Miles of Fegg Hayes, a fireman; Henry Stubbs, a carpenter who lived and worked not a stone's throw from the place where he now lies entombed. Why did our Lord not save these, his servants? True, there are some He spared. Had this mighty explosion occurred not two hours later, four hundred would have perished. And here, in our own village, we give thanks to the Lord for having spared Charles Tanbrey, who survived the explosion which drove the cage upwards as if it had been no more than a bubble at the end of a child's clay pipe. But what of the others? I turn here to Ecclesiastes: There is no man that hath power over the spirit to retain the spirit, neither hath he power over the day of death.' He thrust out his neck as if to defy anyone who thought he'd no explanation to offer. 'How can we know His will? Did He wish to wreak vengeance upon us for sins we might have committed, not knowing we committed them? Harsh judgement, my friends, harsh judgement indeed. For struggle as we might to understand this terrible tragedy, we must fall back on His will. He ordained it. He caused it to happen. We know not why. I know not why. But twenty four men are now free from all searching after whys and wherefores. They have found their answer in the eternal rest which only He can grant. And we will come to know His Truth, as it is known to Joseph and Christopher Beech, to William Lockett, to James Fletcher and William Dean. To all who perished with them so that they should come at last to the Glory. What I do Thou knowest not now, but Thou shalt know hereafter.'

Will went outside. He wanted to go back to the Moel, but the strength had left his legs and he sank on to a bench in the porch. The service had moved him, they thought. He shouldn't have come so soon after the accident; it wasn't so long ago he'd lost his wife. And he was one of the lucky ones. After all, Charlie hadn't suffered bodily. Taking a whistling breath, he lifted his face to the notices pinned across the board: Heath's donation of £50 for the families of the deceased, the Rector of Norton's fund for the bereaved. He'd been through the episode until his mind ached.

He buttoned his coat and went out. Berries lay in raisin-coloured heaps in an angle of the wall, and the hymn faded as he reached the lane. He'd never really forgiven his wife. Even his own children didn't know Charlie was their half-brother. His grudge had festered through the years, his jealousy of the boy's success at school, at Caulton's gift and advice. Charlie had had to pay the price, and it had taken twenty-four dead to bring him to the truth.

14

For two days Will had left the letter unopened, but now he took it out along with a photograph clipped to it. He spent a minute looking at it before turning to the lines of cramped writing.

'Dear All,

I have something to tell you which might come as a shock, though I hope a pleasant one. I suppose you thought I wasn't the marrying type, but I took the plunge last week. My wife's family were from Germany, though she is a natural born American. Her name is Elizabeth Schmelling, and she's thirty seven, which makes her ten years my senior. I met her in the summer, but I didn't want to write earlier in case nothing came of it. We are very happy together and the difference in ages doesn't bother me. Her first husband died in a mine accident.

Now I've got to tell you about the store. It has done really well since I opened up. As I said in my other letters, I wasn't sure I could make a go of it but I have and it brought me a wife into the bargain, so I'm really happy about it all. Liz thinks we might do well getting a bigger place now we are wed and that's something I shall have to think about, the drawback being it seems a pity to move when trade here is so brisk. Liz was in the mail-order business, and at one time she was travelling from the Lakes to the Rocky Mountains. Now she works around South Dakota, but her territory is still as big as Britain. The mail-order people do very well. It's something that might happen over there one day I think. The problem here is the railroads pushing the costs up, and it seems stupid because the fewer people buy the less freight gets handled.

The winters here make the moor look like everlasting spring. Everybody stays put, for if you get lost in the drifts you're a dead man, and anyway there isn't enough people to clear the trails, so I'm writing this while the weather holds with the hope you get it in good time.

Your loving son and brother,

Bill'

Will studied the photograph again. The woman was seated on a bench, Bill standing behind with a hand on her shoulder. He laid the photograph aside, took out pen and paper and began to write, his lips parted in laboured concentration.

'Dear Bill,

Your letter reached here last week. I have to tell you Charlie met with an accident down Whitfield Pit. They blew the pit up but he's all right. That schoolteacher, Caulton was his name, Charlie wrote down to him for years now and that is where he's gone to get over it. The shock was too much for him and he was having a bad time. The schoolmaster's wife was up this way visiting and he went back with her down south to take some long walks and get some air. They lost some men and there is an enquiry so I don't hold out much for the manager's chances – from what I hear he was more concerned about the horses. Anyway, that is the main thing I wanted to tell you. John seems to be doing all right from what little I see of him. I've dropped in on him once or twice and he's been out on business. That young lad of his is growing up but his wife looks strained and I told her she wants to rest but she is pleasant enough.

Well Bill, I am glad you are settled now. From your picture your wife looks like your mother when she was younger. Things go on much the same here and to tell the truth I find it a bit of a struggle sometimes and my chest is no better. I don't see anything of the Benersleys now but if I see somebody that goes their way I will give them a message from you.

Your Dad'

He sealed the envelope and put it by the door to post.

John caught a Sunday train to Macclesfield. It was approaching high summer, and wisps of high cloud feathered the sky. The wheels' rhythm lulled him, and he closed his eyes, letting the events of the last months wash over him. His visits to Nerissa had continued despite an ugly scene during the previous October, when her husband proved himself less of a fool than he'd supposed and sent the maid to Angelica Mullineux's house to check his wife had gone to the theatre with her. Her knock had been answered by Angelica's husband, who'd packed off his own maid, having accused her of bringing flu into the house. Indeed, Angelica had spent the afternoon in bed dosed with brimstone and treacle, and was in no position to give an alibi to anyone. Furthermore, he'd learnt there was no *Heart of Oak* playing in any of the Manchester theatres. When Nerissa returned he'd confronted her. She'd flared up at first, but then admitted the truth. He'd slunk into a chair and said he'd cut her off without a penny, blubbing self-indulgently while snatching glances at her through his fingers. Had she no remorse, seeing another man behind his back? Was it someone he knew? She'd waited for him to calm before she told him. His eyes had started in his head. Not only was she a deceitful hussy, she'd been with a clerk, a bloody colliery employee! At least if he'd been someone of means, a mill owner or something – but this, this Tanbrey – did she make a habit of picking up men out of the gutter?

John smiled to himself, remembering Nerissa's account, and drifted on to other matters. Thompson had been found guilty only of negligence, but Charlie was safe. Charlie, the only person he'd ever felt anything for, inasmuch as he could feel for anybody. Even with Nerissa he wasn't sure of the bond between them, unless it was based on mutual distrust. Ginny would jump through hoops to be favoured with a smile, but Nerissa was like him, engaged in a sort of business deal which suited them both. And his idea. He remembered the time last year when it had come to him in a flash and he couldn't understand why he hadn't thought of it before. He was responsible for the Bull Benevolent Fund. More than a thousand men paid in regularly, and there was a sizeable surplus. Any payments had to go through him. Anyone wishing to examine the ledgers had to consult him first. Men off work through sickness had a full allowance paid for the first month and half the second. Since it was rare for a man to be away longer than three weeks, the fund had constantly increased. Falsification of the accounts would cover any unwarranted withdrawals, and it would take freak ill-luck for the fraud to be discovered. Happening across Heath's letter reduced the risk still further. It was a note urging Heath to take over an ailing ironworks near Tunstall. The present owner was in difficulties and was prepared to let it go to the first acceptable bid. Once added to Heath's industrial empire, the acquisition would prove a valuable asset. Shares had stood at no more than a few pence each, but should Heath decide to buy, these would increase at least fifty fold. John recalled resealing the envelope and dropping it into Heath's tray next morning before the others came to work. He'd bought a thousand of the shares from the fund. A month later, Heath made a successful bid and the value of Tanbrey's holding had increased by seventy times the original amount. He'd paid his profits into an account he'd opened in a Manchester bank under Pandora Enterprises, then returned the money he'd 'borrowed' to the fund. No one had been any the wiser. He now had enough capital for his next venture.

The train pulled into Macclesfield. He named a farm on the edge of the town and instructed the cabbie to take him there and pick him up two hours later. A man emerged from a barn and scowled at him before sauntering across the yard with a whetstone.

'My name's John Tanbrey. I'd like a word, if I may, Mr Wharton.'

'Do I know you?'

'Is there a way in without wading through water?'

The farmer stood at the margin of a pond. 'What would it be about?'

'Something which might be to your advantage.'

The man put his whetstone on the wall and pointed out a path raised above the water by flat-topped stones. 'You're not the parson, are you?'

'Not exactly. Does everyone who comes here have to wade across the pond?'

'It's not a pond, it's a spring what floods. Gives the ducks something to go at.'

'Perhaps we could go inside.'

'I can't see as it'll take no harm out here.'

'It concerns both your wife and yourself.'

'Her's no use with strangers.'

'I've travelled too far to waste your time.'

Wharton shambled into the house and John followed him down a passage puddled with watery mud into a room at the end. The farmer discarded his boots by the door and called for his wife to bring out a pair of toeless shoes. A long-case clock ticked slowly against the wall. Sets of drawers stood wherever there was room, one roughly sawn and rejoined to fit. Before a dull fire lay a large tabby, her family sprawled across the window sill.

'Would you mind if I sat?' Tanbrey began, turning to a chair greased at the wings with use. 'I have a proposition to put to you.'

'And what might that be?'

'Here.' Wharton held Tanbrey's card a few inches from his nose and handed it back, unread. 'As you see, I represent an organisation whose interests lie mainly in the acquisition of land. Our aim is to relieve owners of their obligation to its upkeep, and compensate them by offering generous terms.'

'You mean you want to buy up the farm. The door's behind you.'

Tanbrey felt a flush of anger. 'I'd appreciate it if you heard my proposition before you throw me out. You are always free to choose, of course, but the expense of my journey seems hardly worthwhile if you simply shun the idea before I've a chance to clarify it.'

'Maybe we should hark to what the gen'lman has to say, Ted.'

Wharton glowered at his wife, who began to rock in her chair.

'We can offer a competitive price,' Tanbrey went on, giving a figure twenty percent higher than the best Cheshire dairyland would fetch at auction.

'And what's in it for you?'

'Our clients are only interested in long-term investments, and they have the means to weather any fluctuations in the market.'

'And what are we to live on when I've got rid?'

'Come, come, Mr Wharton, you can't be serious. How many acres do you have? A couple of hundred? We're not concerned with seizing a man's livelihood. From only a partial release of land you could expect to gain far more than it would yield in your life-time. You'd surely find it to your advantage to continue with reduced liabilities, with less need to tire yourself out. Surely you could both make good use of more leisure hours? Forgive my impertinence, Mr Wharton – when was the last time you were in Manchester?'

'It'd be close on ten years since,' his wife said, 'on the occasion of Beatrice's wedding, d'you remember, Ted?'

'I aren't bothered about Manchester nor any other town come to that. I'm selling nowt and now you've done you can leave.'

John gave a regretful sigh. 'I'm sorry we can't reach an understanding. I was hoping to be able to offer our clients – but no matter.' He shook the woman's hand and stepped towards the door as the farmer stood self-satisfied with his back to the hearth. 'Before I go, tell me, Mr Wharton, how much would you say your house was worth?'

'He'll be taking the slates off the roof next, Nelly.'

'I was wondering how much it would cost to rebuild a house of this size. It must have an enormous number of rooms, even a large cellar, I imagine.' A flicker of suspicion crept into Wharton's eyes. Pulling at his cap, he took a step across the sacking. The flea-ridden tabby sprang from the hearth and bit wildly at its fur. 'What amazes me is how it came to be built at all,' John went on.

'What's that supposed to mean?'

'Your house straddles the Queen's highway. Your farmhouse is illegal, Mr Wharton. You know the sort of people serving on the parish. They can do as they please, but they won't allow others the same privilege.'

'Privilege? I'll show you something about privilege.' Wharton stepped back into a corner of the room. At first Tanbrey thought he'd taken a stick, but found himself looking into the barrel of a shotgun.

His wife rose bent-backed from her seat. 'Ted!'

'I'll teach this bloody upstart –' He jerked open a drawer, scattering the contents aside. 'Where's the shot? Where've you put my shot?'

John stood in the doorway. Surely a farmer could lay his hand on a tin of lead without having to search the room. He decided to call his bluff.

'Injure me, Mr Wharton, and it will be more than your house you lose.'

'Don't take on, Ted, you'll have us both hung.'

'What your wife says makes good sense.'

The farmer slammed the drawer, his rheumy eyes filled with sullen hatred.

'If you don't tell him I shall,' his wife said, suddenly worried. 'It were his father had the house put up more than forty years since. He was a cussed devil, and his son takes after him. Ted inherited it. Nobody said owt at the time, and in the end we forgot about it. Nobody had used the road for years anyway. You can see it's nothing to do with us, Mr Tanbrey.'

Wharton had lowered the gun and was leaning on the stock. 'Now her's told you all our business, what are you goin' to do about it?'

'Perhaps we can come to an arrangement,' John said, pulling up his chair again and removing a folder of papers from his case. 'Yes, I'm sure we can.'

The representative of Pandora Enterprises emerged from the house and climbed into the waiting cab. Wharton had signed away twenty acres of land. If Nerissa was right and the County Surveyor did his job, within the year it would be worth many times the amount he'd paid. He congratulated himself on his investigations. He'd taken the trouble to pore over the maps and the track had come to light unexpectedly, an easily-missed path between two lanes meeting in a V some quarter of a mile away.

He'd been unable to discover whether it was still, legally, a public road and he'd chanced that Wharton wouldn't know either. The only thing now was to wait. If the plan to extend the town was ratified, he'd make – he hardly dared tempt fate by reckoning. If, on the other hand, some unforeseen change were to prompt the development of an alternative site, he'd still hang on to it. He'd nothing to lose. Either as farm land or building land, the price would inevitably rise. He sat back, satisfied. His amused smile turned to secretive laughter, and he stifled the urge to laugh out loud all the way to the station. Before the cabbie could thank his passenger for the generous tip he'd just been handed, John had disappeared towards the platform, en route to a Manchester hotel. He sniffed at his newly-purchased carnation and sank back in a first class compartment.

Will drew his chair nearer the hearth. The room felt empty. Edna, Bill, John, Charlie. The world was drifting away from him, and he felt threatened by it. That June he'd seen a steam thresher in the vale, able to do the work of twenty men in half the time. He felt he'd outlived his usefulness. Bill, married and living in foreign parts; John, who seemed destined for better things. But Charlie?' He shook himself free and mended the fire. He was nearly sixty, couldn't get up as he used to, couldn't keep things in his head. He fell asleep in his chair and didn't wake until midnight. When he went to bed he lay for a long time, listening to the comforting rush of wind about the house.

Charlie. Yes, he'd make amends.

PART TWO

REALITIES
1882-1900

There's a divinity that shapes our ends,
Rough-hew them how we will
Hamlet

1

Charlie looked down over the Tunstall terraces. A pewter sky hung over the town, and the whiff of commerce drifted upwards. The last time he'd seen his aunt had been at his mother's funeral eight years before, and he wondered what kind of welcome he'd receive. He lingered for a moment, then took a path through the fields and past the station. He continued to the end of the road, where the market rose above the roofs. Coils of smoke wafted across a High Street of shawled women with baskets; hay carts and coal wagons rumbled over the cobbles. A range of buildings framed the Square, with the Ston Hus – both public hall, fire station and lock up – at its centre and a network of streets radiating from it. He took one of the streets, found the house he wanted and knocked.

'Charlie! Come in.'

Aunt Ethel, his mother's sister, wiped her awkwardness on a stained apron. 'I'll just put the kettle on. Your uncle's not in from work yet, but he's been looking forward to seeing you. Have you had a bite since leaving home?'

'I brought a round of dripping.'

'Well, sit down, we don't stand on ceremony here.' The kettle began to sing and she threw it an anxious glance. 'Cliff's supposed to have cleared the grate but it's smothered as usual. Well, you're looking more like your mother than ever.' She lifted the kettle with a cloth. 'They'll be here in a minute.'

'How are they all?'

'All right, touch wood. Bessie's down Grindley's Pot Bank and Bertha's courting.'

'What about Dick?'

'He's with your uncle down Platt's brickyard.' She watched him sip his tea. 'Have you been on one of them new trams yet? Our Dick says they fair rattle along. They haven't got'em up this end, but they won't be long in coming.'

The door grated, and a man in a clay-smeared jacket came in. He turned a pleasant face to Charlie, and asked if he felt better.

'Much better, thanks, Uncle Cliff, much better than I was. I expect you've heard I went down south for a spell. It's a fair few strides over those cliffs.'

'Will wrote, didn't he, Cliff, said after the accident you'd gone to stay with Mr Caulton, wasn't it? I remember your mother said something once about you going to a do up his house.'

He nodded, quietly encouraged by his uncle. There were a lot of words for what he'd been through, and now he wanted it to drop. 'It wasn't nerves as such, more I couldn't cope with doing anything. I feel more my old self now.'

'I've seen Wilf,' Cliff said. 'He says he'll expect you Monday, then you can look around the place, see what you think.'

'I aren't certain what I'll be looking for.'

'Don't worry, you'll be all right with Wilf.'

Charlie's uncle didn't say much over the table, and after dinner he dozed as Ethel kept up rambling anecdotes tied to her small world. He looked around the cramped living room, with its scrubbed deal table and swilled floor, hemmed in by the parlour which was for visitors only and the distempered wash-room with its brown pitcher sink.

Charlie hadn't seen his cousin Dick since his schooldays, and didn't recognise him at first. After a friendly greeting Dick bent over his paper and scooped up spoonfuls of stew. Aunt Ethel's flow faltered as her daughters came in; Bertha, with her crop of red hair, and Bessie, who greeted him in a breathless whisper while her large grey eyes slid secretively to the floor.

'Our Bessie was only seven when you saw her last. She's grown a tidy bit since then,' Ethel clucked. 'And how old were you when you went to Aunt Edna's funeral, Bertha? About twelve, were you?'

'So you've decided to come into the world of civilisation, have you, Charlie?' Bertha smiled.

'For my sins.'

'And what are you going to do up Wilf Clowes' tileworks? I'd heard you were cut out for better things.'

'Will's a good'un,' cut in his aunt, pouring from the chipped teapot, 'but you saw the letter, from Will, Bertha, asking if Cliff could fix him up with something? Don't you remember? It's that young man o' yours, knocking all the sense out of your head.'

Charlie remembered Will's changed attitude towards him when he'd got back from Devon. He'd told him he'd found him something in Tunstall, and Charlie couldn't understand why he'd gone to the trouble.

'Maybe I can go more into the design side,' he said.

'Well, you'll find out nothing about that from Wilf. Brown marl, that's all he's about.'

'Take no notice of her, Charlie,' his aunt said. 'It'll give you an idea of the business, that's what you want, isn't it? You can sleep in the living room, you'll find it warm enough on the sofa. Bertha and Bessie have the upstairs room, and Dick has the back room with a curtain over it for me and Cliff. We had a lodger, but he kept coming in at all hours so Cliff gave him his marching orders.' She clicked her tongue. 'Anyway, you'll be all right down here, just hang your boots on the pegs so you don't get nothing crawling around inside.'

By ten everyone but Bertha was home. Cliff chatted with him until her boyfriend brought her back from the glee club. But for bursts of rowdy song that came faintly into the room, the house was still.

He awoke to the sound of rain. As his eyes grew accustomed to the light he recognised his cousin Bessie in the doorway. He studied her furtively as she came over and stood in her night gown looking down at him.

'Have you slept well, Charlie?'

'What's the hour?'

'Nearly getting up time. Is it comfortable wrapped up in there?'

'Why are you up this early?'

'I've a throat, I needed a sip of water.' She smiled as if concealing a secret. 'This is your big day.'

'It's only work.'

'That's what my dad says.' She plucked at his blanket, and he felt the touch of her fingers against his foot. 'Come winter you'll be frozen to ice.' He moved on to his back and lay looking up at her, an arm crooked behind his head. ‘How old are you, Charlie?’

‘Just gone twenty one.’

‘Twenty one? I wouldn’t have thought you were that.’

‘What d’you want to know my age for this time of a morning?’

‘Sometimes I can’t get off again if I wake up.’ She giggled behind her hand. ‘You look like a ghost stuck there on the sofa with your head poking up.’ The ceiling creaked and a trickle sounded above his head. ‘That’s our Dick. He won’t use the back way if there’s five extra minutes in bed.’ She stood against the table and yawned, thrusting her body provocatively forward. She held her position as if timing its effect on him before putting her mug on the table. ‘Well, I suppose I’d better try again. They’d have your blood on the bank if you let ’em.’

He lay listening to the patter of rain on the window until his uncle clumped down.

Wilf Clowes’ factory was a jumble of sheds on the edge of town. The owner was wiping his hands on an apron as Cliff went inside, followed by Charlie. Wilf was well into his fifties, with thinning grey hair and the skin thickly folded over the collar of his work jacket. After Cliff introduced them and left for work, Wilf placed a companionable hand on Charlie’s shoulder. ‘Fancy a brew?’

‘Thanks, Mr Clowes.’

‘It’s Wilf, isn’t it, Percy?’ A youth with a crate grunted. ‘He’s my favourite packer, is Percy. Does the work o’ five, all of ’em drunk.’

‘Can’t afford drink on your wages.’

‘See what I mean, Charlie? He’d have the candle off your coffin given half a chance.’

‘When I go down the graveyard, it’ll be in a dust-sheet.’

Will chuckled. ‘Take no notice of my employee, I couldn’t for shame see him begging for charity.’ They went into a dingy office. A kettle wisped on the stove. ‘Right, sit down and tell me what you know about tiles.’

‘Not a great deal.’

‘Well, I’ll show you around in a tick.’ He handed Charlie a mug and drank reflectively. ‘Business is brisk, you know. I’ve had my ups and downs but things haven’t been too bad of late, touch wood. Folks seem to have a bit more to put about than when I started, what with all these new houses going up. Your uncle tells me you come from up Bradley Green way.’

'Not far off.'

'Then you'll know nothing about this new Town Hall of ours. My, there'll be some tiles wanted there – wall tiles, floor tiles, somebody'll be rich.'

'It could be you,' said Charlie.

'D'you hear that, Percy? Charlie reckons I'm all set to make a fortune.'

'I wouldn't be surprised, chance what you take off me.'

'Take no notice of him, Charlie, he gets bitter at times. We don't make enough here to tile the cloakrooms. That'll be left to them as can turn out a quantity, Maws or Dunhills or some such. I bet it's all down on the plans even now. That's what I was trying to tell you, everybody's after tiles nowadays. Hospitals, libraries, baths, schools – you'll be hard put to find a woman doesn't want 'em in her hall. It's a talking point, you see. Wash stands, umbrella stands, shops, publics – the list's endless. D'you see what I'm driving at? Now I can't compete with the big outfits, but I flatter myself I know what folk around here can afford. I've got an iron or two in the fire, so if they want to build another fifty houses up by Furlong, they can come to us and there'll be a dozen crates o' reds ready for carting next day. We aren't about inlays or anything fancy, just plain quarries which'll still be on the ground when you and me're under it.'

'Chance I'll be under it first, with twenty crates to go at.'

'Ignore that soft bugger, Charlie, it must be full moon tonight. Come on, I'll show you around.'

He led the way through the sheds, pointing out the features and functions of the workshops as they passed. Before the tour ended, another employee came in. 'Neville, this is Charlie, come to take over from Jeff. Right, I'll leave you now in Neville's capable hands.'

Neville slapped him on the back. 'Come on, then, young Charlie, I'll initiate you into the mysteries of the tile business.'

He spent the rest of the day pugging clay, and by the time he got back to Calvert Street it was turned seven. He slept fitfully, and in his waking moments wondered if he'd fare any better at the tile works than in the pit. Wilf Clowes' relationship with the men seemed to be that of an older brother. No, he thought, drifting off, it wasn't Wilf but the job, and if Wilf wanted someone to work the pug mill, for the present that would have to do.

It wasn't yet light when he dressed again, and he arrived at the tile works still tired.

*

One weekend Dick introduced him to the monkey-run, and they spent Saturday evening walking the square in their best, Dick chatting to any girl he knew.

'You want to get a good woman, Charlie,' his cousin advised him when the rest had gone to church the next day. 'I can fix you up.'

'I can fix myself up.'

'You want to put yourself about a bit. Tell you what, I know this girl, she's got a friend called Mavis, she'll walk out with a runner's mate for a spoonful o'sugar.'

'What's she like?'

'What d'you mean, what's she like? Who looks at the mantelpiece when he's pokin' the fire?'

'I dare say him with the poker.'

Dick gave a hoot of laughter and clapped Charlie's shoulder. 'You're comin' on, lad. Tell you what, after dinner we'll go up town. She's always there, I'll point her out, see what you think.'

Around three, peeping around the corner of Ston Hus, they saw two girls crossing the square. Dick jabbed his thumb towards them and motioned to Charlie to keep his voice down.

'Which one is it?'

'Her on the left. What d'you think?'

At that moment, the girl at Mavis' shoulder spotted Dick and shouted over. Charlie shrank back. 'I think I'll leave it.'

'Her's all right. Come on, I'll introduce you.'

'Well, don't say anything.'

'Go on, her won't bite you.'

'I'll have to be getting back, Dick, I've to write a letter home.'

Dick's lips framed a question as Charlie beat a retreat to the safety of Calvert Street. The house was empty, and he sank gratefully on to the couch.

Over the next weeks he learnt the habits of the family and neighbours. The town was a hotchpotch of houses, yards, alleys, entries, chapels, pot banks, oatcake shops, taverns, bollards and lamps. It was home to Pick-me-up Jack, who beat his wife on Fridays and Gerty No Hands, who'd crushed her fingers in a mangle. There was Gentleman Jim, who marched the street bawling for everyone to lock themselves in the cellar, the Frenchies were coming; and Salvation Sal, who 'had religion' and blared warnings to the urchins who followed her when they weren't filching apples from Buy-a-Colley as he struggled with his hand-cart. But Charlie missed the quiet, and he'd leave the streets on Sundays for the oases of green which struck through the shard rucks and tile banks. He made his way one afternoon to the remnants of woodland which skirted the town, settled under a birch canopy and closed his eyes. The sound of approaching footsteps roused him and he peered through the trees. It was Bessie. He rooted down in the grass and lay still. When she was a little way off she paused and called his name, and a rush of excitement ran through him. For some reason he thought of the picture of St George slaying the dragon in his school leavers' book. Now the dragon had a high, breathless voice.

'I saw you go in there, Charlie. See? There you are.'

'Is something the matter?'

'I just come out for a walk. It's allowed, isn't it? My friend's visiting today, so I'm foot loose and fancy free.'

'You never told me you came this way.'

'I don't as a rule, I just happened to see you.' She sat by him in the grass, picking at a stalk. Her watchful grey eyes slid down the stem and settled on him. 'D'you like your work, Charlie?'

'It's a wage.'

'I hope you get settled with something you really like. If you hang about, Wilf might give you a leg up. It's the same on Grindley's, I'm sorting crocks in my sleep. They treat you like dirt if you're a young girl.'

'How's that?'

A knowing smile played across her mouth. 'You know what it's like on a pot bank. The older men are worse than the lads. I hate it there, they're always maulin' you.' She began to preen herself, her small hand flapping against the swell of her breasts, making them quiver. 'You shouldn't get in these tangles, I'll have my best dress ruined.' She lay down, looking up at him, her eyes squinting against the sky. 'D'you like butter, Charlie?'

'I suppose so.'

'I'll find out.' She manoeuvred herself up, snapped off a buttercup and held it under his chin. A reflected pool glowed the skin. 'There you are, butterbelly!' She gave her secretive giggle and began to twine a stalk in his hair. 'You'd look well at work, a buttercup in your hair. You'll look like a park garden.' From her dress came the faint scent of glaze. Above their heads a blackbird began an excited trill and darted through the brush. 'Charlie, you're shaking! You're not cold, are you?'

'A bit.'

'Here, get under this wrap with me.'

Her hand was against his own, the yielding fullness of her body pressed to his side. She began to chant:

'Here's a leaf with nine points on, press it to your heart.
The first you meet, the first you greet, will be your own sweetheart..
If he's married, let him pass, if he's single, I'm his lass.'

She gave her quiet, teasing laugh, and as she closed her eyes he felt his mouth against hers. He moved his head away, ashamed.

'What's the matter?'

'It isn't right.'

'What isn't right?'

You being my cousin was what he wanted to say, but said nothing. She looked down at her spread feet, plucking the grass as if some planned exercise had gone wrong. 'Don't you like me, Charlie?'

'It isn't that.'

'Have you never walked out with a girl before?'

'Someone up our way. Not going out, as you call it, more a friend.'

'Who was that?'

'You wouldn't know her.'

She lay back again, her arms behind her head, looking up at him. He looked away, conscious of his growing arousal.

'Charlie –'

Whatever held him back suddenly yielded, and he covered her smile with his lips as she moved hard against him. He knew now what the men joked about. He didn't care who she was, what ifs, buts, all the rest. He tried to release her dress but couldn't and she leaned forward, working unemotionally at her buttons. She lowered her hands as he pulled the muslin to her waist. It was the first time he'd seen a full-bodied girl. He caressed her diffidently, half afraid she might throw him off, but she took his head and began to pull him down.

A crack sounded a short way off. Two men with a terrier were coming along the track. She hoisted up her dress in an instant. 'That's Bert Williamson out rabbiting,' she said, everything forgotten.

'You go on, I'll catch you up.'

'Don't you want to walk home with me?'

'I'll see you in a bit.'

She picked up her bonnet and blew off the stalks. After dusting herself down she went off, Charlie watching from the trees.

Bertha married before the end of the year. He thought he might have to get lodgings if she and her husband moved into the parlour, but they found rooms nearby. Dick borrowed a handcart and he and Charlie moved a wardrobe to the new address. When he got back, there was a letter on the table.

'Dear Charlie,

I've not heard from you for a long time and my reason for writing now is to tell you Bevis is very poorly and has been asking after you. It's his chest like before. If you come up and see him it's certain to do him some good. I don't get off the farm as much as I'd care to and Doris and me would like to see you again too. Have you heard from Bill? Maybe I should have sent a letter but when you are upset the last thing you want is writing letters to the cause of it. Please try and see Bevis, Charlie, he'd really favour a visit.

Your very best friend,

Ellen'

Wilf let him have time off and he left early on the Monday, taking a train to Congleton and walking the four miles to Three Elms. Ellen was carrying a pail to the shippon as he came up and ran to him, catching his hand. 'Charlie! I didn't expect you so soon.' When she unclasped him her face was flushed, the cornflower eyes bright. 'I'm glad you've come. How's your aunt?'

'Happy as a sandboy.'

'Go on, why's that?'

'She likes lodgers under her feet.'

'I think the move must have suited you, you've developed a sense o' humour.' A shadow fell across her face. 'Don't be shocked at him. He took a turn for the worse last night. The doctor was here gone midnight.'

Doris forced a smile when she saw him. 'It's been a long time, Charlie. Won't you have a cup of tea?' He hovered at the doorpost. 'He'll be pleased to see you.'

The window had been shut against the October sun, a gap in the casement plugged with old newspaper. Bevis lay in his made-up bed, his face grey, the flesh hollow below his parchment cheeks. He heard Charlie's voice, and his eyelids flickered.

'How are you, Mr Benersley?'

The farmer ghosted a smile and attempted to raise himself.

'You're all right as you are,' Doris chided. 'Charlie's living down Tunstall way, now, with his Aunt Ethel. You remember Ethel, at Edna's funeral?'

She spoke as she would to a child. The farmer's eyes crinkled to a smile and he poked a bony wrist through the coverings. 'How're you keeping, Charlie?'

'All right, Mr Benersley.'

'I've not seen you.'

'I've been out of the area for a time.'

'I heard about the pit. Are you on the mend?'

'Much improved now, thank you.'

Benersley nodded, smiling. 'And have you found what you were lookin' for?'

'I suppose I will, in time.'

The man tightened his grip on Charlie's wrist. 'I've been wondering about you. I've been wondering all this time.... D'you remember the horse, pullin' the stirk out? Must be gone ten year since. D'you remember, Charlie?'

'Ay, I remember.'

Benersley glanced past him to the netted window and he seemed to see Nat there. 'He did his best, you know. Happen I was lacking in patience.' He turned back to Charlie. 'Your penny must've brought you luck after all, you might have been killed.... have you still got it?' Charlie fumbled it from his waistcoat and held it against the light. 'Bring it a touch nearer. What date does it say? I forget....'

'1870. Fresh minted that year.'

Benersley gave a sigh, and breathed a verse he'd learnt as a young man to the ceiling boards.

'Our place we know, so very low,
'Tis down at the landlord's feet.
We're not too low the bread to grow,
But too low the grain to eat.'

'Don't talk soft, you and your landlords,' Doris chirped, busying with the blanket. 'Your drink's ready, Charlie.' Out of earshot of her husband, she said: 'I think the old man's giving up. Doctor thought he might get inflammation like before, but it isn't goin' that way. Tell the truth, I can't see him pulling through'

'I dare say he'll rally, Mrs Benersley, he's like a cat with nine lives.'

'None of his family lived past sixty. Look at 'im, Charlie, he's wasting to nothin'.'

'What d'you think it is, then?'

'The doctor says his heart. Tell you what, he thinks he ought to have tried more with Nat. You don't know Bevis like me, he takes things deeper than you'd think.' She looked hard at him, as if there was something more she wanted to say. 'How long are you staying, Charlie?'

'Till tomorrow.'

'That's good. D'you know, me and Bevis have been wed these forty years come spring? We've had our times, like the rest. If anything happens –'

'What will you do?'

'Ee,' she suddenly cried, anguished. 'You don't know the half of it, and maybe it's best you don't.'

Ellen came in from the kitchen. Mrs Benersley returned to her work, while Charlie finished his drink and heard about Jane Cowlishaw's new job at the Victoria Mill. He was at his bedside when Bevis died, leaving a frayed chair and a pipe in a discarded rack which could have been a mantelpiece ornament. The farmer's face was empty, but an essence of him still clung to the room like breath in chill air. Charlie felt part of himself had been cast aside, the part that shared the same vulnerability, the same atoms. He had to get out while there was still light to walk the lanes.

The faint chime of the clock at Leek turned him back to the farm. Mrs Benersley was sitting in the firelight by her husband's side. 'There's a slab of cake on the stillage and tea in the pot.'

'I'm not hungry, thank you, Mrs Benersley.'

'Ellen's already in bed,' she said, in a voice he didn't recognise.

'Strange, after all these years, to you I'm still Mrs Benersley. You can sleep in our room tonight.'

'But what about the doctor? What about the certificate?'

'It'll keep till tomorrow. I suppose Bevis isn't bothered now one way or the other.'

He stood looking into the glowing hearth, then went upstairs and pulled up the blankets against the cold. A slab of moonlight fell across the room and the gown hanging from the door. He lay listening to the sounds of cattle, turning over the times he'd spent with Benersley as a boy. Then the darkness paled and the gown had moved towards him. Ellen was at the foot of the bed, her outline smudged against the door. He felt the blankets rise, the warmth of her body at his side, her lips pressed against his own. She took her mouth away and nuzzled under his chin. 'Keep me warm, Charlie.'

He brushed her hair with his lips and listened to her deep, rhythmic breathing as she succumbed to sleep. When he awoke it was daylight and the bed was empty. He went downstairs and found Doris tidying the room. 'Ellen's gone for the doctor. She's calling at the rector's on the way. Did you say you were staying?'

'I'll wait on until after the funeral.'

'As you wish.'

'Doris –'

'Well, fancy you callin' me that after all these years. If Bevis is listening he'll have a right chuckle to himself.'

'What did you mean yesterday when you said I didn't know the half of it?'

She attended to her chores, flapping the cloth and draping it over a chair as if to ward off time passing. 'He was your Dad, Charlie.'

2

Elizabeth Tanbrey, nee Schmelling, stood at the door supervising the loading of a last crate. Her small, well-proportioned figure had thickened since their marriage and Bill complained teasingly about it. But his new status suited him. She was his anchor, filling a void he hadn't known was there. For her part, the constant need to organise her own affairs since her husband's death had begun to depress her. She'd grown tired of speaking to walls, needed someone to be with at the end of a day. She embraced him and stood a little back, tilting her head quizzically.

'I keep wondering if we've done the right thing.'

She drew away. 'After all you've done, leaving your own country, setting up store here and you're worried about a pokey little change like this? What's happened to your sense of adventure?'

'Maybe I left it back home.'

'Too late for cold feet. It's a wonderful day and everything's settled. And if it isn't – well, we'll survive.'

He turned the key for the last time and helped her into the buggy. He looked back at the sign 'W and E Tanbrey, General Store' painted on the planking above the doorway, and for a moment felt he was tempting fate. He shook himself free, joined his wife and set off at a gallop, throwing a powdering of dust across the track. It had been Liz's idea to move south. She'd told him during a heavy snowfall, when the railroads were at a standstill and local travel was hazardous. It hadn't been easy to convince him, and he'd have refused had she not conceded that they lease their store to Jancey rather than sell it. She held him to his promise that spring, when business picked up. Would this not be the best time to let, when sales were booming? Investment, that was the key to sound enterprise; investment and expansion. At first he had a nagging doubt that she wanted to go south not to purchase farm land, but to shed the spectre of her late husband's death. She'd worked hard to persuade him. Ranch millionaires were sprouting like prairie grass, she said. There was wealth in cotton and wheat, fortunes to be made in Californian fruit. The population of Europe was rising with that of the United States, there'd always be mouths to feed. Thinking back to his time with Bevis, the days of drizzle and yards awash with muck, he still wasn't sure. But she could see a house with a portico and their own land stretching into the distance, and as he signed the deeds to the Solomon

Ranch, a day's ride from Kansas City, he saw it too.

He'd heard about the sale from a hand who'd been prospecting in the Black Hills and come into his store for boots one day. Bill had talked to him about his time in England, and the man had said the rancher he'd worked for had made a very healthy life for himself; had a surrey, wife always decked out when they went into town. Why, even his saddles were monogrammed, stitched in yellow thread and made from the finest Spanish leather. He'd spent a life building it up since the time he staked the land way back in the Sixties, adding a pocket here, a parcel there, buying where he could. He had good water, too; you could smell the Republican River from your armchair, and it represented bigger nuggets than the ranch-hand expected to find if he dug the hills till his fingers dropped off. The old man had no family, wanted to spend his remaining years living off the fat, as he called it. The price was no give-away, but whoever got their hands on that spread would get back every cent within a few years. It had taken two weeks for the agent to send the details through, no more than an evening for Liz to be convinced that what they'd been told was bona fide. They'd telegraphed for papers and signed them on the spot. By the time Bill joined her in the gig, he'd sent their entire profits, plus a hefty loan courtesy of the Bank of Chicago, to an agent they'd never met for a ranch they'd never seen.

They spent a few days with some relatives of Elizabeth's near Sioux before continuing their journey by railroad. Through the window, Bill watched the grasslands fade to a blue-green haze on the horizon. Cirrus feathered the sky, the land rising in gale-smoothed hummocks of bluestem to distant reaches of oak and hickory, cottonwood and willow. She caught him looking at the herds speckling the plains

'Home from home,' he said.

'Pardon me?'

'Those Herefords, that's where they come from, England.'

'Thirty years ago there would have been tribes out there, Blackfoot and Arapaho and Comanche. Now your Herefords have taken over.'

'If that hadn't happened we'd not be setting up home and you'd maybe end up the same way as Scott McGoohan. It's the natural order, like the hymn, the rich man in his castle, the poor man at his gate. In another thousand years it might be they'll give us a run for our money all over again. They had it to themselves for centuries, now it's our turn.'

He knew he'd not placated her, and she sat in thoughtful silence until something caught her eye and she jabbed at the glass. The first stalks of Turkey Red were sprouting amid the grasses, planted by farmers who'd set aside speculative areas for grain as well as beef. The sight of the wheat excited her, represented other options; alfalfa, soya, maize. She knew nothing of farming, yet her enthusiasm was infectious. She sat back in her seat and reached for his hand. Tomorrow they'd see their new home. Tomorrow would be good.

Heath barged into the office without knocking and motioned Tanbrey to a seat. 'I can't spend long. Wife keeping all right?'

'She's fine, thank you, Mr Heath.

'And the boy – Matthew, is it?'

'He's well.'

'How old is he, d'you say?'

'He'll shortly be five.... was there something – ?'

'Where are you living at the moment?' Heath asked, cutting him short. John told him. 'Not much of a place, that.'

'It's about all we can manage at present.'

His employer gazed without interest around the room. 'D'you know anybody with a cart? You'll be leaving next week.'

John shuffled some papers. 'Leaving?'

'You know Jack Bellfield?'

'The colliery manager?'

'That's him. Jack's decided he's better back up Yorkshire way. Family connections, he tells me. Must have a job in the offing pays more than me. I only wished he'd let me know earlier 'stead of leaving it to the last minute. Anyway, there you have it.'

'I have what, exactly?'

'Bellfield's place. Better than it standing empty, isn't it? I can always offer it elsewhere.'

'But the new manager, where – ?

'Leave me to sort that one out. You can move Saturday. Bellfield's stuff's already down the station.'

Heath left him staring at Duggan's clock, and he went home with the ironmaster's words still loud in his ears. He said nothing to Ginny, and went to his room after he'd eaten. A small escritoire stood in an alcove, and he unlocked the drawer, took out his journal and began to read through his recent entries. He lingered over a line he'd written a month earlier: *No more cows for Wharton.* Pandora Enterprises would enjoy a substantial increase in the value of land now the surveyor had included a portion of it in his plans. Three acres, with twenty houses to the acre; sixty roofs would shortly rise above Wharton's duck pond. He sniggered into his hand as he read, leaned back in his chair. Should the land be released piecemeal, or as a lot? Should he sell off part and use the capital to set up his own building concern? How would he stand if he were able to build, say, ten homes from the sale of a parcel? He composed his face, closed the journal and locked it back in the drawer. He'd stay with Heath as long as it suited him. He wouldn't starve now if the ironworks and mine closed tomorrow. The secret undertow of his life not only amused, but excited him. And now, the offer of Bellfield's house.

He told Ginny two days after arranging removal. Later, at work, the idea of their second-hand chattels strewn across the cart became intolerable to him. He'd an urge to furnish his new home in a manner befitting his new status and the sale of a small portion of his Macclesfield land would provide him with the means. He'd seen what could be achieved with money. Heath had paid for his taste through the hire of advisers and furnishers, but he'd rather choose the decor and furniture himself, and his choice would be tasteful rather than flamboyant. He wrote an instruction to his solicitor the moment his desk was clear.

Urias Ball's foot had taken the cart's weight, and the bones had knitted badly. His hobbling gait grew more pronounced as the tendons contracted, drawing the attention of a jeering band of youths. But his rage was directed less at them than at John Tanbrey, who he knew was the reason for his misfortune. He'd taken him under his wing as a lad, nurtured him, trained him, and his reward had been brushing dirt and he even struggled with that. Folks had once doffed their cap to him. Now they laughed behind his back and sometimes to his face. The further he plunged, the higher Tanbrey seemed to rise. And now this odious bastard, this cunning shit, was to move to Bellfield's, with half an acre and a coach house. He'd been told of a fine mahogany display cabinet which had recently arrived. How could he afford it? The cabinet, matching table, long-case clock – how? Those drapes and flounces would be enough to dent even a well-heeled wallet – and Tanbrey had no family money – you'd be hard put to swing a cat round in that house of his father's on Moor Top, and not so long ago he was living at the end of a terrace. But, by God, there was one thing – the Bull Benevolent Fund. Yes, Tanbrey knew all about that.

A clerk reported the office keys missing towards the end of the day, and assured Tanbrey she'd get others cut from the duplicate bunch that week-end. Urias kept the keys for three weeks. He chose a moonless night to make his entry, closing and locking the outer door behind him as the clock in Tanbrey's office chimed two. It took a little time to find the key to Tanbrey's door. The lock sprung with a faint click, and he eased the handle down and stood away from the glimmer of lamps, mopping his forehead. Across the yard the lodge was lit, its single window shedding a pallid light across the tracks. He made his way around the key ring, worked methodically until the drawers were all open, then pulled them out and lay them on the desk. He ran his eyes briefly over the notes and papers, then carried the drawers into a windowless store used by the clerks for brewing tea. Closing the door behind him, he lit the lamp and began to sort through the first. Across a block of note-paper were hastily-written memos set out in the bold hand Urias remembered from Tanbrey's time with Bateman. Two of the drawers contained office bric-a brac, an unused writing pad, a box folder, a bottle of ink and notes relating to Duggan's suggestions regarding the benevolent scheme. He turned his attention to the remaining drawers. From the first he drew a marbled pay-book labelled 'Bull Benevolent Fund – Ironworkers Contributions'. He ran his finger down the columns of names and figures; a list of dates for payment and withdrawals headed each page. He leafed through the book, then moved to a similar ledger, dealing this time with colliery employees. Again the figures seemed in order, with regular payments made each week and occasional withdrawals signifying a period of illness. He thumbed through the book with growing agitation and this time noticed a slight indentation which didn't coincide with the inked figures. He turned up the lamp, and faint lines showed through the paper. Taking a pencil, he lightly rubbed it over an embossed disturbance on the reverse. A figure in relief emerged. He flipped back the page and noted the date. The sum amounted to five hundred pounds. And there, something he'd missed; the men's weekly money had been paid late into the bank. There'd been a delay of a week. He noted the date and replaced the ledgers. Dimming the lamp, he opened the door and returned the drawers to the desk.

He felt a surge of elation as he walked home, but by morning his low spirits had returned. What was the figure telling him? He could make no sense of it, yet his instinct was strong. Tanbrey's expensive suits hadn't come from a local retailer, any more than the spindle-back chairs he'd heard about from the plumber who'd installed a water-closet in an unused room. How could the lapse of a week be accounted for? Of course, no irregularity would show if the money was merely borrowed. But borrowed for what? He had to do something to draw the fever from his brain. Pulling the curtain across, he laid out a newspaper and mixed a small amount of flour paste....

John stared at the gummed letters of newsprint before unlocking the pay-book drawer. He turned to the date of his share purchase and immediately found the faint pencil smudge through which the figure appeared. He'd been a fool to pencil in the amount. He'd taken infinite care to erase the sum, and he was rubbing anew. What bastard had the impertinence to rummage through his desk? Was anything else known? He looked again at the words. EMBEZZLER BEWARE YOUR TIME IS DRAWING TO A CLOSE. He gripped the edge of his desk and waited for his head to clear. After a few seconds, he flung open the door to the outer office. 'Miss Redfern, I want to see you now.' The woman made an unnecessary request of a clerk and closed the door behind her. 'I want you to think back to the day you lost the keys.'

'I didn't lose them, Mr Tanbrey, I believe they were taken.'

'Don't split hairs.'

'It was three weeks since.'

'Think, woman, who came into the office that day?'

'It's not easy to pluck names out of a hat, Mr Tanbrey.' He brought his hand hard down, and she sprung to rescue a toppled cup. Her hands shook as she settled it upright. 'What would you like me to do, sir?'

'I want a list of names. I don't care if there are five or sixty. Include all the office staff present on the day the keys were removed. Let me have names on my desk before the end of the day. Whatever else you're doing can wait.'

'Might I ask what this is about?'

'The matter is confidential.'

She left the room tight-lipped. Tanbrey had to go out, and when he returned, shortly before six, he found her list on his desk. Of the thirty names, eighteen were office staff. He quickly ran his finger down the remainder. Eight were unknown to him, and of these four had been asterisked as hauliers, tradesmen and the like who had business on the premises. Two others, according to Miss Redfern, had come to the office to query their wage; a third had asked for a reference for another job. The last name stood alone. He strummed his desk, pushed the paper away and went over to the window, lost in thought.

The following morning he spent a minute looking through the clocking-on cards. Satisfied, he pulled on his coat and informed an office senior he'd be away on business all morning. He'd acquainted himself with the address of the house he intended to visit, knew there'd be no one at home and within ten minutes he was pushing open the back-yard gate. Apart from a mangle, the yard was empty and the back door unlocked. The stench of dirt came to his nose as he went into the living room. There was a threadbare sofa, a cupboard, two chairs and a table whose surface had crazed to treacle. He began yanking open the cupboard drawers, continued his search for an hour before slumping on to the sofa, where his eye caught the grate. A crust of charred newspaper lay on the cinders. He managed to lift it, and it resisted crumbling enough to pick out the faded outline of missing letters.

Urias had been unable to shed any light on the information he'd gleaned from the pay-book. His frustration grew, and his bitterness returned. He was unblocking a drain as a lad came over. 'The boss wants a word.'

'Take yourself off before I shove this rod up your arse.'

'Heath says you've to come up directly.'

He walked off, leaving Urias biting his lip. Heath? He'd thought the lad had meant Tanbrey, if he meant anything. Where were the rest of them hiding? Behind the foundry gate, in the sidings? He returned to his work, but it slowly dawned on him the message could be true. Adjusting his glasses, he turned towards Heath's office, with its bird's eye view of the works. Had he found out about the keys? He'd called at the clerks' office on the pretext of asking if an invoice he'd found blowing about the yard was important. No one had even noticed him, apart from the harridan who kept them all in check when Tanbrey wasn't about. He climbed the stairway and knocked.

Heath put down his pen and motioned Ball to a chair. 'Are you happy here, Urias?'

'Put it this way, Mr Heath, I'm pleased to be doing a bit o' something and not having to rely on charity.'

'It's not the question you were asked.'

'Well, tell the truth, I can't say I'd not prefer my old job down the Grange. Still, beggars can't be choosers.'

Heath lifted a cardboard lid on to the desk. 'Know anything about this?'

'What is it?'

'Take a look.'

The charred fragment of newspaper stared up at him. Urias gave a gasp of understanding. 'It was found in your grate. Newsprint, with odd letters cut out. I'm waiting for your explanation.'

A rumble came from Ball's throat. 'I've nothing to say!' He struggled against a rising tide of hysteria: 'No one's a right in my home but me. It's my house!'

Heath sat impassively, his fingers linked across his desk. 'I once knew a man prosecuted for libel. If he'd made a clean breast before it went to law he might still have a roof over his head. As it was he lost both his house and job and the shock killed his missus into the bargain. Now you can either speak to me – or to some other authority.'

A wild gleam came into Urias' eyes, and his stubby body shook. 'You've all to answer for it! You nailed Christ to the cross and now you want to nail me! That bastard Tanbrey, he doesn't give a cuss for her, I can tell you. Look in his books, Mr Heath, just look in his books. Since when have you rewarded tricksters, eh? Answer me that, when did you last reward a crook?' He was disintegrating. The texture of his cheeks seemed to have coarsened, his eyes starting behind the thick lenses. Patches of moisture oozed from his forehead and smeared a cheek. 'I can prove it! Get his books, I can prove what I'm telling you!'

'Where did you put the keys?'

'You can have 'em back. I only took them to prove a point, d'you see? Nobody on his money can live like royalty. You should never have set him on, Mr Heath, never have set him on.' His voice crumbled in spasms of helpless weeping. Without warning, he swung his crippled leg on to the desk. 'Look at this, just look at it! A bloody cripple! Nowt but a bloody cripple. I could've done his job!'

Heath remained motionless, his eyes fixed on the grizzled head opposite. 'Compose yourself, man.' Urias removed his leg and sat, convulsed by diminishing sobs. 'Now you don't want to make it worse than it already is. I want you to tell me, man to man: did you send Tanbrey a gummed-up letter accusing him of embezzlement?' Ball nodded emptily. 'And you took the keys with the purpose of looking through the accounts and anything else you could find?' Urias inclined his head but said nothing. 'Well, since you've been square with me, I'll be square with you.'

'Don't humour me, Mr Heath.'

'Humouring people isn't my style, you should know that. What I'm telling you is this: Tanbrey came to see me yesterday. He told me he's been to your house and found this stuff in the grate. He tells me he went looking for keys. Well, he didn't find the keys but he found that instead.'

A great lethargy overcame Ball, his speech bubbling through fronds of despair. 'He'd no right in my house, Mr Heath, no right.'

'You'd best not talk about rights in your predicament, man.'

'But he's taken money out of the account, I know he has.'

The man Heath had known for more than ten years wasn't the man who sat bowed at his desk. Ball had always had a greater sense of worth than his position had warranted, but he'd been efficient and trustworthy. Episodes of the man's life ran past him, his visits to Manchester, his injury, his envy for a man half his age who'd ousted him from his job. Every man saw something different in the mirror. Urias' mirror reflected Tanbrey back at him, goading him down the road to insanity. It seemed to Heath that Ball was at a crossroads between loathing and the mad house.

'You should know there's nothing much gets past me, Urias. Whatever your grudge against Tanbrey, there's nothing in the accounts to back it up. Don't you think I've not checked? The books are as clean as a whistle. I know Tanbrey isn't everybody's idea of a good night out, and I don't have to give reasons why I put him where he is, but I'll tell you something –' he leaned forward on his elbows – 'he's got you out of a pickle. He tells me he wants the matter forgotten for the good of the firm.' He straightened, searching what he could see of the man's face. 'Look, you don't want to end up bitter. How old are you, sixty? What d'you want to be clearing out drains for, gone sixty? Take a month off the bank. Take yourself up the Cloud, get over what's buggin' you.'

'D'you mean I'm expendable, Mr Heath?'

'At the end of the day we're all expendable, whether you sit in this chair or you sit in the shit. 'Course you're expendable.' He left his seat and opened the door. 'I'm laying you off for your own good, seeing the state your nerves are in. You've paid into this here scheme, haven't you?'

Urias began to laugh, then stopped abruptly and left without speaking. Heath spent a moment at the window, then jotted a memo to look into extending cover to mental as well as physical breakdown, the episode forgotten. But Urias remembered. A blind had fallen across his world. The empty hearth and unwashed crocks and clanking wagons all merged into a grey void. The threads which had bound him to reality were crumbling. Voices spat at him, Tanbrey's face taunted him with reminders of his failure, street urchins wailed at his window. A vast army marched to his door, their screams growing louder with every step. The noise suddenly stilled. The change in him was immediate.

He'd thought at one time he'd like to kill Tanbrey as he stood with his back to the window, but now such a murder no longer pleased him. Now he wanted to look Tanbrey in the eye. He remembered the Enfield his cousin had brought back from the Crimea. His cousin had used it fighting the Russians at Alma River, said he'd shot twenty men at Inkerman before smuggling the weapon home in his greatcoat. When Urias last saw him, his cousin had confided he'd brought back a couple of rounds too, because his time of danger had taught him the fragility of peace. He'd begun to see society as something which could collapse overnight, when the officers who'd sent men to their graves over a glass of port would be routed by those who'd done their dirty work. When the revolution came, he'd be prepared....

Knowing his cousin's habits, Urias was able to remove both rifle and ammunition from their hiding place. He'd taken them home in a roll of sacking and when he laid the gun on his table, a rare tranquillity had come over him. He threw a bucket of suds across the floor, whistled as he loaded the gun and waited for the kettle to boil.

John Tanbrey was sitting behind *The Times* in his high-backed carver. He had the habit of tilting the paper to one side, so as to have one eye on the paper, the other on his wife and son. Tonight he hid behind the moral right of the British to be in South Africa at the expense of the Boers, but not much else. He saw politics only through the lens of wealth and power. Heath had been a Member of Parliament, and the title had elevated him from ironmaster to public servant and increased his influence. John could see himself playing the same part, though he didn't give a damn about the Irish Question or Gladstone's Liberals. His present concern lay closer to home, in particular the vague sense of unease which had dogged him since Urias had broken into his office.

The click of a spoon broke into his thoughts. Ginny stooped to mop the tablecloth by Matthew's plate.

'Keep him still, can't you?'

She gave no sign she'd heard. Her face seemed older than her twenty-four years, and betrayed her want of sleep. Her son fiddled with the damp cloth. 'Do you want to go, now, Matthew? Then shall you ask father's permission to leave table?'

He put the question as he'd been taught, speaking into his lap.

'Have you anything more you want to tell me?'

Matthew looked towards his mother. 'I think father wants you to –'

'Damn it, must you prompt every word like a bloody ventriloquist?'

She nodded towards the water-stained fabric. The boy picked up her meaning instantly.

'Sorry father.'

'Is there anything more you want to say?'

'I'll try not to be bad again.'

'See to it.'

By the time the boy reached the door he'd broken into a run. Ginny began to clear the table. 'I want you to look for a maid,' he announced from behind his paper.

'There's no need. I can take care of the house, it gives me something to do, and beside, a maid'll cost –'

'I'm not concerned what effect it will have on yourself. I've decided to employ a girl and the next time you go into town you will find one.'

Her cheeks paled, but her eyes remained calm. 'I've been meaning to ask you, John, when I saw that last picture you brought, done by a real artist, and now a maid – where's all the money comin' from?' She seldom addressed him directly, and her question shocked him. She went on: 'I know Mr Heath's been good to you, lettin' you have this house, but you don't run the place, you're not in the gentry class yet, are you?'

He began to gnaw at his lip. How dare she pry into his affairs, an ex-tweeny who'd fettered herself to him like a ball to a convict's foot? Had he imagined the beginnings of resistance in her? The thought unnerved him. Without fear there could be no respect, without respect the edifice of his relationship with her would collapse. The idea she might blab about their life together was intolerable. An image of Nerissa came to him, his dealings with Wharton, Pandora, his fraud, the unrevealed truths of his life – all exposed. She'd bring him down, a word here, there. He'd not forgotten the soft spot Heath's wife had had for her. If her husband were acquainted with some uncomfortable facts concerning their domestic life, Heath might reconsider his position. It was small comfort to know that, with the sale of the first parcels of his land he could ride the storm. Heath had power, and his son Robert, who he saw increasingly about the workplace, would soon carry on where his father had left off. They were still his passport for the time being, the job a useful front to whatever else he might bring to his advantage. He had to keep in with them. How dare she question his decision to take on a maid? Why should he explain to her the need to keep up appearances? He stared coldly across the table. 'Your first job is the running of this house. Your second is to keep your brat out of my way.'

'He's not a brat, John, he's your son. You won't ruin me nor Matthew, you'll ruin yourself. I know me and Matthew are nothing to you. You'll ruin yourself.'

'And what's that supposed to mean?'

'You don't frighten me no more. I'm past hurt. What I feel now is sorrow, some for myself, most for you. I loved you once, I would've walked through walls to catch a glimpse of you. The only thing I've got for my pains is Matthew. This house is full of fine things I wouldn't 've dreamed of five years back, but it's just a shell. Worse than that, a prison.' He raised his arm as if to strike her, but there was no longer any fear in her eyes. 'Hear me out, John.' She took an envelope from her apron. 'This came this morning. It's from my brother. Since we no longer talk I didn't tell you he was in London, tailoring. I've been writing to him these past eighteen months. He knows all about us. I reached the point I had to tell somebody. I'll read what it says.'

He snatched the letter from her, and began to run his eyes over the lines when the bell sounded.

'Do you expect me to answer it?'

She left the room while he put the note in his pocket and made a pretence of resuming his paper. He recognised the man's raised voice, his wife's cry coming from the corridor. He was on his feet as the door burst open. Urias stood there.

'What the hell do you want?'

He heard the words leave his mouth and took a step forward as Ball, empty-eyed, raised the rifle.

'I set you on. Now I'm laying you off.'

Ball's finger closed on the trigger as Matthew came into the room. Ginny, following, screamed for him to stay back. Ball's attention momentarily distracted, Tanbrey lunged forward and grabbed the gun, which went off with a loud report. Seconds passed, it could have been hours, before he heard his son whimpering softly in the corner. There was a chill in the room. He saw that Urias had gone, leaving the outer door open. He was suddenly aware of the clock ticking, the coals settling in the fire. Ginny lay on her side, her cheek pressed to the expensive carpet. He took a step towards her.

'Matthew, lock the door for father.'

The boy went unquestioningly. John knelt and moved Ginny's head to the side. She was quite composed, and the wound in her throat bled only a little. For some reason he recalled their picnic years ago, the paper-wrapped sandwiches. *They used to live up here in the olden days, so they say....* Her smile, the inflexion of her voice, lingered in his eyes and ears like a remembered dream. He rocked her to and fro, kissed her forehead, not knowing why, and as he bent, the note slipped from his pocket. Some compulsion made him read.

'Dear Ginny,

You'll be pleased to know I have been as good as my word and found a position that might suit you. It's with a Mrs Straughan, who wants someone to look after her two children. Mr Straughan travels a lot. I found them by chance in the course of business. There's a room, and they are not averse to a married lady with a child. I had to tell them your husband was in the army. It was all I could think of and they were liberal minded enough to accept it, no matter what they think. You get your keep and some spending. My heart goes out to you when I think what you have suffered at the hands of that man of yours. You should have let me deal with him when I said. You always had a loving heart, and I hope you will find more happiness here than you have known up till now. I'll need to know what you intend by the end of next week, so you'll have to write soon. I know you said you still love him, but I think you should come down now and start again. I've included a little money for your journey, so there's no need to worry about a thing.

Your loving brother,
Sam'

The words swam before Tanbrey's eyes, and he let the letter fall to the floor. Without knowing why, he wept.

3

1887 was the year of the Queen's Jubilee. Australia issued souvenir medals, townships from Vancouver to Quebec were hung with bunting and Singapore lepers were given extra rice. A burial ground in Sind was commemorated to the glory of the Empress of India, and prisoners released from gaol. Throughout the next weeks, the Queen's secretaries struggled to cope with the tide of telegrams to 'she who wore the white flower of a blameless life'. In London, crowds lined the route from the Palace to Westminster and entrepreneurs rented rooms overlooking the procession, knowing they'd recoup their outlay ten-fold. In the Abbey, a riot of colour dappled the nave; military crimson, judicial scarlet, ladies in white, the Persian Envoy in a black lambswool kalpak. The Mayor of London accompanied the Turkish ambassador, whose fez rose from a sea of bonnets. Indian princes took their seats to the strains of the Jubilee March, the Thakur Sahibs of Gondal, Limn and Morvi sat with the Maharajah of Kuch Behar and the Rao of Kutch. The Maharajah of Holkar, resplendent in emeralds, sat beside the Queen of Hawaii, herself accompanied by Prince Komatsu of Japan and the Sultaneh of Persia. At twelve, Dr Bridges struck up Lemmen's *Marche Pontificale*. A fanfare sounded and the assembly rose as the procession began to move up the aisle: the Abbey clergy, the Bishops of London and York, the Dean of Westminster, the Archbishop of Canterbury, then Victoria, with her princes and princesses. The monarch took the Coronation Seat while the Archbishop began to offer prayers for the fiftieth year of her reign. At half past one the service ended, the princes kissed the regal hand, the princesses curtsied, the entourage glided back to their coaches and the Queen waved from her open landau to crowds that cheered her all the way back to the palace under a Queen's Weather sky.

The day after the ceremony, Dick was reading the local paper. 'Hey, listen to this, Charlie:

> Unstained by fraud, by rapine, by blood,
> Be hers the sacred name Victoria Good.
> Then hail auspicious day, for ever clear,
> The moon that ushers in the fiftieth year.

Well? What d'you make of that?'

'What am I to make of it?'

'Well, I'll tell you what I make of it. I think it's a load of rubbish from top to bottom. "Unstained by fraud, rapine and blood"? You want to tell that to General Gordon down at Khartoum. You want tell it to them fuzzie-wuzzies down the Transvaal now they've found gold there.' He skittered his paper across the table. 'I suppose they just sat back in India and Africa and let us walk over 'em, come in, sit down, make yourself a brew. Victoria Good! Victoria the miserable bugger, more like. And I'm havin' to breathe dust ten hours a day to keep her in flunkeys! She wouldn't know a day's work if it bit her in the nose. None of 'em, Gladstone, Salisbury, the lot. Tell you what, you wait till this Local Government Act comes through, that'll take some power off 'em, by God. Rule from the bottom up, that's what we're after.' He gave a sudden grin. 'Have you heard about this do in the Square this afternoon? Let's get up there while the sun's out.'

Charlie retrieved the paper. 'I'll join you later.'

His cousin whistled through the door, while Charlie lay back on the sofa. There'd been a lot of excitement in town over the past week. They'd stretched ribbons across the streets and brought in magnesium flares to light up the new Town Hall. Amid advertisements for Fresson's Purifying Salts and Blood Tincture had been calls to the Jubilee Yacht Race and to Bostock and Townsend's, where flags and banners could be bought for a knock-down price. He flipped over the page. The inmates of Leek workhouse were to be treated to roast beef, plum pudding, beer and tobacco, and in Hanley a ton of meat, two hundred loaves and a hundred and fifty plum puddings had been ordered for the feast in the market. An ox was to be roasted in Burslem, and he wondered if his father would attend the dinner prepared by Sunday School scholars on Moor Top.

He broke from his reading, surprised that after five years the word 'father' could still slip into his mind when he thought of Will. Had it not been for the shock of Bevis' death, he might never have known. He heard Doris's voice anew as he stared through the lines. *'It was just one of them things as sometimes happens between a man and woman, Charlie. I was busy at the time, what with Nat being as he was and Ellen just getting into mischief. I hadn't much time for Bevis once the chores were done. Why dig up old bones?'*

A visit to Moel showed him things had changed. Will's attitude towards him had softened, and he'd struggled to speak.

'You should've been told before, Charlie. Your mother didn't want you to know.'

'I think we'd all have been better making a clean breast.'

'It was me had the weight of it. It were deep waters with your mother much of the time, you never rightly knew what she was thinking. I'm not sure but I should've told you when she passed on.' He'd looked up, the skin slack and liver-blotched. 'Well, it were a long time ago....'

Trumpets sounded from Phoenix Park and Will's voice died. He was past pit work now, and Jacobs had passed the business over to one of his sons. When Charlie had a spare florin he'd go up to Moor Top and leave it on one of his old corkwool teapot stands.... He let the paper slip as his thoughts turned to John. He'd only seen his brother twice since Ginny's manslaughter – once at her funeral, once in answer to his brother's letter. He remembered Ball as a bluff, cheery character whose bark had been worse than his bite. He'd seen him on odd occasions while working for Luke Pointon, thought there were a dozen more inclined to madness than Urias. Yet it was Ball who'd been carried off to the mad house.

'I've got a woman to look after Matthew,' John had told him after the funeral. 'One of the clerks told me about her. She once taught in one of the National Schools.'

'She has him at her house?

'Throughout the week.'

'After all he's suffered don't you think he needs his father?'

'He'll soon get to know her.'

'How old is she?'

'About fifty, I'd guess.'

'And when do you see him?'

'You must understand, I'm at everybody's beck and call. He'd have to be looked after a lot of the time, anyway, and the maid's not up to it.'

'You have a maid?'

'She comes in a couple of hours a day. I think Matthew's better off with Mrs Baverstock. I see him on Sunday afternoons when I can.' Charlie had fallen silent. John had asked: 'Tell me about Tunstall.'

'I had a proposition. The man I work for, he's retiring. He wanted to know if I was interested in renting the place.'

'Does it make money?'

'Seems sound enough. On one side I feel I've been handed an opportunity, on the other I'm not sure I'm cut out for it.'

'Cut out for what?'

'You know.... you and Bill had my share of get up and go.'

'If the man wants to sell -'

'Not sell, rent. He broached it last week. I'm to think it over. I wouldn't be on my own, mind.'

'Oh?'

'There's someone knows the trade better than me. Neville Deakin. I aren't too sure about him, but he knows the business side of things.'

'And why has he offered you this gift of a tile-works?'

'I think he feels he's doing Uncle Cliff a favour, being long-time pals.'

'Is it profitable?'

'It seems to be doing alright.'

'You'll probably find he'll ask an initial payment to put things above board, after that it'll be a monthly sum. Look, Charlie, when you've gone more into it, let me know if you need any help.'

That was a year ago. By winter the transaction had been made and below the board announcing Wilfred Clowes' Tiles, the names of Neville Deakin and Charles Tanbrey had been painted. Neville had taken up the day-to-day running, while Charlie attended to paper-work and supervised the transit of goods. He'd begun a portfolio of tile designs too, and hoped he might be better placed putting some of his ideas to practical use now, if he could persuade Neville.

He wondered about Bill. It seemed impossible he could be on the other side of the world doing the same work he used to do for Bevis. His letters described a world of prairie wolves, summer dust and winds that could drive Arctic blizzards over the Texas border. He wondered about Bill's wife, Elizabeth. Would she have sent Matthew to live with a woman she'd never seen? Had Ellen ever written to tell him what happened to her baby? The last time he saw her she said they'd never corresponded. His thoughts had begun to drift to the rector, who'd recently passed away, when Bessie came into the room.

'Charlie! You gave me a right start. I thought you'd be gone out with the others, a fine day like this.'

'I fancied the morning to myself. I was thinking things over.'

'You're too deep, that's your trouble.' She added teasingly: 'Just wait till you're rich, you'll be able to have as much time off as you like.'

'I'm never likely to be rich, am I?'

She knelt on a chair and looked through the window, the curve of her behind thrown provocatively towards him. Her face had coarsened, but her heavy-breasted figure had hardly changed. 'We could've done with decorating the alley,' she said. 'Might as well decorate a cow-shed.' She twisted her face around, smiling her secret smile. 'You're not going to miss this afternoon, are you, Charlie?'

'I'm not much for festivals.'

'It's the only chance you're likely to get.'

'What will you be doing?'

'Me? Oh, I'll be about. There's a procession, starts at two sharp. They're goin' down High Street, up Sneyd, then into Well Street, then Windmill.' A dull boom sounded and she spun around, her hands to her ears. 'That'll be Durose, firing his cannon. He's been waitin' all year. Hope he's not got it pointed over this way.'

'Whatever way it points'll make no difference, they're only blanks.'

She slid into the chair, her hands cupped between her knees. A heavy stillness had settled on the room, and he found it hard to look at her. 'Why don't you go over and see that Ellen more often?'

'It's a fair way.'

'I thought you said you were friendly.'

'We never walked out as such.'

'What's she up to now, then?'

'Helping run the farm.'

'How old is she?'

'Getting on for twenty seven.'

'My, she'd better get her skates on, she'll be an old maid afore long. Look at our Bertha, twenty-three with one already, another on the way, and she's no oil painting. Is Ellen pretty?'

'I suppose so.'

'What's she like?'

'I don't want to go into all that business. What about yourself, has no one popped the question yet?'

'What a thing to ask!' she cried, her eyes wide in mock surprise. 'You don't have to say yes to everyone knocks at the door. When I get wed it'll be for money, not love.'

'Who's got money around here?'

'At present all I love is the freedom to come and go as I please.' She smiled enigmatically. 'Ah, well, I thought Dick might be about. He said he wanted me to introduce him to someone I know plays the cornet. I don't know why he doesn't go and join the Sally Army.' Her eyes flickered to the kettle and back to Charlie. After a pause, she said: 'I've just remembered what I came back for. I'm just popping up for my sunshade.' He heard her climb the stairs. After a time, she called: 'Charlie, have you seen my sunshade? Come up and help me look.'

Her door was ajar, and he edged it open. She'd undressed and lay on the bed with her legs crossed and a hand cupped demurely over her crotch. She looked up at him, stretched out her hand and eased herself up. His blood began to race. The cannon boomed.

She patted the bed. 'Come on, Charlie, don't be craven.'

'But it's not right.'

'Don't you like me?'

'It's not that, I'm on trust.'

'You needn't do nothing you don't want,' she said, 'come on, just lie a bit.'

He lay awkwardly by her side. 'My fingers're like leather,' he mumbled.

She'd hadn't heard. As he stroked her body, she threw back her head and nibbled the lobe of his ear. He was hardly aware of it, taken up by the swell of her breast and the taut contours of her stomach. Her eyes closed as she lay back, and her breathing quickened in answer to his diffident caresses. He was unprepared for her mounting arousal, and the hungry pressure of her mouth unnerved him. His fingers stole down, and her pleasure disturbed him. He felt his arousal growing with her own, but a distant fear held him back.

'Do you like that? Ooh, I do. Keep doing it.... you can do it to me if you like....' He fumbled with his belt. Into the room came a faint zip of fireworks and again, the dull thunder of Durose' cannon. From Phoenix Park the band struck up a march. 'Put it inside, Charlie, put it in.'

He levered himself on his elbows as Dick pushed open the downstairs door and came in, whistling. He heard the poker scrape in the hearth, then quiet. Dick called, 'Anybody about?'

'Quick, get up!' Bessie thrust him from her and reached for her dress. Charlie was pulling up his trousers as the stair door creaked open.

'Bessie, are you up there?'

'There's no privacy in this house. I had to come back and change my dress. There's no law against it, is there?' She lowered her voice. 'Get under the bed, Charlie.'

Charlie fought with his shirt, stuffing the tail into his trousers as he dived for cover.

'Is anybody up there with you?'

'Yes, it's the Archbishop of Canterbury. Make us a brew.'

'This kettle's already been boiled.'

'There's nothing says I can't have another drink, is there? It's like a furnace out there.' She threw Charlie a warning glare. 'I'll tell you when he's gone.'

She went downstairs, and from below he could hear her ask if Dick had seen Charlie anywhere.

'He's probably taken himself off. You don't expect him to stay indoors on a day like this, do you?'

He lay on the boards until he heard Dick leave and the stair door open.

'All right, Charlie, the coast's clear.'

When he got down she erupted into peals of laughter, the episode no more to her than a forgotten joke. She wiped her eyes. 'Seems we're fated against sin, you and me.'

He went out the back way and began to walk the streets. His dalliance with Bessie had left him frustrated. What other men took for granted had been denied him, and he felt incomplete.

In the afternoon there was a strong sun, the sky fading to haze above the roof tops. He felt conspicuous in his straw hat as he wandered among the crowds decked out in their Jubilee Best. Faint voices carried on the air, and from the lower part of the square came the anthem. Bugles sounded, the bass drum thundered, the bailiff stuck out his chest. 'Now let's have the last verse over again, only twice as loud.'

The procession surged into the High Street, the bailiff in front, members of the Jubilee Committee and massed choirs following. In their wake shuffled Tunstall scholars in the beeswaxed boots and suits it had taken their fathers a month to pay for. After them came the Volunteers in grey melton, then the Fire Brigade in blocks of blue and gold. The line left the square to the crowds, and the boom of the bass drum had already begun to fade as the procession made its way through the fluttering terraces. The crowd gave three cheers for the Queen and meandered towards Phoenix Park, where groups had gathered to watch gymnasts mark the end of the day's celebrations. He'd begun to thread his way back home when Dick came up.

'Charlie! Where've have you been hiding yourself?'

'I've been looking for you since two,' he lied.

'Since two? I've hardly left the square. I've been watching the proceedings. Where were you?'

'In the High Street.'

'I've been talking to a couple o' lasses, and one's got her eye on you.'

'It's not the one you tried to fix me up with before, is it?'

'No, not her, she's fixed herself up. Hey, I've got you something.' He rummaged in his pocket and handed Charlie a ticket. 'That's for the Jubilee Dance.'

'But I don't dance.'

'What's that got to do with it?'

'Where is it?'

'In the market.'

'There's not room to swing a cat in there.'

'Use your loaf! They take out the stalls. You don't expect to start waltzin' round the meat counter, do you?'

'I'll think about it.'

'You've got your ticket, what's to think about? It'll be a good night out.' He gave a cheer for an athlete who'd won a race. 'You might end up with something you fancy.'

At half past nine Phoenix Park was still bathed in the flares of fireworks, and a whiff of smoke hung in the air as Charlie walked to the market with his cousin. The gates had been thrown open, and music washed across the square. A refreshments booth had been set up next to a range of trestles and hired seating. Most men still wore worsted despite the evening heat, leaving the girls to their muslin and fans. A quickstep was in progress. Dick followed his nose to the ale.

'By, it's a fair do tonight. I'd rather be here than down the marl hole.'

He handed Charlie a drink. 'Chance you've got that down, you'll be ready to dance with anybody.' Charlie took a wry pull. 'Best tale I've read in months,' Dick was telling a passing acquaintance. 'You want to read it. *A Study in Scarlet* it's called. This detective by the name of Holmes, he could tell you what you had for breakfast just by glancing at your knife.'

'My favourite reading's the football column.'

'Tell you what, there's a few cherries for the pickin' tonight.'

'I know. I'm off to find one.'

The bandleader shuffled his score. 'Come on, Charlie. It's *Paddy McGinty's Goat*.'

'I'll watch.'

'Come on, it's easy.'

'I'll see what sort of mess you make of it first.'

'Suit yourself.'

Undaunted by a first refusal, Dick found a well-built girl the height of his shoulder. Charlie watched them circle the floor a couple of times, before stepping up to the beer-seller for another pint. The market smelt of tobacco, perfume and cabbage. Stone flags shone in the gas jets, and dismantled stalls lay against the walls – Alice Lowell, Buttons; Francis Hassom, Pork Butcher; John Critchley, all parts for bicycles. His lace had come undone, and as he bent to tie it, another pair of legs joined his under the trestle. He straightened, catching the edge and toppling a glass. He fumbled out his handkerchief with an apology to the girl, mopping at the comma of wine which threatened her dress. 'I'll buy you another. It's not gone over you, has it?'

'It doesn't matter, I'd drunk most of it.'

'No, I'll fetch you another.' He stood, shaking the table again. 'I'm not used to dos like this.'

'In that case I'll have a white wine.'

He pretended to enjoy his drink while studying her over the rim of his glass. Her eyes were dark, and her hair shone jet under the lamps. She had a pale complexion, her brows thick and close above the nose, her features small and regular. She wore a printed cotton dress and a lace wrap over her narrow shoulders.

'I've seen you about town,' she said. 'Your speech is a bit different.'

'I'm staying with relatives. I'm fixed up with a job here.... are you from Tunstall?'

'From Queen's Street.'

'You're not far from us, then. We're down Calvert, just off the square.'

'Who is it you're with?'

'It's my mother's sister and her family. You might know them, the Walkers.'

She gave no sign. 'What's your name?'

'Charlie. Charlie Tanbrey.'

'Mary Ann Heathcote. Nobody uses my second name.'

'Are you on your own?'

'I was with a friend, but she's found a young man. I believe he was with you.' She nodded towards the dance, which was drawing to a close. Dick joined them and turned to his partner. 'Is this the friend you were telling me about?'

'Why? What's up with her?'

'Nowt, from where I'm stood.'

Charlie smiled blandly. The ale was beginning to have an effect, and a pleasurable warmth stole through him.

'I think your friend's had a glass,' Dick's partner observed.

'Him? He's hardly touched a drop since he come through the door. Anyway, Gertrude, it looks as if we're destined to spend the evening together since Charlie's being sociable with your friend and you're being sociable with me.'

'You flatter yourself. There's more than one apple on a tree.'

'I know, but it's not everyone can shake it off.' Dick joggled the glasses. 'What're we having, then?'

Charlie found them uproariously funny, though a voice in his head told him he was making a fool of himself. He tried to imagine Mary in bed, but the image drifted away. The band struck up a Cumberland Reel and she'd gone, Dick and his girl following. Mary's new partner held on to her, and Dick and Gertrude remained on the floor. The hall swam through a haze of swirling couples, and a dull loneliness began to submerge him. He left the table and reached the door, held on until the warm air hit him, and the cobbles swam under the lights. The ale gushed into the gutter, splashing his shoes. He remained stooped, the acrid taste of bile in his mouth, then vomited again. He was wiping his mouth as figures came down the steps, among them Dick and his girl.

'By, you're a sight for sore eyes.'

Gertrude dithered. 'What time is it?'

'Gone twelve. I'll see you back in the house, Charlie. Don't wait up, I'll be late.'

The girl elbowed him with mock severity. 'That's what you think.'

Dick drew her arm through his and began to warble a verse of *Annie Laurie* as they went off. Charlie heard her giggle, then a far-off shriek of laughter. He stood at the bottom of the steps, wondering whether to find Mary Heathcote, but his confidence had gone.

At work the next day, his embarrassment came back to him in sharp bursts. As he walked home in the early evening, he made up his mind to speak with her again. After tea he slipped on his Sunday jacket. He neither knew where in Queen Street she lived, nor if he'd find her at home when he got there. An enquiry at the corner shop pointed him in the right direction. He walked past her house, then turned back and forced himself to knock. No one came to the door. He rapped with greater confidence, but there seemed to be no one about. Both relieved and disappointed, he started back.

He ran into her coming up the street. 'I've just been to see you. About last night.'

'Last night?'

'I didn't have chance to explain.' She began to walk back with him towards her house. She was taller than he'd thought. 'I –' he began.

'I can't invite you in. They'll be back soon.'

'I had a drop too much ....what time did you leave?'

'Gone one.'

He wanted to ask about her partner. 'So you got home all right?'

'None the worse for wear. I hear your cousin's seeing Gertrude again.'

'He didn't say.' He was momentarily lost for words, but found himself asking if she'd like to come out.

'Where?'

'I thought if it's nice next Sunday I could call around, maybe go for a walk.'

She pondered a minute. 'All right, then. Sunday, about two. I'll have to go in now, they're expecting their boots blacked.'

At the bottom of the street he looked back and saw her house imprinted with its own aura, the glances behind the nets no more than curiosity.

4

Cattle froze in twenty foot drifts from the Dakotas to Texas in the winter following Victoria's Jubilee. Some farmers had seen similar conditions before and reduced their herds from twenty thousand to fewer than four, but for the newcomers who'd relied on the prairie to provide for twelve months of the year, what they saved in fodder they lost in livelihood. The weather blew itself out in pneumonia and a cost to insurers of millions of dollars. Unlike his neighbours, who'd been forced to sell their land cheap to stem their rising debts, Bill's loses had been tolerable. Elizabeth had taken a growing interest in the business of the ranch over the four years they'd been there, and though it had proved profitable even after paying freight charges, a niggling voice had whispered they shouldn't put all their eggs in one basket. With reluctance, he'd put some of his acres to hay and fenced in the land. Her foresight had paid off. No longer free to roam, the herds had withstood the blizzards fed and sheltered.

The savage winter hadn't been their only problem. At an age when other ranch wives were rearing eighteen-year-old sons and daughters, Elizabeth remained childless. She fell prey to melancholy moods, when she'd withdraw to a rocking chair on the verandah. She soon brightened, but he knew what the trouble was, and protected her by inventing reasons why the ranch-hands shouldn't bring their children to the house. He learnt from one of his men the name of a German doctor who'd made a particular study of gynaecology, and Elizabeth had taken little persuading to agree to see him. They booked into a hotel in Topeka and the following morning went over to Dr Reitzman's clapboard house in a pleasant part of town. He was close to sixty, his hair still black around the balding crown, the wire-framed glasses exaggerating his dark, intent eyes.

'Mr and Mrs Tanbrey, I hope the journey wasn't too bad. The maid will take your coat, Mrs Tanbrey. Mr Tanbrey, if you would make yourself at home- ' The woman led them into a sparsely-furnished room. 'You care for coffee?'

'That would be nice.'

'And you, sir?'

'Nothing for me, thanks.'

The girl's dark face lit at his accent. 'Pardon for askin', you ain't from these parts, sir?'

'No, I'm from England.'

His answer made her beam. She was the first black woman he'd seen, and the whiteness of her smile amused him as his accent amused her. 'I sure heard o' the ole Queen Victoria,' she chortled, bringing in the drinks. 'And that li'l ole cap she wears on her head, why, I'm thinkin' some day I'll take a boat and go meet her.'

She left with a wobbling gait, chuckling to herself. A few minutes passed, and Reitzman reappeared. He sat informally, pushing his spectacles more firmly on to his nose. 'May I ask, how long have you been married?'

'Just four years,' Elizabeth said.

'And your age, Mrs Tanbrey?'

'Forty-two.'

He made a note and looked up. 'Have you ever suffered a miscarriage?'

'No.'

'And your monthly cycle is regular?'

'Less regular than it used to be.'

He turned to Bill. 'I need to ask a personal question before any treatment can be considered. I must ask you if your conjugal rights are being satisfactorily exercised.'

Bill looked questioningly across at his wife. Reitzman stared tactfully through the window at the picket fence.

'Yes,' Elizabeth said.

'And again, I must ask regarding the frequency.'

Bill said: 'Frequency's no problem.'

'Are any of your blood-relations either without children or have, perhaps, one when they would have wished for more?'

Ellen came into Bill's thoughts. He should have told Elizabeth. He began to regret what he was putting her through. 'Not as far as we're aware,' he heard his wife say.

Reitzman considered his notes, then called the maid from the door. She motioned Elizabeth into another room. When they'd gone, Bill said: 'I've something to tell you, and I don't want it going beyond this room.' The doctor polished his lenses. 'Look, I'm wondering now if I've brought my wife here on a pretext.'

'You needn't say anything you don't want me to hear, Mr Tanbrey.'

'I think you should know – it's done with now. I was already a father. It was something happened back in England. I can't think it'll do anything but harm if Elizabeth got to know. It'd just make her feel worse. A while ago I got a letter from my brother. He told me the baby died within a few days. A girl.'

'From how it sounds you must have left the country before you knew the outcome.'

'I don't want Lizzie hurt. If I could father a child once, I could do it again. It'll save the trouble of another examination, d'you see?'

'I don't want to pry into your affairs. The information you've given me does, of course, throw the light in your wife's direction, though it's quite possible for an almost sterile man to father a child given the right amount of luck.'

'The girl was pregnant right away.'

Reitzman muttered an apology and left the room. Elizabeth was looking through the window as he came in. It was a bright day, and a stiff breeze rustled the orchard. She turned towards him with a fixed smile.

'You were admiring my Red McIntoshes. They're a passion with me, I'm afraid. The secret is to have enough of each variety to ensure survival. Some are susceptible to blight, for example.' He joined her at the window. 'I don't want to give you false hopes, Mrs Tanbrey. Medicine is advancing all the time. Perhaps in a few years we'll know –' He cleared his throat. Adopting a brisker tone, he said: 'You may have your husband present if you wish.'

'I think I can trust you, doctor.'

'I have to do an internal examination. You can leave your clothes behind the screen.' He went out and returned in a smock which smelled faintly of camphor. He rinsed his hands, patted them dry and took an instrument from the table. 'Now, if you'd care to lie back. You will feel some discomfort, but no great pain. It will help me tell if there is anything which might be giving rise to problems.'

Reitzman's breath rasped as he made some adjustments to the dilator. As he'd promised there was no pain, but a sense of indignity which became more acute as his jelly-smeared hand bulged upwards. She felt him burrow deeper, her mouth slackened to the shape of a silent scream. He removed his hand and knelt between her legs. She glimpsed a mirror on a silver stem. He repeated the performance twice, each time grunting his mental checklist. When he pulled the dilator away, the discomfort remained. He washed his hands. 'You may sit now, Mrs Tanbrey.'

'Well?'

'There is no obstruction of the uterus.'

'Which means?'

'The slight possibility remains of a blockage in some other organ. Occasionally the tubes are obstructed..'

'And if there's no blockage, what then?'

'Given your general health is good, we must seek a cause more directly concerned with ovulation.'

'Doctor, I'm not a mind-reader. All I know is the reason I came. It seems to me the most you are capable of is elementary engineering. I'm nobody's guinea-pig.' She reined in a rising tide of anger. 'I'm sorry, I never used to get into a state. I don't know why I said those things.'

'Come, you go back to the waiting room and I'll have your husband along.'

When Bill and he were alone, Reitzman said: 'Few men can understand what being childless means to a woman. A man has his work, a woman has to know she can produce something worthwhile. She needs to do this, and if she cannot, she can feel wasted and useless. She feels less whole. Do you see this, Mr Tanbrey?'

'What're you driving at?'

'I'm sure you have a wife most men would be proud of. You may have to live with her regrets.'

'You've found something?'

Reitzman motioned him to a seat and sat himself. 'I can give your wife the benefit of my experience, the rest is up to you.' He leaned forward, fingers clasped. 'We believe barrenness in women is more widespread than sterility in men. One of nature's cruel ironies, eh, Mr Tanbrey? We must face facts: your wife is nearing the end of her reproductive life. The child-bearing process is no different from any other bodily function. To be frank, I see no cause for optimism.'

'I was hoping for better news.'

'You say you've only been married a short while. Perhaps you can tell me something of your wife's history.' Bill told him that her first husband had died as the result of a mining accident, that as far as he knew there'd been no other serious liaison until he met her. Reitzman enquired the length of her former marriage, shaking his head as if to reinforce his doubts.

'There is one slight possibility.' He left the room and returned with Elizabeth. 'I would like you to consider a course which might seem odd, even unnatural. I've just spoken to your husband, Mrs Tanbrey, about the nature of your relationship. What I would like you to do is act on your pattern of menstruation. Intercourse must take place within four days of the fertile period, and particularly on the day of ovulation. You must rest in bed for an hour afterwards. This is something which can produce a result in some cases.'

'How?' Bill asked.

'We're not sure, it is to do with the cycle of ovulation. Intercourse at various stages can increase or decrease the chance of conception.'

Bill read the disillusion in her face, and reached for her hand. On the way back, she made no comment about their visit. Instead, the empty landscape seemed to absorb her. There was something in the texture of life which had always fascinated her; the bud of an unopened flower; a sear leaf; the soughing of the wind in the barn. He couldn't bear the thought of her vitality ebbing.

'Well, Bill, we'd better do as he says.'

He wanted to say it sounded like hocus-pocus, but spiked his tongue. She made no further mention of Reitzman or the journey.

In the following months, her demands on him grew desperate. She rode five miles to a gully where he'd been fencing and they made love in the shade of an overhanging rock before an audience of cicada. She got him to raise the foot of the bed to make sure, she said, that what went up stayed there. Her black moods grew less frequent now that she felt she had a straw to cling to. He loved her, he couldn't imagine his life without her. The memories of England had blurred, the images of pits and rain, the moorland hills and burbling valleys. He'd grown into the space of this new land, the inaudible thrust of life, the spirit which cut like a blade through the prairies. The child he'd had with Ellen, Dixon's death - they were as remote as stars. His life now was here, his ranch was booming, the omens had never been better. Only his doubts of a second fatherhood clouded the future.

As the weeks passed, Reitzman's advice began to look futile. He became aware of a subtle change in her, couldn't tell what she was thinking.

One evening of fading heat, she looked up at him from her needlework. 'Bill, I didn't want to tell you before....'

'Tell me what?'

'I think maybe Dr Reitzman was right.'

'You mean you're - ?'

The news toppled his daily concerns like a house of cards. He'd grown more resigned to a future without children than she had. Now he felt he, too, had been offered a reprieve. 'We'd best get somebody over. What about Ross's wife, she knows about babies.'

'I'm not an invalid.'

He was on his feet, drumming the boards. 'Or Dirk Halliday's girl.'

'Sit down, don't fuss!'

'I don't know how you can take it this calm.' He went inside and came back with a bottle of whiskey and poured himself a glass. 'That Reitzman got it right, and here's me thinking he's a quack.'

'Isn't a kiss in order?' He came across to her, ran his lips across her cheek. 'Bill,' she said, suddenly serious, 'what shall we call it?'

'Charlie, after one of my brothers.'

'What if she's a girl?'

'Charlie, after my brother.'

She laughed as she used to. 'It'll be a girl,' she said. 'Marian. Marian Tanbrey.'

'Don't I get a vote?'

'You'll not improve on that.'

Later, in bed, he lay awake and put his arm around her. She was sound asleep.

As the months passed, the tension in him grew. There were times when he was unable to give his attention to his work, and handed it over to his foreman, Ross, in his anxiety to get back to her. She went about her routines, easy with her pregnancy, and as the time drew near, Ross's daughter, Rose, came around to help. Soft April days stirred the grama. Soon, goldenrod and black-eyed Susan would grow amid drifts of violet bird's foot. Around the ranch, prairie chickens went through their pairings among the pasque flowers. Lizzie watched the men abandon their chaparejos in the corral, then returned to her needle, the line taut-drawn across the frame. A great tranquillity had settled on her. It was a shock to hear her ask for Ross's wife, Maud. She might have been asking if they'd closed the barn door. A spasm took her, and she held her stomach until it passed. She began to pack her things away, wrapping the thread around the needle, pushing the needle slowly into its cushion. He ran from the room. She sat upright, her head thrown back so that her throat rose stark from her loosened dress. The contraction ended, and she went to the bedroom and removed her underwear. When he reached the shack, Maud was standing by the stove, a cloth folded over one arm.

'It seems as if it's time, Mr Tanbrey. Come on, Rose, or we'll be late for the christening.'

Maud's Irish brogue cut through his turmoil. 'You'd best hurry.'

She gathered a bag. 'When did the contractions start?'

'About five minutes ago.'

'Don't worry, your wife will be just fine.'

When they reached the ranch, Liz was lying on the bed with her knees bent. He brushed a wisp of hair from her forehead and she took his hand. Basins appeared on the washstand; towels, soap. A sealskin had been spread across the bed. 'Don't worry, my dear, you'll soon be as happy a mother as ever drew breath, what with the pair of you, strong as oxes both. Come the morning there'll be a little one, I'll be bound. Mr Tanbrey, did you bring the hot water as I asked? Who wants men around at times like these? You might as well be cursed by the devil hisself. Now, excusin' me, Mr Tanbrey, I know you own the place but I have a little ladies' business to attend to. That lazy devil o' mine'll no doubt have his cards for company....'

He went over to the barn and made a pointless examination of the horses' fetlocks. Maud set a bowl and soap by the bed while she attended to the hot water. 'I'll see to it, Mrs Tanbrey, no trouble, none at all, just plenty of good soap up your back passage. Don't worry, you've plenty of time.' Another spasm. 'Rose, look at these clothes, God bless the little mite. Best hang them by the stove, nothin' like a good airing. You leave the world cold enough, might as well come into it comfortable. Now, Mrs Tanbrey, we'll send your husband for McPhearson, best always to have a doctor nearby, though they only get in the way.' She went out and quickly returned. 'I've never seen a man ride so fast, I swear.'

The contractions increased. Slight sounds registered faintly through the house. She wished Reitzman was there, knew nothing of this other man, except he lived nearby. It was strange, she thought, giving two lives over to someone else, someone you didn't know. There was another spasm, a sharpening of pain. She hadn't finished her sampler. Was that an omen? What was keeping him, what if the doctor wasn't around, where would he have got to?

'I've just boiled a length of linen, all ready now, you'll be right as a summer's day. How're you feelin' now? Tired?'

'A little.'

'Rose, is Mr Tanbrey coming yet?'

'Can't see him.'

'A good heart'll see you through.'

Bill found McPhearson at poker in the saloon. 'You're needed at the Solomon Ranch, my wife's having a baby.' The man looked up and went back to his cards. 'It's urgent,' Bill snapped.

The doctor slowly scraped back his chair. 'We'll carry on some other time,' he said, lowering his hand and following Bill through the door. 'Where you say, son?'

'Got a horse?'

'Wouldn't be much use without one. Wife, you say?'

'It's her first.'

'You gotta learn, patience is a doctor's best friend.'

He spoke in a lazy drawl and tacked his saddle-bag the same way. His whip caught the horse full across the flank.

She cried out as Bill came through the door. Her forehead was clammy with sweat.

'I brought the doctor.'

'That's fine.'

He held her hand. 'I thought you'd have the cot filled by now.'

She struggled up, saw the man's flushed face and sank down, exhausted. 'So this is the mother to be,' said McPhearson. 'Those the ligatures?' he asked, seeing Maud laying out the linen strips on clean paper by the bowl. He stretched one, and it broke. He clicked his tongue in disapproval. 'You'll need something stronger, better see what I got.' He rummaged in his bag and cut two lengths of thread with a pocket knife he'd used to remove a growth from a farmer's rein-hand, knotted the ends and replaced them in a small case which he carried to the bedside table.

'These are strong.'

'I'll boil them, doctor.'

'They're already sterile. Mr Tanbrey, is there any place I can go? I'd like to rest up awhile. No use hanging around while the women are here. When it's time they can give me a call'

A sense of helplessness gripped Elizabeth. Bill left the room to try and busy himself. The contractions were regular now, the pain increasing. As the day faded, she vomited into a bowl, bringing nothing up.

'That's right, dearie, save your strength till later, don't make a rush of things. He'll tell you when he's ready.'

'Or she –'

'He, she; how it is, not what it is.'

Liz caught her breath and clutched the bed-head. 'I think I'm ready.... I feel –'

'Rose, best get the doctor up.'

Rose found McPhearson snoring, his legs thrust defiantly forward. She shook him by the shoulder as another cry came from the adjoining room. A whippoorwill called from the gathering dusk. 'She's started, doctor.'

He made unsteadily for the door.

'You're doing well, my dear. Press down, then rest, bear and rest. Keep holdin' the breath, just as you're doing. Let the pain come out, that's right, let it all come out.'

Waves of exhaustion washed over her. She thought she glimpsed the sky between the blinds and heard an accordion, men's voices singing. She glimpsed the doctor in the doorway, saw Maud's animated face, Rose's lips parted in vicarious pain.

'Bill –'

'Don't you go bothering none about Bill, you just push that little soul into the world, the sooner the better.'

She gripped the rail, her knuckles white, her forehead the colour of putty. 'Is it here, is it here, is it here –?'

'Bear down, my love, you'll soon be through.'

'I see the head, mother!'

'One more push, that's my brave girl.'

Bill heard the scream from the yard, the louder screams which followed.

'The head's nearly out, Mrs Tanbrey. Don't fret, don't worry, your pain's at an end now. Just a little push more. There! Rose, wipe its darlin' eyes will you – no, with the cloth on the side. Dip it in the water. Here we are, Mrs Tanbrey, a darlin' little girl, as darlin' a little girl as ever lived.'

McPhearson let the women get on with it, his eyes wandering idly over the household trappings. The Tanbreys were neither in want nor in ignorance. Perhaps they might one day be a force in the place. He'd be foolish to camp in the wings while a ranch wife performed miracles. The baby's mewling surged to a cry, and Liz reached out to her. The blind-pulls danced against the part-open window, and the scent of the land came into the room. Then McPhearson had his hand on the umbilical cord, waiting for the pulsation to stop, knotting the ligature close to the child's navel.

Maud said: 'I've seared the knife, doctor. Shall I make the cut?'

McPhearson had already severed the cord with his knife.

Maud wrapped the infant in a shawl and placed it in the cradle. 'You'll be holding her in just a minute, my dear, a bonnier baby you never did see, so strike me Lord if it's not the truth I'm sayin'.'

Liz lay back. There was a crack in the ceiling, a web of light illuminating its edge. She wondered vaguely where it came from; the brightness, the lamp scattering all that brightness across the room. The pains returned. A further evacuation emptied her physically and mentally. She closed her eyes.

'Mother, I think it's time Mr Tanbrey came up from the yard.'

'Why not, indeed? Tis all over now.'

Rose called him from the window: 'You have a daughter, Mr Tanbrey.' McPhearson regarded the basin containing the placenta with distaste, prodding it with his knife.

'I'll wash her down, now.' Maud volunteered.

'I'll do it, you get rid of that. Tell him I'll be through, give me a minute.'

Rose gently rocked the cradle, pulled the shawl from the baby's chin. 'Not like Mrs Tanbrey, are you? She's like herself, aren't you, my precious, like yourself and nobody else.'

Maud helped McPhearson with the cleaning, discarding the blood-stained pledgets.

'You got a pad?'

'Everything you need is right here, just wants scorchin' by the stove.'

He held out his hand.'No need for that.'

'Don't you think -?'

'I'm due back.'

He firmed the pad between Lizzie's thighs. Maud left the room as Bill came in, and Rose handed him the baby. He offered it into Liz's spread hands and sat on the edge of the bed stroking the hair from his wife's forehead. She slept heavily and woke in the early morning in a little pain. She ignored it as she'd ignored everything outside the confines of her bed. She felt at peace, with her baby in the cot by her side. On the second day her strength began to return, but the next she awoke at dawn with a high temperature and prodded Bill awake. He dressed in a rush and saddled his horse. When he returned to their room she put a steadying hand on his arm.

'You must go to Maud, tell her to look after Marian.' He couldn't tell what was passing through her mind. 'It's probably nothing, it's probably nothing at all. Go ask Dr Reitzman to come. Will you do that?'

'All right.'

He reached Reitzman's house early the following day and remembered nothing of the journey. The doctor answered the door, a night's stubble shadowing his chin.

'It's Elizabeth.'

Reitzman fumbled with the loops of his spectacles. 'Please - I won't be a moment –'

'I'm worried -'

'Only a moment, Mr Tanbrey. My clothes –'

Reitzman's wife called from the bedroom. He heard a rumble of voices, the closing of a door. The minutes ticked by, and the doctor appeared. 'If you will permit me, Mr Tanbrey – a little less haste, a little more speed, I've always found it so.'

'We've had a girl.'

Reitzman's face plumped in a smile. 'Surely that should be a cause for celebration?'

'Yesterday my wife started with a temperature. When I left she was on fire.'

'When was the child born?' Bill gave him the hour. 'And how was she delivered?'

'One of the men's wives came in with her girl.'

'Does she claim any expertise?' asked Reitzman, his tone hardening.

'We had a local man in as well.'

'McPhearson?'

'We would've liked yourself, but it came on sudden. Where we are, out there, time was against us.'

Reitzman said: 'Was your wife shivering?'

'Not when I left.'

'I'll get the gig.'

'But –'

'No buts.'

Reitzman's urgency infected him. As he walked to the door, Bill grabbed his sleeve. 'It's bad, isn't it?'

'We should treat all infections with respect, Mr Tanbrey.'

They found Elizabeth weakened, her face drained of colour. Bill took her hand.

'Where's my baby?'

'She'll be all right'.

She looked away, distraught. Reitzman and Ross's wife were out of earshot in a corner of the room. Despite his fatigue, Reitzman was acutely aware of the change in her. Now he came over to the bed. 'Mrs Tanbrey, your husband tells me the wonderful news. Have you decided what to call her? It is a her, I believe.' His finger was on her wrist as she gave a hesitant reply. Her pulse raced under the skin, and she shivered a little. He put his hand on her stomach. 'Any pain here?'

'A little....it came on a few hours ago.... is there any risk to my baby?'

He turned to Maud. 'Where is the child now?'

'With my daughter, doctor. She's a good girl.'

'Mr Tanbrey,' said Reitzman, 'Why not make us both a strong coffee, eh?'

Bill left and Reitzman pulled back the cover. The woman's leg was puffed, the veins standing out from the white flesh in hard strings.

'It aches a little.'

He smiled and pulled up the sheet. 'Could you give Mrs Tanbrey some water?'

As Maud brought the glass, he caught her hand and lifted it to his nose.

His action caught her off guard. Ushering her away from the bed, he said in a low voice: 'You realise the danger this woman is in?'

'The poor soul has taken nothing from my hands, I swear to God, nor Rose's neither. There's a good soap here for the usin' and it's been liberally applied. I should think I know my business well enough.'

The woman's face had turned the same angry red as her hair. Reitzman became conciliatory. 'No doubt you do, no doubt you do. Dr McPhearson was present, I believe?' His eyes were as hard as pebbles. She knew what he was asking.

'I didn't like the man, though I shouldn't say it.'

'I'm not interested in prejudice.'

'I told him –' Tears smarted, and she turned to the wall.

'What? Told him what?'

'He'd been drinkin', I could smell it on his breath. I said let me scorch the pad, just as my mother taught me. He wouldn't hear of it. I'm due back, that was what he said, due back. I wish now he'd never come here. I wish –'

Reitzman put a hand on her shoulder. 'Look after Mrs Tanbrey.'

He went downstairs and joined Bill. McPhearson was unfit to practise medicine, he thought. If he had his way, he'd be relegated to the morgue along with those he'd sent there. The thought occurred to him McPhearson might not be a qualified practitioner at all. He considered it his duty to find out. He emptied his mug, washed carefully and went upstairs.

Next day Liz was unable to move without great effort. He encouraged her to sip a watery soup while he held her fever in check through a continual cold sponging. He'd known from the time of her husband's visit there was little he could do. The damage had already happened at the hands of an unwashed quack using swabs any competent practitioner would have balked at. A feeling of revulsion swept over him, not only against McPhearson, but against the fate that allowed a decent woman to suffer while cowhands' daughters spilled babies at the snatch of a rein then left their beds to clean out the stove. A woman of intelligence seldom came into his practice. God knows, she hadn't asked for more than others took for granted.

One of the men was dispatched to tell Reitzman's wife he'd be back as soon as he was able. Maud made up a bed in an adjoining room, leaving Bill to provide what help he could. Reitzman didn't doubt Tanbrey knew his wife was ailing. It showed in his haunted face, his reluctance to let anyone tend her but himself. After falling into a deep sleep, she awoke abruptly and found the strength to hoist herself up. The room had dissolved into fragments. Bill comforted her until she calmed. When she spoke, her voice was little more than breathing. He couldn't bear to look at her. 'Bill, we've not been long together. We've been happy, haven't we?' Dust erupted against his face and he was sitting beside her again on the swaying surrey.

She moved her hand towards him. 'I'm sorry.'

He wanted to cry 'What for'? It didn't matter.

'Let me see my baby.'

He pressed her hand. He hardly knew what he was doing. He crossed the yard. The sky was silver with stars. Rose passed him the child, and he was walking back. He held it away from his wife, its face partly hidden by a fringe of shawl.

'Let me see her....' She reached out, ran her finger across the smooth roundness of the baby's cheek. 'Marian.... let me hold her....'

A comforting warmth suffused her body, draining away the pain. Something of the life-force she'd cherished lit her face. She hadn't known joy could be heard, but the faint onrush of sound told her she'd been wrong. It threw out pictures from her past, a white church, March winds, the double arc of a rainbow across the plains.

She was still holding the baby as she died. Her atoms lingered in the night sky she loved, the hayfield she'd urged him to tend. When the service was over, he sought escape. From what he'd had, from himself. He scribbled a note which he sealed in an envelope addressed to Ross. He cleared the safe and packed his things into a pannier. He remained in the house until late the following afternoon. For a long time he stood at the window, oblivious to the movement of men below. He took his Peacemaker from a drawer. He thought he heard the baby whimpering, but didn't turn. The trail led to a low horizon, and the first stars powdered the sky. They seemed to be whispering *Oklahoma* over and over again.

5

The Institute was an imposing building in a Macclesfield side-street. Gymnastics were carried out in the ground floor hall; the upper rooms housed a laboratory, a library and a lecture theatre. Jane Cowlishaw selected a seat from which she could look down over the spreading lights of the town if she grew bored. The talk was due to begin in ten minutes, and the hall rapidly began to fill. By the time the speaker appeared, only a small number of places remained. Royston Piper, an ex-mill worker whose route to self-improvement had led to his superintending the Institute, rapped for order. 'Gentlemen – oh, I see we have a lady in our midst – Lady and Gentlemen, many of you will be familiar with the name of this evening's speaker, and I'm sure we can look forward to an entertaining hour while Mr O'Rourke tells us all about this new Fabian Society. Thank you, Mr O'Rourke.'

Jane ran a hand through her hair. A light rain pattered against the glass, and from a mantle came the thin fizz of gas. He'd be, thought Jane, no older than forty; spare, straggly red beard, balding crown. As the last clap faded, he lifted his eyes from the bench.

'The Fabian Society, what are we to make of it? A school for scoundrels? An enlightened brotherhood? An organ for bloody revolution? Fabius Maximus, he's the one we should blame, for our movement began with him. His talent lay in avoiding conflict while overthrowing his enemies by subterfuge, or – let us not shirk the word – cunning, thus achieving victory over forces which should have routed his own puny army within the hour. Nowadays, of course, our enemies don't wield swords or shot. Their weapon now is the entrenched prejudice of our rulers.'

He waited for the pattering of applause to fade. 'Was it not John Stuart Mill who said "No great improvement in the lot of mankind is possible until there is a change in their modes of thought"? He spoke true words, my friends, for only by the overthrow of the present order will this country overcome class divide and the injustices which follow from it.' He ran his eyes across the tiers of nodding heads. Jane murmured her approval, unaware she was doing so. He moved to the centre of the bench, resting his arms on its polished surface. 'So this, then, is the aim of our society: change for the improvement of the many; change enshrined in law and government. For Britain can be a fairer place, have no doubt about it. The attitude which condemns men to live out their old age in poverty; that turns a blind eye to child labour; that grants to some unimagined wealth and to the rest squalor – all this can be altered.' He lowered his voice almost to a whisper. 'You think I want to throw out the accepted order of things? Certainly I do, as do those other brave souls who saw this movement through its early stages. But, I hear you cry, surely there has been progress? What of the Factory Acts? What of the grand municipal schemes now taking place in our cities? Can we honestly compare this last decade of the nineteenth century with what our fathers were forced to endure? The scourge of disease, the back-breaking toil of mill and mine? I say to you, yes! For although it would be foolish to deny that improvements have been made, one evil is with us even now: the evil of inequality. We Fabians seek to redress this stain on our national character. Not through the mouth of the cannon, as in France – as may still be the case in Russia – but through the democratic energies of socialism.'

'Before he goes any further, might I ask Mr O'Rourke what my mill hands will do with this democracy when they get it? My own thinking is they'll burn the mill to the ground, then complain they've nowt to put on the table.'

'I suggest to the worthy gentleman that if they had more to put on the table today, our organisation would be defunct tomorrow. As to burning the mill, I doubt they could afford the tinder.' Laughter rumbled along the rows. 'My friends, I do not envisage arson or mayhem. Fabian aims are intellectual, not physical. We see ourselves as oiling the wheels of progress, not smashing them to bits.'

He had a surprisingly resonant voice for so slight a man, Jane thought, as he brought his talk to an end. There was no one in the silk mill where she'd worked for the past five years to provide the stimulus she needed, so she'd looked to the Institute instead. She'd begun to read more widely, but all the books in the world were no substitute for a meeting of minds. She'd come to hear O'Rourke, thinking he'd deliver the usual run-of-the-mill rant she'd heard before, but this man's message was delivered with grace and humour. He didn't take himself too seriously. Royston Piper nodded toward the heads leaving the room. O'Rourke looked up as she passed, fixing the clasp of her hood. 'I'm encouraged to see we have a lady present.'

'Is that unusual?'

'Unfortunately, yes.' He began pulling on his ulster. 'You don't have a local accent.'

'I'm not from Macclesfield.'

'So my fame has spread?' The wisps of red hair failed to hide his smile. 'I must be grateful for small mercies.'

'Excuse me butting in, Mr O'Rourke, but if you want me to call a cab–' Piper said.

'I believe the rain's stopped. I'll walk to the station.' He pulled out a hunter and slid open the case. 'I still have forty minutes. The exercise will do me good. Are you going my way, Miss –?'

'Jane Cowlishaw. I'm going part of the way.'

'Then perhaps you will allow me to accompany you.'

She was slightly taller, and felt less conspicuous after he'd put on his felt hat. Piper stood in the shadows, jangling his keys. The gymnasts had deserted the hall half-an-hour before. 'Tell me something of yourself,' he said as they walked under the lamps, 'and please call me Eric.'

'There's nothing much to tell. I work on one of the mills.'

'Oh, come! A mill lass at the Institute?'

'Royston Piper was a mill hand, and he runs it.'

'I doubt old Royston understood one word in ten of what I was saying.'

'I used to work in Leek,' she said. 'There were a group of us getting ready to form a society, but we all got dismissed on one pretext or another. I knew the line of work, and I came where the word wouldn't be put about. I see good people suffer. I'd like to do more than read books, but I need a living, like yourself.'

The air was damp with unshed rain. The station building lay in a languid light five minutes off. 'Where is it you work?' he asked.

'Down the Victoria Mill. It's just another name.'

'And who's the proud owner?'

'His name's Birkenshaw. He's more interested in shooting pheasants. Most of the work comes down to Jackson, the manager, but he's getting on now. Then there's Birkenshaw's son-in-law. If he gets his hands on the place it'll be downhill all the way.'

'Oh?'

'Partial to the bottle.'

They'd reached the bottom of the slope. A hazy smoke was rising above the roof-tops.

'Would you like me to walk back with you?'

'You'll miss your train.'

'There's bound to be another.'

'At this hour?'

'Yes, perhaps you're right. Here –' he drew out a card – 'have this. We could meet again and put the world to rights.'

He turned to wave, but she was already a distance away.

Roddy Davenport sat at his desk, impervious to the sunshine striking through the grimy panes or the invoices cluttering his desk. He tried to focus on the list of items produced by his father-in-law's firm, but his mind was unequal to the struggle. Jackson could commit a sheet to memory at the wink of an eye, and he'd turned sixty. Yet here he was, half his age and unable to cope. He tossed the sheet aside, slid open a drawer and took out a bottle of Kirschwasser. He was about to put it to his mouth when a knock sounded, and he pushed the bottle hastily out of sight. An office boy appeared, behind him a smartly dressed man of about Roddy's age.

'Mr Proudlove to see you, Mr Davenport.'

The man pumped Roddy's hand energetically. 'I hope I'm not too late. The train was delayed at Stockport.'

'We can't hold ourselves responsible for all the hold-ups on the London and North-Western,' Roddy said, striving to match Proudlove's brightness. 'Please take a seat – if you'll excuse me for a moment?' Davenport went out. A store room at the end of the passage had been converted into a lavatory and he sat like a monarch, pondering the purpose of Proudlove's visit. He'd clearly come by appointment. Just as clearly, Roddy had failed to enter it in his diary. In his effort to recall any correspondence, he eventually succumbed to apathy.

'Ah, Mr Proudlove,' he began, getting back to the office, 'it seems the clerk omitted to enter your visit in the day book, and not for the first time. I apologise for my rudeness in leaving you, but these matters can slide if they're not tackled immediately, don't you agree?'

'I do indeed.'

'Would you care for a little refreshment before we begin?'

'I'm afraid I have a tight schedule. I really wanted to know if the orders are ready for collection.'

Roddy blanched. A slight tremor ran through his hands as he took the sheet from Proudlove. 'You have the better of me – perhaps you could refresh me as to the nature of the business?'

'Excuse my frankness, but I find it hard to understand how an order for ten thousand yards of Sarcenet ribbon could have been overlooked.'

'Ten thousand, you say?'

'Do you mean to tell me you remember nothing of our earlier correspondence? Good Heavens, the orders were posted to you over a month ago.'

'A month?'

'You must have received them.' Roddy began to forage through his cabinet. A film had broken out across his forehead, and he wiped it with the back of his hand. Proudlove clipped his case and buttoned his coat. 'Since the merchandise is not forthcoming, there seems no reason to take up any more of your time. Perhaps you are unaware that my own credibility is at stake, and this is something I prize. Count yourself lucky if we don't go to law. In fact, I'm not at all certain that won't be the case.'

The crash of the door cut short Davenport's attempted apology, and he sunk into his seat as Proudlove left the building. After a time he continued his search through the clutter of papers, and eventually the letter came to light. His eyes blurred. It was worth one hundred pounds. The wholesaler was one of the largest in the North Midlands, with branches in Liverpool, Manchester and the dominions. Manufacturers would fall over themselves for an order like this, and he'd thrown it in a drawer. He was gripped by a sullen lethargy. He knew they only tolerated him. Christ! That a man of his standing should be treated like an office boy! Even the workers smirked when he walked past, and his bitch of a wife laughed brazenly in his face. He hated the bloody mill, the clatter of looms through the office floor. He'd like to be shut of it, leave Nerissa to her whipper-snapper, take his money and go to South America, India, even. There must be somewhere he could be useful.

He delved into his drawer for the bottle and this time took a liberal gulp. Why should he do this job anyway? He, with a degree in palaeontology! He drank morosely. 'Here's to Roddy Davenport, head clerk and entertainer of potential customers. Salutations!' He threw the empty bottle into his drawer and kicked it shut. Rising unsteadily, he drew on his coat and rang the bell. 'You may tell Mr Jackson I'm indisposed,' he told the boy. 'Tell him –' he swayed slightly and gripped the edge of the desk – 'tell him to guard the business while I'm gone. He's to guard it with his life. His very life.' He pushed past the boy and reached his hat from the stand. 'What's you name?'

'Christian, sir.'

'Well, Christian, here's a sovereign for your trouble, eh?' The boy gazed at the coin thrust into his palm. 'He who cannot with his tongue a woman win, I say to you is no man – or no woman either, come to that.'

'Beg pardon, sir?'

'No matter. Tell Jackson.'

The bright sunshine failed to sober him, and he took a long route home until his head was clear, arriving back in the late morning and finding Nerissa out. He called the maid and she appeared at the drawing-room door. 'Is there any meat in this dump? I'm partial to a bit of cold lamb.'

'I don't know, sir. Cook won't be back for a couple of hours.'

'Pop down to the kitchen, see if you can't find me something.'

His eyes drooped. Always out. Never at home for him. Why had he got married? What had he got out of it? Nothing. Not a bloody whit. What was she up to now, the brazen cow?

'I've only managed to find this, sir,' Lucy said, coming in with a plate. 'It's a bit of leg. I'm not sure how long it's been there, but it seemed all right when I sniffed it.'

As he reached up, he caught sight of her well-filled cotton dress. For the first time he saw her as a girl, rather than the owner of a feather duster. 'Lucy.... perhaps you could bring the decanter.' She took a tray from the chiffonier. 'Care for a glass yourself?'

'I don't think I should, sir.'

'Don't be a silly girl. Go and fetch another glass.'

'Well, sir -'

'Or perhaps you'd prefer port. I believe we have some Old Tawny - look, I can see it from here.'

'Well, if you insist, though Missus told me –'

'To hell with what she told you. I'm master of the house, and if I wish to offer a drink to my Lucy, then by God a drink she shall have.' His rush of anger subsided in an instant. 'Tell you what, you can have a glass of amontillado. You're just the girl for amontillado. Amontillado is just for you. I'll get it. Take the weight off those pretty feet and relax. My bitch of a wife works you like a dray horse.' He poured two glasses, handed her one.

'Now, Lucy, what shall we drink to?'

'I don't know, sir. Queen Vic?'

'Damn Vic. Damn all members of royal households everywhere. Let's drink to – I know, we'll drink to the overthrow of marriage. Here's to the abol – abolition – of the holy estate of matrimony.' Lucy wet her lips with the sherry. Davenport took a gulp of whisky, swilled it around his mouth and swallowed. He slid further into his seat, staring morosely at his outstretched feet. 'She doesn't care for me, Lucy, she never has.'

'I'm sure that's not so, sir.'

'She thinks I'm a bore. Can you believe that? She thinks I'm a ne'er-do-well.'

'Surely not, Mr Davenport.'

'She has a man, you know. A pit worker. Nice work, eh, Lucy? The daughter of a captain of industry whoring with a common collier.' The maid digested Roddy's drunken confidences. Before the day was out, Macclesfield would share them. He slid his eyes over her. 'How old are you, Lucy?'

'Twenty-two, sir.'

'And how long have you been with us?'

'This'll be the eighth year, Mr Davenport, almost since leaving school you might say.'

'And how much does she pay you?'

'Fifteen shillings a week, sir.'

'Is that all? Even my dog's worth more than fifteen shillings a week. Even *I'm* worth more than fifteen shillings a week. From now on, consider your wages doubled.'

'Sir?'

'Thirty shillings from now on.' He fumbled in his purse. 'Thirty shillings for my Lucy.'

The girl's eyes opened wide. 'You mean it, sir?'

'Don't doubt I mean it. A Davenport's word is his bond, or her bond, as the case may be, wife excepted, goes without saying.' He held out the coins to her. 'Here you are, some nice, shining shillings to add to the bitch's. Come, take them.'

A sly smile played across her mouth. She came towards him warily, and as her fingers closed on the silver, he grabbed her wrist. 'First, a little kiss.'

'And what if anyone should see us?'

'And who's to see us? There are no eyes in the carpet, as far as I'm aware. Maybe you think there's someone lurking behind the curtain.'

'I'm not sure I -'

'Very well, I'll put my money back. Half rations again, Lucy.'

She turned her cheek. 'All right, but only a little one.'

'No, on your dainty mouth. Just think what a help this will be to your good old mama and papa.' He parted her mouth, tasting the sherry on her lips. 'Now, that wasn't too bad, was it?' She pulled away, and he allowed her to take the coins from his hand and put them into her apron pocket. 'I heard you have a young man.'

'Indeed, sir, Duncan.'

'You can't set up home with nothing. How would you care for an extra florin?'

'And what must I do to earn that?'

'That's what I admire in you, Lucy. You have the gift of quick understanding, whereas I have the gift of lust.'

'What would sir have me do?' she repeated.

'Does Duncan look at you, Lucy?'

'How d'you mean?'

'Has he ever seen you as nature intended?'

'I'm not obliged to say, sir.'

'No time for shilly-shally. Has he seen you without your clothes on?'

'Well, sir, we're shortly to be wed.'

'Then pretend I'm Duncan. Take off your clothes for me.'

'I don't know, sir.'

'Remember the florin.' He sipped his drink with a leg thrown carelessly over the arm of his chair. The whisky had lifted his spirits and dulled the memory of Proudlove's visit. A glow of desire came from the glass. He should have approached her before. The arrangement would have suited them both and leave Nerissa, if she were to find out, and maybe he'd tell her, in no doubt as to her level of competition. If she could cock her rump at a collier, he'd have the maid. 'Well, Lucy? I'm waiting.'

'You wouldn't say no to another florin, sir, only I had to buy a new hat this week....'

'I'm not interested in your excursions into haute couture. Are you worth two florins?'

'It's not for me to say, is it?'

'One florin. Take it or leave it.' She made a move to unfasten her bodice.' Your hair, first. Unclip your hair and take off that silly cap she makes you wear.'

'I don't like this, Mr Davenport, what with me soon to be wed and all.'

'Then you must make the beds or occupy yourself with some other menial task. I'll keep your dowry in my pocket should you change your mind.'

'All right, I'll do it just this once, and not 'cos I want to, mind, only for the silver.'

She stood out of her dress. His eyes smouldered. 'Everything, Lucy. Petticoat and all. Remember our pact.'

'But what if Missus should come back?'

'Missus hardly ever comes back, and if she does I hope she enjoys the view as much as I intend to.' She removed her underwear and stood before him. His eyes slid from her face, already showing signs of coarseness, to the thick hair curled across her throat, to her heavy, drooping breasts, thick waist, sturdy hips and thighs. She began pulling on her clothes.

'No, your dues first.'

'But I'll catch my death, sir.'

'You'll certainly catch your death if I throw you out on the street.' He held the coin before her. 'Come on, Lucy, you've no cause to be afraid.'

'I'd rather you put it on the table.'

He set the coin spinning, and she lunged at it as the reverberations died. She had it in her hand as he moved the table, causing her to lose balance and topple to the floor. As she found her feet, her face crumpled, and she sniffed as she pulled on her clothing.

'Now, now, Lucy, no need for that.' He added, in a harsher tone: 'You are the better off by seventeen shillings, the most easily earned seventeen shillings you're ever likely to get.'

'But I'm to be married soon, and what's to be done if he finds out? He'll be off with another, and I'll be left looking after my family.'

His lust had withered. It was beginning to wane even before her outburst. He didn't think he'd ever be able to comfort a woman again. 'Nobody will know anything, and you will say nothing to anyone. If you do – well, we all know money speaks, don't we?' He left the room and went upstairs to bed.

As he drifted into sleep, Proudlove's face floated in the darkness.

John sat in the lamp-light reading the day's news as Nerissa dressed. London dockers were back at work; there was talk of a Labour Party. He pushed the paper aside. When he'd last seen Charlie, there'd been some girl in tow. Then there was Matthew, nearly twelve, still with Mrs Baverstock though she'd recently made it clear she was shortly to move out of the district and alternative provision would need to be made. He'd rarely seen him, of course, and when he had his mother's doe eyes were looking up at him. He'd soon be sending him away to school; he'd been considering it for months. Then there was Wharton's fields, now in the hands of Pandora with a terrace already built. He was becoming a man of means, what with rents rising and the value of land increasing. He could leave the ironworks and colliery tomorrow without going bankrupt, but his job was still a useful cover, so he stayed. Even so, 'Old Bob' Heath rarely came to the works now he'd retired to Harrogate, and on the rare occasions he returned, he stepped from his landau with the faltering steps of a man of seventy-four. In any case, his visits were more to do with the Grange, whose refurbishment was in the hands of his son Robert. Now all John's dealings were with 'Young Bob'. He blew a smoke-ring and cast his mind back to his wife's funeral. Yes, he'd mourned – it was expected of him – but privately saw his new circumstances as a sign of good fortune. A comfortable home, land sales, rents, a mistress. He'd made a start. What he couldn't understand was that infernal dream, the burning walls, the timbers crashing down from the roof, the acrid stink of smoke which would shoot him upright into the safe dawn light....

He crushed out his cigar and lay back, watching Nerissa at the mirror. She was thirty. She'd noticed a grey hair a week ago and yanked it out. Now she examined her face like a boy looking for spots.

'Something's wrong,' he said.

'Is there?'

'Tell me what's badgering you.'

'I think I'd like to go home.'

'Why?'

She was twisting her ring to catch the gleam of the diamond. 'All men are bastards,' she said.

'Anything else?'

'I've reached the conclusion you're a bigger bastard than most. Would it interest you to know why?'

He moved off the bed. 'I'll take you back.'

'I'm quite capable of taking myself back. I'm capable of doing things you couldn't even imagine.'

He pulled on his jacket. 'If you've decided to have a fit I suggest you put it in your husband's lap, not mine. I'm sure he's better equipped to handle your 'feelings'.'

Her eyes blazed. 'And what would you know of feelings, a man who laughed over his wife's murder and wants to pack his son off to some bloody torture chamber of a school to save him the trouble of an occasional Saturday visit? The only feelings you know are the ones you keep in your trousers.' A strange, pinched expression had paled her face, and when she next spoke her voice was strained and low. 'Look at me, what do you see? I'll tell you, shall I? You see a whore. Not even a whore, since she's paid and I'm not.'

'We can easily arrange –'

The vase brushed his cheek and smashed against a wall. She lunged at him with enough force to topple him across the bed, and he struggled to ward her off. Her movements grew weaker, and she sank down at the side of the bed. 'I'm getting old,' she said, wearily. 'I've had no life.' She became animated, her cheeks flushing. 'I hate luxury! I hate money, it stinks! And that's all I've got. A sordid doss-house of a hotel and the contents of this purse. I'll show you what I think. This is what I think –'

She yanked open the sash, and a rumble of cabs and carts rose from the street below. Unclipping her purse, she held it out and let the contents fall, followed by the purse itself. Now she took up her bag, and he was on his feet, both pulling at the straps. Her powder compact was the first to go, followed by everything else. In a final act of defiance, she let the bag drop and knelt at the sill, looking down at the passers-by, her chin resting on the back of her hands. 'Look at them. The world turns and turns again and it will keep turning for ever and ever and ever. I haven't even the blessing of motherhood.' She got up. 'I want to go home.'

A knock sounded and he went to the door. The hotel porter stood in the passage. 'Everything all right, sir?'

'Why shouldn't it be?'

'Someone came into the lobby saying there'd been a commotion, sir.'

'Well, it isn't from this quarter. Now, if you don't mind, my wife and

I are preparing to go out.'

The man's eyes rested on John's for a moment. 'Just as you say, sir.'

When he turned back into the room, she had on her hat and coat. For once he felt unable to put his thumb on the pulse of things. He tried to put his arms around her, but she moved away. 'I shall have to throw myself on your mercy,' she said. 'I need some train fare.'

'Don't be bloody silly.'

'You'll have your money back, of course.'

Reaching into his wallet, he threw his ticket on the table. 'Here, take it. Enjoy your walk to the station.'

She pushed open the door and left without a word while he stood watching her from the window.

It was dark when she arrived home, and she could hear Roddy snoring through the part-open door. Without lighting her bedroom lamp, she removed her clothing and opened the wardrobe to take out a nightdress. Changing her mind, she put it back and went into Roddy's room. She lifted the cover and got into bed beside him. He snuffled and turned on his back. She lay stiffly at his side, looking at his face. He looked younger in the weak light, almost like the schoolboy she remembered years ago at Heath's ball. His eyelids fluttered. 'Nerissa?'

'Who else?'

'But -'

'But?'

He began rubbing the sleep from his eyes. The idea of their making love seemed absurd to her, but she wanted to punish herself for being unfaithful and punish John for being complicit in her infidelity. The path she'd trod, so firm in her twenties, had begun to disintegrate. Her friends spoke of their children and the grandchildren they hoped to have. Her life was draining away like water from a sink. The only thing left was to swim out of the hole she'd dug for herself, and for reasons she wasn't sure of, the tide had washed her into Roddy's bed for the first time in two years.

'You're – you don't want to –'

'You deserve the occasional treat, don't you think?'

He sat up. A crescent of hair had fallen across his cheek, and he pushed it away. 'I'm not a pet terrier, I don't want to be made to walk the towpath three times a day.'

'Did it come out like that? Poor Roddy.'

'If you're going to patronise me, you can get back in your own bed. I'm not pining, there's too much water gone under the bridge for that.'

'You seem to have an obsession with canals.'

'Eh?'

'We'll start a family, I think.'

'I can't abide being humoured as if I were a – what did you say?'

'It's high time, don't you think? The mechanics might be a little rusty, but I'm sure we'll cope.'

'And what about your fancy man? Don't say you've suddenly developed a conscience.'

She crooked an arm around his waist. 'It's rather late. I'm in no mood for philosophy.'

'I made a mess of things today,' he said, staring up at the ceiling.

'I shouldn't worry, it's common practice for most of us.'

'I wish you'd kerb your bloody cynicism once in a while. I was trying to talk.'

'Oh there, there,' she purred, patting his arm. 'Well, if you're not willing to participate, I might as well go.'

'I can't stand this!' he blurted, sitting like a petulant child with his back to her. 'I wanted to tell you something, damn it.'

She gave a resigned sigh. 'Tell away, my love.'

'Proudlove called this morning.'

'And he is?'

'He's only the buyer for – Christ, does it matter who he is? All that matters is the order he should have had and didn't, that's all.'

'What order?'

'I forgot to dispatch his order. I even forgot he'd placed an order in the first place.' He buried his head in his hands. 'Bloody orders, bloody invoices! Your father's going to have a fit when he finds out.'

'Perhaps if you were to stop whining I'd be able to make sense of what you're trying to say.'

'Holy God, what a mix up, what an unholy mess.'

'You must be the only man in England who can contrast his blasphemies at three in the morning. If you don't want to take advantage of my offer, I'll go back to my room. At least in there I'll be safe from your whining.'

He looked up sharply. 'I wish I'd had the maid this afternoon. She was ready, I can tell you. Don't think I'm not capable. I could have had her down on the floor, only I've got my dignity even if you haven't.' She burst out laughing, laughing to the point of hysteria. At some point she began to cry, for her husband, for herself. 'You might as well cry. I could cry for the both of us. A hundred pounds would bring tears to anyone's eyes. Especially the one who gets the blame, and that's me, if you hadn't noticed. I never wanted the job. I shouldn't have taken it. I was duped.'

'The more I for having married you.' She got out of bed. 'You – with Lucy? You wouldn't know what to do if she gave you a map.'

She slammed the door, but he wrenched it open and came after her. 'You dare say that to me? It's because of you I'm in this bloody state. I'll show you what I can do! I'll show you, you bitch!' He had his shoulder to her door. Her back absorbed the first shocks, but he kicked at the panel, forcing her into the room. 'Whore! A hundred pounds lost and you're the one – you! I'm nobody's laughing stock, nobody's!'

The door gave and he threw her across the bed, his macassared hair draping her face. He made no attempt to defend himself from her flailing arms, but the effort of pinning her down cost him his breath and only his weight finally stilled her. She heard him suck in air with the pain of finding her, but it was an irrelevance to him. He performed like a marionette, came within a few strokes, felt nothing and withdrew. Locking his room, he took from his bedside cupboard a bottle of cognac and opened it. 'I'm nobody's fool,' he repeated to himself, before tipping the bottle back.

He was late for work next morning. The excitement of the previous day had left him with a throbbing head, and he'd been at his desk no longer than five minutes when Jackson came in. 'Just thought I'd let you know, Mr Davenport – Mr Birkenshaw's come in today. I dare say he'll be up directly.'

'Birkenshaw?'

'I just thought you'd want to know.'

'Did he say what he wanted?'

'He didn't, sir.... happen it might be connected with that affair yesterday.'

'What affair?'

'That ribbon Mr Proudlove called about.'

Jackson left the office with a respectful inclination of his head, closing the door quietly behind him. Roddy's palms had begun to sweat. He couldn't understand why he'd allowed himself to be manipulated into a job he didn't want when his family had left him enough to live on and do nothing. Why did he have to pretend usefulness to himself? He leapt to his feet as Birkenshaw came in and held out an arm in greeting. 'Francis! To what do I owe the pleasure?'

Birkenshaw ignored him and sat with his hands on the ivory head of his cane. 'It's no pleasure, judging by what I've heard.'

'Oh? Perhaps you could enlighten me, Francis?'

'Here, read this.' He thrust a paper into his hand and beat an impatient tattoo on the desk as Davenport scanned the lines. 'Well?'

'It was an error, some minor misunderstanding.'

'You call it minor? You've lost this firm a hundred pounds through your blatant incompetence and that's minor, is it? Well, if that's minor, perhaps you'd tell me what the blazes is major, eh? What d'you think it is, a couple of pairs of drawers fallen off the cart? A wench's hair-tie? You've not only cost us the biggest order we've had all year, you've lost us every other order into the bargain. I'll get nothing more from them, and when the word gets out I'll be lucky to pick up owt from anybody else. You call it a minor misunderstanding? I call it a bloody disaster.'

'I'm sorry, Francis. I've – I've – had a lot on my plate lately. I think –'

'You think, you think – I sometimes wonder how Nerissa puts up with you. I blame myself. I should have had more sense than take you on in the first place. Minor misunderstanding! You might have a plum in your mouth, but you've got a sultana for a brain. D'you mean you couldn't even –'

Davenport leapt to his feet with an energy that took Birkenshaw by surprise. 'I don't have to take this, this place was a shambles before I came. If you want reasons, ask your daughter, she'll give you reasons. Did you know you'd sired a slut? Did you know that?'

'My daughter, a slut?'

'Yes, a slut.' Roddy relished the sound of the word, banged his desk with his fist. 'A whore, if you must. If you want to know what's happened to your ribbon, if you really want to know –' A sudden revulsion gripped him. His ranting turned to gibberish, and he sank into his seat. 'I tell you I can't stand it much longer, I can't stand it much longer.'

His chin began to tremble, and he brushed at an eye. 'Are you trying to tell me Nerissa has been unfaithful?' Davenport jammed his knuckles in his mouth and shook his head. 'Are you saying you've been cuckolded?'

A tide of self-pity engulfed him and he turned away to the window. 'I've got more than ribbon on my mind. Ribbon is the least of it. How can I work with all this going on behind my back? Not always behind my back, either. Flaunting, boasting. We haven't been man and wife for –' He made an effort to pull himself together. 'I'm not sure how long it's been going on. It could have been before we married, I don't know the sordid details. She even told me who it is. Cruelty, isn't it, for a wife to tell a husband who she's sleeping with. You wouldn't know, Francis, nobody knows who hasn't suffered –'

'Do I know him?'

Roddy gnawed his lip, finding solace in the pain. 'He's not one of us. He has no money. I don't know what she sees in him. He's a manager, she tells me, a clerk in one of the pits, or ironworks, some such grotesque employment. She didn't even choose –'

'His name?'

'John Tanbrey, that's all I know. She goes everywhere with him, I bet she knows every ceiling from here to Timbuktu.'

Birkenshaw became distant. The marriage had been rooted in money, and there was no sound half as sweet as the jingle of sovereigns. Nerissa's personal arrangements were of little importance. His real concern was that a split could deprive his daughter and any children she might have of a sizeable inheritance. A matter of equal concern was that, in his present state, Roddy was capable of losing him good will. In fact, another fiasco like yesterday's might bankrupt him altogether.

'I'll speak to her,' he said, tapping his stick between his feet.

'She came into my room last night –' Roddy began, then, as an afterthought: 'Yes, speak to her, Francis, I'd be glad if you would. Please don't say –'

Birkenshaw examined his watch. 'Don't worry, this won't be mentioned.' He reached the door and turned back. 'Take a few days off. Jackson can do what needs to be done. As a matter of interest, do you know this Jane Cowlishaw woman?' Davenport blinked up and shook his head. 'It doesn't matter,' Birkenshaw said.

6

Ellen sank into Bevis' old chair before fishing Charlie's letter out of her smock.

'Dear Ellen and Mrs Benersley,
I'm shortly to be married to a girl from Tunstall I met some time ago. The wedding is at half-past two the first Saturday in June and I hope you can both come. Will should be coming too, but I'm still waiting to hear from John. Apart from that, it's just my mother's side. We fixed up to live with Mary's family until we can rent somewhere. I'm not looking forward much to that, but it should give us a chance to get on our feet. I'm sorry I haven't been over to see you, but things are a bit hectic at the moment and there are orders on at the works. I hope you're both keeping well. Will wrote to say his breathing hasn't got any better. He seems to get about, though I don't see as much of him as I ought, John neither. Anyway, if you can be at the wedding we'll have a lot to talk over, so I hope you'll be able to come and if you can't get back afterwards Uncle Cliff says you are welcome to stay with them.

All the very best,
Charlie'

She was glad for him, but his letter had made her more aware of her own situation. Doris was well into her sixties, and her old vitality was ebbing. Without Bevis, she was incomplete. Sometimes Ellen felt the same. The hawkers who came down the track were of no use to a woman of thirty, or the itinerants set on to mend the hedges, or the labourers hired in spring. And apart from these, who was there? She remembered her younger self, a firming girl's figure, seeing a joke in anything. Now her hair was a darker shade of gold and her hips and thighs had thickened. She was what some called 'bonny', others 'past her prime'. But the seasons brought no surprises and there was comfort in routine. She thought of Bill in fits and starts, knowing if he was still single and came back tomorrow she'd reject him because she'd never marry out of loneliness – and perhaps she never felt as lonely as all that. Only occasionally, there'd be a chance meeting with someone she knew, the glimpse of a child playing, a spark flitting between a couples' eyes. And the pang would pass.

She handed Doris the envelope when she came in. 'There's to be a wedding.'

The kettle began to sing. Doris put on her reading glasses. 'Charlie Tanbrey getting wed? I can't see Charlie walking down the aisle for the life of me.' She tutted at Bevis, who at times still occupied the chair. 'I wonder what he would've said? Charlie's younger than you, isn't he, Ellen?'

'I can give him nearly two years.'

'When does he say it is? June? We'd best get over to Horrock's and see what they've got in. If there's nothing we'll have to run something up.' She shook her head incredulously. 'What would Bevis say if he knew?'

As Doris wittered, a question rose with the steam from Ellen's mug. It seemed important suddenly to know who her real mother was. She saw connections being made; Charlie and his girl, couples the world over. For a moment she felt a stranger in someone else's house. She shook herself free. 'Yes, we'll go up Leek this week-end. I've always fancied a hat big enough to maypole around. I wonder what she's like?'

'I can't see Charlie with nobody with a temperament. I thought at one time, you and....'

'No, mother, it's never been like that between us. We're just old friends.' She took the empty pail outside. Doris heard the rhythmic creak of the pump handle and drifted into sleep.

Women watched from their doors; local urchins ran alongside the carriage. There were calls to the coachman and a nod back. And now they were to be man and wife together in the name God. Was he sure this was the right step? Wouldn't it have been better to wait until he was certain? Did he know the constabulary had to walk in pairs up Queen Street of a Friday night, and that they were all Methies up there, forever using their best clothes as an excuse for a carnival? He'd never felt part of the town. He was one of the few who could be found in the Reading Room at the Public Library or attending lectures on The Road to Self-Improvement addressed by a member of one of the newly-formed workers' groups. In the jolting carriage his thoughts wandered to Bessie, who'd got married the year before 'in a hurry', to his aunt, who'd broken off her conversation when he'd unexpectedly entered the room. He suspected his cousin Dick knew something he didn't, but Dick had gone on to marry Mary's friend Gertrude and moved to another part of the town. On one of his visits home Charlie had challenged him.

'Do you know something about Mary?'

'Such as what, Charlie?'

'Gertrude's not been talking, has she?'

'Course she hasn't. She's pleased for the both of you. The only thing she said to me is she's glad Mary's settled down at last.'

Whatever he'd said would have made no difference. From the time of his visit to her house he'd wanted her. The first time they'd been out he'd found himself drawn to the play of light in her hair, her small mouth, her slight but well-shaped figure, her habit of lowering her eyes as she walked. She'd said they had an aunt coming, and she hadn't to be in late. He'd returned to her house afraid to kiss her in case she brushed him off, and left without asking her out again. But she'd broken into his thoughts all that week, and his designs lay discarded in a corner while he sought the courage to ask her out again. The following Friday he'd found her waiting outside the works.

'I've been off work,' she explained.

'What's been the matter?'

'My mother cut her fingers on some glass. I had to clean around the house for a couple of days.'

'How is she now?'

'It was shock as much as anything. I was just passing this way.'

He'd walked back with her and called again the following Sunday. She hadn't tried to draw him out, always held back something of herself, but her company was enough. He enjoyed her walking at his side. A year of Sundays had passed. He'd hold her hand and she'd make a casual remark about the weather as they walked through the drifts of bluebells hazing the patches of woodland. He loved her to distraction.

One Saturday he'd gone into the High Street for brushes and he'd seen her from across the road talking to someone. He followed her into the market, but couldn't see her. Instead of returning home, he'd taken the alleys to her house. No one had been in, but on Sunday she'd come as usual to the door. He told her he'd seen her in town the day before and there was no reaction, not even a flicker of the eye. He'd asked who she was with.

'You wouldn't know him. He's one of the bosses.'

'Have you known him long?'

She'd spun round, her eyes alight. He could see her in his mind's eye now, her head thrust forward, her face on fire. 'I'll talk to who I like, when

I like. You don't own me!'

He'd fallen into a brooding silence, and three weeks passed before he saw her again.

The carriage drew up outside her house. The table had been set the night before; stewed rabbit and onion pie, boiled leg of mutton, beef steak pudding, jelly and blancmange, damson cheese. On a side table kedgeree, treacle pudding and seed cake. Mary's father began to pick his way through the local paper while his wife busied herself with the food. Neighbours and newly-arrived guests flowed into the yard. The journey from Moor Top had cost Will his breath, and Mary's mother finally got her husband to vacate his chair for the older man. Gifts piled in the scullery; a Dresden ewer, a tea service, a toast rack, a breakfast cruet, a tea tray, a slipper bath, a fireside set, smoothing irons, a turbot kettle, a Vienna regulator. The Walkers were there, and Bessie had made her presence felt by tweaking his bottom....

He'd begun to see her throughout the week. Sometimes she'd be out, but she'd always have an excuse, and he no longer pressed her. She'd neither invited nor thwarted his first fumbling attempts to make love to her. He recalled the fringe of woodland, with the trains rattling towards Manchester or London. She'd made no move against him, and when he leaned away, asked him what was wrong. He'd kissed her more forcefully. She'd closed her eyes and her breathing had quickened as he stroked her small breasts. She'd given a low moan, barely audible against the rustle of leaves, and then her arms were around him, her small, full lips open against his mouth. He'd burst like an exploding star and sunk down beside her. He hadn't known what she thought then any more than now, amid the crowd of well-wishers.

'They're treating you all right down at Clowes'?' Bertha asked.

'So-so. Family all right? How old are they now, Bertha?'

'Alice is five and Albert's coming up for two.'

'Have you decided on a name for your next?'

'Not yet, have we, Dennis? Oh, just like a man, never there when you want him.'

Bessie sidled up to him. 'Your great day, Charlie.' She looked over to where Ellen and Doris were sitting. 'I took the liberty of making Ellen's acquaintance. She's nice looking, I'd have expected her to have wed long since.'

She spotted her husband and eased her swollen belly between the furniture.

'You've come, then,' he said, going to Ellen.

'Try and keep us away, Charlie.'

'You've met Mary?'

'We've not been properly introduced. Leave it till she's less busy.'

'Are you – er–'

'I keep telling her to get up to Leek with her best frock on,' put in Mrs Benersley, 'but she won't take no notice. By, you're lookin' smart, Charlie. I only wish Bevis could have been here.'

'I'd better have a word with Will.'

Ellen took him on one side. 'Nat died, I thought I'd better say. It upsets Doris bringing it up. He didn't do too badly, all things considering. It was natural causes.'

'Oh, I'm sorry to hear that....'

'Have you done this before?' he'd asked her.

'You don't think I'm hopping in and out of bed every five minutes? If you think that, there's no point in us seein' each other, is there? You don't want a trollop on your conscience, do you?' He'd protested his apologies, couldn't bear the thought of a rift between them. 'I don't want to bring trouble home,' she'd told him, and he had to be content with that. A girl with a twinkle in her step would have been less complicated than Mary, with a simmering restlessness he couldn't understand, and her moods of impenetrable quiet. He could no more explain her power over him than that of a fakir over a snake. He wanted her because he loved her. He never thought he'd be married to anyone, yet he'd been reaching out for something for so long he ached for it, the order of leave-taking and home-coming, a line of washing across the backs, polish in a wax-stained drawer, winter nights with his paints and summer visits to friends and the rhythm of the daily round – these were every man's right. And Mary, sitting with her darning mushroom and those long, dark lashes that curved at the cheek.

'Speech!'

'Ay, come on, Charlie, let's be hearing from you.'

'Well –'

'Come on, you can do better than that.'

'Well, I'd like to thank you all for the presents out there, I'm sure they'll be a real boon to Mary and me setting up home together. And thank you all for coming. I'm sorry I couldn't fit you all in the carriage, but I could only afford a small horse.' A laugh sprang and died, the planned words forgotten. 'As you know, Mr and Mrs Heathcote – father and mother – are letting me and Mary have the front room until we're on our feet. I seem to spend all my time in other folk's parlours. Anyway, there's plenty on the table so get yourselves stuck in – but not so much as you'll not be able to do any dancing in the church hall later on.'

A clap, a swell of voices. An Irishman squeezed an ancient accordion, behind him the fiddler. They played *Little Brown Jug*, the dancers in beery disarray about the hall until a pattern emerged. They would have danced till dawn, but at twelve the musicians played their last tune. Arrangements had been made. Ellen and Doris were to stay at Cliff's; neighbours had agreed to put Will up together with some relatives who lived further afield. The moths fluttered in the gaslight and he was alone with her for the first time, two pairs of footsteps in the street.

Deakin left the train and took a cab which dropped him at a small inn in the Jewellery Quarter. Shortly after nine, Paskell arrived. He looked around the empty saloon and spotted Deakin in an alcove by the window.

'Care for a drink?' he asked, in a thick, Birmingham accent.

'I've just had one, thanks. Let me.'

Deakin went to the bar while the other man removed his derby and lowered himself into a seat. 'You have them?' Paskell asked when Deakin came back. Paskell smiled. 'Of course you have, else you wouldn't have come all this way.' He took a mouthful of stout, swilling it around his mouth before drinking it down. 'I suggested this meeting with the best of good intentions, Mr Deakin,' he said, examining the froth in his glass. 'You must appreciate, I can't guarantee anything in the way of hard cash at this moment.'

'I was given to understand from your letter –'

'I hoped my letter would indicate interest, but interest won't always add up to hard cash. How many have you brought?'

'I managed a dozen. There's more, it's a case of getting hold of them.'

'While you're rummaging, I'll have another,' Paskell said, and went to the bar, returning with a second drink. 'Don't you think it's a bit public in here for this sort of thing?'

'What d'you mean?'

'All this –' Paskell swept the room with his glass. 'I don't live any great distance away, why don't we see what we've got in privacy.'

He looked meaningfully at Deakin as he drank. It dawned on Deakin what lay behind the stare, the fleshy lips and soft, mobile mouth.

'I think we can do very well here. Anyway, I'll shortly have a train to catch.'

A flicker of disappointment shadowed Paskell's face. 'We'd better get down to business then.'

Deakin unclasped his case and took out a folder, which he laid on the table. 'As I explained, whatever you take will have to be mailed back to me within the next two weeks at the outside. And don't produce facsimiles. Minor variations are what's required. I don't suppose for a minute it would end up in the courts, but I don't want any trouble.'

Paskell sat back in his seat, his fingers linked across his bulging waistcoat. 'Don't worry. Open it up, let's see what you've got.'

Deakin untied the ribbon and spread the folder across the table. Paskell took out a sheet and studied it at arm's length, then in detail. Four squares were grouped around a central motif. A scroll of leaves and hairbells ran across the edge of each square; an arabesque of daisy heads and grasses filled the centre. The details were in cream, the ground a rich copper brown.

'Exquisite,' murmured Paskell.

'Nice in a porch,' Deakin said.

While Paskell, was tracing the intricacies of foliage on the first sheet, he picked up another. 'Now this' – he muttered, almost to himself – 'this is wonderful. You can feel the sun melting through the underside of the waves. I adore the way he's created a leaf from the circle. Very original; the berries here, the tendrils there, just a suggestion of movement. This work is –' His praise attached itself to the next piece, a pair of complementary border tiles. He looked up at last.

'Are they marketable?'

'Perhaps we might do a little business.'

'I thought we might.'

'Tell me, Neville,' Paskell said, touching Deakin's arm, 'you say these are your partner's work?'

'That's what I said.'

'Forgive me for being naîve, but why are you offering them to me in particular?'

'I've already explained, we've no set-up for fancy stuff.'

'Then you should set yourself up.'

'And be in hoc to the banks? I don't think so.'

'If you never take the plunge, you never learn to swim.'

'And if you do you might drown. It's all right for you, you're an employee, it's somebody else's head rolls. The big boys can afford mistakes, they're all geared up. If a line doesn't sell in Birmingham it'll sell somewhere or other. You don't sell to the Queen from a ten foot shed, which is about what we've got, but you can get along if you know who you can sell to, and what. So we stick to reds because there's a demand and they're cheap and we can freight everything we make up the road.'

'And when the world wants no more reds?'

'By then I'll have made my fortune through you.'

Paskell smiled, giving nothing of himself away. 'Tell me about your designer.'

'Does he matter?'

'Since you've decided to act as his unofficial agent – and fleece him into the bargain.'

'You're not exactly as white as snow yourself.'

'It goes on all the time,' Paskell said, in a matter-of-fact tone. 'It's a form of trade, a bit of a squiggle here, a slight alteration there; it'll give me no sleepless nights. Half the stuff in the country started out on somebody else's table. I could have this man of yours over at the works tomorrow and put him in the shop, but then he'd earn a wage. Now he's working for free.'

Deakin said: 'I don't know anything about you, apart from meeting you at the trades stand. But I'll tell you something, I won't be lying on a consumptive's bed come forty. At the first chance I'm off. Hard cash, that's what counts, and anything else is irrelevant. My partner should watch his back like the rest of us have to do. As far as I know, he's up nights producing sheets of this stuff, then it's left behind the cupboard gathering dust. If they're doing nothing, that means they're nobody's property in my book.'

'So you tell him you have contacts, you'll see what you can do to help. You sell his ideas, pocket the money and hand them back with a sorry, no one's interested. And he's grateful you've taken the trouble, poor soul. He should be more wise to the ways of the world.' Paskell took his coat from the stand and flicked the rim of his derby. 'I'll give you two guineas for the lot. Of course, any similarity will be purely accidental – or coincidental.' He put on his hat and fished in his wallet. 'I'll mail them back to you as soon as copies have been made, let's say within a week or so.'

Deakin got up. 'He's not long been wed.'

'And will that make a difference, would you say?'

'It might improve his output, who knows?'

Paskell pushed open the door and they went out. 'You know, Neville, you're a callous fellow. You should go far.'

Deakin hailed a passing cab, and watched him walk away.

As Deakin watched the Birmingham suburbs drift past his window, Charlie was reading a letter from John that, in the excitement of the day, had been left unopened.

'Dear Charlie,

I'm sorry I wasn't able to come to your wedding. I've had a little difficulty since we last met. Perhaps you'd like to bring your wife to dinner shortly, and I'll be able to tell you more. Until then, I wish you all the best for the future and hope the enclosed gift will provide for some of the things you need.

John.'

A banker's draft for ten guineas crinkled under his thumb.

Birkenshaw sat grim-faced, his hands on his cane. He felt depressed, and gave instructions for the landau's hood to be raised against the sunlight. Immediately the carriage halted, he alighted and had already climbed the steps to his daughter's door when Nerissa spotted him from the garden.

'Good morning, Papa.'

He came over to her. 'I've been at the works talking to your husband.'

She continued to snip at her lilacs. 'And what did he have to say? No Earth-shattering revelations?' Birkenshaw sat on a bench without bothering to reply. It was warm, and her spaniel lay panting under the laurels. Behind the remnants of daffodils the kerria were still in bloom.

'The garden's looking fine this year, don't you think?'

'I'm not here to talk about horticulture. I think we should go inside.'

'I do hope I'm not to be lectured. I feel a headache coming on.'

'Act your age, Nerissa. That mamby-pamby nonsense is all right for school girls, it ill becomes a grown woman.'

'I'm surprised at you, Papa! A grown woman, indeed.'

'You might have all the time in the world, but I don't. Could we forget the witty words and talk about something important, like keeping a roof over your head.' He went inside. She found him in a wicker chair in the conservatory. His lips were thin under his open-pored nose. She fleetingly remembered him as he was, a head of dark hair, no waist. 'I'll be straightforward with you, Nerissa.'

'That sounds ominous.'

'This John Tanbrey you're having a – a –'

'Is 'affair' the word you're looking for?'

'It's not a word I'd choose, but since you find no shame in using it, yes, this affair. I want an end to it.'

'I'm not sure how you've come by this intelligence, but you might be a little behind the times. As far as I know, my so-called affair is over.'

'What's that supposed to mean?'

'Exactly that.'

'Look, I don't think you appreciate the effect this could have on the business. Scandal doesn't sell things. I don't think it's ever once occurred to you that –'

'What's never occurred to me?'

'You're old enough to take the consequences of your own indiscretions. It's not that bothers me. I can well understand if – look, I didn't come here to hector; this husband of yours, an hour ago he was in tears. I told him I wouldn't say, but it's got to be said. In the ordinary way I wouldn't interfere, but he made a blunder the other day cost us money, a lot of money. And the reason he made the blunder was this situation between the pair of you.'

'So your concern is with your concern.'

'My concern, since you take it so lightly, is that Tanbrey or whatever his name is stays away and you try and make a go of your marriage. That's my concern. I don't want any more blunders. Unhappy men make blunders.'

'And unhappy women?'

'You shouldn't be unhappy. You have everything you want. A house out here, a husband who'll never have to scrimp like the poor sods down below.' He nodded vaguely towards the town. 'This John Tanbrey, your husband tells me he's a collier. Is that true?'

'I do wish you'd stop referring to him as 'your husband'. He's your son-in-law and he has a name, though it might embarrass you to use it. I'm one of those scandalous women who married for money; it seemed a satisfactory arrangement at the time. Unfortunately Roddy came with the package, and he hasn't turned out to be the asset one would have wished.'

'So you have a - this liaison - with a pit worker?'

'Your friend Mr Heath would be saddened to hear him referred to as that.'

'Heath's in his dotage. What's it got to do with Heath?'

'John worked for both Mr Bateman - you recall Mr Bateman and his orchids, Papa? - and the older Mr Heath - and the younger as a matter of fact, in a personal capacity. I believe he practically runs one of the collieries and iron works. However, as I said, he is now nothing more than a historical event.'

'What you need is children, you've no time for anything else with a family. A woman's work is to support her husband, bring up her children and organise the house. You'd be happier than all this gallivanting.'

'It could be nature has other plans for me.'

'Have you seen a doctor? I can fix you up with a good man. If he can't sort you out –'

'I don't need sorting out, I don't need help, I don't need kindness, I don't need advice, I don't need welfare. I just want to be left alone with my basket of lilacs.'

He took his cane and got up from the chair. Behind the palms the coachman lay sprawled on the lawn, his hat pulled over his eyes. 'Look, Nerissa, I know we haven't always seen eye to eye. If there's anything I can do –'

He couldn't read her expression. The coachman rose to his feet at the sound of the door and attacked the grass on his melton coat. 'Never mind that, take me home.' They turned out of the drive, but as Birkenshaw came to the junction, he changed his mind. 'Take the Congleton road instead. I need to pay a visit.'

Where to, sir?'

'I'll tell you where to when we get there.'

It had been more than five years since Francis last visited the Grange. At that time old Robert Heath had been in residence, but now he'd left the place in the care of servants and Robert, his son. Birkenshaw had moved in the same circles as the 'Old Bob' Heath, and had been a welcome visitor to his house. The son he knew less well, though when they'd met relations had been cordial. His carriage came to rest by the portico, and he was shown into the room where Bateman and Caulton had met, years earlier. Below him the lake glittered, beyond it thickets of rhododendron.

The similarity between the younger Heath and his father was striking. Both had the heavy face, with its expansive forehead and strong nose. But the Robert Heath who stood before him lacked his father's broad shoulders, and had a refined manner of speech his father lacked. He poured drinks and gestured to a chair by the window. 'You're lucky to have caught me in. I'm having the place done up and dropped by to see how the builders are doing. It's best to keep an eye on things. I'm not far away.'

'Let's see, what was the name of your place?'

'Greenway Bank, twenty minutes' away. I'll be moving here in due course, if Laura's health is up to it. You should have been here yesterday, my father was down from Harrogate.'

'How is he these days?'

'Not too well, as a matter of fact. He still thinks he's thirty.'

A kestrel hovered above the trees, then plunged towards the plantation. Birkenshaw followed its descent. 'Bateman's garden's still intact, I see.'

'The old man kept things much as they were.'

'Heard anything about Jimmy Bateman?'

'Still hail and hearty. He moved down to Worthing. I believe he's almost eighty.'

'And still collecting orchids?'

'I dare say he'll die with a trowel in his hand.' A distant flicker crossed his face. Birkenshaw had noticed a similar expression in his father, a sign that it was time to come to the point.

'This isn't so much a social call, as you might have gathered. It's about one of your employees.'

'Oh?'

'His name's Tanbrey.'

'We have one or two Tanbreys. You don't mean John Tanbrey, our office manager at the Bull?'

'What's he like?'

'You may have met him before. He used to work in the estate office. There was another man with him, a Urias Ball. As a matter of fact, he killed Tanbrey's wife, shot her. They brought in manslaughter. You might remember the case. He's in the mad-house now, poor wretch.'

Birkenshaw's eyes kindled. 'I remember your father telling me about it. And Tanbrey used to work here, you say? I don't think I can bring his face to mind -'

'There's no reason why you should. My father gave him his present job when Duggan retired.'

'And somewhere along the line, he met my daughter.'

Heath looked surprised. 'I understood your daughter – Nerissa, isn't it – was married?'

'It hasn't stopped her seeing Tanbrey.'

'Your daughter's having an affair with him?'

Birkenshaw looked into his port and emptied it. 'I have a request, and one I've no right to make, apart from having been a friend of your father all these years. Nerissa's headstrong. Always has been. That's something I can live with. But this – this mix-up – is making her unhappy. She'll not be right until it's sorted out one way or the other. She tells me it's over, but I'm not convinced.' He leaned forward, his large head eclipsing the wall clock. 'I've come to ask you to put pressure on him. I want him out of Nerissa's life for good. You can get to him through his job. No doubt he doesn't want to end up skivvying for a livelihood. A well-timed reminder to tow the line can have a marvellous effect.' He paused to let his words take root. 'I don't want favours. I'm quite prepared to make it worth your while.'

'Good heavens. Francis, I wouldn't hear of it!' Heath's outburst, meant in good faith, rankled with the mill owner. Experience had told him favours never came free. He sat looking at the younger man, who was now standing at the window watching a heron flapping across the lake. 'Obviously, I'd like to help. Between ourselves, it's not an appointment I'd have made. Do you know if all this was happening while he was married?'

'It wouldn't surprise me.'

'If my father had known he'd have been out on his ear. The problem is, he's one of those infuriating people who are a gift to trade. Don't misunderstand me, he's not generally liked; but he is respected – perhaps feared would be a better word – by the working men.'

'So there's nothing you can do?'

Heath reflected for a moment. 'Look, Francis, my advice, for what it's worth, is to let sleeping dogs lie, at least for the while. If your daughter says it's over between them, I think we must take it on trust. We're all allowed an occasional fall from grace.'

'I still think he'll need warning off.'

Heath weighed the circumstances. He didn't want to be involved in a private matter; on the other hand, the Heaths enjoyed a prestige in the area. Appearances counted, and gossip was bad for their reputation. What happened behind closed doors could be brushed under the carpet, but this was different, or could be. 'I'll give it some thought,' he said, bringing the matter to a close. 'Now, I find there's nothing like a breath of fresh air to sort out a problem. Before you go back, you must let me show you what the builders have been up to, then we can take a turn around the gardens.'

Their walk helped Heath make up his mind. He confronted Tanbrey the next day and left him in no doubt as to what would happen if he brought the company into disrepute. He'd left without noticing Tanbrey's simmering anger. Who'd told Heath, and how dare he interfere in his private life? He decided there and then to see Nerissa again. He'd see her that coming Saturday, and to hell with Charlie's wedding.

7

With the massacre of the Sioux at Wounded Knee, the remaining Indian homelands were subsumed under the American flag. A rush for land in Oklahoma had settled two million acres in nine hours, and Guthrie grew from a jumble of shacks to a city of brick and stone within months. When Bill staked his claim, he felt he'd nothing to lose. He'd gone to Oklahoma because of the danger, not despite it. He'd drunk to oblivion, had women as the mood took him. Reitzman should have been there, not some drunken quack. Liz had chanced herself with him, steered him to decisions he wouldn't have made without her and got it right. As the first pangs of grief began to fade, he saw he'd not lost her entirely, but found himself looking at his life through two pairs of eyes and asking what she would have done. One morning he awoke to find her answer in his ears. *At least I'd have looked to Marian. If you cast her aside, you're casting me aside too.*

'Despiertas.' Wake up. The Mejicana grunted in her sleep. He shook her roughly by the shoulder. *'Despiertas'.*

She rubbed her eyes free of sleep. *'Que?'*

'I go back. *Voy a mi casa. Vuelvo a mi familia.*'

'Pero tu no tienes familia.' You don't have a family.

'Mi hija.' My daughter. *'Tengo que verla.'*

He moved out of the bunk and pulled on his clothes. The girl had nowhere else to go and reached up to him. *'Voy contigo.'* I go with you.

'No. Voy solo.'

Her face crumpled, and she knelt on the burlap, her small hands clutching at his vest. *'Lleveme tambien.'* Take me too. *'Yo tambien.'*

The rug she slept in had fallen open at the neck, and her small olive breasts shook in agitation. 'You want make love with me? *No me deseas?'* He tightened his grip on her hands, forcing them away, and she sunk down, weeping.

'Tu vives aqui.' You live here. *'Tengo dinero.'* He pushed a handful of notes into her hand. *'Te enviare mas.'* I will send more.

He'd left her sprawled on the bunk. As he rode home, he felt he was looking into someone else's life. Something had kept him safe, directed his actions. He'd staked a hundred and sixty acres of seer grass no one else wanted. The surging line - families, runners, cripples, children - racing for what they could grab or barter, and he'd staked that. He'd dropped on an empty shack and found the girl in Guthrie. Dorita had bribed her way over the Rio Grande with three other Mejicanas. One had died of smallpox in an army camp at Fort Worth, she'd no idea what had happened to the other two. She'd heard about the opening up of new country and earned her journey there in the only way she knew. She'd arrived as the first of the wooden hotels was being re-built, and there was no shortage of trade from the men who liked her Latin looks. She was seventeen, but looked thirty. Villagers along the Conchos River were starving, and the rest took their chances heading north into the American heartland. Dorita had reached Abilene, then Wichita Falls. At the *Golden Nugget* they ran her up a gitana's dress and pinned a paper bougainvillaea blossom in her hair. It was there Bill had discovered Senorita Dorita, the hostess from south of the border with her almond eyes and a fear of syphilis. She helped him forget, and in return he'd offered her a place in the shack. They'd learned enough of each other's language to pick up the threads of their discarded lives. She didn't expect to trust him, but he represented a meal, and someone to chop the woodpile when the cold set in.

The first thing he noticed was the musty smell, and although it was late he opened the windows. He could look at the empty bed, and wasn't sure he'd be able to sleep in it. Her escritoire was still unlocked, and the lid rolled smoothly back. Envelopes and paper had been neatly laid amid nibs and copper-topped bottles. He found himself holding her pen and thought of the old country. It was something he should have done a year ago but couldn't.

'Dear All,

A year back I lost my wife after she gave birth. I now have a daughter, Marian, but I haven't seen as much of her as I would have liked. Things were difficult at first, but I'm feeling more like my old self now. I suppose you've been wondering what happened, not having had any letters from me lately. The truth is, I've been to Oklahoma. The government was offering free land, and I went there to get away for a while. I'm back at the ranch now, writing this on Lizzie's desk. I haven't had a chance to look around yet, but I dare say everything is as it should be with Ross, my right-hand man, in charge. I wrote him a letter after I went off asking him to keep an eye on things. His wife is a good woman too. Regards to everyone. I'll write again soon.'

As he was sealing the envelope he heard the door creak and turned to see Maud in the doorway. 'Well, Mr Tanbrey, you've come back at last.'

'How're things, Maud?'

'Couldn't be better, Mr Tanbrey, and the baby, growin' up a treat, she is, our Rose lookin' after her as if she were one of her own.' She lowered her voice reprovingly. 'You shouldn't have gone and left the little mite like that, even knowin' what you were labourin' under. A child needs a father or they grow up wantin'.' The small, animated woman with her baggage of good faith aroused a feeling of homecoming in him no amount of chattels could match. He held out his arms and gathered her to him. 'Now, you've not eaten a proper meal all the time you've been away, look at you, the skin hangin' off the bone.' She wiped her eyes. 'Come on with you.'

Ross turned as they entered their shack. 'Nice to have you back, Bill.'

'I'm not bankrupt yet?'

'Well, I tried my best.'

'You must have a magic with you, Mr Tanbrey, encouragin' my husband to have a sense of humour an' all.' She pulled aside a curtain which separated the room from an alcove. 'Go on, have a peep.'

The child lay on her side, her shallow breathing making the blanket rise and fall. He put a finger to the puffed cheek and stroked it gently. 'I don't want to wake her up.'

'Nonsense, I dare say she'll recognise a special occasion. There, now, you're in for a surprise when you open those eyes, my little girlie, and that's for sure.'

When they'd talked and eaten, Ross reached for his briar. He reminded Bill of Bevis, and he was about to say so when Rose entered, followed by a cowboy who hung by the door. She'd filled out, grown her hair to shoulder length. Her obvious pleasure at his return pleased him. She hovered at the table, a high colour in her face. 'This is Mr Tanbrey, Saul. I told you, remember?'

The man touched his stetson, his features hard in the weathered skin. 'Well, seeing as you got company, I'll be on my way.'

Rose followed him out and returned shortly after. 'I've just been telling Mr Tanbrey how well you've been looking after Marian,' Maud said, 'though sure he can see it for himself.'

He'd forgotten the sound of their voices; Ross's drawl, Maud's chatter, Rose's sing-song. He hadn't realised he'd missed it. Ross asked him:

'Something on your mind?'

Bill leaned back in his chair. 'I've been thinking – how'd you like a spread of your own?'

'Are you offering me your ranch?'

'I'm offering you my stake.'

'In Oklahoma?'

Bill drew his seat to the table and pushed the remains of his meal away. 'A hundred and sixty acres of wilderness. If you take it maybe I'll be doing you no favours. If you can't make a go of it, there'll always be work for you here.'

Ross rubbed the side of his nose. 'You're offering me your land?' He watched his wife shake a cloth into the hearth. 'Do you hear what the man's offering?'

'I hear.'

'Well?'

'What would I be knowin' about Oklahoma 'cept what I'm told? You've to make up your own mind, then there'll be nobody but yourself to blame. Yourself and that half-wit daughter of ours, grinning in the corner there.'

'There's no hurry. Sleep on it. It's a notion I had coming back – consider it a thank-you.'

Maud's face clouded. 'For lookin' after the ranch and your baby? What need of thanks?'

'Then count it a gift.'

He returned to the ranch-house relieved. If Ross wanted it he could have it. He'd need a well, some storage. Without more water he doubted the land could support more than donkeys. He'd help. He owed it to them. His mind drifted in the darkened room. Having made the gift, he felt easier with himself, found he could lie on the marriage bed after all. It took him a long time to fall into a dreamless sleep and when he awoke it was light.

The promise of June buoyed him up. He scanned the endless pasture under the brim of his hat and thought of Liz and charged headlong up the slopes of cottonwood and bur oak. When he looked back, his ranch was a white smudge against the enormity of green. A faint jingle came on the air, and a movement caught his eye. He recognised the rider, and when she was within earshot, called out. Rose came towards him without slowing. She was dressed in the chaparejos she'd had from one of the hands, a wine-coloured kerchief at her throat.

'Mr Tanbrey! What are you doing up here?'

'I might ask you the same question.'

The sun splashed auburn lights into her dark hair. Hesitating, she said, 'I'm on my way to Saul's place.'

'You seem to have got yourself well acquainted.'

'Till something better turns up.'

'You sound like your mother.'

'My mother?'

He smiled. 'I meant the way you said it.'

'Can I ask you something, Mr Tanbrey?'

'I wish you'd drop Mr Tanbrey. Even bosses have first names.'

'All right, then, Bill.... what's it like to lose someone close?'

'What makes you ask?'

'I'm wondering what my feelings would be if Saul were to go.'

'But you said –'

'Out here a lot settle for Lukes and Gabriels and Sauls and the rest. My mother and father were lucky, others take what comes along. There's not a lot of choice.'

'So?'

'I'd rather stay single. That's why I wanted to know what it's like to lose a soulmate, not someone you happen across.'

'You got a blue sky and all the space you want, and you're botherin' yourself with puzzles?' She looked disappointed. Points of colour had risen to her cheeks, and behind her the moths fluttered in the oak leaves. He said: 'It's like having a leg off. Every time you take a step, you fall on your face. Then you get a tin leg and learn to walk again. Trouble is, tin legs are not the same as real ones. It takes time to forget you've got it on.'

'I didn't think men still thought like that in 1891.'

'How long have you known this Saul?'

'Not exactly handsome, is he?'

'I'm not going out with him.'

Her smile faded. 'He resented the time I spend with your baby. You don't mind if I carry on looking after her, do you? I know what men are like with babies, they think they can lug them around like a sack of molasses.'

'She won't be a baby much longer.'

She looked out over the land, shading her eyes. 'Why did you run away? You can't run from memories, you just carry them on your back. The only way to forget is to do something else, or meet somebody else.'

'Are you the voice of reason?'

'I'm the echo of your conscience, Mr Tanbrey.'

'Bill.'

He said he'd ride with her. On the crests the breeze caught her hair. A martin wheeled on the currents, and the lowing of cattle sounded faintly across the plain. 'My mother says it's high time I settled down. She thinks I'm in danger of becoming an old maid. An old maid at twenty-two! I wish I'd had a chance of an education. I don't suppose I ever shall, I wouldn't know how to go about it. Did you have an education, Bill? Back in England, I mean?'

'Ay, Moor Top National. Half the time I didn't go in, I'd be stone picking or something. Then I was down the mine at thirteen, shovelling coal.'

'In England?'

'Ay, merry England, the richest country on Earth and half of 'em living in squalor.'

'My mother's from Sligo, Donegal Bay. Six of them came over; two girls, two boys and my grandmother and grandfather. They're all over the place now. I think we still have family in Ireland, we used to get the odd letter. Her mother and father are dead now. Her sister still lives in New York. A lot of Irish live there.'

'I never heard of an Irish woman with only one child before.'

'Mother said she didn't want to put me through what they went through, boiling peelings for broth. She reckons three mouths are easier fed than eight. She was very possessive, kept me in a lot when I was young. I was the only girl with an Irish accent who'd never left America. It's still there, if you listen, but not so much. Guess I won't lose it now.'

'That's no problem. It makes you sound –'

'Irish?'

Saul wiped the sweat from his forehead and looked up from his work. He saw Bill turn his horse back and Rose coming towards him. He returned to his fencing mallet and caught the post a crashing blow which drove it hard into the ground.

*

By the time Bill found time to accompany Ross to 'his place in Indian territory' it was high summer. They found the shack deserted and the roof splayed.

'I thought you said you had a little Spanish surprise out here,' Ross reminded him.

'She could have gone back to the *Nugget*.'

'So this was home?'

'At least when I left the roof was in one piece.'

The remains of occupation littered the floor, a battered bucket, a torn blanket, a tin mug. The makeshift table had collapsed, and the ammunition boxes which had served as seating had been partly stripped of their planking. 'Seems like there's been rough play. Maybe your Mexican girl got into the wrong company.'

'She'd no need for any sort of company. I left her provided for. Whoever came here forced himself in.'

'Or came after she left,' Ross said. 'Maybe some hobo or a guy on the run. There's no sign of a fight to speak of, more rough use.'

They went out into the daylight. The arroyo he'd used for water was reduced to a trickle. 'I should have dug a well while I was at it. Well, what d'you think?'

Ross cast his eyes around from a bar of shade. 'Roof needs fixing, table's broke, and I wouldn't lease the place to a coyote. On the other hand, there's a little water left and a hundred and sixty acres doing nothing. There's Guthrie a couple of days ride away and a nice breeze blowing. On the other hand again, the whole place is overrun by sharks and hired guns.'

'So when are you moving in?'

'It'll need doin' up. It'll need a well and a pump. We'll need some wire. It's gonna cost. I've been puttin' a bit by these past years, not much but a bit. It all depends.'

'On what?'

'On Maud.'

'She wouldn't stand in your way?'

'A woman doesn't like an idea can be a hard woman to please.'

'If you want it, we'll get the papers drawn up.'

Ross gazed in silence across the sunbaked land, took off his stetson and wiped the moisture from his forehead. 'Well, Bill, I'm obliged. Can't ever remember nobody giving me nothing before, leastwise nothing I didn't have to work myself to death over. Maybe I should've joined the rest when they opened this place up. I never thought of myself as no landowner. Guess I'd mapped out my future pretty well, there on your ranch.'

'Best get back and tell your wife.'

Bill stood over Marian's crib, making his repertoire of noises. At nearly eighteen months, her face owed nothing to either Liz or himself, but he thought he caught something of his mother's mouth when she smiled at him. He pulled on his boots, then lifted his daughter and carried her into the kitchen. Sometimes, when he looked at her, he thought of his wife's struggle. At other times Ellen intruded into his quiet moments. When Rose came in Marian reached up to her, and Rose swept her up and began the day's conversation. Suddenly, he glimpsed what he'd known before. Rose was dressing her, easing a smock over the child's thickening hair, the face of both turned towards the door. She lifted the child's hand in a parody of a wave. 'Say goodbye to your daddy, then. We'll take our walk, shall we? I'll see you at dinner, shall I?'

He watched her from the window. He was deluding himself. He was close to his thirty-sixth birthday, and there were fourteen years between them. But she was practical and maternal as his wife had been, and her voice followed him through his morning's work. *The only way to forget is to do something else, or meet somebody else....* When he saw her later, attending to Marian, the spark was bright, and still he said nothing. The next morning there was a heaviness between them, and when she dressed the girl he asked if anything was wrong.

'Saul asked me to marry him.'

'What d'you mean, marry him?'

'Why, what I say, what does marry mean except marry?'

'And what are you going to do?'

'I don't know.'

'I thought you were waiting for something better to turn up, isn't that what you said?'

'I don't know what I said. One day the wind's blowing, the next you're cursing the heat. He talks about going to California, says there's money to be made fruit farming, he just needs to raise a few dollars.' She gave a shrug. Marian caught her mood and began a soft whimpering. 'Now, now, no need for crying, there's no need of tears.' She began to rock her to and fro on the couch until the girl hushed.

'If you wanted him, you'd not be acting this way.'

She looked up, her wide, blue eyes searching his. 'You sound more concerned than my own mother. Anyone would think –'

'What would they think?'

She soothed the child and made ready to go. 'My father told my mother he wants to take up your offer. He's getting everything fixed up, he tells us. Saul wants me to be his wife, and I've a home in Oklahoma if I want it. What would you do?'

'What about my daughter?'

'There are other women. She'll soon be on her feet and you'll have to pay out double the rate, won't he, Marian, double the rate when you start to explore unless he looks after you himself.'

'Don't talk like that! She's lost her mother, what're you trying to do? D'you think your work's over just because this Saul's put his head over the fence?'

'I shall be going, now,' she said.

'Look –' He stood over her as she cradled the girl, looking vacantly across the room. 'Stay. Stay here.' He took his daughter from her and laid the child in an angle of the couch. He could hear his blood singing as he took her into his arms and bent to kiss her. When he spoke, his voice was hoarse with emotion. 'Will you tell him or shall I?'

Marian's cooing broke the quiet of the room. 'I think your daughter's learning the facts of life, Mr Tanbrey,' she said at last, drawing away.

He pulled her to him again. 'I love you,' he said. 'To hell with work, I'm declaring a public holiday. What d'you think, Marian? Rose's father won't mind shouldering the burden, will he? Wait there while I fix up the surrey. Don't budge till I get back.'

They headed into the upland pastures, with tangles of ash and blue walnut patching the slopes as they climbed. When he'd first discovered the place the lush grasses and wooded hills with their pockets of clear water had reminded him of England. Now he wanted to share the place with someone else. He'd finished wandering. He left the carriage and carried their basket to the water's edge. After they'd eaten, they sat in the shade, Marian asleep, Rose on her side looking up at him. He ran a stalk across her cheek. 'I'm old enough to be your father.'

'Should I start calling you father, then?'

'What's a young girl like you doing with an elderly gent like me?'

'You mean an old man like you.'

'That wasn't very kind. As I'm your father, it's my duty to chastise you.'

'Old men can't run.'

He whipped out his hand to catch her ankle, but she'd sprung up, running towards the trees. He caught her easily, spilling her down.

'Old men can be better sprinters than you give them credit for.'

She made a brief effort to free herself before capitulating. Her body rose and fell under her cotton shirt. He straddled her, looking into her fine face with its blue-hazed lids, and in one deft movement pulled her on top of him. 'I bet you didn't think a man of my age could do that.' He kissed her, pressing her to him, his hands exploring the taut swell of her behind.

She felt him hardening against her and pushed him off.

'What's wrong?'

'One thing leads to another.'

'I thought that was the idea.'

'There's a time and place.'

He nodded towards the slumbering land. The afternoon sun burnished the water against the backdrop of trees. 'I would've thought this place was as good as any.'

'That's not what I mean by time and place.'

'What do you mean?'

'I mean a place of my own, and there's to be no man until I'm sure of it.'

'Does it need to be spelt out?' Getting down on one knee, he took her hand and brought it solemnly to his lips. 'Rose, will you be my wife?'

'I don't know, I shall have to think twice before I marry a man bent on molesting me. But then, I suppose we all have our faults. Yes, Mr Tanbrey, I will marry you, if for no other reason than to relieve you of the pent-up emotion you keep in your pants.'

She was laughing, now. He picked her up, made a show of struggling to the waterside to throw her in. Twirling her around, he set her down on the edge and ran, fully dressed, into the lake. His yells woke up his daughter, who began to cry.

'There's no such thing as men,' she told herself, 'only boys, and thank God for it.'

*

Saul left the bunkhouse, deaf to the shouts of card-players and hands returning from the stockyards. He knew the lime-washed church where they were to marry, the spears of wind-bent grass which encroached along the path. From the arched door the land fell to the prairie, the windows throwing slabs of sun across the nave. Opposite the church stood the preacher's house. He tethered his horse and opened the nave door. An elderly woman was kneeling by the lectern. At first he thought she was praying, but when his footsteps made her turn he saw she was holding a tin of polish.

'You after the preacher?'

'Is he about?'

'He went back to the house. You want I should bring him for you?'

'Don't trouble yourself.'

He pulled down the brim of his hat against the glare and went over. The man was at odds with Saul's idea of a preacher, with his rugged face and shock of grey hair. 'What can I do for you, friend?'

'Afternoon, Reverend. I was inquiring after a couple o' pals of mine just got wed, name of Bill and Rose Tanbrey. I thought I'd be able to make it, but my horse got lame. I was wonderin' if you could tell me where they're headed, I'd like to pay my compliments. Close friends of mine, both of 'em.'

'You say you're a friend?'

'That's right.'

'And you don't know where they've gone?'

Saul caught the man's suspicion. 'Now, look here, Reverend, it ain't no idle curiosity. These people I knew from way back.'

'And you are Mr –'

'Like I said, I'm an acquaintance. I called down at Solomon Ranch, thought they might 've gone back there.'

'They didn't tell me where they were going, friend. Married couples don't always take preachers into their confidence. Maybe they took a honeymoon.'

Saul touched his hat. 'Well, much obliged to you anyway. Reckon you're right, three's a crowd. Reckon I'll have the chance of seein' 'em when they get back.'

The preacher watched him mount his horse and laid the revolver hidden under his robe on a side table. He pulled the bolts across.

The night before Ross and Maud's departure rang with wild yells. A fiddler stood by the verandah steps, the accordionist and banjo man behind. The floor had been cleared, hands from other ranches joining the party, girls with print frocks and newly-curled hair. A fire threw dusky shadows across the yard. The trestles were heaped with plates of steak, barons of beef, tureens of hash and bowls of jello. Saul watched from the shadows. He saw Tanbrey, Rose, other forms moving across the firelit space. As the last note faded, Bill went up on to the verandah.

'When I came over from England, I had visions of a place like this, with all the things a man can want. They weren't easy to come by, but when you've got to where you want you learn to put your life in some kind of perspective. There're more powerful things than ambitions, and I'm not speaking through the bottom of this glass when I tell you a good woman's one of them. So before we move on to more important matters, I'd like to propose a toast to someone who's been more support to me than all the heads of beef put together. I'm referring to Rosie. I admire her guts, picking me when there could have been two dozen queueing up, men with hair an' all.' A laugh rang out as he bent to reveal his balding crown. 'Fate's been cruel and kind to me, you all know that. And there's no one here can tell me I've always done the right thing. But there's nothing so bad as can't be mended. Ross started out as just another hand, then he was a partner and now he's a friend. I owe a special debt to Maud, and a thank-you to both of them for producing such a beautiful daughter. Ross, Maud, I know everyone here'll wish you well in Oklahoma, but don't think you'll get rid of us that easy. We'll make certain you get to see your grandchildren. All of 'em.'

Rose's voice rose above the laughter, 'It's not you'll be having them.'

'I'll be sorry to see you go, but it'll be with our blessing and I know you'll make a go of it. It's a fine country you're going to, none better. And as a token of our friendship there's a little something you might care to take away with you tomorrow.'

From the shadows Saul watched him take out an envelope. The embers had dulled, and he made an arc away from the fire glow until he was no more than a few yards from the verandah. He remembered stroking the smooth skin of Rose's cheek, the thick waves he'd run his fingers through.

Ross was awkwardly handling the envelope. 'Well, I don't rightly know what to say. I guess this'll make up for losin' my daughter. Never had a place of my own before, now you're passing on your store in Dakota as well –'

A yellow tongue pricked the night and Bill felt a searing pain and clutched at his shoulder. The boards rose beneath him and their voices faded into darkness. Now it was night, and Benersley's old house lay in darkness. There were scuffles in the byre and a cow lowing. He heard a thud, and Benersley lay face-down on the slabs.

He found himself drifting up through layers of dark sleep. There was a sensation of colour, white sheets. The room sharpened, and Rose was there. He tried to ask a question but couldn't. She gave him water, lifted his head and pummelled the bolster. 'You've been out for more than twelve hours. How's the shoulder?'

'What happened?'

'It was Saul. He shot you.'

He struggled to make sense of it, and a minute passed before he said: 'Saul had a Remington. What use is a Remington, herding stock?' He gave a weak chuckle.

Then he was up, a spoon to his mouth, a stiffness in his shoulder. His strength returned, and he had his daughter on his knee. One morning he felt well again. Rose brought him the lump of lead in his breakfast bowl.

'A souvenir.'

He examined the remains of the bullet, unbuttoned his pocket and dropped the fragment into his shirt. 'My brother Charlie had a good-luck coin given him by a farmer. Must run in the family.'

'How are you?'

'On the mend.'

'My father got it out.'

'I can't remember anything.'

'Saul must have planned it for when we were getting married. The preacher saw him up at the church. They took him there on the cart, but he wouldn't bury him in the cemetery. He should have given him a decent burial. I'd no idea he was so eaten up.' Her fingers were cool under his shirt as she gently peeled away the dressing. 'See? It went in here and out there, ricocheted off the bone. Could have passed clean through your heart. You don't know how lucky you were.'

He held her hand. 'How did they get him?'

Marian had got as far as his couch. Rose started her on a new cirucit.

'It was chaos. Some of the men barged out, most half drunk. You could hardly see a hand in front of your face. He must have blundered into the fire when he heard them. They were shooting anywhere, it's a miracle they didn't hurt each other. Someone hit him in the head. It was more an accident. They brought out the lamps, but he was dead when they got him in.' She reminded him of Elizabeth and her causes, the plight of the Sioux, her sympathy for the underdog. 'It's such a waste! There was no need, he'd have gotten over it. How was I to know?'

He held her close, her sprawl of hair against his lips. 'Maybe he wanted it,' he said, 'he could've killed us any time out there in the plains. He could've stalked us up the hill that day. Put it behind you, it's not your fault.'

She nodded. 'I've felt so alone these past weeks, especially since my folks went. Dad left a note. I'll read it out: "We came to see you every day when you were ill, though I guess you won't know anything of it. You learn to tell when a man's mending, and I know in no time you'll be herding steers again. I wanted to get settled before the weather starts, though me and Maud would have stayed if Rose needed us. She tells me this Jancey who manages your store, he's finishing next year and I can either sell it, find a new man or move up there myself if things don't work out. Thanks ring hollow. The least I can do is make it work. Soon as you're fit, you and Rose come on over. Guess there's nothing much left to say except we are proud to have you in the family, Bill. God willing, we'll meet again soon."'

She let him have the sheet. 'You're a dark horse,' she said. 'If you're not too tired, there are other things needing attention.'

8

Charlie read Heath's obituary again, lowered the paper and peered vacantly ahead. How could one man have achieved so much? Even in death, fate had smiled on him. The storms which had flooded the country had ceased as if by divine providence and the mourners had had a fine October day....

Deakin had been watching him for some time. 'What's taken your interest, then, young man?'

'I was just thinking about Heath.'

He didn't trust Deakin. There'd been an increased demand for patterned tiles from the newly house-proud, and there was more money about. Seaside hotels were springing up along the Welsh coast and public utilities were booming. He'd tried to explain, but Neville resisted with his usual excuses – there were already too many firms jostling for the fancy side; if they set up they'd go to the wall. Charlie deferred to his business sense, but it still rankled.

'I was just wondering how it is some can have that much more than others.'

'You'll be turning socialist next, Charlie.'

'I used to work with his gardener.'

'You didn't say you were a plantsman?'

'Luke Pointon, he used to grow all the stuff for the family.'

'I don't know much about Heath. Lived down your way, did he?'

'Ay, down the Grange. That's what I mean. There's me scrimping along in rooms and he had a mansion.'

'Do I detect a note of bitterness?'

'It isn't his money, it's what he managed to do with his life.'

'Could be luck, old mate. Have you got any more of these designs for me to look at?'

'I've done nothing since summer. I've got little enough time as it is, now Mary's expecting.'

'That's not going to stop you working on your hobby, is it? You know what they say, it's a dull man spends all his time in labour.'

'It'll be my wife in labour, not me. I've given up on the idea altogether. Nobody wants designers, they only want barrow-pushers.'

Neville shrugged. 'I've done the very best I can for you, me old mucker. I've hawked your stuff all over. Trouble is, they've got their own men. Minton, Maw, Boote, Dunnill - it's easier breaking stones down Dartmoor than breaking into that lot. You have to have a lot of luck and a lot of skill. I'm not saying you're short on the skill, but what you need is a gambler's break. Someone on the look-out for the right thing at the right time, like those animal efforts Campbell's are turning out, turkeys and such. I've been told they're selling like hot cakes. That's what you need.'

He might be right. How many others had been right? Harry Caulton, who'd decided at the age of fifty-five to go and teach in France? His brother Bill, who'd written to say he'd found a new wife? But where was *he* going; where was the progression in his life that all the rest seemed to take for granted? Would no job suit him? What good patterns, designs, drawings if they only served to keep him in want? His brothers had moved through their lives with direction, whereas he was planted to the streets, his dreams crushed under the entries which reeked in summer and ran in winter.

His mood persisted through the afternoon, but the reasons he gave himself had nothing to do with his work or any of the other excuses. The problem was his life at home.

The first doubts had set in not long after his marriage. His wife's bleak moods, which had both excluded and attracted him to her, had become a burden, and he came to think he was sharing a house with a stranger. He'd thought he'd be able to learn how to please her as they moved into each others' ways. Instead, shadows clung to her like worn clothing, draining the tone from her voice and diluting her life to sepia. Neither a Christmas gift nor a fine day meant anything, and he couldn't help because he couldn't reach her. When Deakin asked, 'What's taken your interest?' he should have answered the only thing of interest was that Mary release him. Instead, her pregnancy had sealed his fate.

He'd managed to get rooms away from her parents' home shortly after their marriage because he thought things might improve if they were on their own. They'd arrived with a handcart one Sunday, but after a few days he knew the situation between them hadn't changed. Although he earned enough to keep them, he would have liked her to have helped put something by, working while she was able. Wouldn't it be better for the child, not having to scrimp? He knew the answer she'd give before he asked it; she didn't get on with mill girls, they were common company, she had enough to do around the house - and her mother could do with a bit of help, instead of being stuck in all day with a man under her feet.

One day at work he felt unwell. His legs were weak, he had a sick, throbbing headache and in the end he'd had to go home. Mary was out, and he'd spent the afternoon on the couch with a wet rag to his forehead. Finally he'd fallen asleep, and didn't wake until after six. His headache had gone but Mary still hadn't returned. It was the first time she'd been out at that hour, and it crossed his mind she might have gone to bed herself, which she sometimes did. She wasn't there, though the blankets were ruckled beneath the coverlet. As he went down he heard the door scrape and she came in with a bag.

He took the poker and broke the coals. 'Where've you been?'

'You must know where I've been. I've been up mother's.'

'You're late.'

'My housekeeping doesn't run to a timetable. What do you want for your tea?'

'Whatever you've got.'

He watched her knife lard into a pan and bend over the fire. How long before her back hunched like her mother's, with her spine showing through her dress?

He asked, 'Have you been all right today?'

'Why shouldn't I have been?'

'I came home early. I had one of those heads again, like I told you before.'

She sighed and scratched her neck with a thumb nail. 'You want get off to bed at nights, instead of fiddling around down here, drawing till all hours.'

'I've hardly been fiddling around for weeks.'

'Well you must be doing something, not that I care since it isn't my health I'm worried about.'

'There's not much point going upstairs when I can't get to sleep, I might just as well read.'

'You can see 'em reading down the library, not a job between 'em.'

'Happen they're better off without if all there is is cutting clay.'

'And what else is there?'

Her voice faded, as if holding the thread together was too much. A tense quiet had fallen across the room.

'Are you sure you've not been off-colour?' he asked again, to break the silence.

'Where's all this heading?'

'The bed's been slept in, least that's what it looked like.'

Her jabbing at the grate slowed. 'What're you trying to say?'

'Nothing, except the bed was ruffled and I thought –'

Her pasty prettiness crumbled to pinch-lipped rage. 'You filthy dog!'

'I only said –'

'How dare you accuse me of being a whore? Who d'you think you are?'

Her hand went to the pan, and he was too late to restrain her. The lit fat licked the mantelpiece and arced across the tiles, leaving tongues of fire across the floor. As he stamped them out, her voice became brighter, and she changed from monochrome to colour. Within a few minutes the episode would be forgotten.

He left the room and spent the time setting the mouse traps and brushing the yard and outhouse. Where had he gone wrong? Would she have been better off with somebody else, someone who knew about women, who'd give her a back-hander and spend the night carousing with his cronies? Did she treat him like this because he loved her?

She tapped at the window and he went in, leaving the brush by the wall. His meal was on the table, she'd fished it out from somewhere, the fire or floor, added potatoes. An earthenware pot gasped at the window, a pint mug, milk jug, sugar bowl, step-sharpened knife, tablespoon for gravy, platter of bread.

'How is it, Charlie?'

He mumbled something.

'You'll never guess who I saw today,' she said brightly, pouring tea. 'Your Dick and Gerty coming out of the Sally Army with their trumpet boxes. He always was keen on learning to play, you said, now it seems he's converted his wife into the bargain. Potatoes well done, are they, Charlie? They should be all right.'

'And what were you doing down at the Salvation Army?'

'I was next door, having my shoes mended.'

'And did he make a job of them?'

'Look at these.' With a hand on his shoulder, she hitched her skirt to her knee and crossed her leg to show him the heel. The brown cotton folds hung away from her legs, exposing the smooth flesh. As he stroked her calf, she remained poised, like a heron on a stone, watching his hand slide up and down her skin. Gripped by an urge to pay her back for the hurt she'd caused him, knowing her need of him, his confidence returned. She let her foot sink to the floor. She was naked under her dress. He wondered vaguely if she'd removed her drawers while he'd been in the yard.

'I'll lock the door,' she said, her voice husky and still.

'D'you want to go upstairs?'

She began impatiently to unfasten his belt. He prized her small breasts free and entered her awkwardly. He was afraid his desire might wane. He watched her slackening jaw, the ochre eyelids clenched, her breath catching in the creaking stillness. She thrust against him with a kind of desperation. He wanted to delay for her sake, but she was deaf to any kindness he might want for her. Her desire hovered out of reach, and she chased it with a sense of failing, her movements more vigorous and doomed. A warmth rose through him. He fought to contain it, but couldn't. She slowed as she felt him wilt, drooping on to his shoulder. He remained in the chair as she went into the back room, heard the splash of water. He got up and scraped the remains of his dinner into the fire and waited for her to come in. She'd returned dressed. He apologised, feeling wretched.

'Maybe you're trying too hard,' she said in a flat voice.

'But you wanted it.'

She wore an expression he couldn't read. He fought for the normalcy of everyday, but it hovered out of reach.

'You said you'd seen Dick. Had he been to see Aunt Ethel?'

She had no interest. He hunted for something else to say, but the need to comfort her passed. His work didn't fulfil him, and the muse guiding his pencil had drifted away. He had nothing in common with any of it, nothing in common with his wife, who, despite everything, he loved. He reached for his jacket and cap.

'I think I'll take a stroll.'

He left her dabbing at the wallpaper with a rag.

Clusters of stars shone between the racing cloud. He drew up his muffler, pushing the ends into his waistcoat and fastening his jacket against the cold. He stood on the edge of the valley, looking down at the marlholes, the canal, beyond, to the trees dark against the far bank. Now he was down among them, looked back at the dusky scarf of smoke rising from the town, with its cats' eyes of flame.

He turned and walked back to his mother-in-law's house. She shuffled into the living room, her shawl hugged around her.

'Mister out?'

'You won't have to go far to find him, I dare say.' She eased herself into a chair. 'What brings you here?'

'I was just taking a stroll, thought I'd call in.'

'Folks're better off in front of the fire, never mind goin' for a stroll.'

He edged closer to the purpose behind his visit. 'Mary must take after you, she feels the cold.'

'She always has, a pound o' dumplings'd make no difference to her.'

'Has she called today?'

'She called early on for a few minutes.'

He ran his tongue along his moustache. 'This afternoon?'

'Haven't you spoken to her?' she asked.

'I wasn't feeling too well. I came out to clear my head, so I've not had much of a chance to speak to her today.'

'She dropped in this morning and had a bite to eat. She said she was going up town. I'll make a pot of tea.'

Why hadn't she been in at the usual time? What did they know he didn't? What proof had he anything was amiss – a crumpled bolster? She left her rocking chair and carried out the task with the same intensity he'd noticed in his wife; opening the cupboard door, rattling the mugs, an intake of breath as steam billowed, the lull, the pouring. 'You've a job to make ends meet nowadays. It's all right for them as live up Porthill, they can come and go as they please. It's the poor devils round here go hungry.'

'How long has Mary been a regular church-goer?'

'What brought that on?'

'It just crossed my mind.'

'She's always gone. I don't know where she gets it from.'

'I was told,' he said, not knowing why any of it was important to him, 'they were all Methies up this way.'

'Well, you thought wrong.' She eyed him curiously. 'You've come up here for a reason, have you?' He shook his head. 'Are you still doing this painting of yours?'

'I don't have time. I let Neville Deakin have a look at a few, but he reckons we can't tool up down at the shed. He says he's shown them to friends of his, but – well, it were never more than a hobby.'

He toyed with his mug, then got up to leave. She said: 'Neville Deakin? Did our Mary say something about him once?'

'She hardly knows him.'

'I'm sure she mentioned somebody by that name, said he'd called while you were out.'

'She never said anything to me.'

'I dare say it wasn't important.' She sensed his awkwardness. As he pulled on his cap she asked: 'You're all right, the pair of you?'

He left her in the doorway. When he got to his house, the sight of the lit curtain unnerved him and he forced himself to enter before he knew what he was going to say.

At work the next day, he spoke to Neville.

'You say I went up to your place, Charlie?'

'That's what I've been told. I thought it was something you might 've mentioned.'

Deakin's frown cleared and he beamed a smile. 'That's right, Charlie, so I did! I called up a few weeks back. Did I forget to mention it?'

'Why was that?'

'Why was what?'

'What made you call?'

'Oh, what made me call...?' He gave a puzzled laugh and clapped Charlie's knee. 'There's no rule against calling on a friend, is there? I was doing you a favour, old mucker. I called round on the off-chance you'd produced some more works of art for me to hawk about. You want to watch out, I'll be charging commission.'

'Why didn't you see me here?'

'What, at the works? If I recall, I was on my way back from a job when I passed your place. I dropped in on the spur of the moment. By, Charlie, you're lookin' anxious! Has someone been telling tales?'

'About what?'

'I don't know, do I? You know how it is, we've all got neighbours. If there's nowt to talk about, they'll make it up.'

'I aren't bothered with neighbours. I can't understand why you had to call home when we're working under the same roof, that's all.'

'Well, there must've been a reason.' He snapped his fingers. 'I know! I was seeing someone might 've been able to slide a bit of work your way, and I was going straight there. I wouldn't 've seen you back at the works till next day.' His grin slackened, his white, even teeth fading from view. 'Look, if you'd rather me not put myself out –'

Mary bought bedding and begged a neighbour's crib. He looked forward to a fuller house so he'd no longer have to bear her silences alone. He felt he'd at last achieved something. He hadn't the life-worn face of those his own age whose sons were already mould-running, couldn't imagine being responsible for a child, with its needs and want of advice. A reserve between him and others was still there, as it had been at school, Ellen on one side, him on the other. Deakin had said he needed luck with his designs, but there were other kinds of luck - a comfortable marriage, someone who understood, a persuasive personality. All he had was a skill which earned him nothing and a notion of hope against a backdrop of clay. Caulton had presented his paints nearly twenty years ago, and he'd let Caulton down. Yet he could never reconcile himself to a sterile future. He needed to make something of himself, of what he had. Bevis's coin hadn't worked for him yet; perhaps there was still time.

Throughout the rest of that year he produced random ideas at odd moments and continued his reading, sometimes falling asleep in his chair before retiring to bed in the early hours. He became a regular visitor to the local library, discovered Byron and Keats and in Wordsworth saw echoes of his own childhood. He dipped into Mill, Smiles and Darwin and began to see Britain as a rich tub-thumper denying those seeking a stake in its prosperity. At the same time he was proud to be British; proud of Milne's seismograph, Parson's turbine, Starley's Safety Bicycle, Lister's antiseptic – all the glorious threads which made up his country. The more he read, the more he felt apart from the brawlers crowding the Friday night square, the more estranged from his wife and her street tittle-tattle.

Hannah was born during the winter gales of 1894. Nellie helped out during the first weeks, but the joy he felt at his child's birth wasn't shared by his wife, and the pattern of his life went on as before. One morning, waking early, he'd looked through the curtains. The dawn sun had etched sharp shadows across the walls and turned the facing windows to crystal. As he stood looking down the deserted street, the flood of light touched him. At that moment he knew he must cut himself off from her to survive. For some reason he was necessary to her, but he had to cut himself adrift. From then on, Hannah would absorb whatever was in him to give.

When he turned he found her looking up at him. 'What's it like out?'

'Promising a fine day.'

'I slept well. How about yourself?'

'So-so.'

'What time is it?'

'Not getting up time yet. I should go back to sleep if I was you.'

'Aren't you coming back to bed?'

'In a minute.'

He thought there was more than one layer to life: the uppermost, experience; another, just below it, prejudices and attitudes. But there was a deeper seam still, one he didn't understand. He'd felt it in his mother's presence when he'd run to Spring Woods after the funeral, and the shock of Bevis's accident had revealed the strength of the bond between them before he knew the reason for it. And now, standing at the curtain, the certainty Mary knew what he was thinking. When he went back to bed he felt more sure than for months past. He prepared himself for her reaction and knew when it came he could resist it. She seemed more rested than he could remember, her dark hair flowing across the pillow, the almond eyes hooded.

'Charlie, let's have another. What d'you say?'

'I can't say much.'

'Why?'

'I get the feeling you're against mothering.'

'What d'you mean, how am I against it?'

Not caring where it led, he said: 'You don't seem to have taken all that much interest so far.'

'What d'you mean? Where's this leading?'

'D'you remember the time we met, at the dance? When we started going out, I never thought there'd be anybody daft enough to want me. I thought when folks wed, they grew together, like ivy on a tree.'

'Aren't we together?'

'When I was looking through the window just now, it wasn't houses I saw; it was my future. I've been thinking about it a lot of late. Hannah's my future.'

'I don't know what you're talking about. I reckon someone's turned your head, all this talk about the future, what's it all mean?'

'You can work it out.'

'Are you trying to say I don't care for my own daughter? Is that what you're saying?'

'I suppose you do, in your own way.'

'And what's *your* way?'

'You don't bring children into the world to ignore them.'

'Maybe you think we should never have had Hannah.'

'She's the best thing ever happened between us. Maybe she's the only thing.'

Her eyes had filled, the face pinched and old. 'You can't mean it, Charlie. What're you trying to say?'

He couldn't look at her. She was crushing him. But the still voice inside him demanded to be heard. 'Why did you marry me?' he asked, suddenly weary.

'Why does anybody marry anybody? To make a home.'

'I never felt we had one. I'd've died for you once. Now there's something more precious than anything I had with you.' She looked wretched and shrunken, the blanket pulled to her face. He reached for her hand. 'It needn't be like this.... I still love you.'

His last words brought on a violent sobbing. He swayed with her, his hand around her shoulders until she became still. 'I can't help it, Charlie, I've never been no good to myself, nor nobody else. You're right. You'd be better off without me.'

He was still holding her when the first clogs scraped the street and Hannah awoke.

9

O'Rourke lifted the window, gulped the morning air and began his physical jerks. He was a disciplined man, rising at half-past six throughout the week. Now he began his day with star-jumps and press-ups. After his routine, he'd strip, sponge with cold water, dry himself and inhale deeply ten times with the window closed.

Eric's grandfather's haulage business had earned him a fortune. He'd lost the lot through bad investments in South American railways, but not before he'd secured a parish for the younger of his two sons. Eric was one of six children born to the Reverend James O'Rourke and his wife, Emily. By now, the family's income was limited to a modest stipend, but Eric and his brother had been privately taught at a Sussex college which supplied education free to the sons of clergymen. Eric's compensation for his lack of sporting prowess had been a wit which led him, through the debating society and a scholarship, to Oxford. In his final year he delivered a lecture on *Aspects of Equality* to fifty undergraduates, and used his notes as a basis for a piece he sent to the Manchester Guardian. It was the first in a series of articles on themes as varied as the *Noble Pippin* and the *Advantages of the Swallow-tailed Coat*, earning him a following which resulted in a permanent job. Within three years he was sub-editor, editor before the age of thirty. A year later, he resigned his position to return to freelance journalism. This would unfetter him from the system as he called it, and, through the contacts he'd made, provide him with a market for whatever he cared to write. Meanwhile, he had the freedom to pursue other interests, be they an evening with the crew of *HMS Pinafore* or lecturing businessmen on the pitfalls of greed. He became drawn to a political ideal, believing it was only a matter of time before a socialist party was formed.

He spent little time thinking about his past as he enjoyed a leisurely breakfast and read yesterday's Times as egg dribbled from his toast on to his beard. An hour later he left his bedroom wearing a tweed jacket and cap, his corduroys tucked into a pair of Argyle stockings. Collecting a stick from the clothes' stand, he let himself out.

The Manchester pavements were almost deserted, and before long he turned into a cul-de-sac advertising *Horse-drawn Conveyances to Suit Every Occasion*. He emerged minutes later driving a pony and trap in the direction of London Road Station. Jane Cowlishaw's train had arrived from

Macclesfield ten minutes earlier, and he came up behind her, burrowing his fingers under her arms and tickling her through her coat.

‘Oh don’t be soft, Eric! Folks’re watching!’

‘And they’re being well rewarded for it, my delicious pumpkin. Let me bite your ear.’

‘Don’t talk daft!’ She jerked free and turned to face him. ‘A man of your intelligence should have more sense.’

‘If it’s sense you want, you must send for the porter. Hullo, where are your walking shoes? I specifically requested stout footwear.’

‘These are Sunday Best.’

‘Come now, I’m all dressed and ready. I’ve even bought new stockings.’ He hoisted his leg to the back of the bench. A porter watched disinterestedly from the bay. ‘However, if the lady won’t ramble –’ he took her arm and marched her to the rank – ‘behold, your ticket to Valhalla.’

‘It’s not lame, is it?’

‘I should think not, indeed. Finest horseflesh in England.’

Soon they’d left the city, and the Pennines rose above the lush Cheshire countryside. Jane took off her coat, feeling more at ease in her blouse and skirt, and looked out over the land, a hand to the brim of her bonnet.

‘What we really need are bicycles,’ he said. ‘We could get as far as Buxton in a day, and they don’t have to eat.’

‘I’d look well, riding in this skirt.’

‘All the ladies are doing it. I could buy you a modesty version.’

‘I can buy my own bike, thank you all the same.’

‘I’d forgotten, I’m no longer looking at a mill girl, but a section head, no less.’

‘That’s one word for it.’

‘Which means the end of your plans for the labouring masses.’

‘Not at all.’

‘You must learn you can’t wear two hats at a time.’

‘You’re wrong. In a perfect world there’s sense in that, but it’s far from perfect. I’ve learned if you’re a force you can make changes but unless you’re that, you might as well give up. The Victoria’s running down. It has been since I went there, and if it carries on the same way I can see lay-offs come next summer. Birkenshaw’s got no interest in the business. I told you before, his son-in-law couldn’t run a whelk stall. The only one kept it together was Jackson, and since he retired things have gone from bad to worse. The rot really set in after that order for ribbon; Proudlove not only took his business elsewhere but was given promotion, which meant he did us a sight more damage. If it wasn't for paring costs to the bone, we'd be closed by now.'

'Wouldn't the employees find work elsewhere?'

'It's not as easy as you think. It's cut-throat out there. If I can help get the firm established again, I can start looking at the workers.'

'And how do you propose to do that?'

'It's only a matter of time before Davenport's out on his ear. He's drinking more than ever since Nerissa started up with her fancy man again. Sometimes it's as much as he can do to get himself out of bed of a morning.'

'How old is the child now?'

'Nerissa Davenport's girl? Must be close on four. That's something else. Roddy confides in me when he's had a drop. He'll have nothing to do with Flossie, says she isn't his.' She added after a lengthy pause: 'I want his job. If I can make myself indispensible to Birkenshaw, I'll be in a better position to ask favours.'

'And don't you think a union of working men would be better placed to do that?'

'Unions need a leader and folk itching to buy sarcenet ribbon to give them strength. I got involved once, and I will again, but now I'm trying a different tack.'

'So you hope to become an enlightened boss?'

'What I believe in is a week's holiday at the seaside. I believe in not letting good brains go to waste. I believe in the right to a decent living and good health paid for by the government.'

'What, ask the toffs to spend their ill-gotten gains on the workers? You're even ahead of the socialists there.'

'Why not, they slave all their lives, don't they? And why not something for when they retire, so they don't feel they have to produce babies like rabbits to keep them in their old age? Tax the rich, they can afford it, and redistribute the money. They could keep their mansions, maybe sell off some of their prize cattle. It's not so much to ask, is it?'

Though she wasn't yet forty, her auburn hair was slowly diluting to grey. He lay back in the grass, thinking about their time together. They'd become lovers a month after they met. It had amused him at the time, and still did. She, a strapping mill girl brought up in a Staffordshire backwater; he, a maverick radical who lacked her thirst for intellectual fulfilment. He'd never felt the urge to settle until now, knew that if she found marriage lacking, she'd pack her bags. He'd suggested she share his apartment, but she'd said she valued her freedom. His disappointment hadn't lasted, but he was struck on Sunday nights when she caught the last train back with a sense of wishing the week away so he could see her again.

'This fancy man of your Mr Birkenshaw's daughter. Does he have a name?'

'John Tanbrey, Roddy said. He said he was a collier. I knew a Tanbrey once.'

'Oh?'

'He was a collier, too. He'd two brothers, and one of them was a John if I remember right.'

'There's no doubt more than one John Tanbrey in England.' He got up. 'Well, since we're not going on a ramble, I know just the place to visit. It's time you met an old friend of mine.'

'I'm not dressed for visiting.'

'Neither am I.'

The view of the mansion from thc lanc was suddcn and unexpected. 'We're going there?'

'Indeed we are.'

'Eric, let's go back, my hair's hanging.'

'No. I've decided to unleash you on society.'

A servant showed them into an expensively-furnished room overlooking the ornamental lake. Lady Parker-Holt rose from her chair and greeted them effusively. Eric stepped forward and pecked her cheek. 'We were drivng by so I decided to liven up your day. Allow me to present my good friend, Jane.'

The woman held out her hand. 'I do hope you're managing to keep him under control, my dear. Now he's managed a beard, you can pull him along by it.'

Jane said Eric had a mind, as well as a beard, of his own. Her flat northern vowels made her feel awkward. Lady Alice asked if Eric was making her an excuse for lunch. 'You see?' O'Rourke said, turning with feigned surprise to Jane, 'I told you I'd never get away with it. A cup of tea would be very welcome. And perhaps a sandwich of something.'

Lady Alice led the way to a smaller room overlooking a tract of parkland. It transpired she'd been an avid reader of O'Rourke's early columns and had written to the editor asking if Mr O'Rourke could 'do a piece on the history of my house and family'. They became friends, and she'd introduced him to her circle. Her grasp of the social problems thrown up by industrialisation impressed him, leading him to flirt with Fabianism. He'd come to terms with the fact she could enjoy her husband's inherited wealth while espousing socialist views. He'd met bloodthirsty clergy, philanthropic despots, child-loathing teachers and intellectuals hard put to mend a door. That the entire world was one vast paradox amused him. Lady Alice could send a battalion to its death, but still support organisations which threatened the system which had made her rich.

'And you actually work on a silk mill, my dear?'

'I'm afraid so.'

'And who owns it?

Jane wasn't surprised to hear Birkenshaw and Lady Parker-Holt were already loosely acquainted.

'Of course, that was when my husband was alive. I'm afraid I've lost touch.'

O'Rourke said: 'You always hated the nouveau riches, admit it.'

'I shall admit nothing of the kind. You see how he bullies me, Jane? Does he bully you?'

'Bully Jane? Heavens no, she'd make mincemeat of me.'

Their conversation broadened. What did he make of the Jim Crow laws, the plight of the Uitlanders, the deterioration in Engel's health, the reinstatement of Salisbury? What of Gladstone, now in his eighty-sixth year? Would Keir Hardy suffer in next month's elections, or would the electorate vote in his favour? Jane listened from her seat, acutely aware of her ignorance. The question of Wilde's homosexuality came up.

'And what do you think, Jane?'

'I've heard his new play is drawing crowds.'

'You mean the *Importance of Being Ernest*?'

'I suppose when I see it it'll be with the local players.'

'I was fortunate enough to get a ticket for the Haymarket shortly after its debut,' said Lady Alice. 'However, leaving aside the matter of his undoubted genius, do you think the outcome of his trial fair or foul?'

'Fair? Of course not.'

'Oh?'

'He was unfortunate, that's all. He picked the wrong one. There's a couple on the mill, everybody knows about them. No one takes any notice.'

'Really?'

'The mistake he made was not going with this Lord Douglas, but bringing his father up for libel.'

The old lady searched her bag and brought out a packet of Turkish cigarettes. She offered one to Jane, which she declined. 'So you condone acts of sodomy?'

'You're the first woman I've seen smoking.'

'My dear, there's only room for one provocative person. No matter I've given in to the weed, I'm sure Mr Wilde's stay in Reading Gaol is even more tragic. I quite agree with you. If a man wishes to sodomise his friend, the law must allow him that privilege as long as we don't have to witness the fact. That any court should seek to imprison a great artist simply because he finds common norms of behaviour repellant is, in my view, short-sighted. Are you sure you won't have a cigarette?'

'You must credit Jane with having more will-power than you,' Eric cut in. 'And I'm sure she's not totally smitten by Mr Wilde as a person.'

'Then what about Mr Hardy? Surely you've read the critics' lament over his *Jude the Obscure*.'

'I'm afraid I'm too busy for the most part to keep up with novels. What I do is confined to news and politics.'

'But my dear, how careless! There's more to life than newspapers, unless you enjoy government propaganda. Eric – you must take Jane out more and encourage her reading. When you come again, we can have a debate on why Mr Hardy's book has been described as dirt and damnation.'

'Why?'

'Simply because the heroine preferred to live with, rather than marry, the hero. And why not, if that was to her satisfaction? I'm pleased to note you've not been sucked into matrimony yourself. My dear husband was the kindest man in the world. Unfortunately he was a fool, and of very little use in bed. I suppose I'd marry him again, but only for his money.'

'She thinks you're a right card,' O'Rourke said.

'I must read it,' Jane said. 'From what you say, the heroine and me might have a lot in common. There's no reason to suppose marrying is always right just because everyone's expected to do it.'

'I hope you're paying attention, Eric.'

Jane began to relax as she saw their banter as little different from that of the work-place. Lady Parker-Holt and Eric could have been a pair of unionists. Perhaps she could teach her more in a sentence than anything lifted from the political broadsheets. Again, it could be the Lady Alices who wrote them.

'I never found the need of a wedding,' Jane said. 'When my brother died, I moved to Leek. There was someone there had a child by a man who took the first ship out to America. She lost the little girl, though I doubt he'd care one way or the other. I see her from time to time and she's still not wed. She says she's comfortable as she is, just her and her mother.'

'If you're saying women are more resilient than men, I couldn't agree more, though I expect Eric might have some reservations. My late husband had to be dressed like a baby before attending a function, and then his socks always seemed to be odd.' O'Rourke looked at his watch. 'It seems you are about to go. A pity, I was beginning to enjoy myself. I don't see company as much as I would like nowadays.'

'I'm afraid I have to be back with the horse.' He was escorted to his trap by an elderly servant. 'What did you make of her?' he asked, as they reached the road.

'D'you think I was too forthright?'

'In what way?'

'About us, I suppose.'

He jerked the rein and the pony broke into a trot. 'Jane, your views are an open book. I hope one day you'll change your mind.'

Marcus Claire faced Roderick Davenport across the desk. When the solicitor at last trusted himself to speak, he was incredulous. 'All of it?'

'All of it, all except the house. That's one of her father's little investments, damn it, or that would go too. Maybe it's his way of keeping me down. I hate the lot of them.'

'It's not for me to say, but –'

'You're right, it isn't,' Davenport said.

It had been some time since Claire had last seen his client, and he was ill-prepared for the change in him. Davenport's once fine profile had turned flabby, his nose and cheeks bruised with blue-red capillaries.

'But surely, this – this situation –'

'I want everything transferred to this bank.' Davenport took a scrap from his wallet and slid it across the desk. 'Money, stocks, shares, bonds, everything I own. Don't worry, you'll get your cut.'

'This is all very irregular.'

'I need no lectures from anyone on irregularity. It's my affair and my money and I'll do with it as I please.' He rose unsteadily, gripping the edge of Claire's desk. 'I aim to be in Italy by the end of the week. I shall send instructions as to the disposal of anything I've missed from Venice.'

'Mr Davenport, forgive my temerity – does your wife know anything of this?'

'Of course she knows nothing, and you'll favour me by telling her nothing. I've made out a will.' He handed over an envelope. Claire removed his glasses and stared up from the paper.

'This – this woman – who is she?'

'A close friend of mine.'

'Have you taken leave of your senses, man? To cut your wife off without a – a penny, to leave her destitute – and there's a child involved –'

'Now look here!' Davenport's voice had risen hysterically. 'The courts would take a pretty dim view of a married woman carrying on with another man. It's my family's money and I don't owe her a penny. She's never been my wife except in name. Let her lover provide, or failing that her father will have to dig into his pockets, won't he? And I'll thank you not to preach to me about my so-called child. If you knew anything about my relationship with my so-called wife, you'd share the same thoughts as myself on that particular matter. Now, are you going to do as I ask or do I take my business elsewhere?'

He went over to the window and stared morosely out. The roofs below the clerestory window fell to gutters white with pigeon droppings. A cart's shafts rose from a cloud of willow herb. Claire replaced his spectacles. Alright, I'll do as you ask.'

'You do that. My mind's set, and that's an end of it.'

He left the office, stopped at the first inn he came to and sat with a large whisky in the empty snug. He reached home in a bellicose mood and let himself in. The tiled hall seemed more repellent than usual, and he passed quickly to the foot of the stairs. 'Lucy!' He fancied his voice came back to him and repeated the shout. Eventually an upper door opened, and she stood on the landing, Flossie peering through the rails.

'Leave her there, I'd like to speak with you.'

'I'll be down in a minute or two. Flossie and me was just playing.'

'Come down here this instant, damn it!'

The maid whispered something to the girl and retreated with her into the nursery. Christ, how much longer must he suffer this? Even Lucy ignored him. That whore his wife, the bastard she was rearing in his home, they all ignored him. Well, the last laugh would be his. He'd make her pay for the injustices she'd done him. She'd pay, and her father with his blustering incompetence, he'd make them all pay where it hurt most. He'd like to see their faces when they heard about him and Lucy. He'd like to see his wife when she faced Claire across his desk. She thought he was a drunken dolt. He'd make the town ring, might even put the finishing touch to the mill. Whiffs of scandal made for bad business. There'd be no more slaving, no more straining to prove himself a family asset. *Where the hell was she?* 'Lucy!'

'What's all the fuss about?'

She'd reappeared on the landing. Since Davenport's first crude attempts to seduce her, she'd parted with Duncan, concluding the master had a 'crush on her', though her only assets were her figure and a native guile that told her that in Davenport lay her one chance of money. Over the past year, she'd learnt that the odd impertinence did nothing to lessen his desire, and it gave her an immense feeling of power.

'Lucy, I've done it!' He embraced her roughly, bringing his wet lips to her mouth.

'You haven't!'

'I've just come back from the attorney's. It's all in hand.'

'You're teasing.'

'It's true.' He half-heartedly began to knead her breast under the heavy serge. She gave a throaty giggle and pushed him away. 'We're all set, Lucy. Not a word, mind.'

'But I've nothing to go in.'

'Here.' He drew a wad of notes from his wallet. 'This'll tide you over. A little kiss, then you shall have the rest of the day off.'

She motioned him into the drawing room. 'Keep your voice down, you'll have your daughter in the know.'

She felt him tense. 'I tell you she's not my daughter. You don't think I'm such a cad as to leave his own flesh and blood, do you?' He turned away, pouting, and she checked the urge to goad him further.

'Sorry, Roddy, Lucy say sorry to master. Master forgive Lucy?'

She coaxed a pathetic smile from him and removed the notes as he was deciding how to re-establish his mood. Pecking him on the cheek, she turned to the door.

'I'll see you where I said,' he called. 'I've got the papers. Don't be late.'

She thrust out her breasts in a show of provocation. 'You're not to worry, master, your Lucy won't let you down.'

An oppressive silence settled on the house after she'd gone. He poured a glass and sank into a chair. His headache had given way to a dull listlessness. He poured another whisky, and stared bleakly into the glass. When he looked up, Flossie was standing in the open doorway clutching a doll. He fumbled for his handkerchief and blew his nose. 'Well, what are you staring at? I see your mother's out as usual. I suppose she expects Lucy to do everything, including rear her bloody love child.' Flossie dabbed at the doll's glass eyes with a make-believe rag. 'Why aren't you in your nursery doing something useful?'

'Mama gone, Patsy, naughty Mama gone.' Shc offered him the doll. 'You tell Patsy where Mama gone.'

She followed his movements with absorbed concentration, oblivious to her hand on his knee. 'I suppose,' he said, 'I suppose she's gone visiting. She always did enjoyed visiting. I remember going to a dance, years ago. She was wearing a silk dress. Blue suits her, always did.' The doll's porcelain face shone back at him and he recoiled, making the girl start back. 'Go to your room, now. No doubt your mother will be here directly. Go on, up to your room.'

'Can Patsy come?'

'Go now!'

He turned to stare through the window at the daisies at the edge of the lawn. Flossie had gone when he looked back. Snatching his coat from the stand, he left the house.

Lucy emerged from the drapers in a new coat. She'd stuffed the unspent portion of Davenport's money down her blouse, apart from a silver sixpence she'd put in her new purse for luck. There was time to kill before she was due to meet him, and the temptation to show off her new clothes was irresistible. She reached her street as the pavements began to fill with homegoing workers. A swarthy man in a sleeved vest called from a doorway.

'I thought you were out digging,' she said.

'Well, you thought wrong, didn't you?' He came over to her. 'What's this?' She wrenched her sleeve from his grasp and made to move on, but he barred her way.

'Let me pass, Duncan, I've to get back.'

'And where's all this from?'

'I'll dress how I've a mind, we're not walkin' out no more.'

'You're walkin' out with somebody, though.'

'Am I?'

'He must have a deal o'brass to drape it over your back.'

'What's it to you?'

'You can put some my way, since I lost my job this mornin'.'

'Loafing, as usual?'

'I'll give you loafin'.' He manhandled her towards his door. She put up a struggle on the step, but she was no match for a man she'd seen lift a dog-cart. He pushed with his foot against the panel, cutting off the street noise.

'You can't have owt,'cos I've nowt to give.'

He snatched her bag and rummaged through it, throwing aside her compact, comb, purse.

'If you're short of sixpence you can have that. Look at my new bag, half ruined with your dirty mits all over it.'

'You must think I was born yesterday. What's down there?' He pointed to the neck of her dress. Clutching the money to her, she took a step towards the door. He caught her as she reached for the knob, spinning her around and thrusting his hand between her breasts. She struggled with him, her chest partly exposed. 'That were mine, Duncan, you've no right.'

'Been thievin', have you?'

'Hand it back.'

He made a show of folding the money into his belt pocket. She followed his moves, a curled strand dangling over her eye, her skirt creased. When he'd finished, he stood a little apart from her, his large hands loose.

'They won't be back awhile,' he said, referring to his parents.

'It's nothin' to me whether they're in or out.'

'I thought they only let you out of a Sunday.'

'Well, you thought wrong. Davenport's letting me have the day off.'

'And you're goin' home? I'd think that was the last place you'd go.' A sullen petulance came over her. She resisted the urge to tell him the arrangements she'd made with Davenport, her decision to bid farewell to the family who'd put her out to service before her twelfth birthday. She stepped back against the wall. 'What's the matter? Suddenly turned squeamish, have you?'

She struggled against him, but he restrained her, tainting her mouth with the taste of strong tobacco. She made a half-hearted attempt to push him away, ran her lips against his cheek. He moved to draw the door bolt, then took her briefly by the wall. When he'd finished, she smoothed her skirt with exaggerated dignity. 'You can have the money. I'll make you a present of it. There's plenty more where that come from. The only thing is, I won't be around for you to get your hands on it.'

'And where're you off to, Timbuktu?'

'I'll be in Italy.'

'Pull the other one.'

'Wouldn't you like to know.'

He sat to do up his boots. She watched his thick, awkward fingers pulling at the laces, the heavy shoulders moving under his vest. She compared his sturdy frame with Davenport's flabby body. He spoke with the vigour of his class, Davenport with whining self-pity. Duncan, cocky and self-assured; Davenport, flaccid and inept. But Davenport had money.

Whistling, he pulled on his cap and pulled back the bolt. 'Easy come, easy go. Close the door behind you.'

Her temper faded with his footsteps. She adjusted her hat at the mantelpiece mirror and straightened her blouse and skirt.

A pale light frosted the chapel windows. As Davenport's eyes grew accustomed to it, he saw her against the glass. 'Lucy – you found it all right?'

'You might 've warned me about it being so black.'

'What d'you expect at night? It's not a bloody lighthouse.'

'I stubbed my toe.'

'Oh, for God's sake!'

'You're all wound up. You'd better sit down a mo.'

'I prefer to stand, if it's all the same to you.' He sat as he was saying it. 'Where else were we to meet, in the bloody square? That'd look well, wouldn't it, both our faces known. That'd fill a few mouths.' He ran his fingers across his brow. 'I'm sorry, I'll be all right in a minute.' Reaching for her hand, he sat silently, looking up at the dimly-lit beams. Eventually he brought out an envelope and passed it to her.

'What's this?'

'Everything's in there. Hang on to it. I don't trust myself. I think I'll take a little drink, I'll be five minutes, no more than five. I'm all shot to pieces.'

He shuffled along the pew while she listened to the patter of rain on the roof and watched a procession of faces trickle down the glass: her self-indulgent father's, Duncan's, Nerissa's, Roddy's. It was Duncan's face that remained.

Davenport downed two large whiskies. The third he stood on the table, absently twirling the stem.

The voice seemed to come from far away. 'You all right, govenor?'

'Of course I'm all right, damn it, can't a man enjoy a quiet drink without being pestered out of his wits? If you're that interested in my welfare you should have become a bloody priest.'

A second, harsher voice at his elbow: 'He only asks a simple question, no need to be churlish.'

Roddy turned slowly. 'Aren't you used to plain speaking in this doss-pit? Anyhow, what's it to you?'

'Harry here runs an orderly house, bugger off somewhere else if it's not your style.'

'My style is not your concern, and at this moment this place, stinking hovel though it is, suits me.'

'Hear that? The toff here calls it a stinkin' hovel.' The speaker brought his lips near Davenport's befuddled head. 'In that case, we need detain you no longer.'

Davenport was raising his glass as he parted company with the stool and felt himself moving towards the open door. The outer air struck him and he lay for a moment, sprawled over the cobbles, with the door slammed behind him. A narrow street sloped down to the canal, becoming one with the towpath as far as the locks. He tried to orientate himself, gulping the damp air. Turning his face to the spitting rain, he began an awkward descent and reached the towpath without toppling. A ribbon of dark water ran at his feet, and he stood over it, inhaling deeply. He'd clear his mind before he got back to the chapel. Lucy and he would have a good time away from them all, all of this. He wanted colour in his life, a hot blue sky and parasols. If he saw anything made of silk he'd spit on it. Apart from the stockings he'd buy Lucy, of course.

Snatches of song drifted from the saloon. He gazed at the warehouses rising from the canal, gazed at their reflection in the water. What an irony! He, a man of breeding, a palaeontologist, with Lucy, a back-street skivvy. What a hoot! He looked up and caught a flicker of movement by the bridge. It was impossible to see clearly in the darkness, but - yes, he was sure someone was coming towards him. Lucy? He took a step forward as a figure emerged from beneath the arch, and when he looked again it had split into three. He knew straightaway who it was. It was his bitch of a wife with her brat and the other - the other could only be Tanbrey!

From somewhere came the faint sound of a carousel. He desperately wanted something to club them with. He'd finish off the bastard if he swung for it. All three. He'd be in Italy, and they'd never get him back. The undergrowth on the canal bank buckled and snapped as he scrambled up. A post rose from the cutting, but he couldn't dislodge it and slipped back, his collar springing from the stud. Now they were nearer. He could see their faces. It was coming now, giving way. There was a sudden crack as it gave and he found himself toppling backwards down the slope. He fell twenty feet into the lock before the shock of water knocked out his breath. As he went under, he opened his eyes in mute surprise. His fading cries went unheard as he threshed blindly at the walls and a heavy coldness overcame him. He thought he could see figures peering down. It could have been Nerissa, her lover at her side. Then a searing pain clutched at his chest, and their silhouettes merged with the water. They'd turned towards the tavern when one of the three, a bargee, thought he heard a splash. By the time Davenport had been hooked out, it was clear no canal would hold his interest again. They carried him to the pub and lowered him down the barrel ramp into the cellar, where the landlord draped him in a sheet until the doctor arrived.

It occurred to Lucy there might be a connection between the bustle outside and Roddy's absence. She waited for half an hour before easing open the chapel door. The rain had almost stopped, and gas-lit puddles had spread along the gutter. A trap stood a little way off, which she recognised as belonging to a local doctor. As she walked past it, a constable emerged from the crowd.

'Somebody's had an accident, have they?'

'I should go home, miss, if I was you.'

'Oh come on, half Macc'll know by mornin'. Who is it?'

'It's a Mr Davenport drowned, if that means anything to you. Somebody recognised him, son-in-law of Birkenshaw, what owns the Victoria Mill. Now get out of my way before I have you for obstruction.'

She stood shocked for a moment, unaware of figures under the lamps and the distant hum of voices from the tavern. Then the rustle of her skirt reminded her, as if for the first time, that it was new. As she walked over the bridge towards the town, she neither considered how Davenport had met his end nor where she was heading. It would be impossible to go back to his house. No matter where she went, she'd be implicated in some way and it would be only a matter of time before the authorities found out about them. As she mouthed the word, another came to her lips: escape. She began to curse his dying. He'd cheated her, and her day of glory had died with him. All she had to show for it was a new blouse and a feathered bonnet that had made her feel grand, now stupid. Then an echo of his voice came back to her – *Everything's in there. Lucy! I've done it! It's all in hand....* She opened her bag and her fingers closed on the envelope. She clicked the clasps shut and turned towards the street she'd visited earlier that day.

A light shone from Duncan's window. His parents were up, but he'd still be with his cronies. She walked a little way off and stood in a gateway. Fifteen minutes passed before she saw a man and woman approaching. She watched him fumble with the girl's dress and called his name. He turned and stared stupidly at her as the girl, now uneasy, left.

'You'd best sober up or I'm off.'

'What're you on about?'

She took his arm and began to walk him down the street. 'I haven't got much time.'

'Where're we goin'?'

'Italy.'

'Italy? You'd have a job leaving Macc.'

She steadied him in an alley and waved the envelope in front of him. 'I've tickets here and passport sheets and a lot more beside. She flapped the paper across his cheeks. 'They say nobody takes notice of passports and even if they do you can say your name's Davenport, they'll be none the wiser. Come on, sober up! It's the only chance either of us is likely to get.'

He lunged forward, but she pushed him away, her temper flaring. 'I'm not in jest, Duncan. You'd better pull yourself together. Are you coming or am I to go by myself?'

A slow understanding dawned and he followed the movement of the hand. 'By God, you really mean it, don't you?'

'I've been trying to tell you. You'll have to decide now. What's here for you except work and the workhouse? What's here for either of us? A man of twenty-eight shouldn't be living with his parents. You're doing 'em no service staying here, nor your brothers neither. They needn't know. Send 'em a letter when you get there.' Her voice rose. 'We'll be rich! Think about it, Davenport's left it all to me! He won't be needin' it neither, where he's gone.'

'Where's that?'

'I'll tell you later. What'll you do, then?'

His eyes hardened again, his befuddled brain struggling to make sense of it all. He gathered himself together. 'We'll do it. And if you're tellin' me lies, I'll take your head off.'

He went in to change and came out wearing his bowler and suit. She took his arm and walked him down the street.

Nerissa knew something was amiss the moment she saw her unlit rooms. From the darkness came the sound of a child wailing and as she climbed from her cab, a constable was waiting. 'Mrs Davenport? I'm afraid it's bad news, madam.'

10

'What?' Francis Birkenshaw's shout cut through the dusty air of Claire's office. 'This is preposterous. Can't you do anything, man?' The solicitor looked at his desk and shook his head helplessly. 'It's no use waving your head about like a bloody organ monkey. Why in the name of God weren't we informed? Surely you had an obligation to tell us?' Claire said something about ethics, and Birkenshaw banged the table with his fist. 'Confound your ethics! Was it ethical to let him cut off my daughter without a penny? The mother of a young child? Is that your notion of ethics?

Nerissa sat tight-lipped by the window. Roddy's chicanery had at first amused her, but as the truth dawned, she saw that all the raving in the world wouldn't turn the clock back. She also knew she was responsible for her own misfortune. It was a superb irony that Roddy, who'd given hours of his life to berating 'her collier', should have spent his last minutes in a canal lock whilst eloping with her maid.

'I should have scratched her eyes out.'

'Scratch her eyes out, scratch out her eyes,' her father mimicked. 'Scratching eyes'll do no good in your situation, scratching eyes'll not fill your purse.'

'At least I'd feel better.'

Claire interrupted with a cough. 'I'm revealing little in informing you this woman is now living abroad. As the law stands, there is little one can do to alter the matter. Mr Davenport's will is clearly in bad taste, but it is nevertheless binding. The effects were Mr Davenport's before his marriage to your daughter, you understand. Shares in Mr Davenport's name provided a generous dividend and was the principal source of your daughter's livelihood. As for the house –'

'You needn't go on, I know all about the house.'

Nerissa looked across at her father. 'What about the house?' Birkenshaw's eyes slid to the window, then to his cane. 'What about my house?' she repeated. 'It still belongs to us, I take it?'

'I'm afraid, Mrs Davenport, your home –' began Claire.

'All right, it's surety,' cut in Birkenshaw.

'Surety?'

'Against the firm. Against the Victoria.'

'So you're telling me the house I thought was a marriage gift is not, in fact, owned by you after all.'

'It's owned all right. By the bloody banks.'

'So I really do have nothing?'

A lingering silence haunted the room. Claire broke the tension with another cough. 'It would be remiss of me not to... I am empowered to dispose of the deceased's estate expeditiously.'

Birkenshaw said: 'And I suppose you expect her to move back in with me if the banks foreclose, which is more than a possibility with the state of business now. She's no longer a child, or hadn't you noticed?'

'Mr Birkenshaw, you'll gain nothing from being abusive to me. I'm merely here to see to the due process of law.'

'You're here to line your pockets, like every other attorney I ever met. As if I hadn't enough on my plate with his name plastered over the papers. Crooks, the lot of you.' He swept from the room, beating a tattoo along the passage with his cane. Nerissa watched the solicitor shuffle his papers into order, then quietly closed the door.

'I think you should be aware of some facts, Mr Claire. First, my father is not a well man. Business is bad, which is partly to blame, but the main reason is that I have never been able to conform to his ideas of what a daughter should be. My marriage was a sham from beginning to end, and I would be lying if I said I regretted my husband's untimely departure in the slightest. Resented, yes; regreted, no. For many years I've had an escort, a lover if you will, and though for a time we parted, status quo has now been resumed –'

'Mrs Davenport, I have no wish to hear about your private life.'

'I'm volunteering it. I have a daughter, Florence. My beau believes she's his. In fact, she grows more like my late husband every day, which would be a matter of infinite curiosity to him since in that department, as in many others, he was incompetent.'

Claire threw his hands up in a gesture of despair. 'Please, Mrs Davenport, your private concerns are a matter for you and your family. Now if you'll forgive me, there are urgent matters demanding my attention.'

'You don't seem to have grasped my predicament.' Her voice broke, but she collected herself. 'I have nothing of my own at all. Roddy was the one with the money. The mill is in recession and likely to end up in the receiver's pocket.' She paused, white-faced. 'I've managed to squirrel away a small amount, enough to make it worth your while to do whatever solicitors do to secure one's estate for those morally entitled to it.'

'What are you suggesting?'

'It's quite clear, I'm willing to bribe you to look after my interests.'

'But don't you understand? The will is irrevocable. I can do nothing. This, this liaison of yours, it would put you in a bad light in court, and make it all but impossible to implement the new Women's Property Act –'

'And what about my husband's own sordid liaison?'

'It may be unfair, Mrs Davenport, but courts tend to view these matters differently in the case of husband or wife. This is not to my liking, but it's a fact.'

'I intend to contest it.'

'Please believe me when I say it will be futile, not to mention a waste of whatever personal resources remain to you. It is very hard, but even were I to accept your – your – I see no way the will could be turned to your advantage. The terms are quite explicit. Your husband had the right to dispose of his own assets as he felt fit. There is nothing anyone can do.'

His agitation struck her as incongruous in the ledger-filled office, with its sense of order and scent of bees-wax. Slowly, she walked to the door. 'Very well Mr Claire, I shall have to get used to living on the streets. After all, thousands do it every day.'

'But your father –'

He stopped abruptly.

'Yes?'

'You must discuss the matter with him–'

Her eyes burrowed into Claire's lowered head. 'Daddy's house. That's mortgaged to the company, too, isn't it?' She struck the ordered desk. 'Isn't it?' He nodded, his eyes closed. 'Well, Mr Claire, thank you. Thank you for everything.'

She left the office and joined her father in the lobby. From a lowering sky, heavy drops began to fall. She put up her umbrella, but furled it against a squall before they stepped into the carriage.

'I blame you for this. You'll be the death of me, Nerissa. I tell you, you'll be the death of me.'

She made no answer. What her father mistook for endurance was emptiness, and throughout the journey his words rebounded through it like balls of dough. It had been her fault. She'd been a wife in name only. It was because of her he'd lost the sarcenet order. From that point, what little reputation the mill had enjoyed had gone downhill. And still she persisted in seeing this – this man. She was a mother now, a woman approaching forty. When was she going to take bloody stock? His rant reached her through the drum of rain on the roof, and he was right.

John Tanbrey sat behind a copy of the *Times* in the Conservative Club. Scattered about the room were local businessmen and shopkeepers, but 'Young Bob' Heath was absent. It was rumoured his wife was ailing, that he was devoting increasing time to her care. Tanbrey found the gossip irrelevant. In fact, since he was advised more than a year ago that 'his personal life had been the cause of some embarrassment', their relationship had deteriorated. A wise precaution would have been to avoid Nerrisa, or to make sure no one got to hear about any future meetings with her. Instead he'd chosen to ignore his employer, and their relationship had gone on as before. When she told him she was pregnant, he had no doubt he was responsible. That Roddy could be the father was laughable, and he had as little concern for the child as he'd had for Matthew, who, at seventeen was coming to the end of his time at school. His imminent homecoming filled John with a kind of dread. Matthew in the house was Ginny in the house, and beneath his reticence the same quiet courage burned across the years.

Three years short of his fortieth birthday, John increasingly saw his position at the colliery and ironworks as going nowhere. Pandora had put money into his pocket, but no more than his due and less than the sums enjoyed by some of those snoring in their wicker chairs around him. He realised with bitterness that his luck was on the wane, that it was impossible, once someone of Heath's ilk had been antagonised, to regain favour. When Nerissa told him Roddy had drowned, that she and her daughter now lived in a couple of rooms in her father's house and that orders at her father's mill were fast drying up, he felt his guardian angel had deserted him.

A local shopkeeper spotted him and came over. 'Evening, Mr Tanbrey. You heard the latest? Urias Ball died this afternoon.' John lowered his paper, which the man took as a sign of encouragement. 'Softening of the brain, they say. I got it first hand from someone I know works down Cheddleton.'

'The asylum?'

'He knows the warders down there, they come into his place off-duty, like. Ay, softening of the brain. I bet you're not sorry to see an end of him.'

Tanbrey shook his paper. 'The assizes should have strung him up before his delusions took hold of him.'

'There again, leaving aside your own case, he must have been crazed. A normal man doesn't start waving guns about, not around here they don't, anyway.' Tanbrey wondered how this giant of a man had come to run a confectioner's, wondered if he'd ever got his fist stuck in a jar of mints. 'What're you having, Mr Tanbrey?'

'Nothing for me, thanks.' He made a pretence of returning to his reading, but coming back from from the bar, the man continued: 'How're you getting on with Mr Heath these days?'

'As well as any man gets on with his employer.'

'Must be nice to be a millionaire.'

'I doubt I'll have that privilege.'

'Three and a half thousand working for him – and that's just the Bull, let alone all the other irons he's got in the fire.'

'So I believe.'

The man sipped his drink, leaving a frothy moustache winking on his upper lip.

'Walton come into the shop the other day.'

'Do I know him?'

'Butler down the Grange. You'll know Heath's having it renovated before he moves in?'

'I heard something to that effect.'

The man brought his mouth closer to Tanbrey's ear. 'Walton reckons there's enough silver in Heath's safe to keep the fleet afloat.' He lowered his voice to a whisper. 'Says old Mrs Heath left her daughter-in-law all her jewellery. It was settled up who had what before she died last year. According to Walton, the safe near his room's crammed with stuff; tiaras, necklaces, all sorts.... fancy having so much stuff you can afford to risk leaving it in an empty house....'

An image of Ginny at their picnic, years ago, suddenly flooded back. *She's got the number on her box. I clean her room, John, and I've seen it....*

The promise of victory in the Sudan was irrelevant to the colliers leaving their cage at the end of a shift, but their ignorance didn't stem a tap-room xenophobia against impertinent Boers, lazy darkies, untrustworthy Germans and anyone else daring enough to contest British rule. Those to whom Cecil Rhodes was no more than a name in newsprint would argue over his resignation as Prime Minister of Cape Colony and loudly assert there was no likelihood of a British government's involvement in the Jameson affair or any other skulduggery. Robert Heath inclined to a less generous view. The failure of Jameson to kick the Uitlanders out of the Transvaal had caused his African holdings to plummet, and a hysterical press persuaded him it was in his interests to take the train to Manchester, where he could seek his stockbroker's advice whether to sell or sit out the storm. Having to make the decision irked him. The recent weather had been unusually bitter, absenteeism was running high at the works and there were pressing matters to attend to. His father had relied on Tanbrey to attend to his business matters, and the arrangement had worked well enough for him not to want to alter it. However, Heath couldn't rid himself of a growing distrust of the man. He pinned it down to the time of Birkenshaw's visit, and it stuck in his craw on hearing the gossip following Davenport's death that Tanbrey was still seeing Birkenshaw's daughter. Heath the businessman had decided to keep Tanbrey on, while Heath the man resented his decision. Industry won – but not to the extent he wanted Tanbrey involved in his private affairs. Starting today, he'd transact his personal business himself, even though Tanbrey would also be in Manchester on firm's business. He decided on a mid-morning train, where there'd be fewer travellers. Leaving London Road shortly before midday, he took a cab to Connaught Chambers and was shown into an office where a man was sharpening a pencil. He beamed as Heath came in, and told him the decanter was in the usual place.

Nerissa dabbed at her lips with a napkin. 'I've not got used to my reduced circumstances, of course, but Claire didn't get his hands on everything. It's surprising how quickly one can search a house when the creditors are snapping at one's heels. I discovered several little items I didn't know he had, and he had no call on my jewellery. Since Papa agreed to letting me a couple of rooms, I might manage to hold on to it. I'd had visions of hawking it around for what I could scavenge. *Sic transit gloria mundi*, as they say.' She smiled up at him over the remains of their meal. 'Do you find my poverty ennobling?'

'You've had too much to drink.'

A stray ringlet trembled on her cheek, and she smoothed it carelessly into place. 'I do wonder at life, don't you? I had a maid who was going to elope with my husband and now I have no husband.'

'Who's looking after the girl?'

'My father's maid. And at no extra charge.'

'From what you say about your father's business, it seems maids will shortly be beyond the reach of both of you.'

'At least we can fall back on fond memories. What memories do you write in your almanac, John? Pit pony injures fetlock in roof fall?' She laughed mirthlessly. 'Sounds like a headline from the Evening News. Note the alliteration. Perhaps I should become a teacher of English literature.'

'Perhaps you should stop making an exhibition of yourself.'

He lapsed into silence. Waiters passed across the room amid the hum of voices.

'I suppose I shouldn't be too harsh,' she said. 'You're gainfully employed, which is more than my dear late husband could boast. And I have a daughter who has inherited none of your characteristics.'

'And what's that supposed to mean?'

She raised her eyebrows, a smirk playing across her face. A clamour came faintly through the window, taking him back to the time he'd followed Urias through the Manchester streets. He'd promised himself that one day he, too, would be important; and still, despite fortune and toil, he'd only been able to put his foot on the first rung of a provincial ladder. He was still unknown, and it rankled and frustrated him.

'I had the dream again,' he said.

'The dream?'

He lit a cigarette, blew the smoke upwards. 'I always wake up in a corridor. I'm there for a reason.' He turned towards her. 'Do you know my brother in America owns a cattle ranch the size of Cheshire? All he did at home was pick stones out of fields. Don't you think that's ironic, all one huge bloody joke?'

He left a small tip and they went upstairs to his room.

Heath shook hands with the stockbroker and collected his coat from the stand. A whiskering of snow was settling on the ledges as he went out and hailed a cab. The news he'd been given had reassured him; he'd been advised the fall in shares was no more than a blip, and they were expected to regain their value before the month was out. Like his father, he seldom changed his mind once it was made up, and it was a rare impulse which now made him halt his cab some way from the station and get out. He wanted time to think. As he walked, he saw why his feet had taken their own decision. He'd had the trouble and expense of getting the Grange ready for his wife, whose health was failing. The possibility he could be a widower before fifty preyed on his mind, and the worry had sharpened other anxieties. He saw the developing Ruhr as a threat to his businesses. There were whisperings of plans to enlarge the fleets of German merchantmen – worse still, to increase German naval tonnage. In the short term, there was little danger in industrial rivalry, but what of the longer term? Would there be an ironworks or a pit left in Britain? The name Robert Heath had been part of the country's lifeblood for half a century, yet the meteor must eventually plummet, no matter how brightly it flew. Then the problem of Tanbrey, nagging at him like a sore tooth. Not only his philandering, but the simmering discontent which seemed to fester about him. He wondered how long it would be before he ran amok. Had he liked him he could have put his other businesses under his wing. God knows, he had no great taste for a sixteen hour day himself, as his father had. The problem was he didn't like Tanbrey, never had. He was walking past a hotel and on the spur of the moment decided to go in. Apart from a few commercial travellers, the place was deserted. He took a seat and waited for the waiter to some over.

'China or India, sir?'

'I'll have the China – and perhaps a newspaper.'

'I think we have the Times, sir. I'll just go and check for you.'

Heath watched the flakes flurry against the pane. In the glow of the fire, he felt comfortably anonymous. Perhaps he should make this his base whenever he came to the city. The waiter brought a tray. 'I'd also like a veal sandwich, could you manage that?'

He settled to the columns: death of Lowthrie while shooting pheasant.... longest serving monarch.... flickers arrive in Britain. Then a voice caught his ear, and he glimpsed a couple leaving the hotel. He thought he recognised them and in his haste to check knocked over his cup.

'Shall I bring you another, sir?'

'No.' The word came sharp, and as the waiter wiped at the stain he forced a smile of apology. 'No, thank you. Sorry about the mess. I thought I saw an old acquaintance of mine just now.' He pressed a florin into the man's hand. 'Take that for your trouble.'

He hardly noticed the journey back. When he reached home, uppermost in his mind was how to deal with Tanbrey. He couldn't sleep until the matter had been resolved. Not only was his employee still engaged in this sordid liaison – he was conducting it in business hours. *His* business hours. He spent part of the next morning telegraphing the banks, warehouses and customers with whom Tanbrey had had dealings over the previous six months. Finding there was little correlation between his expense sheets and time spent transacting work's business failed to surprise him. He should have looked into it earlier. Infidelity and disloyalty were intolerable to him. Had Tanbrey's private life been locally known, his own character would have been brought into disrepute. Perhaps his father would have turned a blind eye, but to him the theft of the firm's time was like taking gold from his pocket. He recalled his father telling him about the incident with Urias Ball. In hindsight, Ball would have been right. It all began to fall into place. Did a manager's wage really run to new carriages and private education? He had little relish for the task in hand, and anything more trivial he would have handed to one of the other directors. This was not trivial.

It was three the next day before the familiar double rap announced Tanbrey's arrival. When their eyes met, Tanbrey immediately read in Heath's face the reason he'd been sent for. Behind the bland blue eyes lay something deeply hostile. Heath placed his pen in the holder and faced his employee across the desk. 'You were in Manchester yesterday?'

'There was the matter of the delay in freighting the Norwegian consignment to Liverpool, if you recall. It's now in hand.'

'Could you tell me the time you arrived?'

'Shortly after eleven. Why do you ask?'

'And it took you the day to transact the business?'

'The better part of it. Is something wrong?'

Heath drew in his breath. 'I was in Manchester myself and happened to see you leaving the Mosley Hotel in Piccadilly in the company of Nerissa Birkenshaw. I think her name has cropped up before.'

'I do believe it has.'

Heath passed a hotel receipt across the desk. Tanbrey gave it a cursory glance. 'While you'll agree we're reasonably generous with our allowances, this doesn't extend to acquaintances. I've no reason to suppose we've not paid out before for what I politely term your social life. Since the fraud is ongoing, I'm curtailing your employment forthwith.'

Heath returned to his papers. A tension hung like a heavy curtain in the air. Tanbrey stood with a sudden movement, toppling his chair. Heath was about to reach for his bell when the younger man, pale with fury, crashed out of the room, slamming the door with force enough to turn the head of every clerk in the outer office. Later, at home, he received an official notice of dismissal, together with a reminder his house was to be vacated before the end of the following month.

While the Grange was being refurbished, Heath had taken up residence at Greenway Bank, leaving Walton and a servant to look after the empty property. A Mr Hibbins was in charge of the alterations, and Walton was happy to act under his direction until the house was made ready for Heaths' return. At night the butler would visit the local inn and pass an hour reminiscing with his cronies. When he'd had a drop too many, he'd also mention that 'Old Bob' Heath's wife had locked a large amount of jewellery in a safe in the butler's pantry, and that her son had left it there. The combination was known only to Heath and his wife. And to John Tanbrey, who some years earlier had taken Ginny at her word and found a pretext to visit Mrs Heath's bedroom while the family were out boating. Her trinket box had given up the number he'd pencilled in his diary.

Despite his liking for ale, Walton did his duty, making a tour of inspection each night, accompanied by his mongrel. If he got in late, he'd do his rounds in the early hours, and one January night it was almost two before he left an unguarded fire and climbed into bed. He usually slept well, but tonight he couldn't sleep and went downstairs. A light smoke was drifting into the vestibule, and his dog began to bark. He tightened his grip on his candle-holder and quickened his step. As he drew near the Oak Room, he could hear the crackle of burning wood. The smoke was more dense now, and caught at his throat, making him cough. He fell against the wainscot, clutching at his chest and dropping the candle. As he struggled to his feet, he was vaguely aware of footsteps on the stairs. He rose unsteadily, wretching violently and tugging at the handle of the locked door.

'Leave it, Mr Walton. Leave it!'

The servant had an arm around his shoulders and was guiding him to an outer door below the stairs. As they reached the terrace a gush of flame licked through the open doorway, and they drew further back, the dog howling distractedly from the lawns. From one of the windows came a leaping yellow tongue. Walton was the first to find his voice. 'Get the brigade! Heath'll have my guts for this!'

It took thirty minutes for the Congleton Brigade to arrive. Flames tinged the low cloud scarlet, and a bitter breeze fanned the flames. Before dawn the inferno had spread to the central rooms. Half a mile away, the townspeople dressed and followed the clamour of bells.

Tanbrey awoke with a start and drew back the curtain. Through the window a mare's tail of fire hung in the northern sky. He dressed hurriedly and left the house. Pulling down his hat to hide his face, he joined the groups moving towards the glow. Lights shone from the roadside houses, and beyond the church funnels of dusky smoke rose above the trees. He recognised a local constable holding back a group about to enter the grounds. 'Let the lads from the Brigade tackle it, get back to your beds.... there's nothing you can do here.' A figure emerged from the drive and pushed through the crowd, brushing against Tanbrey's arm as he blundered past. John dug into his coat pocket and held out a flask. 'Here, have a spot of this.'

The man took a gulp and wiped his mouth.

'What's the situation?'

'It's too far gone, they might as well throw snuff at it.'

'Is the whole building alight?'

'Only the middle part, yet. All they can do is damp the ends down, stop it from spreading. They're using water from the lake.'

'What of the furniture?'

'They managed to get a piano out. I think they rescued a picture of old man Heath. Broke a Minton vase.... I'm done in, I'll have to go.'

But John was hardly listening. He knew what he had to do. 'Keep the flask, you deserve it.'

He pushed through the bystanders and moved away from the entrance. A hundred yards away the road was clear. A coal cart stood in the lane, and as he was passing it he took an empty bag from the back. Above the trees a shower of sparks danced in a gash of sky. He reached the road which climbed to the moor and pushed through a gap into a moonlit glade from which he could look down on the scene below. He knew the house, each nook, each cranny. Now he'd pay himself back. No one would ever dismiss him again. He turned down the path which led arrow-straight from the Grange to Moor Top. A sulphurous glow etched the deodars Bateman had planted, and as he reached the gardens he could feel a hot breath on his face. The untouched wing faced him. No one would see him. Only a lunatic would risk his life. Maybe he was a lunatic. He didn't know, didn't care. A leafless wisteria clung to the trellis and he climbed it to what was Maria Bateman's first floor room. Standing on the coping, he aimed a kick at the lower pain. A dull warmth struck through the gap as he climbed in. The wall shone a sullen red – or did he imagine it? From the blazing heart of the house came a drone of water, a crash of beams. He took the narrow stairs two at a time, a handkerchief to his face, his sleeves pulled across the back of his hands. The butler's door had jammed, and he kicked viciously at the panelling until it gave. A surge of heat followed him into the room. It didn't matter. Not now. The grey face of the safe shone against the wall. The dial was hot to the touch as his fingers found it. He opened his sack.

It was then he remembered his dream.

11

Deakin waylaid Charlie as he was about to leave. Guessing what Deakin wanted to ask him about, he said : 'I've done nothing recently.'

'What? A talented cove like yourself? I'd have thought you'd be turning 'em out left, right and centre.'

'Neville, I've to be getting back, it's gone seven.'

Deakin grinned. 'You want to get yourself out, enjoy yourself more.' He clapped Charlie on the back. 'Just because you've had no luck to date doesn't mean it's lost, you know. Remember the king and the spider? It's all a case of persistence.'

'It's a case of falling asleep in the chair.'

He left with his partner's 'think about it' following him down the street. Why was Deakin still keen to be involved in his designs? The ones he'd let him have had been returned and stood behind the wardrobe. Either he wasn't good enough, or what he did wasn't wanted. In any case, since his marriage six years ago there were more pressing demands on his time. And Mary had never had any interest in what he did. She might even have resented it; he couldn't tell, with talk between them limited to the odd word across the cruet. He sometimes felt he'd lived a lifetime in his thirty-four years. He'd grown used to his wife's dark lethargy, her relief in bouts of hysteria and the frenzied love-making which brought her no relief. He could have tolerated it had she loved him. Not even loved, but needed. But she'd nothing to give, either to him or to Hannah, and now, in her second pregnancy, there'd still be nothing. He found solace in his childhood memories, toy with the coin Bevis had given him, recall the veins running through the farmer's wrists, the frayed cuffs and eyes narrowed in kindness. Then there'd be Caulton, his high voice echoing through the school room, *On either side the river lie, Long fields of barley and of rye.... Think of the rhythm.... dusky red.... setting sun....* Would anyone miss him? Yes, Hannah would miss him, and for her sake he stayed.

He no longer questioned his wife's absences, but once he'd returned from work to find her out and his daughter locked, soiled and crying, in their room. He'd cleaned and fed her, changed her blankets and lulled her to sleep. When his wife came in he found his thumbs at her throat and five years of misery coursing down his cheeks. She'd been 'walking out', that's what she'd told him. And it was then he realised she couldn't care. She could lead her life, he his, but if ever she left his child again he'd strangle her. Next day he saw a neighbour, who'd offered to send her girl around whenever they needed 'a bit of help'. From then on he'd bought his reassurance for a halfpenny a time.

It was only on Sundays she seemed more settled, taking care to hang out her best clothes the night before, looking over her bonnet and gloves before putting them on the table ready for church. She'd take care with Hannah's feed, chat about events in the neighbourhood. The service was her relief, the rest of the week a pall to be fought through.

When he got home, he knew she was happy. Hannah's clothes lay strewn over the living room and Mary was kneeling on the rug trying to force a doll on her. 'Well, here's daddy, Hannah, say hello to daddy. I'll get us something to eat. What would you like, Charlie? I bought some sheep's brains. I'm spent up. I'll get some tea. You'll never guess what happened here today, would he, Hannah? Shall we tell him? He'll never guess. She said her first numbers. Tell daddy, come on, one, two three. I'd better get some tea. Brains all right, Charlie? Tell daddy, Hannah; one, two three, four....' There was a sense of her tripping, each thought coming on the heels of the next, her movements like those of a small bird. Her heightened mood continued throughout their meal, when she told him Will had been taken ill.

'I thought I'd already told you, Charlie.'

'Of course you've not told me.'

'I've a telegram somewhere.' She sifted through the mantelpiece and brought the paper out. As she handed him the note she began to sing.

'When did this come?'

'Can't remember, Charlie.'

'Late, early, morning, afternoon?' He was already reaching for his coat. 'It's of no account. I'll not be back tonight. You'd best tell Deakin I might not be back tomorrow an' all.' He kissed Hannah. 'You might have told me –' he began, but what was the use? 'Look after her.'

'We'll keep the bed warm, won't we, Hannah, keep father's bed warm. Know what I mean, Charlie?'

She winked suggestively as he went out, slamming the door. Couples were parading along the High Street, and above them the Town Hall flag fluttered in the evening breeze. He'd hoped to find a carrier's cart, but the road was deserted and he'd climbed the hill to Chell before a coal merchant offered him a lift. When he got to Moor Top the light had faded, and as he reached the Moel he saw that nettles had taken over the garden, and weeds were already encroaching along the path. When he pushed open the door, the sickly-sweet smell of damp he remembered from boyhood met his nose. John was waiting for him. A downstairs bed had been made up, and it was an effort for Will to lift his arm from the blankets.

'I'm glad you come, Charlie. Your brother's been 'ere since –' He faltered as he caught his breath. 'Put a shovel on if you're cold.'

His eyes grew accustomed to the firelight. John went over to the window and looked across at the hills silhouetted against the blush of approaching night. 'You know, Charlie, I don't think I've been up to our old room since I left home.' He looked across at his father, now sunk in a rattling sleep, and they went upstairs. Their beds had been sold; old newspapers lay on a cane chair, a saucer with encrustations of wax on the sill. A flush of mist was creeping across the lower land.

'He told me, Charlie.'

'What?'

'Your dubious parentage. Luckily I'm past the age where anything surprises me. I didn't really know Bevis Benersley. Has Bill ever been told?'

'Not as far as I know.'

'At least it proves mothers can be as weak as the rest of us.' He was still at the window. 'He's dying.'

'I know.'

'Three score years and ten. I never thought he'd get so far. How's this tilery of yours?'

'It's a living.'

'And the family? I hardly know them. Mary, the girl?'

'Hannah's fine.'

'And your wife?'

'She's – she's fine, too. What of young Matthew?'

'Look, if ever you're in want –' He took out a card. 'My new address. No use trying to read it in this gloom.' Charlie put it in his pocket. 'Did you hear about the fire?'

'What fire?'

'It seems it was a faulty flue. He's already building again. I expect he's quite comfortable for the while at Greenway Bank.'

'Who're you talking about?'

'Why, Heath, of course. Most of the Grange burned down.' Their worlds had drifted apart. He wondered where their fates lay, John's in wealth and respectability, his in – in what? 'I've no cause to drink his health. It wasn't long since he dismissed me.'

'Why?'

'I don't believe we saw eye to eye. Had his father still been alive, by now I'd have been – well, no matter. I don't suppose you knew Francis Birkenshaw? He's was a sort of – I suppose you'd call him an absent acquaintance of mine.'

'What's an absent acquaintance?'

'One you never clap eyes on. He owned a mill in Macclesfield. Now he's the late Mr Birkenshaw and owns nothing. Seems he suffered a seizure in his carriage. The coachman had travelled miles before he discovered he was the sole survivor of the journey. Apart from the horse, that is.'

'I'm not inclined to joking at a time like this.'

'He'd the good sense to marry his daughter into money and wasn't to know Mr Money would end up in the canal. To add insult to injury, Birkenshaw's mill went into bankruptcy, another fact which no doubt hastened his demise. Both house and mill put in the hands of the receiver and his daughter and grandchild moved to a derelict cottage on what remains of his estate.'

'I don't know why you're telling me all this, I didn't even know him.' They fell silent. Charlie asked, 'Who was it sent the telegram?'

'Ellen Benersley. I'm ashamed to say she called more often than I.'

'She's been here today?'

'She left when I arrived, about four hours ago.'

A feeble hacking came from below. The western flare had died to a gleam, and a stillness settled on the house. The years had been like the firey line on the hill, hemmed in by childhood and an unknown future. Before they turned back to the stairs, John asked: 'Would your wife care for an item of jewellery that came my way?'

'As much as the next woman, I dare say.'

He passed over a box. 'Don't bother opening it now, give it her when you get back. As a surprise.'

They went down. John pulled on his coat. He'd left his trap in a neighbour's yard. If Will's condition worsened, Timmis in the village had said he'd go for the doctor. Charlie closed the door behind him, but despite his weariness he couldn't rest. Behind the glass, squalls were springing up, buffeting the walls with cold. He got up to break a coal, and in the firelight saw that Will was awake.

'I've told nobody but yourself, Charlie.'

He looked at Will's cushioned head and tried to imagine him tending the sturks. 'What about?'

'I've told nobody about the house. The rector wrote it, it's all legal.'

'Get yourself some rest, you'll be running about like a turkey-cock come next week.' Will crooked his finger. 'Something you want, is it, in the cupboard?' He tugged open a drawer. 'Something in here, is it?'

'Top'un.'

Charlie's fingers closed on an envelope. 'Is this what you're after?'

The man nodded. 'Undo it.' Charlie peeled back the flap. The penned lines danced in the candle-light. 'It'll be yours when I'm gone.'

'You're leaving the house to me?'

'It were my father's, now it's yours.'

'But – what of John and Bill?'

'John's all right.... the other's got his farm. I'll rest easier if you have it....'

'They're blood, they've more of a right than me.'

Will tried to lever himself up but slipped back into the pillow. 'You don't want to blame me, Charlie. Them times I took against you.... it wasn't for yourself, understand? It was more me, more against me. I should have reconciled myself to – well, Benersley being your father, it was best forgot.'

There was a further scattering of words, a mention of his wife. When he fell asleep, Charlie went back to his chair. The last thing he heard was the clock chiming the hour.

He rested by a wall, looking out to the distant hills. God didn't live in arches and alabaster, he thought. Where he stood real heavens whirled. He took out John's box and looked again at the silver earrings set in their velvet cushion before putting them back in his pocket. His mind was too full to wonder why John had given them to him.

At the finger post he took the turning to Three Elms. Mrs Benersley was in the yard, switching at a cow, and the hens scattered as he came up. 'Charlie? What're you doing here? Ellen, it's Charlie!' She clanked across the yard on her pattens. 'It is you, isn't it? I can tell you anywhere.' She stepped back. 'My, I don't think we've clapped eyes on you since your wedding. I hear tell you had a little girl. By, Charlie, I never thought I'd see you a father. Ellen! She's about somewhere. Come on in and I'll put the kettle on.'

As she twittered through the door he noticed for the first time the tight tufts of snow-white hair. She held his arm while she put on her indoor shoes. Stalks of straw matted the scullery, a hen pecked at the slope stone. 'Come you in, sit down – no, sit down there where it's warm. Winter and summer are all the same in these sorts of houses, you should know that by now.' A gate creaked across the yard. 'Oh, that'll be Ellen now.' She began to wrench open the window but it had jammed. 'He never did 'em while he were here, so he's not likely to do 'em now, is he? Ellen!' She beckoned urgently behind the glass.

Ellen was unfastening her bonnet as she came in. Her dark, golden hair hung across her shoulder in a plait. The broad face with its pale blue eyes and wide lips would still draw glances.

'Hello, Charlie, I see you've made yourself at home.'

The knowing smile still lingered faintly. He cleared his throat self-consciously. 'I've some news.'

The old lady said, 'It's Will, isn't it? Ellen said he'd not been well.'

'He passed on, Mrs Benersley. I've made the arrangements. It was congestion of the lung. I came as soon as I could. Maybe I should've come to see him more.... it was difficult, what with work and family.'

'You mustn't blame yourself,' Ellen said, 'he had a good few years, more than many. Now I don't know what you're upsetting yourself for, mother.'

Mrs Benersley wiped her eyes. 'I've made a nice sponge. Get him a slice, Ellen. Oh, there's the kettle. Just a minute, Charlie, and I'll get the tea.'

They talked about the time he'd helped Bevis on the farm, their schooldays, the times since. Doris sat in her rocking chair while the cats stretched before the fire, then fell asleep part way through the conversation before waking to continue a sentence. She began to snore.

'Doris didn't know about the telegram, I thought it best not to upset her.'

'It's all for the best. Thanks for taking the trouble.'

'It was no trouble. It's like old times, Charlie.'

'There's a lot of water under the bridge.'

'Not for me. There's been no change for me. I can't see as there ever will be.'

He said: 'You ought to have had a family by now. You ought to have married years ago.'

'Maybe I'm not the marrying kind. I can't see no one leaping the farmyard gate, can you?'

'There must've been someone.'

'All they want is someone to yoke to the cart. I'm better off alone. Anyway, I'll be set up here, I'll be my own boss.' She was thinking of a time when the old woman would no longer be there. 'We get casual men in, we couldn't run without. I don't think there's been a one I could've taken to.' She glanced at the sleeping woman and lowered her voice. 'I go up to Leek every Sunday, never miss. I take a few flowers. She'd be nineteen, now. Just imagine it, Charlie! Quite the little lady.... D'you still hear from your Bill?'

'When I went up Will's he'd sometimes have a letter. He's doing all right. He's got a girl. She'll be about seven, now. He sent a picture. I suppose I'll come across it when I sort out the stuff. You know he married a second time?'

She forced a smile, shaking her head. 'So you never did become that artist, Charlie. Maybe you and me are crossed by the same star, except you're married with a family.'

'Ay, I've got my family.'

He couldn't bear being drawn to talk about his marriage and reached in his pocket for the will, throwing out John's box instead. The silver earrings spilled across the floor and she bent to pick them up. 'My, Charlie, you always were a dark horse. They must have cost a fortune. They're lovely. Are they for your wife?'

'You have them. They were in an old drawer at home, must have been mother's. She would've wanted them to go to someone she knew. She never knew Mary.'

'Oh, Charlie, are you sure?' She tilted her head to clip them on and got up to look in the mirror. 'They're beautiful. Do you know that's the first present you ever gave me? You're sure you don't want your wife to have them?'

'They're yours. I'll bring you a necklace next time.'

She gave her high, knowing laugh, waking up the old woman. 'You still here, Charlie? Ellen's been telling me about that friend of her's, that Jane, living with some man or other. They'd 've shaved her head in my day. Have a bit of sponge, Charlie.'

'He's already had two slices. Are you trying to fatten him up so's his wife won't know him?'

'Has he? You ought to have said. There's some nice rabbit, just wants boiling up. We make do, you know. Poor Will. We'll all be there soon enough.'

'I'll stay till after the funeral, if that's all right. I'll send a telegram home.'

'Will your wife come?' Ellen asked.

'It's not the easiest journey.'

'Leek's your nearest place for a telegram,' cut in Doris. 'There's young Douglas Willowbeck'll run there and back for a ha'penny. I'll get the bed aired.'

When she'd gone, Charlie gave Ellen the will to read. 'So you're a householder. I bet you never thought you'd be richer by a house when you got back. What're you going to do?'

'Maybe I should think of splitting it. John and Bill are more entitled, being blood.'

'You're blood too, on your mother's side. It's yours, Charlie, left to you. You'll have to put it out to rent same as Jane Cowlishaw, it'll bring you something in.'

'I'll think about it. I might sell it. I'll have to give it some thought.' An urge to move away from his own affairs overwhelmed him. 'What's this I hear about your friend giving up the marriage contract?'

'Jane doesn't give a rap what folks think, she'll go her own way, chance what. She's political an' all. She'd have been a Member of Parliament if she'd been born wearing trousers. This Eric's been pestering her to marry him for ages and now she's agreed to share his rooms without the trouble of banns.'

'And is he pleased?'

'I think he'd rather have that than her living miles off. Maybe he's hoping to change her mind. Mother says they're living in sin. What's sin? Just a word to keep us on our toes, that's all. Maybe the mill closing's got something to do with it. She's worked there for a time.'

'What mill?'

'You wouldn't know, it's in Macclesfield. It were never up to much in the first place, according to Jane. There were a lot of funny business at the top, and now he's died of a seizure or something.'

'Who?'

'This Birkenshaw who ran it. I only know snatches. Jane says there's a concern interested in takin' it over, but it's all rumours. Funny name. Pandora. D'you remember the story about Pandora's box, when she opened it all her griefs come flooding out?'

He was going to mention John telling him about Birkenshaw when Mrs Benersley came downstairs. 'It's all ready, now. My, it must've been a tryin' time for you, Charlie. I know he wasn't your real father, but he reared you alongside his own. I wonder if Bevis is listening? Ellen, we'd best get our clothes ironed if we're going to the funeral.' She pattered into the small back room, berating the hens as she would a boy stealing apples. 'I'll fetch some greens out of the garden. Ellen, make sure there's water in the range.'

Ellen asked him what he was going to do with himself, and he said he'd see about the telegram, look around the farm. As she got up, she held out her hands. 'Touch them, Charlie. Hard, aren't they, just like leather. They're more like a man's hands now, and they used to be soft and dainty. D'you know, I think if I'd my time again I'd have gone somewhere. Australia, maybe, or Canada. You get hands like this round here. You can let your nails grow in a telegraph office.'

They sat into the night. Doris snored and woke to continue a point she'd made before while the fire popped and the cats stretched across the hearth. Ellen had changed into a cotton dress. He knew her eyes were on him, knew without knowing how that she had a vicarious image of family. Perhaps she could shut loneliness out, like the threat of insolvency. He knew he'd brought with him a sense of the completeness they both lacked.

'Still got the old coin?

'Ay, still got it. Maybe it'll bring me luck one day.'

'You've had plenty already.'

'It'll be strange, Will not being there.' He stared for a moment into the fire, then got up. 'I've a mind to take a stroll before I turn in.'

'At this hour?'

'There's a moon.'

'Where's your scarf?'

'I don't need one.'

She rummaged in a drawer. 'Put this on.'

He stood to have it tied as if he were a schoolboy, her heavy frame comforting and serene. The dogs padded after him as far as the gate where she'd sung her song years before. The lane twisted in the starlight, the blanched fields shadowed by trees and hedgerows. It took him an hour to reach Rudyard, and he breathed in the solitude, letting the complications of his life dissolve in the lake below him.

When he got back the house was quiet. He pushed the door to and got into bed. When he awoke it was still dark. His ears had picked up a sound. She seemed to drift towards him in the moonlit room. She'd combed her hair loose, and it made a pale halo around her face and shoulders. She knelt by him, reached towards him. 'Charlie, is it as bad as that?'

She'd known all along. He began a muffled sobbing. She brought her head to his, and he caught the dull gleam of silver at her ear. 'I never should have married her, it was a mistake.'

She shushed him like a child, rocking back and forth with him, cradling his head. 'We're two of a kind, you and me. Neither of us realised it, did we? You thought I was more your sister, and I thought you were there for teasing and coaxing.' She turned to him. 'Remember when Bevis died, when I came to you? I knew then, but you didn't. You do now, though, don't you? I saw it earlier, in your eyes.'

He felt her lips on his forehead, then on his lips, the weight of her against him. She drew the gown over her shoulders and pressed his hand to her full breast. Pleasure gripped her immediately, and he reached up to her, to her scent, her body, most to her wanting him; not only to make love to him but to love him after their love making had ended. He took off his trunks and and gently touched her. She let out a satisfied sigh. He could feel her opening beneath him like a flower too long in bud. A steady course, like a level road, opened before him, and he felt a growing warmth, her nails hard against his skin. He came with a drawn sob of orgasm. From outside a cockerel cried.

In the dim light he could see she was smiling; not a smile of triumph or gratitude, but of completeness. He rolled off the bed, pulled on his trunks and sat with his back to the bed-rail, silent.

'I shall have to go back.'

'I know.'

'I've Hannah to think about and Mary's expecting her second.' He felt her hand in his. 'She's in no state to be deserted.'

'Charlie, I know. If you like, just look on what we've done as a token, like the act of a good friend. I know you're married. I know it's a sin in the eyes of the world, but so's being denied what any other woman takes for granted. I don't mean the sex. I mean a soul-mate. I half convinced myself I didn't need one, because I had to. I'm not unhappy. More like a cart without shafts. It'll still bear churns, but there's a part missing.'

She reclipped an earring which had fallen on the bed. 'I don't want to use you,' he said. 'I feel as if I've used you.'

'We used each other. Folks have a right to find happiness the best way they can.' Her hair tumbled across his shoulders. Daylight was strengthening. 'I'll tell you something, shall I, Charlie? I love you.'

'Don't say it, you don't know what you're saying.'

She fell silent, stroked his hand. 'We've never been honest with ourselves. If we had – well....' She left the bed. He could sense her mood changing. She said, with the old amusement in her eyes, 'Apart from anything else, you're better than your brother.'

She left him, but instead of going back to her room pulled on her outdoor clothes and went to feed the fowl. Without wishing to, he slept. When he got up, the sun was already warm and from the hearth rose the smell of frying bacon.

When he got back his neighbour's girl was looking through the window. Hannah ran to him and he swept her up and kissed her, holding her to him.

'Oh, Mr Tanbrey, something's happened, what I don't rightly know. Mrs Tanbrey had to go down the Police Station.'

'What for?'

'I hope it's not bad news.'

He wondered if it had something to do with her brothers, or her father, or his uncle, aunt or one of his cousins. He discarded the idea. He rarely saw them now. What had she done? Hannah clung to his leg until the girl coaxed her away. And Hannah was safe. That was his consolation, whatever else was wrong.

The Police Station lay off the square, with a patch of rough ground in front and a Black Maria parked by the wall. A ruddy-faced officer stood behind the desk.

'I believe my wife's in here. Mary Tanbrey.'

The man nodded down the passage and bent to his sheet. 'Door to your right.'

She was sitting across from two men, one in grey serge, the other in uniform. The urgent clanging of a tram came through the high window.

The man in the suit was scratching his cheek, rasping the stubble. He looked questioningly across the table and gestured to a chair. 'Mr Tanbrey, if you'd care to take a seat.' Her eyelids were red, dark red, almost purple. 'Mr Tanbrey, I look on this as a domestic affair. Are you – do you know the circumstances?'

'What circumstances? What are you talking about?'

'Mrs Tanbrey, if you'd like to speak privately to your –' Mary shook her head absently. 'The fact is, Mr Tanbrey, we've had your wife in to identify a body. We pulled a lad out of a marlhole... it seems there's been an accident. We haven't done with our enquiries yet, but we think he got a cramp. The water's getting on for sixty feet there – '

'Am I supposed to be making sense of this?'

'The fact is, your wife – she's formally identified the lad. I'm afraid there's no doubt about it. He's your wife's son.'

She was staring hollow-eyed at the scuffed dado. At one time there'd been a door, and a strip of dark plaster marked its outline. The man in uniform said, 'If I were you, I'd take your wife home. She's had a nasty shock. We can drive you back if you don't mind waiting till we get a respectable conveyance. It'd not do to be seen in the Maria.'

He heard himself decline the offer. She turned to him, eyes sunk in puce sockets. 'Shall we go, Charlie?'

She rose like an old woman, leaned on his shoulder for support. They left the room and pushed into the sunlit street.

For a week she hardly spoke. He was at his wit's end, didn't know what to do. The act of going on surrounded by the debris of his marriage seemed obscene. One night, as they lay awake, he heard her say: 'I was seventeen when Tommy was born. The father was married with four to bring up. He'd no intention of leaving his wife. It's no one you know. Somebody I met. You've a right to know where I got to.' She grew suddenly assertive. 'I used to go and see how Tommy was bearing up. He never was too strong, but I had hopes he might make something of himself. He'd been taken from me and never should've been. I could've brought him up. It didn't need his wife sticking her oar in, spiteful bitch!' She'd held her hand to her mouth to dull the noise of her weeping. 'They took him off me. He was only a baby. It was all covered up. I kept my respect and he kept his son. Our son! And I was left to scurry over when they gave me leave, set a watch by me, you can see him on such and such at half past seven. They've crucified me, Charlie!

'There was always something I could give him I could never give Hannah. There was always something.' She'd given a reproachful glare. 'When I heard about somebody being drowned, I never guessed it was him. He was a good swimmer, it was the last thing I'd expect. There's no end larking round them marl holes chance what notices they stick up. I don't know what they see in 'em, filthy pits they are, half the works' privvies emptying in 'em. That's what devilment cost him, cost him his life. It was when I saw his father's name in the paper. He'd already been to see him, no mention of me. When I went down the morgue, they wouldn't have it I was his mother. All these years and they kept it close. No one ever knew. I threatened I'd dredge it all up if they didn't let me see him. He didn't want the scandal, did he? Nor her neither.'

He wondered if she was aware of him beside her. 'They'd brushed back his hair and closed his eyes. He had a tinge to his face, but you could see Tommy there – oh, yes, he was there all right, just as if he was about to sit up and give me one o' those cheeky grins of his, "nice to see you, mother, what kept you so long?" Course, it leaked out. The police had to have details. Serves him right. I hope it finishes him off, him and his brazen wife, so hoity-toity, butter wouldn't melt in her mouth. She'll make his life hell. Appearances, that's all she cared about. She didn't give a rap for Tommy. She didn't give a rap for anyone but herself.'

'She must've cared,' he said quietly, 'seeing as she brought him up.'

'That was her way of punishing me. I'd been with her husband, so she'd make sure I couldn't mother my own child, no matter what it cost her. They were all against me from the start....'

As the weeks turned to months, he found himself thinking about Ellen, with her good humour and the placid ritual of her day. He felt no jealousy.

Mary had known the man before she met him. He'd become no more than a prop, someone to prevent her sinking. Why hadn't she told him? What other skeletons were there? She'd destroy him in the end. Yet how could she, when Mr Holmes sat looking up at him from the table? How could he smell the tile-oven's stink when he was trekking the wastes of Africa with Quartermain?

One afternoon he'd called at the stationer's and left with brushes, paper and a new box of colours. At quiet intervals he began again to paint away his life. He didn't seek approval or understanding. A new simplicity echoed the quietness he sought, and he found the energy, sometimes working until midnight when the house was still, to add to his portfolio. The phase passed, and the space behind his wardrobe received its last piece.

He'd toyed with the idea of spending a week-end with Ellen, but couldn't bring himself to neglect Hannah. Mary's absences had grown fewer since Tommy's death, but there were still times she wasn't at home to get his tea after his day's work. The bond between Hannah and himself strengthened. It was he who taught her her words, spooned balsam when she had a cough and applied comfrey to a bruised knee. He was now living a life for himself and his daughter. He hadn't even told his wife he owned the Moel and Will's death was ignored amid the bric a brac of her daily life. His visit to Three Elms, his time with Ellen, Mary knew nothing of any of it and if she had known she wouldn't have cared.

They christened their son Richard. His uncle and aunt, Dick and Gertrude and Mary's mother and father filled the front pew, otherwise the church was empty. Afterwards, the party made its way to his mother-in-law's, Charlie carrying the bassinet, Hannah tottering at his side. After they'd eaten Dick made an excuse to walk off the meal and Charlie joined him. On the far side of the canal the trees were already speckled with the first tints of autumn. A bargees' inn faced a solitary terrace across the water, the road, roughly surfaced with shard and grit, furrowed by lumbering wagons.

'What'll it be, Charlie?'

'Just a small one.'

'Right, a pint and a half and something for yourself.' The barmaid, smiled and levered the pump. 'Well, Charlie lad, how's it feel to be a father second time round?'

'I haven't had chance to find out yet.'

'Your trouble's just beginning.'

'I've enough trouble as it is.'

'You don't know the meaning of the word. Did I tell you I'm in the Sally Army, now, blowing for victory?'

'And what's Gertrude say ?'

'What can her say? I keep telling her, I'm not in your way, am I?'

He downed his drink in a gulp. He was thinner than Charlie remembered, his jacket flapping about his chest like bunting. 'D'you still see Bertha and Bessie?'

'I don't see much of anybody, living over the other end o' the city. Bertha's got four now, so she's not likely to have time on her hands either.'

'What about Bessie?'

'She's down Middleport. Mother said she was having problems with her hands. It's the lead they put in them glazes, you never know what the bloody bosses get up to.'

They went out. A lane crossed both canal and railway. A waste of tile tips and broken cables struck through the hawthorn, with disused quarries cut from the hillside. For a time they shared a tense Sunday quiet, until Dick said: 'Come on, spit it out. What's on your mind?'

'You heard about Mary's lad, this son of hers who got drowned?'

'There's not much doesn't get 'round in the end. Look, you mustn't take it amiss what I'm tellin' you. We knew the Heathcotes, just nodding terms, living nearby. Well, like I said, the word gets around. It always does.'

'What word, Dick?'

'What's the point in raking over the past? We might all be dead next week.'

'You knew, didn't you? You knew about this lad of hers?'

'There was talk.'

'More than talk.'

Dick turned to face him. 'Charlie, I'll be frank with you, and don't take it the wrong way. There was talk your wife had a – a reputation, like. No one wanted to say. It could have been tittle-tattle, anyway. Would it have made any difference?'

'It might.'

'Be honest. You were smitten, like many a man before. It would've made not one jot chance what I said.'

'Maybe you're right. Shall we go back while it's still light?'

They walked on in silence. 'You'll have to come over some time,' Dick was saying, sensing the heaviness between them. 'I'll teach you how to blow a cornet.'

'I should've learned a while back, it might have kept me out of mischief.'

By the time they returned, a chill was creeping up from the valley.

Since their first meeting, Deakin had fewer designs to put to Paskell and what had been a mutually attractive deal was floundering. Deakin's wife, who hadn't known what was going on and even if she had would have condoned it, had welcomed their move to the better side of town. Her husband had enough irons in the fire to shore up his income and had never been averse to fanciful accounting and the odd batch of tiles which went astray. Even so, it peeved him that the business he'd floated on Charlie's back had come to a close, and that his wife was now having to work in the offices of a local pot-bank. She'd sacrificed a family for a nice home and a piano neither of them could play, looked on Deakin to provide and sulked when he didn't. He was surprised when Charlie told him unexpectedly he'd taken up his brushes again and showed him his latest ideas, but his smile turned quickly to disappointment.

'Is this all you've got, Charlie? Where do you hide the *real* stuff?'

'That is the real stuff.'

'You'll have to get him to do better than this, Mrs Tanbrey.'

'It's nothing to do with me, he's enough to do around the house without wasting his time on that.'

Deakin flicked through the sheets while Charlie watched him curiously. 'You don't seem very impressed.'

'It's not that I'm not impressed, it's not that at all. Well, tell a lie, it's – well, I can't bear to see a talent thrown away. I only wish I had a tenth of your skill with a brush. This'll never see the light of day. Can you see it in somebody's kitchen? Or this?

'If I'm as good as you say I'd be doing it for a living by now.'

Deakin shook his head. 'Knock some sense into this man's head, will you, Mary? It's just a matter of time, Charlie. Keep on and you'll get there. It's no use blowin' hot and cold. You've to know the market and keep everything steady, one or two a night, then everybody knows where they stand. That's business, young man. Be businesslike, give folk what they want.'

'What're you going on about, Neville? I can't see me making a fortune, chance what.'

'Well, you've hit the nail there, Charlie. I'm interested, like I always have been. Designs are no use to us, not being set up for the fancy end, but there's nothing to stop you freelancing and making a bit extra while we're turning over the reds, like I always told you. I promised you I'd hawk your stuff around and I'm still trying to get your feet on the ladder. I thought that's what friends are for, but I'm wasting my time with this. Get back to your flowers and your cottage gardens and such, that's what folks're after. I bet the last time most folks saw real flowers was when they got wed, so they want them on the wall instead so they don't need watering.' He gave his laugh. 'There was somebody I met at the last trade do showed a distinct interest in your stuff. If their order book hadn't been full, I don't doubt I could've got you a start. I'll try'em again, but not with this latest stuff of yours, flowers that don't look like flowers and orange trees like lollipop sticks. You might as well tear 'em up and start again. Not that they're no good in your eyes, Charlie. Maybe only brilliant artists can see it, hey, Mary? But sales aren't made to brilliant artists, they're made to Joe Scroggins with a dog cart down the road. Isn't that so, Mrs Tanbrey?'

Charlie watched him go from behind the parlour nets, then went to mend a broken chair.

12

'Shh, class, Marian has something she wants to say.' Miss Whittle, a prim, erect woman in her early thirties, waited for the hush. 'First, put up your hand anyone thinks they know Marian's secret.' Miss Whittle allowed her eyes to wander around the room, Ten Rules for Christian Living pinned to the pine walls, Prairie Grasses We Collected gummed to a deal table, a flip calendar on the desk. 'Yes, Isaac?'

'Her Pa gone down sick.'

Marian shook her plaits.

'I'm afraid you're wide of the mark there, Isaac, you must have a melancholy turn of mind. What about you, Nicole?'

'Ma'am, I –' The girl turned away, sniggering into her hand in embarrassment. The class grew more attentive.

'Well, Nicole, when you've recovered from your hysterics?'

'Beg pardon, Ma'am, Marian's gonna have a baby.'

It took a second for the roar to erupt. Marian sat impassively, a half-smile on her lips. 'I think you got that wrong, Nicole, but we all know what you meant to say.'

The girl whispered the correction into her lap. Miss Whittle smiled thinly. 'I'd say that's one hundred percent better. And do you have any idea what your Mommy's going to call her new baby, Marian?'

'She's not made up her mind yet, Ma'am. She says she doesn't mind what so long as it's all right.'

A boy raised an arm. 'Please, Ma'am, does Marian know whether it's gonna be a boy or a girl?'

'Why, no one knows. Do you know whether a cow on your father's ranch is going to have a bull calf or a cow calf?'

'We sure know after it's been born.'

There was further disorder from those who understood the joke. Miss Whittle let it run its course. 'So I want you all to be thinking about a gift for the new baby when the day arrives. I already know what my gift is going to be.' She quelled their questions. 'No, I intend to keep it a secret, and you must keep yours a secret, too. Now, the history of great American Presidents. Jacob Wallis, have you learnt your Presidents? Come out here and you can tell them to class.'

A straw-haired boy went over to the box Miss Whittle kept in the corner, stepped up and fixed his eyes on the furled flag. 'Well, Ma'am: George Washington 1789 to 1797, John Adams 1797 to 1801, Thomas Jefferson 1801 to 1809, James Madison 1809 to 1817.... I kinda forgot the rest....'

Marian went out into the hot afternoon sun. It was the part of the day when time slumbered and insects hummed in the verges, the time of day she pondered the world. She fancied her father was a little in awe of her. She knew Rose wasn't her mother, but there could be no mother more real, and she was too pragmatic to waste more than an odd moment wondering what her real mother had been like. She could talk to Rose like an eight-year-old adult. Her father didn't figure in their conversations, but she always listened to his talk of brothers and the green lands he'd left behind. She wondered if she'd soon have a brother too.

Rose was in the kitchen when she got in. The girl twitched her nose, said hello and went to her room. She came back in her dungarees and took a teat from the drawer.

'You going to feed the lamb?'

'Uh–uh.' A pet lamb was sick. Marian had made one of her decisions. She poured a little milk from the can and worked the teat back over the neck of the bottle.

'Had a good day at school?'

'Uh–uh.'

'And what've you been learning about?'

'Not an awful lot. Jacob Wallis thinks he's clever knowing the names of a few Presidents. It's taken him nights through the week.'

'Well, don't begrudge him.'

'And there's another thing, Miss Whittle says she's got a present for the new baby.'

'Oh? What is it?'

'She didn't say.'

The lamb lay in the barn between slats of sunlight. She knelt down and crooked its head under her arm. Pushing forward the teat, she forced its mouth open as her father had shown her. It gave a tentative suck, then began to drink. When the bottle was empty she lay the head back in the straw and left, dropping the bar across the gate.

'Should you be working in the kitchen like this, Mommy?'

'Why?'

'Daddy says you're not supposed to work in your condition.'

'My condition's just fine.'

'I heard daddy say he's sending for grandmama to help.'

'And when was that?'

'Just after he got the letter from England to say my other grandaddy died and Uncle Charlie was going to have his house an' all.'

'D'you spend all your time listening to grown-ups' conversations?'

'Not all the time.'

'It's a long way for grandmama to travel.'

'I know. She's gotta catch a train and a coach and the journey takes days, but you still shouldn't be making blueberry jam in your condition, Miss Whittle says so.'

'I wonder what Miss Whittle knows about it.'

'She's a woman. She ought to know.'

Rose transferred the mixture to an earthenware jar, holding the saucepan handle through her apron. Marian found a book and began to make a list of unfamiliar words to ask Rose about later. She'd never seen a black face, but knew from the book these black people were shipped over from Africa to work in the cotton fields. She began a page entitled *My Thoughts on Being a Black Girl,* and was still writing when her father came in and skimmed his stetson across the table and stood over her, scrutinising her efforts with mock seriousness.

'*My Thoughts on Being a Black Girl*? I thought being a white girl was more in your line. Is this something your teacher asked you to do?'

'It's something I'm doing for myself. I've been reading all about it in my book.' She lifted it for him to see. 'I'm just imagining. Miss Whittle says imagining's good for you. She says poets have imagination, and musicians. I got to imagining myself as a black girl, only I don't know what black girls are called.'

'How about Clarissa?'

'Clarissa's not a black girl's name. That's the name of a princess.'

'Victoria, then.'

'She's the Queen of England.'

'You'll have to call her something that'll make 'em sit up and take notice. How about George?'

'You're no help at all, daddy, all you do is make jokes.' The child in her was fading. She looked up at him, his skin the colour of tobacco, his thinning hair now threaded with white, the silver moustache, shirt and pants speckled with dust. 'Tell me the news.'

'What d'you want with news?'

'I just want to know, and I don't mean how many rabbits you dug out of the alfalfa, I mean real news.'

He sat in a thinker's pose on the arm of her seat. 'Tell you what, they found big gold.'

'Where?'

'Klondike.'

'Where's that?'

'In the Yukon, way, way up north. You got to have nerves of steel and a good stove to see you through, otherwise you're dead meat.'

'Have you ever been there?'

'Not as far as I know. They got grizzlies roaming around – they squeeze you to death as soon as look at you.'

'I suppose people shoot them for fur.'

'You need special bullets to shoot grizzlies. Gold bullets. A grizzly can catch an ordinary bullet between its teeth. I can just see them prospectors now, huskies tearing down the Chilkoot Trail and through the White Pass with water foaming like a witch's cauldron.'

'Water doesn't foam like a witch's cauldron.'

'It does up the Yukon.' He got up as Rose called from the kitchen. 'That's imagination for you. You can leave your black girl while we have a bite.'

Although Ross's ranch was little bigger than the shack he'd shared with Maud on Bill's spread, it had been built against the extremes of the seasons. He hadn't prospered, neither had he suffered like other ranchers struck by sickness or hardship. When the arroyos were flowing, there was enough for a modest herd of Herefords, which provided him with a small margin after paying railroad dues. He'd refused more help from his son-in-law. Bill had helped him enough, and it was up to him to make it pay even though that meant working a seven day week. Maud was not impressed. 'Had the Almighty intended workin' on the Sabbath, he wouldn't have given us Sunday.' Tis the way to an early grave for the both of us here in this heathen place, without a soul to give us the time of day.'

'Things're improving. Maybe this weekend I'll get around to that well.'

'And I suppose you'll be diggin' it yourself, three hundred feet deep and more. I'm too old for wells and so are you. We should have been in Dakota now, selling blankets. I know you've got a bee in your bonnet. I'm too old.'

'It's gotta be done. We need more water.'

'We could've stayed on at Bill's ranch, it was steady work we had, not this back-rackin' day after day. How're we goin' to manage when our joints go? Pride's fine in a younger man, in someone your age it's for idiots.'

'I expect the Lord will provide.'

'I wonder how my girl's doing? I hope it's not trouble she's havin'.' Tears fell and were forgotten. The telegraph from Rose was waiting when Ross next went into town. 'You go,' he said, 'I'd best stay here.'

'Men are all the same, useless when you need them, useless when you don't.'

He took her to the station. It was dusk before he got back.

Bill drained his whiskey as Marian ran downstairs. A wave of panic swept over him. 'I got a sister, daddy! Grandmama sent me to tell you. She says to tell you mommy's fine.'

He followed her upstairs and took a deep breath before pushing open the bedroom door. Rose sat propped on pillows, a high colour flushing her cheeks. Her mother bustled around the room, bundling soiled sheets and looking over her daughter's shoulder at the baby's crumpled face. He stood there, a hand on the bed knob and thought back to Elizabeth and McPhearson. There'd been no doctor this time. Maud pulled down the baby's blanket. 'A nice little one, God bless her soul, aren't you, a nice little one. Well, three days in bed then we'll have the pair of you up and doing, there's no reason encouragin' lazy habits, none at all.' She noticed Marian, who'd been standing at the foot of the bed. 'Here, young lady, make yourself useful and help me carry this lot down.'

When they'd gone, Rose held out her hand to him. 'How's it feel to be a father the second time around?'

'Well I was hoping for a lad to help around the ranch but I suppose a girl will have to do.'

She smiled drowsily and drifted into sleep.

*

As autumn ousted summer from the prairies, Bill felt an urge to visit his brothers again. He wished he'd seen his father before he died, but he hadn't known the old man had been ill, and by the time Charlie's letter arrived it had been too late. As the zephyrs stirred the pasture, he began to feel part of him had never left England, and how easily the lowing cattle or a gust of wind could awaken memories. But the onset of colder weather occupied his mind, and when he and Rose saw Maud off he wondered whether he'd done Ross a favour or whether the coming spring would end his misgivings.

As it happened, the winter was mild that year. By April Ross and the itinerants he'd hired had begun a well. The future of his spread depended on a regular supply of water, and the last thing he wanted was to admit defeat. The nearest substantial supply was on the Denver brothers' land, several miles away. He'd tried to strike a deal, but they didn't take kindly to trespass, the older one had said, while the other stood at the door polishing his Winchester. But what they could do was make him an offer on his land and stock. He'd told them he wasn't interested. They'd advised him to think about it, and his answer had been to begin the well. If that failed, he'd give the land away and set fire to his ranch rather than sell it to the Denvers.

He might have been too rash. He knew Maud yearned to go back, changed his mind and decided he'd take up the Denvers' offer if the trickle of water on his own land dried up and there was no improvement in his circumstances that year. He couldn't easily reconcile himself to failure, and though he could move up to Dakota after Jancey's lease ran out and run the store, the land was his life, always had been. In any case, his son-in-law already had a new overseer, and he couldn't see himself swamping out the men's quarters.

He let the men go at the end of the month, and Maud echoed his feelings of defeat. Was there a life that didn't squeeze the last drop from your veins? Was there such a life in the world, or was it just a fancy notion put about by book-writers? Why was the Almighty unforgiving, and was it always to be like this, clouds across the plain and no sun rising?

Her words followed him outside. Peering into the shallow cut, he picked up a stone and let it fall. A soft, sweet smell rose up. Throwing his stetson on the ground, he hoisted a leg over the boards. The improvised ladder shook as he made his descent and a faint whiff came to his nose. He caught the pale points of light webbing and dissolving, prodded the mess with his boot. He found himself laughing, a long, echoing laugh which rebounded off the timbers and drove upwards into the dusty air. Maud heard it from the window, shook her head and continued her darning.

She looked up as Ross came through the door in his bare feet.

'I just been inspecting the well.'

'Where's your boots?'

'I left them outside. We made a strike. We got oil.'

'I say you got oil, I'm seein' it all over the floor.' She asked guardedly: 'And what are we to do about that?'

He slumped in a chair, removed his hat. 'I need a rag or something.'

'You can't expect me to get those pants clean, wash 'em till doomsday and you'll be toilin' for nothin'. You'd better get them off. Here, this is the best place –' and she threw his pants on the fire, putting up a mesh against the blaze. 'I've not got ten pairs of hands. Oil!' She followed her routines around the room. 'How much oil?'

'Must have seeped up. I don't recall seein' anything on the surface, usually shows on the surface.' She toured around him in agitated silence. 'Might be a few drops, sometimes happens I've been told. Folks bankrupt themselves setting up rigs, then nothing–'

'What're you goin' to do?'

'Haven't had chance to think.'

'Maybe it's not worth it.'

'Maybe it's not.'

'We don't have the money to go giddyin' around for the sake of a barrel.'

'We don't.' He shook his head. 'We sure don't.'

'How much would we –'

'Could be nothing. Probably is nothing. There again, folk make strikes, been making 'em forty years since Titusville. When I was in Pennsylvania there were more rigs than trees in some parts, looked like a forest. Some rich folk up there, ridin' around like lords. One I knew had his own boat. His own boat, Goddamit, with the crew all done out in braid! All from outa the ground, he told me, sure as I sit in this chair. The boat came outa naphtha and kerosene. Naphtha, for pity's sake! You could blow up a bank with naphtha! Know what he told me? Crude – that's what he called it – crude's the fuel of the future. Said this guy Rockefeller got rich knowin' that. This rich guy, the one had the boat, he sold out to Standard Oil. Made him four million. They reckon it's all about cars. He tells me they'll soon be everywhere. You got the car, there's no roads to run it on – well, up north they got asphalt, and that's from crude, like gasolene. I don't know, except this guy had a boat outa oil, so maybe we got enough for a couple of new lamps, maybe....' Maud left to hang out the washing. When she came in, Ross was still sitting in his chair, gazing at his feet. 'We're going to need a licence. I gotta find out more. We need a drill.' He leapt up. 'I need new pants, I gotta see somebody, gotta get my hat.'

The town lay still in the heat. Ross pushed open the shack door and went in. A bull-necked man with cunning eyes looked up from his desk. Waller was the only local man who had drilling experience and knew the legal codes even if he flouted them. Hoisting a leg on to his desk, he ignored Ross and bit into an apple.

'Looks like you'll be busy for some time, so if you'll excuse me –'

Waller aimed the core at a drum. It hit the mark with a dull thud. 'You can't get 'em plumb in the eye, you employ tactics. Like I was sayin' the other day to a partner of mine, give our boys enough steel and they'll whip them Spanish bastards out the water. We oughta kick their asses right outta Cuba, the bastards got no call t'come sneaking up on other folks' back yards.'

Ross said: 'I come on business.'

'And what business might that be?'

'One might be to your advantage.'

'It'll cost.'

'I only have so much.'

'I don't negotiate.'

'I think it'll be too much for me, no matter what,' Ross said, moving back to the door.

A flicker of interest registered in Waller's eyes. 'Wait on. I was gonna say I don't negotiate with *anybody*. Care for a slug?' He took a bottle of rye from a drawer and tilted it to his mouth.

'I'll come to the point. Mr Waller. I got a tract of land, thought I might try a little prospecting.'

'You mean oil, or salt? What're you talkin' about?'

'There's been strikes here and there, thought I might try my luck.'

'You're speakin' through your ass. Ain't got a chance in a million.'

Ross flicked the dust from the stetson he was holding. Waller sank into his chair, studying the man through lowered lids. 'You got oil, ain't you?'

'I'm a farmer, that don't mean I'm only interested in grass.'

'Tell you what, Mr–'

'Name don't matter.'

'I'll drill your well for free.'

'And?'

'I get ten per cent of what comes out.'

'Not interested.'

'You got nothin' to lose. You know how much it costs settin' up a rig? You gotta get the goddam thing there first, then you gotta buy in a team knows what they're doin'. All for a million to one we don't find enough to fill an injun's jawbone.'

'I got a better proposition: you give me a figure, I think it over and let you know.'

Waller leaned back, an elbow resting on the curved back of his chair, the brain behind the small, unblinking eyes calculating its next move. 'Tell you what, I'll drill your hole, all steel bit that'll bite your ass off – hey! What sort o' land you got there? We're not talkin' rock or basalt or any other shit that's gonna take a year –'

'Clay all the way. Some shale.'

'Clay, huh? It'll cost you a thousand bucks. Take it or leave it.'

'I'll pay seven hundred. Three now, four when the job's done.'

'When d'you want to start?'

'What's wrong with now?'

Ross stood at the door, adjusting his hat against the sun. It seemed to him his visit had marked a watershed in his life. He'd lived steady years, taking reasoned chances. He'd neither prospered nor starved, and Bill had promoted him for his knowledge of the land. He could be relied upon to do his best and to give his best and it was out of character for such a man to throw caution to the winds. But now he'd staked what he owned to drill oil, and that meant he'd parted with his best stock and a year's rent from the store. If he didn't strike, the only winner would be Waller, who'd have the satisfaction of more dollars in his bulging pockets. As he went out into the torpid afternoon heat, he couldn't shake off an impending sense of unease.

*

Bill sat in the kitchen reading a letter from Charlie which had been sent from England a month earlier:

'It's some time since I last wrote, but I've had a lot on my plate and couldn't get round to it. A lot has happened over the year, the chief thing being I've left my wife. I needn't trouble you with all the goings-on, suffice it to say we've not been man and wife for a long time. It's all taken its toll on me, and the situation is I've given over my share of the business and moved back to Moor Top. I'm living at Moel with Hannah and Richard, making a living odd-jobbing on the farms, but not much. Mary didn't care whether they came with me or not. I think she preferred it. I see Ellen from time to time and Mrs Benersley still hops about the place. I don't see so much of John, though. He owns a factory in Macclesfield now and when I last saw him he hinted at getting married. I always feel for that lad of his, Matthew. The last I heard he'd left school and taken himself off to London to look for work. As I said, I've left Mary to her own devices, and it took a long time to reach a decision since she's not responsible for herself and I felt a duty to stay despite what it was doing to me. I didn't tell you earlier but I found out by accident she already had a son I knew nothing about. I feel as if a load has been lifted off my back, just being able to breathe fresh air again uplifts me.

'I've got nowhere with the fanciful ideas I've had over the years and I've more or less given up hope of ever getting on in that direction. Ellen had the notion I might try for a schoolmaster, but I don't know if I'm cut out for it, or if I'm bright enough. Pits and tileyards aren't the best recommendations for that sort of position, let along being separated from your wife. Anyway, that's enough of my problems. When I get the chance I'll have a photograph sent out of the three of us. You can send one back, and let me know how things are with you.

'Well, Bill, that's about all for now. All the best to you and yours.

Charlie.'

Of the three of them, Charlie had been the one with the talent. What he didn't have was the driven tenacity of a successful man. He didn't have the belief in himself. He wished he could leave Charlie some of his own luck, if not the struggle which went with it.

Rose came in, and he handed her the letter. After a sympathetic comment, she passed it back. 'You get a letter from England, yet no word from my folks in two months.'

'Probably too busy now the weather's come. If they feel anything like me after a day, they'll be hard put to hold a pen.'

'But it's not like my mother.' The baby was reaching for a jar of molasses. Bill moved it out of reach and reminded Marian it was time for school. Rose's voice rose in exasperation. 'Marian, you forgot again!'

The girl composed herself. 'Thank you Lord for what this table has provided and can I go now?'

'You'll have the good Lord strike you dead if you treat Him like that. Watch you remember next time.'

When they'd gone, she lifted Colette from the chair and sat her down in a corner of the sofa with a rattle. 'You stay put, madam, mommy's going to be busy some. After, we'll take a turn outside, get some of this air into your lungs.'

Whenever she rolled back the lid of the bureau she'd a sense of having made the same move and thinking the same thoughts as the woman who'd preceded her. Now, as she took out an envelope and paper, the guilt of intrusion settled on her again. Shrugging it off, she addressed an envelope and completed a hurried page. If there was no reply by the end of the month, Bill would have to make the journey and find out what was going on.

A month passed with no reply forthcoming. Now Bill, too, found it hard to disguise his misgivings. Leaving his stockman in charge of the ranch, he left one day at first light. In the late afternoon he reached the rail head. He fell asleep listening to the locomotive wailing in the dusk. When he awoke, the prairies were bathed in the ashy light of a risen moon. An oil lamp swung silently from a hook, and he watched it for a minute before lowering his hat against the weak light. Again, tiredness overcame him, and his last recollection was of figures draped in sleep.

When he awoke, the train was clanking into the station. He found a hotel and had a long drink. The foreboding which had trailed him since he set out persisted, and he wondered whether his anxieties were due to Rose's conviction something was wrong or to his own. After a meal he hired a horse and continued his journey. A fierce midday heat swallowed the noise of the town. It hadn't rained for weeks, and the ruts ran with a fine ochre dust which the ground-eddies scattered among the sparse grass. Maybe the drought had been responsible for them hearing nothing. No, if their difficulties had been as great as that, Maud would have got in touch.

It was late when he came to the familiar line of low hills. Streaks of madder suffused the cloud as the light weakened. He reined in his horse and took a drink from his canteen. Slowly, he clicked his horse forward. Ross's shack came into view, but he struggled to make sense of it. There was no mistaking the three black towers that pierced the fading sky. He heeled the horse to a gallop, his mind feverish with explanations. Ross had wanted to spring a surprise, to turn up out of the blue decked out, Maud in a new bonnet.... or was he ashamed oil had taken over from farming? He'd soon know the reason. Oil! It was like digging up gold nuggets. Now he could see barrels in the compound. How many, thirty? Must be close on fifty. Fifty barrels waiting for the morning cart.

And there was Ross! Bill dismounted and lifted an arm to the figure, but Ross had moved out of sight. The feel of the place was different. He tried to put his finger on it. It wasn't the rigs, or the barrels, but an odd emptiness. He walked towards the door, expecting Maud to greet him, but recognised the click and swung around. The youth, no more than seventeen, had the Winchester pointed at him from a corner of the house.

'You're on private land.'

A hard lump rose to Bill's throat. 'I came to see my in-laws, name of -'

'Don't live here no more. You ain't from round these parts, can tell by your manner of speech.'

Bill turned towards him. The youth took a step back and braced the gun.

'I just want to know where they went.'

'Sold out to Gulch Oil. Guess they went north, maybe got a place in Tulsa.'

They'd never do that, they'd get in touch. He was lying.

'All right, I'll try the post, maybe they'll know something.'

'Makes sense.'

He held the rifle steady as Bill walked back to his horse. In less than an hour it would be dark. When he reached the track, he didn't turn until he'd cleared the higher land. There was little point trying to make it back. He made camp close by an arroyo and lit a fire of dry twigs. He was middle aged and responsible, a man with a wife and young children. Yet he reached a decision he'd have balked at as a younger man, wondered if the fate that befell Dixon those many years ago was already in the wings waiting for him, too. He fitted his forefinger into the curve of the trigger of his Colt. He kept the gun by him as he kicked dust over the fire and pulled his blanket up against the chill. Sleep was slow to come, and he lay with the comforting steel against his cheek....

The century drew to a close. Victoria was as helpless as her subjects to resist the currents of time. Some believed her empire would crumble under its own weight, that the cost of maintaining her dominions was too heavy a burden to bear. Fresh breezes were sweeping through Europe, bringing jubilation tinged with uncertainty while other winds blew through the hearts of those who'd made the West their home. Bill had a leg in American loam and a foot in English soil, and he was at one with the destiny of entrepreneurs, risk-takers, crooks and idealists united by a dream. But for John the map still shone red, and when he left his new office the thud of looms symbolised an enduring land with the Queen at its helm and trade in its veins. Why trouble with America when SS Britain was still afloat on the high seas?

Charlie's concerns were detached from these universal currents. The day he'd parted from his wife was more firmly etched on his mind than the newspaper rants against Boers and Prussians. What he remembered was the crumple of Deakin's jaw as his fist struck home and a crushing sense of defeat which bore down on him at the canal-side. He remembered the splash Bevis's coin had made as he hurled it into the water. *Leave her. Take the children. Leave the place, the yard, the entries and the stink of smoke, leave it all.* What did Mafeking matter when his heart was bleeding? The Moel wore the stamp of neglect, but it was his and the farms about might offer work. He'd try to make a go of it and send her what he could afford.

Even now he couldn't see her sink.

PART THREE

RESOLUTIONS
1900-1924

Tis all a chequer-board of Nights and Days
Where Destiny with Men for pieces plays
Hither and thither moves, and mates and slays,
And one by one back in the Closet lays
The Rubaiyat of Omar Khayyam

1

Higham Sparling pushed back his spectacles and addressed his flock: 'Friends, I often think back to my first days as new rector of Moor Top. I knew I'd have a difficult task following in the footsteps of my predecessor, but in my own way I have endeavoured to shed as strong a light on the Christian principle as he did, and, like him, I firmly believe Christ's teachings should be made relevant to the age in which we live.' Glancing at the occupants of the first pews, he went on: 'We have much to be grateful for. We heard not long ago that our gallant army at Ladysmith had been relieved, and now we hear about Mafeking. I must tell you that Mafeking is not a modern city, but little more than a collection of huts. I doubt anyone here would have heard of it had the name not been trumpeted across the newspapers. So why was the relief of Mafeking so dear to us?' A lens caught a shaft of light, and the rector's eye flashed white. 'The answer is contained in a single phrase: the fundamental grit of the breed. I think that goes to the heart of the matter. It's more important than the news from Ireland and the political squabbling in London. Fundamental grit refers to the character of the people of these islands: courage, steadfastness and loyalty to the cause of right. We must be proud of it.

'And let us not forget mercy. For did our Lord not tell us: Blessed are the merciful: for they shall obtain mercy? Justice, mercy and grit are the qualities God has seen fit to bestow upon us. Will He safeguard our nation until the end of the next millennium, or even the end of this present century? I think about this often. I read only the other day that two brothers have flown a device across some wasteland in America. They no doubt believe these so-called gliders will shortly be carrying men through the skies at impossible speeds. What arrogance! Had the Lord intended men to fly, he would have provided them with wings, and they wouldn't be of rag. We treat God as a bystander; yet the machines we build would be impossible without His help, for it is He who provides man with the ingenuity to develop His sciences under His direction. Only a short while ago, Mr Marconi sent the first telegraphic transmission from Dover to Wimereux. It was with the Lord's help he sent it, for without Him there would be no Mr Marconi, and no Mr Wright, and all their wonders would be as nothing.' Someone coughed, and the rector strove to reconcile the end of his sermon to his opening remarks. 'We must give thanks to God for the age in which we live. We have food; we have homes, and fuel to heat them; we have schools to banish ignorance and hospitals to banish pain. These are worldly realities, yet through them all we see God's shining face, for He is with us to the end. Amen.'

Ellen followed the congregation into the May sunshine. She was about to set off for home when she changed her mind and took the lane to the Moel instead. She looked forward to Charlie's surprise, but the surprise was hers as she walked up to the door. When she'd last paid a call, the garden had been rank with nettle and vetch. Now the weeds had been cleared and the shrubs cut back, bringing light to the budding clumps of gentian. She peered through the window into the living room, then went around to the back. Charlie was sawing at a branch far down the slope while Hannah sat on a bench with Richard, pointing out pictures in her book. Hannah looked up and tugged at her father's jerkin. Charlie stopped work, and Ellen went down to him, holding her bonnet against the breeze.

'Charlie! I thought you'd be in your Sunday Best.'

He grinned. 'Been up to church, have you?

'It does me good once in a while, though I don't know what he's on about half the time. Still, it's nice to sit in peace sometimes, don't you think?'

'The nearest I get to relaxation these days is sorting out the garden.'

A wood fire sent the smoke billowing across the field. Richard, bleeding from a small cut to his knee, was tugging at his trousers. 'Hannah, take him in and wash his leg. You'll find some lint in the drawer.'

She took her brother by the hand and led him to the back door. Ellen watched them go. Something of the day, with its quiet blueness and familial movements touched her.

'How're you coping?'

He put down his saw and wiped his forehead. 'Hannah's up at school now. I take Richard up to one of the mothers when I have to. She already looks after two for women working down the mills. School might take him next year as well.' He heaved the lopped branch up to the fire. 'Are you staying?'

'For a bit.... have you heard from Mary?'

'She's gone her own way and I've gone mine. Best see what Hannah's up to.' He shook his head, smiling the smile Bevis used to give. 'Proper little woman is Hannah, cleans through like a new pin.'

Ellen was already part of his daughter's imaginary household, and sat with a collection of drawings in her lap over the make-shift meal.

'Of course, you wouldn't know, Charlie.'

'What?'

'It's a while since you last came down. It's Doris - I think she's starting with softenin' of the brain. She's beginning to forget things. I feel guilty about leaving her.'

'I'm sorry to hear that.'

'She's turned seventy, you know.'

'I've been busy of late, or I'd come down more. You know how it is on farms this time of the year.'

'You can give us a hand down the Elms when you've a minute to spare.'

'Come on, Richard, eat up all your dinner, it'll do you good,' Hannah coaxed.

'Ay, tell him it'll put hairs on his chest.'

Ellen envied him his content. Doris would get worse. He had his home and his children, and she asked him vindictively how the authorities would react to his taking them away from their mother.

'She ought to have thought of that earlier,' he said, making Hannah's ears prick. 'Anyhow, a good father's better than –' He gave his shrug. 'I was wondering about the pit again, save me scraping by here. I heard there were jobs going in the lamp house.'

Her bitterness erupted. 'You've denied yourself all your life. Don't you think you're better than pit work? You're not a labouring man and never will be. Caulton told you that more than thirty years since. You're got brains, Charlie. Like I told you before, you want to find out about schoolmastering, you'd have folks doffing their caps when you walked down the path. You'd not have to be up of a winter's mornin' picking straw off the pump. The schoolmaster now, he's got his own trap.'

He prodded the grains of salt sprinkled across the table.

'Are you going to be my teacher, dad?' Hannah inquired solemnly.

His lips twitched, and Ellen, defused, spluttered into laughter. 'You know Jane relented and got married? She says Eric might try for the government. I went to the wedding. They had a photographer as well, and gentry.'

Hannah cleared away the dishes. He caught her hand. 'Why don't you take our Richard for a walk when you've done the washing up? Tell you what –' he slapped a coin on the table – 'buy yourself a ha'penny o' liquorice from the shop.'

'Can we have a bag of fudge, dad?'

'Ay, go on, and don't scoff the lot, the pair of you. And save me and Ellen a few bits.'

His awkwardness was further from the surface. She thought he'd become more comfortable with himself, reconciled himself to misfortune and survived. She'd once enjoyed seeing him shuffle, but the game no longer held any attraction for her. When the children had gone, he took a pipe from the mantelpiece and tamped the tobacco in a way so reminiscent of his father she was moved to turn away.

'D'you still love her, Charlie?'

'I don't wish her ill.'

'That's just like you, forgive and forget.'

'I dare say none of us can change what we are. We come out fully formed, chance whether we like it or not.'

'What's she do for money?'

'I post some down once a week. I managed to put a bit by from the business. I never hear from her. She might go back in with her mother, though I can't see that lasting.'

'This Neville Deakin you told me about, have you heard anything more about him?'

'What am I supposed to have heard? Neville was just one, I dare say.

I can't see any point raking it over again.'

He saw himself, that afternoon, a band of agony pulsing behind his eyes and his head screaming for a pillow. He'd blundered upstairs and found Mary naked and Deakin in his unbuttoned shirt. His fist enclosed all the injustices of her past and only when he felt it smash against Deakin's jaw did he know he'd struck him. He carried with him mental snapshots, like the separate frames of a magic lantern. He thought back to the disturbed bed shortly after his marriage, the designs Deakin had called for, his excuses. He'd found Hannah and Richard coming back from an arranged errand. If Deakin hadn't managed to get out the back way, he might have killed him.

The fire fell, the image shattered.

'She's still their mother.'

'She's not fit.'

'But she is their mother.'

'You wouldn't understand.'

'This other son of hers,' she persisted, not knowing why. 'She must've had some good in her to keep on seeing him.'

'There's things defy explanation. Mine were brought up by me and the next door neighbour.' His pipe had gone out, and he banged the dottle in the hearth. 'It's water under the bridge, anyhow.'

She looked for a moment into the embers, remembered the night they spent together. He felt her restlessness hovering just beneath the surface. When he looked up, her eyes were full on him. 'I'll be forty in two years,' she said.

'I'm not far behind.'

She held out her hand to him, her skin hard, but her face, framed by the dull golden hair, still soft and clear. 'Charlie, you've not forgotten? I don't want you to forget. Don't you want me?'

'I don't want anything at the moment.'

'You did before.... I know you did.'

'It's nothing to do with you, it's in myself.'

'We're not all the same. There's women and women like there's men and men. You don't have to be afraid of me. This Neville, he only did what we did.'

'It wouldn't be any good, not yet. Give things time to settle.... it was different, him and her.'

‘That’s you all over, give things time. If you’d given things less time you’d not be ditching for farmers, you’d have been in an office somewhere instead of letting it all go to waste on her. I haven’t got any time left. You and your harebrained ideas, and where’s it got you? Twelve years on a tile bank and a broken marriage.’ Her squall died to a whisper. ‘You could’ve had me, I would’ve made a good wife for you. And now you’re wed and there’s nothing to be done about it, split or not.’

Her words evaporated, leaving her upset and him hemmed in, wishing she’d not come. He thought of the unfinished work in the garden and wanted to be there, poking his stick in the fire. She brightened as if aware of what he was thinking. ‘You must come back with me, Charlie. I’ll have to go because of Doris. Why not come down with the children, it’ll be a treat?’ She began to pull on her coat and took her hat from the dresser.

She’d brushed aside her mood as she followed him into the back room. A hob-black bike leaned against the wall. ‘It was Joss Randle’s,’ he said, ‘he gave it in lieu of what was owing.’

‘It could do with a clean-up.’

‘I’ll get around to it. It’ll need tyres and the brakes seeing to.’

‘Good Heavens, Charlie, it looks ready for the knacker’s. How old is it?’

‘What’s age matter when you’ve transport? It’ll save me hours of foot-slogging.’ He grinned. ‘All right, I’ll come back with you.’

Hannah and Richard returned. Hannah complained of a sore throat, and Richard said his throat was sore in sympathy.

‘I’m not surprised, it’s all those sweets you’ve been eating. Got an outing for the pair of you. We’re going to Ellen’s for a spell. Hannah, get your best bib and tucker on – and get Richard’s coat, don’t want you both freezing to death down there in the Land of Lap.’

‘What’s the Land of Lap, dad?’

‘Have you never heard the poem about the Ancient Mariner? *The ice was here, the ice was there, the ice was all around....*’

She joined in: ‘*It cracked and growled and roared and howled like noises in a swound!*’

‘ Who told you that?’

‘We did it with the mistress. It’s about a sailor who brings bad luck on his ship by killing an albatross.’

‘And he lived in Lapland, is that it?’

'Don't be silly, dad, he'd freeze to death up there.'

The day was pleasantly warm, and the hills glowed with light. Along the lane, blackthorn were bursting with leaf, the slight breezes carrying with them the scents of early summer. Three Elms lay in its sheltered cleft, its windows bright against the sun. He watched Hannah and Richard wander off. 'Keep him out o' them byres, Hannah, and don't go near the pond!'

Doris was standing at the door, her body bent under a tweed shawl. The bird-like movements he remembered had gone, and her head, crowned with a shapeless bonnet, seemed to precede her into the room. Only after Ellen had helped her to a chair did she look up. 'You've brought along a young man, Ellen.'

'It's Charlie. You know Charlie, don't you?'

Her face was vacant. 'Charlie.... Charlie who?'

'Charlie Tanbrey. He's come to see us, he's brought Hannah and Richard.'

Doris closed her eyes, murmured something and opened them again. 'D'you have a morsel o'bread? I've a strange taste in me mouth.... What's his name again, Ellen?'

'It's Charlie. You know Charlie? You've known him ages.' She smiled helplessly at him. 'I'll get her a bit of cake. D'you want some, Charlie?'

'I'm all right for the moment, thanks.'

'Look, she's dozed off again. This is how it is now.' She covered Doris with a blanket as the white head drooped and the mouth began to snore. 'Hey, I've something to show you.' He got up to follow her, but she pushed him away and came back with a wicker basket. 'Now what d'you think's in here?'

'It's not a brace o' pheasant, is it?'

'D'you give up?'

'All right, I give up.'

She lifted an old newspaper and rummaged inside. 'Shades of old times, eh, Charlie,' she cried, holding up a tile. 'Here, what d'you think?'

Oblivious to the shadow which had fallen across his face, she chattered on about wanting to make something of the place, keep the scullery clean and the beetles at bay.

'Where did you get them from?'

'I bought them up Leek. Why?'

He took a tile from her, turning it around in his hands.

'What time's Nat due back?' piped Doris.

'Nat's not here no more, mother. Nat died.'

'Died, you say?' She fell asleep, mouth agape.

'See how it is, Charlie?' Her exuberance faded as she noticed his expression. 'Don't you like them? I thought they were really pretty.'

'They're mine. My work, my designs.' He left the chair and tore the paper back. 'This. And this – all mine.'

'Are you sure?'

'It's a poor sod doesn't know his own work. There's been some alterations, a line or two here and there. They must think I've fallen off a cart.' He glared at the pieces as if to smash them, then moved back to his seat, the tiles fanned in his hand like playing cards. 'Bloody Deakin!'

'It could just be a coincidence, and –'

'He never seemed to be rattling round for a bob like the rest of us, now I know why!'

'I was going to say,' she interjected, raising her voice above his tirade, 'it proves a point. It's no use going off at the deep end. I was going to say it shows you've done the right thing after all. Why don't you go and have it out with them down this factory? You can see who it is on the back. If this Deakin can sell 'em your ideas, they must have some merit. Why don't you confront them? You've still got your sketches, haven't you?'

'It'll be one of his cronies. He wasn't content with my wife, he was filching my bloody work into the bargain!'

She sought to console him, but he was deaf to anything she might say. In his anger, he hadn't heard his children come in, and his disgust lit on Doris buckled against a pillow, a trickle of saliva weeping from her mouth. Hannah put her hand on his knee, her face flushed. He thought she'd worked up a heat running around the farm.

'I don't feel well, dad, it's my throat.'

'You've still got it?'

'It feels sore.'

She put her hand to her neck, and Richard followed suit. Charlie's rage hung in limbo between tiles, Deakin and his daughter. Hannah clambered on to his knee. A clammy sweat had broken out across her forehead.

'She's got a fever,' Ellen said. 'It looks as if she's picked something up.'

Charlie pulled her coat around her. 'I think we'd best get you to bed, young lady.'

'I'm all right, dad.'

'Seems like it. Cow heel broth, then bed.'

'Can I have some broth as well?' Richard asked.

'You've got a throat an' all, have you?'

'Hannah's having some.'

'Hannah's poorly.'

'Stay if you like, Charlie, I'll warm the bed.'

Hannah moved closer to him, drowsy in the heat of the room. 'Thanks for the offer, but I think we'd best go home.'

Doris stirred as he was putting on his outdoor clothes. 'Bill? I thought you were in foreign parts.'

'That's my brother, Doris. I'm Charlie. I've to take Hannah back home, she's not feeling well. We'll call again, have a bite with you next time.'

He'd forgotten about the tiles. The vale lay calm in the blue light of evening, and a thin smoke veiled the stars. Ellen came in from the stables. 'The cart's having a new wheel, but you can take the horse and Richard can stay here the night. He'll be all right with me. Hannah can't walk with a temperature.'

She stood by the door, watching them along the track. The sky had darkened to a rich sapphire beneath which the dark uplands rose. The horse plodded against the last fragments of sunset and the flare of mares' tails in the west.

He ran to the trap as the doctor climbed down and came to the make-shift bed, the evening chill on his clothes. He removed his coat and set his bag down on the table. 'How long has she been like this?'

'It came on in the afternoon.'

He ran his fingers over Hannah's neck, looking past Charlie as he touched the swollen tissue. She lay inert, her face pale and still. 'Any sickness?'

'She said it was her throat.'

'Would you bring up the lamp?'

He held a lens to her mouth. Taking a spatula, he parted her lips and caught her throat in a beam. She arched her back and gave a weak cry of discomfort. The throat was red and swollen, and around the tonsils a yellow membrane had begun to form. The doctor moved the light away and stood back. 'Your daughter has diphtheria, Mr Tanbrey. I have to go back, there are things I shall need.' He was pulling on his coat. 'Keep her warm. Don't move her.'

Charlie watched him from the doorway. An image of his portfolio came to him. He wanted to destroy it, to hurl it from him. Without it he would have had more of himself to spare. He'd have to be rid of it if Hannah were to survive. If anything were to happen he'd be to blame. He'd taken her from her mother, carried her off to a hovel reeking of damp. He was the one to blame. He sat at her bedside, helpless, stroking her hand. Her pulse was the flicker of a blown leaf, the face burning under a wan skin. 'Don't worry, we'll have you well, I won't let anything happen to you, you know that, your dad'll take care of you...'

By the time the trap returned, she was struggling for air. The doctor removed his coat and necktie with restrained haste. Hannah was sinking, her eyes rolling under the closed lids, her hands clutching at the blanket. He held up the lamp and examined the leathery membrane. 'Are you a brave man, Mr Tanbrey?'

'What's to be done?'

'I have to help her breathing. I have to make an incision.' He unclipped his bag and fumbled for an instrument. 'This should have been done in a hospital, man. You don't perform operations on someone's hearth. You should have called me earlier. It's running rampant. You must have heard..'

'For God's sake, I got a lad to fetch you as soon as I could, I thought it was a sore throat....'

'I know. I know.' He took out a vial and sprinkled the contents around the table and over his hands and arms.

'She's not going to feel anything? You've got something to help her?'

The doctor's eyes shone in the beads of light. Time was passing, he wasn't sufficiently practised, had to cope. 'She'll feel a prick, nothing more. Bring her to the table as gently as you can.' Charlie laid her along the scrubbed boards. 'Do you have clean linen, something to slip under her back?'

He dislodged the drawer in his haste, scattering the contents. The doctor held the lancet upright, twisting it in the light. 'She won't feel anything. Keep her head still and hold fast to her arms.'

Turning to the girl, he pulled the skin of her throat taut and made a shallow incision below the larynx. A comma of blood oozed into the wound. His eyes met Tanbrey's briefly. A kind of horror held Charlie, and in desperation he tightened his grip on her arm as the knife cut deeper. Hannah convulsed, her back bowed, her thin body fighting for air. *He had to go deeper, deeper.* The doctor firmed his grip on the lancet and sliced the tissue with a hard, searching stroke. The trachea rose palely into the cavity, and he slit it open. Her chest heaved with the inrush of air. He stole a glance at the father. Her face was already losing its dusky tinge. He took a catheter and carefully inserted it into the windpipe. Hannah winced as he stitched the wound and applied a bandage to the site.

'You can lay her back on the couch, Mr Tanbrey. It was a near thing. Yes, a very near thing.' He turned to the father. 'Well, now....'

Charlie sat, still stroking his daughter's hand, his eyes glistening. He hadn't the words for thanks. Words would break him down. He offered his hand, and the doctor grasped it. 'I've nothing worth giving,' he said, gathering himself. 'You'd be welcome to anything I had.'

'No time for that now. When the sickness has passed, I'll mend her throat. There'll be nothing but a small scar. Now, there's something I'd like you to do for me. Go and leave a message for my wife. Tell her I won't be back. She'll have to get the locum to answer any calls until I've finished. And ask her to leave a message with Nurse Allen to come up here as soon as she can. I'll wait until she arrives.'

'It's not over yet?'

'Just to keep an eye on things. When you get back, I suggest you take a rest.'

The sky had paled with approaching dawn. He took a last look at his sleeping daughter. 'I'll be back as soon as I can, Doctor'll look after you.'

Gossamer silvered the fields to either side the track. He rode with a briskness he didn't feel, heard a voice at his side, whispering she's well over and over again.

He came back in full light. His legs felt weak, and his conviction to rid himself of the portfolio strengthened. He felt he'd been granted a reprieve, but only if he kept his part of the bargain. He worried about having thrown away Bevis' coin. It had been a worthless talisman, but he'd tempted fate in casting it from him. He had to make amends, had to avoid cracks in the paving. He was going to take up Ellen's suggestion. When Hannah was fully recovered he'd visit the schoolmaster and find out how to go about it. When she'd got back her health he'd.... His thoughts strayed back to Ellen. His children had a mother in name only. Better someone who cared, someone who'd make a family.

He set the horse in the field and took the path to the house. He pushed open the door and went into the living room. At first he didn't understand; the doctor's posture, perhaps... something in the drooping shoulders, the silence. He could hear someone speaking, there was nothing I could do, it happens sometimes, the struggle weakens the heart, you see; voices, speaking. With infinite care he peeled the sheet from her face. Her eyes were closed, her lips pressed in her way, *let me do it dad, you know you're no good at this kind of thing.* She'd always been willing to do her chores, works like a little woman, she does. Hannah.

He left the room, the house. The scents of morning suffused the air. A solitary sycamore stood on the height, and he leaned against it, looking out across the spare blue hills. The pond she'd helped him dig was still turgid with winter debris. She was standing there. *I'll catch a newt for you, Richard....* Something of his childhood he heard, he thought. They'd sung it at school. A hymn. A home for little children. Yes, a home for little children.... above the bright blue sky.

Slowly, like a man bent with years, he turned back.

2

John Tanbrey gazed across the roofs from his office window. It pleased him to go over the last few years in quiet moments when he was alone and listening to the looms stuttering below. He enjoyed his reminiscences, and smiled to himself as he saw anew a thief dragging a coal bag away from the blazing house. Then he was in London, seeking out dealers who were happy to do business with no questions asked. There were the dowdy fences in Birmingham, too, and a medley of accents came to his ears, each calling out a figure. The whole thing would have been dealt with by the insurers, anyway. That's why there'd never been anything in the papers. As far as they were concerned, everything had gone up in smoke. And anyway, Heath's wife had died during the rebuilding and the family silver had found a more useful purpose sunk into Birkenshaw's mill. That was the good thing about reminiscences. You could cover time and distance in the wink of an eye. Now he saw Birkenshaw's cortege. And now Nerissa in her labourer's cottage. He savoured her fall from grace every day. Birkenshaw had died bankrupt and he'd bought the house, grounds, cottage and mill and still had money concealed in Pandora. The thing that delighted him most was Nerissa's shock on discovering the identity of the new owner. He'd always cherish the memory of her mouth, drawn into a ring of disbelief when she found out. She'd been reliant on her father, then on her husband. Now she was reliant on him, down to the tenancy of her hovel.

Then there was the time at the Union Club he'd had the good fortune to run into Barrington. The MP had been drunk at the time, but his ramblings had formed the basis for the present satisfactory state of Tanbrey's bank account. Silk, Barrington had told him, was finished. 'The dandies have had their day. Wait till the socialists take over, there'll be bugger-all silk then. Smart mills will sell up while they can, or change to lines that provide a future.' He'd leaned forward, tapping his nose. 'Uniforms, that's what we need, uniforms.'

He'd toppled at that point, but Tanbrey's curiosity had been aroused. He'd called a cab and seen the man back to his home. Barrington had sobered surprisingly quickly. 'The war in Africa, the bloody Boers! Any time now, the whole lot'll go up.'

'And would a supply of uniforms be subject to a Crown contract?'

'Most certainly.'

'And if I were to submit a tender?'

'It might be looked upon favourably. There again, it might not. It all depends.'

'On?'

'On any number of things....'

'Perhaps you could be more specific.'

'I could be. Yes, why not? There's no reason why a right-minded person shouldn't obtain a contract for the duration.'

'And by a right-minded person, you mean one willing to grease a right-minded palm.'

'You have the matter in its entirety.'

'Yours?'

Barrington had smiled, nodding his head like a mandarin. 'Consider it a sale. You're in business. For a paltry few hundred you can receive a contract officially ratified by the House....'

That had been more than a year ago, and still the war showed no sign of flagging. He'd found someone who could see to the installation of new looms and within the month consignments of greatcoats, spats and night-caps had been making their way to Aldershot. It seemed nothing he did could tempt fate. With his tenancies and the Victoria Mill, his estate and the amount growing daily in the bank, he was already wealthy. Only one detail clouded the horizon, and that was Nerissa's daughter. Now seven, she seemed to grow more like Davenport every day. He'd never been able to admit to himself that the child was not his own. It seemed Davenport had been equally convinced, and had hated her. Had he realised that by some thousand to one chance he'd managed to produce an heir, would he have absconded? Birkenshaw's house and mill would have passed to his creditors and Davenport would have employed expensive lawyers to assure his divorce, with custody of his daughter, and Nerissa would have fared the same. His thoughts strayed briefly to his son. He'd heard nothing of Matthew since receiving a short letter from London nine months ago, and was mildly curious as to what he might be doing....

As if to free himself of his son's unwelcome intrusion, he rang the desk bell. While he waited, he was struck by the idea he might invest in one of the new electric telephones Barrington had been talking about.

'I've been intending to speak with you for some time,' he said when the woman came in.

Jane O'Rourke, nee Cowlishaw, disquieted him. Some men might have found her attractive. Few women in their forties were unscathed by hard work, yet the years had dealt kindly with her, and the silver threads running through her hair lent her a maturity which might prove useful to him.

'Tell me, how long have you been here, Mrs O'Rourke?'

'Mr Birkenshaw set me on when Mr Jackson retired.'

'And you've worked in this capacity since?'

'Yes.'

'Tell me something of your life before you came.'

She wondered how much he knew. Ellen had confirmed what Jane had already guessed, that this was Bill's brother. 'It's not been particularly exciting. I worked in Leek for a time, then I came here.'

'Why was that?'

'I was made redundant. I have a house I let, so I had enough to tide me over until I found another job. There was work to be had in Macclesfield. It seemed an obvious choice.'

'A house to let? Where?'

'In Bradley Green. I used to live there.'

'So did I. Or at least, close by.'

There was a lengthy pause. She asked: 'Can I ask why you've sent for me?'

He leaned back in his chair. 'My background has nothing to do with textiles. You could say I acquired the Victoria through default. What I've learnt I've picked up along the way.' He moved back to the window, his back to her. 'I feel your talents are being wasted. The administrative side need some strengthening. I'd like you to work as my personal assistant.'

'Are you offering me promotion?'

He turned. 'You've been here long enough to know the wrinkles. I need someone who's au fait with the market, at the same time able to command the respect of the workforce.'

'My ways might not be yours, Mr Tanbrey.'

'Then we shall have to resolve the situation. Sleep on it, if you wish.'

When she'd gone he sat tapping his pencil. He knew she was the wife of Eric O'Rourke through occasional references in the press. He was sure if he met him he'd detest him on sight, as he detested every liberal idealist.

However, the man had friends. His name had appeared alongside that of Lady Alice Parker-Holt, Lord Ratcliffe, Sir Eustace Croxton and the rest. There was no reason to suppose this same brood wouldn't find themselves in charge of the country, given a fickle public and the right degree of resentment. If that happened, he might need friends in the right place to ensure his continued success. O'Rourke, he believed, was not particularly well-off compared with his wealthy friends. If, as was rumoured, he aspired to Westminster, the increase in his wife's wages would be the sort of thing he might remember with gratitude....

Eric was suspicious. He was happy Jane had been offered the job, but wondered about Tanbrey's motives. He knew little about Tanbrey, but the rumours Jane had heard puzzled him. It seemed the man had gone from colliery manager to owner of one of the largest mills in Macclesfield, with no family wealth and no history of working in the textile trade. O'Rourke had never met him, and his life had been too busy to consider him except in passing. Now, however, their worlds might draw closer. He voiced his views to Jane after dinner one evening, when she asked: 'You think he's got something up his sleeve, don't you?'

He reorganised the utensils in a gesture of resolution. 'Perhaps. Take it. See what happens.'

'D'you remember what I told you about when I worked in Leek? I told you I was involved with the union. Well, since I've been at the Victoria I've kept out of it. I've done my best for the women, but I've not been involved. There's so much needs doing.'

'Quite.'

'I know what I've said before, but what I'm thinking is, if I take this job I'd be even more removed from the floor. I don't know if I want that.'

'My dear, only you know what you want.' He dabbed at his mouth. 'But let me say this: never believe the bottom-up pundits. Rule by the labouring man will never succeed. The only thing that will work is top-down. Alter the way the bosses think, and the rest will follow. Try it the other way, and you end up with anarchy.'

'You've changed your tune, Eric.'

'No, my sweet, it's perfectly to the point. As you yourself once said, if you have power, you have influence and without power you have none. Hence my aim to become a Member of Parliament. As an overseer, you're nobody; as Tanbrey's right-hand woman – well, who knows? In due course you might even whisper' conditions of service' in his ear. He might even take notice.'

'You think so?'

'Well, perhaps not. Look, why not accept the offer, see how it goes?'

She nodded reluctantly, her mouth set. 'If I hate it, I shall know who to blame.'

'I remember we had all this heart-searching over whether we should tie the knot, and that's turned out to be a resounding success, hasn't it?'

She smiled wryly as he left the room.

Before the year was out, John and Nerissa married. He'd once provided the local rich with amusement, but no one would laugh at him again, least of all her. They'd enjoyed each other over the years. He'd been her bit of rough, an hour's escape from the constraints of etiquette. Marrying her would confer any residual status she had to himself, and she hadn't refused because there was nothing she could do to avoid the shame of debt. She'd be a social asset, cultivated, intelligent and urbane. She'd be useful to him. Owning everything her father once had gave him great pleasure. His life began to take on new patterns of deceit. He was a generous benefactor, a ruthless employer, a dutiful husband and a self-interested schemer – depending on who was asked, and who was sacked. Above all, he was a force to be reckoned with. And he'd developed a taste for young girls.

One afternoon in late November, he'd caught the train to London. His favourite haunt was Whitechapel. The squalor of the place, with its drab brick and seedy life, excited him. He especially liked the autumn fogs which hung like a miasma across the river. The streets shone with drizzle as he took the cab from Euston. Through the window he watched the charcoal sky seep across the rooftops. The girl was sheltering in a doorway, her feathered hat the only splash of colour in the otherwise colourless street. He lowered the window and she came up to the cab, sheltering under a small umbrella.

'D'you have somewhere to go, sir?'

Her polite cockney amused him. He stopped the cab and she stepped inside and sat opposite, her thin face pinched with cold. He lit a cigar and sat back, his eyes bright in the shadow, watching her movements. She was pretty, but already her skin was growing coarse. He tapped his cane and the cab turned into the next street.

'It's 'alf a crown a go, sir, a crown if you want the night.'

'And what could you possibly do that would take the night?'

She giggled demurely. 'Oh, there's plenty of things to please a gentleman, it's the knowing of 'em, that's all.'

He could imagine her using a docker's penny to put clothes on her doll. 'Here.' He flipped over a sixpence, which she retrieved from the folds of her coat. She dropped the coin into her purse like a thrifty housewife. 'D'you want me to do something for you 'ere in the cab, sir? Some gentlemen prefer doin' it in a cab.'

'No,' he said, speaking through a haze of smoke. 'But you can earn your sixpence by showing me your pretty legs.'

'You won't see much in 'ere –' He reached over and lifted the hem of her skirt. 'All right, sir, I'll show you if you like.' Without finesse, she hoisted it above her knees. He made a movement with his cane, and she pulled her skirt over her drawers. 'It'll cost extra to that sixpence if you want to touch me privates, a shillin' if you want me to touch yours.'

'You should run a whelk stall, you'd make a fortune.'

He found the second girl loitering outside a pawnbroker's. Her poinsettia lips were slightly smudged, and her tightly-curled hair stuck to her forehead in dark worms. He beckoned, and she came over. He'd never told Nerissa about his bolt-hole in the warren of streets between Paddington and the Grand Union Canal, the white stucco villa tucked inconspicuously into an unlit cul-de-sac.

'Do you know each other?'

The first girl giggled. The other, more assertive, said they'd seen each other 'on the rounds, so to speak'.

The house had been empty for some weeks. He lit the vestibule lamp.

'It ain't half cold in 'ere,' the bolder girl said.

'I wouldn't want you to catch your death on my behalf.'

'How long will it take, Mister, only my mother says – '

'Don't trouble yourself.' He drew the sitting room curtains and lit the lamp. 'You'll be home before they send out the specials. Here.' He pressed a coin into each girl's hand. 'And there's more before you leave. If you're good girls, that is.'

A woman he employed to look after the place had left a scuttle of coal.

He lit the sitting room fire, and the gas heater which supplied hot water to a newly-installed bath. Pouring himself a cognac, he offered the girls a large gin.

'I fink he's tryin' to get us drunk, gal,' the dark one said, her mood heightened by the plush novelty of her surroundings. Her companion sat vacantly twisting the stem of her glass.

He scrutinised them over the rim; the first girl, Cathy, sharp, pale with mousy hair carelessly done up at the back; Daisy, who'd run to fat in a couple of years. The room began to lose its chill. Cathy stood in silence, sipping her drink. Daisy lay back on the chaise longue.

He said, 'I'd like us to be together for a while. A cab will call for you at one. I'll see to the fare, of course.'

'Be together, eh?' Daisy drawled tipsily, her pneumatic lips framing a knowing smile. 'What d'you think he means by that, girl?'

'I'm not green, you know.'

'I suggest you take a bath.'

'Cor, you got a bath?' The excitement on Daisy's face turned to petulance. 'I'm not dirty, you know. There's nothing wrong with me, if that's what you think.'

He got up. 'I'll light the way.'

The bath stood on a dais in what had been a large bedroom. He adjusted the valve until the water was running comfortably hot and watched the girls undress through the steam. 'I'll just watch you enjoy yourselves. Then we can all have some fun...'

'I must impress you with a warning,' he said, as they stood in the vestibule shortly before one. 'The money isn't just for a few hours' romp. It's a reward for keeping your traps shut. You can now forget it ever happened. Should I need your services again, I think I know where to find you. And I'm sure neither of you will put yourselves at risk troubling to find this place again.' He looked at his watch. 'Here's the cab. Be good girls, and you'll find more where that came from.' He closed the door behind them and turned down the lamps. Shortly afterwards he retired to bed.

He got up and dressed shortly before five. He felt depressed and for some reason needed the consolation of the empty streets. He decided to take a circuitous route to Euston and an early train back. He enjoyed the calm before the onset of day. A costermonger trundled a handcart towards Covent

Garden; a wagon rumbled over the sets, its driver in oilcloth against the early morning air. From the river, came a mournful hoot, an answering whistle from Paddington. He passed a constable, a group of road menders, a dray. Lost in his private world of shadows, he failed to notice the figure until it drew alongside. When he looked up he found himself facing his son.

'We seem fated to meet,' he said, finding his tongue. 'And where are you going at this hour?'

Ginny's doleful eyes swam up to him. 'I'm working, father. I have a job.'

'Where are you working?'

'I found employment with a printer. Nothing too ambitious, I'm afraid. I suppose there'll be opportunities, I don't know when.'

'Are you a journalist?'

'Oh, no, I'm training to be a compositor, that side of things.'

Tanbrey looked beyond the plane trees, their branches tinged in ashy light.

'I'm married, now,' Matthew said. 'My wife's a seamstress, Bernadette.'

'Is she Catholic?'

'A practising Catholic, yes.'

Tanbrey said: 'I don't believe in mixed marriages.'

'I didn't expect you to. That's why I didn't tell you. I'd better go now, or I'll be late.'

'Where are you living?'

'We have a room off Edgware. It's convenient for us.'

'I'd have thought an expensive education would have equipped you for more than a room with a seamstress.' Matthew held his eye steadily, and he could feel Ginny there. 'Anyway, it's none of my business.'

'No. No, it isn't.'

Tanbrey tugged at his glove and moved away. 'I'll leave you to your job.'

When he looked back, his son was out of sight. As he walked towards Euston, the low mood which his walk had begun to dispel descended on him once more. He wondered, as he had throughout his life, if the Cosmic Jester was hiding behind the Doric columns ready to pounce on him as he made his way to the platform.

'Someone called for you,' Nerissa told him when he got in.

'Who?'

As she handed him a card, he smelt the cigarette smoke on her clothes.

'Need you light those infernal things every time I go through the door?'

'They're my consolation.'

'Then go and console yourself elsewhere.'

Taking the holder from her mouth, she blew a defiant ring and left him. He followed her into the adjoining room. 'When did he leave this?'

'Yesterday. When you were attending to your so-called business concerns.'

'You know how it is, important matters need a prompt response.'

'A response in a bodice?'

'I don't think there's anything to keep me happy here, do you?'

He shaved and changed. He'd intended to go to the mill, but the name printed on the card had aroused his curiosity. He'd seen Ebenezer Hodson at local functions but had never been introduced. He was the owner of the Vulcan, a local foundry, and as far as he knew made a reasonable living. His small workforce had been with him for some years. He wasn't sure what they actually made...

He was shown to the office by one of the gatemen. Hodson looked up over a pair of wire glasses and extended a grubby paw across the desk. 'You've found me in a clutter, Mr Tanbrey. Your wife said you'd not be back before tomorrow.'

'I managed to conclude my business sooner than expected.'

'This seat's more comfortable.' He cleared a chair of its debris of paper. 'If you'll bide a minute, I'll get us some tea.'

He hovered around the table as if trying to recollect why he'd asked Tanbrey to come. Tanbrey studied his features; the hairless, skull-like head, deep-set eyes, loosely hung frame. Hodson went into the adjoining store and returned with two mugs. He handed one across the desk.

'I'll come straight to the point, Mr Tanbrey. I need to expand, and to do that I shall want capital. I don't like the banks, usurers, the lot of 'em. What would you say to a partnership?'

Behind the eyes flickered a hint of something. Cunning? Shrewdness?

'Why should I want to part-own a foundry and a few engineering sheds?'

'I know we've never been formally introduced,' Hodson said, 'but first let me say something to you. I know more about this business than anyone around here. I built what I've got from scratch and I've taken some knocks along the way. As you should know, comes a time you either get bigger or go to the wall. The time of small's over. You'll never cost under the big boys, chance what. Well, it's teachin' granny, you know what I'm on about. It was Barrington put your name to me. He said he'd given you a leg up in your own line, you might see your way to investing in mine.'

Tanbrey had met Barrington on several occasions since he'd dropped the contract for uniforms into his lap, but he'd never mentioned Hodson to him.

'Barrington has a share in the business,' Hodson went on. 'Just a toe-hold – but, well, we're both men of the world, I needn't spell it out. He could be as useful here as he seems to 'ave been down your mill.'

Machinery clattered faintly through the walls. A peripheral blur of office chaos intruded. Tanbrey asked: 'Why me?'

'When you came here, Birkenshaw's place was a laughing stock. You've turned it on its head. Makin' allowances for folks killin' themselves out in Africa, facts speak for themselves. If I'd had the capital before that lot started I could've supplied the bloody army and navy too, I'd be a millionaire by now. What am I doing? Makin' pit tools. When the next lot goes up, I could be doin' far better than that – if I get some help.'

'Couldn't Barrington see a way to increasing his stake?'

'Lawrence has a lot of irons in the fire. What he tips down his throat'd buy this place up. That, and his floozies.'

Tanbrey probed. Was Hodson reliable? Had he and Barrington contrived something between them? What did he know about either of them? What did he really know of Hodson's business? The war wouldn't end tomorrow, despite Salisbury's khaki election. The Queen was said to be in poor health. She wouldn't last for ever, and his looms were already set for the trappings of mourning. He had venture capital to risk, and diversification was a wise precaution. There'd been peace in Europe for thirty years; if it ended, the demand for steel would go through Hodson's roof.

'I'll have someone look into your books.'

'They're ready any time.'

In the yard, men were loading a wagon. Hodson's face hovered at his shoulder. 'Pit-tub wheels, the bodies follow on the next cart.' He pushed back his cap, ran a finger across his scalp. 'Don't take too long, Mr Tanbrey.

And I'd be grateful if it were just between us and the walls for the while.'

'If – and I say if – I agree, what will be my part in the scheme of things?'

'As little or as much as you want. Sleepin' partner, if you've a mind.'

Tanbrey left with the smell of manoeuvrings in his nostrils.

Lawrence Barrington lounged in the committee room of his club and looked across at Tanbrey, sitting on the couch opposite. His gravelly voice cut through the banter of the room. With his fat neck, overflowing gut, florid face and wet lips, he epitomised debauchery. Tanbrey thought he was fortunate to have met him.

'John, did I ever tell you about the woman from Pimlico?'

'I don't believe you did.'

'Wife of an earl. When he was off shooting grouse, she was making feathers fly at home. Liked army men. Thighs like a couple of plucked partridges. Couldn't get enough of it. Next day, she'd be opening a fete, not a hair out of place.' He moved his bulk conspiratorially. 'You know what she liked best? She adored dressing up as Joan of Arc and –' At that moment Hodson pushed through the door. Barrington completed his anecdote as the ironmaster came over. 'Ah, Ebenezer, old fellow, thought you'd fallen into the forge.'

'I was detained. Anyone runs a business nowadays wants their head looking at.'

'Oh, come now, it's not as bad as that, surely? John and I have been having an interesting conversation about the delights of the Metropolis, haven't we, John? We've been discussing the disgraceful moral laxity therein. Here, have a glass of this.'

The glass didn't suit Hodson's fist and the wine didn't suit his temperament. He cast a look towards Tanbrey.'You've looked at the books?'

'Everything seems to be in order. Your accounts show a regular, if unexciting, profit.'

'We were talking just before you came,' Barrington broke in. 'I'm persuaded against my better judgement, Ebenezer. I see a third each way, me and John sleeping. I'll stump up enough to get me there, John contributes likewise.'

'Thirty-three and a third each,' Hodson said impassively.

'That's it, and if anything's going in the nature of ironmongery, I'm sure we'll be well placed to push something your – our – way. Should the conditions arise - which I'm sure they will - I shall want my name in invisible ink, of course.'

'That sounds fair trade,' Hodson said, holding out a leathery hand. Barrington was slow to release it.

'We'll do some business, Ebenezer. I've got all the contacts you need for a full order-book. We'll make you a captain of industry yet, just like John here. Get those plans in. It's expansion time for you.'

He raised his glass.

'To a finger in every pie,' Tanbrey proposed.

'And a hand on every thigh,' Barrington growled, flushed with drink. 'Come on, Ebenezer, favour us with a little mirth, old fellow. You've just struck the bargain of the century. What say I propose a further toast. To the unsurpassed –'

'Unsurpassable –' Tanbrey said.

'Highly profitable –' Hodson added.

Barrington gave a bellow of laughter. 'To the unsurpassable and highly profitable Hodson and Partners!'

3

Bill put up a token resistance to Marian's insistence he have his fortune told.

'What're you afraid of, daddy?'

'It's a load of mumbo-jumbo I'm paying for.'

'You could buy the fair, if you'd a mind.'

He squinted under the brim of his hat. Yes, he probably could buy it; tents, carousel, engines, ground, bunting, band and all the inhabitants of Tulsa.

'What's she got under her bonnet this time?' Rose said, coming over with Colette.

'She's trying to persuade me against my will.' His daughter tugged him towards the tent at the edge of the field. *Luisa Fuentes: Your Destiny for a $1.* 'All right, I give in.'

He parted the flap. Flies buzzed against the canvas. A bangled woman faced him across a small, draped table, took his dollar and nodded to a chair. A jangling banjo broke faintly through a blur of voices.

She peered down at his palm, said in strongly-accented English. 'You come from Europe. Please, you no need resist.'

'Resist?'

She met his eyes, bent again to his hand. 'You have good luck in life. You also have the bad. *La buena suerte y lo malo.* I see three children and a loved one missed.... I see others, they are dead. *Los muertos....*'

What was he doing, listening to this clap-trap? Any one of a hundred could have given her his life story. Which dead? His first wife, Elizabeth? Of course he'd have known somebody who'd died. By the time a man reached forty-seven, it was obvious.... and a third child?'

'Tell me why you come to America.'

'To seek my fortune, like the rest.'

'I see a dark place. It is grey, grey hills. There was death in this place. You were near to this death.'

A sudden confusion ran through him. Dixon? Could it be Dixon?

'But you are also a wealthy man. *Un rico.*'

'*Ud ha visto mis ropas. Y mi reloj de oro.*' You've seen my clothes and gold watch. It was facile, all this, a charade. Did she mean Dixon?

She ran her finger along the line of his palm. 'You speak Spanish good. This is the line of life, *la linea de la mortalidad.*'

'Meaning what?'

'The length of the line, it show you 'ow long is your life.' She studied the creases intently, then sat back and folded her hands across her lap.

'Well?'

'It is nothing. I cannot read. Some days I cannot.'

'You want more money, is that it?'

'No me importa dinero.' He picked up his hat and made a move to go. 'All right, I tell you. It is not always written so I tell you.'

'Go on.'

'I see water. A big ship. You sail on a big ship, *un vapor grande.*'

'What about it?'

'You go, now.'

'What about this ship?'

She shrugged. 'You ask, so I tell you. The sea....*el mar.... El vapor grande significa la muerte.'*

'You trying to tell me I'm going to drown, is that it? I paid a dollar for you to read my death warrant? I'll have to speak to the sheriff, see what can be done about charlatanry. You can keep the money for your cheek.'

He came out looking shaken. Rose said, 'You don't look like you enjoyed that.'

'Let's take a turn on the carousel.'

Bunting fluttered in the air. The band struck up *Camptown Races*, black musicians, probably from Georgia, bow ties and striped blazers. Rose took his arm. 'Well? You've not told me what she said.'

'Just a load of rubbish. She said I'd had three children for a start –' and as he spoke, the memory of Ellen and the baby came back to him.

'What else?'

'She talked about a ship sinking and I'd be on it. At least I think that was it. It's all mumbo-jumbo anyway. Ships sink every day. There'll be an earthquake somewhere, somebody'll fall off a cart loading grain bags and the moon's made out of green cheese.'

She squeezed his hand. 'It's a living. Everyone has to make one. You probably got it all wrong anyway.'

An echo of the woman's premonitions persisted throughout the week. The word *muertos,* the dead, had been pushed into a quiet corner of his mind. She'd raised spirits he'd hoped had been laid to rest. Elizabeth, Ross,

Dixon, Maud, his first child. He stood in his office looking over a city of crowds sucked in by oil. He'd heard they were making the first people's car, everything hush-hush, but the word was this man's Model A would sell for less than $750. They were aiming to pitch it up to thirty miles an hour. If it all went through, he'd snap one up. And all because of the derricks stretched around Tulsa. But despite his good fortune, *Los muertos* plagued him, none more than Ross and Maud. He drifted back to the time he'd gone to Ross's homestead....

He'd waited for nightfall before riding back to the shack. Leaving his horse in a gully, he'd edged towards the gated enclosure of Gulch Oil. The man who'd pointed the rifle would be in the house somewhere. He'd edged up to the window. What had driven him to take the risk? He didn't know then, had never known since. He remembered hearing the door splinter, could still smell the stench of fear on the man's breath as he stood over his bed and pressed the Colt to his temple. The barrel of a Winchester had protruded from the pillow. He'd whipped it out and sent it clattering across the planking.

'What you want with me, mister?' The reedy voice. He could hear it now, clear above the rumble of carts below.

His hands had stopped shaking. Who'd find out if he killed the man? He deserved to be shot. He deserved his death. Maybe Ross and Maud were having the time of their lives, taking a vacation, tomorrow they'd arrive in a gig, Maud with a hat box on her knee....

'Where are they?'

'Who?'

'Don't trifle with me, I'll put the first one through your guts. Where are they?'

'You mean –?'

'The couple had this place, what happened to them?'

'I don't know, I swear I don't know, mister, honest.'

He'd crashed the muzzle hard on the twitching head. A ribbon of blood had oozed downwards into the staring eye. 'Tell me, or I'll do for you. I got nothing to lose in this hell-hole.'

'It wasn't me, mister, honest to God you gotta believe me, it was that bastard Weller, him an' the Denvers that done it. I'm just a guy lookin' after the pumps, you gotta believe that.'

'What did they do?'

'Shot 'em both, mister, sure as I lie in this bed. Bart told me. He was drunk, didn't know what he was sayin', told me where they'd gone there'd be no more problems. Said he'd offered for their land, but they weren't biting, now they're bitin' dust. It was Bart Denver told me, sure as my name's Clem Firstone.'

'Where're the bodies?'

'For Christ sakes, mister –'

'Tell me!'

The spreading stain cut out a segment of the man's chin, making his face look curiously skeletal in the moonlight. 'They buried'em in the arroyo. He took me up, showed me the place. I didn't want to go, mister, but he forced me. I got no stomach for killin'.'

'That's why you keep a loaded Winchester under the pillow?'

A thread of weak light had caught the man's eye. 'You're not goin' to kill me?'

Bill had relaxed his grip on the Colt. Why didn't he feel anger? Why hadn't he smashed the conniving face? There was a rapid movement under his hand, at the same moment a searing pain in his thigh. His gun had gone off and the man had fallen back with a bullet graze to the shoulder. Bill had wrapped his leg in torn sheeting and bound the man's hands. In less than two hours it would be dawn.

'Right, can you hear what I'm saying to you? I'm taking you with me. Try another trick, it'll be the last, you understand?' The man nodded dully. 'Right, get up. I'll be behind you all the way.'

'I won't. I'm goin'.'

'You're going, all right. Going all the way to the gallows.'

The man had stumbled to the door, faint with loss of blood. The knife wound in Bill's thigh had made him limp, and he wasn't sure how deep the cut was. They'd reached town at first light. The man seated before him on the horse was on the verge of collapse when they reached the Sheriff's office. Within weeks of Bill's visit to Gulch Oil, Waller and Bart Denver had been strung up. The younger Denver, Ryan, and Firstone, had been sentenced to five years labour for withholding evidence. Bill's deeds relating to Ross's homestead and the Dakota store had been produced and verified by his bank and forged papers found in Waller's house exhibited to the jury. The exhumation of the bodies had clinched the proof. Both bore shot marks to the head, and the calibre of bullet removed from the skulls was found to match Denver's gun....

The silver cigar case under Bill's hand came into focus and he turned from the window. The Remingtons on the wall, the Turkish carpets, the fancy china, it all stemmed from that first barrel of oil. Ross and Maud had paid with their lives for what was now his. They'd meant more to him than his own family; Ross with his stubborn modesty and strength; Maud, who'd delivered his daughter and railed against his first wife's death. Now he and Rose were the custodians of their fortune.

When the trauma began to fade, he asked Rose what she wanted to do. She'd asked him to sell part of the oil rights to a newly-formed company that was already carving inroads into Standard's markets. He had the papers drawn up to give him concessions in the Shell company. His suite in Tulsa and the cigar box under his hand proved the wisdom of her decision. As Shell's fortunes mushroomed, so did theirs. His heart still sang to the whisper of zephyrs, but oil - oil that had cost four lives, that would one day oust the horses from the street below. Oil had given him what only a man in a million could dream of.

On the other side of the Atlantic, a woman lay on a soiled mattress listening to the voices in her head. One told her her name was Mary Tanbrey, the other screamed Mary Heathcote. She emptied the bottle of gin, let it fall to the bed and pulled back the blanket. She searched her face in the mirror and a hag with tea-darkened hair stared back at her. For the past year she'd shared her pillow with lice and her bed with anyone who had the price of a day's rent. She lived above a barber who'd told her to use the back way for fear of upsetting his customers. Lately she'd begun speaking to herself. People noticed, but they couldn't see what her eyes told her as she walked down the street.

The door opened and the barber came in, a foam-flecked razor in his hand. 'Someone to see you.'

He turned and went down. Two men stood there; a constable and a slight, suited man with an air of officialdom. The policeman took her by the arm. 'Better get some clothes, missus, you'll fare better with someone to take care of you.'

'I've got a husband to take care of me and he'll be here directly.'

The man in the suit coughed and took a step forward. 'I'm a medical officer working under the authority of the Board of Guardians for Wolstanton and Burslem Union Workhouse. It's come to our notice you're without means and –'

His words flew with his bowler across the floor, and before he'd recovered she'd gouged twin furrows down his cheek. She resisted the constable's arm with a show of strength which toppled them both. He wrenched the blanket from her bed, and draped it over her head. Downstairs, the barber ushered his only customer out of the shop. The upstairs door crashed back, a boot found the first tread. She bit through the policeman's sleeve, breaking the skin. He jerked her head back, manhandled her into the entry where a van waited. It took the strength of both men to carry her inside.

Terraces rumbled past, cobbles patched with shard and clinker, posters pasted to the walls: Wiverill's Pianolas, Epsom Salts, Charlie Chan, the Great Illusionist. Tradesmen's houses, with gothic windows and ornate barge boards. A hotel, a Methodist Chapel, the Big House where the Wedgwoods once lived. At Tunstall, shreds of bunting still clung to the Town Hall. Was it really a year since the African war ended, or were they from the previous year, when the black horses had trailed a lament for the dead Queen down the High Street? She pondered. Bunting for rejoicing, not funerals. That must be it. And the market hall where she'd met him at the dance sixteen years ago. He'd knocked over his drink and gone, taking Hannah and Richard with him. Neville Deakin should have taken her away somewhere, not gone off with his wife to Cannock, the tile works all sold off.

As they rounded the corner she saw it on the hill, a grey block with grey windows. Now it was hidden behind the rows, each house higher than its neighbour. She pummelled the boards, shrank to the floor, and when the doors opened she seemed to be standing in the shadow of the workhouse gate. They led her into a hall and from there to a high-ceilinged room. There was a leather-topped table, chairs to either side; a plaque, 1838; a list of the Board of Guardians in red. Two men were whispering in a corner of the room.

'I've brought the woman.'

'Booked her in, have you?'

'There's no one about.'

'Best leave her in the Waiting Room.' One moved reluctantly to the door. 'He might 've left the book open, I'll take a look.'

The man took her down a passage and through a further door, which he bolted behind her. A single-barred window overlooked the lane. She sank to a bench and pulled her blanket over her ears to block out the screaming which broke into her cell from a distant part of the building. She climbed to the window and looked out. A hearse creaked through the gate and down the lane. She kept it in sight as it turned on to a track and disappeared down the slope.

A pauper woman came in with a bundle of rags. 'Get these on while you're 'ere, everyone 'as to wear the same and they're all the same size.'

Our Father, which art in heaven –

A man came in. 'Get yourself covered up so we can book you in.'

Hallowed be Thy name, Thy kingdom come –

He snatched the blanket from her and threw it across the floor. She shivered, her shrunken breasts partly exposed through the open shift. He struggled to get the wrap over her head. A button broke off, and his temper flared. 'This'll go straight in the boiler. Now come in the office and look sharp.'

Somewhere a door opened. She was standing before a high desk, drawers each with an ivory knob and a safe and a frayed chair. There was a clerk dipping his pen.

'Got one for you, Harry.'

The pen scratched. He took a blotter to his list and lifted a file in silence. 'Name?'

'Mary Ann Tanbrey.'

'Married, widow or spinster?'

'Married. You won't keep me in this hole long. My husband'll be round.'

'Maiden name?'

'Mary Heathcote I was.'

'Next of kin?'

'Mr Charles Tanbrey.'

'Your legal spouse?'

''Course he's my legal spouse, what d'you take me for?'

'Names and ages of your natural children?'

'Hannah died, I read it in the papers.' She added, grandly: 'I was unable to attend due to pressing matters.'

'Other children?'

'One left. That's Richard. I've scarcely seen him, I've been otherwise engaged.'

'Age?'

'Richard'll be coming up for eight. Or maybe he's gone eight.' She began to whimper. 'I can't keep up with it all, I can't, I can't....'

He waited for her to calm. 'Do you have parents?'

'Both dead, now, their luck.'

'Siblings?'

She reeled off segments of a dimly-remembered past, forgetting her answers as she gave them. When she'd gone, he addressed a note to the local constabulary: Admission of Pauper: Mrs Mary Ann Tanbrey, estranged wife of a Mr Charles Tanbrey, believed living at Moor Top. We request the husband be brought for a hearing inasmuch as it appears he has neglected to support his wife, now resident at Wolstanton and Burslem Workhouse situate Chell.

He dropped the note into a tray as the next inmate arrived.

Jane left the Manchester train and took a cab to a house in Nelson Street. A girl opened the door.

'I'm Jane O'Rourke. I believe there's a meeting?'

A woman appeared, her hands outstretched in welcome. She led the way into a large Drawing Room. A grand piano had been pushed against the wall, together with other items of furniture. The vacated space was taken by rows of chairs occupied by women. A journalist, the only man in the room, sat by the window, polishing the edge of a boot with his finger.

'Ladies, I want you to meet Mrs O'Rourke, the wife of one of our prospective MPs. Jane, I believe you've already met Lady Alice. I'm sure she won't mind if you join her.'

Lady Parker-Holt patted a cushion. 'I'm so glad you could come, my dear. I'm not really convinced I should be here. I cannot for the life of me see that I can be of any use at my age.'

'How're you keeping?'

'As well as might be expected of someone on their last legs. And how's dear Eric? It's so long since I've seen you both. You must come and have tea with me soon.'

'I'm sure he'd be pleased,' Jane said. 'To tell the truth, my employer doesn't know I'm here. I sent a note saying I was off sick.'

Lady Alice leaned forward conspiratorially. 'I must give you a little advice to pass on to your husband. You must ask him to give up his wilder fantasies for the while if he wishes to become a politician.'

'What d'you mean?'

'Tell him he must espouse the Liberal cause.'

'But –'

'Socialist power is inevitable, but I believe the Liberals will steal their thunder. As a Liberal politician, he'd have a far better platform than he would lecturing to colliers at the local institute.'

Jane flushed. 'I'm not sure I could dissuade him even if I wanted to.'

'Now you're angry with me. I can't say I blame you. But, you know, we have these Tories on the run. Now that Salisbury's dead, I scent a whiff of change. I have it on good authority that Ramsay McDonald and Herbert Gladstone have something up their sleeves which could well work to Eric's advantage.'

'And what might that be?'

The old woman dropped her voice to a whisper. 'A plot has been hatched to give Labour candidates a clear run in constituencies unlikely to vote Tory.'

'To give Labour a chance in a next Liberal government, you mean?'

A sharp tap interrupted their conversation. Heads turned to the animated figure of Emmeline Pankhurst. As the applause died, she stepped into the window-light. 'Ladies, welcome. I see before me the unheard voice of Britain. Thank you for coming.' There was another rumble of applause, which she allowed to run its course. 'Ladies, the time has come to cast off the mantle of wife, mother and daughter and to raise with pride the sceptre of female radicalism. The time has come to make no further plea for emancipation, but to demand it as a right, and if our demands are not met, to take it.' Cheers rang out. The reporter's pencil hissed in the following silence. 'Suffrage is not in a politician's gift, to be handed out to whomsoever men deem fit. If the drunk and the cad can vote merely on the basis of gender, why cannot a woman, even a gifted woman, be allowed a cross on a slip of paper? Ladies, the hour has come. From henceforth it shall be deeds, not words.

'Of course the struggle will be hard. And perhaps it will be brutal. There is no point in relying on the Tories to support us. They will not. We might have friends in the Liberal Party, should they come to power, but can we trust them or will it be the usual empty words? We stand under the united banner of women's reform and we owe it to ourselves and to the nation to translate our beliefs into a cause. Universal suffrage is not a privilege, it is our birthright – more than that, our duty.

'Some will say there are more pressing causes to occupy our time. Events of great moment fill our lives. We have a monarch who is no ally of the Liberal view. We have a half-starved and illiterate populace. There is dissent at home and uncertainty abroad. Yet it is despite these matters, indeed because of them, that women must make their voices heard. Away with persuasion! Deeds, not words! I see a women's social and political union whose aims are to secure for women the parliamentary vote and to use their power to promote social and industrial well-being. Look around at my daughters, seated there by the window. What would I wish for Christabel, what for Sylvia, what for all of you gathered here today? I tell you. I wish you the right to be recognised as men's equal. I want your voices to be heard. Loud, clear voices, proudly proclaiming the power of your womanhood. That is my wish.'

A brief silence hung like a curtain over the room. Then someone clapped, and within an instant the chamber was filled with a euphoric clamour. Arrangements were made for subsequent meetings, volunteers sought to publicise the Women's Social and Political Union, and to produce ideas for raising funds. A contribution box was taken from under the piano and passed around.

Lady Alice stayed behind with Jane after all but Emmeline and her daughters had left.

'You mustn't over-burden yourself,' Alice told her, 'and you mustn't expect miracles. After all, the fight for suffrage was going on when I was young. Well, who am I to throw cold water, my dear? I wish you every success. With you and your daughters at the helm, I'm sure the movement will leap ahead.'

The maid came in. 'Your cab's here, madam.'

Lady Parker-Holt pulled on her gloves and swished into the passage. At the door she turned to Jane. 'Perhaps I can take you somewhere?'

The streets were crowded. Alice watched the passers-by with lazy interest as the horse clip-clopped through the traffic. 'I'm glad I wrote to you about the meeting,' she said. 'I know Eric's passionate to get things changed. He's always been a staunch supporter of women's rights. Let's be perfectly honest, Jane, women have had more power than they care to admit since the world began. Any woman who can fill her bodice starts with an advantage. The trick is to convince the man he has the whip-hand while you're holding the reins. I beg your pardon, my dear, rambling on like this. One rarely has the opportunity to say more than half a dozen words nowadays, and the servants ignore them anyway. Where are you going to, did you say?'

'I think back home. If we could go to the station?

'I was hoping you'd join me at the Free Trade Hall. They're performing Elgar again. He has a marvellous talent, much better than that mawkish Russian, Tchaikovski. Whenever I hear him, all I want to do is cry. I like to smell the hedgerows. Elgar makes me feel secure.'

Jane let the old woman's thoughts wander through the thoroughfares. If anyone was an enlightened despot, it was Lady Alice; pompous, self-effacing and utterly generous. Someone not quite at home in a rapidly changing world.

The farm buildings merged into a pastel winter afternoon, and a thin wreath of smoke hung across the trees. Ellen had stayed up till late polishing the fender and leading the grate. She'd set vases of holly on the sills, swilled the path and tidied the yard. She could have done more, but her pregnancy at forty-two had exhausted her. Many years had passed since the last gathering at Three Elms. Bevis had never been one for social occasions, and Doris had always seemed content with visits to Leek with local farmers' wives. Ellen glanced at her, snoring by the fire. Now she walked aimlessly, her white head thrust forward, her shoulders hunched in a dowager's hump, once familiar routines forgotten, her days crumbled into vague images lacking sense or chronology. With a characteristic mental sweep, she cleared her mind. She'd the well-being of her unborn child to consider; that and Charlie's going to the college -- and the greater problem of his wife. They'd be here soon. She'd wear the silver earrings Charlie had given her, and the new dress she'd bought. Doris opened her eyes and sat staring into the fire.

'Do you want a drink?' The old woman struggled to rise. 'You want to go the back way? It's always when there's work to be done.'

She supported Doris as far as the privvy, and when they got back fed her a little meat stew. Doris pushed away the spoon without petulance. 'Is Charlie here?'

'Not yet. He'll be here soon.'

'Is he still at that painting of his?'

'He says he's stuck them all up in his attic.' The woman nodded without understanding. 'He's doing no more, he's shoved 'em all in the roof. He's to be a schoolmaster, like Mrs Caulton who taught us hymns. I told you before. It's no use telling you nothing if you forget all the time, is it?'

It was no use telling her about the child, either. She'd tell no one but Jane.

Charlie came on his bike after the service. Since Hannah's death, he'd got into the habit of going to church. During the sermons, he'd fix his eyes on the rubric which followed the chancel arch. It was here he felt close to his daughter, sensed she was by him in the pew. He usually walked with Richard, but today he'd wheeled out his bike and left it in the porch and when the service ended he'd set his son on to the cross-bar for the ride to Ellen's farm. Since Hannah's death, he'd developed a fear of losing him, had made an arrangement with Ellen to take the boy if anything should happen to him. He'd lost touch with his wife. Her elder brother had written asking that the allowance Charlie sent each week be forwarded now to his address; they'd lost rack of her, they'd pass it on when she called.

Responsibility for her still nagged at him. He'd deserted her, as she'd deserted him and her children. He couldn't go back even if there'd been somewhere to go back to. He'd written to her brother and sent the date of Hannah's funeral to the local paper and she still hadn't come. He could neither forget nor forgive, and it was the certainty that it was over that had brought him to Ellen. And now she was bearing his child. His marriage had been a disaster. No use trying to atone for it by sealing his portfolio in the roof. What had that achieved?

He'd moved towards a fresh beginning. Come September, he hoped to start his teacher training. He'd rent out his house, and Ellen had offered to look after Richard. But that was before she knew she was pregnant. She'd been right. Teaching was better than labouring on the farms, but if they found out about his personal life, who'd employ him then? Was a man who'd deserted his wife fit to educate others' sons and daughters?

A mild breeze blew away his anxieties. To either side the jolting bike dipped the winter-green fields, and below the finger post webs of smoke curled from her fire. Richard got off to open the gate, then ran after him as he jolted, feet off the pedals, down the track.

Eric O'Rourke was standing with his back to the fire holding an empty plate. 'I really do think these suffragettes should think more democratically – thank you Ellen, I will have another very large slice of your excellent cherry pie – instead of coming out with all this twaddle about a new militarism. Militarism is bayonets and grenades. What a dreadful thought.' He took an enormous bite from the pie and continued provocatively: 'Be blowing up the Houses of Parliament next. Think what happened to Mr Fawkes.'

'It's all right, Ellen,' Jane said, 'he's just trying to rile me up. I don't know why he wastes his time.'

'I protest! I was merely expressing a view. What do *you* think, Charles?

'I can't see why anybody should be denied the vote.'

'We all want that. It's merely a question of how we achieve it. I mean, d'you think my wife should start knocking off bobby's hats?'

'Only if the bobbies knock her's off first,' Charlie countered.

O'Rourke spluttered into his pie. 'Very good, I like that one. Mind you, I don't think there's much fear of that. They wouldn't be able to reach it for a start.'

He erupted again. Jane said: 'Well, there's one thing for certain, they could squash you without lifting a foot. I do believe he's shrunk since I married him, Ellen. He never was that tall to begin with.'

Undaunted, Eric produced two panatellas from his top pocket, one of which he offered to Charlie as the women cleared the dishes.

'I don't recall smoking one of these before.'

O'Rourke lit a spill and puffed out a thin blue cloud. 'Now's your chance. A generous helping of filet de boeuf, a cigar and a good talk. What could be better than that?'

'I hear from Ellen you're trying to make a go of politics,' said Charlie.

'A little bird's been whispering.'

'Can I ask what kind?'

'An acquaintance has suggested I stand for the Liberal Party at the next election. I thought she was wrong. I saw my lot with the Socialists. There you have the party of the future. Now I'm not so sure. Not that there won't be a Labour Party. There most certainly will. The question is, when?

It's somewhat like myself – small, but significant. I'm forty seven. If I have anything to say, it has to be now. At least the Liberals will go part way, and there are others who'll join their ranks. Besides, I daren't offend this elderly lady. It's partly through her financial support I'm able to pursue these madcap ideas at all.' Richard had fallen asleep, his quiet breathing interrupted by Doris's snores. 'Tell me about yourself. You're going to be a schoolmaster, they tell me.'

'It all depends whether I get the qualifications.'

'Your son, he's not yours and Ellen's?'

'No.' Charlie wondered how much he knew. 'No, his mother isn't about at the moment.'

O'Rourke changed the subject. 'Jane thinks your brother may be her employer.'

'I wouldn't be surprised. I don't see that much of him.'

'And you have another brother – in Canada, did Jane say?'

'America.'

'What's he like?'

'He used to be a bit of a tearaway. Now he's a family man, and a rich one at that.'

'Oh?'

'Last I heard, he'd given up farming and gone into the oil trade.'

'Where?'

'Oklahoma.'

O'Rourke puffed reflectively. Out of the blue, he asked, 'What d'you know of these French painters?'

'You mean Delacroix, David?'

'No, I'm not talking about those awful pictures of Napoleon done up like a god. Have you heard of Renoir?'

'I can't say I have.'

'There, you see! There's a pack of 'em – Renoir, Monet, Pissarro. When I was down in London some years ago, I had my first glimpse of their work. The gallery was owned by a Frenchman, Durand-Ruel. No one was buying. Do you know, I find that extraordinary. There were these beautiful canvases, going for a song.'

'I can't say I've heard a lot about them. I study where I'm able, but there's only so much time.'

'Full of light and colour, different from anything I'd ever seen. Glowing with spontaneity. I scrounged what I could and bought a couple. I don't give a hoot whether they're fashionable or not. You must come over and see them.'

'Did Jane tell you I was interested in painting?'

'I expect Ellen must have told her.'

'I don't do a lot, now. I've done nothing since – well, if I get a schoolmaster's job –'

He saw the attic. The dust would already lay thick on the sleeve. From the kitchen came a clash of crockery. For a time, the women's conversation continued the theme of Jane's letters; her aspirations for Eric, enthusiasm for the women's movement, rumours of the true state of her employer's marriage, that he mentioned Flossie more than his own son.

'You're losing your accent,' Ellen was telling her. 'Not like me and Charlie. I've told him he wants to start speaking right if he's to be a schoolmaster.' She pushed the door shut, lowered her voice. 'Jane, I'm expecting.'

'I know. You're all right?'

'I'm fine.'

'What about his wife?

'It's a right mess, isn't it? He doesn't know where she is. You don't know the half of it. She was a right trollop, and I know that sounds well, coming from me. Charlie found out she already had a son. Then he found her in bed with a workmate of his.'

'What are you going to do?'

'Can you get off work when the time comes? No one need know down here. We go weeks without seeing a soul – apart from labourers, and most of them aren't local. And Doris doesn't know what day it is. I'll need help, just for a few weeks, then I'll cope.'

'When's it due?'

'End of July.'

'Wouldn't you be better off with a doctor?'

'It'd be all over the moor. I understand it's a responsibility, especially after last time.'

Jane fell silent, then a flicker of a smile played across her mouth. 'These Tanbreys certainly get about. All right, I'll see what I can do. Again.'

A knock sounded.

'Probably those two,' Ellen said, but her ear had picked up a slowing in the faint rhythm of speech from the next room. 'I bet it's mother woke up, I'd best go and see.'

The man was already standing in the room. She saw Charlie's face, dough-white and haggard. 'It's Mary.' He was pulling on his coat. 'I've to go to the workhouse at Chell. Would you keep Richard for the night if I'm not back?'

He managed a nod to O'Rourke and the women, and followed the man into the yard.

4

The light was fading as he reached Chell. He found himself dithering through cold and fear – fear of the place, of what they'd say, leaving her to suffer in that hole, taking her children from her. Fear of that. The cab moved off, its lamp casting a bilious film across the sets.

'I've come to see my wife.'

'And who might that be?'

'Mary Tanbrey.'

The gateman yawned, took a lamp and opened the door. The building reared into the darkening sky, its windows flaring in the western light. From the town, faint pulses of sound swept upwards. They paused at an entrance, the man struggling to open the heavy door. Iron beds lined either side a dimly-lit hall. A severe hacking came from one, from another a name called in terror. He followed the man. 'Your wife's in the next room, the venereal, we call it. She's in there, the last bed.'

The light-band widened as he went inside. He passed down the aisle until he heard a voice call his name. She was barely recognisable in the weak light. She struggled to turn, opened her mouth in a parody of welcome. 'You'll have to take me home, Charlie.'

'Nobody's been able to find you.' His words caught like barbed wire in his throat. 'Nobody knew where you were.'

'You're the only one to come. My brothers haven't come, I've not seen any of them.'

Her voice came to him from a distance. She lifted an arm, let it fall limply on the bed. He took her hand. She could no more help what she'd become than a tree could change its bark. 'I'll have you out of here, don't fret, I'll see you get out.' He brushed helplessly at his eyes.

'How's Hannah going on, and our Richard?'

He looked up in his distress. 'Hannah died. You must know, I wrote to your brother.'

'Not a bad girl, Hannah.' Her grip on his fingers tightened. 'Charlie, they brought me here under false pretences. I'm not to blame. It wasn't me did anything. I can't help it if men come calling on me all the time–'

Her speech had deteriorated to an empty rambling. *It was not her fault, not her fault, he should have stood by her.*

'Mr Tanbrey? Can I speak with you a moment?' A middle-aged man was standing behind him. Charlie let go her hand and followed him into a recess. 'My name is Henshall. I'm employed as a doctor to oversee the paupers by the Board of Guardians. Mr Tanbrey, your wife.... your wife is suffering from syphilis.' He waited for a response, but there was none. 'Unfortunately the salts of mercury we use in such conditions has proved ineffectual. I have to tell you that the disease has invaded the organs.' Charlie heard a profound sigh well up and up, and knew it was his own. When he looked again at the man, his eyes were empty. 'I believe one of the officers brought you here earlier. Whether you face a hearing for the neglect of your wife is not within my sphere. I have to tell you she has little time left.'

'I'll take her out.'

'I'm afraid it's too late for that.'

He smarted with pity; pity for her, for himself, for Hannah, for every memorial to the wretchedness of life. 'She can come back with me. I wouldn't let a cur die here. She'll not go to a pauper's grave while I'm alive.'

'To move her now would only hasten her end. Far better to pass away quietly than suffer further anguish. You may stay with her if you wish.' He left the room. Charlie came slowly back to her bed.

'What does he want, Charlie?'

'Just.... just formalities.'

'I'm not a fool. Shall I tell you something? I'm not afraid, you know. I went to the church all these years. I'm not afraid to go. I think it's for the best. What do I have to fear? I'm going to see Tommy again, going to see my Tommy....'

In the morning a sheen of drizzle clung to the roof tops. He pushed through the iron gate, oblivious to the water on his face or the envelope in his hand. Part of him had died with her, as part of him had died with Hannah. She'd been no wife and he, latterly, no husband. He was overcome by a sudden, overwhelming sense of futility, and went to an ale-house and drank by himself in a corner. Instead of oblivion, the liquor brought her face back to him. As if to cut out the sight of it, he took out the envelope and read the summons to appear at court. It meant nothing. He crumpled the paper and went out. When he reached the Moel, a great lethargy came over him. He lay on the couch and immediately fell asleep.

A mob of women had gathered outside the Free Trade Hall. A brick struck a banner stretched across the railings. *Give Women the Vote. Deeds Not*

Words. Barrington halted his cab a little way off. The police had broken through, and as he watched a constable seized one of the girls by the arm. Her companion lashed out with a rolled umbrella to a roar of approval. As he drove on, another woman was being dragged towards a waiting van. He recognised Christabel Pankhurst.

He lit a cigar and released the smoke in a vindictive cloud. Let them torture their pretty bodies in hysterical displays of exhibitionism, they'd tire of it in the end. The only place for a woman was on her back. Yet he had to watch his step. He'd advised the House that to continue to ignore the women's vote would be to play into the hands of the militants. There was a limit to the length of time a government could stand against this onslaught. The Tories were already in a precarious state. If Balfour were to resign and a Liberal government were elected, these so-called suffragettes might win a victory and promote the fortunes of the moderate Right into the bargain. Barrington hated the moderate wing of his own party even more than the socialists who draped their opportunism under a banner of reform. They'd landed the country in a mess in South Africa. The Boers should have been sent packing within weeks, instead of the drawn-out saga it had all become. The one consolation was money. War made a lot of it, and he hoped after this week-end he'd see more of it coming his way. A belching motor-lorry passed. He wondered how long it would be before every tradesman had one, and a man could hunt in vain for a decent butler.

At the station he stepped into an empty first-class compartment, and when his train slowed at Macclesfield caught sight of Tanbrey gliding past the glass. He called out, and John took a seat beside him as the train moved away. Barrington produced a hip flask and put it to his lips. 'Now, my dear fellow, the weekend lies ahead. Care for a brief snort?'

Tanbrey leaned back in his seat. 'It's too early for me.'

Barrington put the flask back in his pocket. 'You've never been to one of Whimpie's little dos before. I don't know where you've been hiding yourself.'

'Perhaps after this weekend I'll be hiding myself permanently.'

Barrington laughed and clapped his leg. 'You're a cool customer, dammit.' He leaned forward in his seat and tapped his nose with a fat finger. 'I'll wager you're not such a temperate scoundrel where the fillies are concerned, hey?'

The countryside drifted past at a leisurely pace. Barrington talked about imported food taking its toll on the British farmer, about the lack of machinery in the manufacturing process. Tanbrey, listening with half an ear, was wondering what the weekend would hold. He'd got to know Barrington well over the last three years. They'd a lot in common. Both wanted power, and both enjoyed a blameless public life at odds with their personal licentiousness. Barrington's inherited wealth meant he'd been able to use the time Tanbrey had spent climbing the ladder in carousing with the rich and famous. He was on intimate terms with many of the gentry, who, together with a growing band of third-generation industrialists, made up the country's elite. Lord Whympinger was the grandson of a shipbuilder who'd made a fortune supplying vessels for the Orient run and Barrington had known him since Eton. This weekend it was Whimpie's turn to host a party of politicians, industrialists and nobility to whom Lawrence Barrington was a notable addition.

They changed to a branch-line train which puffed through the sleepy Oxfordshire countryside en route to Compton. Barrington fell silent, his eye fixed on the tapestry of fields gliding past the window. 'It will be a shame if all this goes,' he murmured. 'No other country has anything like it, you know.'

'I don't follow.'

'We've had these sparkling summers, haven't we? England at its very finest. *Sumer is icumen in, lhude sing cuccu* and all that. How long before the storm, would you say?'

'Mob rule, you think?'

'Oh, not the mob, John, no, no. There'll be the odd strike of course, nothing that can't be dealt with. A little stick, a little carrot, and donkey plies his trade. No, I'm inclined to the view our Teutonic brethren might wish to flex their muscles. And with the current shambles at the War Office, they might well flex them with some success. I suppose they have their axe to grind. After all, they never seemed to get their place in the sun. They've overtaken us, you know, in all but coal.'

'So have the Americans.'

'But they have space, my boy, no need to antagonise anybody. Most of them came from here, anyway. But our European friends – no, that's an entirely different kettle of fish, I'm afraid.'

'I can't see it. Not for a while.'

'Would I had the gift of self-delusion. You're hoodwinked, my good friend. Beneath the pond the eddies wax strong. Mr Kaiser is hiding under the stones like a wise old trout. He'll suddenly leap out, then woe betide all those little flies disporting themselves in the sun.' They came to a wayside station, and Barrington rose energetically to his feet. 'Enough of that. Come on, our stop.'

A hot afternoon hush had descended on the platform and the fields beyond. The train puffed away, the smell of steam mingling with a faint scent of mallow which grew against the station wall. A car was waiting in the lane. The chauffeur came over and touched his hat. 'I trust you had a pleasant journey, Mr Barrington. Master sent me to bring you on up.' He stood aside as they stepped in and cranked the engine.

'So Lord Whympinger has acquired a Rolls Royce?' Barrington growled.

'He has a Sunbeam as well, and a Lanchester for picnics. Trouble is all the dust they kick up, 'specially when you're gettin' up to twenty.'

'Maybe we should have kept it at four.'

'Oh, I don't know about that, sir, you're hard put to hold the old lady at twenty. She'd fly like a bird if I let her.'

The lane widened as they reached a crossroads. Stone pillars framed the entrance to Whympinger's estate, a belligerent eagle perched on each. The driver crossed the intersection without slowing and continued up a beech avenue under a pulsating sun. Whympinger's pile appeared suddenly between the trees.

'There it is,' Barrington said, 'Compton, in all its Gothic excess.' Tanbrey gazed at the building but made no reply. He had a long way to go, and he'd probably never get there. 'My dear fellow, don't be crestfallen,' Barrington said, patting his knee. 'Success is a will o' the wisp. What you see is three generations and a lot of luck.'

A reek of stale smoke persisted throughout breakfast the next day, despite the maids having opened the dining room windows. A row of lamp-warmed dishes had been prepared; ham tongue, galantines, grouse, pheasant, partridge and ptarmigan. Bowls of fruit and jugs of lemonade were set on a side table, together with China and Indian tea. Tanbrey and Barrington arrived to a silent assembly of diners. Barrington muttered a greeting and helped himself to a bowl of porridge, while John had a generous helping of ptarmigan. The politician settled himself by a silver-haired man in his sixties, who grunted through a mouthful of grouse. He eventually washed it down and addressed a remark to the table napkin. 'Shares down again.'

'Yours or mine?' asked Barrington.

'Everybody's, I should think.'

'Tanbrey, meet Colonel Sir Julian Smythe. Smythe, a friend of mine, John Tanbrey.'

'Pleased to meet you. What are you, Civil Service or something?'

'Not yet.'

'I hope you're not one of those bally politician types, like Barrington here. It used to be a decent country before the professional put-it-righters came along.' He dabbed at his mouth and rose unsteadily. 'Too much port last night. Must inspect the sanitary arrangements. Coming for the shoot later, Barrington?'

'I can't see why not. Tanbrey will join us, I hope.' Barrington watched him as far as the door. 'Silly old buffer, wouldn't you say?'

'You're going to tell me something.'

'He knows more about what's going on than anyone in the house, and that includes Whympinger himself, when he deigns to put in an appearance. Family connections, old man. A brother in public service, could even be the secret service for all I know. There's not much gets past Julian. Octavian too, come to that.'

'His brother?'

'Julian's the adjective, Octavian the noun. Their father was a classicist, I'm told.'

'Do you people ever grow up?'

'Schoolboy dreamers, always reaching for the helm. And sailing the ship, of course.'

After breakfast some of the men went out in an open carriage. Everyone but Tanbrey wore caps and tweed jackets, and his isolation grew as the voices around him assumed a warm familiarity one with another. One of the party looked his way. 'You're not shooting, then, Mr –?'

'John Tanbrey. I'm afraid you have the advantage of me.'

For a moment the possibility he was speaking to someone he should know struck him. He chose to ignore it. 'Name's Tremaine.' The thin lips moved in the skull head. 'You've come with Barrington, I see.'

Barrington came to his rescue. 'This is all very remiss of me, I should have introduced you earlier. Mr Tanbrey is here to spend a pleasant weekend with us before he returns to the rigours of commercial life. Unfortunately, and I know he won't mind my mentioning this, Mr Tanbrey's things were stolen by some felon at the station. His man gave chase, but I'm afraid we don't know the outcome since the train departed before we could apprehend the blackguard. He is now in the unfortunate position of having only the clothes he stands up in.'

A sympathetic buzz ran around the carriage. Barrington's eyes twinkled.

'Oh, bad luck, old chap.'

'You should have asked old Whimpie to set you up, he's brimming with stuff. The gun would have been not the slightest trouble.'

'You're welcome to share my shooting, old man, no buts about it.'

'I'm afraid that will be impossible,' Tanbrey said, forced to enter further into the scene Barrington had contrived, and which would keep the politician and his cronies amused for years. 'In struggling to apprehend the thief, I twisted an arm. I'm afraid I'd prove a disappointment. I'm quite happy on this occasion to watch.'

Later that day, Compton's game room groaned under the weight of the shoot. Tanbrey had had little chance to talk with Barrington privately, but after dinner he followed the politician up to his room.

'I have a bone to pick.'

Barrington lowered his bulk on to the bed. 'I'm sure you have, but before you pick it let me tender a little advice.'

'You should have advised me how to survive that bloody soiree earlier, then this morning's fiasco could have been avoided. I'm not a social experiment. Had I been born with a silver spoon in my mouth, no doubt I wouldn't need the tuition.' His squall died. 'What did you ask me to come here for? My education, or your amusement?'

Barrington slackened his tie and lay back. 'A little of both, John, a little of both.' He tilted a carafe towards his glass and took a leisurely sip. 'You might also add opportunism.' He settled himself luxuriously on the counterpane. 'You remember our friend, Hodson?'

'What of him?'

'Hodson and all the other Hodsons are pick-and-shovel men. The world is overflowing with pick-and-shovel men. That is what they do, that is what they are. What the Hodsons need is a wily soul, or in our case two wily souls, to propel them into a post-Hodson phase. Now a post-Hodson

Hodson doesn't concern himself with nails and tub wheels. He concerns himself with much grander things. It's the wily souls who must see that he gets them. His job is to do, ours to think, and to instruct. Opportunism is the key, and opportunities don't fall from trees. One has to put oneself into a position where they're most likely to occur. If you want to get struck by lightening, then you must climb the conductor.' He chuckled to himself and took another drink. 'This gathering of fools and bumblers who comprise this country's elite fortunately provide such opportunities. Forget Westminster. We're just a pack of donkeys, braying. This is tomorrow's almanac, this is where the bloodhounds are let off the leash. It's a big game, and the rules are written in Chinese. Unless you have an interpreter, you'll never understand how it all works. Think of it as a game of charades. It's them what gets the answers carry off the spoils.'

'D'you know, I believe you're trying to tell me something.'

Barrington turned his pale eyes on Tanbrey, who'd taken a seat at the foot of the bed. 'John, we understand each other. If I don't spout this bullshit, then who will? I want you to join us. It's like being back at school, I can teach you what to say. You have your mill and a third of a back-street foundry. You may have more, I don't want to know. You consider you've done well, and who can blame you? You have your house in the country and you're well off. Let me tell you this, old man; these people have enough on their wine racks to buy your house and everything in it. Everything's relative. If you really have a mind to go to the top, as I know you do, this is where they make the greasy poles.'

'You've not explained why you thought today's little episode necessary.'

'A severe jolt can work wonders. On the other hand, it can end a good friendship.'

'Why are you taking this trouble with me?'

Barrington smiled broadly. 'Why, because you're my protégé, of course.'

'And you're a patronising bastard.'

'Without doubt, and a cunning one at that. Now, if you'll excuse me, I'm rather tired.'

Tanbrey returned to his room and lay on his bed. The politician was slippery as an eel, but he'd put work his way at the Queen's funeral and

Edward's succession and introduced him to Hodson's business. Whatever the outcome, and even if there were no outcome, he'd be unwise to disregard the path Barrington had set out for him. These people held his rein, and with their merest nod could send him back where he started.

Later, while the rest were playing bridge, Barrington gave him a wink and John followed him into the adjoining room. Seated facing each other across a small table were Julian Smythe and Whympinger, both comfortably flushed. It was the first time Tanbrey had been close to his host. With his macassared hair and tilted nose, Whympinger was the caricature of a story-book nob.

'Oh, here's Barrington and Tanbrey come to join us at cards,' he said. 'In reality, the only things worth playing are the women on the back, don't you think? Tanbrey, you'd care for a tot?'

'Perhaps a small whisky.'

'You must call me Whimpie, like everyone else. It's derogatory, of course.' He handed him a glass. 'Barrington tells me you've left your wife at home. A good thing, too. One never knows what entertainments might present themselves. Wouldn't do to have one's spouse snooping around the corridors.' He lay down his cards. 'Well, sorry I can't stay. Must attend to my duty, or my own good wife will be coming in here to sort me out. Toodle-oo for now.'

Smythe left the table and slipped into an easy chair. His eyes began to bat, and Barrington kicked his ankle. The colonel started up. 'Oh, beg pardon. Must have dozed off.'

'You were giving us a most valuable insight into the state of the country's naval strategy,' Barrington said.

'Was I? I don't remember. Well, there *is* no strategy, as you call it.' Smythe struggled up, his voice growing more assertive. 'It's a bally shambles, Kitchener and that blighter Curzon, squabbling like ferrets in a bag. Minto's no use, either. Only one with anything between the ears is Jacky Fisher. The man can actually think. I'm amazed they made him admiral, let alone Sea Lord. You've heard of this new ship, Barrington?'

'I've heard some mention of it.'

'Don't know much about ships. Always been landlubbers in my family. They say it'll make everything else obsolete, twice the fire-power, greater range than anything anyone else has got. Fuelled by oil. Blessed if

I can see why. Didn't have it all his own way, had to fight tooth and nail to get it up and running.' He lowered his voice. 'Argument is, once this thing's launched, the whole fleet might as well go to the breaker's. Then where's your advantage, hey? See their point, I suppose. Pour me another, Barrington, there's a good chap.' The politician poured a liberal measure, while Smythe stared at Dreadnoughts through the fire-screen. 'Twelve–inch guns. That's fire-power for you. Stick one of those up a Prussian's arse, soon teach him his manners.'

From the next room came an arpeggio, a female voice shrill above the piano. Smythe, flushed with wine, waved an arm in time to the song, humming a melody which he made up as he went along. Barrington flicked a glance at Tanbrey, and moved the chair a little nearer Smythe's.

'Julian, there's something I'd intended to speak with you about. As you might have heard, John and I have acquired part of a modest business concern. An ironworks to be exact. It provides no more than a modest return. Obviously, we'd both prefer it to do a little better. I wonder if your brother could help? Your talk of battleships makes me feel we're somehow trailing behind.' Smythe cleared his throat and looked shiftily over his shoulder. 'This isn't the House, Julian. There are no strangers without. John's a friend.'

'Perhaps you'd feel less restrained if I joined the singer,' Tanbrey said.

The colonel broke into a bumbling apology. 'No, no, no, no, no. No need for that, old man. A friend of Lawrence is a friend of mine. No, it's not that. Barrington knows enough about tendering for contract, as well as do you, no doubt. The work is well advanced, Barrington. The thing will be launched next year.'

'But armaments. A little plate, a few gun cases - crumbs under the table. You know the sort of thing.'

'That must be a job for Woolwich.'

'Not totally. Not necessarily.' Barrington beamed at Smythe's silky head. Moving to the mantelpiece, he propped himself on an elbow and lit a cigar. 'Do you recall that mineral line, about four years ago? If I remember rightly they wanted ballast, and they were prepared to blast an entire hill to get it. It was a very desirable hill, from a scenic point of view, and your house looked on to it.' He paused, blew a ring of smoke. Smythe's head appeared to shrink into his shoulders. 'I spoke on the subject at some length in the House. It was a close-run thing, fighting all that tosh about the needs of the state exceeding the unpatriotic demands of the individual. But your hill is still intact, and the grouse are happy – as I'm sure are you, Julian. At least for the while....'

'I'm not the noun, old boy, only a mere adjective.'

'But Octavian –you know, younger brother and all that....'

'All right, you unctuous devil, I'll see what I can do. I can't promise anything, mind.'

'What more could a man ask?'

'And if the matter of quarries comes up again, you can see to it it's resolved in a permanent fashion. I'm sure there are any number of views they can ruin away from my neck of the woods.'

'Should the matter come up again, I shall do my utmost to see they are ruined irredeemably. Another drink?'

Shortly before midnight, the first guests went to their rooms. By one the house was quiet, but for the occasional faint rattle of doorknobs and, from Barrington's room, a subdued slapping.

Charlie brushed a crumb from his moustache and left the table. The sun was already streaming through the window. As he took his coat from the peg, he felt his collar stud hard against his throat. He made an adjustment, fixed his cycle clips and pulled on his cap.

'You've forgotten your lunch.'

'It's tied on the bike.'

'Your big day, then, Charlie.'

'I'd best be off.'

Ellen watched as he pushed the bike up the track. When he was out of sight, she turned to clear the table. 'You'd better be getting ready too, Richard. Shame you're not going to the same school, it'd save a lot of trouble. You hear? No use sticking your neck into books this time of a morning. Keep your eyes on Vicky while I take these in the scullery.'

He put down his book and tried to scoop milk into Victoria's mouth. The spoon slid down her cheek, and milk dribbled on to her bib.

'She'll have no more,' Ellen said, coming back and lifting the girl out of her high chair. 'Go see if Josh wants anything doing before you go to school.'

The boy went out, leaving the door open. He spent a minute talking with the dairyman, then came back in. 'He says he doesn't want anything.'

'Then get your clogs cleaned up. And get some bicarb on your teeth, they're stainin'. Come here!' He came over and stood as she straightened his jersey. 'There, that's better. I want to see my face in them clogs before you go.' She lifted her daughter from her chair, wiped her face and removed the bib before undoing the child's smock. 'Come on, my precious, can't have you all covered in slops, can we? Mother'll put you on some nice, clean clothes. You stay quiet or the pin'll stick in, like yesterday. You finished, Richard?'

He presented himself for inspection, then left the house with the book sticking out of his pocket. When she'd finished her chores, Ellen sat with a mug of tea. From today Charlie was a schoolmaster, teaching at the same school they'd both attended thirty years before. A lot had happened in the past three years. Charlie had decided to sell his house to help put himself through college, catching a daily Manchester train while Ellen looked after Richard. Doris had died of a stroke before Victoria was born. She'd missed her a lot at first; now she'd never know who her real mother was, nor anything more about the circumstances which had brought her to the Three Elms.

She and Charlie had married before her pregnancy showed, choosing an anonymous Manchester church in the early morning to register their vows. The only witnesses had been Jane and Eric O'Rourke. It had been a time of worry for Charlie, who was still wrestling with his conscience over Mary and thoughts of the Magistrate's Court. It was a relief to hear that the matter of neglect had been subsumed into workhouse business, that Mary's older brother had confirmed Charlie's regular payments had been entrusted to his care and that his sister had left the district and couldn't be found. The local paper hadn't reported the proceedings, so there'd be no wagging tongues. The uncollected payments had paid for a burial and headstone in the Municipal Cemetery, and he took comfort from the fact Mary was spared a pauper's grave.

The rector's power over appointees to Moor Top school had lessened with the passing of the new Education Act, and this had worked in Charlie's favour. The man who interviewed him was not from the area, and the one question put to him by the rector had been: 'Tell me, Mr Tanbrey, who are your favourite hymnists?'

After a slight hesitation, Charlie had answered: 'Well, there are the Wesleys.'

'Which one in particular?'

He'd tried to focus on one of last Sunday's hymns. 'Charles,' he said.

'Indeed. Your namesake, in fact.'

Half an hour later he'd been offered the post of assistant teacher. 'I'm sure the managers will join with me in wishing you a very happy and rewarding time here. We are confident you have all the qualities needed for a successful career at Moor Top....'

Ellen could imagine him tongue-tied, hands fidgeting on his lap. A schoolmaster! Folk would doff their hats! Why, it was almost on a level with the rector. He should have done it all along. It gave her a flush of pride to feel settled with him. She'd spent her young days laughing at him, and now she'd spend her middle age caring for him. Charlie, a schoolmaster!

He stood a little to the side of Russell, a teacher given the task of introducing him to the class. Russell stood brandishing a cane as the boys trooped in. Some were new to the school that September, others less inhibited; it was one of these who became the first victim of the new term. Russell made a lunge for the tuft of hair above the boy's ear and pincered it between his thumb and finger. 'Talking, Barnes? Talking as we enter the hallowed precinct, mm? And on the first day of a new term? Is this the example we wish to set for the uninitiated? Have we learnt nothing from our time here?'

Two things struck Charlie. The first was Russell's dapper appearance. With his neatly-combed head, clipped moustache and small, even teeth, he looked more like a mannequin than a teacher. The second was his habit of addressing the boys as 'we', as if he, too, were involved in a conspiracy he nevertheless had to quell. He accompanied each question with a downward yank of Barnes' head. By the time he reached the last, the boy had bent double in an attempt to escape further torture, forgetting Russell's trick of a sudden, upward jerk.

'Well, and what have we to say? Have we an apology here, mm?'

'Sorry, sir.'

'We're sorry too. We didn't catch that.'

The shorn head travelled again towards Russell's shoes, and Russell's head followed.

'Sorry, Mr Russell.'

The master let go the boy's hair, rubbing his fingers and thumb together with deliberate squeamishness. Barnes rubbed his temple, his eyes streaming, his cheek roughened by Russell's sleeve. The remainder of the line shuffled in and stood behind the desks, the knees of some wedged between the desk-top and seat. 'Sit. STAND! Too much noise. A bedlam. Too much clanging of desks, mm? Now, sit.... quietly.' They eased on to the plank and waited, the bolder ones with their eyes on Russell, the rest looking at their desk lids. 'We may now rest our arms on the desk top, a hand loosely grasping the opposite wrist. Now today is not only the start of a new term, it is also time for you to meet your new master.' Faces turned to Charlie, who inwardly cowered under the weight of them. The memory of Caulton came to him, and faded. 'We have NOT been told to look anywhere but at myself, and the next person who looks anywhere but at myself will receive his reward from the cabinet behind, mm? Those we have entertained before know what we're referring to.' Charlie's eyes moved to the cupboard, and he saw Francis Gordon there. Russell was locked in his private world. 'We seem to recall some faces, some familiars. Mr Tanbrey will no doubt acquaint himself with the more troublesome among us. That's right, isn't it, Mr Tanbrey? He will no doubt be referring miscreants to Mr Cupboard, who will see to it as only he can, mm?'

He chose monitors to issue pens, ink and copy books. While this was being done, he stroked his moustache and glared at the class. 'We shall write our names on the covers. On the first page we shall print the Ten Commandments, which we see here.' He tapped a chart on the wall without looking at it. 'If Mr Blot happens to appear, one stroke. If two Mr Blots appear, two strokes. That's our rule, mm? Yes, that's our maxim.' Now that each pen was safely scratching, he returned to Charlie. 'Now, Mr Tanbrey, you have all you need. Chalk, such books as there are. If there's anything else, we're behind the partition, mm?' He lowered his voice and lifted the lid of his high desk, where a timetable had been pinned. 'Don't be frightened of them, that's the thing. It's the first day that counts.' He lowered the lid, nodded meaningfully to Charlie and made his exit.

Their nibs scratched ominously. Twice Charlie raised his desk lid and studied the blurred outline of his timetable. The first boy finished his work. Russell's voice sounded through the partition. More children put down their pens. The word 'History' swam up to him from the timetable. More had their eyes fixed on him, first from one side, then the other. He felt himself to be in the grip of some strange lethargy. A whispering broke out at the back of the room, and he allowed the sound to continue unchecked. Some were still writing; others, aware the silence had been broken, joined the disruption with cunning glances up at him. Two boys began to mutter in voices intended to catch his ear. A boy in front turned to talk to them, raising his desk lid, making it rattle.

Charlie cleared his throat. 'Turn around, please. Stop talking.' His voice seemed to leave no trace. Without waiting for the noise to lessen, he began: 'We're going to talk about the Romans this morning.' He cleared his throat again. 'The Romans sent their armies two thousand years ago. They conquered what we call England up as far as Scotland, then made a–a wall to keep out the Scottish tribes.' The words disintegrated in his throat. 'Who can tell me,' he persisted, 'who can tell me who built the wall?' Some grinned. Others were menacingly mute. He crushed the strain of silence under his rising voice. 'Emperor Hadrian was his name. He was a sort of king.... king of all the Romans.'

'Did 'e build th' wall 'issel'?' a voice bawled.

Heads turned, smirking. Charlie said:' 'His soldiers built it.' The boy nudged a newcomer at his side. 'When we say Hadrian built the wall, it's the same as saying his army built it.'

'I wouldna say me father built the cow shed if it were me uncle did it.'

He could feel their restraint buckling. Their taunts came faster. 'I'd like to carry on. The Romans had already taken over most of.... of Europe and Hadrian was one of their Emperors. The man who conquered us was – does anybody know who conquered us?'

'Was it Napoleon?'

'Napoleon Boggypart.'

'Noggie the boggie!'

Ink spattered a cheek. The spring-seats clattered, and a crash erupted above the general clamour. He started up. He could stand their horseplay but not the indignity of being ignored. Russell had been right, it had to be like that. There was no other way. A trestle lay on its side at the back of the room, and one of the boys was making a burlesque of hauling it upright, while his cronies mouthed encouragement. The anxiety which had threatened to overwhelm him melted away. Even before he spoke, the class had begun to quieten.

'You four, out here.' The shadow of Francis Gordon reared by the easel. They made their way past the rows. 'Line up. Here!' They lined up shoulder to shoulder, hands clenched. He swung back the cupboard door and flexed a cane. 'You three, by the easel. You, step up here.' A lad moved sullenly forward. Charlie stood before him. A great sympathy welled up in him, for the boy's resolution not to let himself down before the class. He felt part of the same ritual, both he and the scholar left swimming for survival in a storm–tossed sea.

'You deliberately knocked over the table.'

'It were Boothy, sir, I –'

'Don't answer me back!' He faced the class. 'D'you think I'm here for fun? The next one opens his mouth gets a dose of what he's about to get, only twice the strokes dealt twice as hard.' He levered up the boy's hand with the cane. Russell's head came briefly into view, a silent mosaic behind the frosted glass. The lad's face was inscrutable as a slab of meat. Charlie saw his own boy there, brushed away the image and swept downwards. The tip of the cane caught the boy's field-hardened fingers at the joint. He didn't flinch. Charlie brought the cane down on his other hand, striking a pulpy finger. The boy held his eye, made no attempt to rub his fingers. If he didn't rub his fingers, he'd not lost. 'Next.' He flailed downwards as the rest looked on in silence. The last withdrew his hand twice. Finally struck, he yelped, tears streaming down his cheeks, burrowing his swollen fingers in his armpits. Charlie motioned the boys away. 'Mr Russell gave you the Ten Commandments to write. We'll forget all about the Romans since you're too ill-mannered to listen. You can write your commandments out again as punishment for this bedlam. And if they're not done to perfection, I'll beat the whole class.' He left them with their heads bowed and went into the cloakroom. Nausea overcame him, and he grasped a hook, breathing deeply. When he went back, they were still bent over their copy-books.

He went to Russell's rented cottage in the lunch hour, and found him in shorts and plimsolls, pumping a dumb-bell. He invited Charlie into his small front room. Like Russell, it was neat and precise, with little more than a settee and rug. A photograph of a football team hung above the mantelpiece; a shelf nearby bristled with trophies.

'We keep ourselves up to the mark, Tanbrey. Won't be a moment. You've had something to eat?'

'A sandwich. I thought I'd come and explain about this morning.'

Russell had resumed his exercises, grunting in time to the lifting of weights. After a few minutes, he began a vigorous on-the-spot running, lifting his arms almost to chin height.

'I'll go, shall I? I dare say it'll keep.'

Russell motioned him to stay. He finished by striking from side to sternum with the blade of his hand, hung like a rag doll for half a minute, took a deep breath and towelled the sweat from his face. 'We need food. You've eaten, you say?' He came back from the kitchen with a dish of cold shepherd's pie and a tumbler of water. He put the glass on the mantelpiece and stood by the drowsing fire, picking at his plate. 'We heard it all this morning, Charles, don't think we didn't. Quietness reigned after that, mm? Sylvan silence. That's the way of it. Just as we train a dog, no different. They'll be quite happy now they know which side their bread's buttered. Won't be able to do enough for you.'

'I don't like using the stick.'

'Necessity the mother, unfortunately.'

Charlie looked around. 'You've got this place up nice.'

'A place for everything, everything in its place, otherwise we can't cope.'

'I came about the lessons. I didn't stick to the timetable. By the time they'd settled, it was too late.'

'Timetable, mm? What's it got to do with timetables? We're not standing on ceremony. See that? Our time with Bradnop. Recognise me?' Charlie studied the picture showing a football team and picked him out. 'No change, mm? Instantly recognisable. How old would we be then?'

'I don't know, twenty?'

'Correct. And that was taken fifteen years ago.'

'I'd never put you at thirty five.'

'We keep on top, keep it at bay. It's having the drive. Nature can be stopped in her tracks with the right signals, mm? Your body's your slave, there to be of service.'

'Another morning like this'll stop *me* in my tracks, never mind nature.'

'We have our baptisms. Another week, you'll be eating 'em for breakfast. Forget timetables. Do as we like, mm? Your first job, you'll find out.'

'Find out what?'

'Education, it's for the boys on top. For the rest, schoolmastering's for the

Peelers. We're just holding the fort. A bobby's job, keeping them out of mischief. Just amuse them. The rector doesn't care, hardly ever puts a nose in.'

Charlie looked at his pocket watch. 'Look, Mr Russell –'

'Russell K Russell. The K is for Keith.'

'I just wanted to say I'm sorry if I disturbed you. I knew they'd try it on. I just didn't expect it to be so soon.'

Russell wiped his mouth and put the plate down. 'You're new to the game, no need to explain. They're on about building a new school up the road, have you heard? It'll be bigger than this, dare say they'll appoint a new head.'

'Will you apply?'

'We might. Can't say. Other things in life, mm? Moor Top isn't the universe.'

'What will you do?'

'We've no ties. We budget. A single man has the advantage of flexibility. You're married, Charles?' Charlie nodded. 'Flexibility, that's the card to play. Now, time for a tea before the bell. We'll go in the next room.' He went out, calling through the door: 'Hear you came here yourself, Charles, as a scholar. Bet it's not changed one iota.'

'That was in Caulton's time,' Charlie said, raising his voice. 'He taught in my room. The rector at that time was Francis Gordon. He had no qualms about using the cane.'

'Sound man. What about Caulton?'

'Last I heard, he'd gone to France. I suppose he's getting on for seventy, now. I kept in touch for a time. You know how it is, trying to keep up with people.'

Russell came in. He'd put on his trousers, shoes, and shirt. He handed Charlie a mug of tea. 'We heard all sorts of rumours about you. You seem perfectly normal to myself. You don't mind my saying, you're a trifle late to come into this game. We're surprised they took you on.'

'It's a long tale, Russell. I was lucky enough to have a house to sell, and my wife helped. I can't say I had any credentials, not unless you include the pit and working on a tile bank. I was lucky. I got in at the right time, when they were crying out for teachers.'

'Schooling, the big project. Expansion at all costs, mm?'

'I sat a test, and I've read a lot. Anyway, you might not think so, but I like children.'

'Really? How curious.'

Charlie wondered how much he knew about his life. They chatted desultorily while Russell fastened a collar to his shirt, the reason for Charlie's visit forgotten by both of them. When they went back to the school, Russell immediately began tugging at the bell rope, his lips set in a determined line.

Charlie settled into a routine. There was no repetition of his earlier confrontation, but it was some months before he learned a more comfortable familiarity with his class, and even then his confidence could wane and he'd become acutely aware of his responsibility for them. It sometimes felt as if he was making amends to Hannah by helping other children. He knew it was a harmless nonsense. Sometimes his mind went back to the day Caulton had taken them sketching on the moor, and into the room poured the golden light, the schoolmaster striking through it in his straw hat. He thought of his own work, shut up in the attic of a house which now belonged to someone else, a foolish talisman against the hubris of ambition.

He rarely heard from Bill now, and John's last letter talked about the manufacture of castings for gun mounts to be used in the new ships. The three of them had lived in isolation from each other for so long that letters, when they came, seemed somehow irrelevant. Then, a week after Campbell-Bannerman's Liberals won their landslide victory, he came home to find an envelope on the table.

'Guess what, Charlie? Jane's husband's an MP. What d'you think of that? Eric O'Rourke an MP, and he's been eating at this very table. Here, read the letter.' He scanned the lines, written in Jane's bold hand.

'You never mentioned her being in gaol.'

'That's what I was going to ask you. I'd like to visit her, if that's all right.'

'I thought all this suffrage business would be over by now.'

'You'll not douse a blaze with a cup o' water. Jane'll be in and out of prison every day till she gets her own road. Shall I write back, tell her I'm coming?'

'Ay, if that's what you want.'

'I do, Charlie. I'll write tonight.'

A week-end was the only convenient time. Taking a cab from Euston, she reached Holloway tired and confused. It was the first time she'd been to London, and the traffic's constant clatter unnerved her. She could see no bell-push, and there was no answer to her knock until, finally, a door within the gate swung open and she was admitted into a cobbled forecourt. A guard escorted her down a passage which smelt of vomit and she was admitted into a large room, partitioned from the prisoners by a high grill. She found Jane on a seat at the end.

'How're you coping?'

'You shouldn't have come all this way on my account – but it's lovely to see you, all the same.'

'I showed Charlie your letter. We're really pleased for Eric. Has he been in?'

'This is the first day they've allowed visitors, and there's not many turned up so far. Eric's up to his neck. I didn't want him to come.' She reached further forward. 'I had a letter.... he's had tea with David Lloyd George.'

'I think I've heard the name somewhere.'

'You'll be hearing more. He's out to steel Labour's thunder.'

'I can't understand how you can talk about politics, cooped up in here. What happened?'

'There were eleven of us arrested for inciting a so-called riot outside the House of Commons.'

'What an embarrassment. For Eric, I mean.'

'Eric's all right. The whole thing appeals to his sense of humour. He doesn't take us seriously, like any other man. We all refused to pay a fine. Sylvia Pankhurst's here, and there's Emily Lawrence at the end. We'll do it again, you know.'

'But what about your job?'

'I doubt there'll be a job when I get back. It's bound to get out. All your brother-in-law has to do is put two and two together, all the odd days off, all the excuses. How's the family? Charlie's settled, is he?'

'He gets tired. He seems to be getting on well with his class.'

'And how're you, still beavering away?'

'Ay, still beaverin'. No, that sounds ungrateful. I've never felt better, touch wood. Vicky's into everything now, takes up all my time.'

'What about Richard?'

'We get on famously. Got a lot o' Charlie in him, what with him enjoying his own company, into his books and such.'

'How old is he now?'

'Just gone ten.' And for a moment she was back home, watching the mist smother the byres in droplets.

'I'm committed, you know. Before, I was always flirting with this and that. Now I feel fulfilled, I suppose you'd call it.'

'Do they treat you right, Jane?'

'Some do, others aren't so particular. The powers that be hate intellectuals. We're classed as that. Anyone can see further than their nose is that. I've been lucky. They haven't force-fed me yet.'

'Whatever do you mean?'

'Some have starved themselves. The authorities can't abide a martyr, so they stick a tube up your nose and pour food down it.' A warden caught Jane's eye. She brought her mouth closer to the grill. 'You'd be surprised how many ears these walls have.'

'I don't know why you're going to these lengths, making yourself miserable for the sake of a vote. They'll do what they want, no matter who gets in.'

'It's the principle, Ellen; you know me and my principles.'

'You'll do nothing to alter things until they're ready to alter, chance all the principles in the world. You can't afford principles, turned fifty. Best leave 'em to them with a bit of get-up-and-go. You'll be catching your death, stuck here with this lot.'

'Perhaps you're right, who knows? At least it's something I can believe in. And there's plenty of fight left in these old bones, even if I do look decrepit.'

A voice called for the visitors to vacate the building. The prisoners filed out under the scrutiny of the wardens. Once through the gates, Ellen inhaled deeply, as if to rid herself of the stink of the place. Hailing a cab, she passed the rest of her time in the station buffet until her train arrived.

5

Tanbrey looked up as Jane came into the office. She guessed why he'd sent for her, and was surprised he'd not sent for her before.

'Would you say I've treated you unfairly in any way?'

'Not as far as I'm aware.'

'Then perhaps you'd favour me with an explanation for this.' He tossed a newspaper across his desk and watched her glance at the headline.

'What sort of an explanation would you like, Mr Tanbrey?'

'I was led to believe you'd taken time off through illness – not to carry out subversive activities in my time.'

'If you choose to put it like that.'

'Is there another way? And to add insult to injury, you've served a term in gaol.'

'As a political prisoner.'

He glared at her, the muscles of his neck taut. 'As a criminal who seeks to disrupt the legitimate business of Parliament.'

Something had held him back from an earlier confrontation, and it came to her that her husband was the reason. Tanbrey had suspected Eric might one day have power, and it wouldn't do to upset his wife. Moreover, public opinion was fickle. Rest assured Tanbrey didn't give a damn whether women had the vote or whether they went to hell. What did matter was how the public might view them next year, the year after that. Today's hysterics could be tomorrow's martyrs. Already they were attracting influential support. That's why he hadn't sacked her. He was afraid she could do him harm. He was afraid Eric might do him harm. But then, why see her at all? Why not simply keep up the pretence that once in a while she'd be ill for a day or two and leave it at that?

'What will you do?' she asked.

'I value your work. I've no wish to lose you.' He toyed with his papers. 'Forget this stupid business, we'll pretend it never happened.'

The moment he spoke, he knew he'd said the wrong thing.

'You call women's suffrage stupid?'

'I'm not concerned with your political view. My function is to make sure this place doesn't grind to a halt. That's why I promoted you. All the libertarians in the world won't keep the looms turning.'

'But they might entitle those running them to a vote.'

'I couldn't give a damn who has the vote as long as it doesn't affect this firm.'

'I'm afraid it will affect this firm, and thousands more beside.'

'Oh?'

'You seem surprised, Mr Tanbrey. You shouldn't be. It won't be long before women get the same pay as men. And why not? They work their fingers to the bone for it. Nothing less than full emancipation is what we're after.'

'I take it from your little speech you have no intention of curtailing your activities?'

'If it means compromise, you've hit the nail on the head. I'll come to the office and do my stint, but my views are my own and neither you nor anyone else will alter them.'

A carter's shout came faintly through the glass. He looked down on the yard, coldly angry. Had it been anyone else they'd be out by now. Yet he'd grudgingly developed a respect for her integrity. She was the least venal of all the people he'd known. And he thought of Barrington, who'd first commented on 'this Liberal upstart's wife who provides occasional amusement for the House and hopefully embarrassment for her husband'. If he were to get rid of her, what might follow? Barrington had wormed out the orders which had put a lot of money into Tanbrey's pocket, but Barrington was getting old. Perhaps he'd soon be a fading star and Tanbrey might need to look elsewhere for his contracts. The Liberals were now centre-stage, could be playing to a packed House next month, next year. On the other hand, his business could suffer if his employee's activities continued to make their appearance in the local papers.

Jane wondered what was passing through his mind. As the seconds ticked, her impatience grew. What right had he to patronise her? He owned her labour, nothing more. His only quibble was her lying about her absences. And why had she lied? To protect her work? To avoid the issue? Suddenly, she saw what she'd known inwardly for some time. The job was no longer important to her. She was past being owned, past being efficient. She might be dead within ten years. She no longer wanted to hire herself out.

'There's no need to ponder further. I've decided to leave. It'll save you the trouble of sacking me.'

He'd already turned from the window and was on the point of reconciliation. Instead he said: 'As you will.' She'd reached the door when he called her back. 'I find it ironic that a woman fighting women's causes should have overlooked her own well-paid position while continuing to wallow in her victimhood. Nevertheless, I'll keep your job open for one week. If you reconsider –'

She held his eyes in silence for a moment, then left. He knew she'd won.

Eric's earnings as an MP and his freelance work kept them comfortably off. At times, the movement's lack of progress depressed her. Private bills foundered, and it seemed women were no nearer achieving their aims. A fault line had developed in the Women's Social and Political Union, born of the frustration and a growing resentment of Mrs Pankhurst's hectoring style. Despite this, their angry mood prevailed, and was made angrier still by the imprisonment of Emmeline and her daughter on a charge of Breaching the Peace by inciting members of the public to rush into the House of Commons.

The government was aware of growing support creeping through the social ranks. Even so, the most optimistic of suffragists expected no more from the new Liberal Prime Minister, Herbert Asquith, than from his ailing predecessor. However, he was shrewd enough to promote Lloyd George as his successor at the Treasury, thus stealing Labour's radicalism in a welter of reforms. The People's Budget provided a pension for the first time. National Insurance followed.

'It's all very commendable,' Barrington rumbled. 'Unfortunately, the money has to come from somewhere, and that includes yourself. Sixpence in the pound. That's one fortieth part of your income to prop up the feeble, the idle and the decrepit. Even death isn't exempt. Not even your honest tipple. Lloyd George is a bastard, and I hope he rots in hell. Unfortunately he's a clever bastard, and is therefore unlikely to do so. There is a crumb of comfort. Despite official protestations to the contrary, everyone is pleased we at last have rearmament. Uniforms, shells, guns – that should be of some benefit to us, hey, John? Smythe did us proud before and he will do so again. Then we can pay this government's trifling tax.'

'So you think it will be a substantial programme?'

'My dear boy, we're gearing for war.'

'With whom?'

Barrington arched his eyebrows. 'John, I sometimes despair. You really ought to get out more often. With whom? With the bloody Hun, who else?'

'But if we re-arm –'

'If? When. War is inevitable. It's simply a matter of time.'

'We've had this sabre-rattling from Germany half my life. Perhaps I'm less convinced than you.'

'John we've had this conversation before, and I know nothing I say will convince you. I must say I'm rather surprised. I'll tell you this, treaties make wars. Wise men draw them up and rub their hands with glee, ho, aren't we clever, we've saving the world. The trouble with a balance is, a finger in the tray and all your sugar falls out. And I tell you this. When it comes it will devastate Europe. These old coves with their walrus moustaches, what do they know? Half of them propping up the decanter and rambling about their half-remembered days in the Crimea. Things have moved on. We're no longer talking about a few flag-wavers storming the kraal. Most of Europe will be under arms when it happens, all clambering aboard the trains. You could get every man alive to the war in a matter of days. Think about it.'

'I see you've worked it all out.'

Barrington beamed. 'What does an old gin-soak know about anything? Leave it to the young. It's their time now, worse luck. As long as we make a bit out of it, eh?'

Despite meetings by landowners to protest at 'this Draconian cut in our standard of living', the government prevailed, and the reforms Barrington both detested and welcomed were made law. With the accession of George V, the political rifts began to deepen. The lag in workers' wages accelerated a demand for more powerful unions and strikes paralysed large sections of British industry. At the same time, Jane grew more disillusioned with the mechanisms of power. After almost seven years in the WSPU, hardly anything had been achieved, though clashes with the police had became commonplace.

Eric regarded the headlines with his usual provocative humour. 'Jane, listen to this – it's from a distinguished bacteriologist. "Militant suffragettes are sexually and intellectually embittered, comprising the excess female population who would have done better to have gone abroad to find their mates".' Jane bridled as O'Rourke continued: '"A government requires physical force, intellectual ability and an appreciation of standards of abstract morality. I believe women to be deficient in all three qualities".

What d'you think of that?'

She snatched the paper from his hand and glared at the article. 'Distinguished bacteriologist? I'd like to shove a few bacteria down his throat –'

'He is distinguished, remember.'

'Self-appointed experts!' She threw the paper back. 'I'd like to cut his balls off.'

'Hear, hear, cut them off by all means. Sexually embittered? He obviously isn't familiar with my wife's carnal appetites, or I'd make him eat his words.'

She sat, simmering. Wouldn't he ever take things seriously? Of course, she hoped he never would. Intensity in a man was something she couldn't abide.

It had been some time since Charlie last had word from Bill. His letter now came as something of a shock: 'We've booked a passage on the *Mauretania* and if all is well we should see you in the spring. Rose wants to visit some of Europe first, but we've only worked out a loose sort of schedule. I'll send you another note when we've got our plans right. Rose is looking forward to meeting you, and so is Colette. Surprise John with the news, will you? He always was a dry stick, and this might give him something to jump about.'

He passed the note to Ellen, unaware of the brief shadow that had crossed her face. 'Well, Charlie, it seems as if the wheel's turned full circle. He must be making a lot of money. Europe? My, if we get as far as the farm gate we're doing well....'

She watched him manoeuvre his bike up the track, as he did each work-day morning. Richard had already left. If he missed the carrier's cart it meant a four mile trudge to his new school at Leek. He'd been one of the lucky few to be selected, and she was as pleased as Charlie was for him. She hoped Vicky would follow the same route. To give them a start, not having to sweat as she'd had to. But she'd been lucky. Lucky in Charlie, lucky in her health. She'd made no effort to hold back the comfortable spread of middle age, and her hair was almost free of grey. Charlie's years showed more; in his grizzled moustache, his often tired eyes and colour-washed hair. As he grew older, he reminded her more of Bevis; the same tolerance, like a cushion in an easy chair. They'd moved into each others' ways. She'd grown content with her cleft in the moor, felt safe and secure.

But Bill's letter had awakened demons, and as she read it a second time, the sweet smell of hay seemed to come to her nose. Again she felt the chill seeping through the damp walls of her Leek room, heard again the pigeons cooing in the church tower. What would it be like, seeing him again after all these years? She put it behind her. She'd always been able to ignore what she could do nothing about.

Rose said: 'You're sure you don't want the maid along? They said they'd hold a berth till tomorrow.'

'You think I'm not capable of getting us through, is that it? We want no maid, she'd only get in the way.'

'Of what?'

'Of.... whatever we decided to do.'

She pushed him away. The excitement of the journey had infused her with a child-like happiness. He'd wanted to make the trip for years. They'd wrangled over it and concluded their itinerary must include a visit to Bill's brothers in England, her late mother's family in Ireland and at least Paris, Athens and Rome. Money was an irrelevance. Their share of oil receipts grew by the month, and new fields were being discovered all the time. Rose's ambition to go to university had been vicariously fulfilled when Marian graduated from Radcliffe with a degree in geology. She'd inherited her father's resilience and humour and her mother's level-headedness. She enjoyed study, but had no misgivings about seeking the crowd when the mood took her. She'd grown tall and slim but had no desire to 'settle down' despite an army of callers. Through her father's connections she'd moved to the first rungs of the oil business, living an independent life in her own rooms within the Tanbrey household. It would have been no problem to have taken a trip with her family to Europe, but it could wait. She preferred to stay behind and work. Colette had no such qualms, and they'd made an arrangement to postpone her final year at school. The best teachers in the world couldn't compete with what she'd learn on the trip.

Bill looked out at the receding New York skyline until the Statue of Liberty slid into the mist. Flicking his cigar butt into the spume, he went to join his wife and daughter in their stateroom.

He could sense her joy when she set foot on European soil for the first time. She felt she was visiting a dimly-remembered relative to catch up on a lifetime's news. Though her mother had never been outside Ireland before joining her family in America, she'd given Rose a feel of the old places which seemed far removed from the new country.

They spent a little time in their Paris hotel, and when they weren't planning, Rose and Colette would make pointless purchases at the local market in order to polish their French.

'Je voudrais le cygne d'argent.'

'O, le beau cygne. D'accord.'

'Ca coute combien?'

'C'est dix franc. Vous etes anglaise?'

'Non, je suis americaine de l'etat d'Oklahoma. Je vous presente mon mari et ma fille.'

They spent Christmas in Rome before taking a boat from Brindisi to Alexandria, where they joined a steamer for a two-week voyage up the Nile, their companions wealthy Europeans who lazed on the deck watching the desert drift past. They rode camels to the Pyramids and sent echoes through the ruins of Karnak. Their cabin took on the look of a bazaar, with its trophies, its photographs of Abu Simbel and Luxor. In the dusk they sat on deck listening to the boom of bitterns and a tenor singing from a gramophone somewhere across the water. Bill's tan had deepened to leather by the time they reached Cairo. Rose and Colette, under their parasols, remained untouched by the sun apart from a rash of freckles which had broken out across Colette's forehead.

The ship docked at Pyreus, and they travelled to Athens. It showered for the first time, but the rain was welcome after the heat of the last weeks. For two days they remained in their hotel. On the third, the sky cleared and in the warm sunshine they and a local antiquarian climbed the Acropolis to the Parthenon. By the time they returned to their hotel, Bill had begun to tire, and he was content to leave them to their visits while he chatted with the other guests over a glass of Retsina. At night, Rose would pore over the books and pamphlets she'd collected on her travels. Did he know the Parthenon was almost intact before the Turks used it as an arsenal in 1687? Did he know the friezes were originally painted?

When they arrived back at the French capital, he wrote to Charlie: 'We'll be leaving Paris in a couple of weeks. We're going to spend a little time in Ireland with Rose's family, if we can trace any. That should give us some entertainment, since nobody knows about us coming and there might be nobody to see when we get there. With luck we'll be in Liverpool early April. When we get there, I'll send a telegram and you can get ready for a family reunion.'

The cart creaked to a halt in a narrow street of low-roofed houses near the Leitrim border. Rose sat in silence for a moment, looking across the patchwork of fields towards the River Moy and beyond to the faint hills. The breeze carried the tang of the sea, and she sniffed, her eyes closed, as if savouring memories of a distant childhood.

'My wife's looking for some of her family might live around here.'

The man seemed not to hear. Rose said: 'My mother – she went to America with her parents. Two girls, two boys.... her maiden name was O'Mara.'

The man looked up, removed his hat, scratched his thinning hair. 'Not Maud O'Mara, went over and married a farmer?'

'That's her! That's my mother!'

'Well, well, well, well, well. Well, I never did. Let's see, that was more than fifty years ago. Well, well, that's what I call a surprise. To see you, your mother's daughter an' all.' An elderly woman was walking past them. 'You know this one here's an O'Mara? You recall Maud O'Mara, we used to play with her when we were no age? Well, this is her girl.'

The woman lowered her pail and clasped Rose to her. 'You've got a place you're stayin'?'

'No, we were looking for somewhere....'

'You'll be lookin' no further, you're stayin' with me. Ah, if that's not your girl....' She embraced Colette, pecked Bill's cheek and turned to the carrier. 'You tell the others. Tonight they'll be comin' to the ceilidh. You bring them over.' She turned to Rose. 'You'll be lookin' forward, no doubt. I'll off to the pump, then you'll be restin' a while. All the way over the sea! Well, your man's burnt to a berry! Wait till I tell them, wait now....'

As the light faded, they arrived. Colette strained to hear from her bare-boarded room. The woman came in with tea. 'Come now, you must be wearin' somethin' nice for the ceilidh. I brought you this for your hair, a present to remember.' A violin wailed. She thought of the barn dances back home. 'Your mother and father are about now. You'll be all right, have your tea now.' She set down a tray. 'We heard about your grandma, killed in that heathen land.'

She dabbed at her eyes. 'She's with the Lord now, no doubt telling him to wipe his feet on the rug.' She handed Colette the cup. 'There, have your drink and come along down,'

Chairs had been arranged for the musicians. A girl danced a jig while onlookers clapped in the dark and hens pecked across the threshhold. One of the men took over from the girl, unfaltering despite the effect of drink. Rose protested she didn't know a step, but they pulled her on anyway. A thick, mild night came on. Lamps streaked the small windows and pricked the fields where the wail of fiddle and pipe merged with the waves in washes of sound.

'To Rose and Bill and their daughter Colette, a fine Irish name.' A wild cry broke out. 'And to Marian, three thousand miles across the seas. May they come and visit their poor folk once again before the Lord calls. And to wish them joy in their lives, and much life left to live.'

Rose looked up with brimming eyes. 'I can't tell you what this has meant to me. I feel I've found my roots at last. I know those of you who knew my mother, her relations, now my relations, have been shocked at the way she died. I've not gotten over it myself. Perhaps I never shall. Her and my father. But although her life was hard there as it was here, I know she was happy. And if she's looking down now, she'll be happy for us. I feel somehow I've done what she always wanted. Wherever you are, mother, God bless.'

The hour chimed, the gathering began to disperse; a great uncle she never knew she had, an eccentric cousin chasing a pig he'd brought along to listen to the band, the granddaughter of another uncle, with Colette's colouring and snub nose....

They left late next morning, with many hands to wave them off. The village twins came shyly forward with sprigs of heather. 'For the journey. Wear them with you.'

The salt breeze bore away their last goodbyes.

Charlie didn't know Ellen had ordered furniture until he got in from work and she showed him the new double bed in her mother's old room.

'Charlie, we had a telegram saying your brother would be here the day after tomorrow. I put a pound down. We can afford it, can't we?'

'What've you done with the old bed?'

'I got one of the men to cart it off. They could've taken it back home for all I care.'

'Are beds all you've been buying?'

'Well, there's the sheeting. I'll use some of my savings. It's for a special day, isn't it? Can't have guests to a pig-sty.'

She'd had a compulsion to re-order the house, to throw unused items on the cinder-heap and remove others to the shippons and put them under canvas. Her rag and broom kept up a relentless pace, until the quarries blinked with suds and the fender gleamed. She'd finished in the bedrooms, waxing the floors to a sheen.

'Charlie, how about the front door?'

'Doesn't it open right?'

'The graining looks as if it's lost its colour.'

'It's a bit late in the day.'

'Can you give it a going over?'

'He's my brother, not gentry. They'll have to take as they find.'

'I'd best wash the curtains. Wonder if they'll dry?'

Her desire for order hid her disquiet at seeing him again, the man who'd abandoned her. Charlie had seen them together in the hay barn all those years ago and never mentioned it since. But she'd not forgotten.

The engine clanked into Congleton Station. They were the only passengers to alight. Bill looked about him as the train moved out. The countryside was as unchanging as the chugging engine and the horse plodding over the tracks. A few miles away, the Cloud jutted over the fields he'd rambled as a boy, with the same birch thickets climbing the slopes. A pony and trap clattered into the station yard, and the figure holding the reins raised an arm. Bill waved his hat. 'Charlie! Over here!' Charlie got down from Russell's loaned trap and made his way towards them. 'You've shrunk! It's all that schoolmasterin' doing you no good!' Though Bill still towered four inches above his brother, Bill's once lean body had thickened, the swarthy skin darkened to umber. He saw in Charlie an older, frailer man. 'This is Rose and my daughter Colette.'

Charlie raised his cap and shook hands.

'Pleased to make your acquaintance,' Rose said, pecking his cheek. 'We've heard a lot about you.'

Colette examined him with quizzical shyness. 'You look nothing like my dad.'

He helped them across the line with their luggage and flicked the rein.

'The Old Country, eh, Charlie? You'd not believe the time we've spent planning this visit. I'm pleased to see things haven't changed.'

Charlie turned the pony into the lane. Primulas were already budding in the verge. During the climb to Moor Top, Bill looked across the remembered landscape and wondered if Ellen had changed as little over the years.

Three Elms couldn't accommodate everyone, so they'd hired a hotel room. The party was set for a Saturday, and Charlie had spent the previous week worrying about its cost. But Ellen was not to be put off. The occasion was worthy of celebration.

They set off in the late afternoon in Russell's trap. Charlie felt uncomfortable in his new suit and spent the journey running his finger under his starched collar. Bill, Rose and Colette said they'd wait at Three Elms until John arrived in his new car with Nerissa and Flossie. The O'Rourkes were coming on the six o'clock train, and Charlie's relatives had written to say they were hiring a charabanc.

Russell gave the reins a flick. 'Fine spring day. Winters awful, full of bronchitis and murk. This is the order of the day, mm? Plenty of brightness, none of those wretches back there.' He nodded towards the school. 'And you, Mrs Tanbrey, aren't you glad to be alive?'

'I might be if you didn't drive as if there's a fire.'

Russell made a sound in his throat which could have been a laugh. 'We enjoy a brisk trot now and again. Sometimes get as far as Ramshaw, Buxton once in a while. Charlie tells me you've never set eyes on your sister-in-law before.'

'Which one?'

'The American lady, Rose isn't it?'

'The cart doesn't stretch to America.'

'Just so. It's a place we've always wanted to visit. We read a lot, you know. Motion pictures, there's the game. That's where it's starting out. Motion pictures. Better than teaching, Mrs Tanbrey.'

'Don't you think it's time you called me by my first name?'

'Certainly. Ellen. What d'you think, Ellen?'

'Think about what?'

'Moving pictures? Just the thing. Keeps the masses on the mark. Better than religion.'

Russell's awkwardness of speech intensified when he spoke to women, although his pupils seemed to have no trouble understanding him. He coaxed the pony around a hairpin, narrowly avoiding a column which had been set up to celebrate the end of the Boer War. 'Come on, you heathen creature, best hoof forward. Not too hard by the plinth, sir! We abhor animals, better as tripe....'

A print of the late queen overlooked the trestles. Ellen was inspecting the place settings as John's car pulled up outside, scattering grit. Rose and Colette came into the room, with Nerissa and Flossie. Charlie had seldom seen Nerissa. He wasn't sure what to make of her marriage to his brother, but he could see her in her daughter, the pale and pretty face framed by thick, dark hair. Outside, his two brothers and Richard were looking under the bonnet of the car. Above the growing babble he heard the faint whistle of O'Rourke's train....

Charlie sat in a mellow mood. John stared without expression at the wall. Bill's laugh boomed down the row. Dick and Gertrude, with their children, were seated alongside Bessie, who'd made an attempt to disguise her weight under a generously-cut blouse. Her husband, a rough-cut miner, had spoken scarcely a word since their arrival. Jane and Eric sat near the door, Eric's tongue holding forth as Jane's eyes meandered from table to table. A mill-owner, an oil millionaire, a Member of Parliament, a suffragette, two schoolmasters and an assortment of wives and labourers. A crash rang out, and heads turned to Dick as he rose unsteadily to his feet.

'It always gets 'em, that, a tray across the knee. Never fails.' John sat stony-faced; Bill leaned back, prepared to be amused. Nerissa fitted a cigarette into an ivory holder. 'Never thought we'd be gettin' a visit from our illustrious cousin again, did we Bessie? Isn't that right, Bertha? And now here he is, bold as brass before our very eye-balls.'

He grasped the edge of the table, began to lean, righted himself and leaned again. 'There's a few faces here this evenin' I've never seen, and some I've not seen for many a year and that's not altogether a good thing to my mind. It's get-togethers like this make family, never mind meetin' up for weddings and funerals. This should be regular, a regular thing for all of us.'

'The poor fellow's maudlin,' O'Rourke whispered behind his hand. 'I think we should tie him to the wall before he collapses.'

Rose caught Colette's eye and they exchanged a smile.

'Now this here do is in cele-celebration of a very shpecticular man.

You all know what I mean. We might talk about what we're about, but Bill here's the only one what's got off his - his -'

'Chair?'

'Seat?'

'All right, call a spade a bloody shovel, got off his arse and done it. He's done what we'd all like to do. He's taken the chance and got somewhere. And when we moan about our lot, if we'd had the same spirit we could've done likewise instead of pullin' our faces. And I'm not just speakin' for you lot, I'm speakin' for myself as well.'

He tilted precariously, a hairsbreadth short of imbalance.

'Sit down, you soft sod.'

A roar followed his wife's reproval. 'As I was saying before my conscience here interrupted me, Bill took the ball – bull by the horns and now he's come back a man of means, and who can blame him? I only hope 'e can see 'is way clear to puttin' a bit my way before he leaves.' He swayed again, his wife mirroring his movements with a supportive arm. 'By, I don't know what they put in this stuff, but whatever it is makes your toes curl.'

'He'll be havin' one off come tomorrow,' chimed Gertrude. 'Sit down, man.'

'Cart 'im off 'ome, Gerty!'

'Tuck him up in bed.'

Dick waved them away. 'What's that grand ship you're sailin' back on, the *Titanic*?'

'Why, are you coming back with us?' Bill shouted over the din.

'I've my work cut out keepin' a roof over my head here, let alone fortune-seekin' at my time o' life. Well, all I wanted to say is the best of luck. If you 'ave any more of it you'll be makin' John there jealous. What 'ave you got in your branch of the family? Thank God for Charlie. At least he restores my faith in the human condition, which is about our level, hey duck?' Gertrude gave him a warning stare, and Dick held up his hands in submission. 'All right, all right, present company excepted. Now I'm going to give way to Bill, but before I do – no, before I do, I'm goin' to tell you a joke: a burglar breaks into a house, and it's pitch black inside. He 'ears this voice, "Jesus is watching you, Jesus is watching you." He thinks: "Funny, wonder who's sayin' Jesus is watching you?" So he lights the lamp and there's a parrot sat on a perch. So he says to this parrot, "What's your name?" and it says, "Percy". He says, "Percy's a funny name for a parrot." The bird looks him in the eye and says, "I know, and Jesus is a funny name for a bulldog."

Gravity finally got the better of him, and Dick pitched forward into the remains of his dinner. The roar which followed was not shared by John, who looked stonily ahead. Colette played a rag, and a prolonged applause ended Bill's speech. The O'Rourkes had to catch the last train. Eric clasped Charlie's hand. 'Wonderful, not enjoyed myself so much in years. That cousin Dick of yours, put him on the boards, he's a natural. Charlie, you must pay us a visit. I've collected a couple of paintings by Adolphe Valette, very interesting stuff, I can tell you. You must cast your expert eye over them when you come up. I'd better look sharp and say my goodbyes.'

'Russell will give you a lift to the station,' Charlie offered.

'Wouldn't dream of it. The walk will do us good. Must remember that joke. Maybe I can use it in the House. "Funny name for a bulldog –"' He turned away, chortling to himself.

'A bit fuller than I used to be, hey, Charlie?' Bessie cooed, out of earshot of the rest. Her breath smelt of gin, and her eyes simmered with the same Jubilee-Day guile.

'We're both a bit longer in the tooth.'

'And you've gone up in the world, Charlie.'

'Ay, half way up the first rung.'

'It's nice to see you've got over your misfortunes.'

'I think they're waiting to go,' he said, and she pursed her lips towards his cheek.

The driver cranked the engine and the charabanc moved off, John's car following. Russell helped Ellen into the trap. 'Nice do, Charles. We have no family, always pleasant to join someone else's. Just a mo while we light the lamp. See there? The first hawthorn leaves. Spring at last. Spring at last!'

Bill came around the corner of the cow shed, making her jump. She turned towards the house, her pail splashing milk across the flagstones, and he took it from her.

'Ellen, it's the first chance we've had to talk.'

'I thought you were busy packing.'

'Look, we're not kids no more. I'm fifty-six. There's things need saying, just to clear the air. I don't want to go back with a taste in my mouth.' They reached the door. He'd be sailing in two days. Rose and

Colette had gone to Leek, the others were at school. 'I know you've been avoiding me. Jane hardly spoke during the dinner either. Have I got plague or something? Sit down. Please.' The chair arm needed darning, and she began to pick at the threads. She wished he'd joined his wife, or gone walking. 'Ellen, Charlie wrote and told me about the baby. I'm sorry. I know it was years back, but I never forgot. I left you to cope and I can't forgive myself for that. Look, I don't know what it is, but I feel I've got to set the record straight.'

'What for?'

'I don't know what for.' For a moment he sounded helpless. 'I was awake most of the night. I have to clear things between us.'

'If it's the –'

'Ellen, I killed a man. I've told no living soul before, not even Rose. That's the reason I ran.'

'What d'you mean?'

'It was an accident. When I knew about you having a child, the only thing I could think about was packing up and getting out. I left Nat money for you and the baby. I got as far as Whitfield and saw a man I used to work for. He picked a fight and he fell on a spike. It was an accident. The spike was just sticking up out of the waste, like they do. I panicked and buried him, then I ran. Ran all the way to the States. It wasn't for the baby, see? I'd have done some thinking and come back next day. It was Dixon. I'd have been strung up. I had to get out.'

She recalled the column in the local paper. The conclusion had been Dixon had had an accident. The land was full of old shafts and discarded workings. How deep would he be now, buried and forgotten?

'It was *you*.'

'I didn't want trouble. He fell, and that was it. That's why I carried on running.'

He sounded defeated. She said: 'Seems to me you're drawn to violence, what with your in-laws, now this Dixon.'

'Look, there's only one way I can make amends. I'm better off than any man has a right to be–'

'Me and Charlie don't want your money.'

'And I'm not offering it you. I know you wouldn't take it. I'm offering it to young Richard and Vicky as a gift. You can't refuse. It's their futures you're lookin' at.'

'You've no need to buy yourself. You should never've brought it all up again. It was dead and buried years back.'

'Ay, like Dixon.' He pulled uneasily at his chin. 'There's another reason for offering. I can't explain. It won't make sense to you, me neither. I feel somehow this is the end of the match. The whistle's gone, and that's it. Maybe it's because of going back, I'm a loss to say what it is. I'd just be grateful if I could make them a gift. It's a sort of pact. With myself, if you like.'

'You'll have to see Charlie when he gets back.'

He seemed relieved. 'He's a good sort, our Charlie. One of the unsung heroes that keep it all ticking over.' He felt he'd said the wrong thing. 'Look, Ellen, about Dixon – it was in confidence....'

'Then you shouldn't have told me.' He looked at her in alarm. Thirty years ago she would have taunted him. 'Who'd want to know anyhow? As you say, it's in the past.'

He'd hoped his visit would put things right between them. If he stayed he'd be a celebrity and enter the local folklore, a fearless adventurer who'd made his fortune in foreign parts and returned a wealthy philanthropist. But he no longer belonged there. He knew he'd never come back.

6

Bill watched the crowds making their way along the embarkation dock. He'd booked two cabins, and Colette had already made herself at home.

'Daddy, is it true they call this the Millionaires' Special?'

He said he was going to look around and get his bearings.

'What do you suppose is wrong with daddy?'

'I expect he's tired,' Rose said. 'It's been a long trip. Have you enjoyed it?'

'Sure. Wait till we tell Marian. Won't she just wish she'd come!'

'Maybe she'll be along next time.'

'You mean we're coming again?'

'Who knows?' Voices came faintly through the glass. 'Your Uncle Charlie and Aunt Ellen were nice, weren't they? You'd better write them when we get back.'

'I'll write on the way. And you can as well – to grandma's family in Ireland.' She lay back. 'I think I'm going to rest a while, mommy. I feel like I've been around the world a dozen times.'

Rose returned to her own cabin and sat on her bed, running a brush through her hair. Bill was still on deck as the ship pulled away. When he came into their cabin, he recited the wonders he'd seen, the gymnasium with its mechanical camel, the rowing machines. The Astors were on board, someone had mentioned Guggenheim. Next he'd go on the car deck, explore some more. He sat on the bed.

'Is anything wrong?'

'Should there be?'

She lay down her brush. 'Would you have preferred to stay at Charlie's a while longer?'

'It's nothing to do with family.'

'Then what?'

He stood looking out at the receding quayside, the figures passing on deck. 'I don't knowwhat's wrong, I don't know what it is.'

'Colette's gone to bed, maybe you should do the same. We've been over half Europe. You're just tired, I guess. When we get back, you must see the doctor if you feel no better.'

He slipped his hand inside his jacket and brought out an envelope. 'I want you to have this.'

'What is it?'

'We have more than we know what to do with. Charlie's kids.... it's a little something for each of them. Give it to the bank, they'll put it through.'

'Why give it to me?'

'Charlie wouldn't take it. You don't mind, do you?' His earnest manner was alien to all she knew about him. He raised a smile. 'You know what I'm like with papers, I'd probably lose it.'

'Mind what?'

'Helping them out. He's the one never seemed to.... well, you know. I left a note for your side, too. They must have something. Hand them both over to the bank, they'll sort it out.'

She put the envelope in her bag and lay on the quilt beside him, listening to the distant throb of the engines. He reached for her hand, and fell asleep holding it. He awoke much later and went back on deck. A song lilted faintly across the calm sea.

He was glad when they went down to dinner. They spent an hour with an insurance agent from Washington who stubbed out his cigarette in a palm pot before lurching back to his quarters. Rose went into Colette's cabin to say goodnight, and when she came back Bill was sleeping, lines of fatigue etched across his face.

He felt better after breakfast. While Rose and Colette took the air on deck, he took a Turkish Bath and tried to relax before joining Rose for lunch. He seemed to have come to terms with whatever had been troubling him – most probably, she thought, leaving England.

'I didn't know what to make of John,' she said, feeling she could now talk about the last week. 'What's he really like?'

'I never had much to do with him, despite living in the same house. He'd shut himself in, or you out, I'm not sure which.'

'Now, Nerissa – I think I could make a friend of her, but she's holding back. Did you sense that?'

He shrugged. 'Didn't seem a match to me. We never got to see his son, neither. He's married and living in london, I'm told. Seems as if he's lost touch.'

'And that pretty girl, Flossie, she was so quiet.'

There was so much that intrigued her about them. She'd found the accent difficult, but the moors were just as she'd imagined them. And

Ireland, with its endless greens amid the squalls of rain.

'We're coming again, daddy – mommy says so.'

He broke into a smile. 'If it's possible, we will.'

'We could come every year, you said so yourself. We can afford it.'

He was desperate to change the subject. 'But you might get married. Your husband can bring you.'

'We'll all come together. Marian doesn't know what she's been missing. I know! Let's send a message home. I was speaking to a boy told me you hand it in to the radio room and they'll send it down the wire.'

'And what's your message?'

She thought for a moment. 'I know. "Safe and sound in the middle of the sea".'

An iceberg warning came through Jack Phillips's headphones. He passed it to his assistant, Harold Bride, who took it up to the bridge. Captain Smith nodded and Bride returned to the radio room.

It was cold and clear. Bill stood at the stern, looking down at the trailing spume. Passengers relaxed in their deck chairs, a man exercised in a walking run, groups lazed by the rail.

'He didn't seem bothered,' Bride told Phillips. Phillips shrugged. Not long after, he received a second warning, this time from the *Caronia.* Other guests were handing in messages, and he took Colette's from the list. Bride took the new warning to Smith. Far below, fireman Harry Senior wiped the sweat from his forehead, took a gulp of water from his bottle and drove his shovel into the coal.

It was late afternoon. Rose pulled a woollen wrap about her shoulders and went to her cabin to change for dinner. Bill wasn't hungry, so she and Colette joined the others on their way to the First Class Dining Saloon where a celebratory dinner was being prepared for Captain Smith.

At 7.30, Bride took a further warning. He found Smith at the head of the table, his trimmed grey beard prominent beneath the strong nose. They'd begun the third course as Bride passed the message over. Smith took it and resumed his meal. At nine, he made his excuses and went up to the bridge. From the forward funnel, a dusky plume drifted into the starlit sky. The cold was intense, and the few on deck were muffled against its bite.

'Keep your eyes peeled. I'm going to turn in.'

Smith went to his quarters. In the radio room, Bride sank on to his bunk, leaving Phillips to cope with the incoming calls. Nineteen miles to the north, the *Californian* lay trapped in an ice field. Her captain had sent out a warning that more icebergs had been sighted. Phillips, overwhelmed by the messages coming to him, cut off the *Californian*'s radio operator.

Fred Fleet leaned against the crow's nest and waited for his relief to arrive. He wore a thick coat, a woollen scarf and a double layer of underwear. Behind him dark wreaths poured from the ship's cavernous funnels. It was eleven thirty at night, and the deck was deserted. He swung his arms vigorously in an attempt to keep warm and thought longingly of his bunk and a hot drink. Strains of music floated through the air. *O Danny Boy –*

A pale wall of ice reared from the water. The next line froze to his lips.

Bill started up with such force the bedclothes fell in a heap to the floor..

'Bill, what is it?'

He held his head, whimpering. She pulled his hands away. 'It's just a bad dream, something you've eaten.'

The cabin stilled. He took a deep breath. 'It was about the worst nightmare I ever had.... that fair we went to in Tulsa.... that fortune-teller – she was under the water, half her face gone.' He shook his head. 'What time is it?'

'I suppose around midnight.'

'That fortune-teller – I just remembered what she said.'

'Hush, now. I'll get you a drink.'

A blade of ice had sliced through the hull, popping the rivets. The plates buckled with a continuous thunder, sending jets of saltwater into the boiler room. Harry Senior's ears picked up a distant roar against the throb of machinery.

'We just hit something.'

Fireman Edward Self stopped shovelling. 'What, in the middle of the bloody ocean?'

Harry let his shovel clatter to the floor. 'I'm going to see what's afoot.'

Jack Thirlwell skimmed a chunk of ice across the deck, then picked it up and dropped it over the side. It hit the water with a satisfying plop. This seemed to amuse his cronies from the Third Class, and he scooped up another piece.

*

Rose said, 'Hasn't it gone quiet?'

'The engines have stopped.'

'Why?'

'Maybe there's a fault.'

'Will they be able to fix it?'

He shrugged. Footsteps sounded outside the cabin. 'I'll take a look,' Bill said.

Harry pounded back past the boilers. 'The mail room's under water, the bastards've shut the doors! It's bloody floodin' in!' He kicked a shovel across the floor. 'I'm getting' out'

Bride rubbed the sleep from his eyes. The first person he saw was Captain Smith.

'Call for assistance.'

Phillips began tapping out the Morse Code. Smith turned at the door. 'What's that?'

'CQD,' Phillips said.

'Sir –'

They turned to face Bride, now on his feet. 'Well?'

'There's the new SOS signal....'

Smith snapped: 'Put it through.'

'There's trouble. Get your clothes on, I'll get Colette.'

'What sort of –'

'There's no time.'

'But –'

'For God's sake do it!' His face had turned to putty. She stared at him in disbelief. Colette stood at the door. 'Don't worry, it'll.... it'll be all right.'

He hustled them out. A steward stood in their way. 'Life jackets if you please.'

They joined the First-Class passengers standing on deck in evening dress.

Bride flat-handed the desk. 'We're bloody sinking! Look at that ship out there! What's it doing, for Christ's sake? Why don't they answer?'

Phillips wrenched off the earpiece. 'Must've switched off the set.

We're on our own now, lad.'

'Are you bloody mad? They won't let us drown!'

'It's miles off.'

Phillips made a helpless gesture and retrieved the headset.

Harry Senior reached the deck. Knots of passengers stood by the davits, many hastily attired against the bitter cold. A tense hush had settled over the ship. He turned to Edward Self, who'd followed him up. 'I'm not going back down. Not bloody likely.'

'What're you going to do, Harry?'

'It's every man for himself.'

'It's not that bad, is it?'

'You stupid bastard, there's only boats for half that lot. Who'll be on 'em, the bloody stokers? It's arse-hole to the bloody steerage. You do what you want, I'm not goin' down.'

The Gondoliers floated across the dark expanse of water. The Third Class berths and forward boiler rooms were already submerged. Bride and Phillips continued in the radio room as Smith gave orders to start loading the lifeboats, women and children first. Some clung to their husbands and fathers. Sixty feet below, the Atlantic slapped the ruptured hull. On the bridge, Smith ordered guns to be issued to his officers.

Bill's forehead was clammy with sweat despite the cold. Fear numbed him. Strange how some had a window on the future. Maybe time didn't travel from A to B. Maybe some saw into a time not yet arrived. *Los muertos....* el mar. The sea. What would it be like, that last, slow, sinking into oblivion? He couldn't help himself, couldn't help them.

Rose looked up at him, her face pale in the flares. 'You mustn't give up. You mustn't.' Colette buried her face in his chest, sobbing silently. 'It's not written. It's not!'

A hand on her shoulder: 'Your turn, Missus.'

'You mustn't die, Bill, you mustn't die.'

He prized her away. 'I'll be on the next boat. Colette, you take care of your mother–'

He bit his lip until he tasted blood. He didn't know what to do. Firemen stood by the davits, smoking pipes, wearing life-jackets, silent.

The pulleys squealed. Rose dipped below the rail, her eyes never leaving his face. He held fast to the bar, waving, saw an arm raised in reply.

The Third Class passengers burst into the First Class section and swarmed on deck. Harry had split from the others and was clinging to a vent. Smith struggled across the tilting deck to the radio room. Phillips was still at his desk, 'No power, no bloody power.'

Smith stood by the door. 'You've done your duty. Abandon your post.'

Phillips smashed the set hysterically. 'Come on, come on!'

Water crept up the deck. His feet were sunk in lead. When he got up, Smith had gone.

The great ship's stern rose sheer from the water. There was an unnatural silence. A priest gave absolution to a weeping man, to a group by the rail. A woman babbled incoherent Italian, implored someone to take her baby. Bill turned away. When he looked again, they'd gone. The screws hung against a glittering sky. Men were sliding noiselessly down the deck as the ship cracked. He held fast to the rail until the cold froze his fingers and he let go and felt himself falling. The rush of water crushed the air from his lungs. He rose through a dark cavern, thought he saw Dixon's lifeless form floating downward. Cries of horror echoed across the water. A sort of warmth infused his body.

Harry Senior fought his way on to an upturned lifeboat. A rocket pierced the dawn sky. *The Carpathia* was steaming ahead at full speed.

Spring returned. Along the rills, the dew-spangled celandine basked under a benign sun, a rabbit-tailed willow nodded from the heights and from the valley a languid smoke drifted upwards. When he reached school, he found Russell in an excited mood. Would Charlie come over tonight? He could bring his wife if he wished.

'What's it all about?'

'Can't say, sorry. I'll put my culinary talents to good use.'

For the past five years Charlie had taught in the new Council School, with a proper office for the head and a wind-whipped yard for the scholars. Russell had decided not to apply for the new headship, and it had been given instead to a man well-known in the district. The staff had grown to include three women. Soon, the youngest had become engaged to a local stonemason and resigned, her place taken by a prickly middle-aged spinster, Miss Hobday. His cane cupboard was now rarely opened except to take out books. Some days seemed to drift on the summer haze, the scholars' whisperings part of the tranquil fabric of the afternoon before a sudden caprice would prompt him to break the silence. 'Would you care to hear about –?' and he'd name a character in some story he'd read the night before, or recite a favourite poem.

'Does the road wind up-hill all the way?
Yes, to the very end.
Will the day's journey take the whole long day?
From morn to night, my friend.
But is there for the night a resting place,
A roof for when the slow dark hours begin?
May not the darkness hide it from my face?
You cannot miss that inn....'

And he thought of Bill and Bevis and Hannah. 'Now, let's say it together. Speak up so we can all hear. Does the road.... '

Their voices would fall through the bars of sunlight, and he'd open the windows to the drowsy air.

'Mr Tanbrey, would you please find out who it is keeps playing on the pipes?' Miss Hobday had asked, one break.

'What pipes?'

'The heating pipes. What d'you think I meant, the bagpipes? Someone in your grade keeps banging them with his boots.'

He squinted down at the scrawny woman perched on her hard chair, her feet barely touching the floor. 'I'll look into it.'

'It's every lesson alike, I can't get on with anything with the pipes being kicked every minute of the day.'

She reminded him of a malevolent gnome. He always thought of her as gnarled. The pupils called her the Old Witch. Someone had drawn a crude picture and left it in her desk.

'I didn't think I had a pipe running along the back.'

'Of course you have pipes along the back, Mr Tanbrey. We've all got them, or how else is the place to be heated?'

'By the radiators, I should think.'

She opened her lunch, the crustless bread cut into small squares, a pippin which she wiped against her slight bosom. She began to nibble at the edge of her sandwich. 'It isn't the radiators being kicked and scuffed, it's the pipes. You should attend more to what goes on in your class.'

One of the other women broke in, brightly: 'What a lovely day, and we're stuck here! Just think, I could be rambling over Morridge.'

'That's just wishful thinking,' her companion said, and for the moment the tension was defused. The monitor rang the bell for the next lesson.

Ellen turned down Charlie's invitation to go with him to Russell's that evening.

'He's all right when you get to know him.'

'I think he's strange. You go and have a night out.'

'He might 've put on extra food.'

'I dare say you'll finish it off between you.'

He cycled to Russell's cottage. The door was ajar, and he knocked and walked in.

'What, no wife?'

'She's not feeling too well, Russell, touch of belly ache.'

'We're sorry to hear it. Kaolin and morphine, have you tried it?'

Russell motioned him to a seat. His eyes were bright with restrained excitement. Unable to contain himself any longer, he said: 'We've something important to say, Charles. Do you want to hear it?'

'If it's that important, I suppose I'd better.'

'We're leaving Moor Top. We've decided to make the break, mm?'

'Where to?'

'Here, read this. Go on, read it.'

Charlie read the letter. 'Well, Russell, I don't know what to say.'

'What is there to say? New opportunities beckon. Fresh horizons.' He began to pace the room. 'It's the thing of the future, motion pictures. We make no pretence to be a great Thespian. Dare say we could, given the opportunity. Fascinating business, Charles, fascinating business. We're not green, you know. Amateur dramatics, glee clubs, we've done them, we've kept at it. No pretensions, though, mm? They want gymnasts for their stunts. Well, that's my forte. Before it's too late. I'll learn what they want. Horse riding, fencing. Eight years left, Charles. Eight good years. The man behind the mask, that's what we'll be.'

'What're you on about, Russell?'

'The letter!' He snatched it up and held it like a proclamation. 'It's all down there. We report to the studios at seven. They need the light, you see? No need for music-hall experience, not in our game. We're a stand-in, mm? Who can tell? America, Europe? Goodbye to Moor Top and all who dwell therein. Pastures new.' He opened a cabinet and produced a bottle and glasses. 'Drinks, that's the order of the day! The finest Madeira, none other. Wish me well, Charles.'

'You said *me*.'

'What?'

'It doesn't matter. All the best, Russell.... I'll be sorry you're going.'

'Just the two of us, Charles, no one else worth inviting. Not that crew up at the school. None of them know, and good riddance. Good riddance we say. To a better life!'

'A richer life?'

'Richer in spirit, if not in pocket, mm?' He lowered his glass. 'Say nothing. We're just going to go. No thanks, no speeches, none of that specious horse-dung.'

'You mean you're just going to walk out without a word?'

'Certainly. Correct.'

'But – your contract. You have to put in your notice. You'll lose money.'

'We're contracting, all right, contracting out. We're glad to see the back of it. A fool's game, always thought so. What use is it, what benefit?'

'It's a living, some would say a good one compared with the pit.'

'Strictures and boundaries, codes and ethics. A straight jacket. A dumping ground for the nation's scoundrels, mm? Intelligent people don't need schools. Schools stifle them. Intelligent people can pick it up from books. A good library, Charles, that's all. Control, that's what it is. Control and propaganda. Now, motion pictures, that's real. That's real education. Something done, something accomplished. We do it, we see where we've been.' He drained his glass and refilled it, his grey eyes aflame.

'Maybe I should have done the same. It's too late now. I shouldn't be too ungrateful. There're some pleasant souls.... There was something else I'd have liked to have done, though.'

'Mm?'

'I tried for a while to get design work.'

'Design?'

'Tiles, crockery and stuff. I think I was good enough. I know I was.'

'What happened?'

'It's a long story. I trusted people and made a mistake. They used my work, but I didn't get a penny. Have you ever felt you were tempting fate?'

'In what way?'

'I got to thinking I was rising above my station, and, well, things happened to punish me for presuming. I ended up sealing everything I'd done in the attic.'

'Really? How curious.' Russell toyed with his empty glass. 'I hear you had dealings with the Old Witch, Charles. Remember the uproar about that sketch she found on her desk? It was myself who did it. We felt like it, silly cow. Sorry we weren't there to share the excitement. What she wants is a good man. A man with a good erection.'

'*You* did it? Maybe you should stay on.'

'Good God, not for us. No interest in women. Don't understand them. Too demanding. Too scheming. They squeeze your life into moulds. Come on, we'll eat.' He whipped a cloth from the platter with a conjuror's flourish. 'Not to worry, Charles, not to worry. And say nothing, mm? Not a word.'

Eric O'Rourke's speech drew to a close. 'My Honourable Friends on the benches opposite will agree this present government has done more to halt the drift of our population to the dominions than all the governments of my Honourable Friend's persuasion have attempted before. The Honourable Gentleman's blustering will do little to attract the House to his view.'

Taking his seat, he smoothed his beard in anticipation of Barrington's response. Barrington rose to his feet, his gut bulging through his part-open waistcoat. 'I am indebted to my Honourable Friend. While his rhetorical skills might show a little improvement, the same cannot be said for his arithmetic, whereby he is able to subtract 284,000 from 464,000 and arrive at a figure close to zero. As he is well aware, over 464,000 of His Majesty's subjects now leave these islands every year, compared with a mere 284,000 in the first decade of this century; at which time that part of the House I represent enjoyed a majority which they're bound again to do in the very near future.' A chorus of hear-hears echoed around the Tory benches. Barrington continued: 'Perhaps my Honourable Friend is trying his usual ploy of deflection. He's more full of red herrings than the Irish Sea. I recall an urgent debate on the illegality of the Irish Citizen Army when he threw up the demise of Captain Scott. At another time, he demonstrated his support for the National Insurance Act when the topic in question concerned the Chancellor of the Exchequer's acquisition of £1000 worth of shares in the American Marconi Radio Corporation.'

This was greeted by a jeer from the Liberals, as Lloyd George, now cleared of fraudulent involvement, looked impassively towards the speaker. 'I also recall that my Honourable Friend has attempted, through stratagems ranging from bluster to what I believe is called wit, to divert the attention of the House from the hysterical behaviour of the suffragettes to whatever takes his fancy. He has good reason to do so, no doubt. I'm sure even Miss Emily Davison would have been impressed by his tactics had she still been with us. However, I'm assured that the House is unanimous in its denouncement of these ladies. Why anyone should wish to burn down a railway station and ignite Kew Gardens is a puzzle to a mere man. I'm of the opinion that common acts of criminality should result in a custodial sentence, rather than universal franchise. Be that as it may, what the honourable gentleman's red-herrings have failed to address is the coming of war.'

A tired groan went up. Barrington waited for it to subside. 'Yes, I realise I'm old and laughably out of touch. We all want to wallow in our deck chairs and leave our neighbours to their own devices. Not good enough. We need more than a navy. We need an army. A very large, bullying army. More than that, we need to appreciate why. When we accept the why, we shall have the will to do what is necessary to avoid conflict. Peace is never cheap, but war is dearer. Fortune never favours the feckless. It favours the strong. Before it's too late, I call upon the leader of His Majesty's Government to raise the necessary levies for the protection of his subjects, among whom I number my good self.'

Barrington sat to a patter of applause. O'Rourke once more rose from his seat. 'My Honourable Friend omitted to reveal that I am a clergyman's son. I am sure the nature of my father's vocation is of utter indifference to anyone, including myself, and I allude to it merely because his stance reminds me so much of my father's. My father went to great lengths to prepare a sermon that would uplift his flock. He was rarely at a loss to use the pulpit to great effect. Unfortunately, no matter how diverse he intended his themes to be, he inevitably came around to decrying Papery. I hasten to add that he had nothing against the Catholic Church. Indeed, many of his friends were of the Catholic persuasion. Nevertheless, for some reason best known to himself, railing against the Pope was all that sustained him for the better part of three decades.'

Cries of 'get to the point' rose from the benches opposite. The Speaker intervened. O'Rourke continued: 'The analogy I wish to make is that the Honourable Member follows my father's footsteps to the letter. No matter what the subject under scrutiny, he can be relied upon to bring us his news of impending war. Is he not aware that our navy is more than a match for the German navy? Does he not realise that Britain has long ruled the seas, and will continue so to do? At this rate, the Honourable Gentleman will become an embarrassment not only to himself, but to the party he purports to represent.'

A clamour of support rang in O'Rourke's ears for a time after the House adjourned. Members of all parties enjoyed a drink together in the Commons bar, but there was something about Barrington he couldn't stomach and the two avoided each other wherever possible. It was known that Barrington had interests which would benefit from a European war, and that he had a nose for trouble, as well as a knack for turning it to his advantage. The smell of war was strong in his nostrils, and O'Rourke was sure he'd acquainted John Tanbrey with his view. O'Rourke cast his mind back to the time he met Tanbrey at Rudyard. He'd made no mention of Jane's departure, and neither had O'Rourke. But Tanbrey had let it slip that Barrington was a friend of his. O'Rourke remembered feeling both men could, under the right circumstances, prove dangerous.

Such thoughts came to him often in his rented London apartment near Vincent Square. He usually caught a train from Euston to arrive home in the early evening, but occasionally had to delay until the following morning when a late sitting kept him up. He'd come to the conclusion he wasn't cut out for high office. He enjoyed the irrelevant theatre of it all. He looked forward to each new morning, exercising his slight frame needlessly, deriving daily amusement from the thin white legs bobbing under his chin and ignoring the patch of worn carpet under his window. Some of his friends had other women; he'd heard Barrington had several. But O'Rourke had no need of a double life. His occasional pleasure was a visit to the races. It amused him that he was a member of the party which had denied universal suffrage and it amused him more when people like Barrington brought up the subject of his peculiar matrimonial arrangements in the House. He relished the gossiping corridors and took neither Barrington's threat of war nor Jane's causes seriously. He still believed in the Fabian ideal, but time was too short for passion. In Westminster, passion was the refuge of the cynical.

Jane mellowed with him. She'd disengaged herself from the WSPU. After ten years, the suffragettes had got nowhere. She'd begun to believe that public sympathy was on the wane, that continuing acts of vandalism alienated them from potential sympathisers. She still believed in the cause, but wouldn't the WSPU gain more credibility if it adopted a more conciliatory approach? Surely, then, the press would have nothing to gripe at? She'd reached the age when the intensity of women's causes had begun to stifle her. In three years she'd be sixty. Any resolution would come at its own pace. Throughout her life, she'd done as she wished, and the trait had become ingrained. She now felt as little allegiance to the Pankhursts as to John Tanbrey.

7

Ellen said: 'It's addressed to us both, so I'm going to open it, Charlie.' He followed the play of expressions across her face. 'Well–look at that!'

He took the sheet from her and read: 'I know I should have written earlier, and I apologise for having taken so long to reply to your kind letter. As you'll understand, it was lonesome at first and I couldn't get used to not having him around after all our time together. I had a lot to deal with, though, and that kept me pretty busy. Now that awful blackness has lifted somewhat, and I'm so grateful I have the girls with me. I have to tell you Marian's walking out with a young man with whom she works. I don't think she'll marry too soon, though, she has all sorts of ambitions which don't fit into making a home. Colette's different. She was very close to her father, and she's taken his death much harder. We've been a great comfort to each other in this time of sorrow.

'I'm running on too long! You must get in touch again soon. I'm writing as if Bill's death meant nothing to you, and of course we've shared the same grief. How are Richard and Vicky? I hope they're doing well – which brings me to a point of concern to both of them. I don't know whether you believe in premonitions? Looking back, I'm sure Bill knew he was going to die, and it was important for him to help his family in some way. Please don't be offended, Charlie, your brother was a very generous man. He wanted to make provision for your children, to help them with their schooling and what have you. I know he broached it with you and you wouldn't accept a gift from him, and maybe I'd feel the same, I guess. But it was dear to him to pass on some of his good fortune, and as a favour to me I'd like you to accept the enclosed banker's draft to be spent on Richard's and Vicky's future in whatever way you wish. He insisted on sending an equal sum to my mother's remaining family in Ireland, which I've done also. It will make me so happy if you'll accept, this time, as I know Bill would be too.

'I do hope we meet again. I still dream about the sinking. I guess I'll never entirely get over it. You know what I think? It was all because of money. The ship had to be the fastest and they cut down on the life-boats. Those poor people, I'll hear their cries to my dying day.

'I'm getting maudlin again. Can I end by saying, write soon? Please give our regards to everybody we met, even the cows.

With our best wishes, Rose'

'I told Bill I didn't want charity.'

'So did I, but maybe we were wrong. Remember the golden ball, Charlie? It's supposed to roll once at everybody's feet? Now it's our turn.'

'But –'

'No buts. You've earned it. You deserve it.'

'Earned it?'

'Through enduring. We both have. Put it in a bank and thank your stars. Send it back, the children'll never forgive you.' He stood, undecided. 'It's not for you or me, we wouldn't know what to do with it we've been so long trying. You start them off right, our Richard and Vicky, and then their children'll have a start too. It's their time now.'

He stared down at the envelope, then picked it up and smiled at her.

Miss Hobday faced her class, her mousy hair loosely swept into a bun. Her pupils sat with arms folded behind their open snap-tins. She slowly paced the first row. As she passed each desk, she nodded and the lid of each tin snapped down. In the middle row she stopped and pointed at a box which lay open on the desk. 'What's that?' The girl immediately shrank into herself. 'I asked you a question. Speak up!' The eyes of the class were fixed on her, some showing relief, others vicarious fear. 'It looks to me like offal. Your mother has given you offal.'

'Yes, Miss.'

'The unclean parts of a beast, not fit for human eating. It looks like an ox tongue with bread. You know what can happen to you if you eat offal? Do you know what will happen to you?'

'No, Miss.'

'Who can tell her? Well?'

'Please, Miss, you get ill Miss.'

Miss Hobday ignored the reply and returned to her victim. 'Offal is the food of sluttish creatures. Any child who eats it is despised of God. I'm shocked. I'm shocked your mother sends you to school with offal!'

'Please, Miss, her mother's dead. She lives with her aunt.'

The voice sprang from a corner of the room. The speaker, realising his error, recoiled. The schoolmistress's shadow fell across the girl's desk. 'Stop snivelling! Stop snivelling and whining!' Miss Hobday's bun broke loose and a strand hung on her cheek. 'Offal eater! Even the beasts of the fields know better. Shut up the box. I'll shut it up for you! Never, ever eat in my presence again. Do you hear me?'

The deranged voice froze the girl into submission. Outside, a game was in progress, and shouts broke through the open windows. At length a bench creaked and someone dared to cough. The moment of dread had passed. With the bell, Miss Hobday repinned her hair and went out .

In the lunch-hour the head teacher came into the staff room. 'Has anyone seen Mr Russell? A scholar told me he left his class in the middle of number work. I found them still sitting there after the bell.'

The staff looked from one to the other. 'Perhaps he's sick,' one ventured, then, looking across to Charlie, who had his head down: 'What about the lavatories?'

Charlie went through his part in the charade, returning when he'd composed himself. 'He's not there.'

'I wonder if I should go to his house?' the headmaster asked himself. 'Miss Hobday, you've not seen Mr Russell, have you?'

'I saw him pass my door.'

'When?'

'At twelve o'clock or thereabouts.'

'You don't happen to know where he was going?'

'I'm afraid he's never taken me into his confidence.'

The head went out. Twenty minutes later he returned. 'It's most irregular. Mr Russell seems to have vanished. I looked through the window of his house and the room had been cleared out. Mr Tanbrey, you're a particular friend of his, do you have any idea where he could have gone?'

'I'm afraid not.'

'Well, if he doesn't turn up for afternoon school I shall have to inform the authorities.'

'That's not very helpful, Mr Tanbrey,' Miss Hobday said, when he'd gone. 'Still, it's no great loss. They never did much in his class, anyway.'

An uncharacteristic boldness came over Charlie. Having only recently come to terms with the death of his brother and already regretting Russell's departure, he had a rare urge for confrontation.

'How d'you know?'

'How do I know what?'

'How do you know Mr Russell did nothing?'

'You don't have to be clairvoyant to know that. I wouldn't expect you to agree, of course. Thick as thieves, the pair of you.'

'How do you know?' Charlie persisted, levelly.

Miss Hobday bridled. The others took refuge behind their needles. 'Don't ask me how I know, Mr Tanbrey. I've been teaching long enough to recognise types like Mr Russell – and you yourself, come to that. Teachers? Humph!'

Some demon goaded him on. He heard himself say, 'I think you're an evil old witch who hasn't a good word to say about anybody. If you were teaching children of mine I'd have them out of here in two shakes of a cow's arse.'

One of the women yanked her wool from the ball, while the others spoke brightly about the wild flowers collected for the week's nature table. Charlie ate his sandwich. Miss Hobday sat bolt upright, her mouth twitching. Charlie finished: 'You're like something out of a Grimm's Fairy Tale, only madder. I think I'll spend this afternoon banging the pipes, just to rile you up.'

He left her stunned into silence. That afternoon, the head called him from his class. Had he used an expletive whilst addressing Miss Hobday – to do with certain parts of a cow? It had been a punishing day. He felt he should have stayed at home, what with Mr Russell's disappearance and Mr Tanbrey's outburst.

When he walked to Miss Hobday's room to deliver his apology, he found the head in charge of her class. 'Now Miss Hobday's gone home! She complains of feeling unwell.'

The shadows of his life were beginning to lose their strength. As summer came, a golden heat burnished the fields and sounds came faintly on the torpid air. The countryside was drowsing, and he drowsed with it; and through the high windows drifted the fragrance of hawthorn and mown grass and he thought of Caulton striding under the tumbling clouds.

Richard had developed a facility for languages. He'd been offered a place at Oxford, and Bill's generosity would secure it. He was already looking forward to vacations in France, said that to gain a good career he'd have to be fluent in more than one language. At times, casting a glance at his son bent over his books, Charlie's thoughts strayed to Hannah. But Hannah without pain; a memory, sometimes poignant, always companionable. And Vicky, with her broad, freckled face and the same straw coloured hair her mother used to have before the years streaked it with grey. He wondered at times what had happened to Matthew, who must be in his thirties now. John had said he was in London. Was he still there? Why was he estranged from his father? Why was John ruthless with anyone who crossed his path –apart from Charlie himself. And his marriage to Nerissa – what sort of life did they have together?

His children had completed the circle of his life. He'd survived the death of his parents and his child and brother, the tragedy of a first marriage and the unfulfilled promise Caulton saw many years ago when he gave him the paints. He'd survived the shock of knowing the reality of his parentage and cheated death where others had lost their lives.

When the long summer days lit the sky, he went on rambles with his son. Soon, Richard would be gone. Perhaps he'd hardly ever see him again. They'd climb the Cloud in companionable silence, listening to the bees in the gorse. Ireland made the headlines, and drifted by. What mattered was the arching sky and the chirp of crickets. Not Ireland, nor the assassination of an archduke in far-off Serbia. The here and now. That's what mattered.

O'Rourke threw down his paper and turned to Jane. 'It pains me to say so, but Barrington was right. I think we're in for it, my love.'

'I suppose we are.'

'Your noble causes will sail into the sunset. In a month the vote will be an irrelevance.' He kissed her cheek. 'Along with Parliament and most of the populace, of course.'

'It was a foregone conclusion, and we must ensure it works to our advantage. I believe I mentioned this before.' Tanbrey squinted through the smoke at Barrington. The club was deserted apart from a couple of members dozing in a corner. 'Your looms are turning, uniforms for our fighting men, braid by the yard. You're a lucky man, John. Lucky you met me.'

'The luck is mutual.'

'I'm sure you're right. Tell me, do you remember our visit to Whympinger's place?'

'How is he?'

'I haven't the remotest idea. Do you recall Smythe?'

'He's still living?'

'If he were not, it would be necessary to resurrect him, along with his brother. Particularly his brother. Fortunately, there's no need. I spoke to them both only last week.'

'And?'

'We came to an agreement.'

'Another agreement?'

'One can reach any number of agreements so long as one knows the right people.'

'You're going to tell me something.'

'It seems we might get a contract for helmets.'

'Helmets?'

'You must know helmets, John, they help keep one's head in place.'

Tanbrey blew a ring at the ceiling. 'Does Hodson know?'

'All in good time.'

'I suppose,' said Tanbrey reflectively, 'there's always the chance of a settlement?'

'There's always a chance pigs might fly. No, there are no more Bismarcks, and the Kaiser can't afford an ignominious retreat.' Barrington leaned forward, his rheumy eyes lit. 'The Schlieffen Plan will be pursued with the usual vigour, I dare say. The Germans will go for the French jugular, then turn back on Russia while France lies a-bleeding. The Germans have to strike first. Surprise tactics, millions on the trains. It would take a genius to undo it once the thing's been put into operation.' He raised his glass. 'In less than a month we'll be embroiled in the biggest fiasco in military history. Cheers!'

He drained his glass and called for another.

Three weeks later, Sir Edward Grey rose to address Parliament. 'Last week I stated we were working for the peace of Europe. Today, events move so rapidly it is exceedingly difficult to know the actual state of affairs. In the present crisis, it has not been possible to secure the peace of Europe, because there has been very little time, and there has been a desire – at any rate in some quarters – to force things rapidly to an issue. As we now know, the result is that the policy of peace, as far as the Great Powers are concerned, is in danger.'

Grey's nose dipped towards his papers. After a pause, he continued: 'I telegraphed both Paris and Berlin to say it was essential for us to know whether the French and German governments were prepared to respect the neutrality of Belgium. The French are fully resolved to do so. The German

Minister for Foreign Affairs doubted he could answer at all. Now I note from news which has recently come to me, that an ultimatum has been given to Belgium by Germany, the object of which was to offer Belgium friendly relations on condition that Belgium facilitate the passage of German troops. For our part, we cannot bargain away whatever obligations we had in Belgian neutrality.' An intense hush had fallen across the chamber. Every eye was fixed on the speaker. Someone coughed. 'We are going to suffer terribly in this war, whether we are in it or not. Foreign trade is going to stop because there is no trade at the other end. Even if we stood aside, we should not be able to prevent the whole of the west of Europe falling under the domination of a single power, and I am sure our moral position would have lost us all respect.'

His speech drew to a close. There were no questions. Later that day, a new meeting was convened. Again, Grey, looking pale and shaken, faced a full House. After a lengthy silence, he picked up the communication he'd just received from the Belgian Legation in London. 'Germany sent yesterday evening at seven o'clock a note proposing Belgium allows them free passage on Belgian territory, and threatening, in case of refusal, to treat Belgium as an enemy. A time limit of twelve hours was fixed for the reply. The Belgians have answered that an attack on their neutrality would be a flagrant violation of the rights of nations. Belgium is firmly resolved to repel aggression by all possible means.' He lowered the sheet and looked across the rows of faces. 'The Government is prepared to take into grave consideration the information it has received. I make no further comment upon it.'

Richard came in and threw his jacket over a chair. 'I've just enlisted.' Ellen asked superfluously what he meant. 'I've joined up. I'm going to fight the Hun. I've done it, not two hours ago.' Charlie heard himself ask why. 'To wear the King's colours, of course. Look!' He took out his armlet, emblazoned with the royal crown. 'It's worn on the sleeve.' He fixed it and waved his arm with exaggerated pride.

Charlie shook his head. 'You had a future any young man would have dreamed of and you've thrown it away on a spur-of-the-moment notion the papers talked you into?'

'I don't call fighting for my country spur-of-the-moment.'

'I know you mean well, but–'

'It's too late, I've done it.'

A wave of tenderness swept over Charlie. 'You should at least have spoken to us first. Why didn't you speak?'

'I guessed what you'd say.'

'You're throwing away the chance of a lifetime, a chance I never had.'

'You mean university? I'll go next year, there's plenty of time. I'll perfect my French and amaze them all.'

'It's war, our Richard,' Ellen said, 'men fighting each other with guns. It's not a holiday.'

'The Hun deserves a bloody nose. How can you stand by while Belgian babies are being nailed to doors? It'll all be over in a month or two, anyhow.'

'You don't want to believe everything you read in the papers,' she said.

'Our teacher says it could go on for longer than anyone thinks,' put in Vicky.

'Is your teacher an authority?'

'She says there's too many soldiers now, they'll all have to fight.'

'That's what armies are for.'

Charlie moved to the window and stood, looking out. 'There's no need to have left your education. Some would give their eye teeth for your chance. There's professionals can fight, they're paid to fight. You've got your whole future ahead.'

Richard shrugged and went out. On an impulse he'd decided to return to Leek. He found the crowds swarming through the streets, some singing *Goodbye Dolly Grey*. A contingent of riflemen were guarding a gun carriage which had been set up in the square. There was an electricity in the air, and his spirits soared. A sense of the destiny of his country rose through the summer heat; the Huns were bullies, barbarians; the British decent, brave, doing the right thing. He looked across at the cheap flags fluttering from the windows and pushed past a group of girls towards the gun carriage. He was passing the grocer's as an old man caught sight of his armlet.

'Answering the call to arms, eh? Where're you going?'

'I'm still on reserve.'

'You'll be off to foreign parts. I wish I was young again, I'd be going with you.'

The gun carriage had been cordoned off. An officer was speaking to the crowd, the riflemen moving between questioners.

'How long will it take?'

'Not long.'

'Where's Kitchener?'

'With his feet under the table if he's got any sense.'

'What about grub?'

'What about it?'

'Is it fit for eating?'

'Just like your mother bakes, only twice as hot.'

The world seemed lit like a flashing carnival. Within a day his planned future had been unravelled, its place taken by a euphoria he'd never felt before. Daily troop trains clattered through the station. Moor Top sermons paid tribute to the honour of the nation, and the pulpit was draped in the Union flag. Britain was to be purified of the sloth which had submerged the land. For the first time the fundamental things that mattered could be seen. War pageants whipped up a fever of suspicion, with here a foreign waiter with a strange room plan, there a German barber about to cut an English throat. Were we to give in to the barbarian, the country among whose illustrious sons were Drake, Nelson and Wellington? Across the land, thousands answered the call to arms, fifty-four million posters in windows everywhere, and everywhere Kitchener's accusing finger. Your Country Needs You. Enlist Now! Rally around the Flag! Forward to Victory! Answer the call of your race! And the parks overflowing with khaki, drilling....

As he stood on the step, the reality of his decision hit him. It was not yet six, and a pearly mist shrouded the woods below the farm. Charlie handed him his case. It promised another hot day. He thought perhaps Richard should carry his coat and Ellen thought the same. Vicky stood in the doorway in her nightdress, scraping her toe against the step. He felt ill-at-ease. He'd no business going; he was letting them down. What did he know about fighting? He was too young to be....

Ellen smoothed his collar. 'There's food in your pocket. Make sure you keep up your strength.' And now his father, the early disapproval buried, the faintly stubbled chin, the thinning hair, the grey-flecked moustache.

'All the best, son.'

'Well, time to be off, I suppose....'

'You're sure you don't want me to –?'

No, he preferred to walk alone, it wasn't far, plenty of time....

He turned at the end of the track and waved. Back before Christmas. That was it. Back before Christmas.

An excited line formed around the Town Hall; labourers, clerks in their bowlers. He joined the queue and shuffled forward. Trestles had been set out, each occupied by an officer. He waited until a seat had been vacated.

'Name? Address? Sign here.'

Some struggled, others made their marks. Then they were outside, the pigeons cooing from the finials and a barrel-chested sergeant marching the new recruits to the station.

'Strip.' He disrobed in a cubicle acrid with sweat. 'Richard Tanbrey!' He came naked from behind the screen. One of the doctors was scribbling something on a form. A second looked with brief disinterest as he filed past. The third made a rudimentary check; teeth, chest, back, hair, and then on to another table where they tested his sight, made him skip and jump. The last doctor applied a stethoscope, nodding expressionlessly. The shambling line passed through. He joined the others for bully beef and stewed tea. The reek of cigarette smoke filled the air. He was summoned to the regimental depot and issued with tunic, trousers, puttees, boots, helmet. The tunic was heavy and the trousers chafed his legs. In the morning a lance corporal yelled instructions in marching, turning and saluting. Next an issue of underwear, kit bag, entrenching tool, water bottle, haversack, comb, razor, an ammunition pouch.

He was drowning in a khaki sea. He felt himself turning into a machine. Now he knew how to salute the paying officer before and after receiving his six shillings and sixpence; how to keep his tunic buttons bright and his belt polished. He learnt how to handle a Lee Enfield, how to rise on the dot at the quarter-to-six reveille, how to perform his physical jerks without drawing the PT sergeant's attention. He grew used to the drab order of barracks' life, trapped in an endless routine of service, with its structures, endless ditties, endless swearing, unwashed crockery, typhoid inoculations, mock trench warfare and the clamour for cleanliness. Weeks passed before he began to see his companions as individuals. They might use their week-end passes for a pub-crawl, but they were moving towards the same destination as himself.

One day, after church parade, a bandy-legged cockney nudged him. 'Heard the latest?'

'What?'

'Heard a whisper. Home service is abolished as from nah. Gonna be a draft unit instead.'

A sombre Welshman said, 'That means we're going abroad, then?'

'Just a whisper.'

'That's why we're here,' Richard said, with feigned enthusiasm. 'I don't suppose we can complain.'

A two-day burst of bayonet practice followed a week's musketry. They were issued with an identity disc and addressed by the Brigadier General. 'Men, you will shortly be going overseas, most of you for the first time. Your country is proud of you. You have done your duty in service to your king. I wish you all a safe journey and a safe return. It is to men like you that our country will owe a debt of gratitude in the years to come. We wish you all a fond farewell.'

Active Service Pay Books, rifle-oil, pipe, tobacco, writing pad. The unit marched under the gas jets to the station. It was mid-night when the train moved out. The regimental band struck up *Tipperary*, its jaunty notes fading into darkness.

John Tanbrey took out his wallet and flourished a wad of notes. 'I shall begin by offering a token of my own. Colonel Collinsworth will count it while we consider to what purpose our donations may be put. Those of you who have sons fighting in France will know the dangers to which they are increasingly exposed. The lack of high-explosive shells for our lads at the front is scandalous, and it is hoped Mr Lloyd George will very soon put his energies to good use in righting this appalling shortfall. But he needs help. Your help. Our help. How much do we have, Colonel Collinsworth?'

'A little over £50.'

'Fifty pounds, that's a start. That will buy a few minutes' respite for our boys. Those of you who value the life of a son, a brother, or a husband – join me. Offer what you can. There's no excuse. You're all in work. The ladies among you, I'm addressing you especially. A million of you are now engaged in full-time employment. Spare a little of your good fortune for the lads in khaki. They're protecting you from the Hun. They're our only defence, a thin line pledged to fight to the last man to keep our island free. Free from tyranny, free from bloodshed. They need shells to do the job. Here!' he delved into his wallet again. 'Have more! Buy another shell, a rifle, parts for a Lewis gun or something for a Bristol Biplane – even if it's just the shine on the windshield. How much now, Colonel Collinsworth?'

'It now stands at £75.'

'Let's make it £100. Who will help make it £100? Yes, a gentleman over there. Over there, corporal!' Three corporals pushed through the crowd, donations clinking into their helmets. The helmets were returned to the podium and emptied. 'Well done. We certainly know generosity of spirit here. I don't know about the folk down south, but I'm sure they're not a patch on us. Colonel Collinsworth – do you have the figure there?'

'I do. We've finished the count and we're pleased to announce we've made a collection of £105.10s 6d. A very creditable sum. That will give the Hun something to put in his pipe. Well done! Well done!'

The crowd dispersed. Collinsworth, a white-haired veteran of the Boer War, helped Nerissa off the podium. 'Mrs Tanbrey, you must be very proud of your husband volunteering his services at this very busy time. It was a good show today, a jolly good show.'

Nerissa smiled and lit a cigarette. He was at pains not to show his disapproval. 'You aren't used to ladies smoking,' she teased him.

'Each to her own, ma'am.'

'But you don't really approve?'

Tanbrey had been listening with half an ear while talking to a reporter. 'I'm sure Colonel Collinsworth has other things on his mind than your smoking, my dear.' He led her to the car.

'Perhaps we could do the same again,' Collinsworth said, opening the door for her. 'You can't imagine the difference it makes, having a local figurehead on the stand with us. Well, no doubt I shall see you soon, Mr Tanbrey.' He held out his hand. 'Mrs Tanbrey.'

As they drew away, a winter gust blew against the hood. Nerissa wrapped her stole more closely around her shoulders and gazed emptily at the whitening road. She lit a cigarette from the old stub.

His reflected face glared palely at her from the screen. 'I wish you'd get rid of that infernal thing.'

'Does it disturb you?'

'You disgust me! Trying to get off with Collinsworth – Christ! Flirting at your age, revolting bitch!'

'Master doesn't approve,' she wheedled, her hands shaking. He mimicked her. She knew how to rile him. It was the only power she had left and a substitute for everything she'd lost. 'You were very free with our money today, dear.'

'You don't have any money.'

'The boys over the briny will be most grateful.'

'Why don't you shut up?'

'Still, I suppose it makes a change from handing it to whores.'

'One finds one's pleasures where one can.'

'I suppose you feel you're safe in your little cocoon of probity. Unfortunately, truth has a nasty habit of popping up when you least expect it.'

'What're you babbling about?'

'What should I be babbling about? It's only a trophy speaking, only a tarnished old worthless old trophy. I expect you think I welcomed the chance to grace the platform. I wonder what our amiable army buffoon would say if he knew? I wonder if his outrage would run to returning the cash?'

His eyes started with loathing; loathing of her nicotine-stained fingers, the grey strands of unkempt hair brushed carelessly about her ears. Their respectability was like being fettered to the ground by the weight of public approval. He couldn't stand her intrusion into his life, and she preferred hatred to indifference. The money he'd so eagerly parted with had been collected from his workers the day before. She'd found out from a chance meeting in town and told him so.

He gazed morosely through the screen. There was a pattering of rain against the glass. She began a thin warbling. '*We all go the same way home, all the whole collection, in the same direction....*'

When they got back, Flossie was still up.

'I thought you'd be in bed,' he said.

Nerissa yawned. 'I'm going upstairs, anyway, I'm tired.'

Flossie looked up. 'No, Mummy, there's something I have to tell you.'

'That sounds terribly important. I'd better pour myself a nice large gin to help me concentrate.'

Tanbrey turned away. Flossie stood behind the chair. He'd never been able to tell what she was thinking. Even before she spoke, he knew she was going to say something that would shock him.

Her mother fitted another cigarette into her holder. 'Don't leave us in suspense – spill the beans.'

'I'm going to be a nurse, Mummy. I wanted to be sure before I told you. I've said I'd like to go overseas.'

Nerissa's hand trembled as she lit her cigarette. Flossie had never been away before. Nerissa saw a future isolated from her husband and cut adrift from her daughter. She'd dreaded the day she married. But the end would be the same. She'd have no one.

After a strained silence, Tanbrey said: 'There's nothing glamorous being a VAD. I'm surprised you've even considered it.'

'It's something I want to do.'

'Why do you want to do it?'

'Because –' she shot a glance at her mother – 'because I need to get out of this house before I'm driven off my head. This house is dead.'

A sigh welled up in his throat. 'When do you intend to leave?'

'I packed while you were out. I've ordered a cab for six in the morning.'

Nerissa took the remains of her cigarette from the holder and crushed it into the tray. She left without looking at her daughter, and when she'd locked herself in her room she began to weep helplessly. In the morning, she stood at her window watching Flossie manhandle her case into the waiting cab.

8

'Some good news, John. Can't say too much over the telephone. Perhaps we could meet?' Tanbrey suggested a time. 'Excellent idea. I'll contact Hodson, I think he should be with us.' Barrington hung up. He'd booked a private room at the Connaught, and had been there only a few minutes when Tanbrey and Hodson arrived. Barrington beamed at them over his glass. 'Can I get you something?' Tanbrey wanted a scotch, Hodson a pint of mild.

Hodson turned to Tanbrey. 'Hear what happened last night?'

'I wasn't in town.'

'You've heard o' Steineke's ironmongers, just off High Street?'

'Go on.'

'The old man had his window put through by this mob. Bloody Steineke! I've known the family twenty years, wouldn't harm a fly. Bloody papers!'

Barrington came back and set down the drinks. 'Never a waiter these days.'

'That's because all the waiters are fighting the Kaiser. I was just telling John here about the Steinekes. Some bloody ruffians starting a rumour about 'em being German spies. German spies! They've been here since the year dot. The old lady, spying? It's as much as she can do hang a set o' net curtains.' Hodson snorted into his drink. 'Are they going to arrest my overseer? He's the best man I've got, and his mother's German and his father's Italian. Pepe Lorenzo. Why not arrest him and close us down? The whole bloody country's gone crackers, ask me. Papers, whippin' it all up. How many Zeps have *you* seen? Read the papers, you'd think the place was crawling with Germans.'

Barrington wore his accepting face, nodding as Hodson's indignation ran its course. He said: 'Something's come up, might be of interest.'

'If it's more work, we're hard put to manage what we have.'

'A small project. If a go can be made of it, I dare say there'll be more in the pipe-line. What I've been asked to do is to see if it can proceed on a limited basis, at least for the while. I'm told the ordnances aren't involved.' He tapped his nose. Tanbrey sipped his drink blandly.

'What is it?' asked Hodson.

Barrington twirled the stem of his glass reflectively. 'You'll know the Austins? They've had some success, a good motor. The Ministry has the idea of extending their use. The present thinking is for the vehicles to be used as a basis for a fleet of ambulances. Everywhere else is stretched to capacity. We've got a couple of empty sheds, I dare say there's enough plate to make bodies for a few hundred, maybe a thousand. It's excellent business.' He leaned back, drained his glass. 'I know bugger all about machinery of any sort, I'm just a facilitator. I'll find out the details later. The thing is, to build these things on the Austin chassis. It's all confidential at the moment. Why the top brass should slap on confidentiality orders is a mystery to me. I shouldn't think the Hun would be interested if we plated every ambulance on the globe. I put it down to hysteria, myself. But there you have it.' He lowered his voice theatrically. 'The Ministry's prepared to pay well, which is jolly good news, don't you agree?'

Hodson ran a worried finger down his cheek. 'But what of the other orders? There's twenty thousand helmets this month gone to the painters. The way things are going it could be a few million....' He tailed off. In a brighter tone, he said: 'I didn't tell you, did I? My son joined up the week just gone. I told him, wait your turn, lad, there'll be conscription soon enough. Well, that's me being old fashioned. King and Country – and they're coming out o' Parkside gibbering with neither arms nor legs.'

Tanbrey asked: 'Is there a date for all this, Lawrence?'

'I was hoping very soon.'

Hodson's eyebrows arched. 'You'll be lucky to start at the end of next year. You don't seem to –'

'We need shifts,' Barrington cut in.

'The buggers need a rest. They're already down at the works gone five.'

'Bring in the ladies.'

'Have you ever tried mauling a wagon load o' sheet? It takes a man all his time, let alone a wench.'

'They'll work for less and work harder.'

'But what about the lads? Their nose'll be right out once I bring in girls.'

'They'll be too busy building ambulances to worry about that.'

Hodson scratched the rough skin under his collar with renewed vigour. The war and Barrington had been good for him, yet he'd always felt a sense of discomfort. He felt pressured. That's how it all seemed when he was pressured. But ambulances – at least the idea would protect lives, not destroy them. And his son had just joined up....

'It's not what we do, as a general rule.... I didn't think the top brass'd run to the cost of it, working behind the lines.'

'We must assume,' Barrington said solemnly, 'that some spark of humanity still resides in the Governmental soul.'

'Ay, and we must assume it keeps the tills ringing,' countered Hodson without irony. 'I'd better be getting back. I don't know about casualties in the trenches, there'll be a casualty here if I have to put many more hours in. I'll have to go.'

Barrington gave a token laugh which died as Hodson left. 'Wife and family in good shape, John?'

'As far as I know.'

'You're not sure?'

'There's a lot I'm not sure about.'

'Not to worry. The Noun's decided. He's had a little trouble, but he's behind us all the way. There is a detail I didn't mention to our friend Ebenezer, however.'

'Which is?'

'The ambulances are to be armoured as a trial. Octavian is very keen on this project. You see, his son was killed in one of these contraptions not long ago. You can see the interest.' Barrington leaned forward, again lowering his voice. 'The project will pay handsomely – even more handsomely, if the sort of substantial plate he has in mind cannot be procured in these straitened times. And who would know?'

'Hodson might.'

'Hodson might.... but the specifications he receives might not necessarily be the ones envisaged by our boy in his London office. As far as Ebenezer is concerned, it's just another job. Forget the armouring, just a straight-forward job.' He leaned back. 'Another drink, John? And we keep it to ourselves, eh?'

'Don't you have enough money?'

'One never has enough, especially when one falls foul of the roulette wheel. No, it should get me off the hook for a while – and generate a useful addition to your own meagre income into the bargain. Never look a gift horse, John. I'll fix it for the both of us. But not a word, eh?'

'About what?'

'That's the idea.'

'Bloody war!'

'Tut-tut, I'm surprised you're so involved. You're not considering a career in politics?'

'Flossie's gone. She's decided to nurse.'

'Oh. Unfortunate.'

Tanbrey fell silent for a moment. He said: 'Do you ever wonder what life's about?'

The politician blew a ring, watched it rise and disintegrate. 'Yes, I've given it a great deal of thought over the years. It's all about avoiding the clap.'

A fortnight later, Barrington paid a morale-raising visit to his constituency. He'd insisted he'd 'show his face' at a large motor firm which now produced vehicles for the war effort. He joined the director on a platform overlooking the intense activity taking place below. Buses, ambulances, trucks and limbers stretched in lines along the shop floor, each with an attendant group of men and women in dungarees.

'Marvellous effort. I'm most impressed. This is an all-day operation?'

'Twenty four hours a day, seven days a week.'

'And how're the ladies bearing up?'

'Productivity's never been higher. I hope they stay on when it's over.'

'I'm interested in the procedures, how the thing goes from order book to completion. I suppose for each type of vehicle you have some kind of blue-print to work from?'

'That's correct. If you'd like to come with me, I'll explain how we go about it.'

The director led the way into a wood-panelled office. Barrington opened his briefcase and took out a small notebook, which he laid before him on the desk. 'You must excuse my ignorance, technical matters have always eluded me.'

'That's no problem, Mr Barrington. I'll show you a current spec, and how it works. Any particular interest?'

'Well, let's see. Off the top of my head, I suppose an ambulance is a good place to begin.'

The man opened a drawer in the filing cabinet. 'We keep copies of the specifications in here. We have around six of each, saves us the trouble of printing more for the various departments. Here we are. Ambulances –or an Austin chassis destined to become an ambulance.' He spread a sheet across the desk.

'So these lines and figures represent an ambulance in the making?'

'It's just a van really, with a slightly different body and a cross painted on it. They were using carts a lot at first, but that's water under the bridge now.'

'And would these be the same kind of specs, as you call them, as for an armoured car or something of that sort?'

'More or less the same, except, as I say, these vehicles are just run-of-the-mill, no heavy plate involved.'

Barrington poured over the drawings, writing the odd word in his notebook as the man continued to explain. 'I think I'm beginning to grasp the essentials.' He looked up. 'Well, this visit has been both fascinating and enlightening. Unfortunately, I'm on rather a tight schedule, and I'd like to do a brief tour of the works before I get back, if that's all right? Speak to the workers, that sort of thing. I do think it's important to keep up civilian morale, don't you?'

'We do it all the time, works wonders.'

'I might need to shout a bit, with all the activity going on. Do you have a glass of water handy?'

'I'll see to it.' The man disappeared into an outer office, leaving the door ajar. Barrington crossed to the still-open cabinet and quickly extricated a sheet, which he folded into his case. The man returned, glass in hand. 'Here you are, Mr Barrington, a glass of the finest.'

Barrington took a sip and stood up. 'That's much better.' He folded his notebook, placed it alongside the specification sheet and fastened his bag. 'Right, I'm ready to face the troops.'

The director cleared his desk and closed the filing cabinet. 'If you'll just follow me, Mr Barrington.'

They left the office. A secretary came in and took the glass. She spent a minute in the office then went out, closing the door behind her.

The following evening Barrington made a telephone call to Tanbrey. 'John? Lawrence. Do you recall our project?'

'The ambulances?'

'Exactly.'

'Is there a problem?'

'On the contrary, our little plan is about to bear fruit. I hope you'll be pleased.'

'As long as nothing gets out. I'll leave the details to you. You've had plenty of practice.'

'You sound a little edgy.'

'You've not called to talk about my nerves.'

'No, no, that's for your physician to worry about.... remember, John, stay mum, eh?'

'Is that it?'

'For the while. I'll leave you to your cocoa.'

Barrington replaced the receiver. The sense of annoyance Tanbrey felt at having been drawn into Barrington's drama over the phone continued as he went upstairs to his room. In the lounge, Nerissa put down her pencil and folded a hastily-scribbled note into her dressing-gown pocket.

The letter arrived, bearing an American stamp. Charlie immediately recognised the small, neat hand.

'Dear Charles,

We're writing on the off-chance, knowing this might not get to you. We've been working on a 2000 footer. That refers to the reel length of the film. You won't see me, though. We sprained an ankle, so now we're making the props with the carpenters. This film is called *The Woman.* We're working under Mazy, who's in charge of painting the scenes. Chaplin's the real genius. No doubt about it, he's got the energy and no end of ideas. Have you seen *Laughing Gas*? If you don't know him now, you soon will. He worked for Fred Karno. You'll have heard of him, of course.

This is the life, Charles, better than working. The air over here's golden, which is just the thing for this line, and it has the advantage of being six thousand miles away from the war. If we come back to England we'll visit you, but since the *Lusitania* went down, no one is taking the chance.

Regards to your good wife and family, and take a tip from a reformed man – get your paint brush out again. Can't help thinking back to the day I walked out of school. You must tell me what the Old Witch said. She'd be ideal on a set – a touch of paste and you've got a corpse.

Well, Charles, all the best and if there's still a postal service over there, send a letter to the address above and let me know how things are.

Kind Regards,

Russell'

PS We might have found an understanding woman'

Charlie passed the letter around at work. Miss Hobday had left the school a year ago, and the head confined his amusement to his office. In the afternoon, as Charlie was getting ready to go home, he waylaid him. Did he know of Russell's intentions all along? No? Well, he must keep them informed of any further developments on the Mr Russell front, it sounded most interesting.

He pedalled back, the sun warm on his back. He paused, as he always did, on Moor Top road, looked out over the grey-green uplands and the cloud-dappled sky whitening on the horizon.

Ellen greeted him at the door. 'Charlie! Richard's home!'

The news filled him with pleasure. He found him in the front room, talking to Vicky.

'Hello, dad. Still alive, you see.'

'But – why didn't you tell us you were coming?'

'Only had the papers the day before yesterday. A fortnight's leave.'

'A fortnight? D'you hear, Ellen? Two weeks leave!'

His son's unpacked bag lay against the wall. 'I've just been telling Vicky, I've had promotion. I now have to arrange other deaths than my own.'

Charlie ignored his cynicism in a flush of pride. Ellen asked: 'And what did you have to do for that, our Richard?'

'I think they found out I could read and write.'

She spread a clean table cloth. Later, as they were eating, she said: 'You've not told us what it's like, yet, Richard. I hope you've been behaving yourself.'

'No opportunity to do anything else.' He continued his meal in silence.

'Is it bad?' Charlie asked quietly.

'So they all say. I'll let you know. We'll be going overseas when I get back.' He studied his cup, stroking the handle absently. 'I'm afraid it's not as glamorous as we were led to believe. From what I've been told it's – it's a bad show.' He added, with false brightness: 'That's the best meal I've had all year.'

Something of the spark had gone from him, and Charlie learnt, on their walks, to talk about the strike of Welsh miners, the cessation of demands by the suffragettes, Lloyd George's promotion to Minister of Munitions, anything but the war. On the last day of his leave, Ellen went downstairs to find he'd already gone. He'd left a copy of *The Thirty-Nine Steps* on the table. Charlie picked it up and a note fell out. 'Sorry to rush out like this. Keen to do my bit, you see. The mud on the cover is not any old mud, but the finest army mud. Cheerio for now. I'll write as soon as I join my unit.'

He put the note in his pocket. When Ellen came in, she found him reading the lines anew.

Matthew had thought that before George Rand, the printer for whom he'd worked since coming to London, retired, George might make him an offer of the business. The two men had always enjoyed each others' company, Rand had no family and Matthew had taken responsibility for much of the day-to-day work now that George had turned sixty. It was a small press, employing no more than half-a-dozen men, but the atmosphere was cordial and Matthew had no regrets about his time there.

His last meeting with his father had been an embarrassment to him, and he didn't care if he never saw him again. He'd told his wife about his family. They'd almost given up hope of having a child when she found herself pregnant at the age of thirty. A year after Teddy was born, she gave birth to Alfred. The first time they'd celebrated with a visit to the Gaiety Theatre to see the *Sunshine Girl*. The following year he'd bought her a locket.

With the war, more work flowed in. Besides the usual bread-and-butter lines, enlistment posters, Bairnsfather cartoons and endless postcards kept the presses running into the night. It was while he was printing cards for the No Conscription Fellowship that his vague attitude to the war hardened. He'd reached the conclusion it was more important to work for his family than to risk his life in fighting, and he'd heard there were others like him in Germany being cajoled into doing their bit for the Kaiser. Those with an interest in promoting the war were safely behind the lines, making shells and giving orders. His conscience pricked him. Each month he saw fewer young men through the omnibus window. Had he imagined disapproval on the faces of those he saw travelling home? Was he a slacker, a dodger, an idler, a traitor? Who were the heroes – the women with their hands yellow from cordite or he with his palms inked? To kill a stranger for a reason you didn't understand – how could that be right? His contact with the No Conscription Fellowship gave him the security of knowing others felt as he did. In May, when married men were conscripted for the first time, he told

Bernadette what he was going to do. She knew there was no point in arguing. He wouldn't fight. He could find no moral defence for it. The war wouldn't last for ever, but now the country was crying out for women. If he was locked up she'd have to move away from inquisitive neighbours and get work until it was over. Yes, it would be hard for both them and the children, but they'd survive.

Bars of sunlight climbed the hall walls. A flag-draped table occupied by four men and a woman stood under a scroll listing past officers of the borough. The man at the centre wore a Captain's uniform; to his right, a matron of the Charing Cross Hospital and a Church of England vicar; to his left, a grocer and a banker. A clock ticked intrusively. The grocer's smile died as the door opened and a corporal marched Matthew in. The officer coughed and made a play of examining his papers. 'Matthew Tanbrey?'

'Yes.'

'Yes, sir.'

'Yes, sir.'

'You're not a Quaker, I see?'

'No, sir, an Anglican.'

'Confine yourself to the question.'

From the open window came the rasp of a lorry. The Captain pushed his file away with an air of boredom. 'You've received your papers?'

'Yes, sir.'

'And you refuse to fight for your country.'

'Yes, sir.'

'On what grounds?'

'On the grounds I do not believe the Government has the right to expect one man to slaughter another.'

The grocer stared ahead. 'You say it's not right for the Government to expect you to fight. Suppose the enemy was attacking your wife and kids? Suppose he had rape in mind. You'd invite him in, would you?'

'I hope I'd do my best to protect them.'

'Then that's fighting isn't it?'

'Protection is not the same as murder.'

'Are you such a coward as you wouldn't bear arms against an enemy what came at your family? Suppose you killed him protecting them? What would your answer be then?'

'He probably hasn't had your experience, Harry,' interrupted the banker, 'he's like all of them, green as grass.'

The officer plucked at the end of his moustache. 'Now see here, young shaver; thousands of young men like yourself see it as their duty to fight for the flag. You seem an intelligent sort of chap. How would you like to see your country usurped by foreigners, your way of life shattered and your family murdered in cold blood? There's no need for that to happen. We can drive the Hun back. Together, with strength and determination. We're defending the lifeblood of Britain. Everyone must play his part. I haven't the time for conchies, someone else doing their work for them. Service life will make a man of you. You'll be able to stand four square before your children in the years to come, knowing they owe their lives to you. Have you ever seen a person murdered in cold blood?'

'Yes, sir.'

'Could you explain that?'

'My mother was shot.'

'Could you elucidate?'

'It happened a long time ago. The man was deranged.'

The grocer cut through the awkward silence which followed. 'That's all the more reason why you shouldn't be in front of this tribunal now. You should be shouldering arms like the rest. If your mother was attacked now I dare say you'd have had no qualms about shouldering a gun.'

'Perhaps what I saw put me off.'

The man threw up his arms while the officer exchanged glances with the woman. She looked up at Matthew, her eyes pale behind the wire glasses. 'Mr Tanbrey, we feel some sympathy for your family circumstances. However, the purpose of this tribunal is to weed out bogus claimants to conscientious objection. The words are quite explicit. Conscientious. Of the conscience. Now, you say you are an Anglican. Do you regularly attend church services?'

'Not often.'

'If we assume a religious belief to be the basis of conscience, and you are not a practising Christian, it surely follows you have no Christian conscience and cannot use your so-called conscience as an excuse,' broke in the clergyman, indignantly triumphant.

'I have a conscience irrespective of any religious belief.'

The military man threw down his pencil. 'This is getting us nowhere. I agree with the parson. You have no conscience. You have no religion. I'll be blunt, sir. I think you're a cowardly malingerer. Perhaps you would allow me–' he said, addressing the desk, – 'to quote from some lines I read recently:

> The man who is born of a nation,
> Who shrinks in her hour of strife,
> In a contest for freedom's salvation,
> No longer is worthy of life.'

'What d'you say to that, hey?'

'The writer is entitled to his view.'

'I advise you not to bandy words with this panel,' snapped the vicar. 'You clearly do not realise the seriousness of your situation. Do you have any idea what your refusal will mean for your family? I need hardly tell you the country will exact its due in no uncertain terms. Is that what you want? To have your wife and children fear to open the door, to suffer bodily harm? Surely you cannot look forward to breaking rocks and cleaning out latrines? Think of it, man. All this, set against an honourable duty to your king and country. Do you really want this humiliation?'

The clergyman's eye began a spasm. A street vendor called from the pavement below.

'Well, what d'you have to say about that?' the grocer barked. 'It'll be all over the *Herald* this time tomorrow.'

'I have nothing to add.'

'So you're an absolutist!' sneered the Captain, shaking his head. 'I'd rather greet a cut-throat than a yellow anarchist any day. You'll wish you'd never been born! You'll be praying for a glimpse of trench mud, I promise you. Corporal! Take this man away, he's a bloody absolutist. Strict prison law for him!'

The corporal began to march Matthew through the bars of dusty light.

'Wait.' The matron gestured him back to the table. 'Captain Hodder referred to you as an absolutist. Is that the case?'

'I don't know what the word means.'

'You say you're not prepared to fight. Can you drive?

'I drive a van for the firm sometimes.'

'Would you be prepared to drive an ambulance?'

'Yes, I would.'

The group at the table fell together like a pack of cards. The Captain leaned forward and cleared his throat. 'You'll hear from us within the week. Good day.'

He closed his file, conferring in whispers with those to either side. The grocer grinned at something the banker said. The corporal nodded to Matthew, who followed him out of the room.

A thin dawn light paled Richard's billet. An hour later, they were rumbling across the border into Belgium, the shell-torn towns stirring with the first signs of life. As the day brightened, farm waggons and limbers shared the streets with motor ambulances and Service Corps vans. Beyond the last buildings, a poplar-lined road ran to the horizon. The countryside was deserted, and they moved at a snail's pace through the day. As dusk came on the convoy decamped. Early the next morning Richard joined the column marching along the railway track. The sky was white, and he felt a sprinkling of rain against his face. Geese made a wheeling delta above the stubble-fields and disappeared into woodland stained with the first bronze of autumn. They passed a ruined cottage, its slates smashed into an upper room. A collapsed trench snaked through an entanglement of barbed wire. Corroded spikes pierced the verge like rushes, with here and there a wooden cross. They marched in silence, the soles of their boots sucking at the soft ground. Shell bursts plumed a distant sky, answered by the faint clatter of batteries. The Engineers had converted a ruined chateau into a store. An order came for fatigue parties to carry the rivetting frames to the reserve trenches a few hundred yards away. Work continued for the rest of the day. In the evening the men marched back to camp.

Before nightfall, his draft was ordered to stand by. He hoped the rain or the tanks whose early promise had reached them would mean a sudden end to the war. He hoped throughout the evening, when the stink of cigarettes drifted through the huts. He slept dreamlessly and awoke to a four o'clock call and a ten mile march to the railhead. They climbed into cattle trucks, thirty to a truck. He sat in a corner, seeing the bluebells and campion on the sill at home, smelling their scent in the glades. He drifted into sleep as the train clanked through the lichen-green countryside. At the halts, the men made tea from water scrounged from the engine driver and slept overnight in sidings. Most were still asleep as the train started again, and when the doors slid back the flat land had given way to birch-crowned hills. In the early sun lanes spread on either side the track, with clusters of red roofs among the tracts of woodland.

They pulled into Albert as night came on. Rubbled buildings overflowed into the main street and the cathedral rose above the ruins, its Virgin and Child caught in a motionless descent, the streets awash with slurry. A blue evening sky darkened the road. The column continued in silence. He felt he was marching to a starlit oblivion, and into his mind again stole memories of his father's face and Ellen's, the shaft of a trap, a moonlit lake. A voice whispered '*wear the king's colours, king's colours, king's colours....*' over and over again.

Matthew brought his ambulance to a halt behind the others at the quayside. He remained in his cab, watching the gulls fighting for scraps thrown out by the troops. A line of commissioned buses, armoured cars and vans stood by the wall, each vehicle at the centre of a knot of smoking soldiers. There was a consignment of tanks on railway wagons. There'd been talk of a 'big push', a lot of gossip, nothing definite. *Our noble fighting men on the Somme.... tremendous enemy casualties....* Some correspondent, earning his keep writing what he was told to say. Suppose the Kaiser did overrun Europe, what difference would it make? They'd praised Pax Romana and Pax Britannica, what was wrong with Pax Germanica? That would bring the peace. Peace from Britain to Russia, from Norway to the Levant. But they didn't want peace. They were in a grocers' shop war, a contest for spoils. And behind it all, unseen faces, plotting. Some of those patches of khaki wouldn't come back. If he were to tell them, they'd call him a traitor. The message on both sides was black and white: kill the Hun, kill the Englander, before he kills you.

A column of mud-smeared ambulances began to chug towards the ship with their cargoes. He felt easy with this. This gave him a sense of usefulness. He'd never been an absolutist, but if the choice lay between slaying a man and doing nothing, he'd have done nothing for the rest of his days. Now there was help he could give. There were children in his street who scavenged lumps of coal because their fathers hadn't the price of a fire. He'd scavenge too. He'd pick up the remnants of a life. This made sense to him. This he could do.

A corporal hopped on to the footboard. 'Foller 'im in front.' He got down and moved to the next vehicle with the same instruction. The locomotive hauling the tanks began to clank away. The first ambulance honked. He stepped out, cranked the engine and drove out of the yard.

The man passed in and out of consciousness, his shattered femur piercing his shredded clothing. The ruptured flesh reeked of putrefaction, the swollen thigh green with gangrene. Flossie injected morphine into the wound. The surgeon scored a thin line in the sound tissue, then cut firmly to the bone. A thick tongue of blood welled into the gash. The man jerked as the saw bit into the bone. The amputation took three minutes. The surgeon swiftly cauterised the veins, swabbed the stump with antiseptic. Two orderlies removed the man as Flossie washed down the bench with a chlorinate solution. The severed leg was wrapped and trundled away by a whistling porter to the lime pit. The van reeked of pus which the surgeon could no longer smell. He stepped outside and lit a cigarette. A muffled boom sounded faintly beneath the cheeping of coal tits.

'Come for a stroll?' She hesitated. He was already walking towards a wood beyond the field. He said, 'As you wish,' and hunched his shoulders in an attitude of disregard. Not much over thirty-five, the last year had aged him. He looked Italian rather than English, she thought, thickset and short with the first powdering of grey in his dark hair. Perhaps he hadn't noticed she was just behind. She wondered what his unfocused eyes actually saw. 'He'll be dead by the time we get back,' he said. 'I used to come here as a boy. The *Hotel Napoleon*. You won't know it, of course. I wouldn't have called it the most hospitable of places even then. My father liked the walking and the family just trotted on. We were all very long-suffering.'

He pushed through a clump of brambles which tore at his legs. She was looking for a way around. 'There'll be a path somewhere. There. Try over there.'

Shafts of sunlight dappled the ground through the trees. He looked incongruous in his soiled smock, she in her gown. He said, without turning: 'Tell me about yourself. What made you come to this hell-hole? Wouldn't you have been better off in a knitting circle, balaclavas for the boys and all that? Or should it be balaclavae?'

'Probably for the same reason as you.'

'And what's that? For the glory of England? To see what it's really like?'

'Why do you sneer?'

He flicked his cigarette into the brush. 'A good question. I suppose I sneer because if I didn't I'd go mad. At least sneering's constructive. It shows there's still something left behind the eyes. I see you've put yourself down on the transfer list.' She nodded. 'You want to move to the hospital, I mean a hospital of bricks and mortar, where one might operate on a man without killing him?'

'I'm restless.'

'I shall miss you. If you go, that is.' He lit another cigarette and exhaled noisily. 'We should have met before in more profitable circumstances, as they say. I'm not much good, I'm afraid. I'd ask you to come to bed, but I've lost interest. Nothing personal. If we're both still –' He shrugged. 'Anyway, you wouldn't want me. I'm not your type.'

Guns boomed through the birch. 'I wonder how long they're going to keep it up?' she said.

'You'd better ask Mr Haig. I wish he'd give us a break on Sunday, at least. He's disturbing the birds.'

'I think we should get back.'

'You go, I'm going to sit on this log and brood.' As she walked off, he called after her, 'Bring me back a leg. A couple of arms will do.'

She caught a last glimpse of his smock between the trees.

Richard's unit disbanded. Huts were scattered throughout the remains of a wood. Troops moved between the buildings, part of the supply system to the front. The new arrivals lolled about, cursing the lack of provision after a march of twenty miles from the railhead. A patter of rain blew at intervals from the south west. They were too exhausted to notice. Some had removed their boots and sat in their stockings. Others rubbed at their toes and heels. Richard sat on a wall, smoking a damp cigarette, oblivious to the activity from the depot. One of the men approached him.

'What is it?'

''Scuse my askin', sir, when are we goin' to eat?'

'I'll try and find out.'

'Only the men are ravenous, as you might expect, sir. We understood there'd be a meal at the end, like.'

Richard crushed his cigarette into the rubble. 'So did I.'

He went off, trying to find someone. He saw a superior striding towards an armoured car and began to put his question. The man hastened by without returning his salute. 'For God's sake don't bother me with that now. Bloody arsehole show, the lot of it. Ask someone else.'

There was no one. The soldier who'd put the question had already merged into one of the groups huddled, shivering, under canvas and makeshift coverings. Some of the men had found a length of tarpaulin and improvised a shelter to keep off the spitting rain.

'Not so bad as it might be.'

'Yeh, just like the Savoy, innit?'

'Bleedin' Frog's weather. We've prob'bly all 'ad it anyhow.'

'That's right, cheer us all up, why don't you? Bloody Job's comforter, him.'

The dull thunder of artillery was answered by short, jarring bursts from a howitzer behind the lines. By late afternoon it had relapsed into silence. Richard and a fellow officer, Owen Bradall, reconnoitred the camp. On the edge, collapsing trenches had cut a swathe through the marl, and the ground had been churned into a mire of barbed wire and mud. From a dug-out rose the nauseous stench of the dead. A squirrel ran across the rim of earth and disappeared along a rusting spike.

'How long will it be d'you think?' Owen asked.

Richard said, 'Pretty soon.'

'Have you written home?'

'Not yet.'

'Look, my sister's sent these.' Owen pulled a glove from his pocket. 'Seem to have lost the other. We spent most of the time quarrelling. What about you?'

'My sister's too young to knit. She's only twelve. Mind you, that's not too young, is it? When I write I'll tell her I want three gloves – one for you, two for me.'

'Shall we get back to camp?'

They turned in unison. Richard asked: 'Are you jittery?'

'No,' Owen said. 'I'm in the pink. Tell the truth, I'm shitting myself.' He assumed a sham brightness. 'Serves me right for joining up.'

Dusk came on. A gramophone sang *If you were the only girl in the world*. Richard uncapped his pen.

'Dear All,

This might be the last time I write, because soon we'll be in the thick of it. It's very pleasant country around the Somme, and we're giving the

Boche a run for his money. At the moment everything's calm, and the lads are taking a well-deserved break and writing letters home, like me. Don't worry about me, I'm indestructible. As soon as this lot's over, I shall demand my place at university and spend my lovely inheritance. I hope you're all well.

Your loving son,
Richard.'

Orders came through to join the battalion in the trenches, and they picked their way through the stumps of a wood. Across the ridge spurts of earth burst upwards in a series of muffled detonations. The dug-outs were already overflowing, and Richard ordered his men to bivouac where they could. As night came on, he and Owen slept in their greatcoats in a shell hole. He awoke, stiff with cramp, to rain and men hacking. A ration of cold porridge was passed around, a torn loaf, broken biscuit, dab of butter, tasteless beef stew. He began to stink. There wasn't enough water for washing, and the chloride of lime made it all but undrinkable. He gathered wood with Owen and lit a fire. They were joined by two other officers – Finney, a nervous southerner, and O'Connell, a Scot.

'If it happens, it happens,' Owen said. 'The odds are in favour of survival. You have to keep that in your head the whole time.'

'But survival on what terms?' asked O'Connell. 'I don't think I'd want to celebrate the end of the war legless, unless through imbibing immoderate amounts of whisky. And you'd always be dependent. I couldn't bear that.'

'I bloody hate papers!' broke in Finney, agitatedly. 'Don't show me a paper. Bloody propaganda, all those bloody cliches, how well we're doing, got the Boche on the run. It's all bollocks. There's more truth in a Grimm's fairy tale.'

Richard poked in the fire. 'Won't be long.'

'You joined last year?' Owen said.

'I did a stint in England. It's not what I thought it would be. I must have been mad.'

'It's an experience you won't forget,' O'Connell said, quietly, 'and the worst is the acting, pretending to keep your head while all about are losing theirs.'

The firelight flickered on their downturned faces. Finney asked with stifled desperation: 'When d'you think it'll be over, O'Connell?'

'Who knows? When the last gun fires. Could go on for years. No one knew just how right Kitchener was.'

Finney's rage, always festering, boiled over. 'Bloody load of bollocks, the lot of it. Bloody Haig, the madman. Poor sods!' Turning, he dashed the remains of his tea into the dying fire. 'Sorry, O'Connell, berating your countryman like that. It's just – well, it's all so bloody pathetic.'

Mills bombs and Very lights were issued next morning. Rumours of movement had increased but still no order had been given. Some passed their time hunting for souvenirs amid the debris. The day was drawing to a close when the command came through. Richard felt a dull nausea in his stomach, could taste the bile on his tongue. Nights of rough sleeping had taken their toll. The column spread along a rutted track through remnants of woodland pock-marked with water-filled craters. He made a futile attempt at briskness. Keep it up, lads, best foot forward, keep going, keep going.... The line thinned, the more agile running ahead in the hope of a better bivouac. The track descended through blasted thickets to new lines of trenches. Artillery thundered across the space, and vivid plumes illumined the darkening sky. There was a stuttering of shells close by which sent up fonts of mud and from the mire rose a sickening stench. He found a dug-out and sank down. As night came on, the mail arrived. Vicky had made him a cake. He felt a sudden urge to cry. He broke off a piece for Owen, who'd joined him.

Sleep evaded him for a long time. Someone was playing a mouth organ. A German, perhaps, perhaps one of his own men. It didn't really matter.

9

October had turned cold, and Ellen insisted Charlie wear warm clothes when he went out on 'one of his jaunts' as she called them. Now in her mid fifties, she'd grown heavy of frame and her wide face had loosened. The gold was fading to grey, but the cornflower eyes still sparkled. He'd walked the fields as far as the railway at Rudyard. The line clung to the water's edge, hidden in the copper-tinted woodland among boat houses and cabins. It was Sunday, and the rumble of an approaching train snuffed out the distant whisper of bells. He watched it pass over the bridge and turned back.

In the afternoon his arm ached. He shouldn't have gone on the walk, should have sat instead, especially after a week at school with all the children bothering him. Ellen had lost none of her strength. She was always on the go, attending to the farm and men, cooking and cleaning. The pain passed. 'You know, I swear I smelt pipe smoke when I came in. Has anyone been ?'

'Not unless we had burglars.'

'It was plain as day. Tobacco, in this room. It's gone now.'

'Well, you gave up your pipe and there's nobody else smoked here since Bevis died,' she said. 'Charlie, I do believe you're imagining things. I hope you're not going the same way as Doris, that would never do.'

He smiled in his easy way. Victoria had gone out with a friend, and the house was quiet. Ellen said: 'Do you feel better, now, Charlie? Shall we go upstairs?'

'I thought Sunday was the day of rest.'

A heavy sensuality clung to her. He followed her to their room, removed his clothes and lay on the counterpane watching her undress. She went into the next room and he listened to her splashing at the wash stand. She came back and got into bed beside him. 'I've bought a new scent. D'you like it?'

'I can't smell anything.'

'It's cold. Let's get under the coverlet.'

She entwined herself around him, making her small sounds of satisfaction before brushing his lips with considered kisses. Her arousal grew and she began to rub herself against his thigh.

'O, Charlie, d'you like that? Touch me.' She lifted his hand to her breast. 'Come on, Charlie, come on top, come on top.'

Desire rushed through him. He approached her gently, eased himself part in, withdrew and entered her again.

'I'm going to come.' She moaned insistently.'Keep it inside me.'

She pulled him to her and he entered her thoroughly. She stretched her arms through the bars of the bed, her face taking on a look of discomfort, almost of pain. 'Keep on. More. More. Do me, do me as hard as you can.'

The bed click-clacked against the wall, but she was oblivious, crying as if in distress. A release shuddered through him. He lay still, then removed himself from her.

'We got there in the end, Charlie. I'll make us a cup of tea. My, look at the time. Vicky'll be back.' She dressed. 'Stay in bed if you want. I'm going to do a spot o' mending.'

He heard her go down. From his pocket he took Richard's letter and read it again. He lay back with it still in his hand.

The lead ambulance jolted over the ruts. There were six vehicles in the convoy, moving at a snail's pace through a ruined landscape. In the afternoon they came to a halt on the outskirts of Amiens. An officer rapped on Matthew's door.

'Don't lose the man in front. Half an hour at most.'

He stepped down and moved to the next vehicle with the same message. Matthew got out and stretched his legs. The convoy moved on.

Flossie sat with her tea in the nurses' room. The growl of engines woke her from the constant tiredness which had plagued her since her transfer to the Abbaye St Omer. She followed the progress of the new arrivals from the window as the convoy moved slowly down the drive, then turned back to study the leaves in her mug. The door opened, and the whiff of iodine came into the room. Sister stood in the doorway. 'Nurse Tanbrey, could you give Nurse Marlow a hand?' Flossie put down her mug and rose tiredly. 'Yes, I'm sorry, I know your rest time's due, but we've suddenly been inundated.'

'That's all right, Sister.'

Flossie followed her down a corridor which led into the cloisters. L'Abbaye had once been the home of an order of nuns, and the Abbess had offered the building as a hospice for the duration of the war. The nuns had been given the opportunity of remaining as nurses, or of transferring to an institution elsewhere. The only problem was a lack of space brought about by the intensification of hostilities since the summer. A nun with the voice and complexion of a schoolgirl greeted Matthew and the other drivers in strongly-accented English.

'You get the water 'ere at thees pump and you share thees room when you are not doing driving. You come around, I show you the rest of thees place, yes? You are free to go over the grounds if you want. You breeng up the wounded soldiers from the fields hospitals and in 'ere they get well again, we 'ope. Come, I show you around.'

The day was mild, and men were convalescing in the open air. Those who'd lost a leg occupied wheelchairs grouped in a semi-circle inside the cloisters, and the blinded sat bandaged and upright in wicker chairs set out on the grass. Further afield, along the web of paths running through the estate, walked a group with head injuries, accompanied by a nurse on unremembered tours. At night the nurses worked by oil lamps, and although the Abbaye had a telephone, there was neither electric light nor gas. As the weather grew colder, fires were lit and an enormous stove occupied pride of place in a corner of the refractory. Matthew found it hard to sleep despite his journey. He wrote a letter to his wife, then shortly after midnight, put away his pen.

A heavy rain had fallen during the night, whipping the lane into a thin mud. Matthew kept in second gear, the engine making a tortured whine against the distant crump of shells. The steering bucked under his hands as the wheels slid into old furrows. The medical officer in the adjacent seat had removed his helmet and was swinging it by the strap. Below the rise, a scattering of huts and tents came into view, separated from the battle zone by a stand of undamaged woodland. Matthew followed the signs to the Casualty Clearing Station. The injured sat in silent groups under canvas. Some had fractured limbs and shrapnel wounds; one of the men had lost an eye and part of his cheek bone. The grass had been scuffed to a plastic marl. He and the officer stretchered those unable to walk to the ambulance, shunting until dusk between field and L'Abbaye. Shells were still pounding as night came on. From his billet he watched the sky flare. He fell asleep wondering if there was more he could have done.

Richard ran a finger across his grenades. The same gripes he'd had earlier had given him a sleepless night and continued as he leaned by the trench wall, checking equipment he'd already accounted for. He moved to the foot of the ladder. Blotches of khaki merged with marl. The duckboard was half hidden under mud, with ridges of washed-down clay across the slats. The men were motionless but for an unconscious turning of a head or the shifting of a foot. He leaned against a stave and heard the beating of his heart. A whistle sounded, and his legs carried him up the rungs and out into the open. A pumice plane rose gently to a near horizon. Sweat had broken out across his forehead. Behind the reserve, a green wash of fields ran like a tide to the rim of shattered land. He could see the men fanning out, crouching, see the top of their helmets, the tip of a nose. He heard himself give the order to follow. Ahead of him stretched the endless grey waste, the black lava mushrooms exploding upon the land like gigantic rain. He began to run, crouched low, tilted to the side; smaller, smaller target. His boots slapped the ooze, boots at home, in the field; steady, don't slip. Shrapnel fizzed into the mud, but he heard nothing but his own mute cries of desperation. The horizon receded as he ran towards it, and a vast sky filled his vision. He felt utterly alone, yet the slap of his footsteps bore him on. He motioned the men to a depression. An earth blanket rose up, and he fought for breath. 'Down here, chaps. Follow on, chaps....'

They gained the support lines. From the forward trenches, a battalion of Light Infantry was engaged in a battle for Bapaume. Machine guns chattered through the whitening sky, through the cries of men falling. He fought to blot out the sound, his eyes searching the sides of the trench for the fascinating horror of human remains; a finger, heel, button, knee, boot. He picked out a bullet, put it in his pocket, felt he'd stolen a relic and dropped it. An incessant rattle gave way to a continuous, stuttering volley. Along the front, Vickers' guns spewed across their lines. The tumult split the air, seemed to thicken it, turn it black. Rain lanced down. He realised his teeth were chattering, caught snapshot glimpses of his men huddled against the marl in shallow dug-outs, any hole, any refuge, brick or stone or scoop of slime. He closed his eyes. *You next. You.* They reached a support trench. When would his turn come again? What time did darkness fall? Seven? No, before that, six-thirty. Last night it was hardly that. Should be safe. Should be safe. *Let them die. Let them die, not me, not me.*

At dusk the din stopped. Along the trench came the wounded, their blood-saturated dressings grey in the fading light. A man spun like a top, blubbering. Then bloody heaps with uniforms reduced to sacks from which motionless arms protruded. A scattering of German prisoners-of-war had been herded at the rear. The first he'd seen.

Eric O'Rourke leaned against the rail at Epsom. The gap between the horses widened. The crowd roared and he roared with it. 'Come on, *Sunny Jane*, come on, girl.' He turned to the man next to him as his horse crossed the line. 'Splendid race, splendid. An excellent animal, strong of sinew and fleet of foot.' He should have found it amusing that a man as comfortably off as he, with his press activities, a parliamentary income and a generous inheritance willed to him by the recently-deceased Lady Alice Parker-Holt, could still rave over a win which wouldn't buy a decent dinner for two, but never gave it a thought. Now he felt more at home on the back benches, where he could fall asleep if he wished. He no longer needed to pipe the party tune. What was going on in the Somme? Was the carnage worth it? Should not the government sue for peace? At other times he'd demand the battle be waged until the last drop of blood had been spilt if by that civilisation would be 'freed from the tyranny of German aggression'.

'I can see it coming,' he told Jane, handing her his win in the shape of two theatre tickets.

'What?'

'I can see Asquith receiving the order of the boot.'

'What made you say that out of the blue?'

'I've been thinking about it all the way back. David will be at the top within a few weeks. All it needs is a little bit of wheeling and dealing with his Tory friends.'

'What about Asquith?'

'Yesterday's rising star, tomorrow's shooting star.' She marked the page and shut her book. He noted the cover. 'Since when did you take to reading Forster? What happened to the battle for democracy?'

'My hair's gone grey fighting battles. It's taken me sixty years to realise you might as well throw snuff on the fire for all the difference you make. We're all a hostage to fortune, and that's it.'

'Where's the old fire, weavers' rights, votes for the ladies? Don't tell me you've given up. If you're reading Forster there's no hope for us.'

'You're a fine one to talk. I doubt I'll see you delivering lectures on Fabianism any more. Let's face it, Eric, you've been bought by gracious living like everyone else. It used to be socialist this, socialist that. You all come out like gingerbread men in the end. I might not have the old fire, but I can still be useful to myself. That's why I signed up to work. I've got a job supervising down Woolwich.'

'You mean the arsenal?'

'Since we spend most of our time in London these days, I might as well.'

'Making shells, you mean?'

'You want us to win this war, don't you?'

'Blowing people to pieces? Not like you.'

Her mouth set hard, the expression accentuating the heaviness of her face. 'What alternative is there?'

'You could have nursed. They're bringing them up by the train-load. I could have fixed you up.'

'No, Eric, I've thought of that, and I'm too old for it. I'd be taking orders from some matron half my age. It'd never work. They could all be sons of mine. I want to help give them something to fight with. The more the arms, the quicker it'll all be over.'

He was going to remind her of her earlier commitments to the working man, to the vote. For as long as he could remember, she'd espoused the cause of good. It seemed she'd suddenly become a stranger to him. For the first time in his life he was unable to sleep. At two he got up and went downstairs to make a drink. Snatches of their conversation came back to him as the clock ticked in the silent room. They could all be sons of mine. Now he understood. When he returned to bed, he fell asleep.

Matthew found it a relief to walk beneath the dripping boughs. The rain calmed him. He enjoyed the burbling brook and the grey blurring of sky. There was an erasure in rain. He could let his mind wander back to his wife and children in London.

The gully overflowed into a series of ponds. Green scum had formed away from the turbulence, and duckweed grew among the stones at the bank. The area was bordered by rhododendron and silver birch. Flossie was standing at the water's edge as he came up.

'I've just seen a badger. It disappeared there, under the bushes.'

'I expect there are all sorts in here,' he said. 'Foxes, deer – they'll all be down after dark for a drink.'

She looked up questioningly. 'I feel I've seen you before somewhere.'

'You probably have. I spend time here, as well as at the field hospitals. He looked up at the unbroken cloud. There was a faint booming. 'If this keeps up we'll both be kept busy.'

'You drive an ambulance. I thought I'd seen you somewhere.'

'Yes.'

They left the wood together, walking back towards the Abbaye. 'Did you –'

'I volunteered to drive. It seemed a useful thing to do.'

Two nurses appeared, arm in arm. One girl was jovial, round and fair. She nudged her companion. 'And who's your friend, Flossie?'

'A fellow badger-spotter,' Matthew said. 'I've still got some time left. I think I'll carry on a while.'

'You'll catch your death!' the girl called after him. She smiled at Flossie. 'Well, aren't you a dark horse.'

Shells burst through the rain, sending up geysers of mud. They stumbled down the trench, barging against a corporal dragging a casualty behind them. A stretcher-party came through, carrying a man. His sleeve was empty, and now a leg came away. The carriers, destabilised, fell. Richard vomited into the side of the trench.

An NCO came up. 'Leave him, he's dead.'

A shell whined into the clay, sending up a cloud of debris.

'That one's close.'

'They're getting' a fix.'

'Christ!' One of the men began a low, repetitive cry of horror. 'Christ, Jesus, mother, mother....

Richard looked back. A sick fear threatened to paralyse him. The earth erupted and he cringed by the clay wall. He felt he was going insane. They must see it in him, they must.

'Steady, men.'

A senior NCO was gesticulating towards the enemy lines. It was time again, again, time again. He heard himself echo the order, and the men straggled out, some carrying boxes of grenades, cans of water. The sky had darkened, and the first flares lit the land in harsh chiaoscuro. Some of the men let their ammunition fall into the mud. A numbing grey mist absorbed his mind, leaving behind a colourless putty. The battalion they'd been sent to relieve crawled from the shadows and disappeared towards the rearward trenches. A drawn silence descended over the battlefield, and he sank to the ground, sleeping where he lay.

A setting sun shone fitfully through the mist, and the noxious stink of cordite drifted on the air. He stared up at the sky, then down at his dew-covered blanket. A rat scampered away as he pushed it back. He rose unsteadily, took a *Black Cat* out of his cigarette case. A little way down the trench, he recognised Owen and Finney and went to join them.

Owen said brightly: 'Coffee's just made. Got a fag?'

Richard passed him one.

'O'Connell bought it,' Finney said in a matter-of-fact tone. 'Copped a direct hit, lucky sod.'

Owen passed over a tin mug. 'Nasty do, yesterday. They're planning something. They always are when it's quiet.' Richard looked down the trench. A sentry was eating a sandwich, his periscope raised above the lip.

'Quite a number copped their lot, apparently,' went on Finney.

Owen said: 'I wonder what they're up to?'

A sergeant major barked down the line.

'Better go,' Richard said.

The guns began a thunderous hail. In the trench the men fixed their bayonets. Above them, currants of shrapnel hissed into the mud. Some of the men cowered against the wall, others huddled in a dug-out. The sky flushed with flares, and sparks spat from the Vickers' guns. Richard stood at the head of the line. The moon shone faintly through a clearing haze. A senior NCO was threatening anyone who refused to go over the top. The men began to crawl up the ladders and disappeared into the darkness. There came an endless crack of rifle fire and the cries of the wounded. Richard called up the second wave and stepped over himself. Against the hills he caught faint glimpses of crumpling silhouettes. To his side, a man collapsed, screaming. Now he saw no one. He stumbled into a water-filled depression and flung himself down. A body floated in the pool It might have been a bundle or rags or filth sculpted in the parody of a man. He staggered to the next hole, collapsing alongside two men already there.

'What do we do, sir? We'll be killed if we go on, sir.'

'Go on. Go forward.'

'Sir?'

'Move!'

The men rose to the lip. The first fell on his own bayonet. The other seemed to have melted into the land. Meaningless words welled up from his throat. A figure loomed against the flare of lights. He pumped his Enfield and watched the shape crumple. He fell, sobbing, into the remains of an old trench and lay there.

A dawn mist drifted upwards like steam. A hush had fallen across the battlefield and he thought he could hear a bird singing. He peered back towards his lines. Stretcher bearers were picking their way towards him. When he felt their hands on him, he tried to burrow into the mud. Someone might have spoken. He thought they were being fired on. It wasn't yet light. He tried to stand, but there was no strength in his legs.

Matthew reversed the ambulance behind the reserve and went out with the stretcher bearers to pick up the wounded. There was a German and four Tommies, including an officer. All but the officer had been wounded. The German had been shot in both legs. Three of the other men had been badly hurt. He didn't think they'd survive. The British officer would be sent to rest, perhaps, depending on the MO's report.

At six o'clock the Germans sent up a barrage. Matthew began to move off. The road was firm, but a skim of mud made the going hazardous. Richard looked around the cramped interior of the ambulance. The German he'd shot gazed at him with feverish eyes, his legs wrapped in a blood-stained gauze.

Matthew's voice came through the partition. 'Won't be long, soon be out of range. We'll clear this stretch, then it's all plain sailing.'

Richard took comfort from the voice. There was something familiar in it, something half-remembered, reassuring. Then the voice exploded, and he was falling over a precipice into darkness. Daylight came through a gash in the roof. The vehicle had lurched into a ditch. The German was unconscious, and the decapitated head of one of the injured lay against his feet.

A rear door had been blown away. Richard crawled through the gap. The driver sat at his wheel as if preparing to move on. Richard reached up to him, and Matthew toppled, still sitting, into the shell hole. He stared at the medical officer's empty seat, holding his hands to his face as if vaguely troubled. The road was completely exposed. The stump of a tree vanished in a cloud of debris. He stumbled up and staggered towards the spurting fountains.

Half a mile ahead, children were working in the fields.

'I will replace twenty with five,' Lloyd George confided to his mistress. 'Of course, I shall need to work with my Chancellor. Mr Bonar Law will be a tough nut to crack, but crack him we will. I see no point in huge committees. The war will go nowhere with the kind of squabbling you get in the larger group. No, five is just right. We'll have this war over. The people won't stand for it much longer. I feel it in my bones. It'll get worse, and they won't stand it.' He got out of bed, put on his shoes and turned to run his fingers gently down the woman's back. 'A beautiful skin you have, all those passionate little vertebrae. I feel I should come back to bed. I have to go.'

She turned over, spreading her arms across the pillow. 'Must you?'

'Yes, I'm afraid I must. Ffarwel, my precious.'

He watched the Strand slide past the window of his landaulet. He'd need everything in his power to keep the factories turning. There had already been reports of revolts in Germany and Russia. It was imperative the war end soon, before the revolutionaries had a chance to tear down the flags at home. Already the first drab winds of winter were coursing through the streets. Each lost ship would bring the country one step nearer the begging bowl. How much longer? But oh, those creamy, creamy thighs....

Law hailed him from his Whitehall office. The Welshman said: 'Can't really hang about, Andrew. Anything out of the normal?'

'I don't expect you to,' Bonar Law replied. 'But there is something you might like to know about.'

'What is it?'

'You know Lawrence Barrington?'

'It depends what you mean by know. I'm not in his circle, if that's what you mean. I always took him for a cynic.'

'I agree he has that in his favour.' Bonar Law took up a position with his back to the fire. 'Probably wrong to talk about it, might have been helpful to delay it till after the war. It's not the time to put our trust in Joe Public, David, he might run amok.' He lit a pipe and puffed a grey cloud which hung against the cornice. 'This is confidential between the two of us.'

'Go on.'

'Lawrence is one of those irritating men with not only one iron in the fire, but an entire blacksmith's forge....'

'A typical Tory, you mean.'

A bank of glowing coal collapsed with a slight rush. Bonar Law walked to the window and addressed the London skyline. 'It seems he has some sort of partnership. He cottoned on to some war work armouring ambulances.'

The Welshman sprang up. 'I know nothing of this. I know nothing about armouring ambulances. Who gave him this bloody contract?'

Bonar Law turned back into the room. 'There was no contract. Officially, that is. A secretary was checking the registers against the dates of procurement meetings. She came across this inadvertently. We seem to have a rogue in the requisition office who took it upon himself to order some armoured ambulances off his own bat. I suppose he thought the order could be hidden among the usual red tape.' He knocked out his pipe, scratched his head. 'The order was placed with a company in Macclesfield with which some legitimate business had been done in the past – helmets, casings, that kind of thing. Lawrence and a couple of others are partners there. That's as far as we've got at the moment, without spoiling the scent.'

Lloyd George paced the room with a mercurial display of anger. 'Double-dealing again, always bloody double dealing! A man has to have eyes up his arse. I tell you this, when this war's over I'll personally see to it any swine who's made so much as a dishonest farthing will live to regret it. I'll ruin him. What's more, I'll let everyone know why I ruined him. I'll feed him to the bloody hounds all right. Just a minute. Isn't that Smythe's arena, Octavian or whatever his stupid name is? Well, he's due for a visit.'

Law rekindled his pipe and threw the vesper in the hearth. When the Welshman had gone, he sat for a minute at his desk before ripping the top page from his jotter and tossing it in the fire.

The surgeon made an incision in the German's thigh and parted the flesh. Using a pair of forceps, he sought a grip on the disc. At the third attempt, he felt a satisfying tension and pulled out the bullet. He went through the same procedure on the other leg, this time removing two. He dropped all three into a tray.

Sister asked, 'Any bone damage?'

'It seems not. Got there in time, I think – unlike the other poor sods.'

'He lost some blood,' she said, as the soldier's wounds were being attended to. 'Even the ambulances aren't safe, it seems.'

He nodded to an orderly, who wheeled out the sedated man. 'They brought the wreck around the back. Seems to have sparked some curious interest. Yes, I think we can save him.'

The German awoke four hours later. The adjacent bed was occupied by Chalky, a chirpy East-Ender who viewed his own fractured pelvis as a stroke of good luck. On the rare occasions he wasn't calling across the ward, he was planning to buy a butcher's shop. 'Oy, oy, Fritzie, wakey wakey toime is it? 'Ow're ya feelin' maite? Ya stiw got the owd pins, ah see.' The German gave a thin smile. 'Don't worry, owd china, they fixed ya up proper. Blady good these surgeons, be walkin' on air in no toime.'

His comments drew a response from a Geordie opposite. 'Let the poor bugger sleep, man, instead o' pesterin' the poor sod an' he's half unconscious, like, yer daft bugger. Chalky by name and chalky by bloody nature.'

His comments set up a banter which reached the usual consensus – that the day Chalky got his butcher's apron and buggered off for good couldn't come soon enough.

'That's jast what ya can expect from these blady sheep-shearers ap norf, Fritz. No sympathy for the enemy. Blad-firsty lotta bastards. Oi reckon it was them got us inta this shit in the first place.' Flossie came into the ward, and Fritz took second place. 'Oy, oy, sweetheart.'ow'd ya like t' see me 'am shank?'

'Send the bugger back to Blighty, pet. Get'im on the next boat and let 'im show 'is shank to somebody daft enough to look at it.'

Flossie turned to pull the curtain around the German's bed. 'It makes no difference to me, I'm a vegetarian.'

Working at the hospital had drawn her out of herself. The wounded were arriving daily from the Somme. The men joked their way to survival, while the nurses kept their sanity by joining in the ribaldry which kept the wards going. The German slowly regained his strength. At Christmas, when the howitzers had stilled for the day, he shuffled along the corridors on crutches. The nurses had set a tree in each ward and decorated the windows with improvised streamers. There was no enmity between the British and German troops. They'd shared the same hell. They all hoped the war would end before they returned to service. The Abbaye became a refuge against the world, their real enemy not the fellow-at-arms but the fellow-at-home, still being persuaded of a cause.

Fritz's bellowing laugh could soon be heard above the banter. Flossie partnered his first excursions around the grounds, and continued to partner him when she knew he was able to take his exercise alone. His uncomplicated view of life had struck a chord with her. Before, he'd been a patient, but now she saw him as a man; a man with a strong head and the glint of laughter always shining through his eyes. He wasn't Fritz. He was Johannes Maarling, the son of a timber merchant who lived near Lahr in the Black Forest. He was a happy man with brothers and sisters who was destined to take over the family business.

'I never want fight. Your Tommy, he don' want fight. We both the same.' A pause, a schoolboy frown as if struggling with a complex equation: 'You know, the one who shot me, I see him before, then in the van. He go mad, I think. I wonder what happen to him?'

'I was told they all got killed, Johannes'

'I hear the noise, I know nothing, then I am here. I lucky to be alive. Nobody tell me nothing about the others, their names.'

'I don't know either. I suppose I could try and find out.'

'No, sometimes I not want to know. Now I just glad. You see! I walk now, no crutches. Nurse Tanbrey, you make me walk again. You like Jesus. No, Mary. You make me walk on water.' He broke into his loud, hearty laugh as if telling a joke against himself. 'I do not like this nurse name. I call you Flossie.'

'Don't let Sister hear you.'

'Who is this Sister? *Sie ist eine blode Kuh.*'

'And what does that mean?'

'It mean she don't count. She only want husband, yes? He make her happy.' They walked through the snow. Frozen fans bowed the branches in a white tracery. Away from the sun, a haze chilled the air. 'Flossie, you know I get better all the time. I not go fighting no more. I not go kill your Tommies.'

'I know.'

'They take me somewhere, you know. I go for the prisoner of war, I out of the fighting. Where I go, Flossie? No. It wrong to ask it. I ask nothing. I get you in trouble. If the others hear me asking, I get you in trouble.'

'I don't know, Johannes. Work on the land, I suppose. I know there are camps in England. Should I ask one of the doctors?'

'It does not matter. I'm alive, you see? Soon I be running through the woods. Soon I be lifting the trees with my bare hands. You watch.' He made a burlesque of hoisting a toppled branch and sank back, feigning exhaustion. 'Not ready yet, Flossie, I think. I stay in hospital a little longer.' After gauging the effect of his joke on her, he said: 'Flossie, if I don' see you in a little time, you have this, you remember old Fritzie, *ja*?' He took her hand and pressed a package into her palm. 'Go on, open it.'

She took out a ring carved from smoothed beech. Part of the ring had been fashioned into a sapphire.

'I tell them I do it for my sister, but it for you. It is a gift. I have nothing else. I know about wood, it is our trade, you see? I see a man painting, I ask him can I use your paint, only five minute? So I mix the blue. It come off, I suppose. It does not matter. You try it on. If it too small –' She slid it absently over her finger tip. 'If it too big, I make another. Or if I go, you keep it in a box, *ja*? When you look at the ring, you think of me. But you keep it safe. I don' want your children use it for toy in five years. Flossie, now I upset you! You do not like. See, it fit your middle finger. The middle finger, it strange place for a ring.' She was unable to look at him. 'You only supposed to say thank you. You supposed to be pleased.'

'Thank you, Johannes, it's very pretty.'

They walked back. Two days later, his bed lay empty.

'Gorn for a swap, old Fritzie,' Chalky shouted across the ward. 'Exchange, they calls it. Good old Hun, was Fritzy. Better'n that Geordie any day. Well, what's on the menu today, nurse?'

She pretended not to hear, and hurried out.

10

David Lloyd George's feet beat a furious tattoo along the corridor towards a door with the words 'Octavian Smythe, Military Requisitions' printed on it in bold red letters. Without bothering to knock, the Prime Minister strode in, his face already warning of the approaching eruption.

'David, what an unexpected pleasure –'

'I want a word in private.'

'Of course. Phyllis, perhaps there is something you need to attend to?' Smythe's secretary closed the door behind her. The Welshman turned the key in the lock and faced Smythe across the desk.

'Who gave you permission to contract armoured ambulances?'

'I was under the impression that's my job, ordering things.'

'Don't try any of that public-school nonsense with me. You order things through committees, using the procedures laid down in committees, you don't play God. You wouldn't even be behind that bloody desk except as a favour to keep your mates on side. You and that bunch of toffs, we'd be better off without the lot of you.'

'All right, I've been rumbled. What more can I say?'

'You're not in a position to say anything. I can't have this in my government. With a war on, for Christ's sake? You're going. Off the bank with you, boyo.'

Smythe studied his blotter. 'Care for a tot of whisky?'

A sudden sense of futility welled up in the Prime Minister. Would he ever be rid of these people, this powerful old money he couldn't do without and couldn't abide, with more tentacles than an octopus?

'I take your silence to be a no.' Octavian replaced the decanter in the cabinet and sat with his drink. 'I don't know whether you know, but I lost my son six months ago in Verdun. He was an only child. He'd been struck in the leg, but was expected to make a full recovery. His ambulance took an indirect hit from a German shell. I believe he died instantly. At the time the allies were taking five yards a day, and the following day the Huns took it back. I lost my boy for fifteen feet of mud –and an ambulance which might as well have been made of matchsticks.' The man took a slow drink, gazed into his glass. 'I needed to do something, and do it quickly. For my sake, for his mother's, for his, for all the other poor devils who.... well, you know.' He looked up. 'Why didn't I put my idea through a committee? You can hear them now. Not enough ambulances being hit to justify the expense. Put under 'future considerations'. All the red tape and meanwhile my boy's just another statistic. Then I thought of this small firm which had done good work in the past and might be just the place to produce vehicles that don't blow up at the sight of a squib. I hid the order as best I could, and no, I didn't defer, or refer, to anyone.'

'By "good work" I suppose you mean the helmets you just happened to get passed on to your friend Barrington who just happens to be a director of this so-called foundry.'

'You've heard. Then you'll know that was passed by committee and done at a good price.' He finished his drink and toyed with the glass for a moment. 'Unfortunately, I'm not the only one who's been caught double-dealing.'

'Meaning?'

'The ambulances were not built to plan. In fact, they were not armoured at all. The technical boys recommended half inch steel plate, with protection for the driver, not the usual quarter inch or so. Any more than half an inch and you need a different motor, or more wheels, so they tell me. I passed the specifications over to Barrington. He didn't use them. And he received a considerable amount of money for a job he didn't do. And his partners too, if they were in on it.'

'How do you know this?'

'The vehicles were dispatched along the front. I had a few trusty scouts in place to keep an eye on them. Managed to get them into the hospitals. The old boy network has its occasional uses, as you know. One ambulance got blown up. Men were killed. When it was taken in for examination, it was found to be made of thin plate, with no driver protection. To add insult to injury, the firm had stamped its name on an inside panel. I couldn't care less what happens to me, I'll survive. But I'd like to see my erstwhile friend brought to book. Quite frankly, I hope he rots in hell.' He poured another measure. 'I've become rather an expert in tracking people with dubious motives. I might as well tell you about it, seeing we're speaking man to man – so to speak. It wasn't too difficult to get hold of Lawrence's recent wanderings. His secretary never bothers to lock the office, and his diary's usually on the desk. Sometimes open, in fact. It appears he paid a visit to a firm in his constituency on a so-called morale boosting initiative. They used to make cars, now it's the war effort.

'He must have passed on to his partner – or partners – a conventional specification from somewhere. Did he get it from this firm, I asked myself, and when I telephoned the director the answer seemed to be a resounding 'yes'. Apparently our MP asked to look at plans for the conventional ambulances. The director recalls Barrington asking for a tumbler of water before he spoke to the employees, which the director had to leave the office to get. The secretary in the next room saw Barrington rummaging in the drawer. She saw his reflection in a cabinet, apparently. In fact, she'd told her boss of her suspicions even before I began to make my own enquiries. That, together with the fact she'd made a tally of all the plans for the various vehicles only a few days earlier, and now there was one missing.'

'And this firm of yours has received extra money for the armoured vehicle, is that what you're saying to me?

'Puts my little pecadillos in the shade, doesn't it?'

'And you purposely chose the firm Barrington's mixed up in?'

'He was a school chum, wasn't he?'

'All this bloody jiggery pokery behind my back – I suppose Accounts paid up, nothing said?'

'They did, unfortunately. Too busy to check the fine print, the old boys.'

'The old boys! I've heard it half my life. Look, I don't care a tinker's cuss what happens to you. It's my head on the block if this gets out. My reputation.'

Smythe said: 'I have a solution. Would you like to hear it?.

'Go on.'

'You're quite right, David. You have to avoid a scandal, and there may yet be a scandal. The Prime Minister not in control of his own office, communists at work in the corridors of power; the press would have a field day.'

'Get to it, for God's sake.'

'It's rather obvious. Why not say you took it upon yourself to place the order for the armoured ambulances? I'm sure you can make it retrospective. Offer the requisitions committee a few gongs, something to shut them up. Think of the high moral principal, saving the lives of our unfortunate wounded, bringing our boys back home safe and sound. It would be a feather in your cap. It would then give you the chance to order a formal enquiry into the whole sorry affair and to come out of it smelling of roses.

What d'you say?'

'I don't like being forced into corners by a con-man.'

'David, I do understand, believe me, but if the press were to get hold of the story as it stands, they might get hold of other equally unpalatable facts about your private, even your political life which, though of course I'm well acquainted with various newspaper people of rank, I can do nothing about.'

When the Prime Minister next spoke, it was as a chess player who'd parried, bluffed and come to respect his opponent. 'These men who were killed. Do you know their names?'

'Would it make any difference?'

'Their names must be kept out of the public domain for the time. Family only, and no mention of any ambulances. Let sleeping dogs lie until it's convenient. Barrington's partners, were they in on it or not?'

'There's always a chance Barrington passed over the plans he'd filched and they'd be none the wiser. Probably thought the job was well paid, but didn't ask questions. He must have got them to sign the real plans on completion of the schedule. I have them in my drawer, signed by a Mr Hodson, the firm's owner, I believe.' He took out a couple of folded sheets, passed them over. 'You see, it says 'modified' on the cover, and the one he stole didn't. He probably just swapped covers until the appropriate pages were signed, the usual trick for busy men. Or maybe Hodson and the other partner, I believe by the name of Tanbrey, were in on it. All partners stood to gain whether or not.'

Lloyd George rose from his seat, his former rage forgotten in this new turn of events. 'Alright, next of kin to be informed, but not how they died – yet. Don't want to draw attention to these ambulances outside this room. If by some chance Barrington finds out we're on his tail, I'll get him arrested. In the meantime, I'll get someone to do some detective work on Mr Hodson and – what's the other one called?'

'Tanbrey, my spies tell me. John Tanbrey.'

'We'll see if we can get something on him as well. We'll have the bastards flayed. Keep it quiet for a month, and if nothing else turns up we'll get the police around, starting with that pompous bastard Barrington. I've wanted to nail him for a long time and even if it has to wait until this war's over, nail him I will.'

He stood to go. 'Do I still have my job, David? No more fraud –

scouts' honour. Play your cards right, this could help keep your coalition on the road a bit longer. Anyway, the Adjective is the brains of the family. I'm a mere Noun.'

'Coalition my arse. If you do anything like this again, I'll have you roasted on a spit. Because I'm the Conditional Bloody Verb.' He unlocked the door and snatched it open. 'Sorry to hear about your boy. It's a sorry business.'

Octavian's secretary was returning as the Welshman left.

'Ah, the pretty Miss Phyllis is back....'

He stepped aside to let her in, then closed the door sharply behind him.

Charlie had left his bike at home, for the skeins of unmelted snow had made cycling impossible. He paused to look across the land as he always did, hoping the familiar scene would lift the unease he'd felt since Christmas. He'd tried to convince himself it was the greyness of winter, but the real reason was he'd received no letter from Richard in more than a month. At school, the children were muffled in hand-me-downs, some of the boys allowed to wear miniature uniforms under their coats. The new rector came in once a month to 'keep the fires lit' as he called it. He'd read the Roll of Honour, a pair of Scouts would blow the bugle and play the drum, and the school would sing a patriotic song taught by a retired piano-teacher who donated her service for free.

There's a land, a dear land, where the rights of the free,
Are as firm as the earth, and as wide as the sea,
Where the primroses bloom and the nightingales sing,
And an honest poor man is as good as the King.
Home of brave men and the girls they adore;
Westland, best land, my land, thy land,
England wave-guarded and green to the shore,
God bless our Empire and king ever more....

There was a minute's silence before the first winter coughs and Charlie led his class away. The head had insisted one half-day a week be devoted to the study of an Allied country, and he'd fixed a rota listing the countries to be described. Today was French Day.

'French Day, that's what we're doing today.' A groan went up, which he allowed to run its course. 'Who can tell me about France? Anything? Anything at all? Yes – Donald Brown.'

'They say they eat frogs' legs, sir.'

'And snails–'

'Frogs and snails, is that all? What about cities? Who can tell me the capital of France?'

'Sir! Sir!'

'Wendy Wiltshaw?'

'Please, sir, London, sir.'

'That's England, dunce, dunna tha even know that?'

Hands waved, reckless with enthusiasm. 'Tommy Bourne?'

'Please, sir –Paris, sir.'

'Correct. London is the capital of England as Paris is the capital of France.' He drew an outline on the board. 'Who can put a dot where Paris is?'

Half a dozen made their mark. Charlie selected the nearest and drew a circle around it while the class argued who'd made it. 'Paris, the capital of France. Does anyone know the names of any other cities? Has nobody ever heard of Marseilles? What about Rouen?' He marked them in. One of the scholars, a small boy who rarely spoke, raised his hand. 'Yes, Michael Birch?'

'Calais, Amien, Albert, Cambrai, Ypres, Abbeville –'

A surprised silence followed the boy's mispronounced outburst. Charlie smiled. 'Well remembered. Where did you get them all from?'

'Me dad reads them out of the paper, sir.'

'Can you tell the class what they're all to do with?'

'The Tommies are there.... my cousin...' He couldn't be drawn further.

'Well, France is our ally. That means it helps us in our time of strife. Their men fight alongside our own. They're all in the trenches together, fighting the enemy. They don't talk like us. They don't know English, most of them. When we say *yes* they say *oui*. When we say *no* they say *non*. But you all know something about the French. You've all heard about wine and champagne. If you find yourself rich one day, you'll be able to buy champagne from up Leek. You might even drive there in your car. It doesn't come cheap, and neither does the wine. France is famous for its wine. It's grown in the vineyards, and in some parts they still crush the grapes underfoot.' He had to explain, the girls affecting squeamishness, the boys holding their noses. 'You don't say Mister and Missus. Who knows what they say for Mister? Yes, Emma?'

'Please, Mr Tanbrey, they say *Monsieur*.'

'Right, only we say it 'Miss–your' otherwise it sounds like a drain.' No one understood. 'And the ladies are *Madame. Monsieur et Madame.*' He wrote down the numbers to ten, which they copied. One by one their stick pens clicked down and a hush fell across the room. The head's face appeared behind the glass-panelled door, behind exhortations never to fly kites in case people thought you were in league with the enemy. Charlie gave instructions for powder paint to be mixed. He didn't want to talk about France and the war. He wanted a France with blue skies and the reflections of red boats in blue water and men in straw hats. He wanted the France he'd seen in Eric O'Rourke's pictures. He'd turn French Day to his advantage. The real France now, not trench France. 'There's a France none of you will have heard of. I'm talking about its artists, the painters who live there. Before my son went to the fighting, we used to go up Manchester to the Art Gallery and see some of the paintings by the great French artists. No one here knew about them not so long ago. I didn't know about them, either. I'll tell you some names: Degas, Renoir, Monet and Manet. I always mix the last two up, because they sound nearly the same. All these painters brought France alive. They told you more in a brush-stroke than five weeks in a classroom like this. Some of you might not like what they painted if you saw it. Some of you might think: what are all those blots and blotches? He can't paint right, thing's aren't like that in real life–'

A rap sounded. The head pushed open the door. 'Mr Tanbrey, could you spare a moment?'

There was a pulse of silence. They began to chatter as he left the room. The head took his place at the desk. Ellen was sitting in a corner of the office as he went in. He knew. *He knew.* She managed his name, held out the black-edged envelope. He was her heart's song and her soul wept for him; for his small successes, his frailties, his shyness, his kindness, his loss. He held the unread sheet before him, but his eyes were empty.

'This came too, Charlie,' she said, holding him. He opened the letter.

'Dear Mr and Mrs Tanbrey,

Just a line to tell you how upset I am about Richard. There never was a better man, and I want you to know he played his part well. We were friends all through. He always talked about you. I found out a lot about music and books listening to him. I want to offer my condolences in your time of loss. I hope we can always keep him in our hearts. I'd like to meet you after this war is over, God willing. I'm sorry, I can't tell you anything about how he died because I don't know myself, but I know he would be doing his duty.

Again, my heartfelt condolences,

Owen Bradall

Charlie went back to his room, still holding the letter. They were talking about something, he might have said something, received a reply, no, I'm all right, I'm better off here. He faced a void of faces, heard the magpies croaking through the high windows.

'As I was saying, they call them the – the impressionists, and....'

Did it matter when his heart was breaking? He had to get out to that high, cloud-shadowed land where he might be able to touch the face of his son. It was dark when he found himself back home. He couldn't remember where he'd been.

Bells pealed through mills, alleys and bunting-decked homes. The heroes have won! Our glorious sons have vanquished the blond beast! Hurrah for England! Long live the King! In London maroons marked the moment or armistice. From offices showered forms and papers, yesterday's memoranda, tomorrow's engagements. Horns hooted, tambourines shook, Dominion soldiers lit a bonfire at Nelson's column. Across the square dancers tried to keep step with the rattle of stone-filled kettles. A drunken dog joined its drunken owner dancing to a hurdy-gurdy, while outside the Palace a huge crowd gathered. It was over.

The same evening, Nerissa sat at her window watching rockets spill stars across the Macclesfield sky. Her husband was reading thanksgiving at a local church. In a few minutes her cab would arrive, and she once more fumbled in her purse and drew out the note she'd scrawled some months before. Holding it under the lamp, she read what she'd heard of her husband's words again. *The ambulances.... Is there a problem, Lawrence.... as long as nothing gets out.... I'll leave the details to yourself.... you've had plenty of practice....* Maybe she was on a wild goose chase. Maybe that's why she'd taken months to decide what to do. Maybe the end of the war was her last chance to – to do what? Consolidate her position? Prove she wasn't altogether spent? Nail the man who she'd heard speak those words into the telephone, there, in her house? Was she making a fool of herself, and if she was, did it matter?

The clock chimed. She took another sheet from the bureau and hurriedly transferred her pencilled scrawl into coherent lines written in ink. A honk sounded outside. She crushed out her cigarette, pulled on a winter coat, screwed the pencilled note into a loose ball and threw it at the fire. It bounced, unnoticed, off the fender on to the carpet. The town roads were full of men in uniform and cavorting girls. The driver turned into a dimly-lit suburban street. She pushed open a gate and walked up the path.

'Mrs O'Rourke?'

'Won't you come in?'

The change in Nerissa shocked Jane. She'd last seen her six years ago at Bill Tanbrey's leave-taking, and although at the time she'd remarked on her gaunt appearance, it hadn't prepared her for the woman who stood before her now.

'You'd best sit by the fire. I'll take your things.'

'That's very kind of you.'

'I'll just get Eric. I won't be a minute.'

Nerissa fitted a cigarette into her ivory holder. Her eyes rested on the book Jane had been reading, and she was flicking through the pages when O'Rourke and Jane come into the room.

'I didn't know you had an interest in Dr Stopes.'

'Of course,' said O'Rourke. 'Jane believes in harems for married men and free love all around. It's some time since we met. How are you, Mrs Tanbrey?'

'Might I trouble you for an ash-tray?'

He gave her a saucer and sat opposite, his thin face animated by the business of the evening. 'I think she's rather sensible,' Nerissa said, referring to the book. 'Anyone who produces ten children must be content with a life of poverty, wouldn't you say? I should think birth-control can't come soon enough. I have a daughter who's been away so long I'm hard put even to remember her name, let alone nine others.'

O'Rourke's offer of tea did nothing to curb his wife's indignation. 'I think how many children a woman has is up to her and her husband, nobody else.'

Jane went into the kitchen. Nerissa glanced around the attractively-furnished room. 'Mr O'Rourke, where are your servants?'

'Put it down to war shortages. My wife doesn't hold with conventional ideas of service. I must say that to a certain extent, I agree with her. Now let's see, you contacted me, something personal you wanted to talk with me about.'

Nerissa delved into her bag and took out the sheet. 'I think you might be the best person to look at this, since you and Mr Barrington are both in the same game. The police would probably think I was barking.' He cast an eye over the lines, stroking his beard. 'It's from a telephone conversation my husband had some months ago. I'm assuming it's Lawrence Barrington he's referring to. As you probably know, John's a partner with him at Mr Hodson's works. He did let it slip they were making ambulances for the war. I can't think why he told me. He doesn't usually tell me anything.'

'You're suggesting this telephone conversation is evidence of some kind of malpractice?'

'One develops an instinct for subterfuge, especially when one has a husband like mine. *Is there a problem.... as long as nothing gets out....* It doesn't sound too wholesome, does it?'

'What would you have me do?'

'Come on, Mr O'Rourke, I bet there's more tittle-tattle in the House of Commons than in a ladies' sewing circle. What I'd like is for you to see what you can find out of Mr Barrington's and my husband's business venture. Ambulances. That seems to be the key. Maybe they were doing something naughty, and you can find out what it was.'

O'Rourke got up and stood by the window. An eruption of silver sparks flashed across the night sky. He put coal on the fire and replaced the japanned scuttle as Jane came in with a tray.

'Do you take sugar, Mrs Tanbrey?'

'No, thank you. It looks as if I shall grow into antiquity without a single sweetening feature.'

Eric's mind was ticking. What was this woman really after? Revenge on her husband? Was she to be trusted? He thought back to the time of Jane's resignation. Did he himself harbour a grudge against the mill-owner for that reason? Did he see this note as a chance to pay him back?

'I can see you're wondering why I'm anxious to implicate my husband,' Nerissa said, as if reading his mind. 'Well, I'll tell you. He and I are, as they say, man and wife in name only. It's important for successful men to be happily married for the sake of appearances, don't you think?' She looked at Jane. 'I believe you worked for him at one time. Upright, decisive – any adjective will do. You see, I could put up with his little ways if– if....' She inhaled deeply. 'The honest citizen, forever serving his church and country, master of probity, salt of the earth.... In fact, he's rather a cad. And I'd be surprised if his pal isn't a cad too. That's why I came. I want him exposed. Even at the expense of exposing myself.'

Bells pealed across the town and the surrounding hills. Eric slapped his thigh. 'Well, at least the war can safely be consigned to the dustbin of history. I wonder what the poor devils will do when all the excitement's died down?'

'He has women, you know. I found out through one of my venturings into his bureau. He thinks he has the only key. Now that in itself is strange, wouldn't you say? What's a wife for, if not to rifle through her husband's belongings once in a while. My daughter Florence served on the Western Front as a nurse, you know. I'm very proud of her. She's not John's daughter, of course. You may have heard my first attempt at matrimony fell into a canal while eloping with the maid. It was in all the papers. Old Roddy couldn't even make a success of that. Flossie's his child, you see. I only have myself to blame, I should never have married him. I admired John's strength. Our affair, I suppose that's what you'd call it, went on for many years.'

She seemed to lose the thread of what she was saying, her eyes drawn to some distant point in the past. Jane asked: 'If you didn't love each other, why bother?'

'Power, my dear. I really don't want to relate the ins and outs of it. Suffice it to say he took over the family business and I was part of the package. You see, John started from nothing – but I believe you already know something of the family history?'

'The question is,' interrupted O'Rourke, 'how did he become rich?'

'Now that, I really can't say. It all belongs to his murky past – and his murkier present, if the sheet you're holding is anything to go by. See what you can discover, Mr O'Rourke. I need a little power of my own.'

'I can't promise. As you suggest, the House is full of secrets, but they don't always come my way. In fact, you're lucky to have caught us, we spend so much time in London these days. I'll spcak frankly: are you simply asking me to help you avenge yourself on your husband?'

'I really do hate him, you know. I'd hire a private detective, but I no longer have the means. You know Barrington, you've met my husband. I want to know what's happening. Is that too much to ask?'

Eric looked into the flashing sky. 'We're entering a new era, ladies. Health, education, the Trades' Unions.... our firey Welsh orator will win next month's election, and my darling wife will be first in the queue to register her vote.' He swung around. 'I'll see what I can do. Could be no more than schoolboy games. You must understand that if I act on this, you could find yourself in the public eye at some later stage. For the while, let's say you came here to discuss some matter of local interest.'

Nerissa stood. 'In that case, I think it's high time you did something about the state of the local roads.' Jane brought her hat and coat. At the door Nerissa turned. 'The trouble is, I never seemed cut out for the normal boredom of life.'

They watched her walk to the end of the path. 'Better keep things to ourselves, whatever game she's playing.' O'Rourke said.

'You mean don't tell Ellen.'

'He's Charlie's brother. If anything comes of it, he'll know soon enough.'

Returning home before Nerissa, John saw the paper ball on the floor. Perhaps it was more than idle curiosity which prompted him to pick it up and read his wife's words under the gas jet. He felt a sudden vulnerability, which quickly turned to anger. Folding the scrap into his pocket, he picked up the telephone and asked to be put through to Barrington's London number.

'Something's happened. We need to meet.'

'You sound agitated. It must be important.'

'Tomorrow. I'll get an early train.'

'Can't we speak over the telephone? Your good lady wife isn't lurking in the shadows, is she?'

'Expect me before one.'

'Well, I am rather busy at the moment–'

John cut him off and picked up the whisky decanter. By the time he heard his wife at the door, he was mellow enough to say nothing.

Tanbrey took a cab to Barrington's Kensington address, and his sense of foreboding grew as he neared the block. The politician must have been looking out for him, for the front door to his apartment lay open. As

Tanbrey went inside, Barrington appeared and showed him into a large drawing room. 'Now, John, you realise you've taken me from my business. I hope you're not wasting your time. As well as mine, of course.'

'She knows.'

'Knows what, and who is *she*?'

Tanbrey unfolded the scrap. 'Look at this. She's on to us! You and your bloody calls, why didn't you conduct your business face-to-face like any other crook? She'll take us all to the bloody cleaners.'

Barrington glanced at the creased paper and studiously filled a glass without offering one to Tanbrey. 'You really should exercise more control over your family, John. I have felt a certain sang froid in certain quarters of late. Perhaps you're right. Things don't look too rosy and someone might have spilled a few beans. I fear a visit to court might not be entirely out of the question.'

'What about your so-called friends, won't they gallop to the rescue?'

'They might. In fact, I'm sure they will. Of course, your little note is just one part of a conversation you might have had with someone on the end of a line. Who that someone is will be left for others to decide. There are plenty of Lawrences, one's as good as another.'

'You're a bastard.'

'Born in the gutter, looking at the stars. Well, not quite the gutter. You see, there's a tacit agreement between my friends and myself. It goes something like this: if I go down, you go down. It's all a case of knowing where the bodies are buried. And of having friends in high places, of course – including the judiciary, if it gets that far. Unfortunately, you might not have that luxury.'

Tanbrey's face had drained. For the first time in his life he felt trapped.

'Come, now, John, you don't seriously think I'm a loser, do you? As far as I'm concerned I'm a very sleeping partner. I don't know one end of an ambulance from another. How was I to know you and Ebenezer were making a bit on the side skimping contracts? Anyway, we'll have to see how things go, won't we? Perhaps we'll find it's all been a storm in a teacup, who knows? If not – well, you'd better get your story straight. A provable story, that is – which can be difficult.'

Tanbrey was incandescent with rage. 'You'd drop your mother in the shit for a whore's smile.'

'It's a tough league, old boy.'

'If I'm nailed, you can rest assured there'll be a few whispered names and yours will be top of the list.'

'Which, as I say, will have to be proved.' Barrington hauled himself upright. 'John, John, I've put my name to nothing. Who's to say I instigated this whatever it is? You see, you're a little short on the pedigree side, whereas I'm not. You must always watch your back. I've spent my life watching my back. That's what the House is all about. Ninety per cent watching your back and ten per cent music hall.' The stench of drink came strongly on his breath. 'I seem to have taught you nothing, and there's me, thinking you were my Eliza Doolittle.' He shook his head with mock resignation. 'Anyhow, I'm sure you have important matters to attend to.'

Tanbrey went out, slamming the door behind him. The cold outside air did little to stifle the fever raging in his brain, and he spent the rest of the afternoon in a hotel lounge. By the time he got back to his train, he'd decided on a course of action. There was someone he needed to see. He didn't intend to be a loser either.

11

Charlie awoke from a bad dream. The bedroom was bitterly cold, but a feverish heat burnt through him. Ellen sat up. 'What's the matter?'

'I don't feel too good.'

'Would you like a cup of tea?'

He left the bed and stood for a minute, gently massaging his arm and looking out across the moonlit hills. He knew it was his heart, and so did she. He said it might be indigestion. She berated him for eating too quickly. 'Why don't you pack up school altogether, Charlie? We'll survive, especially now Vicky's got the job in the Post Office.' She peered at the bedside clock. 'Why, it's only just gone one. I'll get us a drink.'

When she returned he'd fallen asleep, and when he awoke shortly after dawn the pain had gone. Ellen made a fire and swathed him like an invalid. As he dozed, she wrote a reply to a letter which had arrived a few days ago.

'Dear Rose,

Thank you for the invitation to your daughters' weddings. Two together make a good show. You say Marian is nearly thirty and Colette is just twenty-one. My, your Marian left it a bit late, but from what you said before she was the one who wanted to work her way up, so it seems she's had a change of heart after all. It's six years since we last saw you. Doesn't time fly!

I know you've had your share of misfortune, but the sad news is Charlie's son Richard didn't come back from the wars, and Charlie's taken it really bad. He's had a bad time of it one way and another, what with his elder daughter dying and all the trouble with his first marriage, and it's taken a toll of him. What I want to say is, I don't think Charlie's up to a long journey. I'd love to come, I've hardly been off this farm since I can remember, let alone England, but I don't think it would do him any good and I couldn't leave him on his own. He doesn't know about your letter and I'm writing this while he's asleep in his chair. I can't say how grateful I am, you offering to pay for us. You are often in our thoughts, but I think travel would be bad for him.

I hope the weddings are a beautiful day for everyone. Our Vicky is fourteen now, and just starting in her work. Next time you write, maybe it will be wedding bells for you too, Rose. I think no one should be lonely in this life. I've known that myself, and it's not to be recommended.

I hope we can keep in touch.

With kind regards,
Ellen'

As she sealed the envelope, she found herself wondering if Rose had ever known about Bill and her and the baby. She turned and found Charlie looking at her.

'You've been busy.'

She slipped the envelope into her apron pocket. 'Just a letter to Jane. We've not seen each other in ages. 'D'you feel better?'

He pulled back the blanket. 'Must've cured something. I think I'd better not go in today, all the same.'

'I told you, there's nothing like rest to put you right, it's better than all the doctor's pills and potions. Why not take a stroll? It'll do you good.'

'I've a mind to visit the Moel, see how Harris is getting on.'

'Whatever for? You want to go down Rudyard. They say the lake froze over. You don't want nobody to see you around Moel, especially having taken the day off.'

He relented until he reached the lane, then decided to go anyway. He took a wide sweep around the village, coming out on the track past his old house, and rested on the stile. The air was clear and still. When he was a lad, there'd been the reassuring clatter from Heath's ironworks in the valley, but now the hammers were silent. He'd heard the family were going to sell off parts of their estate now the slump had set in and war-work had come to an end. He remembered the Heaths had dug out a boating lake in Spring Woods. Richard would have been seven then. That one family could have so much, while his old teacher, Harry Caulton, had had to content himself with –

Harris Pargeter's shout broke into his thoughts. 'Hello, Mr Tanbrey, out walkin', then?'

'I've not been feeling too well, Harris, I thought a stroll would put the sparkle back in my cheeks.'

'I heard about your boy, Mr Tanbrey. It's been a bad do. D'you fancy comin' in a bit?'

'I don't want to take up your time.'

'Nay, come in, I'll put the kettle on. Missus's just gone down her sister's for an hour or so. Come on in.' He followed the man into the familiar living room. 'Sit yourself down there, I'll just get a brew started.

My, you've brought some weather along. When you sold me this place, you never said I'd need a coal cart an' all.' He went into the kitchen while Charlie stood at the window. 'It hasn't changed much, has it?' Harris shouted. 'Tell you what, when them south-westerlies blow, hang on to your hat, what? First year, I thought I'd find the roof down below in Bradley Green.'

By the hearth, ash had discoloured the wallpaper. Harris tottered in and thrust a mug into his hand. 'I've made a few alterations here and there. Missus can't abide draughts, so I blocked up the trap in the attic with a bit of beading. You can still feel it a bit, but I've done the job so now she doesn't bother no more.'

His portfolio had been sealed in. 'Found nothing of value up there, Harris?'

'Tell you the truth, I wasn't bothered about lookin'. Come now, I'm hardly likely find a crock o' gold am I, unless you put one up. You didn't, did you?' He gave a chuckle. 'I'll tell you what, we're in fine voice up yonder.' He meant the church choir. 'On wings of love my heart is borne, and o'er the wide sea ranges....' Charlie found himself laughing. Harris laughed with him. 'Some music up there, Mr Tanbrey. Purcell, Mendelssohn, all them old masters. My love hath lost the bloom of youth, so fair, indeed was she....'

Harris sang on while Charlie's shoulders shook with grief and silent laughter.

'It is entirely right that our resources be put at the disposal of those treating this most virulent outbreak of influenza. No one would disagree with my Honourable Friend that prompt action is necessary. However, perhaps the Honourable Member should for once adhere to the matter in hand and condemn these unlawful strikes. Will he please make his views clear to this House?'

Eric watched Lawrence Barrington sink into his seat. He'd become grossly fat, his small, malevolent eyes glowering from a bloated face. His command of the chamber had by now ceased to have any impact on O'Rourke, and he sat thinking over what had happened since he last saw Nerissa Tanbrey. It was surprising what could be discovered poking about solicitors' offices, especially solicitors who owed you a favour. His starting point had been the mill. It was in the ownership of Pandora Enterprises, not John Tanbrey. Once he had the name, it had been a straightforward matter to look through the trades' directories to see what else Pandora owned. A third share in Hodson's foundry and works came to light, and a dozen rented houses on the edge of town. Eric studied dates. Pandora first appeared as a building concern in 1883. How old would Tanbrey had been then? Mid twenties, nothing more. Eric discovered he'd been working for Heath at that time. Until 1896 Tanbrey had been employed as Office Manager of the Bull Colliery and Ironworks. His salary could never have been enough to create Pandora. There had been no link to Barrington until much later, when his name cropped up as part-owner of the foundry. How had Tanbrey made his money? Something must have happened before Pandora, but what? Why should a man of means remain with an employer who could only have paid him half his yield in rents? Whatever the source of his wealth, it had enabled him to buy the Victoria Mill. An inheritance was unlikely, given Tanbrey's background, and he knew his brother Charles had only modest means. His money must have been a stroke of fortune. At this point Eric had had to concede partial defeat. The man was plainly wealthy, but no evidence seemed to exist to tell how, and a subsequent visit from Nerissa had failed to throw further light on his investigations. At that point he'd decided to concentrate on Barrington, and to look at their connection from a different viewpoint. Miss Carlisle, a former secretary in the Prime Minister's office – she was the one to see....

The session ended. O'Rourke joined the others moving towards the exit. Outside, the smoky air caught at his lungs. A procession of omnibuses was crossing Westminster Bridge. He hailed a cab and gave the driver directions to Miss Carlisle's Lambeth apartment.

'I shouldn't really say anything, Eric. Such matters are confidential, as you well know.'

He sprawled across her couch, the cake-stand within easy reach. His small talk gave her time to sharpen the axe he knew she wanted to grind. Middle-aged women didn't take kindly to being usurped by girls half their age. 'Oh, come now, Sybilla, it's water under the bridge, surely.'

'Then why are you so keen to know? Isn't the forthcoming election more up your street?'

'A foregone conclusion. David in, Asquith out. Goodness, I'm naturally curious, that's all! The war didn't wipe out common curiosity , did it?'

'You've not come all the way here to talk about your curiosity. You can't fool an old hand like me, you know. I smell a rat.'

'You're entitled to smell what you like. Come on, no one tells me anything.'

'You're sure there's something to tell?'

'You know more than the League of Nations – well, more than Lloyd George, at any rate.'

He'd pressed the right button. 'All right, for what it's worth. I can rely on your discretion?'

'I'm insulted.'

'I still don't trust you. I don't trust any man.'

'A wise precaution.'

'It's nothing much. I don't know the whole story.'

He scratched his chin, allowed his eyes to glide over her Landseer print, the aspidistra under the window. 'A comprehensive summary will suffice.'

She brushed a crumb from her bosom. 'It's about ambulances. Some directive given to armour a hundred or so. It happened when David was Minister of Munitions, but apparently he knew nothing of it. It came to light the steel plate or whatever they put on them was too thin, and someone was making money out of it. I'm out of my depth, you understand. Lawrence Barrington's name has been whispered, but I don't know how he was involved. The whole thing was going on behind David's back. I think it was that put him in a mood. You mustn't take my word for it. I might have it all mixed up.'

O'Rourke ran his tongue across his lips. 'Who gave the order for these vehicles?'

'You're going to get me into hot water.'

'I've never seen you before in my life.'

'Oh, come, now, Eric. I'll tell you what I've been told, which is not the same as saying you can rely on it.'

'Oh, rubbish. They should have you working for the *Mail*.'

'Well, obviously, it was a war requisition, so I'll give you a clue: the person who was in charge of requisitions. I met his secretary on a couple of occasions and we had a chat.'

'I bet you did.'

'What's all this about, Eric? I'd have thought horses were more in your line these days.'

He shrugged with indignation. 'There's no need to bother yourself about any indiscretion on my part, my lovely; mum's the word. It's just a little constitutional matter.'

'It's irrelevant to me what you do with it. I've had my marching orders. I'm a nobody, and that's official. Now tell me, have you taken Jane to see *Pygmalion* yet?' He said he hadn't. 'You should, you know. Mrs Campbell's Eliza is simply divine.'

He nodded enthusiastically, his mind on other things. Two hours later, he emerged from the block flushed with Miss Carlisle's sherry and made his way to Hyde Park to feed the ducks.

Octavian was zipping a travelling bag when his secretary announced O'Rourke's unscheduled arrival. In connection with what? O'Rourke would rather not say – but it was a matter of some urgency. He was shown into the office and offered a chair.

'I think I've seen you around the corridors,' Octavian was saying, putting his bag down and sitting. 'And what's so important now the war's over?'

'It's about ambulances.'

'In what connection, Mr O'Rourke?'

Eric fished out Nerissa's copy, which he laid on the desk. Octavian read the lines without lifting the paper. 'And where's this from?'

'Someone with a connection to the matter.'

'You mean connected to Lawrence Barrington?'

'Indirectly.'

'I see.' An adjoining door had opened, and a man entered the office. 'Take no notice of my brother, Mr O'Rourke. I was about to take a few days in Devon, and he's here to see I pack my toothbrush. Julian, Mr O'Rourke'

'Eric,' O'Rourke said.

'Julian, look what Eric's brought in. What d'you think?'

'You're the Noun, I'm only the Adjective. What do *you* think?'

'I think we should trust Mr O'Rourke if he'll trust us.'

Half an hour later, Octavian went to see the Prime Minister, leaving his travelling bag, Eric and Julian in the office. Julian sat in the vacated chair. 'Bloody fool, Lawrence. Always lived too much life, if you get my drift. Too many gals, too much drink. I'm afraid he's torn it this time, along with this Tanbrey fellow, it seems. The Noun tells me they were waiting to see what turned up with Tanbrey. Let Lawrence loose for a time, a sprat to catch a mackerel, that sort of thing. You've done a good job. I expect the legal boys will sort it all out. They'll both end up in the dock, this other feller too, I shouldn't wonder, the one who put his name to the sheets. There's no secrets between me and Octavian, you know. Never has been. I suppose David'll make sure it all comes out in the wash, just in time for this election. No doubt give him a boost, guardian of public morals and so forth, though it might go the other way, for all that. They're getting unpleasant out there, don't want to hear about wheeling and dealing in high places.'

Eric got up. 'I'll have to go or I'll miss my train.'

'Certainly, old boy. Now I hear you're a horse man, and here's a little tip to help you on your way. *Bayuda*. Three thirty, Ascot. A cert, dear boy, you'd be a fool to miss it.'

O'Rourke left wondering if he'd done the right thing. His mood was uncharacteristically thoughtful as he made his way along the corridor Lloyd George had paced earlier. He stood at the door for a moment, pulling on his gloves and watching the snowflakes flurry above the pavement. As he stepped out, he almost collided with a colleague heading in the direction of Whitehall.

'Eric! Have you heard?'

'What?'

'It's Barrington, he's had a stroke. He was having a bite at our table not half an hour ago, next minute he's choking. He's had it.'

'Dead?'

'He's with the angels, now. Never expected Barrington to go like that, I don't know why.'

John Tanbrey heard his wife's footsteps in the hall and called out to her.

'Can't it wait?'

'Do you make a habit of listening to other people's telephone conversations?'

'Is this another of your delusions?'

'You bitch, making up lies like some Fleet Street hack.'

'I see I've been rumbled.'

'Who else knows?'

'I'm not really at liberty to say.' His lips were pinched with rage, and she thought he'd strike her. She said: 'I suppose you've seen the headlines?'

'I'm not in the mood for drivel.'

'Your friend Mr Barrington's dead. No one to hold your hand now, my dear.'

He got up and left the room. She could hear him fumbling at the pegs for his coat. Smiling, she made her way upstairs.

It was late when he turned into a street in a poor area of the town. He knocked at one of the houses and waited until the rumble of a sash drew his eyes upwards. A woman's head appeared above the ledge.

'I'd like to speak with Pepe.'

'It's Mr Tanbrey, isn't it? He's sound asleep, sir, can't it wait till the morning?'

'No, it cannot wait until morning. What the devil d'you think I'm doing here at this hour, taking the air?'

'Just a minute, Mr Tanbrey, I'll get him up.'

The head retreated, the door opened and Hodson's overseer stood on the step, pushing the flap of his shirt into his trousers. 'Yes, Mr Tanbrey?'

'Get dressed. We're going for a walk.'

Lorenzo came out and closed the door softly behind him. As they walked off he glanced up at his wife's shape against the window. The air was still and sharp, with a cold mist rising from the cobbles. They walked in tense silence, Tanbrey saying nothing until the last of the houses fell back.

'Pepe, you've been here a few years now. How long? Ten years, more? How long ago was it your father came to England looking for work?'

'I forgot, Mr Tanbrey. Twenty year, maybe, when I was very young man.'

'And then the war came, and you're working for Mr Hodson.' The man fell silent. 'Pepe, are your mother and father still living?'

'My mother, yes, but she not well. My father, he die. Mr Tanbrey, I don't know why you get me out of bed to ask these questions.'

'I'm going to say something to you, Pepe. I have the power to send you back to Italy if I chose to do so. I know the people who can do that. I know the magistrates. But I'm quite happy for you to be here. I know you want to stay.'

'What you mean, Mr Tanbrey, I go back Italy? I British person, I have English wife and baby, another coming. Why I go back, you tell me?'

'I've already told you, there is no reason for you to go back. You have a good job at Hodson's, a responsible job. You're one of us.'

'What you talkin', Mr Tanbrey? I don' know what you talk about.'

The little man grew more agitated, threw out his arms against the leafless hedgerow. Tanbrey said: 'When I was in London, I made up my mind to see you when I got back home. It's about the ambulances. You remember the ambulances? In the works, in the war? Do you remember?'

'Of course I remember. What wrong, something happen?'

'Do you remember Mr Barrington, he used to come in from time to time?'

'I see him, what of it?'

'I'm afraid Mr Barrington is no longer with us, Pepe. There's just me now. Me and Mr Hodson. And you're very important too, of course. Mr Hodson tells me your mother is a German lady. Is that true?'

'Yes, my mother come from Berlin. Why you speak about my mother?'

Tanbrey rubbed the warmth into his hands. 'It was a bad war, with many men lost on both sides. In wars, there are spies everywhere. You weren't spying, were you, Pepe?'

'What I want spy for?'

'To help your German mother. To help your cousins in Germany win the war. Maybe that would be a good reason to spy, or to commit acts of sabotage.'

A haunted look came into the Italian's eyes. 'I not spy, or do this other thing. I help no one in the war, just do my job. Ask Mr Hodson, I just do what he say.'

'I don't doubt it, Pepe. I'm not accusing you of anything, you know that. But there are other people who might not know you as I do. They might wonder if you deliberately sabotaged the ambulances by putting the wrong plate on them so our Tommies would get killed. Thinner plate.They might think that. I don't, but they might. They'll say your mother wanted the Tommies dead and you wanted the Tommies dead. And if they think that, well, you can guess the penalty, can't you? Goodbye wife, goodbye bambinos, goodbye England, goodbye Pepe Lorenzo and his mother.'

'I don' understan' what you mean, what you talkin' about, Mr Tanbrey?'

'I found something out, Pepe. I found out Mr Barrington and Mr Hodson were up to something. I found out they were fiddling money getting you to put thin plate on the ambulances instead of thick plate. You wouldn't know, how could you? You just worked from the plans, that's all that was required of you. But Ebenezer and Mr Barrington, they knew. Mr Barrington is no longer here to answer for himself, but Mr Hodson is. And you were too late to stop it once you knew.'

'I not know this. What you mean, all this business with the plans, I don' know what you mean.'

'But you do, Pepe. After the job was done, you heard them talking in Mr Hodson's office. Don't you remember?'

'I don' remember nothing.'

'I think you do. You were waiting outside the office, ready to go in with the forms when you heard them. You heard Mr Barrington say "The fools will never find out we fixed the ambulances. You did a good job, Ebenezer. We'll make a good sum, and no one will be any the wiser." Then you heard Mr Hodson say "No one will ever find out, that's the good thing. What about John, though?" And Mr Barrington said: "The fool knows nothing about it." And Mr Hodson laughed at that. Then he saw you at the door and realised you'd heard them talking. Mr Barrington grabbed you by the throat and threatened you with violence if you ever said a word about what you'd heard. And Mr Hodson said the least that would happen would be the sack, and you'd never work in town again, and the worst would be –' Tanbrey crossed his throat. 'That's what you heard, Pepe. And that's what you'll tell the authorities when you are sent for.'

'I hear nothing. Mr Hodson, he not a crook. He never do this thing. He gave me job, he trust me. I not lie, Mr Tanbrey. I cannot lie.'

'Then you must suffer the consequences, and Mr Hodson will still find himself in court to answer his case, because a little bird tells me the attorneys have already got wind of what has been happening, and the full weight of the English law will be hard to bear, particularly if it seems you have been involved in any way. And Mr Hodson might say that you were. I might say that you were. Remember, a German mother, an Italian father, both foreigners in a foreign land. Things won't look good when the jury see a foreigner who's sabotaged the Tommies' ambulances. They'll say you're a traitor and have you shot. Unless you tell the truth. Unless you tell them what you saw.'

The little man, beside himself with terror, began jabbering in rapid Italian. They'd reached a canal bridge. A disturbed bird rustled the reeds. 'Of course, nothing may happen. Maybe no one will find out about Mr Hodson's secret, and there will be no court, and no judge in a white wig. We'll have to wait and see. Maybe things will go well for you, and your wife will keep her job – she works for me, doesn't she, on my mill? There might even be something better for her. You should both prosper, I don't see why not. It's up to you. Say what you saw, then no jail. No going back to Italy when you come out. If you come out. An old man, no family, no future, begging for scraps. Just remember what you saw.'

He began to walk away. Pepe hung back, shivering in the pre-dawn air. 'Think about it, Pepe,' he called over his shoulder.

Flossie left the train at Waterloo and hailed a cab. The streets had been full of soldiers, and now they were full of scurrying clerks. The driver stopped outside lodgings off Tottenham Court Road and helped her in with her bags as she hunted for a tip. The small room contained a frayed carpet, some cheap furniture, a ewer and towel, a peeling mirror and a couple of prints. She hung her clothes in the wardrobe, and after sponging her face lay down, falling asleep almost right away. She didn't wake until late afternoon, then ran a comb through her hair and went out.

Four years of iron rations had honed her appetite. She found an inexpensive restaurant near Charing Cross Road and ordered Dover Sole and boiled potatoes, with apple pie and custard. She couldn't go back home. She wouldn't allow herself to be trapped again. She needed to earn a little money in London while she planned what to do. When she got back she wrote a letter to her mother and began another, taking time with the address since German was unfamiliar to her, and putting the letters by the door ready for posting.

In the morning she got up early to look for work. She found nothing that day, and after a fortnight her savings had dwindled. Her thoughts strayed reluctantly back to nursing, only to find ex VADs had filled every vacancy. On the Friday of the following week, she resolved to make a last attempt to find something, anything. Walking past a florist's, she almost missed the card advertising 'permanent vacancy, flat above'. Within a few minutes of her stepping inside, the card had been removed from the window.

She went back to her lodgings for her case. A newspaper seller was calling above the din of omnibuses. *Military ambulance fraud.... Read all about it!* She bought a paper and folded it into her bag. Later, sitting in her flat, she spread the paper over her bed and began to read: John Tanbrey... Ebenezer Hodson....pending trial....if found guilty will receive lengthy prison sentences....

She gazed at the haze of words, then tore out the page and burnt it in the hearth.

The man leaving the courtroom would have seemed preoccupied to a casual observer. Those who knew him better were shocked. Though less than a year had passed since Flossie sold her first carnation, John Tanbrey already looked bent with years. He carried himself like an old man, the fire gone from his body, the skin sallow and taut. An hour earlier, the lawyer famed for his ability to free wealthy crooks on a technicality had done his work well. What did the so-called evidence provided by a vindictive wife prove? What merit lay in this scrap of paper? For all he knew, it could have been a forgery, and if it wasn't, what then? In what tone were these words uttered, if indeed they were uttered at all? A reasonable tone, a humorous one, even? Was the phrase – 'As long as nothing gets *left* out' – merely that of a concerned partner who wished to make sure the correct procedures were followed? Or, if it really is 'As long as nothing gets out', what might have been the question? Perhaps it was something like: 'The War Office is worried about the effects on civilian morale if the people believe an increase in the production of ambulances means an increase in the number of dead'? Was that it, to which a throw-away remark was provided by a man who had his work cut out making clothing for our boys at his mill, and couldn't be expected to attend to every detail at the Vulcan as well? Does any of it mean anything, except that Mr Tanbrey has been hauled before this court on the flimsiest of evidence while his partners, Messrs Hodson and Barrington, the latter now conveniently deceased, wheel and deal behind his back? As Mr Maynard Keynes has recently stated in his forecast of economic gloom, 'There are a lot of men who look as if they have done rather well out of the war'. Isn't that just the case here? Mr Tanbrey had received his dues for the job he had no reason to believe had not been done. Perhaps he was negligent. Perhaps he was naïve, or stupid or both. But was he a crook? On the strength of a supposed telephone call from an almost estranged wife? If you believe this, then you must find him guilty. I see no evidence for it.'

The feeling of relief that swept over Tanbrey on being acquitted hadn't lasted long. The sight of Hodson being led, protesting, from the court, of Pepe Lorenzo's outburst and tears, had soon passed. Because he'd heard for the first time. He hadn't wanted to hear, had never given it a thought. But now, in summing up, the judge had allowed the victims' names to be revealed to the press. *Richard Tanbrey. Matthew Tanbrey.* The next of kin had already been informed of their grave loss. Tanbrey had sat, stunned, seeing nothing until he felt the constable's hand on his arm and the court was almost cleared. Matthew. Why hadn't they seen the connection? He never knew, never thought. And Charlie's accusing finger, pointing at him, Ginny's...

He reached his house not knowing how he'd got there. His acquittal seemed irrelevant. He'd like to have seen more of Charlie. Now he'd probably never see him again. The court might have found him not guilty, but that was only the court, and Charlie – what would he think? Charlie, who had something he could never have. He wondered what it was. Then it came to him. It was the gift of love. John had never loved anyone. Not even himself.

The maid came in from the back room. 'Madam asked me to give you this, sir.'

He took the envelope. 'You can go. Go into town, whatever it is you do.'

With great lethargy, he opened the flap.

'Dear John,

You will be pleased to hear I am relieving you of my company. Flossie has written to say she is shortly to marry a German soldier she nursed in the war, and I am going to live in Germany. Things are bad in the cities, but we will be far from the madding crowds. A foolish thing to do at this point, you might think, but there again I've never been noted for my common sense. If I had, I would never have married you.

I've taken quite a lot of money from the safe. I found out the number one day looking through your things. I suppose it's money no one is supposed to know about, so I don't expect the police will be involved. Even if it isn't, it wouldn't do your public face any good to tell everyone you've been robbed by your loving wife, would it, especially coming so soon after the mock trial you've just gone through? (Or left by her, come to that.) Ah, well, such is the stuff of life, as they say.

By the way, there's been a trunk call from someone claiming to be your son's wife. She says she found our address looking through her husband's effects. Life is full of surprises.We talked about the trial, and I told her you were guilty as hell and would have absolutely no qualms about that poor man Hodson being fingered in your stead. She's going to get in touch.

I asked a mutual acquaintance to help nail you, and we are both disappointed you didn't end up behind bars. Still, what the hell! Enjoy the rest of your life, preferably alone and miserable. By the time you read this I shall be far away.

Your adoring wife,

Nerissa.'

PS Do you know, this time I really suspect I've won!

He screwed up the letter and hurled it from him. For a moment he was undecided what to do. That night he was unable to sleep. The envelope was waiting on the hall carpet when he went downstairs, and he ripped it open with such force he tore part of the enclosure. He struggled to focus on the sloping black characters running across the sheet.

'Mr Tanbrey,

You might be surprised at my writing to you. You never had anything to do with Matthew, and so you never knew he'd died in the war. And why should I have told you? I've never met you, and you won't know anything about your grandsons either. He spoke about you sometimes. I think he felt sorry for you. Why did you hate him? He was a fine man, a good husband me and the children will miss every day of our lives.

I do not know who was responsible for his death, I only know what the courts say. If it is true, you have nothing to recriminate yourself for, except you were never a father to him and the courts are not always right. There is nothing more I want to say. I'm sure if Matthew is looking down on you, he will forgive you. That would be his way. It is not my place to do the same.

Bernadette Tanbrey.'

He staggered to the chair. Somewhere in the room a dark pulse seemed to beat. The enormity of his crime bore down on him like a pain. His son, his only son. He'd killed him. And Charlie's son. He'd killed them both. The courts had acquitted him but he could never acquit himself. The rhythm of the day faded into silence, and the telephone had been ringing for some minutes before he lifted the receiver. Had he forgotten he was due at the Charity Ball at eight? They were looking forward to welcoming him back.

His acquittal had been a mere formality. Everyone knew it. A celebration was in order....

He let the receiver fall, opened the French windows and went out. A steady rain was falling, and he sank to a bench, letting the comforting drops course down his face.

Andrew Bonar Law, came into the room.

'You've read the papers?' said Lloyd George.

'You mean Ireland?'

'No, not Ireland. They'll soon be under martial law, might knock some sense into the lot of them. And it's not the bloody miners either. No, I mean this ambulance fraud. Have you read it?'

'For what it's worth, I wouldn't be surprised if they'd got the wrong man.'

Lloyd George smiled faintly. 'Possibly true. In the greater scheme of things, does it matter? We got somebody, I made sure of that. And we got it in the papers. Along with the names of the dead. People always want to know the names of the dead. It gives it a personal touch.'

'And, of course, you can build on that.'

'If we're going to get in again, we shall need all the help we can get.' The Prime Minister retrieved his newspaper from the desk, lowered his glasses. 'I like this, Andrew: "The Prime Minister has always been most explicit in his dealings with what he calls crooks and fraudsters – particularly at a time when our valiant men were giving their lives in service to their country. He is extremely encouraged that justice has been done." Well, what do you think?'

'Barrington should have served time. He always was a lucky sod.'

'And the other one, the crafty bugger who hired someone as crooked as himself, I hope it bankrupts him. Anyway, enough of all that.' Lloyd George folded the paper. Linking his fingers together, he brought his head closer to the other man's. 'Andrew, I'm worried.'

'Is it your wife again?'

'It's no laughing matter. I'm still worried about this Versailles fiasco.'

'You said you'd squeeze the German lemon –'

'–till the pips squeak. I know. But this, this French demand. Christ, you can't humble a proud people like this, all these bloody reparations they want. We'll have to fight another war in twenty years at this rate.'

'That's your opinion, is it?'

'Not only mine. In fact, it's stirring up already.'

'Perhaps.'

The Prime Minister lowered his voice still further. 'Keep your eyes on this National Socialist German Workers' Party. And this man Hitler.... we must keep our eyes on him as well.' He leaned back, smiling. 'I'm in the mood for a good lunch. Come and join me.'

12

At the beginning of the Summer Term, 1921, Charlie pedalled his bike steadily along the lane, his cap pulled down against a faltering breeze. He made his ritualistic stop along the top road he was sure was Roman, though he could find nothing in the library to say so. He looked across the land; east, to Morridge, north to where the Pennines folded hazily towards the plain, west, towards Mow Cop and Congleton Edge. Almost sixty, he allowed life to flow over him in a gentle stream. The staff thought of him as an unthreatening eccentric. Maybe they considered him stoic, or too enmeshed in his own world to care much what happened outside it. His bouts of remorse were less frequent now, and dulled when they came. There were days he'd hardly think of Richard. Then he'd find himself going back to the times before the war when they'd rambled the hills together in companionable silence and some trivial thing would jog his memory, the sight of a barge on the canal, perhaps. He couldn't shake off the conviction that John had been one of those responsible for Richard's death along with that of his own son. He couldn't help wondering how a just God could have caused such a malicious coincidence. There'd always been a bond between him and his half-brother, and now it was shattered.

He usually arrived early. He liked to get things in order before his class arrived. The caretaker would join him and they'd talk about the weather, and then the first scholars would appear in the yard half-an-hour before the bell. Sometimes a child would be there before him, playing a solitary hopscotch until the yard began to fill. What had become of Russell? Was he still in America, or had he returned to some grimy school up north? Where was Neville Deakin, who'd used his work and his wife; and his cousins, Dick and Bessie and Bertha? What had become of the red-haired boy whose tear-stained face he could still see, his hands smarting from Francis Gordon's cane? And Caulton and his wife, who'd both be in their eighties if they were still living? Why hadn't he kept in touch? Why hadn't they? So many faces, such a rushing life. Sometimes he imagined it was like a railway shunting yard. A pull on the lever, a change of points, and the train took another line with a different cargo. Who were Ellen's parents? Had they followed her throughout the years, hidden from sight along the lanes?

Increasingly troubled with angina, he was going to finish that year. Ellen thought her infusions of foxglove might be too strong, and now she bought tincture of hawthorn from one of the farmer's wives. She was right, of course, he'd have to give it up. In a way he felt he'd come down to his class, thought he understood them better than when he first started. He never had to use the cane, now. There were offences he chose not to see, of course, but he enjoyed their childhood with them.

'Ivy, Grace, give out the poetry books.' A murmur of approval from the girls, dissent from the boys. There'd be the rhythmic clump of books and they'd be waiting; starched pinafores, scrubbed faces, snotty noses, threadbare jerseys, rickets, coughs, ringworm, the growl of a lorry beyond the window. 'Has everybody got a copy?'

'I haven't got one, Mr Tanbrey.'

'You can share. What shall it be?'

'Sir! Sir!'

'Yes?'

'Fear of little men, sir.'

'What's that?' he pretended.

'He means that one about not going hunting, Mr Tanbrey.'

'Who wants to read first?'

'Sir! Sir!'

'You can all read together. Girls can read the first few lines, then the boys can have a go. We'll see who's best.'

He tapped the lines on his desk, the laggards catching up, the speeders reined in; blank faces, animated faces, shy, stumbling, mumbling, expressive....

'Up the airy mountain, down the rushy glen
We daren't go a-hunting for fear of little men–'

'And now the boys–'

And Caulton was there before him, swishing his cane in the sun, Launcelot's shield blood-red in the sun–

'Wee folk, good folk, trooping all together
Green jacket, red cap and white owl's feather'

And at the door, Francis Gordon brandishing his stick. *I must beg forgiveness. I was leaving the school, then I discover I've blundered into a cage of monkeys. I think I must be in a zoo. A human zoo, full of foul-mouthed –*

Creatures. He looked up. The class were silent, looking at him. He seemed to see them for the first time. 'I'll read a poem now. No, I won't. Henrietta, you can read it, your voice is better than mine. I'm beginning to croak like an old frog.' They giggled in empathy. 'It's a poem by a man who lived in the country, like you. Like me, for that matter. Some of his poems are about the countryside he knew. A sort of imaginary countryside, in a way. But in another way it's about time passing. Passing years.'

The girl reminded him so much of Hannah. There was the same smiling openness about her. How old would Hannah have been? Twenty-eight? Twenty-eight! And no doubt with a family of her own. Still smiling at what might have been, he said: 'Page 136. Have you found it?'

The girl waited for the pages to settle, the coughs and shuffles to subside. She spoke in a low voice, with a mixture of pride and bashfulness.

'Into my heart an air that kills, from yon far country blows:
What are those blue-remembered hills, what spires, what farms are those?
That is the land of lost content, I see it shining plain,
The happy highways where I went and cannot come again'

He hadn't wanted a fuss. He explained to those who didn't know that he hadn't been in the profession very long, not in comparison to some in other schools who'd taught three generations and would still be at it now, given the chance. His excuse wasn't good enough. He was worthy of celebration and something like a child himself.

'We've already booked the room, Mr Tanbrey, so you can't give us a no for an answer.'

'We'll get your wife to bring you.'

'What am I to wear?'

'Your best suit. The invitations are for your wife and daughter as well. Does she have a young man, yet?'

'If she has, she's said nothing to me about it.'

'Don't flatter yourself it's just for you, it's our end-of-term as well, you know....'

The head chinked a spoon against his glass. A soft night air came into the room through the open windows. Charlie was older than any of them, though they all seemed senior to him. They'd come out with the latest educational methods, leaving him behind, and he was too old for fads. They'd always seemed together, like one unit, whereas he'd never been more than himself. A further rattle of the spoon brought silence.

'Now, Mr Tanbrey – Charles – I think we can safely use his first name now he's leaving us –Charles has been with the school for many years as a teacher and before that as a pupil just down the road. I know he's not going to make a grand speech, but he's not going to get away lightly, either.' A moth fluttered against the light, and Charlie watched its faltering progression. One of the women was fanning herself with her hand, her cheeks pink with heat. 'An occasion like this would be incomplete without some reference to Charles's life before he became a teacher. I've taken the liberty to go behind his back and tease out one or two scraps of information from Mrs Tanbrey. How many of you know, for example, that Charles's first ambition was to be an artist, or at least a designer? And how many realise how useful he is around a farm? We know him as an unassuming member of the school, always first here, never late, but how many know of Charles Tanbrey the painter, Charles the designer, or collier, or gardener? Enough occupations there for half-a-dozen dozen lives, I should think. No doubt in his modest way, Charles was accomplished in all.'

It was pleasant in the room, listening to the summer echoing outside. In a sense none of it seemed relevant to him. It seemed only five minutes ago he was making his corkwool and peering out from the hollow in Spring Wood. So much had happened, and as he sat there listening with half-an-ear, the images became as gauzy as dreams. He was aware of himself patting the pockets of his jacket as he got up. He'd seen Bevis do the same. Out of the corner of his eye he caught the blur of Ellen's face. She knew how he hated it.

'Well, thank you for those kind words. I'm sure they're not altogether deserved. I don't want to say much, but I'd like to thank you all for the food and company. I'd like to thank you, too, on behalf of my wife and daughter for all your kindness over the years. I thought I'd just go out with a pop, like pulling a cork out of a bottle of Dandelion and Burdock, and not have to make speeches, which I'm not over-good at....' He let their protests run their course, cleared his throat. 'I never thought I'd end up a schoolmaster. There's been no teachers in my family. Plenty of colliers and mould-runners and even button-makers, but no teachers.' His tongue began to loosen. 'I suppose you've got my wife to thank. She's the one advised me when I most needed it, and she couldn't have been more right. I must be one of those who actually like children....' His voice seemed to fade, as if a membrane had been drawn across the sound. The room sharpened, their faces flushed with laughter. 'And so now every time I feel irritation getting the better of me, I bang the pipes instead and get my own back on Miss Hobday. For some, retirement is the end of life. I hope it won't be that way for me. There's so much to do. I feel I haven't scratched the surface yet....'

Again, a distortion of his voice, his colleagues' faces shadowy among the tables. He felt an urgency to get out.

'And we thought this might be just what you'd like in your – we were going to say 'retirement', but we'll call it a change of direction and leave it at that.'

'Come on, open it up.'

'Don't keep us all in suspense'

He drew from the wrapping a box of paints.

'We're indebted to your good wife for her suggestion. She believes it's time for you to begin again where you left off. Please accept them as a token of our regard and thanks.'

Now you can turn out masterpieces by the score. He's got potential, Mrs Tanbrey.... he's got potential....

'Thank you,' Charlie said. 'I used to have a box like these.'

The moon bathed the fields in quilts of light, and from the woods behind the barns an owl hooted.

'You're tired, Charlie.'

'It's been a long night.'

'Best go straight to bed. You sounded a bit distant earlier, when you were making your speech.'

'I had a turn.'

'You're all right now, though?'

'A touch of nerves, that's all.'

'Have a good night's rest, you'll be up with the larks.' He was still standing by the door. 'What're you doing there, why don't you go up to bed?'

'I don't know.' He pulled his cap back on. 'I think I'll take a stroll.'

'What, at this hour? Where to?'

'I won't be long.'

He opened the door and the smell of mown fields came into the room. 'Don't wait up, I'll not be long.'

He climbed the stile and found himself taking the path to Rudyard. The meadows glimmered and from the woodland the owl continued its low, mournful call. He'd no idea why he was walking. The clock at Leek sounded the hour, the chimes clear against the singing becks. He climbed another stile, quickened his pace. He could see the next stile against the blur of foliage. The shapes didn't look like cows. Were they poachers, or mill hands out with their terriers? The figures were plainer now. He could hear their voices on the air. He could hear the swish of the girl's dress. They were almost on him and he knew, perhaps he'd always known. He lifted his face. Time shrank to a single beat.

'Dad?'

He tried to articulate the name, couldn't.

'Le pauvre, le shoc c'est trop....'

A sudden weariness bore him down. 'Richard?' His fingers strayed to his son's jacket. 'Richard?'

He fell forward, sobbing.

'Tu pleures des larmes de joie.'

'I knew there was something....I....'

'Shall we go to the house, dad?'

'What will they think? What will they think?'

As if for the first time, he saw the girl.

'This is Madeline, my wife.'

'Je voudrais recontrer ta femme,' said the girl. I'd like to meet your wife. She added: *'Je vais t'appeler papa.'* I'd better call you father.

She linked an arm through Charlie's and they went back.

Richard's story lasted until morning. He was slower than before, and Madeline had to jog his memory. He'd been unable to recall what happened for many months. He could remember the ambulance, the German soldier, but only as snapshots. He must have been thrown into the road, found a dead soldier lying nearby. The man had been terribly mangled, but his identity disc still hung around his neck. He might have cut it, untied it, tied his own disc in its place. Desertion was a capital offence, but it hadn't mattered to him whether he lived or died. There were plumes of smoke above the ridge, more dead soldiers strewn across the lane. He'd blundered through them into some trees. He'd slept in fits and starts, watching the flares light up the trees, and woke at dawn aching in every limb.

He'd had no idea of time, only self-preservation.. He'd emerged by a field, picked up the sound of running water and drank from the stream. Afterwards he'd shed his puttees and cap. He remembered he no longer felt tired. He had to get away from the shells. He had no map, a few francs. He wasn't far behind the line, two miles at most. He'd dropped the dead man's disc in a hole in a tree. He'd have to be French, think in French. He'd seen the farm across the field, its jumble of sheds and farming implements. Dawn was some way off. He'd approached the buildings crouched in shadow. He'd tried the door of an outbuilding, then an empty cowshed. A door led to the milking room, and in the trickle of light he'd seen a farmer's smock and leggings hanging from the wall. He'd emptied and stripped his uniform and put them on. They fitted well enough. He found a tam rolled into a pocket, put that on too. His uniform he buried under the straw heap.

He'd put five miles between himself and the farm by the time the sky began to pale and set out his possessions in a glade: four eggs, a dixie of milk. He broke an egg into his milk and drank. He dropped his revolver and dixie into the pouches of his smock. As dawn came up he'd moved to the open lane....

Charlie sat in silence. Ellen said, 'Well, what an adventure.... eh, Charlie?'

'Il pense que ce n'est pas sur.'

'Madeline says I think it's not safe,' Richard said.

'From what?'

'I'm a deserter. A marked man.'

There was a lull. Charlie asked, 'What happened next, son?'

Richard reached out his hand to Madeline. 'My guardian angel must have been with me. I had my French, of course. Sometimes I'd bump into some other peasant, and I could see they were curious about my accent. I made out I was from the south, come to help out on my cousin's farm now labourers were in short supply. I got by. I even managed to steal a map from a station master. He was more interested in his boules than attending to his job. I saw it in his office window and helped myself. I managed to steal all manner of things, even a bicycle. I rode it all the way to Meaux before it was stolen from me. You can't trust anyone nowadays.'

He fell silent. His wife prompted him. He told them about the work he'd found on a vineyard near Esternay. The locals had told him it had been a poor year. They were short-handed, with the men fighting. 'I invented a Spanish mother married to a French father living in Orleans. I'd been a student at Salamanca. My mother had been ill. I had leave for a month. I'd run out of cash. My family had lost their money due to the war.' He shrugged. 'I bought some better clothes. Nothing too obvious. I tried to keep up with the news. I thought maybe they'd win the war without me. I grew a beard, of course. Then I reached Lemont, not far from the Swiss border. It was there my luck nearly ran out.'

'My father –' Madeline broke in, in heavily accented English.

Richard smiled. 'Monsieur found me asleep in his barn. He was looking for rats and found my revolver instead. I awoke staring down the barrel of his gun. Luckily for me, he wasn't too friendly with the local gendarmerie, something to do with his poaching on land belonging to the Mayor of Troyes. He questioned me across the kitchen table with the family looking on. How had I come by the Webley? I told him I'd bartered it with my cousin for a fishing rod. Where's your fishing rod now? It broke. I threw it away. Fortunately he took to me, and so did his daughter. I worked for a year in his joinery business. You'd like Lemont. A few old houses, the River Aube. You could catch anything in that river. Trout, carp....

'By the time he knew I was a deserter Madeline had made it impossible for him to give me up. He developed a malicious pride in harbouring me from Le Authorities. Le Authorities were *merde*. Especially the police and the Mayor. Then the war ended. A priest he drank with got together some papers, some business about a deceased Monsieur Tanbreye from another town whose certificate his widow was happy to produce in return for a new pine chiffonier. I am now a Frenchman, married to a French woman, residing in France.'

'And tonight?' Charlie asked.

Richard drew in his breath. 'I couldn't write. I wasn't even sure when the war ended if the deception would hold. I knew you'd be told I'd died. I felt ashamed, dirty. For a time I developed a stammer. I'm afraid I went through a bit of a bad patch.... I wanted you all to know I was still alive. It took me two years to risk getting a passport. By then you had to have your photo stuck in it, but by then I'd filled out a bit and I was Tanbreye with an 'e'. Even so, every knock – well, I won't bother you with the details. Madeline insisted, and I said it would have to be this dead of night stuff, the night ferry, locked in a hotel in Victoria the next day, another night train here. It was like being on the run again.... pity about university. Maybe I'll try again some time. In France, of course.'

Ellen shook her head. 'It's like a dream, isn't it, Charlie? Vicky, isn't it like a dream? We'll use the spare room. Richard and Madeline can have our bed.'

Madeline was unclipping her bag. She passed a photograph to Ellen. 'Richard and me, we 'ave baby, see? Jean Claude Tanbreye age one year old. He with my parents.'

Charlie stared at his grandchild in bewildered silence. In his mind's eye he could see them erecting a plaque to the fallen in Moor Top church. What was he to do? Did it matter, now that his son was alive. He'd never been to France, nor Ellen. Now the world seemed less threatening. And he had money from his retirement. Maybe next year. Maybe.

They stayed around the farm for a week. It was off the track, and nobody would know. They intended to set up in business selling the family's furniture in Troyes. Bill's money would help....

John called on Charlie's sixtieth birthday. In the three years since the trial, he'd lost weight, and there was a flatness in his speech which hadn't been there before. It was as if he no longer felt. He enquired about Ellen, Vicky. If they needed help, he had only to ask. He was doing well, others had gone to the wall, but.... 'I never had anything to do with it, Charlie.'

'It's in the past. How's Nerissa?' He could no longer shut him out. It wasn't his way. But he'd say nothing about Richard. Not yet.

'I didn't tell you, she's gone to live in Germany with Flossie. Flossie married a German casualty she met nursing in France. I'm on my own now. How do you fancy a stroll down Spring Wood?'

They walked down the lane, past the spring tumbling through the stone-strewn gutter. 'I suppose,' John said, 'you get out of life what you put in. Perhaps we'd alter ourselves if we could, but no one is given that chance. We inhabit a shell, and just peep out from time to time. Don't you think so, Charlie?' The setting sun lanced through the trees, and a crimson band clung to the roof of the rebuilt Grange, now a hospital. 'Perhaps our only chance of innocence is our childhood. After that, it's – well, you know what I'm trying to say.' They paused to look at the house through the trees.

A filigree of branches etched the flaring sky. 'And that's where it all began. A scuffle on the dance floor.'

He preferred not to stay the night. When he'd driven off, Ellen said: 'You can't take all the world on your shoulders, Charlie, best let him be.'

It was the first Sunday in May, and the sky was bright with the coming summer. The past week had been wet, with no washing dried, or Ellen and Vicky wouldn't have been struggling with it now. He cranked the mangle and watched the sheets billow across the yard. Sunday washing broke a rhythm, like stopping your ears to the sound of bells. On an impulse, he stopped cranking and said he was going to church.

'Church, Charlie?'

'Ay, I think I will. Do you want to come?'

'What, with this lot?'

'Let Vicky finish off. Get the crows to hang 'em out.'

He changed into his best and wheeled out his bike. He was late and unable to make his accustomed stop and admire the view. He'd stop on his return, for the ritual had become talismanic over the years, and he felt uncomfortable when he couldn't spend a moment in the airy quiet. On the heights he always felt part of a rhythm, part of the trilling of birds and the vibrating chorus of life.

The bell stopped pealing as he reached the door; the choristers were already leaving the vestry. He found his thoughts straying unbidden to the girl at school. *You read it, Henrietta. Your voice is better than mine. I'm beginning to croak like an old frog.* He found himself chuckling, and his lips formed the shape of his inward smile. For some reason he felt immensely happy. *What are those blue remembered hills, what spires, what farms are those?* So like Hannah. So like Hannah, that girl.

He lifted his eyes to the rubric, picked out in red above the chancel arch. *Come Unto Me And I Will Give You Rest.* There was a sense of lightening, a whitening of light, of weight, a brightness shining from the wall. He wondered what Ellen would do when he'd gone. And Vicky. What would they do? He seemed to have risen, glimpsing Hannah among the choristers. He could see her at the side, her hymnal half-lowered. It was difficult to tell whether she was beckoning or waving. He thought he heard Durose's old cannon, the soft plop of spilt liquor through the trestle. A bright cone passed across the chancel and its rubric, over the singers and the hymn they sang.

'What's the matter, Mr Tanbrey, don't you feel well?

Hannah stood in the light. *Yes, beckoning.* He moved forward, almost stumbled, and she caught him. The rector joined the others around the pew.

'He just fell forward,' one of the women was saying. 'It must be his heart. I do believe he's gone, rector. I do believe he's gone Home.'

A sudden wind soughed and burred, scattering last year's leaves by the vestry door. And there was no spite in it.

EPILOGUE

THE GRANGE, MILLENNIUM EVE, 1999

Sir Paul Tanbrey stepped from a Schweizer helicopter into the enclosure and took the stand to a pattering of applause as the council leader rose to his feet. 'Ladies and gentlemen. Sir Paul has kindly agreed to take time off from his busy schedule to honour us with a whistle-stop visit to the Grange. He needs no introduction from me in his capacity as Director of Central Services, but some of you may be surprised to learn he has strong links with this area. His great grandfather was born on Moor Top, not a mile from here, and actually worked in the Grange under the estate manager. That was many years ago, of course, when it was owned by the Bateman family. However, enough said: Sir Paul Tanbrey.'

A slight current lifted Sir Paul's white hair. 'Ladies and gentlemen, I'm honoured to have been invited to open these important celebrations which, I am reliably informed, will last until midnight, thereby bringing to a close a century of staggering achievements. As you've already gathered, my visit today will be for me, personally, a fulfilling one. John Tanbrey, my great grandfather, did indeed work in this house under both the Heath and Bateman families. I welcome this opportunity to look around the building where he spent so much of his time. So, without more ado, I declare this celebration well and truly open.'

The crowd dispersed. Sir Paul, flanked by members of the council, walked towards the house.

IN MEMORIAM

In Memory of Laura, the dearly loved wife of Robert Heath of Greenway Bank who died May 5th 1897 aged 47 years. Also the above Robert Heath, who died February 23rd 1932 aged 81 years. Blessed are the dead which die in the Lord. Rev X1V (also see below)
Memorial Stone, St Lawrence Church, Biddulph

Signorina Lucy Morris, an Englishwoman living in the Via Fuseli, is reported to be the latest victim of a typhus outbreak effecting the area. Police have tried unsuccessfully to trace the man with whom she was living shortly before her death.
Il Giornale, 3rd August 1921 (translated)

Frau Nerissa Elizabeth Tanbrey, the estranged wife of English industrialist Lord John Tanbrey of Overton, died at the Sister Teresa Hospice near Lahr on the 27th March 1926 after a brief illness. Frau Tanbrey was 69
Mitteldeutsche Zeitung, 29th March 1926

The decapitated body found beside the main railway line near Poynton Station has been identified as that of Mr Ebenezer Hodson, former owner of the Vulcan Foundry, Macclesfield. Mr Hodson, who served a term of imprisonment for the fraudulent manufacture of sub-standard vehicles in the war, had been described by his wife as 'not particularly depressed' shortly before his suicide. Mr Hodson's only son, Steven, served as an officer in the Cheshire Regiment until his death in Canberry in 1916.
The Mercury, 24th February, 1928

Mrs Jane O'Rourke, who died earlier this week, will be mourned by many. Mrs O'Rourke, a former member of the Amalgamated Society of Textile Workers and an early convert to the suffragette cause before the Great War, will chiefly be remembered for her novel *Tied to the Mill*, which she wrote in her seventieth year and which drew heavily on her experiences of factory life in the last century. She was also a respected contributor to various periodicals, chief among which was *The Northern Star*, where readers eagerly awaited her weekly column. She is survived by her husband, the Honourable Eric O'Rourke, MP.
The Times, 2nd September, 1936

'My father Harry had cancer of the jaw, and that's what got him. They say it was chewing tobacco that did it. They had to do that to keep their mouth free of dust, you see, stoking boilers in the ships. He had a fair old life after he left Doncaster. He was only 13 then, and he got work on the sailing ships. The things he used to tell me about! He said he'd been a cowboy in South America, and a ranger in Australia and a gold miner as well. That was in South Africa, I think he said. That's apart from

the Titanic. After that went down, he ended up in the Merchant Marine, defending cargo boats in the war. After he'd got it all out of his system, he ends up working as a docker in Tilbury.'
From May Senior's account of her father Harold's life, after his death in 1937 (transcript 1996)

We might refer to Eric as Discourse, Dissent and Horses. Of the three, I think he will chiefly be remembered for the latter. I'm sure there's more than a few who have benefited from his weekly tips; I certainly have, even if they were given on a Sunday.
From Eric O'Rourke's funeral service, conducted by the Rev. Wilbur Hotspur, 1st April, 1941

I miss you dearest Mother,
More than words can say,
The memory of your kindness,
Will never fade away
In Memoriam: For my mother Ellen Tanbrey from her loving daughter, Vicky. The **Evening Sentinel, 16th January, 1942**

Lord Tanbrey of Overton, the industrialist and benefactor, died at his home near Macclesfield in the early hours of Friday morning. It is believed that his son's widow Bernadette and his grandchildren will be the chief beneficiaries of his will. Lord Tanbrey's generosity in support of local causes is well known, particularly towards women who had lost sons and husbands in the Great War. The Tanbrey Hospice will be a lasting memorial to Lord Tanbrey's altruism.
The Times 15th August, 1943

Victoria Tanbrey, of Three Elms Farm, near Leek, will be sadly missed. A gifted amateur pianist and founder member of St Edward's Ladies' Choir, she worked for many years in the Post Office, eventually attaining the rank of Deputy Cashier in the Hanley branch of the GPO. (telephonic services) She held this post until her retirement through ill health. Miss Tanbrey was 48.
The Evening Sentinel, 10th September, 1952

Robert Heath, son of the above of Greenway Bank who died April 1st 1954 aged 78 years. **Memorial Stone, St Lawrence's Church, Biddulph**.
(See above and below)

Mr Russell K Russell passed away peacefully in his sleep last night. Russian émigré and long-time companion Natalia Solovyov, who has an adjacent apartment, says Mr Russell had retired to bed shortly after watching the Beatles interview on the Ed Sullivan Show and enjoying his nightly meal of Shepherd's Pie, a favourite dish in

his native England. Mr Russell had been a bit player and stuntman in the silent movies, but is best remembered for his book *Make Your Body Your Slave*, which sold widely in the Twenties. He was 91.
LA Star, February 10th, 1964

Robert Edward Heath, of Greenacres, Grange Road, Biddulph, died 7th December 1971, aged 70
Register of Burials: St Anne's Church, Brown Edge.
(Author's note: this last surviving member of the Heath family who lived locally moved from Greenway Bank Hall to Greenacres shortly before his death.)

We are sorry to announce the death of Richard Tanbreye earlier this week. Until his retirement, Monsieur Tanbreye worked in the furniture business established by his late father-in-law early this century. Monsieur Tanbreye will be sadly missed by his wife Madeline, their daughters Fleur and Bridgett and son Jean Claude. Monsieur Tanbreye was 77.
Le Journal due Centre, 3rd April 1973 (translated)

Frau Florence Beatrice Maarling (nee Tanbrey) died of broncho-pneumonia on Monday. Her husband Johannes believes her death to have been caused by a recent accident sustained when she fell from a step-ladder while attempting to change a light bulb. Frau Maarling leaves a son, Franz, a daughter Mae, and seven grandchildren. She was 80
Sudkurier, 12th January, 1973 (translated)

Jean Claude Tanbreye, Professor of Mathematics at the Academie de Grenoble, passed away yesterday. Professor Tanbreye, considered by many to be the outstanding scholar of his generation, will chiefly be remembered for his seminal work *The Value of Zero*. Professor Tanbreye, who was unmarried, was 83.
Le Figaro Rhone Alpes, 10th September 2006 (translated)

Contractors working for Nimmo-Sharma Roadstone exposed a human skeleton yesterday while excavating tip waste near Brindley whilst completing the latest phase of Brindley Country Park. Forensic analysis has confirmed the remains are those of a middle-aged male, and are not of recent origin. A heavily-corroded spike, a legacy no doubt of 19th century mining activity in the area, was found within the rib cage, suggesting the man had been the victim of a tragic accident.
The Sentinel, 22nd June, 2020

END NOTES

We have been directed to prepare for the sale by auction of over 2000 acres of farms and woodland belonging to Mr Robert Heath. The auction will take place at the North Staffordshire Hotel at 2pm on March 5th, 1920
Notice issued by H Steele and Son, January 1920

Quite recently, the Cripple's Aid Society has received a most munificent and great offer - an offer made spontaneously by that generous-hearted gentleman Mr Robert Heath, to give over to use as a country hospital for our cripples his magnificent residence, Biddulph Grange. **From an after-dinner speech by Mr Eric Young, Consultant Surgeon to the North Staffordshire Cripples' Aid Society, 10th November, 1921**

Since acquiring this property, Lancashire Education Committee has undertaken extensive improvements to the heating and lighting systems of the existing hospital. Part of the stable block has been converted to a laundry equipped with steam and electric machinery. The mansion itself forms the administrative area and contains an exceptionally well-appointed operating theatre. **The Preston Guardian, on the sale of the Grange Hospital on 1st April 1926 to the Lancashire Education Committee.**

I joined the staff in 1949, when the Grange came under the control of the North Staffordshire Hospital Management Committee.
Recollections from Mr Denys Wainwright, Consultant Surgeon, 1976

Fight to Save the Grange Hospital
The Chronicle, 14th October, 1983

We intend to spend £12000 saving the beautiful gardens of the Grange from vandals.
West Midlands Regional Health Authority bulletin, October 1984

The gardens are deteriorating at an alarming rate. The Chinese Temple is now a ruin, the tunnel which leads to the garden is in a dangerous state. Parts of the garden suffer regularly from unchecked vandalism.
From article by Mr Peter Hayden, 23rd November, 1984, in 'Staffordshire History'

The Council has bought the Grange Estate. The National Trust will take over responsibility for the formal gardens and we will be approaching the Countryside Commission to see if they will create a Country Park in the undressed grounds.
Notice issued by Staffordshire Moorlands District Council on 9th April, 1986

Grange Hospital is to close next year. A question mark hangs over the future of the house.
The Chronicle, 1990

Black Bull Colliery Demolished:
The Chronicle, 28th October, 1983

There is evidence to suggest there is more than a grain of truth to this Lady Chatterley story. According to some historians, a titled lady visitor to the Grange had been in the habit of visiting Mr Bateman's gamekeeper, and not necessarily to talk about his whippets. Her amorous exploits are revealed by a local man who informed our reporter that the story was passed down through the family and probably originated from his great-great grandfather who was a coachman to the Batemans. It was rumoured that the secret liaison produced a daughter who was adopted by a family living near Moor Top. This has never been confirmed. **Local News Article, 15th May, 1997**

If you wanted to examine a superb collection of Victorian tile designs, the attic of a derelict moorland house might be the last place you'd look. 'They were in a folder covered in dust,' said Bob Daintry of Heritage Renovations, Macclesfield. 'They were all signed Charles Tanbrey and dated.. I've no idea how they came to be there.' If any of our readers can help unravel the mystery, please get in touch.
The Chronicle, April 20th 2018.

Chell Workhouse is now completed as far as to be fit for the reception of the poor, and by the end of the week the inmates of the old workhouses at Burslem and Wolstanton, about 220 in number, will have been removed to it.
The Staffordshire Advertiser, 28th March, 1840

Tutor Andrew Dobraszczyc's current series of local history walks have ended with a visit to the old Chell Workhouse. The remaining buildings are due to be demolished later this year. **WEA Information, summer, 1993**

Tunstall Calver Street (formerly Calvert Street)
Clearance Areas Compulsory Purchase Order: Dwellinghouse and rear yard - No 12 Calvert Street, together with adjoining entry. **Recollections of the 1960s - author**

Mrs Rose Tremaine, formerly Tanbrey, widow of ill-fated oilman William Tanbrey, married Francis Bamber L Tremaine in Tulsa on Saturday. The ceremony was attended by Mrs Tremaine's daughter Colette Ullan and her husband Jose Manuel, and her step-daughter Marian Deaville and husband Andrew, together with a few close friends.
Tulsa World, 18th July, 1921

Carmen Lopez, aged 53, walked into the offices of Shell Oil yesterday claiming she was the great-granddaughter of William Tanbrey, a founder of the company. According to Lopez, the English farmer got rich through oil in the 1880s after having had a brief liaison with her Mexican great-grandmother Dolores Anita Sanchez. The woman gave birth to a male, Ricardo, who, Lopez claims, was her grandfather. She says the story came from a Cherokee squaw who attended to Dolores shortly before Dolores' death in 1923. Carmen is set to issue a writ demanding that Eleanor Parker, Director of Overseas Development and a descendent of said William Tanbrey, submit a DNA profile for independent analysis along with her own. Stay with this frame.
CNN Radio Newscast, 10th July, 1998